BOUND FOR GOLD

BOUND

for

GOLD

WILLIAM MARTIN

A TOM DOHERTY ASSOCIATES BOOK

New York

BOUND FOR GOLD

Copyright © 2018 by William Martin

All rights reserved.

A Forge Book
Published by Tom Doherty Associates
175 Fifth Avenue
New York, NY 10010

www.tor-forge.com

Forge® is a registered trademark of Macmillan Publishing Group, LLC.

The Library of Congress Cataloging-in-Publication Data is available upon request.

ISBN 978-0-7653-8421-8 (hardcover)
ISBN 978-0-7653-8423-2 (ebook)

Our books may be purchased in bulk for promotional, educational, or business use. Please contact your local bookseller or the Macmillan Corporate and Premium Sales Department at 1-800-221-7945, extension 5442, or by email at MacmillanSpecialMarkets@macmillan.com.

First Edition: July 2018

Printed in the United States of America

0 9 8 7 6 5 4 3 2 1

In Memory of

KEVIN STARR
my Harvard mentor

and

STEVE MARTELL
my oldest friend

ACKNOWLEDGMENTS

Back in 1975, at the University of Southern California film school, I took my first screenwriting class. Our big assignment that semester was to write a treatment for a feature-length film.

Though I had little writing experience, I had already rejected the advice that you should write what you know. I believed then, as I do now, that you should write what you *want* to know, or where you want to go, or who you want to meet when you get there. And operating on the principle that I should go big or go back to Boston, I decided to follow my ambition. I would write something historical and as big as I could make it.

But whenever we write, we *are* writing what we know, because to create believable characters, we draw on our understanding of human nature, which emerges from experience and observation. I remember looking around at my USC friends and thinking that all of us had come to California to chase the Hollywood dream, but now we were learning to face the hard realities of making our way. Some of us would succeed. Some of us would be disappointed. And in that, we were a lot like the men and women who had been coming to California since 1849. We were living our own Gold Rush.

Out of that sense of connection with the past grew the adventures of two characters named Spencer and Flynn in a screenplay called *The Mother Lode,* and out of that screenplay has grown this novel, four decades later.

Though the screenplay was not produced (the fate of most screenplays), it won the 1976 Hal Wallis Screenwriting Fellowship, which meant that my name appeared on the cover of *Variety,* I signed with an agent, and for the first time in my life, people other than my wife called me a writer. So, while I should thank the legendary producer of such classics as *Casablanca* and *True Grit* for offering that fellowship, I must first thank my wife. She called me a writer long before there was any supporting evidence.

Chris was there in 1975 and she's still there today, my best friend then and now, ready to put up with long weekends of work, ready to share a nice dinner and a good bottle of wine when the work day is over for both of us, and always ready for research trips, which can be a lot of fun if you do them right.

Like Peter Fallon, I believe that by visiting the places where history happened, I can feel the vibrations and maybe make sense of it for all. I also like to write books about places where our children live. When I wrote *The Lincoln Letter,* set in Civil War Washington, our daughter was living there. Now, both sons live in California, so we got to see a lot of them during the writing. Indeed, all of the Martin-related young people—Bill and Virginia, Dan and Keri, Liz and Will—have offered support, insight, expertise, commentary, companionship, and enthusiasm, especially in our explorations of California vineyards, San Francisco restaurants, Gold Rush historical sites, and the High Sierras.

And our first research trip was our most fortuitous. It brought us to Sutter's Mill, where gold was discovered in a tailrace on a January morning in 1848, and where we met Ed Allen, one of the most knowledgeable site historians I have ever encountered.

Soon, Ed and his wife, Joanne, were welcoming us into their home, offering us their gracious hospitality, and devoting days—yes, *days*—to showing us the gold country that they know and love so well. We visited placer sites, hydraulic sites, mine shafts, head frames, dry gulches, tailing piles, and the stone foundations of mining towns long since dried up and blown away. We felt the heat. We heard the silence. We saw the ghosts. And I took a lot of notes. In the towns that survived and thrived, we also enjoyed some nice meals. If you feel the landscape in this book, if you see that world of a hundred and seventy years ago, it is in large part thanks to Ed and Joanne Allen.

Since Amador County winemaking also figures in this tale, we just had to do our share of tasting, and wineries like Renwood, Terra d'Oro, and Deaver provided wonderful experiences. But I must mention William Easton, owner of Easton/Terre Rouge wineries, who took the time to give us a fascinating tour of his vineyard and discuss the work of growing Zinfandel in Gold Country.

There are many others to thank, too.

First, a few institutions, organizations, and sites: the California Digital Newspaper Collection, a project of U.C. Riverside, which has digitized a window onto the daily life of that distant era; the California Historical Society, where the librarians brought me document that amazed me; the

Carson Pass Ranger Station at the El Dorado National Forest, which offers on-site lectures on the struggles of the overland immigrants; the Columbia State Historic Park; the Doheny Library at the University of Southern California, where I read so many Gold Rush journals so long ago; the Marshall Gold Discovery State Historic Park in Coloma, site of Sutter's Mill; the Old Sacramento Historic District and the Sutter's Fort State Historic Park in Sacramento; and the San Francisco Maritime National Historical Park.

Among fellow authors: Deborah Coonts checked out San Francisco locations for me when I couldn't get there myself. David Morrell, cofounder of the International Thriller Writers and the man who gave the world the character called Rambo, saw that important research material landed on my desk. Willie Nikkel took me gold panning on the American River, just a mile or so downstream from Sutter's Mill. I still have the gold flakes in a little bottle.

Others from across the country: Joseph Amster, who gives great tours of San Francisco in the character of the Emperor Norton; Christopher Brewster of Washington provided insights into foreign investment in the United States. Margherita Desy of the Naval History and Heritage Command and Gary Foreman of the U.S.S. *Constitution* Museum offered details on the handling of a nineteenth-century sailing vessel. Over lunch in the famed Tadich Grill, Mike Green of San Francisco discussed international gold funds. And Steve and Mary Swig of San Francisco welcomed us into their handsome Victorian home, a pre-earthquake classic, showed us their grand city, and provided copious primary source materials.

A few old friends: Rick Jewell, a retired USC cinema professor, read the screenplay four decades ago and never stopped telling me that I should turn it into a novel. John Hamilton and Joe Riley, whom I met in high school long ago, are still dispensing wit, wisdom, and humor. Tom Cook does the same thing, with the added insights and commiserations of another lifelong novelist.

In publishing: Robert Gottlieb has been my agent of thirty-four years (and there aren't many writers who can say that). Tom Doherty and Bob Gleason, my publisher and editor at Tor/Forge, and their team of talented professionals keep me in print in the digital age. It was Bob Gleason who said a few years back, "You know, Bill, there's a great story in the California Gold Rush." I said, "I've been thinking the same thing for a long, long time."

And finally, a word about the two men to whom this book is dedicated:

Kevin Starr was perhaps California's most famous historian. At Harvard, back in 1970, he taught a course that opened my eyes to the connections between American history and literature, and he later became my thesis advisor. We renewed our friendship when I started this novel, which led to long lunches and pleasant dinners with our wives, visits to the Bohemian and the Pacific Union and the other clubs where Kevin was a member, and a powerful sense that when I sat with him, I was sitting at the fountainhead of San Francisco history. He was a beloved teacher, a prolific writer and scholar, and the grand possibilities of California and of the America dream were always evident in his writing and his outlook.

Steve Martell was my first friend in high school, which made him my oldest friend. He was godfather to one of my sons, as I was to his. He was a sounding board for my story ideas and a cheerleader for my books, and no matter how long you have been at this work, you need cheerleaders. Steve and I talked often about this Gold Rush adventure. More than once he said, "Bill, if we were alive back then, we would have gotten on a ship and sailed to California, right along with your characters."

Both of them were in line to receive the first draft of this book. I wanted their opinions before I rewrote. But on one sad Sunday in January of 2017, I learned that both had passed away, one in Boston, one in San Francisco. I think of them often and miss them both. But, as I hope this book demonstrates, while life may be fleeting and fragile, friendship is not.

WILLIAM MARTIN
October 2017

JAMES SPENCER DID NOT sleep well in the hours before dawn. Old men seldom did. So he was half awake when the first shock struck.

It came from somewhere out in the deep Pacific. It rolled in under the Sutro Cliffs, then ran along California Street, rumbled through the foundation of his big house, climbed the grand staircase, and vibrated right into the springs of his four-poster bed.

Everything shook, as if the ice wagon had missed the porch and backed into a corner post.

Nothing more than a good, hard jolt, he thought. Just part of living in California.

But that was not his only thought. In the fitful darkness, James Spencer's mind worked like one of those cheap Chinatown kaleidoscopes. Every twist of his body on the bed and every turn of his head on the pillow brought a new image to his brain.

Was it the jolt that woke him? Or the dog barking down in the street? Or was it the dream? The recurring Boston dream? The nocturnal journey to the Arbella Club, where James Spencer's father hung forever in a full-length portrait. He could see the eyes scowling down from that portrait even then, even there, three thousand miles and almost six decades away.

And why *were* so many dogs barking now, up the hill and down and inside the house across the street?

Then he realized what had awakened him. Not the dogs. Not the dream. Not the jolt. He had to piss . . . again. The never-ending need of an old man to piss was a merciless thing.

And what time *was* it, anyway? Still too dark to see the clock by the bed. But a little after five, he figured, because the sky was brightening. It was springtime in San Francisco, which meant it was springtime in the Sierra, too. The rivers would be running fast, pushing gold flakes over the gravel as they had for thousands of years, long before a sluice-tender plucked a pea-sized nugget from the tailrace at Sutter's Mill and brought the world to California.

Maybe if he thought about those rushing streams, if he imagined the sound of that flowing water, it might help him to piss.

Then he could get dressed and go down to the office and spend a few quiet hours with his Gold Rush journal. He had been transcribing it, and the transcribing had become rewriting, and in the rewriting, an eighty-three-year-old man had found what might be his final purpose. He would tell his descendants about himself and his wife and their role in the building of California. He would tell them about the Chinese. He would tell them about the Irishman who lived now like a spirit in his memory. He would even tell them about the Irishman's lost river of gold.

But first he swung his feet onto the floor and slid his toes about in search of his slippers. He could not find them. No matter. Cold feet might help him to let go if visions of fast-flowing snowmelt failed. So he picked up the chamber pot and, following the principle that men always pissed standing up, he stood.

That was when it hit him, hit him so hard that it took the legs out from under him, hit him as surely as if someone had smashed him in the back of his knees with a shovel.

The chamber pot flew into the air. James Spencer flew onto the bed. And a night's worth of cold urine flew everywhere. The bed seemed to rise, then drop. Spencer rose with it, then *he* dropped.

That jolt had been just a foreshock, followed by maybe half a minute of quiet before the infernal engine humming deep in the earth had loosed a flywheel that spun off its mounts and whirled upward with the force of a hundred million steam locomotives.

Now the light from the streetlamp was dancing on the wall because the streetlamp was swinging in the street. And the window itself was moving because the walls were moving. And the bed was moving because the floor was moving, too.

James Spencer sank his fingers into the mattress and held on.

The bedroom door flew open and the shadow of Spencer's servant, Mickey Chang, appeared. "Mr. James! Mr. James!"

"Stay there!" shouted Spencer. "Stay in the doorframe. Hold on!"

Chang braced himself against the rocking, his eyes wide white in the half light.

The roar grew louder, the shaking more violent.

The bed danced to the terrible symphony of sounds playing now like a prelude to the moment when the whole house would collapse in a thunderous cataract of wood and plaster and chimney bricks. The room echoed with the woodwind shattering of glass and china, the mid-range groan of nails and studs and floorboards straining to hold onto one another, the percussive clanks and bangs and rattles and booms of doors and drawers slamming open and windows shaking loose and furniture toppling, and beneath it all, a deep, relentless, terrifying *basso profundo* rumble rising from the core of the earth itself.

And over the close-by sounds came the noise of something collapsing up the street, something big.

And bells were ringing everywhere, ringing above the roar and below the shattering, ringing in a range of tones and rhythms so wide that it sounded as if every bell in every church in San Francisco was trembling with the fear that God had deserted them, as if every steeple was swinging like the lampposts on California Street.

The bed jerked to the middle of the floor, then jerked back again and banged into the wall. In another room, something fell over. On the street, someone was screaming and the dogs were still barking. And just outside the window, something was snapping. A tree was snapping. Many trees were snapping. But there were no trees on California Street. What was snapping? What the hell was snapping?

And before he could answer, it was over.

The roaring receded, like a train rumbling off into the darkness.

The shaking settled to stillness.

Spencer lay silent and listened as, one by one, the church bells stopped ringing. Now he heard only the barking of the dogs and the whimpering of Chang's wife in the attic bedroom above. He glanced at his bedside clock. He could just make out the hands: five thirteen. The earthquake had lasted an eternity in not much more than a minute.

Mickey Chang still stood in the doorframe, arms braced, eyes wide.

James Spencer spoke as calmly as he could, "Put on the light, Mickey."

The servant's eyes shifted from side to side and rolled upward to watch a trickle of plaster dust drift down. Then he slid his hand along the wall to the faceplate and flipped the switch. Nothing.

"Damned electricity." James Spencer sat up and began fishing under the bed.

Chang scurried over and found the slippers, which had done their own dance across the floor. "Wet. You piss on them again?"

"There's piss everywhere, Mickey. We'll clean it up later. Go and see to your wife."

"Wear your slippers . . . or put shoes on." Mickey Chang had served James Spencer for decades and stood on no ceremony. "I bet we got broken glass downstairs, too."

James Spencer slid his feet into the slippers and went to the window. In fifteen or twenty minutes, the rising sun would illuminate the devastation, but from his bedroom on the corner of California and Gough, with Van Ness below and Pacific Heights above, he could already see it.

To his right, up the hill, the brick façade of a new house had simply dropped off, and three stories of masonry now lay in the street, shrouded in a fog of dust.

But to his left, just down the hill, the Colemans' fine mansion stood foursquare and stalwart. That gave James Spencer some hope, because the same craftsmen had built his house.

Then he squinted down at the tracks and the steel plate in the middle of the street. He cocked an ear to listen for the hum of the cable that started spinning at precisely 5:00 A.M. at precisely 9.5 miles per hour, but he heard nothing.

As for the utility poles climbing up from Van Ness, every last one of them had snapped off, snapped like saplings. Now a great Aeolian harp of wires, the copper-alloyed symbols of modernity that carried electricity, telegraphic messages, and the telephonic sound of the human voice, lay in long, slack, useless strands. One of the wires was sparking on the pavement, sending up a little cloud of blue smoke.

A door opened across the street. Spencer's neighbor, Matt Dooling, in bare feet and nightshirt, staggered onto his veranda and looked about, as if to convince himself that it was not a dream. Then he scratched his bald head and went back into his house.

And James Spencer turned to his daily routine.

He made an effort to refill the chamber pot, which met with some trickling success. Then he dressed in the brown suit that Chang had set out for him the night before. He chose a red cravat because red would project confidence when he sat for breakfast at the Bohemian Club. But he did not call for hot water, because on Wednesdays he took a shave in the barber shop in the Spencer Building, and he expected that by eight o'clock, the city would be getting back to normal. So he would do his part.

JAMES SPENCER'S MORNING ABLUTIONS took twenty minutes and included two aftershocks. Then, fully and finely dressed, he went to the top of the stairs, looked down, and decided that he and his wife had built well. The staircase rose straight and undamaged. The oak pillars that supported it and the oak balusters that separated it from the foyer all appeared plumb upright.

But at the bottom, he saw how the earth had throttled the mansion known as Arbella House. The chandelier had fallen from the fifteen-foot ceiling and smashed into a thousand pieces. The wires holding up the huge, gilt-framed mirror had snapped. The mirror remained miraculously upright, leaning against the wall, but the glass had shattered.

James Spencer straightened his shoulders, tugged at the points of his vest, and smoothed the broken reflection of his cravat. Then he turned to the library at the front of the house.

His collection of books, his California histories, including the complete works of H. H. Bancroft in red morocco, the rare books he had bought from the old Spanish missions along El Camino Real, and all the works of San Francisco's "local color" school—his Bret Hartes, Jack Londons, and Mark Twains—had all been jolted from their cases. Books now covered the floor.

He picked up the volume at his feet—*Roughing It*. He glanced at the inscription: *To the Spencers, who knew where to find the* real *gold. Best Wishes, Mark Twain.*

He did not inventory the damage. There would be time enough for that later.

He turned instead from the dark woodwork and heavy draperies of the library to the other side of the foyer, to the bright sunlight and golden walls of the parlor. He glanced at the portrait above the fireplace. It had not budged because it was screwed to the wall. It was like its subject. It endured.

Janiva Toler Spencer wore a proud expression and a green dress in the portrait, the expression formed by raised chin and arched brow, the color carefully matched to the tile surround on the fireplace. She had planned it that way, he thought. She had been an excellent planner.

"Well, my dear," he said, "it seems we've had a little shake."

She answered, but only inside his head, and only for him.

Then he heard the pantry door scrape open. Something new, he thought. That door had never scraped before.

Mickey Chang pushed through with a tray: coffeepot, cup, newspaper. "In here or in conservatory?"

"The conservatory, as usual."

Mickey just stood there in his black mandarin jacket and silk hat.

James Spencer knew his servant well. Mickey Chang's hesitations and movements and grunts and silences all formed part of the unspoken language of master and man.

James Spencer said, "Is the conservatory—?"

"Maybe in here. Not so much broken glass in here."

Spencer felt the weight of the day pressing on his chest. He gave the portrait another glance and went into the dining room.

As Mickey poured the coffee and opened the *Chronicle,* the house rattled with another aftershock.

James Spencer pretended to ignore it, like the seasoned San Franciscan he was. He sipped his coffee, read the news, then turned to the review of *Carmen,* which had premiered at the Opera House the night before, featuring the legendary Enrico Caruso. Spencer had considered going. He still liked to be seen out and about in the city he had helped to build. But a heartburn had kept him at home, and it was starting up again.

He was studying an advertisement for Bromo-Seltzer, wondering if it might put out the fire in his chest, when the back door banged open and Mrs. Cooney's brogue filled the kitchen. She was his cook. Every morning, she rode the California Street cable car all the way from the Slot, the tough neighborhood on the other side of Market Street. Ordinarily, she got straight to work. But today, she pushed through the creaking door and right into the dining room.

James Spencer barely looked up. "Good morning, Mrs. Cooney."

"It ain't a good mornin' at all, sir, I hate to say."

"Did you see much damage, then?"

"I did indeed. Damage everywhere. But it ain't the damage that's been done, sir. It's what's comin'."

"Coming? What's coming?"

"Fires, sir." Grace Cooney stepped back, as if she had delivered a blow. "There's . . . there's fires breakin' out everywhere."

"Fires?" James Spencer felt a new thump of pain in his chest.

Mrs. Cooney wiped the sweat from her forehead. "Must be half a dozen last time I looked. And there's gas hissin' somethin' terrible, sir, all over town, right out of holes in the ground it's comin'."

James Spencer had feared that. Fire, not earthquake, had always been San Francisco's greatest enemy. He went back into the parlor and looked east along California Street. And yes, gray smoke was fogging the sky beyond Nob Hill.

Mrs. Cooney said, "The fires is all south of Market Street, sir. But the thing of it is . . . they're spreadin'. That's why we rode up here in the horse cart, me girl and me. We loaded up what we could and come over the hill. It's for certain the fires'll burn through everything south of Market, sir. Then . . . well, before long, it'll be just one big fire."

"Calm yourself, Grace," said James Spencer. "The best fire department in America is right here in San Francisco."

"That may be, sir, but the thing of it is . . . there's no water."

"No water?"

"I seen the lads openin' hydrants all over, and nary a drop did they get. Busted mains, I'm thinkin'. And you can't put out a fire if the hydrant's as dry as a fence post."

James Spencer looked again at the distant smoke, then turned to Mickey Chang, who had been listening to every word. "Start the Ariel."

"The Ariel? Where we goin'? Not to the fire!"

"To the office. To get our papers. And my journal. I must get my journal."

James Spencer always rode in the front passenger seat and let Mickey Chang do the driving. He liked to watch the world speed by, and he liked the looks they got when people saw his chauffeur, looks that said, "Who knew a Chinaman could drive an autocar?"

And the Ariel was fast. It had a big four-cylinder engine that could push the car along at forty miles an hour. But that was not why James Spencer had bought it. Nor did he buy it because it was built in Boston, as his friends suggested. And he did not buy it for the rich forest-green color, the seats of tufted brown leather, or the distinctive horse-collar grille. He bought it because of the advertising: *As fast on the hills as most cars are on the level.* That, he said, made it a car that was *made* for San Francisco.

While he waited for Mickey, he stood on the porch and studied the sky. The sun was up full now. The morning air was warming. The breeze came out of the northwest, so he did not smell smoke. But he knew that he had to hurry. He kept the business records of Arbella Shipping and Mercantile in fireproof safes, but he had locked the original journal and transcription into his desk on the fifth floor. And oak desks burned.

He took off his homburg and waved impatiently at his servant. The Ariel coughed and came puttering out of the barn. Spencer gripped the handrail, pulled himself into the seat, and said, "Don't drive over any live wires. And don't dawdle."

"I never dawdle." Mickey had replaced his indoor silk cap with a felt fedora. Had he added a suit and cravat instead of his mandarin jacket, thought Spencer, he might have passed for a white man. He said, "Just don't be givin' so many damn orders when I drive."

There were no other cars on the street, but people were everywhere now. Some had come out, half dressed or still in nightclothes, to move as aimlessly about as sleepwalkers. If they glanced at Mickey Chang, they did not register shock that a Chinaman was driving. They had no more shock to give. Others were standing on sidewalks, gazing toward the columns of smoke rising beyond Nob Hill. Still others, the industrious ones, the ones made for crisis, the ones who had built the city and would rebuild it, too, they had shaken off the shock and were already attacking the rubble.

As the Ariel rolled through the intersection of California and Van Ness, James Spencer looked left and right. The fine big houses that lined the avenue had survived with little damage, despite the heaved sidewalks and uprooted cobblestones.

But another block brought them to Polk, a business street that served the wealthy of Van Ness and Pacific Heights. And here James Spencer saw devastation. Bricks littered the street. Plate-glass windows had exploded from storefronts and sprayed shards everywhere. Other storefronts had simply collapsed onto the sidewalks.

They passed a man sitting on a broken curbstone. He was weeping. In front of him lay a cart, and still attached to it, a horse killed by a falling chimney. The man looked up and said something in a foreign language. It sounded like Italian.

James Spencer told Mickey to keep driving.

But they could not go quickly because there, in the swale between Nob Hill and Pacific Heights, it seemed as if the earth had actually split open. Great chunks of pavement had broken and heaved like tide-driven ice floes in some frozen East Coast harbor. And the steel rails of the cable track had twisted right up out of the ground.

At the intersection of Hyde Street, the views north and south were the same: buildings knocked off their foundations, power lines snapped and sparking, choppy rivulets of cobblestone and pavement, puffs of smoke, and people struggling to make sense of it all beneath a brilliant blue sky.

Mickey Chang wheeled around a chest of drawers jolted from the second floor of a building that had lost its entire façade. James Spencer could look into all four rooms—neat parlor, dining room, two upstairs bedrooms. An old woman was sitting in a rocking chair in the parlor, staring out at the street and rocking . . . and staring . . . and rocking. . . .

Just below Leavenworth, they came upon a group of men digging with bare hands into a small mountain of bricks that muffled a woman's cries for help.

Mickey gave a look. Should they stop? James Spencer pointed ahead.

So the Ariel climbed to the top of Nob Hill, where the mighty mansions, side by side, proclaimed that this was a place beyond wealth. The richest San Franciscans sought the heights. The richest men built their homes where the views were majestic and the breezes fair and others of their breed had built, too.

Names like Crocker, Stanford, Huntington, and Hopkins—the Big Four—echoed from the earliest days of the Gold Rush. Their fortunes, born of the picks and shovels they sold to the miners, had matured into unassailable, unimaginable wealth when the Transcontinental Railroad made them titans.

James Spencer had done business with all of them. He had been welcomed into their homes. And he had welcomed them to Arbella House, the envy of any who visited, unless they visited Nob Hill first. Here was a fanciful world of turrets and towers, of marble and brownstone, of Italianate palazzos and high Victorian castles, houses so huge that they competed for grandeur with the new Fairmont Hotel, perched on the edge of the summit. But beyond the hotel, columns of smoke were rising, gray and foreboding.

Mickey said, "Maybe the fire will follow the smoke and burn toward the bay."

"Let's hope so." James Spencer pointed ahead. "Keep driving."

Mickey steered across the top of the hill, avoiding piles of rubble, a cornice that had dropped from one of the houses, holes that had opened around sewer covers and water lines. At the intersection of Mason and California, with the glittering Fairmont on their left and the Mark Hopkins house on their right, he pulled the brake and stopped.

Below them, hundreds of people were surging up the steep California Street incline, fleeing the fire with their belongings on their backs. Hundreds more were watching. A few had even set out chairs, as if the scene were part of some grand opera that would all be over in a few hours.

James Spencer brought his hand to his chest. Mickey asked if he was all right.

"Just keep going," said Spencer.

So down the hill they went to Dupont Street, then Mickey turned right and wove through the jam of horse carts, autocars, and fire engines, avoiding the chunks of broken pavement and debris, and made it all the way to the corner of Post Street, where the fallen façade of a six-story building finally stopped them.

Directly ahead, on Market, the gray granite Spencer Building still stood. The cornice had fallen seven stories and lay in chunks on the pavement. The plate-glass windows that welcomed customers into a street-level barbershop, haberdasher's, and bookstore had all shattered. A huge crack ran up the side of the building. And in the sky beyond, a new column of smoke was coming to life, as silent and threatening as a snake.

Mickey looked up at the buildings and said, "You think all this burn?"

"I don't know. But the fires are closing in." James Spencer felt the impulse to run, to go as he had when he was a young man, in the days when he first saw this city, when it was nothing but shacks and tents and mud. So he jumped down and went.

Mickey turned off the engine and ran after his boss.

James Spencer was still steady on his feet. He credited his rock-ribbed New England ancestry, the hard work he had done in the gold fields, and the daily walk he took on the hills of his adopted city. He scrambled over the brick wreckage, ignoring the sound of someone screaming deep down in the rubble. Whoever they were, they were doomed. So he kept going, straight for the arched entrance of the Spencer Building.

To its left, the Palace Hotel gleamed in the sunlight, seven stories of glorious fancy—pillared, bay windowed, crenellated. On the roof, men were looking over the wrought-iron railing, looking down at the street, looking up at the smoke, preparing to fight for the grandest hotel in the West, using water drawn from a seven-hundred-thousand-gallon gravity-fed tank suspended above them.

So, thought James Spencer, his building would not ignite from that side. And to the right rose the eighteen-story Call Building, tallest structure in the city. Its steel frame construction had withstood the earthquake, and its modern fireproofing, Spencer hoped, would withstand the coming conflagration.

He took a deep breath, ignored the pain in his chest, and stumbled out into the middle of Market Street. It appeared as if an underground river had rolled in from the bay, run under the city's grandest avenue, flowed all the way to the other side of the peninsula, then receded, leaving instead of ripples in the sand, great rolls of earth; instead of gravel pockets, piles of broken cobblestone; instead of random boulders, huge deposits of fallen brick and finished stone; instead of dead trees, a tangle of twisted trolley tracks and utility wires.

"Hey, boss! Careful!" cried Mickey.

James Spencer looked down at the trolley track in front of him, took a step, and the cobblestones collapsed. His body tumbled toward the sinkhole that opened, and he would have dropped into the depths, but for the track rail. He straddled it, hit hard, and cried out. Mickey grabbed him by the collar before he tipped headfirst, then dragged him back and leaned him against a pile of rubble.

James Spencer felt as if he might vomit from the pain shooting up through his groin and into his kidneys.

Mickey squatted next to him. "Boss, you all right?"

"Yes, come on." James Spencer tried to stand.

"No. You stay. You as gray as the cobblestones."

"But Mickey—"

"I'll go. I know your desk. And I can run."

"But Mickey—"

"No more *buts.*" Mickey grabbed the gold chain on Spencer's vest.

The old man watched his servant's fingers work through the keys until they found the one for his desk and slipped it off the ring. He gripped Mickey Chang's hand. "The transcription is in the long ledger . . . and the notebooks. You know the seven notebooks. They're all in a single box."

"I know, boss. I know. Don't worry."

"If I don't . . . If I'm—"

"Come on, boss! If you *what?*" Mickey looked up as flames exploded from a store at Stockton Street. He wiped the sweat from his forehead and said again, "If you *what?*"

"If I don't make it through this—"

"Just stay here. I be right back."

A fire engine came careening around a corner. The bell was clanging. The hooves of the horses were pounding, thundering, sparking on the cobblestones and sending up great clods of dirt where the cobblestones had come loose.

James Spencer thought the engine might roar right over them, or hit a hole and fly into the air and land on top of them. But it sped past, though for all its energy it would be impotent against the unfolding disaster.

Spencer grabbed the baggy sleeve of Mickey Chang's jacket. "Give the transcribed journal to the historical society. The original chapters go to my children. Their names are on the folders . . . and—" He clutched his chest, as if he could hold in a sudden burst of pain.

"And *what*? What else, boss? I gotta go."

"Mickey, do this, and I will reward you."

"Ah, you're always sayin' that." Mickey jumped up and scrambled across the street, leaped over the broken stones on the sidewalk, and disappeared through the arched entrance of the Spencer Building.

"Reward you with a chapter of your own," said James Spencer, almost to himself.

A moment later, the ground shook again. Another aftershock. Two women on Market Street screamed and ran, as if aimless movement would protect them. Other people looked up, covered their heads, scattered. From somewhere back on Dupont came a roar and an explosion of brick dust. Spencer hoped that nothing had fallen on the Ariel.

As the shaking continued, the pain in his chest seemed to widen and deepen.

Then the huge sign above the fourth-floor windows of the Spencer Building broke off and came crashing down, turning once in the air before hitting the sidewalk and flying into a thousand pieces. The huge gilt letters had read Arbella Shipping and Mercantile.

ONE

Tuesday Morning

THE TEXT CAME IN overnight.

Peter Fallon read it when he got up around six thirty: "SFO to BOS. Redeye, boarding now. Early biz in town. Breakfast, Arbella Club, 7:30? JetBlue Flt 2034. LJ"

LJ was his son.

They had named the boy after his grandfather, who had been known in the Boston building trades as Big Jim Fallon. So it was only natural that they would call the first son of a new generation *Little* Jim. And when Little Jim topped six foot one, along about the time that Big Jim passed, they started calling the kid "LJ."

LJ Fallon was now an associate in the San Francisco law firm of Van Valen and Prescott. And he did not do things spontaneously. Every step he had ever taken—from the colonial in West Roxbury, where he grew up with Peter's ex and a stepfather, through Harvard, then law school, all the way to an office in the Transamerica Pyramid—had all appeared as part of a plan.

A surprise night flight across the country and an early breakfast with Dad? That defined "spur of the moment." Not like LJ at all.

Something was up.

So Peter showered and dressed, threw on a tweed sport coat, and grabbed his scally cap. Donegal herringbone, perfect for an autumn-crisp morning and the kind of cap that a smart-ass Boston guy might put on to proclaim his Irish heritage at Boston's oldest, most Yankee-fied social club, named for the ship that brought the Puritans to Massachusetts and renowned for its unrelenting prejudice against the children of the Irish potato famine, at least until the presidency of John F. Kennedy.

It puzzled Peter that LJ had joined the Arbella instead of some other Boston bastion, like the Harvard Club or the Somerset or even the Club of

Odd Volumes. Something to do with a girl, or with impressing the girl's family, but the girl had left the picture when LJ left for Boalt Hall, the Berkeley law school. This disappointed Peter on two fronts. He liked the girl, and he did not like the distance between Boston and Berkeley. At least the kid had a real job. He'd also kept his club membership, so maybe he might move home someday to use it.

Peter hurried along Marlborough, across the Public Garden, up Beacon Hill to Louisburg Square, a living monument to the three "b's" of nineteenth-century Boston architecture—bricks, bowfronts, and black shutters—encircling a fenced park where locals with gate keys could clean up after their dogs while inhaling all the high-toned history, too. Charles Bulfinch, famous Federalist architect, had lived on the square. So had the Alcotts, William Dean Howells, Robert Frost, even former Secretary of State John Kerry. The last house to sell here went for twelve million.

Peter sometimes thought he should have gone after the big bucks in Boston real estate. But he never regretted the path he chose. He had a long list of adventures, a longer list of clients, and one of the great brokerages for rare books and documents in America.

When someone needed a volume appraised, they turned to Peter. When someone needed some cash and decided to sell a presentation copy of a Mark Twain or a signed Lincoln letter, they turned to Peter. When someone learned of a lost first draft of the U. S. Constitution or some other treasure that needed finding for the good of the country and the wider world, they turned to Peter, because Peter . . . got it.

History mattered. The documents that let us touch it mattered. The buildings where it unfolded mattered. The whole parade of human beings in general and Americans in particular mattered. To study the past was to light the way to the future. That's what Peter liked to believe, anyway. That's why he did what he did. And he was good at it.

He was also good at going anywhere in Boston and looking like he belonged. He could stop for a quick shooter in some Southie bar, where they talked about sports, politics, and money and knocked back buck-a-bottle Buds at three in the afternoon, or he could visit the Arbella Club, where they talked about money, sports, and politics and sipped Far Niente Chardonnay at lunch, and he always fit in.

So he didn't bother to make a big flourish with the scally cap.

He climbed the Arbella Club stoop, rang the buzzer, and admired the polish on the brass door knocker. He also noticed a little hand-lettered sign in one of the sidelights: *No soliciting. All deliveries in the rear.* He imagined the *No Irish Need Apply* sign pasted discreetly into that spot a century before.

When the door opened, he removed the cap. But before he stepped in, three men pushed out. He made way. Exit before entry. Simple good manners.

He nodded, but they barely acknowledged him. This would not have surprised him with some members of the Arbella, except that these were not the usual Arbella types. One was black, one white, one Asian. All wore dark suits. Dark expressions, too. And the first two seemed, by their bulk and manner, to be working for the Asian. Security? At the Arbella Club?

Times, Peter concluded, were changing.

He stopped in the foyer to let his eyes adjust. The tall case clock chimed once for 7:30. In the library, two men and a woman were talking about something that sounded important. On the staircase, a waiter in a crimson jacket was carrying a coffee service. At the coat check under the stairs, a man was collecting his briefcase.

Peter approached the reception desk and said, "I'm a guest of Mr. Fallon." He liked referring to his son as "mister."

The maître d', in blue blazer and tie the same color as the waiters' jackets, gave a polite, "This way, sir," and led Peter into the dining room.

The sun poured through the east-facing bowfront, burnishing the mahogany furniture, illuminating the mural of old Boston on one wall and the portraits of old Bostonians on the other. Coffee cups and silverware chimed and chirped, but wall-to-wall carpet, patterned after the green and gold original, muffled the sound. So conversation merely murmured—business talk at some tables (but no work papers, please), leaf-peeping chitchat at others, where out-of-town reciprocals planned their foliage tours. It was morning in Boston. And there was no better place to enjoy it than the Arbella Club, or so this room would suggest.

LJ Fallon was sitting with his back to the door, reading *The Globe* sports page.

The waiter was clearing one round of plates and setting out another.

Peter said, "The Patriots need cornerbacks."

LJ looked up and brightened.

Peter remembered the expression. It said, *Dad's here.* It would always say that. And it would always give Peter a little twinge of pleasure and pain, because it was the face that greeted him whenever he came to collect the boy for a weekend visit. The divorce had been hard on LJ, and even now, after all these years, Peter still saw the same mixture of hurt and hope when he looked into his son's eyes.

He also saw the resemblance. From the day LJ was born, people said that he was a Fallon. He had the black hair, the strong brow, the wiry build. He was taller than his father, but that was as it should be. He was also smarter, as Peter would tell anyone. LJ could handle math and physics, subjects that Peter had ducked. So . . . smarter, yes, but short on experience and maybe a bit light on common sense, as every father who'd ever taken pride in a son's brains had reminded the boy at least once.

LJ glanced at the scally cap. "Nice touch."

"Subtle." Peter was pleased that his son got the joke. It meant that six years in San Francisco had not entirely drained the kid of his Boston attitude. Peter sat and slipped the cap onto the empty chair between them. "So . . . how was your flight?"

"Got some sleep, landed at five thirty, came straight here. Used the weight room, then showered." LJ's hair shone in the light, still a bit wet.

"You could have showered at my place."

"I didn't want to bother you so early, especially if Evangeline is there."

Peter shook his head. "She's in New York. She and I are—"

"On the outs?"

"Taking a break."

"Again?"

"There's a reason we're not married. A reason we live in different cities. We have lots of fun together. Then we don't. So—" Peter shrugged.

"I think you're pretty well suited."

But Peter didn't want to talk about Evangeline. Talking with your son about your girlfriend was just . . . wrong. Like kids imagining their parents having sex, or vice versa. He gestured to the coffee stains on the tablecloth. "You already had a meeting?"

"Yeah." LJ laughed. "No rest for the weary."

The old waiter returned with a coffeepot and a fresh cup. LJ thanked him by name. The waiter smiled as if not everyone remembered his name. Then he filled the cups and asked if they would like to order from the menu.

No. Father and son would take the buffet, thanks. But first, some chitchat.

Peter asked, "How's this new girlfriend?"

"She's one of the things I wanted to talk with you about."

"Oh?" Peter took a sip of coffee.

"No spit takes, Dad. But . . . I think she's the one."

Peter swallowed and set down the cup. He always proceeded with caution in conversations like this. He liked everyone who came into his son's life, until he was told not to. "You *think*?"

"Oh, hell, I know." LJ broke into a grin. "I gave her a ring last week. We've been living together for three months."

So that was why LJ had crossed the country, to tell his father about his engagement. He wasn't in trouble. He hadn't lost his job. No one was suing him for malfeasance or misfeasance or any other kind of feasance.

Peter relaxed for the first time since he'd seen that text. "Congratulations. If she's the one, I'm happy for you."

"You'll like her. She's smart. Pretty. Funny. And . . . she's also half Chinese."

Peter noticed his son's eyes shift. The little boy again, telling his father something that he was not certain would meet with approval.

Peter said, "Just half?"

"Her late mother came from an old Chinatown family. Her father's white."

Peter said, "I can't wait to meet her." He almost asked what the kid was so worried about. Chinese, Japanese, Indian . . . it didn't matter to Peter. He had dated plenty of women from outside the Irish-American gene pool. A gorgeous black history professor who wrote a book about Lincoln. An Algerian beauty he met at the Paris Book Fair. And of course, a daughter of old Boston privilege named Evangeline Carrington.

But Jimmy was popping up, as if relieved to have that business out of the way. "Let's get some food. I'm starving."

The buffet stretched along the wall, beneath portraits of the club presidents. At one end, above stacked plates and bowls, loomed the face of the eighteenth-century founder, far less famous than his portraitist, John Singleton Copley. At every stop, cold New England faces looked down on warming dishes of bacon and French toast, a bubbling pot of "porridge," bowls of fruit salad, and Danish pastries in raspberry, apple, and, of course, prune.

Thaddeus Spencer, wearing a brown cutaway and red silk cravat, hung over the scrambled eggs. His jaw was set hard against whatever wind was blowing in his face. He looked like a man of business, and not only a man who was good at his own business but one who could, if called upon, make it his business to mind yours.

Peter whispered to LJ, "Do you think he'll complain if I take an extra sausage?"

"He may be the smartest guy on this wall. He persuaded the board to buy a double bowfront on Louisburg Square in 1836. This building's worth twenty million."

LJ dropped a few more sausages onto his father's plate and said, "I'm here to talk to one of his Boston descendants. And I want to talk to you about his San Francisco son."

So there it was, thought Peter. Something *was* up.

THE STORY SPILLED OUT over breakfast: At the behest of senior partner Johnson "Jack" Barber, LJ was overseeing the liquidation of the Spencer estate.

"I thought your specialty was corporate stuff, mergers and acquisitions—"

"When a senior partner asks you to do something, Dad, you do it. It's how you climb the ladder."

Peter popped a piece of sausage into his mouth and said, "How can I help?"

"Appraise the Spencer rare book collection. James Spencer was the son of the guy on the wall behind me. He went to the Gold Rush, had adventures, did well. His company lasted until the 1990s, when corporate raiders dismantled what was left of it. Now the family is liquidating the estate, house and all, including the Spencer library."

"How many books?"

"Maybe two thousand. All good stuff. A complete H. H. Bancroft, signed Mark Twains, old Spanish manuscripts."

"A few days of work, but a few days in San Francisco? Hell, yeah. I can get the Hangtown fry at Tadich's and the Shanghai soup dumplings at Great Eastern, go for a hike in the Muir Woods, *and* meet my future daughter-in-law."

LJ took a sip of coffee and said, "It's a little more complicated than that."

Peter was not surprised. "It always is."

"Spencer kept a journal."

"He was part of a literate generation. They saw the Gold Rush as the great adventure of their lives. So a lot of them wrote about it."

"He transcribed his and gave it to the California Historical Society. But about a year ago, it disappeared."

"And you want me to find it?"

"I want you to help me reconstruct it. The last great-granddaughter, named Maryanne Rogers, died without issue. She put a codicil into her will that before the liquidation of the estate, all seven original sections of the journal, scattered among the heirs, should be gathered and digitized, so that—I quote—'the world may read a document essential to California's history, even if it starts another gold rush.'"

"Another gold rush?"

"She was a little batty."

"But another gold rush? That sounds like a big deal." Peter took a sip of coffee and looked into his son's eyes.

The little boy flickered for just a moment, only to be replaced by the level gaze of the young man on the rise.

The father said, "There's more here, isn't there?"

"Well, the heirs have their own agendas."

"Heirs always do." Peter leaned across the table. "If memory serves correctly there is a certain Spencer heir named Sturgis. Is he in on this?"

"He's in on everything." LJ looked down again, a bit guilty. "But Dad, you're the man for the job, no matter *who* else is involved. So, what about it?"

"Another gold rush . . . difficult heirs . . . strange codicils in a batty old woman's will. How did she die?"

"Hit in a crosswalk."

"Wait, wait, don't tell me. Hit-and-run, right?"

"Don't be sarcastic." LJ sipped a little coffee. "But, yeah. She lived in the old family mansion on California Street. It's called Arbella House, believe it or not."

"So this James Spencer remembered his Boston roots."

LJ cut into a sausage. "Every Thursday, Mrs. Rogers doddered down California to Van Ness, then three blocks to the House of Prime Rib. She always ordered two martinis and a big plate of beef—"

"House Cut or City Cut?" said Peter.

"You've eaten there?" LJ laughed. "When it comes to food, Dad always knows."

"And when it comes to hit-and-runs, Dad's always suspicious."

"She was hit in the crosswalk at Sacramento. White panel truck. They never found the driver."

"Anybody else with her?"

"Mr. Yung, the butler. He survived."

"Witnesses? Other than the butler or Colonel Mustard?"

"Come on, Dad, don't be sarcastic. My boss, Johnson Barber, was waiting for her in front of the restaurant. She liked it when an important San Franciscan of the masculine variety escorted her around town."

"A full-service law firm." Peter looked again into his son's eyes, then up at the eyes of the portraits on the wall. The eyes in the portraits did not shift, unlike his son's.

"So," said Peter, "it was either an accident, or somebody wants to get this journal reconstituted quickly, and offing the batty old heiress was the only way to do it?"

LJ sipped his coffee, as if to say, *Point made.*

Peter buttered his croissant. "Has anybody told you what this new gold rush would look like?"

"All I know is that we are trying to find seven notebooks that created the finished version of James Spencer's journal."

"Put them together and you get . . . what? A treasure map? The location of a buried gold stash? Or is it a gold vein?"

"Maybe all three. Maybe something international. But yeah, there's more to this than meets the eye."

"There always is," said Peter again.

"If I find the notebooks, my treasure is the goodwill of Mr. Johnson 'Jack' Barber, senior partner at Van Valen and Prescott."

Peter did not need to think it over or ask any more questions. He loved a challenge, like reconstructing a Gold Rush journal. He loved to go after something with a bigger story, and between the Revolution and the Civil War, there was no bigger American story than the Gold Rush. He also loved searching for a pot of gold, and here was real gold, maybe in a real pot. Most importantly, he loved helping his son, even when the son's eyes said he was hiding something. So, Peter offered his hand. "Deal."

And LJ's cell phone buzzed. Half the people in the room jumped. LJ fumbled into his pocket, pulled out the phone, put it on silent. By then, the maître d' was beside him. "Excuse me, sir, but cell phones are—"

LJ put up his hand, apologized, and stood, "Dad, I have to take this."

The maître d' gestured toward a door at the end of the buffet. "The cell-phone booth is that way, sir."

LJ told his father, "Check your email. I sent you the first section of the journal, just to whet your appetite. Passed down from Maryanne Rogers, typed by my secretary."

"So that means we only have to find six?"

"See? The job is already easier than you thought."

Peter took out his phone and saw first that he had a text from Evangeline: "RE: weekend. Driving or AMTRAK? And what ETA in NYC?"

After a two-month "trial separation," Peter and Evangeline were planning a weekend in New York. Plays, museums, dinners, all on her turf.

Peter didn't want to blow her off. But his son almost never asked him for anything. So he texted back: "How about trip to San Fran instead? Doing job for LJ."

Text answer: "Are you lying? No using son as excuse."

"No lie. Come along. On me. Separate beds."

"Side trips? Just pitched article on California old-vine Zins."

"Side trips to old-vine vineyards, yes. Side trips with old-vine boyfriends . . . up to you. Although a certain boyfriend unavoidable."

That boyfriend would be Manion Sturgis, Spencer descendant.

Her answer: "OK. I'll book the Mark Hopkins. Separate beds."

"Drinks at the Top of the Mark, on me."

Then Peter clicked to the email, opened the link to the journal pages, and saw the beginnings of a grand national adventure. Sixty pages, starting on January 10, 1849. He glanced up at the portrait of Thaddeus Spencer, who would have been hanging right there on that very day, then he began to read. And to his astonishment, the first entry brought him to exactly where he was sitting. . . .

The Journal of James Spencer—Notebook #1
January 10, 1849
My Iliad Begins

The day had come. I had made my decision. I would do what drove me and not what tradition prescribed.

I know that this displeased my father. Thaddeus Spencer may have passed on to the heavenly counting-house where God now provided him with ledgers to balance and coins to number and then to balance and number again, like Sisyphus on holiday, but his eyes still stared down upon me from his portrait, as they would upon any who ever again called for a plate of oysters or a tureen of duck liver pâté in the Arbella Club dining room. And those eyes did not approve . . . of anything.

I had determined, as our friend Richard Henry Dana had put it, to serve my time "before the mast," to live fully in the world of men, visit our distant shores, and write of my adventures. I would "see the elephant" before settling down to a life as remunerative and yet as unremarkable as my father's. And so, on that bright, cold Wednesday, I had invited to the Arbella Club my brother and five women whom I loved or merely tolerated— sometimes simultaneously—so that they might hear the words of two men named Samuel, one who always encouraged me and one who left me quietly intimidated.

I had not revealed that last bit to my mother. I had forewarned her of my announcement, so she was unhappy enough already. She took her seat at the round table, with her husband's portrait peering over her shoulder and her other children flanking her like an honor guard, and she pursed her lips at me in long-suffering disappointment.

To her left sat Diana, the slightly more cheerful of my siblings.

Beside Diana, the portly Samuel Batchelder, editor of the *Boston Transcript*, admired the champagne bubbling into his glass. To his left, his wife, Hallie, maintained a stream of happy chatter about the depth of the snow in Louisburg Square, the beauties of the new Boston mural on the wall behind me, and the miracle of the even newer, green-and-gold Belgian-loom carpet on the floor.

My brother, Thaddeus Jr., sat at Mother's right like the Spencer prince regent, a title that was his inheritance by virtue of his place in the birth order and his due by virtue of his efforts in the family business.

His wife, Katherine, a meddlesome ninny with a crinkling eye and an irritating laugh, was crinkling her whole face in my direction, as if the prospect of planning a spring wedding appealed to her almost as much as the prospect of spring itself.

The object of her speculations, Miss Janiva Toler, sat next to me.

Our recent appearances about town—at museums, musicales, and poetry readings—had set Boston to wondering. Would this be the young lady to capture James Spencer? The answer would be no . . . for the moment. And when I returned from my adventure, the answer might still be no . . . forever. It was a chance I had to take.

Until she graced you with her smile, Janiva usually presented a dour expression to the world. But on this day, her jaw seemed to have grown so heavy with disappointment that she could do no more than keep her mouth tightly shut, or it might drop open, causing her to resemble one of those old women who wears lead-matrix dentures and goes about looking as if the weight of the world may not be on her shoulders but is surely in her mouth.

The heaviest weight at the table, however, the true force of gravity, sat opposite Sam Batchelder, between my sister-in-law and Janiva. He did not make much in the way of small talk but greeted each guest cordially, then took his seat and allowed the conversation to flow around himself as the rock allows the stream.

While the ladies were most solicitous of him, the coolness of his demeanor suggested that he did not find female attentions unusual. Of course, the ladies would have been solicitous even if he were not, as my sister whispered when he entered the dining room, "as darkly handsome as Byron himself, in black velvet cutaway and gold waistcoat." Samuel Hodges's wife had died eleven months earlier, leaving him with two small daughters. So ladies were inclined to see tender bereavement beneath his black brow. I saw the rock and the rock-hard surety of an experienced man.

The waiters—in crimson cutaways and breeches—finished pouring the champagne. Then the two Samuels exchanged glances, and Batchelder raised his glass.

"A toast," he proclaimed, "to the monthly ladies' lunch and our female guests, who bring to this masculine space a refinement that inspires us all."

"Here, here," said Hodges, and we gentlemen concurred.

Hallie Batchelder, who was happily taken in by her husband's charms, gave a giggle, took a drink, and said, "Oh, Sam, you're too kind."

My mother, who had never been taken in by charms of any sort—which may have explained her attraction to my father—barely touched her glass to her lips.

"And now"—Sam Batchelder aimed his glass at Hodges and me—"to the Sagamore Mining Company. May they pass safely to California and leave there a bright example of New England democracy . . . while leaving with all the gold they can carry."

It was plain that this toast brought consternation to the table.

My sister, easily consternated, said, "Who are the Sagamore Mining Company?"

"*We* are," I answered. "Samuel Hodges and I and ninety-eight more, a joint stock company going to the Gold Rush on the ship *William Winter.* We leave Friday."

"The Gold Rush?" said my brother.

"That crazy thing in California?" said my sister.

"The very thing," said I. "And a *real* thing. So says the president of the United States."

"But the wedding," said Katherine. "I thought this was about the wedding."

And Janiva broke her silence. "There's not to be a wedding . . . at least for now."

"Oh, James," said Katherine, seeing her spring plans fade, "how could you?"

"A fair question." My mother pursed her lips even more tightly.

Hallie Batchelder tried to change the subject. "I . . . I love champagne, so decadent in the middle of the day, and so icy cold."

"Chilled out in the snow, my dear," said her husband.

"From the faces I see around me," said Samuel Hodges, "we might have chilled it right here at the table."

"Forgive us, Mr. Hodges"—my mother haughtily raised her chin—"but I had hoped for news of my son's engagement to Miss Toler. Instead we learn that he is bound for a barbarous shore and foreign country."

"The territory of Alta California is now an American possession, ma'am." Hodges spoke neither aggressively nor defensively, as if facts were facts and needed no adverbs. "It's been so since the Treaty of Guadalupe Hidalgo last year."

"I daresay," offered my brother, "had Mexico known of the gold, they might have driven a harder bargain."

"I doubt it," said Hodges. "They are an inferior people."

"How do you come by such knowledge, sir?" asked my brother.

I explained that Hodges was supercargo for the Boston Leather Works. "So he's been to California many times to procure hides."

"They called you Bostoños, do they not?" asked Sam Batchelder.

Hodges nodded. "When word goes out that a Boston ship has entered the great bay, the rancheros slaughter their cattle by the thousands to trade."

"What leads you to conclude that they are inferiors?" asked my sister.

"Why, their indolence, miss. They take only the hide and leave the rest to rot in the open country . . . sirloin for the vultures, rump steak for the dogs."

The plain-speaking Mr. Hodges was bringing a harsh new level of discourse to the ladies' lunch. "These Spaniards and their Mexican serfs are not worthy of California's bounty. I'm glad we've taken it from them."

"All I know," said my mother, "is that California is more than six months away."

"There's no time to waste, then, is there?" said Sam Batchelder.

My mother turned her eye onto our old family friend. "What are you after, Sam?"

"Dispatches from the Gold Rush," I said, "And I'm going to deliver them. I've always wanted to be a writer, Mother, not a businessman. This is my chance."

My sister said, "What makes you think you're even half the writer that Dickie Dana is? You've never written anything more than a love letter in your life."

I was tempted to say that she should not comment on love letters, as she had received so few of them. But I would not see her for a very long time, so I refrained from hurting her feelings and said, "I know that I've written too many ledger entries."

And Hodges took my part. "Your brother will chronicle our efforts, miss, to show New Englanders how a noble band of their own kind shapes a world-historical event."

"Noble?" My brother scoffed. "How noble can a shipload of fortune hunters be?"

"How noble?" Hodges swung his big head at my brother, like an ox swinging a horn at something that annoyed him. "In California, we will demonstrate the quality of our breeding, sir. A hundred Christian New Englanders, all signing articles of incorporation, all putting up bonds of three hundred dollars apiece for tools, food, and provisions, all prepared to confront the disorder and chaos of California—"

"Just a moment"—my brother raised a finger, a gesture of pure pomposity learned from my father—"James can make his own decisions about where he goes and what he does. He's twenty-four. He's of age. But if he's pledging company funds—"

"You are a small-minded man, Mr. Thaddeus Spencer, Junior." Hodges's tone could have chilled a jeroboam of champagne, let alone a few glasses.

Sam Batchelder tried to thaw things. "Now, Thaddeus, the fact is that the *Transcript* is putting up the bond for your brother."

"If you think it's such a good idea, Sam, why not go yourself?" asked my mother.

"Someone needs to stay and edit your son's dispatches. Besides"—Sam patted his belly—"I'm too fat."

"You get seasick, too," said Hallie.

"So does James," said my mother.

"Seasickness passes," I said.

"Death does not," answered my mother.

"Oh, Abigail," said Sam Batchelder, "they're picking up gold by the fistful out there. A series of dispatches from one of our own? It'll be a sensation."

As my elders batted my fate about like a shuttlecock, my eye was drawn to the waiter filling Hallie Batchelder's water glass. He was new and was doing something unheard of on the staff. He was listening to our conversation, listening with such rapt attention that the glass came close to overflowing.

But no one else noticed him. They never noticed the waiters. They were all listening to Sam Batchelder tell my mother, "Half the young men in

America are headed west, half of Europe, too. Don't keep James from the story of the century."

"The story of the century," asked my brother, "or the myth?"

"The myth, yes"—my sister rolled her eyes—"the myth of the Golden Fleece."

I was beginning to think that I should have left without saying good-bye to anyone but Janiva. So I asked them, "If Miss Toler understands, why can't my family?" I took her hand, which rested on the table beside mine. And her touch told me that she did *not* understand . . . or approve. It was limp and cold. And suddenly it was wet.

The waiter had reached between us to fill her glass, which overflowed and spilled onto her sleeve. He snatched the towel from his arm and sopped the water on the table. Then he began daubing at Janiva herself.

She pulled away. "It's all right. It's quite all right."

Hodges said, "Pay attention to your own business, mister, or I'll have your job."

"Yes, sir. Sorry, sir." The waiter hurried away.

But something about him annoyed Samuel Hodges, whose dark eyes followed him all the way to the kitchen door.

Sam Batchelder, however, kept talking. "This is no myth. A tea caddy containing two hundred and thirty ounces of fine gold, carried across the continent by military courier, put on display in Washington? *That* is evidence of glittering reality."

My brother scoffed. My sister rolled her eyes. My mother pursed her lips.

CONVERSATION CALMED AFTER THAT, perhaps because even when upset, the Yankee stomach is always ready for chowder, which was soon emerging from the kitchen.

An ancient waiter named Jonas led with a silver ladle and a towel on his arm.

The new man followed, holding the tureen with the grandest of cere-mony, extending it to arm's length, moving with a measured gait, not tak-ing his eyes from it, as if by watching it he could keep from sloshing it. But he was not only ceremonious. He was slow. And the tip of his tongue peeked out of the corner of his mouth, proclaiming that he was nervous, too. What-ever experience he had gained from life had plainly not come in service. Nevertheless, he arrived at the table without spilling a drop.

I gave him a nod, as if to let him know that I approved. He winked, as if to say that he had just put one over on all of us, except perhaps for me.

Ladies first, Jonas ladled, and the aroma set my mouth to watering.

But our new waiter seemed distracted. Jonas had to give him a hard jerk of the head to bring him along from my mother's place to my sister's and so on.

Sam Batchelder watched the chowder fill his wife's cup as a child watches the cutting of his own birthday cake. "Hurry, Jonas, before the ladies' chowder cools."

"I can't wait." Hallie Batchelder dipped her spoon.

My mother pursed her lips at the woman she sometimes called "Hungry Hallie."

Jonas stepped to Janiva's shoulder and again jerked his head.

My brother said, "Our new man's a bit of a laggard, Jonas. What's his name?"

"It's Michael, sir," answered Jonas.

My brother flicked his eyes at the new man. "Where do you hail from, Michael?"

The waiter said, "Unh . . . I . . . I hail from . . . the . . . the—"

"Come now, man," said Hodges, "you must know where you were born."

"The British Isles, sir."

By now, everyone had noticed his accent.

Hodges gave a snort, as if deciding whether to charge. "*Which* British Isle?"

Through clenched teeth, old Jonas whispered, "Go back to the kitchen, Michael. You're wanted in the kitchen. Go back. Go."

"*Which* British Isle?" repeated Hodges, as if he already knew the answer.

My brother stroked his beard and said, "The second largest of them, I suspect."

"That would be Ireland," said my sister, forever proud of her geographical knowledge, though she had seldom traveled much beyond Boston Light.

"You mean this fellow's Irish?" said my mother. "Irish? Call the club secretary."

"Hightower!" shouted my brother. "Mr. Hightower!"

Mother grumbled, "Bad enough that we have to put up with them on our streets—"

But for the muffled sound of Hightower's footfalls on the new carpet, the dining room had gone quiet.

Jonas reached for the tureen. Michael pulled it back, sending creamy hot chowder sloshing and splattering. I jumped up to avoid it and snatched Janiva out of the way, too.

Hallie Batchelder gave out with another, "Oh, dear." And while she was distracted, her husband slid her chowder over and spooned some into his mouth.

I might have found the whole scene hilarious, except that Hodges had picked up his butter knife and was wiping it off so methodically that it appeared something he had done before, with sharper knives. Skinning knives, perhaps.

So I put myself between Janiva and the Irish waiter and told him to hand over the tureen.

He looked into my eyes, then into the chowder, as if deciding whether to give it to me or throw it at me. He was slightly shorter than I, not much older, with black hair and refined features quite unlike those of the ape-like Micks caricatured in the newspapers. He glanced at Hodges, then he grinned and proffered the tureen, "If you think you can do a better job, sir—"

By now, the cadaverous Mr. Hightower had reached our table. "Back to the kitchen with you, Michael. There's dishes to be washed—"

"—and debts to be paid." Michael Flynn plunked the tureen on the table and retreated.

Hightower pulled Janiva's chair out and invited her to sit again. He told Jonas to get a damp towel and sop up the splatters. He invited Hodges to enjoy another bottle of champagne "compliments of the club secretary."

"Never mind the champagne." Hodges dropped his butter knife on his plate with a rattle. "I want that Mick out. Out today. He was listening to our conversation."

The Irish waiter stopped at the kitchen door, his back to us but his ear cocked.

Hightower was saying, "He claimed he was a Scot, sir. We hired him to wash dishes, but today we needed—"

The Irishman turned on his heels, as if he had come to a decision, and announced, "I ain't a Scot. I ain't a Brit. And I ain't the sultan of Turkey." He stalked back. "Michael Flynn's the name, and as Irish as Paddy's pig I am, a poor refugee—"

"Be quiet," said Hodges.

"—from the rocky fields of Galway, where the potatoes turn to black mush and the people die from starvation." He pushed past Hightower and grabbed the ladle from Jonas. "And I can see that I've been called by the Good Lord himself to save all you fine folks from the same sad fate. So I'm needed right here. Not in the fuckin' kitchen!"

"In the *what* kitchen?" said Hallie Batchelder.

"Cover your ears, dear," said her husband.

"So I'll finish chowderin' up the lot of ye's, or you'll all think less of me and me race!"

"We could not think less of you than we do," said Hodges.

"Then let me change your mind." Michael dunked the ladle and splashed chowder into Hodges's cup. "Eat that. It'll take the edge off your temper."

Then he splashed another measure into Hallie Batchelder's cup. "You, too, darlin', but get it down quick before your fat-guts husband steals it all."

My brother jumped to his feet, "We don't want your chowder. We don't want you in our club. We don't want you or your kind in our city."

"And I don't want to be here," said Michael Flynn, "but life don't always work out, now, does it? I'm payin' the debts me sister owes for makin' the mistake of dyin' in a miserable room in a miserable hovel called Hightower House, in a miserable Boston slum called Fort Hill. Until I work off them debts, Hightower's weasel of a brother is holdin' all her property, includin' the only thing dear to me in the world."

"Be quiet," whispered Hightower.

The Irishman looked at my mother. "'Tis a fine daguerreotype of me and me sister and our own dear mother, taken a month before she died."

My mother pursed her lips and looked away, as if she could not care in the least.

"Oh, yes, ma'am," said Michael Flynn, "we Irish have mothers, too."

"*Dams* is a better word," said Samuel Hodges.

"Dams? Dams, is it? A dam is a female breed horse, sir. Not a human person."

Hodges leaned back and folded his arms, as if to say that was exactly his point.

"If you're callin' me sainted Irish mother a dumb animal, I'll be askin' you to step outside. And we won't be fightin' with butter knives. Bare knuckles it'll be, to the count of ten."

Hodges pushed back his chair to stand.

But the Irishman grinned. He seemed well-skilled at starting fires, then throwing water on them. "Of course, if you're callin' her a fine thoroughbred, which is usually what it means when you put a sire to a dam in the sport of kings, I accept the compliment. So take your seat and eat up. You'll need your strength for your long trip."

Flynn splattered chowder into the remaining cups and called out as Hightower slipped away, "No need to be sendin' for the constable, there, Mr. Club Secretary. I'm done. Let these fine folks get back to plannin' the conquest of California." He dropped the ladle into the tureen. "I just might head out there meself. So you can keep the family picture. That way you'll recognize me when I come back a rich man."

He had seized the moment and made it his own. I was impressed and secretly entertained.

Then his eye fell on Janiva. "And may I say, miss, if your handsome beau won't marry you and take you along, I'd be charmed to offer you protection on the voyage. You'll get no sneaky-fingers or bloomer pullin' from me—"

Hallie Batchelder gasped. She knew what that meant.

"—for I'm as honorable as any man in this room. And there's no reason why ladies shouldn't see the world and have a bit of adventure, too, is there?"

I was shocked. This waiter had just said to Janiva what Janiva had said to me when I told her I was leaving. I stiffened my spine and said, "You're done, mister. Best hurry for the next ship." Then I prepared to defend myself.

But Michael Flynn answered with a courteous bow. "I apologize, sir, if I've offended you or your lady. You seem a right gentleman, despite your upbringin'."

Yes, he could start a fire and put it out, all in a sentence or two. Then he turned smoldering ash into a conflagration by reaching his arms around Hallie Batchelder, and before anyone could react, grabbing the table and flipping it at Hodges. Amidst screams and shouts and gasps of shock, the tureen, chowder, glasses, silverware, dishes, centerpiece, and my ninny of a sister-in-law went flying.

Flynn snatched the bottle of champagne before it toppled, took a swallow, pivoted on his heels, and stalked toward the cloakroom, shouting, "May the lot of ye's rot under the gaze of all the dead Boston bastards on these walls."

Though the table was gone from in front of her, my mother remained motionless in her chair, pursing her lips. Hallie Batchelder seemed to be having a fit of hyperventilation as her husband fanned her with his napkin. My sister stared at the dinner plates now spinning on the floor with eyes almost as wide as the plates.

But Hodges took action. He flung the table off himself and sent it flying at me. Then he scrambled to his feet and hurried toward the cloakroom.
A moment later, all two hundred pounds of him staggered back into the
dining room, turned once, and collapsed onto an unoccupied table, setting
off another explosion of glass, cutlery, and club-monogrammed china.

The Irishman, wearing someone's fine winter cape and a familiar brown
hat with a leather visor, poked his head through the door and shouted at
the unconscious Hodges, "One-two-three-four-five-six-seven-eight-nine-
ten. Out!" Then he pivoted and strutted down the hallway.

I hurried after him, reaching the foyer just as the front door slammed.
Then, from the outside, Michael Flynn's gloved fist smashed through one
of the sidelights.

"Good God!" shouted Hightower. "Somebody should shoot that man!"

"Let him go," I said.

"But sir, he just stole your hat."

The Irishman was singing as he bounded down the steps. Something
about a "wild colonial boy."

"My hat?" I said. "He can keep it. Wherever he's going, he'll need it."
Then I picked up the card that had flown into the foyer with the broken
glass. Neatly lettered upon it were the words *No Irish Need Apply*.

January 12, 1849
Farewelling

The air smelled of snow on the morning that I gazed for the first time upon
the vessel that would take us to California. The *William Winter* loomed over
Long Wharf, a wall-sided Atlantic packet with raised decks fore and aft,
false gun ports painted into a white strip along her side, and three mighty
masts piercing the clouds.

I stepped from our coach directly under the gaze of Reverend Winter
himself, a North Shore minister so beloved of his parishioners that they had
named a ship for him. He appeared seven feet tall, exquisitely carved in black
robes, with his Bible clutched to his chest and his god-like mane of white
hair blown back in the imaginary breeze, a fitting figurehead for a boatload
of high-minded Christian adventurers like us.

But this wooden minister paid no mind to the Sagamores farewelling
with friends and families, or to the bustle on the nearby wharves, where
other crowds were gathering and other ships readying for California. And
he did not cock his ear to the band playing light airs by the gangway. His

gaze reached beyond all of us, beyond the harbor islands, out to the gray sea that would soon be our highway to wealth and fame.

Let others have the wealth, I thought. I would take the fame of writing it all down.

Then my mother interrupted my reverie. "You're not going to California in *that* little chamber pot, are you?"

"It's as seaworthy as the *Constitution,* Mother, and almost as big."

My sister leaned out the carriage window. "Has it ever gone around that thing at the bottom of South America?"

"The *Horn,*" I said. "It's called Cape Horn. And this ship has crossed the Atlantic a hundred times. She can weather whatever comes at Cape Horn."

"I wouldn't sail to Cape *Cod* in it." My sister climbed out after me. "And why do they call it a 'she' if it's named for a man?"

"Let's ask the captain." I helped her down, then reached up to help my mother. "I'll introduce you both."

"Where is he?" asked my mother.

"He's standing by the taffrail, that man in the black sea cape and the top hat that looks like an upturned plant pot."

"Taffrail?" said Diana.

"The stern rail," I said, "at the very back of the ship."

My mother looked at him. "Stern rail and stern face."

"Like you, Mother." And I noticed two men sniggering at our conversation.

One was Christopher Harding. He was an old Harvard chum. He had even squired my sister to a cotillion in college. He could be forgiven.

The other was Deering Sloate, whom I had disliked from the day that the alphabet made us neighbors in a classroom at the Boston Latin School twelve years before.

Was it any wonder that I had asked my mother and sister not to attend our departure? I had no desire to see this voyage turned into a floating boys' school, complete with the cliques, grudges, and the needling insults so common in such places. And no one had more skill at sophomoric needling than Sloate, especially where mothers and sisters were concerned. So I decided to needle first.

I said, "Hello, lads. Ready for me to write about how brave you think you are?"

"Jamie, old boy! I was hoping you'd be with us." Christopher's skinny frame fairly quivered with excitement. "There are half a dozen of us from the Class of Forty-five."

"We can start a Harvard Club, then," I said.

"What fun!" said Christopher, who had a naïve innocence and absolutely no ear for sarcasm.

"Fun." Sloate laughed, though it was unclear if he was laughing with Christopher or at him. "He thinks it's going to be fun, Spencer."

I gestured to the big Walker Colt that Sloate wore in a holster at his hip, like a badge of manhood. "That gun won't help against twenty-foot seas."

"You're not bringing pistols?" Sloate rested his hand on the gun. "Just your pen?"

"I can do more damage with my pen. Be careful, or I might turn it on you." Then I turned my back on Sloate.

I had packed a brace of Colt Dragoons, a gift from my brother, but as my mother's first glimpse of them in our parlor had caused her emotions to overflow, I was not wearing them on the wharf. I did not want another scene. I also wanted to board quickly, so I ordered our footman to fetch my sea bag from the boot.

The bylaws of the company, acceded to by all members when they signed articles of incorporation, stated, "Each man shall be allowed one sea bag, not to exceed seventy-five pounds weight, the contents being the equivalent in bulk of a single sea chest, dimensions $36 \times 48 \times 24$. For reasons of space, no chests shall be allowed, except those belonging to the company physician and assayer."

I had weighed, measured, and packed my bag, based on this list:

1 oilskin for rain
2 hats—1 broad-brimmed black felt (which I was then wearing),
   1 straw
2 pairs of boots (1 new, 1 broken in)
3 each of flannel shirts, heavy twill trousers, suits of small clothes
1 blanket, 1 sheet of India rubber for ground-sleeping
10 reams of foolscap, 7 notebooks, 100 pencils, 5 pens, 20 nibs,
   20 bottles of ink
5 books—Shakespeare, Virgil, Dickens, Fielding, the Holy Bible
2 Colt Dragoons, with powder horn and lead mold

In addition, I was wearing my winter cape over my tweed suit. It was a rig that could stand up to Boston's weather, so I was certain that it could handle the worst that the ocean might hurl at us.

When the footman handed me my sea bag, my mother's eyes filled with tears. She pretended to shiver and said, "Oh . . . I hate a raw winter day."

And I was glad that Janiva and I had already bidden our farewells. . . .

I HAD RIDDEN THE day before to her home on Blackstone Square, to take tea under the watchful—and baleful—gaze of her parents.

Mrs. Toler was a sweet and perceptive woman. Mr. Toler was better known for bluntness. He owned the Roxbury Cordage Company and boasted that there was no more important industry in Massachusetts, as his ropes formed the shrouds and fashioned the lines that held Boston masts in place and kept Yankee sails aloft in the heaviest gales in the farthest reaches of the watery world. I had never disputed this statement, as Mr. Toler did not invite disputation.

While the mother had made lively small talk, the patriarch had said little, and by his scowl had reminded me—if I did not already know—that he disapproved of my continued presence in both his parlor and his daughter's affections. A spurned father, it is said, can be even less understanding than a spurned daughter.

At length, Mrs. Toler had made an excuse to draw her husband from the room, thus providing her daughter and me with a moment of privacy.

Once alone, I had taken Janiva's hand and assured her, "If I could bring you, I would."

"Then why don't you? Women deserve a chance to look beyond the horizon, too, just as that Irish waiter said."

"I wouldn't take my life's philosophy from Irish waiters."

"Even when you know it to be true?" She had slipped her hand from mine.

"When I return, I'll take you to Italy. We'll visit the antiquities."

"Is that meant to be the proposal my father has been expecting?" This had burst from her so angrily that I was glad to see Mr. Toler reappearing with my cape and hat, a wordless invitation for me to be on my way.

Janiva had then escorted me to the foyer, where she pulled from her sleeve a red neckerchief with a yellow paisley pattern. She said it was silk and so would warm me in winter and cool me in summer and dry quickly when I washed it, which she hoped I would do often.

After a glance into the parlor to make sure that her father was not watching, I had embraced her. And even through the heavy layers of wool that I wore and the lighter cotton and petticoats that encased her, I had felt enough to make more than my heart leap up. She had then shocked me by taking my face in her hands and giving me a kiss longer and more profound than any I had ever enjoyed.

"My parting gift," she had said with a mixture of loving ferocity and cold anger. "I won't be there tomorrow. I won't play the heartsick lover for all of Boston to see."

"Nor would I ask you to. We sail on the morning tide. It ebbs at eight thirty."

"Far too early for my delicate constitution." She had added bitterness to her tone.

And her father's voice had echoed from the parlor: "*Good-bye*, Mr. Spencer."

Now the ship's bell was ringing—eight times for eight in the morning.

The first mate spoke through a brass trumpet while the captain stood, arms folded at his back, projecting an air of imperturbable calm. "All Sagamores to board immediately. Those not registered in twenty minutes will be left behind."

This brought a wordless moan from the crowd and a burst of movement on the wharf. Mothers held their sons. Fathers hid their tears. Lovers kissed. And a group of young men—full of life, energy, and optimism—gathered their gear and pressed for the gangways, all to the band's accompaniment of a jaunty "Yankee Doodle".

I embraced my mother and sister and turned for the ship before either of them started weeping.

I tipped my hat to a group of tradesmen who were passing a bottle in the cold air: the Brighton Bulls, six former butchers from the abattoir on the Charles River. Their leader introduced himself as Fat Jack Sawyer, whose fat looked more like muscle to me.

I dodged a Negro rolling a water cask to the forward gangway.

Then I fell in behind Jason Willis, whose wife could not bring herself to leave her husband's side. Willis was a classmate of my brother's and generally a decent fellow, but not one who believed that the rules ever applied to him. As if to prove that point, his servant was carrying his sea chest while Willis carried his bag and his wife clung to his arm.

At the top of the gangway, the second mate was checking each name and weighing each bag, so Willis and I had time to talk.

He said, "Looks like we'll be sailing with darkies, James."

"If the crew doesn't mind, why should we?" I asked.

"Indeed. Why should we mind darkies if we're asked to tolerate Micks? From all the brogues and blarney I've heard, there's a few of them in the fo'c'sle, too."

I had never considered Jace Willis worth the energy it took to argue with him. So I smiled and turned to the man behind me.

He was a burly fellow, with a sullen brow and dark eyes. He wore the clothes of a tradesman, which may have explained his discomfort, considering that so many of us were dressed like dandies out for an afternoon of pistol-shooting fun. He carried a sea bag in one hand and a large canvas sack in the other. I offered my hand.

He dropped the sack, which clanked, pulled off his glove, and enveloped my hand with his own. "Name's Dooling. Matt Dooling."

"Well, Mr. Dooling, I hope you're ready for adventure."

"Ain't expectin' adventure. That's a word with a ring of fun to it. Ain't expectin' nothin' but a hard voyage and hard labor in California."

"If I may ask, then, why have you decided to join us?"

"Every man has his moment. Every man has to take his chance when it comes, or he'll spend the rest of his life wonderin'. That's what I told my wife and kids."

And a line from Shakespeare popped from my mouth: "There is a tide in the affairs of men, which if taken at the flood, leads on to fortune."

"Didn't tell 'em that, exactly. Just told 'em, if I sold the blacksmith shop, I could pay the bond and get a berth on one of the first ships leavin' for California. So here I am, aimin' to work hard and send every nugget home."

In the face of such simple sincerity, I was embarrassed at showing off my book-learning. So I said, "It will be a pleasure to sail with you, sir."

Then we were distracted by raised voices at the head of the gangplank.

"I'll have your name," Willis's wife was saying. "My husband is on the board of this company."

"Name's Kearns, ma'am, Sean Kearns. And these is your own rules. No sea chests allowed." Kearns spoke with one of the brogues that Willis had alluded to.

"But an extensive library," said Willis, "will benefit everyone on a six-month voyage. An exception can be made."

"I ain't the man to say."

Samuel Hodges was standing by the mainmast, in much the same authoritative attitude as the captain on the quarterdeck. Now he came to the side. "Trouble?"

Willis said, "Samuel, this fellow won't allow me to bring a few books."

"No sea chests allowed," said Hodges. "It's in the articles."

Mrs. Willis said, "But, Samuel, surely a few more books will—"

"Madame," said Hodges, "in California, we will need only what we can carry."

"This is ridiculous," said Willis.

"Ridiculous?" And Hodges revealed how quickly his calm might blow up a tempest. "I'll show you ridiculous." He grabbed one of the handles of the chest on the servant's shoulder, gave a sharp tug, and flung it into the water.

Both Willises gasped as if their child were in that trunk.

"Now, come aboard with your sea bag," said Hodges, "but *not* your wife, or the two of you can stay here and fish your Fenimore Cooper out of the harbor."

The wife tugged on her husband's arm, and a red-faced Jason Willis turned and pushed back down the gangway.

Hodges called after him, "Don't delay if you plan to sail, Willis." Then he turned to me and his mood changed in an instant. "Good morning, James."

"Good morning, Samuel." I glanced at the chest sinking into the harbor, then spelled my name for the mate and handed over my bag for weighing.

"Give him a good billet," said Hodges. "He's the most important man on the ship."

"I'm hardly that," I said.

"Nonsense." Hodges turned for the quarterdeck. "We're making history, Spencer. You can't make history without a historian."

"First cabin, berth four, larboard." Kearns waved me aboard and turned to Dooling, who had fit his tool bag into his sea bag. "Bag on the scale and state your name."

"Matt Dooling's my name, and my bag's fifteen pounds over."

Hodges spun around and approached again.

I interceded. "This man's a blacksmith, Samuel. He's brought tools. That's why his bag's over the limit."

"Is that true?" said Hodges.

Dooling nodded. "I brung hammers, tongs, hand bellows—"

"A blacksmith may be valuable in California," I added.

Hodges thought that over, then told Dooling, "You should have filled out a request. But Spencer's right. We can use your tools. Come aboard."

As we descended the companionway, the blacksmith said to me, "Matt Dooling never forgets a favor."

SOON, A HUNDRED MEMBERS of the Sagamore Mining Company assembled on the deck in a swirling snow flurry. And what a grand mix of men we were—merchants, mechanics, shopkeeps, schoolteachers, lawyers, six butchers, a new-minted doctor, and one ambitious writer, all bundled against the cold and warmed by the mix of emotions that boiled in every breast. Most of us were in our twenties, prime age for adventuring. But some, like Dooling, appeared to be in their thirties, the decade when men must either accept their place in life or take a final chance to change it. And a few, like Hodges, had reached their forties, already successful yet hungry for more.

While California beckoned, we would first hear from Reverend Stone, pastor of the Park Street Church. He took to the quarterdeck, raised his hand, and the band stopped playing. This caused the buzz of conversation to cease on both the ship and the wharf.

The first mate brought the speaking trumpet to his lips: "Seamen, stand by!" And twenty sailors stopped in their tasks, wherever they stood.

As the wind puffed from the west and pushed the snow sideways, the austere young minister looked up into the flurry and said, "Almighty God, you who made the sweeping seas and the craggy mountains, look with favor upon this company of Christian men. Guide them through the dangers they will face and the temptations they will encounter."

And from somewhere forward came whispering. I could not see the whisperer's face as his hat was pulled low, but I recognized his brogue . . . and the hat.

Reverend Stone continued, "When the great winds blow on your ocean sea or the dark impulses course through your human creations, keep these men in your grace." Then he lowered his gaze to us. "As for all of you, I charge you to bring your values, your culture, and your Christian faith to California. Implant them there to grow and flourish."

I was listening to the reverend, but I could still hear that Irish waiter whispering to one of his mates by the anchor capstan, "When these Yanks get to the diggin's, they'll be no different from the rest of us. They'll knock down any who get in their way."

Just then a carriage came clattering onto the wharf and caused me to forget both the whispering Irishman and the droning minister. Seeing the Toler footman at the reins, I knew that Janiva had come after all! For a moment, I considered leaping over the side to embrace her and surrender straight away to the life of domesticity I was fleeing.

But just as suddenly as she appeared, our leaving-taking accelerated.

It started with a slight motion beneath our feet and a gentle *whoosh* of water along our hull. Slack tide had ended. The ebb was begun. And neither time, tide, nor Captain Nathan Trask would wait for any man, not even the pastor of the Park Street Church. The reverend was reaching his conclusion, "In the name of Almighty God—" when Trask cried, "Amen! Amen, Reverend. Amen."

The crowd answered, "Amen."

The captain shook Reverend Stone's hand and directed him to the gangway while dockhands scrambled and the first mate called through his megaphone, "Drop anchor!"

Yes. *Drop* was the order. Our longboat had hauled a light kedging anchor into the channel. Once it dug into the mud, the men at the capstan would crank the ship onto it, repeating the process until the *William Winter* was well away from Long Wharf. The captain did not seem to favor the newfangled steam-driven tugs puffing about Boston Harbor, perhaps because no tugboat would be waiting in California. Our crew would know how to warp ship and leave a dock the old-fashioned way.

The anchor splashed, and the first mate cried, "Away all lines!"

Now rose another cry, almost a wail, from the families on the wharf, as if they were at last accepting the truth that we would be gone for years and might return as different men, if we returned at all.

Somewhere in the crowd, a little girl cried, "Daddy!"

Samuel Hodges took off his hat and waved it at her. "Be good to your sister, and mind your Aunt Nell!" I thought that I saw him wipe away a tear. I could not be certain.

The reverend stepped off the gangway and nodded to the band, which began to play "On Jordan's Stormy Banks."

But I was watching Janiva push through the crowd, her eyes searching. I squeezed between Christopher Harding and Jason Willis and called to her.

"James! James!" She waved. "Godspeed, James Spencer. Godspeed!"

"I'll write. Every week. I promise."

People in the crowd and in the company were now taking up the old hymn.

"On Jordan's stony banks I stand and cast a wishful eye . . ."

The mate cried, "Lay on the capstan."

"To Canaan's far and happy land, where my possessions lie . . ."

Eight men held bars fitted into the capstan-head like spokes in the hub of a wheel. As they pushed clockwise, seven hundred and fifty tons of *William Winter* almost miraculously began to move.

"All o'er those wide extended plains shines one eternal day . . ."

As the Irish waiter cranked past, he said to me, "Are you sure you don't want to take her along?"

"Are you sure you don't want to sail on a different ship?" I answered.

"Quiet at the capstan," shouted Kearns.

Yes, I thought, quiet at the capstan. There would be time enough for you later, Michael Flynn of Galway, time enough for Samuel Hodges to make your life miserable.

"There, God the son forever reigns and scatters night away . . ."

Janiva was standing now beside my mother and sister, and they were all singing:

"I am bound for the Promised Land, I am bound for the Promised Land . . ."

Then my mother turned away in tears. My sister brought her hand to her mouth to hide her quivering chin.

"Oh, who will come and go with me?"

But Janiva kept her eyes resolutely on mine, as if she would not allow me to see her weep. And through the falling snow, her lips formed the words, "I love you."

"Isn't that sweet," whispered Deering Sloate. "She loves you."

I ignored Sloate. There would be time enough for him later, too.

"I am bound for the Promised Land."

I pulled off the red and yellow-paisley neckerchief that she had given me and waved it.

I waved it until the *William Winter* had twice kedged the length of her cable and turned into the channel. I waved it until we had shaken out our t'gallants and made for President Roads. I waved it through three choruses of the old hymn and prayed that when we returned, I would find no irony in the lyrics, that I would come home to tell of a true promised land on the far side of our vast American continent.

But I did not deceive myself. We were not bound for the promised land. We were bound for adventure, bound for danger, and bound for gold, however we could get it.

BY LATE AFTERNOON, THE *William Winter* was running before a brisk northwesterly that pushed the morning flurries far to the east and brought down a cold that was deep and bracing and filled a man with a sense of his own existence, even as it froze the tips of his ears.

I reveled in the rhythm of wind, water, and wooden hull, and I understood yet again why men would leave all that was warm and domestic to sail the endless and unforgiving sea, for here was a domesticity all its own. Our ship was like a great birth mother, rocking us, rocking us, up and down, down and up, over and over, with a soft yet certain hand, holding us to her bosom like the living thing she was . . . never mind that a third of the company had taken seasick before we crossed Massachusetts Bay.

I feared that belly-churning head-spinning spew, feared it like a broken bone, feared it for the misery of it, and feared it for on this ship, the sick ones would only give the needlers another reason to needle.

But much to my satisfaction, the chief needler sickened before anyone else. We had barely passed Boston Light when Deering Sloate lurched to the rail so suddenly that he did not have the time, or perhaps the knowledge, to determine which was the better side for puking. So he did it straight into the wind, with the expected effect.

By the time we cleared Cape Cod, two dozen men, green-faced and groaning, had stumbled like drunks to the side.

Just after four o'clock, eight bells and the beginning of the first "dog watch," we made the turn south. By then I had found a spot on the weather side, away from the vomiteers, where I could watch the sun dip toward the horizon and hear the hiss of the water along our hull, all without their retching and wretched accompaniment.

I calculated that we would pass near two hundred seaborne sunsets before reaching San Francisco. I resolved to observe each one and celebrate nature's unending variety even as it unfolded within the proscenium of her comforting predictability.

Then I sensed beside me a man who embodied the predictability of ancient hatreds within the discomforting proscenium of an explosive Irish temperament. I gave him the corner of my eye and said, "A fine hat."

"Best I could find in the cloakroom. I like the leather visor." He tugged at it.

"Did you know that the Sagamores were sailing on this ship?"

"Didn't know and don't much care. I'll steer clear of the big Hodges feller, but it ain't him you need to be worryin' about. It's the captain. He's the hard case on this ship."

"Where did you learn to sail?"

"Never said I did. But I can haul a line and climb a rope. The rest I'll learn." He looked up at the canvas bellied round in the booming wind. "Better than ladlin' chowder for Yankee swells in a club where everybody has a broomstick up his ass."

The bosun's whistle sounded three notes that cut through the roar of wind and sea, and the first mate shouted into the speaking trumpet, "Ship's company, all aft!"

With alacrity, the men responded, and in minutes, the midships was crowded with Sagamores, while nineteen sailors, all save the helmsman, stood before the rail separating us from the quarterdeck and the captain, who studied us with a kind of interested detachment, as if examining a tray of oysters and deciding which one to pop into his mouth first. Then he nodded to the mate, who began:

"I'm Hawkins, first officer and last man between you and the captain. Before you speak to him, you speak to me. I will determine if your words are worth his time."

The captain turned toward the setting sun. His face became all angles and edges, sharpened by reddening rays skimming low across the sea.

"Now, you Sagamores," Mr. Hawkins went on, "if you're seasick, don't vomit belowdecks. It'll stink for months. And don't vomit on the weather side. Get to the lee. If you don't know the lee, look to the sails. If the sails belly to larboard, puke to larboard."

And as if it had been planned, Christopher Harding, who had been swaying by the mainmast, suddenly brought his hand to his mouth and turned toward the setting sun. The mate shouted, "The *other* side! Leeward, I said! Puke to leeward!"

Christopher made it just in time, generating loud amusement from the Sagamores. The crew, however, knew to stand stock-still and silent when assembled.

"The captain don't usually speak so soon in the voyage, but all this pukin' means we're full up to the scuppers with landlubbers. So you need a talkin' to right now. So . . ." The mate stepped back, leaving the stage to his superior.

With one sweep of his eye, the captain fixed his gaze on every man. "I am Nathan Trask." His voice was high and harsh, sharpened by a lifetime of cutting through storms and stiff Atlantic gales. "I have sailed the Boston to Liverpool run for nine years without incident. But the owners of this vessel see greater profit in ferrying fortune-seekers to California."

He paused, as if to let the contempt in his voice settle upon us like a mist. "It will not be an easy journey. We will cover seventeen thousand miles. There will be storms and cold and heat to cook your nuts if you sit too long on the deck."

No one cracked a smile now. It was plain that nothing this man said was meant for laughter.

"At Cape Horn the wind'll blow so hard, you won't be able to breath it before it jams down your throat. And the waves'll run as high as the mainmast. Every man'll get wet and stay wet for as long as it takes to clear the danglin' prick of South America."

I was glad that I had brought my sea cape.

"In the Pacific, we'll run the Roarin' Forties, ride the Southeast Trades, and fall into the doldrums. When we are becalmed, it'll be boredom and heat that do you in. I tell you this because I tell you the truth, which you may not have heard until now. But I tell you this because we are New Englanders, and no race has rounded the Horn as regular as we. That's why you're running for riches on my ship instead of on the back of a mule pulling a wagon."

He strode right, then left, looking into every eye like a minister before a sinful congregation. "It don't matter a fiddler's fart to me whether you find gold or not. I will get you where you're going in six months, more or less, so long as you follow the rules. Mr. Hawkins, tell them the rules."

"Aye, sir." Hawkins affected similar chin whiskers and gaunt appearance, a captain in waiting. "There's only one: obey the captain in all things."

Trask nodded. "Let any man violate, deviate, or hesitate when an order is given, and I will have that man spread-eagled before the next sail change. I'll waste no breath on you Sagamores. Obey your leaders. You elected them. But you did not elect me, any more than you elected He who rules above. And on this ship, He is my only superior."

I was beginning to doubt that Captain Trask believed even that.

He said, "I can condemn you to hell or take you to the Promised Land in that song. It's up to you. Is that clear?"

The Sagamores mumbled and nodded, though a few scowled and shot angry glances about, as if insulted at such a talking-to.

Captain Trask looked at Hodges, who had put himself on the quarterdeck, though respectfully to windward of the captain. "Speak for your people, sir. I want to hear it. I want to know that I am making myself clear."

"As clear as the sunset, Captain. We hired you to take us to California. We will obey your orders and trust your experience. Once there"—Hodges looked out at the assembled company—"the president and board of directors will determine our course."

Trask studied Hodges, as if deciding whether this answer was suffi-
ciently subservient. Perhaps he recognized that Hodges had to project leadership, too. Men in power usually understood one another, and so long as one
man's power did not challenge the other's, all would be well.

But if any aboard doubted Trask's supremacy, he was about to disabuse
them. "You veteran seamen, you know what's expected. The rest of you, pay
attention. Seaman Flynn, step forward."

We had not yet crossed the forty-second parallel, and Michael Flynn
had already crossed an imaginary line. He hesitated a moment, then obeyed.
I could not see his face, so I watched as Hodges glanced at him, then looked
more closely, then stared as if he were seeing an Irish apparition. Then he
turned and said something into the captain's ear.

The captain ignored Hodges and proclaimed, "Seaman Flynn, while at
the capstan, you showed disrespect to Reverend Stone. In so doing, you
showed disrespect to the ship's company, to the Sagamores, and to me. After
obedience, I demand respect, because disrespect is the forerunner of dis-
obedience. A dozen lashes."

"A dozen lashes?" cried Flynn.

"Make that fifteen. And another for every word out of your mouth."

"But—"

"Sixteen. Ship's company to witness punishment. Mr. Hawkins, seize
him up."

"Aye, sir." The first mate signaled to a pair of sailors who grabbed Flynn
and wrestled him to the starboard side, where they raised a hatch grate and
trussed him to it. Then they stripped his shirt. The white skin of his back
against the grate looked like fine Irish linen set down on a black frying pan.

"Mr. Kearns, fetch the cat," ordered Hawkins.

We all knew of the cat-o'-nine-tails, nine knotted strands of rope attached to a handle, a simple yet diabolical instrument of discipline. And we
had all heard of floggings. We had expected to see a few before the voyage
was done but not on the very first day.

And I could rightly say that the next few minutes chastened any man
who might ever have considered back-talking Captain Nathan Trask.

"One!" cried First Mate Hawkins.

Flynn grit his teeth and clenched his jaws.

Whistle, snap, and "Two!"

Flynn straightened up as if he would shake off the pain.

Whistle, snap, and "Three!"

Blood appeared on Flynn's skin.

Four more lashes, and Flynn's back began to resemble rare beef, purpling, bruised, blood-blistered. But still he kept silent.

Deering Sloate joined Christopher Harding at the rail, and others followed, because this was a sight to sicken any man.

Two more lashes and a line of blood droplets splattered across the deck, as if to describe the arcs that the whip strands were taking with every swing.

"This is getting inhuman," I muttered and turned my eyes toward the sky that was itself blood red.

"They been doin' it since the Romans," whispered Matt Dooling from behind me. "And you was ordered to witness punishment. You can't turn away."

So I watched and tried to concentrate on the motion of the ship, but the maternal rhythm seemed now to be keeping pace with the infernal swinging of the whip and the snapping of the ropes against that white Irish flesh.

Up, whistle, down, snap. Up, whistle, down, snap.

After a dozen strokes, the captain made a small motion of his hand, and the second mate stopped swinging. The captain announced, "We will forego further punishment. Cut him down and salt his wounds."

Released from the grate, Flynn wobbled, trembled, but instead of collapsing, pulled himself up straight and defiant, like a man who had taken a beating before.

The captain said, "Have you learned your lesson, seaman?"

Flynn glared toward the quarterdeck.

"Belay that cross look, mister," said the captain, "or I'll seize you up for another dozen. Have you learned your lesson?"

"I have the utmost respect, sir, for you." Then Flynn turned his eyes to Hodges.

Hodges moved closer to the captain and said something else in his ear. The captain did not even shift his eyes in Hodges's direction.

A man pushed forward, George Beal by name, Sagamore physician. He had recently completed studies at the Harvard Medical Annex and, like so many of us, saw this voyage as a chance to test his mettle in a world not made by his parents. He would test it first on lacerations made by a knotted rope. He asked permission to tend to the sailor's back.

The captain eyed him and nodded.

As the doctor led him to the companionway, Flynn glared at me. "I ain't like you or your friend up there. When I fight a man, I fight him and we're done with it. I never had a man flogged for beatin' me fair."

I was shocked but reminded myself that a man who had endured such punishment might lack clear-headedness. I watched him stagger to the companionway, with Doc Beal close behind, then I asked Willis, "May I borrow your flask?"

BELOWDECKS, A POT OF stew bubbled on the cast-iron caboose, the ship's stove. The heat and hefty aromas made this dark, low-ceilinged space feel like the sailor's home it would be for six months. The forecastle, or "fo'c'sle" in seafaring jargon, occupied the space forward of the mast, snug in the bow. Eighteen wooden berths, in stacks of three, lined the bulkheads. Lanterns swung over the table and the benches affixed to the deck. Here the crew ate, slept, sang, and kept warm.

Flynn was sitting on a bench, his shoulders hunched, his head down.

Doc Beal was mixing something with a mortar and pestle.

The cook, a burly Negro in a white apron, was examining Flynn's back, saying, "Ain't so bad. More bruise than blood. Second Mate go easy on you."

Flynn said, "It ain't the pain botherin' me, Pompey. It's the singlin' out."

"The what?"

"Hodges and his nancy-boy friend singled me out, told the captain I'm a troublemaker, which I ain't."

"Nah." Pompey shook his head. "First day, the cap always pick on somebody. But I ship with him for three years and he never yet listen to no passenger 'bout nothin'. He's a hard man but fair. If he say you done somethin', you done it."

Flynn seemed too pained to argue. He just bowed his head.

And from the shadows, I said, "I can't speak for Hodges, but I had nothing to do with this."

Flynn looked up with anger in his eyes.

I preferred to look into them than at his back. I asked him how he was feeling.

He laughed, though he could not be amused at anything but the stupidity of the question. "I feel like a peeled potato."

I offered the flask. "A little painkiller."

"I never touch the stuff."

Now it was I who laughed. But he turned away and stared into the shadows. So I offered the flask to the Negro, who took it eagerly and poured a shot down his throat. With his apron he wiped off the mouth before handing it back to me.

Doc Beal told Flynn, "If you've never touched it, you might want to start, because this is going to hurt."

Flynn looked into the mortar. "What's that?"

"Salt mixed with vinegar."

Pompey peered over the doctor's shoulder. "I use plain salt."

"Salt dries the wound," said the doctor, "and that's good. But vinegar cleans it. The mix stings just as bad but works better."

Flynn snatched the flask, took a long drink, and said, "Lay on."

And for the next few minutes, Doc Beal dipped his fingers into the concoction and spread it delicately across the lacerations. Flynn kept silent, though the pain was surely excruciating. I watched with such awe that I did not take a swallow from the flask until the salting was done.

Then Flynn growled at me. "You got somethin' else to say?"

"Only this." I paraphrased his own words: "When I fight a man, I fight with my fists. I never had a man flogged for fighting me fair."

"A fine speech." Flynn slipped a clean shirt over his skinned back. "When I'm up to it, you can take a swing at me to prove you ain't a nancy-boy. Now get out."

I shoved the flask into my pocket and returned to the main deck. If I had nothing else to say to that Irishman on the voyage, I had said my piece.

January 14, 1849
Our First Sunday

The ship makes a steady eight knots that will bring us in two months to S 8′03″ W 34′52″, just off the Brazilian coast, where we can finally make a turn west. As the great belly of South America bulges far into the Atlantic, some thousand miles east of Boston, we must sail away from our goal before sailing toward it, but that seems always to be the nature of travel by sea . . . and through life, too.

Little intercourse between sailors and passengers. Much settling in. Many routines established, including my writing. I conclude that some days will require long passages rewritten into the past tense. Others will make little impression but for their monotony. . . .

January 18–20
Seasickness and Storms

Overnight, the northwesterly that had driven us began to shift. By six bells, we were banging hard against a headwind that sent cold sleet into our sails and slammed relentless waves over our bow. This "hulling," as the sailors call it, produced a motion that I could neither ignore nor tolerate. Soon I had joined a dozen or more Sagamores at the rail to "cast and scour," as ye olde Pilgrims put it, much to the amusement of the seamen who warned us yet again not to puke into the wind.

But after two days, good sailing returned, about the time that I stopped vomiting. Pompey told me I was now "cleaned out good," so I might tolerate a bit of salt pork and biscuit. It eased me, and now I can truly say that I have got my sea legs.

January 24, 1849
A Dispatch for the Transcript

We hove-to when a northbound ship appeared on the horizon, the brig *Pemberton,* carrying a cargo of molasses and hemp after trading lumber and codfish in Barbados.

It is a cordiality of the sea that passing vessels often reach out to one another. The exchange may be simple, as when we sighted our first sail: "Ship Ahoy!" "Halloo!" "What ship is that, pray?" "The bark *Virginia*, from Le Havre, bound for New York. Where are you from?" "The ship *William Winter* from Boston, bound for California, five days out." Unless there is leisure or something special to say, this is seldom varied from. But if there is time or need, men who might never have call to communicate on land become, in the great blue void, as brothers. And if one asks another to enact the role of Winged Mercury, to convey a message that will calm a worried wife or assuage an uncertain family, it will be done.

So, we exchanged news with the *Pemberton* and delivered a satchel of mail, including my first dispatch for the *Transcript:*

> We have been cruising a dozen days and neither the temperature nor the angle of the sun give promise of the warmth that lies ahead. It is as cold as if we were wandering the White Mountains of New Hampshire rather than the white caps of the Atlantic.
>
> Captain Trask issues no order without certainty and maintains strict discipline. He punished a sailor the first day and has found no further need to let the "cat out of the bag." The sailor in question now goes about his duties gingerly, avoiding any eye contact, thereby avoiding any further difficulty.
>
> In truth, every sailor is kept busy through every watch. There is always work to be done—replacing lines, holystoning the deck, drawing out yarns

from bundles of rags and junk (of which the owners buy up great quantities) to be used for chafing gear and caulking, and a thousand other daily chores, all in addition to steering, reefing, furling, and pumping. Our wooden mother demands constant attention, assuring that her children are too tired to cause mischief.

As for the Sagamores, we have organized into "watches," like the crew, so there are no more than thirty-five of us on deck at a time. We eat at appointed hours. We hold formal meetings to discuss company business. In the evenings, some engage in Bible study while others enjoy lively debate on political or literary subjects, with topics such as, "Is the Death of Slavery Imminent?" and "The Novel v. the Epic Poem: Wherein Lies Greater Truth?"

The British wit Samuel Johnson may once have said, "Going to sea is like going to jail, with the added danger of drowning," but as this vessel formerly plied the Atlantic passenger trade, we enjoy certain comforts. My own billet, in the first cabin, contains a berth separated from the main saloon by a door fitted with shutter blinds for ventilation. Once I am settled, I am as comfortable as if I were in my own bed on Beacon Hill.

The saloon, between mizzen and mainmast, features a table and benches fixed to the deck. We enjoy natural light from the skylight and gratings, which we may open for ventilation but may batten down when the weather—in sailor's parlance—"turns dirty."

On the deck below are members who chose "second cabin," thereby saving forty dollars. Below them is the hold, containing the supplies that will stand us in good stead in California. And therein lies our only controversy.

A contingent of Sagamores, led by Jason Willis, has raised the possibility of operating as merchants rather than miners. He comes from a mercantile family—his father is one of the owners of the *William Winter*—and he theorizes that goods will be scarce in San Francisco, so inflation may turn a well-stocked hold into a gold mine of its own. Board President Samuel Hodges opposes this idea.

I shall elaborate upon the dispute in the weeks ahead. But for now, the way is clear and the winter sea has calmed.

Yr. Ob't Correspondent,
The Argonaut

January 28, 1849
Another Sunday

Psalms in the morning. Brisk sailing through the day, an invitation to dine at the captain's table in the evening.

Other captains, I had been told, entertained passengers every night. But Nathan Trask appeared to have taken the lonely responsibility of leadership into his very soul. When he came on deck, he held himself aloof. Some days, he spoke exclusively to the mate, who conveyed his orders to the rest of us. Some days, he appeared only to take sightings and return below. Some days, he appeared not at all.

His cabin impressed me in the fashion of an orderly set of rooms at the College, with a tight berth to starboard, a privy seat and sink-stand to larboard, a mahogany table beneath the skylight that formed the roof of the aft deck house. Charts hung in a rack on one bulkhead, sextant and chronometer in cherry boxes on the shelf above his berth. Railed cases along the hull held books: novels by Dickens, Maury's *Wind and Current Charts*, and other scientific works. A learned man, then, despite his manner.

That evening, he welcomed myself, Samuel Hodges, Jason Willis, and our "quartermaster," the corpulent Charles Collins, former food broker from Quincy Market.

Hodges offered a toast, "To our illustrious captain and our first two weeks at sea."

The captain raised his glass. "Pray that your last version of that toast is as warm, for we're likely to be another six months at sea."

"James here will run out of things to write about," said Willis.

As we talked, we were passing bowls and filling plates with a concoction of beef, potatoes, and carrots prepared by a cheerful Portagee steward who buzzed about, serving, topping glasses, and generally seeing to our comfort.

Feeding a company of gentlemen—who expect something more than a bit of salt beef for supper—is a tall task on a long voyage. But Collins had done an estimable job. He had loaded a hundred barrels of beef and pork. He had taken aboard two dozen egg-laying hens, a pair of breeding pigs (the sow being pregnant), fifty barrels of peas, fifty of kidney beans, root vegetables, and apples to last four months, by which time we would have reached the bottom of the world and turned north again.

"Rounding the Horn," said Trask, "is a thing that no man forgets but that few have adequately described. It will give Mr. Spencer plenty to write about."

Hodges turned to me. He was growing whiskers like black adze blades on the sides of his face. "So, James, have you written about the efficacy of a good flogging?"

"The incident on the first day was—" I searched for a word.

Willis provided it: "Powerful."

"Powerful indeed," said Samuel Hodges. "And may I say, Captain, that you made a good slam among the men by flogging an Irishman who surely deserved it."

"Deserved it?" said the captain. "Had that Irishman gone whispering a few days later, I might have ignored it, for by then I would have found someone else to punish."

Hodges cocked a brow, the first time I had seen him perplexed about anything.

The captain leaned forward. "Punishing one man focuses every man. Do it early but do it mercifully. You'll achieve many goals at the expense of one man's back."

"One *unlucky* man," I said.

The captain turned to me. "Ever gone aloft in a heavy blow, Mr. Spencer?"

"No, sir."

"You should. Then you might understand."

I felt my face redden. I had never climbed anything higher than the ladder leading to the second tier of bookshelves in my father's library. I asked, "What, exactly, would I understand?"

"The simple physics of fear. The motion of the deck is multiplied on the mast. Like so." The captain held his knife at my chin and pivoted his wrist, so that the tip augured toward my nose. "The mast is the lever, the deck is the fulcrum. The higher you go, the wider swings the mast. Imagine climbing eighty feet of icy shroud, sidestepping along a thin footrope to the end of a spar, then reefing a tops'l while the deck pitches and the mast spins and the wind grabs at your collar like Satan's own crimp, press-gangin' you to hell. Imagine that, and you'll know the physics of fear."

Hodges scoffed. "But, Captain, an ignorant Irishman knows nothing of physics."

"I do," answered Trask. "I know that his fear of climbing those shrouds must needs be less than his fear of the stripes I'll put on his back if he refuses."

"I think Seaman Flynn is a slow learner," said Hodges. "I would have punished him a *second* time for his cross looks."

"Flynn served his purpose. And you, sir, are to have nothing to do with him. I recruited him at the Bell-in-Hand. I took the measure of him and gave him the quill. Whatever went on between you two in Boston is of no matter to me."

Hodges said, "May I remind you, Captain, that I am the president of the company that has hired you, and so long as we are contracted, we expect certain—"

The captain's cutlery clanked onto his plate. "Certain *what?*"

Wherever his next remark was to have taken us, Samuel Hodges showed the good sense to reconsider. "We expect a smooth voyage to San Francisco, sir."

"Where some of us"—Collins spoke for the first time, taking an opportunity to change the subject—"would like to enter into a business arrangement with you, Captain."

"Business arrangement?" The captain shifted his eyes to the other side of the table.

Hodges said, "They would start a trading house in San Francisco, sir."

"A more traditional means of money-making than the gold pan," answered Trask.

"So it is," said Willis. "The *William Winter* would make a fine vessel for ferrying goods from the East." He had conducted himself with icy disdain for Hodges ever since the immersion of his library. It surprised me that he would even dine at the same table. And now, he pressed the captain, "We may be sailing in the real gold mine, sir."

"I have told you," said Hodges, "we seek more than gold. We seek timber, fur, hides, tallow. We seek to clear land. We seek, in short, to *conquer* California. But an empire needs a cornerstone. And the cornerstone is gold."

Empire . . . a word to reckon with. Hodges had not used it before in my presence. But I suppose that any man who had seen as much and dreamed as grandly might use such words.

The ship rocked, and the timbers groaned. We had become familiar with the motion and the sound, but at times, the sea would assert itself, as if to provide a rhythm for our talk or a punctuation for the uncomfortable silence that settled now upon us.

At length, the captain lifted his decanter and refilled our glasses. He did not smile, though he seemed amused. "I'll not worry about conflicts between the Sagamores and crew, when such fundamental conflicts exist among the Sagamores themselves."

Hodges lay his gaze on Willis and Collins for a few moments, then he said to the captain, "There will be no conflict between the Sagamores and your men, sir. You have my word. And none within our group."

I was not so certain. While Hodges dreamed grand dreams, Willis and his compatriots were sons of New England, men from the measure-twice-cut-once school, who sought their advantage in the simple arithmetic of wholesale over retail, who pursued their wildest dreams by electing directors and hiring lawyers. And around the edges of the company lurked the loners who would happily pursue their dreams on their own . . . charters be damned.

February 7, 1849
A New Season

Near four bells of the larboard watch—two in the afternoon—the sun emerged as if from hibernation. The temperature leapt up and with it our spirits. We were another week closer to the equator and also to the equinox. The ocean, slate-colored for so long, appeared suddenly as blue as Boston Harbor in July. Flecks of golden sunlight danced on its surface, and warmth seemed to radiate into every soul.

Around six bells we fell in with a school of dolphins that announced by their presence that we had reached happier seas. They circled back, swept around the hull, and sped along in the bow wake, leaving white wakes of their own as they went. But when Pompey produced a harpooner's lance and began muttering about fresh fish for dinner, the dolphins disappeared, as if by some magic they had heard the conversation.

There was magic in the glorious southern sunset, too. Like a painter I studied the layers of red, pink, purple, and amazingly, green, that shimmered on the horizon.

After dark, the off-watch sailors gathered for a "sing" on the foredeck and filled the air with the scratchy jauntings of fiddle and hornpipe.

I listened to their tunes and stared up into a sky so thick with stars that they appeared as a fog of light in the blackness. And it crept into my mind that I would have loved to show Janiva this marvelous sight, but I banished thoughts of her as quickly as I could, so as not to dwell on feelings that often asserted themselves in physical ways, no matter how hard I tried to ignore them.

I stopped beside Willis, who was likewise staring into the dark, perhaps thinking of his own loyal wife. How much more difficult must it have been for him on such a romantic evening as this, given his knowledge of intimacy?

Once a man has enjoyed nightly connubial pleasure, it must be even harder to ignore the need.

"A fine evening," I said.

"I would be reading, but my library is edifying the crabs in Boston Harbor."

"You can borrow my books or perhaps the captain's. I think he favors you."

"The captain favors efficiency." Willis leaned close to me. "He is a close-hauling man, Spencer, the perfect partner for a long-range trading company."

Just then, a roar rose from the sailors. The music had stopped because someone was telling a story. I glanced toward the noise, wanting to slip away from this conversation and join that, because I knew where Willis was headed.

But he gripped my elbow. "If it comes to it, are you with us?"

"If it comes to *what?*"

"If we take the company away from Hodges. If we recast the charter. Your brother would leap at the chance to invest."

That was not the thing to say to me, and surely not when Hodges was watching from the starboard rail, worried perhaps that "the most important man on the ship" was conspiring against him. I removed Willis's hand and said in a loud voice, "You are forgetting one thing."

"What?"

"I am not my brother." And letting on not at all that I had noticed Hodges, I ambled toward the crowd of sailors near the bow.

Michael Flynn was standing on the raised forecastle deck, like Reverend Stone on the quarterdeck three and a half weeks before. But here was no holy solemnity. Uproarious laughter answered the Irishman's scatological preachments:

"So I find meself on a window ledge three stories above Broadway. Barefooted and damned near bare-assed, I am, whilst in the bedroom, the delectable Delia Dunphy is tellin' her husband there ain't no one else there. But her husband's a disbelievin' man. He's tearin' the room apart, sayin', 'Where is he? I can smell him!' And he goes lookin' in the closet and under the bed and even between her legs—"

The crew roared at that. These were young, virile men, cooped up for six months on a ship where randy stories were as close as they would get to the amorous adventures that all of them craved. Whatever they were thinking—or longing for in their private moments—the best reaction was to laugh.

And Flynn had the gift, punctuating his story with swooping arms, pivots, pirouettes, voice changes, and accent changes, too. "All the while, her husband's mutterin', 'I'll find that Irish bastard and fix it so's he never fucks another man's wife again.' Now, below me, a crowd's gatherin'. And someone shouts, 'Jump! Jump!' Nice folks, them New Yorkers. Anyways, that's when the husband sticks his head out the window and says, 'Aha! I found you!' And he points a big old flintlock right at me nut sack and says, 'Stand still, 'cause I'm gonna shoot your pecker off, you black Mick bastard!'"

"Black!" shouted Pompey. "You ain't black. I'se black!"

"He meant it metaphorically, me African friend. But"—Michael Flynn's eye fell on me—"there's times when the high mucky-mucks and their minions make us *all* feel like the sons of slaves. I'm lookin' at one of them now."

I do not remember if I took a step into the shadows. Perhaps I did.

Flynn leaped from the forecastle and pushed through the crowd of sailors to stand in front of me. "A few weeks ago, I promised this Sagamore swell that I'd let him take a swing at me once I was feelin' better. Well, sir, me back's healin' up nice, and here I be."

The Irishman was challenging me, directly, publicly, tauntingly.

He offered his chin. "Go ahead. I ain't got this far in life with a glass jaw." Then he closed his eyes and let his mouth go slack, like a man who knew how to take a punch.

Every sailor was watching now, to see what I would do. If I walked away, I would be marked. If I took the taunting and struck, that would lead to other difficulties.

But on a crowded ship, a man needed to hold his head high. Momentary conflict was preferable to months of ignominy. Those thoughts, however, did not come to me in an orderly fashion. I simply decided that the best thing to do was to punch this smart-aleck Mick, but slack or not, his Irish jaw might break my fist.

So I pulled back my right, prepared to deliver my knuckles to his nose, and someone grabbed my elbow. Then a voice growled into my ear, "None of that."

Flynn's eyes popped open and brightened at the sight of Samuel Hodges, who had me by the arm. "Well . . . speakin' of glass jaws."

Hodges ignored him and kept his mouth close to my ear. "Remember my promise to the captain. No conflicts with the crew."

"A good idea," Flynn said. "No conflict. Besides, I ain't after givin' free punches to every fancy-pants Yank aboard. Just one. And it ain't you, Mr. Sam the Glass Jaw."

Like any man finding himself in a fight he doesn't want, I was happy to let Hodges pull me away.

"Don't dirty yourself," Hodges told me, "or hurt your writing hand."

"Oooh, your *writing* hand." Flynn made a gesture with his own right hand, mimicking one that men on a long voyage might be tempted to use in the middle of the night. "Mustn't hurt that."

The sailors roared.

Hodges said to Flynn, "Keep it up, Mick, and if there's trouble, it'll be on your head. I might have the captain cut your grog rations."

This caused the laughter to stop as suddenly as if someone had dropped a boulder from the crow's nest.

But Flynn hopped back into the lantern light atop the forecastle and got back to his story. "As I was sayin', the richest man in New York wanted to shoot off me manhood, so I did me best to protect the jewels"—Flynn clapped both hands over his groin—"while the crowd kept callin' for me to jump."

The sailors were laughing again.

"I asks him, 'How can you shoot me pecker off when I ain't got one?' The feller's eyes go wide, and he says, 'Ain't got a pecker? Where'd you lose it?' I says, 'I got it shot off in the war.' 'War? What war? There ain't no war.' He had me there, so I had to think fast, so—"

A part of me was curious to hear the rest of the story, but Hodges was leading me toward the gangway. "I know you'd love to wallop him, James, but—"

Hodges stopped in mid-sentence and looked to the larboard side, near the mizzen shrouds, where Willis was now in deep discussion with Collins, two former schoolmasters, Selwin Gore of Brookline and Hiram Wilson of Dorchester, and Tom Lyons, who styled himself the company attorney.

Hodges released his grip on me and strode across the deck. "May I join you?"

"Why, of course," said Willis with false sincerity. "We're just discussing early Renaissance sketching."

"Indeed," added Collins. "So many nights to talk between here and California."

I wanted no part of this, lest I be drawn into choosing a side, so I descended the gangway and bumped into Matt Dooling, coming up.

"Evenin', Mr. Spencer. I'm for a bit of air. Gettin' stuffy down there."

"There's plenty of hot air above, too," I said.

"Whatever there is of it, there's more belowdecks."

"Put a hundred men on a ship for long, hot air and hot talk become the currency."

"Aye. But hot talk is just paper money. There's plenty aboard who believe in nothin' but specie. Hard coin. And the hardest money is gold, to be got however we can get it. That's what the men are sayin' down there."

So, above and below, mutiny was in the air. And we still had months to go.

February 10, 1849
Target Practice

We now went about the deck in shirtsleeves, enjoying summer in February. All the hatches and skylights lay open, admitting fresh air deep into the ship and alleviating for a time the growing tension.

About six bells, eleven in the morning, the lookout sighted a whale carcass to larboard. Someone said that it would make a fine target, and within minutes, a dozen Argonauts had produced pistols, many boxed since the beginning of the voyage. I considered bringing out my Colt Dragoons but decided that this was an event worthy of description rather than participation.

The deck quickly became a dangerous place with so many excited young men waving weapons about. Some were shooting for the first time and had so little clue as to the proper handling of a pistol that muzzles were flashing and bullets flying about like a swarm of lethal insects. Most of the sailors went scrambling up into the rigging. But I concluded that the safest place was *behind* something, not above. So I put myself behind the longboat stowed amidships, took out my notebook, and watched.

Christopher Harding accidentally fired a round into the deck. It ricocheted back and blew a hole right through the brim of his hat. He shrieked and jumped a foot into the air.

Second Mate Kearns hurried from the quarterdeck and warned the shooters to point the guns overboard or target practice would be prohibited.

Deering Sloate answered by aiming his big Walker Colt over the side and haphazardly discharging it. "Like that?"

"If you want to waste bullets," said Kearns. "But no more shootin' into the deck."

"If I'm so careless as to waste bullets, take care that none of them hit you." Sloate sneered, so that his features, enhanced now by a goatee, made him resemble ever more closely the rats reproducing down in the hold.

I had done my best to avoid Sloate, but as he was also firmly with Hodges in the dispute over our stores, Hodges considered us both allies.

He turned back to the men at the rail and shouted, "A contest, lads. Who's first?"

Even the poorest marksman thought he had the chance to hit that great mass of wallowing blubber. So they all crowded the rail, and as each man squeezed off his shots, the others responded with shouting, joshing, laughter, and a few groans, too. From a distance, we must have made a strange sight on that bright, blue sea, with the little white puffs of pistol smoke blowing off into the wind and the gray, shark-chewed carcass floating by.

I took notes, filling three pages before a pair of polished boots appeared on the deck beside mine. I looked up to see the smoking barrel of that huge Walker Colt and Sloate smiling behind it.

He said, "Write this: 'In the first shooting contest aboard the *William Winter,* Deering Sloate of Dorchester has won with five hits on a dead humpback at fifty yards.'"

"I'm sure your friends back home will be very happy."

"You are an insincere little scribbler, James Spencer." Sloate took the cylinder out of the pistol to dump the spent percussion caps on the deck.

But a voice dropped from above: "Belay that!" And Michael Flynn dropped from the ratlines. "Dump your trash over the side, mister. Me and the lads holystone these boards every day. We'll have no little pieces of metal stickin' in our knees when we do."

"Certainly not." Sloate flicked his wrist, so that the metal caps dropped into the sea. "Don't want to hurt the knees of a man who spends so much time on them."

I could see anger in Flynn's stiffening posture and in the half-step he took toward Sloate. Then the memory of his flogging seemed to temper him.

Sloate laughed, goading with the skill he had been honing since grammar school.

I said, "You'd best reload, Sloate. This fellow's got a short fuse."

"His fuse was cut the first day." Sloate looked at Flynn. "Just stay on your knees, Irish, and the captain will stay off your back."

Flynn watched Sloate saunter back to the shooters on the lee side. Then he said to me, "A fine lot of friends you're travelin' with."

"They're not all friends."

"Then you shouldn't be travelin' with 'em. Travelin' is for friends."

After six weeks, I was sifting carefully to determine who my friends were.

February 24, 1849
Crossing the Line

We had now reached S 0′1″ W 45′4″, which meant that the sun at noon was directly over us. I sat on an empty hogshead, basked in the warmth, spread my papers on my knee, and prepared another dispatch for the readers of Boston. It began thus:

"And now, we are sons of Neptune. In keeping with seafaring tradition, we enjoyed a raucous ceremony last night. Second Mate Kearns, who has crossed the line more often than any man aboard, played the King of the Sea, complete with false beard and long hair fashioned from a deck mop. Dressed in a breechclout, armed with a harpoon, attended by two Negro sailors, he sat on his "throne"—the winch capstan on the forecastle deck—from whence he announced that he would choose one crewman and one Sagamore to represent all aboard who had never before breached the equator. 'They will be shaved with a dull razor, usin' tar for soap and oakum for towel. By their sacrifice they'll earn for all—'"

A shadow appeared above me as I wrote: Michael Flynn, off watch. "An easy way to make a livin', that, sittin' down all day stringin' words together."

I said, "Sometimes, I'd rather be working in the rigging."

"Not in a big wind, you wouldn't." Flynn's face showed the cuts and scratches of a dull shave, for he had represented the crew in Neptune's barber chair and had taken it all in great good humor, though clumps of tar still clung to the hair on the sides of his face.

I suspected our King Neptune knew that Flynn would do well when he selected him, just as he knew that Christopher Harding, the representative—or victim—elected by the Sagamores, would provide fine entertainment when he squirmed and squeaked as Pompey scraped the peach fuzz from his face and the sailors roared.

Christopher had retreated to his cabin afterward and had not appeared since.

During the night, I had heard him whimpering and had knocked on his door, but he ordered me away. So I said, through the shutters, that he had taken it like a man and done us all proud. "Even Mr. Hodges agreed."

I didn't mind a small lie in service to a friend. I hoped for him to regain his pride, or he would soon be known as a nancy-boy, to borrow one of Michael Flynn's more inelegant phrases.

Now the Irishman leaned over me and said, "Outside of the Bible and some damn-fool pamphlets on gold minin', there ain't much to read in the fo'c'sle. How about you let me have a gander at what you're writin'? I'll tell you what I think."

"Some of what I write is for people to read. Some of it is for me to re-member so that I can write it better later. Someday I'll give you some. How's your face?"

He ran a hand over the nicks and scratches. "I give the lads a good laugh, so it was worth it. Easier to ignore pain when the lads are laughin'."

"That shave was not your first time ignoring pain, I'd bet."

Flynn leaned against the rail. "Ignoring pain is a lesson you learn when life hurts you here"—he jerked his thumb to his flogged back—"or here"—he gestured to his heart.

"Your sister?" I asked.

"Long before that." He looked off to the northeast, as if he could see all the way to the land of his birth. "When you're a boy and your da dies tryin' to move a boulder so's he can till the rocks beneath . . . when the potatoes turn black, and your ma loses heart 'cause she's got no hope of feedin' you and your sister . . . when you steal a lamb and they catch you and flog you. Them things make you hard and bitter, rebellious-like."

Flynn fixed his eyes on the whitecaps. "Comes the day you join the Fenians—fellers lookin' for a way out, fellers who think things should be different. And one night, one of you takes a shot at the resident magistrate—I ain't sayin' who—and an informer whispers, and you spend a month in custody whilst the law tries to beat more names out of you. Well, in a life like that, you learn how to ignore pain."

"Were you convicted?"

"If I was, I'd be rottin' in Kilmainham Gaol this very day. But here I am, runnin' for riches just like the lot of ye's."

Eight bells rang. High noon. Time for Flynn's watch.

I said, "About what I told you in the fo'c'sle—"

He chuckled, as if my earnestness amused him. "*You* didn't put the cap-tain up to anything. I know that. What I don't know is, why do you care a damn for what I think?"

"It's a small ship, and I care for what any man thinks about me."

"A small ship, aye. A short life, too. Best not waste it carin' about what men who don't care about you are thinkin' about you." Flynn gave me a salute and headed off.

He made sense, in a roundabout way.

But my thoughts were drawn to a splash in the water. Christopher Harding had come on deck and had thrown something over the side. I went to the rail and saw that it was a split of stove wood. Then he pulled out his Colt and began firing madly at it.

Sloate, who'd come up close behind him, whispered, "Squeeze, squeeze the trigger."

Christopher, as skinny as a shroud, with arms no thicker than rat lines, held the pistol with both hands. The barrel quivered. The arms shook. He drew back the hammer and . . . *Bang!* A bullet struck the floating wood. Then two more shots, two more hits.

"Good boy," whispered Sloate like a proud teacher. Then he noticed Hodges watching, and he said, "We'll all be deadeye shots before this cruise is over, Samuel. I promise."

"Every man a marksman," said Hodges. "That will do us well in California."

Every man a marksman? Marksmanship is a talent like singing or painting. Some men are born to it and some are not. But every man would be *something* before this cruise was over. And the one thing we surely would be was *changed*.

Peter Fallon read "The Journal of James Spencer" whenever he had time, all the way to the JetBlue gate at Logan. He skimmed over the weather reports and shorter entries. He slowed and settled in for the narrative.

The William Winter *pounded south, encountered more dolphins, sighted sperm whales, and cruised through schools of albacore that the sailors caught and Pompey cooked into a fine chowder. They collected enough rain in barrels that they never put in for water. They grew tired of salt beef. They grew tired of each other. Petty disputes festered, and the larger dispute was never far from any conversation.*

Spencer wrote about the tensions. But he also observed the heavens and tracked the constellations. A few nights after they crossed the Tropic of Capricorn, just as Dana had promised in Two Years Before the Mast, *they saw the Magellanic Clouds, a glowing cluster of two nebulae named for the first explorer to run the treacherous straits at the bottom of the world.*

Soon they felt the chill and put on their winter clothes again. They navigated between the cold coast of Patagonia and the fog-shrouded Falklands. They spied a majestic albatross following their wake. Sloate told Christopher Harding to shoot the bird, but Spencer grabbed Harding's hand and reminded him of his Coleridge. Harding laughed and fired, and the bird fell into the sea. Someone, Spencer wrote, would be cursed for that.

On they sailed until the Southern Cross, brightest constellation in the hemispheric sky, passed directly overhead. That meant they had reached the latitude of Cape Horn. But the wind held fair from the northeast, and the men began to wonder what the worry had been. As Spencer wrote for the Transcript*:*

Captain Trask shaped a course to ride the friendly zephyrs as far as possible. And all was well until the afternoon of April the eleventh, when a cloud the color of coal dust rose on the southwest horizon. Soon it was racing toward us, consuming daylight and blackening the sea. Then the northeast wind shifted and swung round, as if the Lord had deemed the *William Winter* sturdy enough to form the pivot point between two mighty currents of water and moving air. The first mate cried, "All hands ahoy!" The captain, who seldom spoke from the quarterdeck in more than a whisper, shouted for reefed tops'ls. But before our sailors could climb, the sea leapt up with the fury of an Appalachian catamount. The sudden turbulence knocked me off my feet, and the sudden wave that rolled over us drove me halfway down the deck. . . .

TWO

Wednesday Morning

BONG!

"This is the captain speaking. We're in for some turbulence, folks. So please return to your seats and keep your seat belts fastened."

Peter lifted the flap of Evangeline's jacket.

They'd lucked out and gotten a row where the third seat was empty. Plenty of room to spread out. Evangeline took the window. Peter wanted the aisle. She'd been sleeping. He'd been sipping coffee and reading on his iPad.

She woke up. "What? What are you doing?"

"Checking your belt. Don't want you flying around like Sandra Bullock."

She yawned, stretched, lifted the window shade, looked out. "Where are we?"

He tapped the screen in the seatback and brought up the animated airplane crossing the continent. "Somewhere over Nevada."

"All desert down there."

"The great Humboldt Sink." Peter leaned over and gazed down onto the brown, sun-baked nothingness.

They had not been this close in months. She leaned back to give him a better view. He pretended not to be enjoying the proximity. She pretended not to be aware of it.

He said, "Imagine walking from Missouri, across the grasslands, along the Platte River, over the Rockies, then you have *that* facing you."

"With the Sierras still to come." She angled her head so that she could see the silver and white mountains, rising like a wall before them.

"That's why New Englanders went by sea. No mountains. And—"

She gestured to his iPad. "Where are the Sagamores now?"

"Getting close to San Francisco."

"Like us."

"It takes us just over six hours. It took them over six *months*. The second half of their passage has been pretty uneventful, but rounding the Horn . . . man, that was brutal. It starts with a black cloud on the horizon, then a wave almost washes Spencer overboard. Then he says, 'In minutes a heavier sea was raised than I had ever seen, and our ship became no more than a bathing-machine, plunging half-submerged, then rising, then plunging again into the ice-green water.'"

"A bathing machine in brutal cold," said Evangeline.

Peter kept reading, "'The sea was pouring in through bow-ports and hawse-holes and over the knight-heads, threatening to wash everything and everyone overboard. But the crew, including novice Michael Flynn, sprang aloft with a kind of bravery that on land would defy description, and . . .'

"It goes on like that for four pages, eleven days, 'a relentless pounding misery of snow squalls and sleet in a hatch-battened coffin so clammy and wet, some men sprouted boils and carbuncles while others saw their very skin slough off with their clothing. When word passed that First Officer Hawkins had gone overboard and was riding the black sea toward his everlasting reward, there were those in our saloon who spoke with outright envy rather than sorrow.'"

Peter looked up, "A man can write like that, we owe it to him to reconstruct his journal."

The plane hit an air pocket. Evangeline smacked her head against the window. Peter grabbed his coffee cup. They dropped, then rose, then dropped again. Whatever wasn't strapped down went flying, including the coffee, which sloshed out of Peter's cup, floated for an instant in the air, then splattered all over his trousers.

"Peter puts on khakis . . . stains sure to follow," she said when the plane settled.

"At least it's not red wine."

"No red wine snark. If not for red wine, I'd have stayed in New York."

"It's not the red wine I'm worried about. It's the red wine*maker*."

"Manion Sturgis has set out to grow the best Zinfandel in the Sierra foothills. So if I'm writing about Zins, I'm interviewing him. He's a master vintner."

"Master vintner, master womanizer, major asshole."

Evangeline pulled a clump of Kleenex from her purse and gave it to Peter. "Sop up the coffee. It won't stain as much. And you're breaking a personal rule."

"What rule?"

"Never speak ill of someone who does your kid a favor. If not for Man-ion, LJ might never have gotten a job with Van Valen and Prescott."

"He might've come back to Boston or New York. Plenty of work there."

The plane hit another rough patch and vibrated like a pickup pounding on frost heaves. Everything rattled, the seatback trays, the overheads, even the window shades.

When it stopped, Peter said, "Besides, Sturgis only did it to get back into your—"

"Don't say 'into my pants.' *That* never happened. He's just a friend."

"But he'd still love to get into your—"

She raised a finger. *Don't say it.*

"—good graces."

The plane hit a sinkhole in the sky and dropped right into it, dropped as if the engines had stopped. Someone screamed. Something banged in the galley. A flight attendant hurried aft to stop the banging, lost her balance, and landed on a passenger.

Evangeline reached across the open seat to Peter.

He took her hand and held tight.

They were dropping like an elevator, which was better than nosediving. If they started nosediving, he might scream himself.

Then the plane bounced off another layer of air, rose, dropped again, then seemed to go up like a glider and vibrate a bit more until finally it found a cushion of air. The ride settled, then smoothed.

Captain Intercom crackled: "Now you see why the seat belt sign is on, folks. We'll be keeping it on all the way to San Francisco."

Evangeline let out a deep breath and tried to pull her hand away.

But Peter held it a moment longer.

She said, "This is a business trip, Peter. Separate beds."

"Separate beds." Peter sat on his and bounced a few times, then tried hers. "Not as soft. You can share mine if you want."

"It should be separate *rooms*, but the hotel is full." Evangeline was standing at the window, bathed in tones of peach . . . walls, bedspreads, carpet, draperies, all subtle complements of the color *peach*. "And I like the hotel."

They were in the Mark Hopkins, on the seventh floor, enjoying one of the few things they still agreed about—San Francisco.

After their own cities—Boston for him, New York for her—they loved San Francisco. Small enough to navigate, like Boston, grand enough to rival New York . . . innovative but a bit hidebound, like Boston, brimming with big money and big ideas for spending it, like New York . . . built by a lot of the same people who built Boston—Yankee shippers, Irish and Italian immigrants—but more cosmopolitan, like New York, with an Asian influence that you couldn't find anywhere on the East Coast.

The truth was that San Francisco wasn't like anywhere else. It was all its own.

And for those who had first seen it as young lovers, it was all theirs. Even lovers who'd never been west of Cleveland dreamed about the City by the Bay. The hills, the fog, the romance . . . no chamber of commerce flack had ever come up with a better pitch.

Peter and Evangeline had been in their twenties the first time. They had just lived through the crazy Back Bay business and didn't know where they were headed, alone or together. They stayed across the street in the Fairmont tower, in a room with a view of the Golden Gate Bridge. Way too expensive but worth every penny. When they raised their heads from whatever they were doing between the sheets, they had the glorious sensation of floating, floating out the window, floating across the hills, floating over the Bay and into the fog. And when they took a break from bed and got dressed and went for a walk, there were all those great vistas . . . and beautiful buildings . . . and amazing restaurants.

And they fell in love.

Then they fell out of love, married other people, divorced, and fell back into love of a more *mature* sort. Now they were having . . . difficulties . . . growing apart, living apart, spending more time apart because sometimes *apart* just seemed like the best thing. So a San Francisco weekend could go either way. They might push the beds together, or one of them might move over to the Fairmont.

Down on the street, a cable car bell clanged.

Peter said, "I love that sound. Reminds me of our first afternoon here, back in—"

"Even if I *was* inclined to stir up memories, Peter, we're due at Arbella House."

"So . . . no time for a quickie?"

She growled and stalked toward the bathroom door. "I need to freshen up."

"We'll take the cable car," he said. "I hear that after it stops at Arbella House, it climbs halfway to the stars."

She tried not to laugh, but he could always make her laugh. If he was hoping she'd leave her heart in San Francisco again, getting her to laugh was a good start. And she laughed. Then she said, "Dream on, boy. Dream on."

He heard the shower. He undressed and threw on one of the hotel robes so he could jump in after her. Always good to go to a meeting steam-cleaned and sharp.

He sat on the bed to check his iPad, and the hotel phone rang.

What? Who used the hotel phone anymore? Old school, hard-wired, no caller ID? He let it ring again, picked it up, said hello.

"Mr. Fallon?" The voice was a male.

"Who's this?"

"A San Francisco friend. Just want to warn you to watch out for white panel trucks and hit-and-run drivers. This is a dangerous town." *Click.*

The guy sounded friendly, like he might even grab Peter and pull him out of the way if that panel truck swerved around the corner. But when it came to money, especially gold, everybody was friendly . . . until they weren't. So the game had started. Someone was already playing Peter Fallon. That meant they were playing his son, too.

He glanced at the bathroom door. Shower was still running. Let it. And let this go a bit longer before raising red flags . . . with Evangeline or anyone else.

In the lobby, a young woman was reading the paper on one of the set-tees. As Peter and Evangeline came by, she got up, put on her sunglasses, and followed them out into the cold wind that was pumping wisps of fog along California Street.

Peter noticed her because she was a redhead, five-ten, trim, chic, red lipstick, pricey shades. Evangeline noticed her because Peter did. As they crossed the street, the woman turned down the hill with her phone at her ear, and Evangeline gave Peter the eye.

"What?" he said innocently.

"You can never *not* look when a redhead walks by."

"Did you notice anything unusual about her?"

"Her lipstick was too bright? Her legs were too long?"

"For a girl who looked so well turned out, that jacket was awful loose. Like she was wearing something on her hip."

"A gun? Don't start, Peter. You're here to appraise an old book collection and reconnect with your son."

"And find a journal that may start another California Gold Rush."

The bell clanged, and the cable car stopped in front of them, with the whole city framed behind. He almost took a picture.

Evangeline noticed someone rush up, an Asian guy wearing a hoodie over a Giants ball cap. She elbowed Peter. "He looks like a guy at airport baggage today."

"And you recognize him because?"

"That hat."

"Half the people in this city wear that hat, like Red Sox hats in Boston."

"So now *I'm* imagining things?"

Peter gave the guy a sidelong glance and whispered to Evangeline, "Maybe it's the same guy. Or maybe it's just *some* guy, some guy running for the cable car."

"I'm just trying to think like you, Peter. Seeing the world through your eyes."

Not many people riding west. So Peter and Evangeline got seats on the outside platform.

The guy in the SF cap sat on the other side, took out his phone, started texting.

The gripman threw his big lever, and the gears grabbed the cable running under the street. The car jerked, then rattled on past the Pacific Union Club.

Peter pulled out his phone. "Let's put ourselves in the history, with the P.U. Club and the Fairmont for background, the only two buildings left up here after the fire."

"Oh, Peter, no selfies." She pretended to be annoyed, but when he held out his arm, she gave the screen a big smile.

He angled the iPhone so the guy in the Giants cap wouldn't be in the picture, but the guy moved his head just as Peter pressed the button. Accidental photo bomb. But a re-shoot? Peter didn't even ask. Evangeline would only tolerate one selfie at a time.

The cable car rolled past the Grace Cathedral, then down, past apartment houses and businesses, into the swale between Nob Hill and Pacific Heights.

She said, "Can you see the history here? The Earthquake history?"

"Smoking ruins. Broken sidewalks. Twisted cable lines. Once the Great

Fire got going, it burned from downtown, up and over Nob Hill, all the way to Van Ness."

That was also where the cable line now ended. The guy in the Giants cap jumped off and hurried toward Polk, making a call as he went.

Peter and Evangeline walked to the corner of Van Ness, three lanes on each side of a tree-lined median, the most direct route from the Bay Bridge to the Golden Gate, always jammed with commuter traffic. Add local businesses—car dealerships, restaurants, groceries—and it was always jammed with local traffic, too.

Peter pressed the "Walk" button on the traffic light. "This is where they set up the dynamite line."

"Dynamite?"

"To create firebreaks. They made a last stand at Van Ness. They'd declared martial law by then, so soldiers from the Presidio just came in and threw people out of their houses and started blowing them up."

"The poor always get screwed," she said.

"Poor? Not on Van Ness. This was a street of dreams in 1906."

Evangeline stepped into the crosswalk, and Peter grabbed her elbow.

"What?"

"Be careful. Maryanne Rogers got run down a few blocks from here."

"And got this whole business started?"

"The 'lost journal' business has been going on for longer than the hit-and-run business, I think." Peter looked both ways, then up California Street, because the Rogers hit-and-runner had come down the hill and around the corner.

All clear. No white panel trucks, no speeding cars, just an Asian kid in a hoodie curb hopping on one of those small-wheeled Dahon bikes. So across the street they went.

"Did they stop the fire at Van Ness?" asked Evangeline.

"Two miles of fancy mansions made the supreme sacrifice to protect Pacific Heights, although the fire jumped Van Ness at California and burned up to Franklin."

"Had to make room for Whole Foods." She pointed up the hill, on the left.

But Peter and Evangeline were going farther, up to a block of rarefied old Victorians standing oblivious behind wrought-iron gates and hedges just above Franklin. Apartment buildings rose around them and the traffic roared like a ceaseless river, but that fantasy island of turrets, gables, pillars, and Palladians defined *old* San Francisco, a mythical place that had all but disappeared during those three awful days in 1906.

They passed the Coleman House, once owned by an Englishman who bought a played-out mine and built a fortune. Then they came to Arbella House, Queen Anne gone wild, with matching turrets on the front, little balconies, arched windows, and a bouquet of colors—yellow clapboards, mustard trim, red highlights. Evangeline hoped it was as beautiful on the inside. Peter squared his shoulders and rang the bell.

A MOMENT LATER, THEY were standing in a foyer as big as an indoor tennis court. A chandelier hung from the high ceiling. A staircase descended from the left, as if pursuing the rays of sunlight pouring through a stained-glass window on the landing. And at the foot of the stairs, an enormous gilt-framed mirror reflected the colors right back up.

Evangeline glanced into the parlor, all bright yellow. Her eye went to the portrait of a woman in green silk over the fireplace. And beyond, in the dining room, was the portrait of a man in a brown suit, butterfly collar, and red cravat.

LJ Fallon came up behind the stern-faced Chinese butler, Mr. Yung. Long past was the son's resentment of his dad's girlfriend. He gave her a hug and led them into the library, where a Tiffany pendant chandelier hung above a Mission-style table. Books lined the walls. Heavy draperies kept out the light. A desk filled the turret at one end of the room. At the other, an arrangement of leather furniture beckoned readers to the fireplace.

Johnson "Jack" Barber was admiring a painting above the mantel. He pivoted as they entered. The key light on the painting glinted off his bald head. He wasn't tall—five-six, maybe—but his quick movements filled the space around him.

"One of my favorites," he said. "'The Mother Lode, Viewed from El Dorado.'"

"Looks like a Bierstadt," said Evangeline.

"Very good," said Barber. "Thought to be lost in his studio fire but right here the whole time. You must be the on-again–off-again girlfriend."

Way to start off on a bad note, thought Peter.

Evangeline shot a look at LJ, who rolled his eyes as if to say, *Sorry, he's my boss.*

Barber came around the sofa to offer a fake grin and dead-fish hand-shake.

Evangeline smelled Aramis, big stuff back in the seventies, when men's colognes were a thing, along with double-knit suits and male permanents. She wondered if this guy ever had enough hair for the disco 'do.

Peter, however, was noticing the bespoke suit, a true fashion statement. And the statement was, *I can afford a $3,000 suit. Can you?* Gray glen plaid with subtle red stripes and a red tie to highlight them. Nice.

Barber offered the dead fish to Peter, who dead-fished him right back and said, "I have no skill at appraising paintings."

"I do," answered Barber. "It's worth about seven million. It's the view that the Gold Rushers had as they crested a ridge and looked across the Cosumnes River toward the Sierras. James Spencer actually saw that view. But . . . you're here to appraise the books."

"That's what my son said."

LJ stood by the library table and watched his father and his boss mark their turf.

Barber strolled over and patted LJ on the back. "Your son is a fine young man."

Fathers liked hearing that, even from guys they had taken an instant dislike to.

Barber said, "He also assures me you're the best in the business. Are you?"

"Am I what?" said Peter.

Beat. Beat. Evangeline watched Peter.

"The best?"

Peter's eyes shifted. *Beat.* He licked his lip. *Beat.* He leaned forward, just to emphasize that he was taller than Barber, whose name was appropriate for a man who shaved his head on what appeared to be a daily basis.

Evangeline jumped in before it turned ugly. "Peter Fallon is the best or you wouldn't have asked for him."

"She's sticking up for him," Barber told LJ. "I guess she's on-again."

"So," said Peter, "let's get down to business."

"Not until the executor gets here," said Barber.

"But we can look at the books," said LJ.

"An amazing collection," said Barber.

LJ handed his father a copy of *Roughing It.* "Twain's adventures in California."

Peter looked it over. "Morocco with a gilt stamp. There are only two first editions of this book in this binding."

"Three," said LJ.

Barber gestured to the book. "Now, open it."

Peter saw the inscription. "Very nice."

"How much?" asked Barber.

"With a Twain signature, in a rare binding, a presentation copy inscribed to an old Gold Rusher? Sotheby's would love it." Peter closed the book and gave it back to his son. "Of course, there are a dozen Bay Area booksellers who could tell you this."

Barber nodded. The light glinted on the place where his skull bones meshed.

Peter said, "I'm not here to appraise paintings or books, am I?"

Barber looked at LJ. "Your father is very sharp."

"Tell me about the journal," said Peter.

"We may not be able to determine who stole the transcription," said Barber, "or why, but Maryanne Rogers believed that we owe it to California to reconstruct it."

"Is Maryanne Rogers the lady in the portrait in the parlor?" asked Evangeline.

"That's Janiva, James Spencer's wife," said Barber, "and Spencer himself is in the dining room . . . both painted by John Singer Sargent."

Peter and Evangeline looked at each other and thought the same thing: Bierstadts, Sargents, Tiffany, and all those books? This was a museum, not a house.

Evangeline asked, "Is there a portrait of Maryanne Rogers?"

"In her sitting room, upstairs." Barber flicked his eyes toward the ceiling and his voice dropped, as if she was still up there. "She married at twenty. A naval lieutenant, killed in Vietnam. Never remarried. Never had children. Became one of San Francisco's leading citizens, patroness of the arts, prime mover in AIDS charities, dowager queen to a generation of descendants . . . a wonderful woman."

"Too bad she had to die in a hit-and-run." Peter threw that out and watched for a reaction.

"She died as she lived," said Barber. "Enjoying her life in the city she loved."

Smooth, thought Peter, as if Barber had said that before, maybe in a eulogy . . . or a witness report.

But Evangeline said, "Nice to hear you drop the smart-ass lawyer act."

Barber looked at LJ. "She sees right through me. She knows I'm just a big softie."

"Softie. Yes, sir."

"And Mrs. Rogers would be unhappy if I didn't offer you a bit of refreshment after your flight. Tea? Coffee? Something stronger?"

Evangeline said, "I'll have a white wine."

A voice entered the library: "It better be *viognier* from Manion Gold Vineyards." In the doorway stood a tall man with silvering hair and a tan more suited to L.A. than the City by the Bay. He was wearing a double-breasted blazer and linen slacks, and he entered a room as if he expected that everyone knew exactly who he was and why he was there. He swooped straight for Evangeline, kissed her cheek, then held her at arm's length. "As gorgeous as ever. And so dignified. So . . . so *Boston*."

"I moved to New York almost twenty years ago."

Manion Sturgis said, "You can take the girl out of Boston, but you can never take that strong Yankee bone structure and sharp eye out of the girl."

She shot her sharp eye toward Peter.

Manion swung a hand in the same direction. "*And* you can take the Boston boy out of Southie, but"—Manion turned after the hand—"you can never take that chip-on-the-shoulder attitude out of the boy."

Peter gave the hand a long look before he shook it. "I'd say it's a pleasure, but we pride ourselves on honesty in Boston, too."

"Don't confuse 'opinionated' with 'honest,' Peter," Sturgis said. "Now . . . I hear you've come to put the humpty-dumpty journal back together again."

"Maryanne Rogers had a different opinion," said Barber. "And who invited you?"

"Sarah Bliss. She should be here soon."

As if on cue, the doorbell rang, Mr. Yung answered, and in came an old San Francisco hippie. That's what she looked like: about sixty-five, frizzy gray hair, long peasant skirt, just as gray and almost as frizzy, striped socks and Birkenstocks encasing wide feet, backpack over an orange hoodie with the SF logo on the front. She dropped the backpack and announced, "I am executor of this will, and I call bullshit."

Barber pressed the intercom to the kitchen. "Mr. Yung, I think we'll need something stronger than white wine."

"I'll bring in the whole cart, sir," answered the disembodied voice of the butler.

Sarah Bliss waddled a bit when she walked and filled the room with a presence quite different from Sturgis's. He was a polished surface. She was all lumps and bumps, and she made the leather club chair sigh when she sank into it.

Barber sat down next to her and flipped open the folder on the table. "You'll have to sign these documents so we can hire Mr. Fallon."

Sarah Bliss twisted around and looked at Peter. "I'll bet you're expensive."

"You're getting my friends-and-family rate," said Peter.

She looked at Evangeline. "And the pretty lady? Does she work cheap?"

Barber offered her the pen. "Your signature, please, Mrs. Bliss."

Manion Sturgis said, "That's probably how he did it with poor Mary-anne. Just shoved the pen at her when she didn't know what she was signing."

Barber said, "Maryanne's will was witnessed and notarized."

"Any undo influence by her lawyer?" asked Manion.

Barber said, "You're giving our visitors the wrong impression."

"No," said Peter, who had drifted over to one of the bookshelves and was perusing the volumes, "I'm finding it entertaining. But I'm easily entertained."

"You mean easily distracted," said Evangeline.

"Ooh, banter," said Sarah Bliss. "I love banter."

"Families squabbling over leatherbound books," said Peter, "a laugh a minute."

Sarah Bliss said, "This is no little squabble. This 'find-the-journal' codicil is signed in May, and Maryanne is killed in June."

"In a traffic accident," said Barber. "I witnessed it. It was terrible. But these things happen."

"Damn fishy to me," said Sarah, "and to my Benson, and *he's* a lawyer."

"Your Benson." Barber scoffed. "Defending enviro-radicals who link arms around eucalyptus trees to protect them—even though they're an invasive species filled with so much oil they explode in fires—that's not estate law."

"Those trees are living things," said Sarah. "They have rights."

Peter and Evangeline looked at each other. One look said, *We are now on a fast train to crazy town.* The other said, *And it's gone off the rails.*

Barber said to Peter, "I hope your son gave you fair warning."

"My lawyer agrees about undue influence." Sturgis leaned against the mantel, as if trying to improve the Bierstadt. "Especially since my brother was the signing witness."

"See what I told you," said Peter to Evangeline, "family squabbles."

Barber said to Sturgis, "We know you don't trust your brother. What about young Fallon here? You recommended him. And he's all-in on this journal hunt."

"A smart boy," said Sturgis. "No need, however, to drag his father way out from Boston to appraise the books."

"You took the words right out of my mouth," said Peter.

"Reconstructing a family journal when you can't get the heirs to cooperate is a waste of time. So"—Sturgis picked a book off the shelf and put it into Peter's hands—"while Evangeline comes out to Amador County to taste my wines and write a nice article, stay and play with these."

Peter looked at the book, then at his son, then at Evangeline. He had decided on *cool* as the only way to play this, for LJ's sake. Cool and close-mouthed.

Mr. Yung wheeled in the liquor cart: tea, coffee, bourbon, an ice bucket with the neck of a bottle poking out of it.

Sturgis walked over and lifted the bottle. "Sturgis Napa Chardonnay."

"Your brother makes fine wines, too," said Barber.

"You drink it, then." Manion looked at Evangeline. "The helicopter is under repair, so a car service will get you at nine tomorrow. A two-hour drive, a nice tour, a even nicer vineyard lunch." Then he said to Peter, "You can come, too, if you behave."

After the door closed behind him, Peter said to Evangeline, "Pick you *up*?"

"Banter's getting heavy now," said Sarah Bliss. "Mellow out, people. Have a drink. Or"—she pulled out a neatly rolled blunt—"smoke a joint." She fished for a light.

Mr. Yung appeared under her nose with a flame in a Bic.

The others watched her inhale, then she offered a toke to Evangeline, who shook her head. "Munchies make me fat." So, to Peter. He said no and gestured to LJ. "None for him, either, not in front of his dad."

"Or his boss," said Barber.

Mr. Yung poured Chardonnays, except for Barber, who took a tumbler of Wild Turkey and said, "If the executors don't authorize it, Mr. Fallon, we can't hire you."

"And the executors don't," said Sarah Bliss. "So . . . nothing to do but go home."

"Glad we didn't get a suite," said Evangeline.

Barber said, "The estate discretionary funds can pay for two nights at the Mark Hopkins, three if you decide to work pro bono on behalf of your son. But if you decide on doing some vineyard hopping or touring, you're on your own."

Peter said, "I may stick around for the entertainment. And"—he took a sip of wine—"the Chardonnay."

"Or the *viognier*," said Evangeline.

"I was hoping you'd say that," answered Barber. "There were seven notebooks for seven sections. Spencer had six children, spread around the country."

"That's why I was in Boston," added LJ, "tracking down a descendant who had the second notebook, the one who called me while we were in the Arbella Club, Dad. It's still being transcribed."

"Some of the notebooks are easier to find than others," said Barber.

"But we need to find all seven," said LJ.

"Otherwise?" said Peter.

"Otherwise"—Barber rattled the ice in his glass—"the estate cannot liquidate. This house and its amazing contents cannot be sold. The proceeds cannot go to the charities selected by Maryanne Rogers."

"And the second Gold Rush cannot start," said Sarah Bliss. "That's what you're really after, isn't it, Barber? A mythical river of gold up there somewhere in the Sierra foothills."

Barber rolled his eyes and took a sip of bourbon. "I am just doing my job."

Sarah Bliss grabbed her backpack and headed for the door. "Come and visit me over in Sausalito, folks. We live on a houseboat. We call it the *Tree Hugger.*"

"The *Tree Hugger,*" said Barber. "She calls her boat the *Tree Hugger.* Is it any wonder she's such a pain in the ass?"

CHINATOWN. IN SOME CITIES, an afterthought . . . but in San Francisco, the center that held, right on the flank of Nob Hill.

After the 1906 fire burned the city to charcoal, they tried to push the Chinese out and grab the real estate. But the Chinese would have none of it. The enclave they had built in those first wild years—when white men sought the favors of Chinese courtesans or the muscle of Chinese laborers—*that* Chinatown was the place where Asian roots sank deepest in America. From there, the Chinese had gone forth to become part of the national story. And nothing, not the 1906 disaster, not the eternal greed of white men who coveted those streets, not the thuggery of Chinese tongs who fought to control the neighborhood, none of it could move the people off their turf.

Peter and Evangeline arrived at the Hunan Garden House on Washington Street a few minutes ahead of LJ and his fiancée.

A classic Chinatown dining palace. Foo lions flanked the front door. A big aquarium—featuring the fish featured on the menu—separated the reception desk from a high-volume dining room with big booths along the sides and two rows of tables in the middle. Chinese prints in red lacquered frames covered the walls. Painted screens covered the service areas. White cloths covered the tables and deadened the sound.

"Lots of tourists." Peter slid into the booth. "But lots of Asians, too."

Evangeline glanced at the menu: Chinese characters, a little English. "Good odds for a good meal, especially if one of those Asians is your future daughter-in-law."

LJ and his girlfriend were arriving now.

Her name was Mary Ching Cutler. Chinese on her mother's side, Anglo on her father's, with slender height inherited no doubt from Dad, long black hair and almond-shaped eyes from Mom, a confident gait that was all twenty-first-century American girl.

Evangeline whispered, "Nice-looking couple."

Peter had decided to let the afternoon business simmer. Meeting Mary was more important. So it was hugs and chitchat and a welcome from Howard Ching, Mary's cousin and owner of the Hunan. Then came a chef's choice banquet of pork belly dumplings, sizzling rice soup, lobster steamed in ginger scallion sauce, Hong Kong dry-cooked shrimp, lamb chops in hoisin, garlic green beans. And with every course, they drank Tsingtao beer and small talked and got to know each other.

The flight from Boston?

A little bumpy, but we had an extra seat. . . .

The weather in Boston?

Hot for October. Nice to be back in the blowing fog again.

And how did you two meet, exactly?

At AT&T Park. Interleague play, Red Sox against the Giants. LJ wore his "hanging Sox" Boston cap, Mary her Giants cap. They came with friends. They left with each other, each wearing the other's cap. Very cute.

"Opposites attract," said Peter, especially since Mary had nothing to do with the law. She was a budding fashion designer.

"It shows." Evangeline admired her blue silk jacket decorated with gold Chinese characters, set off with a white silk blouse and black slacks.

Mary said that she had started her own mail-order house, a small operation that had taken off after some good online reviews.

Yes, they were living together . . . in an apartment on Jackson, in the same block as the Cable Car Museum, in one of those San Francisco sweet spots where you could walk a few blocks downhill for a good meal in Chinatown or climb a few blocks up for a fancy night at the Top of the Mark. A big apartment, LJ boasted, with an option to buy. Two bedrooms, Mary added. One for sleeping, the other for an office, LJ's desk on one side, Mary's design table on the other. And . . .

. . . conversation went so well that it was pay-the-bill time before Evangeline asked Mary about her father.

As Peter snatched the check, Mary said, "My father is in the gold business. A geologist. Cutler Gold Exploration."

Peter raised his head from calculating the tip. "Gold business?"

Evangeline saw the look that Peter shot at his son. She said, "Pay the bill, Peter."

He gave it another glance. "They didn't charge for the drinks."

"A courtesy," said Mary. "Cousin Ching always buys drinks for family guests."

"But make sure you tip for them," Evangeline said.

"Of course I'll tip for them." Peter went back to calculating. "Sometimes, it's like we really *are* married."

"You're too much of a loner." Evangeline looked at the kids. "He's too much of a loner."

"And you're too much of a wanderer," said Peter.

"So we won't be settling down anytime soon," added Evangeline.

Mary gave LJ the corner of her eye, as if she wasn't quite certain what to make of this. LJ gave her just the slightest shake of the head, as if he had seen it all before.

Peter signed the check and asked Mary, "Where does your father live?"

"Placerville, the crossroads of the Mother Lode country."

Then Peter asked LJ, "Have you told him about this journal? This Spencer project that's supposed to trigger a new gold rush?"

"Jack Cutler knew about it before I did."

"Oh?" Peter searched for a word. *Interesting?* Too bland. *Suspicious?* Too . . . suspicious, for the moment.

LJ nudged Mary to take over.

She explained, "There was a woman named Ah-Toy, who arrived in 1849 from China as the concubine of an American sea captain. She made a lot of money satisfying the needs of the Gold Rushers, including an Irishman named Michael Flynn."

"Wait a minute," said Peter. "Flynn's the Irishman in the journal. This is getting very—"

LJ said, "Just listen, Dad." And he nodded for Mary to keep talking.

She said, "Ah-Toy lived to be a hundred. She died in 1928. My great-grandmother took care of her at the end. Ah-Toy would talk of her customers, including the Irishman. She liked him because he liked to talk. And he talked about 'the Chinese gold of Broke Neck, the first trickle from the lost river of gold.'"

"What's Broke Neck?" said Evangeline.

"An old Gold Rush camp," said LJ.

"And your father is looking there for the Chinese gold?" asked Peter.

"He's a geologist, so he's always looking," answered Mary.

"This Chinese gold," said Evangeline. "Is it a real river or a big bag of it?"

LJ looked from Peter to Evangeline, as if gauging how much to tell. "Either one . . . or both. That's what the journal might tell us. That's what the 'second Gold Rush' means."

Peter said, "So my son finds himself at the end of not one but two streams of historical memory about the Gold Rush, and they both seem to be leading to the same place. Why didn't you tell me all this before I flew out?"

"It sounds a little coincidental, I know, but you're always looking for the connections, Dad, the bridges, the things that tie us to history. That's what I'm doing."

"It sounds like you're courting conflict of interest, too."

Evangeline noticed that Mary was blushing. Uncomfortable conversations should be conducted away from the eyes of strangers or cousins who ran restaurants. She elbowed Peter, "We ladies need some fresh air."

OUTSIDE, EVANGELINE WENT TO work changing the subject. She said she wanted to see Chinatown through Mary's eyes and find a new angle to write about.

So Mary led them down Washington Street toward Portsmouth Square.

But Peter took LJ's elbow and stopped in front of a Chinese market. Dead chickens hung in the window, above trays of spices, roots, and crinkled brown mushrooms. Peter said, "You have some explaining to do."

"There's a lot going on, Dad. Just go with the flow."

"Are you planning to give your future father-in-law inside info if we find this journal about some dead Irishman's river-of-gold tall tales?"

"Of course not."

"Are you in some kind of trouble?"

"Challenge, Dad, not trouble. And like you always say, challenge means opportunity. I can't say more. So just do what I ask, okay? That'll be a big help."

Peter tightened his grip on LJ's elbow. "Somebody called my hotel today and told me to be careful crossing streets. Who would be doing that?"

"There's an old joke, Dad, where they ask you a question and you say, 'If I told you, I'd have to kill you.'"

"Old joke," said Peter, "seldom funny."

"But sometimes appropriate. We're all on a 'need to know' basis here."

"What kind of trouble are you in?"

"There are dangerous people in this town." LJ looked at the girls, who were half a block ahead, chatting away. "Maybe you and Evangeline should go back to Boston."

"Not happenin'. Not now."

"Dad."

"You asked me to come out here and help you. So I've come. Evangeline, too. She even got an assignment. But she really came because she likes you."

"I like her." LJ pulled away and started walking down Washington Street. "But it was a mistake to get you involved."

"Well, mistakes happen." Peter went after LJ, grabbed him again by the arm, turned him around, studied those eyes, and saw that look again, the one that said the kid was protecting something deep down—a hurt, maybe, or a disappointment, or a dark secret. It was plain that LJ didn't want to say, "Dad, I fucked up" or "Dad, I let the schoolyard bully push me around." It was also plain that he wanted help, but on his own terms. So Peter decided to be a dad, which meant supporting his kid, no matter what.

He said, "Mistakes happen, son, and I *am* involved. I'm not going back to Boston. I'm not leaving you out to dry. I'll help you find these seven installments. Just promise me you'll tell me what I need to know when I need to know it and that you'll be careful."

"You be careful, too."

THEN THEY HURRIED TO catch up to the girls.

At the corner of Washington Street, Mary stopped and made a sweeping gesture: "They call this Chinatown's Living Room. Portsmouth Square, cradle of San Francisco."

A wide, paved plaza opened before them. Traffic grumbled on the surrounding streets where tourists studied menus in restaurant windows. Locals trundled along with shopping bags and little kids in tow. And just down the hill loomed the worst and the best of American architecture: the postmodern neo-brutalist tower of the San Francisco Hilton and the gloriously futuristic fancy of the Transamerica Pyramid.

All across the plaza, on the benches, beneath the big red pagoda-style gate, under the little trees and the lantern-shaped streetlamps, groups of Chinese—mostly men—talked, smoked, played chess, dealt cards, did business, sometimes in the open and sometimes in the deeper shadows where things always looked a little suspicious.

Mary gave her group of Anglos a quick history as they crossed:

Here, in 1846, a U.S. Navy captain named Montgomery, commanding the *Portsmouth*, rowed ashore, marched up the hill to the ramshackle quadrangle of wood and adobe, and raised the American flag to claim the whole peninsula from Mexico.

Here, on a May day in 1848, a Mormon merchant named Sam Brannan started the worldwide insanity when he held up a jar of yellow dust and shouted, "Gold! Gold! Gold from the American River!" But Brannan didn't care about the gold. He sold picks and shovels and meant to sell a lot more of them once he got everyone headed for the diggings.

Here, the entertainers and gamblers and "soiled doves" went to work in 1849. Here, on an October afternoon in 1850, Californians celebrated statehood, achieved more quickly than any territory before or since. Here the Vigilantes hanged their first victim in 1851, and San Franciscans built their first city hall, first school, and first post office.

The Chinese who settled on the surrounding blocks had adopted Portsmouth Square back when it was a gently sloping greensward. Now an underground parking garage accommodated the tourists and commuters. The locals got restrooms, trees, shrubberies, a pretty playground, and a nice bricked footbridge over Kearny Street to the Chinese Cultural Center in the Hilton.

By the time Mary was done, they were halfway across the square, and most people were paying them no mind at all. But wherever he went, Peter tried to tune himself to whatever frequency was vibrating in the air, and he noticed eyes cast in their direction. An indifferent gaze, a sidelong glance, an outright glare. An old guy on a bench never took his eyes off them.

Maybe they looked like some kind of high-end walking tour, since the girl doing the talking was Chinese. But tourists didn't spend much time in Portsmouth Square at night. Maybe that's why people were watching.

The only other non-Asian that Peter noticed was a woman in black sweats, ball cap, and pricey shades. She had jogged into the square from

Washington Street right after them, went past, and . . . shades at night . . .
odd.

Then that old guy on the bench was getting up, coming toward them,
in and out of shadows, past a table of mah-jongg players, past two old
women arguing in Chinese. He was wearing the basic uniform of the Chinatown elder—sneakers, khakis, windbreaker, plaid shirt. And he was
moving with purpose, maybe even anger.

"Hey! Mary Ching Cutler!" The old man pointed his finger.

Other people looked up from their games and conversations.

Two young guys got up from a bench. One was tall, all in black, with
long hair down the back of his neck like a mullet. The other was big all over
and wore a traditional Chinese mandarin hat pushed down over his wraparound sunglasses. Young guys watching their turf, oozing attitude.

The old man said, "I told you don't come around no more. Where you
father?"

LJ grabbed Mary by the elbow and said, "We have to go."

They tried to step around the old man but he got in front of them and
called to a group playing chess under a streetlamp. "Mary Ching Cutler.
Her father Jack Cutler. He cheat me. He cheat you. He cheat everyone!"

"He never cheated anyone, Uncle Charlie," said Mary.

"Let's just go," said LJ, "straight into the Hilton." He pointed to the
footbridge beyond the big red gate with the pagoda roof.

Peter said, "I don't want to be caught on a footbridge."

"Caught?" said Evangeline. "No one is catching me."

"There's Tong Boys all around," said LJ. "Like the guy with the mullet
over there. If they want to catch you, you'll be caught."

A few more old-timers were getting up, coming toward them. Others
were gawking.

"You father promise us gold!" said Uncle Charlie.

Mary said, "You invested and lost. It's like gambling."

"We're sorry, Uncle Charlie. We really are," said LJ. Then he whispered
to Mary, "I thought he went back to Hong Kong."

But Uncle Charlie was right there. LJ tried to move around him, but
Uncle Charlie kept blocking the way, saying, "I no got money go Hong
Kong. I broke 'cause of Jack Cutler. Me and half the peoples in Chinatown.
So you and your friends, go. Go. Get out."

Peter put his hand out to hold off the old man and pushed Evangeline
forward.

Uncle Charlie looked at the hand as if it had struck him. "You no touch. No touch!"

"I'd be careful, mister." Mullet Man sauntered up. "Uncle Charlie knows kung fu."

"Get lost," said Mary to Mullet Man. She wasn't backing down.

LJ tried to push everyone toward the footbridge, with the growing crowd of Chinese following him.

Then Mullet Man stepped in front of them. "Hey, these people are pissed. They want some talk. So"—he folded his arms as if this were the last word on the matter—"you stay and talk . . . or pay to leave."

"I'm a tourist." Peter stepped around Mullet Man. "I don't owe them anything."

The guy in the wraparounds joined in. "My pal wants you to talk to the people who been screwed by Jack Cutler."

"If they read the prospectus," said Mary, "they knew what they were getting into."

Uncle Charlie shouted, "Tell them go. Tell them get out Chinatown."

Wraparound looked at LJ. "What about it, big boy. You gonna run?"

"No" Evangeline pulled out a can of Mace and pointed it at the sun-glasses. "We're gonna walk, right out of this square."

Wraparound said, "Whoa, lady. We're bein' friendly here. Or we *were*."

"I'm friendly, too," she said, pushing past as Peter, Mary, and LJ quick-stepped after her.

They were halfway over the footbridge, with the traffic on Kearney roaring beneath them, when another Chinese guy got up from a concrete bench and blocked their way. He wasn't too big, but his slick black suit, black shirt, black tie, and dark sunglasses announced that he was the big-gest man in Chinatown, or thought he was.

Mary stopped, then the others did, and the crowd caught up.

But this guy gave a little gesture with his walking stick and jerked his head to Mullet Man—get them out of here—and the whole crowd began to retreat. Uncle Charlie stood a moment longer, then even he backed off.

This guy said to Mary, "You pretty stupid, comin' down here ten o'clock at night."

"It's my neighborhood, too. I live three blocks up the street."

"Not your neighborhood no more, not after your father get all your relatives to go for bad gold stock. You think they know better. But they stupid, and he cheat them."

"That's an unfounded rumor," said Mary.

The guy grinned at Peter and flashed a gold tooth. "Feds call it affinity fraud, like what Madoff do to his Jews. Now, who the hell are you?"

"You first," said Peter.

"Your someday-daughter-in-law, she know. She know Willie Ling. Everybody know Willie."

Mary told Peter, "They call him Wonton Willie, which his grandmother named him because he liked to eat fried wonton so much."

Wonton Willie nodded, as if he took no offense at the nickname. "I come from Hong Kong. Little boy. Now I the new mayor of Chinatown."

"Who elected you?" asked Peter.

Willie studied Peter, then asked LJ, "This you father? From Boston? He some kind of wise guy?"

"Not sure he's wise. But he's smart," said LJ. "The original smart-ass."

"Well, he not smart enough to know Chinatown, if he don't know the mayor."

LJ leaned closer to his father and stage-whispered, "He's self-appointed."

"Yeah. Self-appointed, hey. You come America, you say what you are, then you *be* what you say." Willie pointed his walking stick at Peter. "What you are?"

Evangeline was getting annoyed. She said, "He are with me. And I are holding this." She showed him the can of Mace.

Wonton shook his head. "No, no, no. You no point that at me. Point at Wraparound. That okay. But Wonton get mad. You no want to make Wonton mad. Just ask Chinatown peoples. They know."

"We'll do that," said Peter.

Wonton stepped out of the way. "But tonight, you get a free pass."

THEY HURRIED ACROSS THE footbridge and took the Hilton elevator down to Montgomery Street. Only after they were walking down Washington Street, did LJ start to talk:

"Wonton Willie is a small-timer trying to go big. The Feds took down the Wo Hop To Tong a few years ago, indicted twenty-nine people, including a local legend named Raymond 'Shrimp-boy' Chow. Wonton has been building his power ever since."

"He's a punk," said Mary.

"A punk with muscle," said LJ.

They went past the Transamerica Pyramid, heading for the Embarcadero. Peter slowed at every intersection and scoped out every car. There'd be no hit-and-running on his watch.

LJ kept talking. "Don't piss Willie off. And stay away from Uncle Charlie, too."

"Which brings me to this father of yours," Peter said to Mary.

"Dad," said LJ with a note of warning in his voice. *Don't upset her any more.*

So they went another block in uncomfortable silence until something on the sidewalk caught Evangeline's eye, near the park at Davis Street. "What's this?" She pointed to a shiny curve of metal implanted in the sidewalk, like a giant outline.

LJ said, "It represents the bow of a ship. The original shoreline ran along Montgomery Street. Portsmouth Square overlooked a shallow bay called Yerba Buena Cove. Most of the financial district sits on landfill, and a lot of ships are buried in it. Whenever they build another building, they find another ship and put another outline in the sidewalk."

He pointed to a nearby plaque: "'Site of the *William Winter,* arrived from Boston, August 1849. Uncovered during excavations in 1969.'"

"That's the ship the Sagamores sailed on," said Peter. What a connection. He loved connections. He gazed up at the Transamerica Pyramid and all the traffic speeding past and said, "Imagine how it looked the day that ship arrived."

LJ said, "You can read about it in the material I sent you a few hours ago. The second installment, all transcribed and ready."

The Journal of James Spencer—Notebook #2
August 2, 1849
Hell on a Hill

Hard through the Golden Gate we sailed, chased by the fog that rode like a phantom on the cold Pacific wind, close-hauling past the headlands and the ruins of the old Spanish fort and into a bay the enormity of which was exceeded only by its beauty. All of us, Sagamores and sailors alike, crowded forward to set our eyes upon that expanse of blue water, bejeweled islands, and golden hillsides glimmering in the sun. And for a few moments, we forgot both the travails of the journey just ended and those that surely lay ahead.

Samuel Hodges had described it for us. But a man had to see San

Francisco Bay to appreciate or perhaps even to comprehend it. It stretched five miles inland to a wall of hills that in New England we would have called mountains. It extended north and south for many miles more. And any who looked upon it would have to conclude that it was one of the wonders of the natural world.

A cannon shot from the fort startled us out of our contemplations and proclaimed our arrival. Then a sailor pointed to the top of a bald hill, where men with spyglasses were studying us and, by means of a telegraphic semaphore, were signaling our ship-type and other particulars to the city beyond.

With a few deft sail changes, Captain Trask rounded that hill—soon thereafter named for the telegraph—and warped the *William Winter* into Yerba Buena Cove, where we were presented with a sight such as no man could have imagined anywhere on earth before that time and place, in the month of August, *anno domini* 1849.

Hundreds of vessels lay bow to stern, beam to beam, none more than a cable's length from its neighbor, a forest of masts and spars that surely held more timber than all the hills around us. We counted old whalers and new schooners, sloops and big packets. And amongst the larger vessels swam schools of longboats, lighters, cutters, and rafts, carrying cargo and men across the muddy shallows or up to the wharves that reached out from solid ground like long, rickety, wooden fingers.

San Francisco appeared to be the magnetic pole for half the world's iron anchors and the ships tethered to them, but in truth it was no more than a plank-and-canvas collection of huts, board houses, and rope-staked tents, the most insubstantial city that ever erupted from the earth or crowded a shoreline or climbed to a little square where the American flag flapped in the wind. Spreading out from that square and onto the hills all around were more tents and shacks, some lined up orderly along wagon ruts that aspired to be streets, others plunked down wherever the plunkers found it convenient.

A pall of smoke and dust hung above it all, but fog was dribbling in over the hills, like a head of ale overflowing a mug, and it would soon drown smoke and city both. It might also deaden the noise that reached us even in the middle of the cove, the din of thousands of shouting men (for I did not see a single woman) and hundreds of clanging hammers (for San Francisco was a-building, even as we dropped anchor) and scores of banging pianos and banjoes and squeeze-boxes (for as many saloons and gambling tents were visible right from the ship).

"Goddamn," grumbled Matt Dooling, "but it looks like a shantytown."

"Or a boomtown," said Jason Willis. "A good place for a blacksmith to set up."

Dooling gave Willis a look, then moved farther down the rail.

Willis whispered to me, "A chap like that, I can understand. His main chance is in the diggings. But you're from a mercantile family. You know what we could achieve here."

I reminded him of the vote. In a contentious meeting the day before, the company had cast 61-39 in favor of holding together and retaining Hodges as president.

Willis looked at the men crowding the rail. "The company may be more fickle than you think, or more willing to listen once they see the opportunities right here."

I was not so sure. Men were gazing at San Francisco with as much emotion as they had displayed upon leaving Boston. But it was not nostalgia for what they were abandoning. It was anticipation. They were swelling with anticipation. They were fairly bursting with it.

On the voyage, men had let their beards sprout, so facial hair was in full flower, but in the days before landfall, many had begun to spruce. Some had visited the ship's barber for a shave or trim. (I shaved regularly, as was my custom.) Most had brought out their flannel shirts, a good choice in the surprisingly cold wind. And all had put on their heaviest belts to hold the pistols and Bowie knives that now they might wear in earnest.

Add to their anticipation their vigor. Captain Trask had kept a safe, disciplined ship. Though the first mate had been lost in the pounding misery of Cape Horn, no one else had been seriously injured. Moreover, Doc Beal had insisted that all Sagamores consume a daily measure of lime juice, with or without rum, to fight off the scurvy, while Samuel Hodges had ordered that we engage in at least six hours of exercise a week—fast walks around the deck and gyrations known as squat-thrusts, push-ups, and sit-ups—to preserve our muscle and wind.

But while we had fared well physically, the boredom of almost seven months at sea had allowed small conflicts to magnify and larger issues to fester, making the *William Winter* a floating cabinet of distrust, disagreement, and outright hostility.

Arguments and fistfights had erupted only occasionally and usually over small matters . . . a man taking too much space at the mess table or spending too long at the head when others needed to hang their bottoms in the bow ropes. But we had settled most disputes as civilized men will do, in a civil manner, so our competing factions had mingled cordially enough during the voyage, as they mingled now at the rail.

I could not understand why any of them would surrender the chance at a glittering gold claim to sit in a San Francisco tent, behind a pile of ledgers, with a cold fog seeping in, and do no more than they had done in Boston.

But our "halfway" adventurers seemed willing. They had come to a new place, where nature—both the divine and the human—would demand new attitudes. Yet they could not think like anything other than what they were: New Englanders who believed that cost defined value and value trumped experience. They reminded me of my father.

Everyone, however, obeyed when Mr. Kearns ordered them to the stern to hear the captain's "arrival" speech.

Trask did not offer any eloquence. He jerked a thumb and said, "There it is. They call it San Francisco now. Used to call it Yerba Buena, whatever that means. Maybe they'll call it somethin' else next week . . . Hell on a Hill, from the looks of it. We'll run the longboat till eight bells, midnight, so you can see for yourselves. But any Sagamore not aboard by noon tomorrow, we'll leave you here. Any sailor not aboard by six bells of the morning watch, we'll find you and hang you for a deserter."

I glanced at Michael Flynn, who stood with the rest of the crew.

He was looking around at all the other ships, which should have been sailing back to Boston or New York but instead lay abandoned with crews gone, paint peeling, masts stepped down. Two vessels had been beached, and men were dismantling them for lumber. Another, anchored at the end of a wharf, was covered over with a shed that made of it a huge floating warehouse. Desertion seemed epidemic.

Samuel Hodges planned for the company to stay a day in San Francisco, hear the talk in the town, determine the location of the newest gold strikes, then take the *William Winter* as far as the inland rivers would allow, either north on the Sacramento to Sutter's Fort or south on the San Joaquin. Then we would head overland for the diggings.

As for Trask, he planned to turn his ship around and sail back to Boston.

But if crewmen were tempted to jump now, how much worse would it be when we were just fifty miles from the mines?

Hodges stepped forward and opened his Bible. "As we left Boston with a prayer, let us arrive in San Francisco with—"

"Ahoy, the *William Winter!*"

Hodges glanced over the side at a man standing uneasily in the stern of a rowboat.

"My name is Jonathan Slawsby. I'm here to do business."

Hodges ignored him and read: "The Lord is my shepherd, I shall not want.'"

"I say ahoy the *William Winter*! I'm agent for Sam Brannan, biggest merchant in San Francisco. I'm here to buy whatever you've brought."

Now half the company was looking at the man in the black suit and beaver hat.

"'Yea, though I walk through the valley of the shadow of death—'"

"Say, are you deaf or somethin'?" shouted this Slawsby, who threw a glance at half a dozen other boats rowing fast in our direction, then said, "I'm here to do business."

Hodges looked up from his Bible and shouted, "Not interested!"

"I'll pay triple for whatever you've brung, whatever you paid for it in"—Slawsby looked at the transom for the name of the port—"Boston. Triple. A fine profit, sir!"

Now it was Willis's turn to shout: "If you can pay triple, you can pay tenfold."

"Not interested!" shouted Hodges.

From another boat, a man shouted, "Ahoy, there!"

"Go back to your whorehouse," said Slawsby to the new boat. "We're doin' honest business here."

"'Whorehouse'?" whispered Michael Flynn. "Did he say 'whorehouse'?"

The man in the second boat shouted, "Do you got any women aboard? Marryin' women, loose women, young women, old, pretty, ugly, it don't matter—"

"There's no women aboard this ship," said Trask. "Now move away."

"Hey, Mr. Captain," answered the man, "you may be king cock on that quarterdeck, but in San Francisco, you're just another bearded dick. So damn your orders. We need women and we'll pay plenty for 'em!"

"You'll need more than women if you don't get away from my ship," said Trask. "I'll turn the four-pounder on you."

"We need goods!" shouted Slawsby. "Goods *and* women. Here's the prices." He pulled a sheet of paper from his pocket. "Pork, fifty dollars a barrel. Flour, twenty-five—"

"Fifty dollars for pork?" whispered Collins. "We only paid ten in Boston."

"We pay in gold!" shouted Slawsby. "But them prices won't last. There's more ships comin' in every day, carryin' smarter men than you, and if they sell, prices'll go down faster than your Boston breeches in a Frisco whorehouse."

Collins whispered to Hodges, "Half the pork is spoiled. We could sell 'em that."

"Such a fine Yankee gentleman," muttered Michael Flynn.

A man in a third boat shouted, "If you've brung shovels, we'll top any price! Especially Massachusetts shovels! Ames shovels! Best damn shovels made!"

Willis looked at me and said, "Are you not related to the Ames family of Easton?"

I was. But I did not say so. It would only encourage him.

A man on a fourth boat asked if we had egg-laying hens and offered seventy-five cents for every egg. A man on another boat topped that with a dollar.

"A dollar for an egg?" muttered Thomas J. Lyons, attorney-at-law. "Impressive."

Another topped that with fifty dollars for every hen.

I could see men making eye contact and whispering. These were powerful inducements. Perhaps we really *had* brought the gold.

Hodges shouted to the Sagamores, "Remember your charter, men!"

While this was happening on the starboard side, another boat was bumping up to the larboard. No one noticed until a grappling hook snagged in the mainmast shroud.

An instant later, a broad belly of a man sprang onto the rail with all the skill of an acrobat. He balanced himself, then shouted, "I'm Big John Beam, and I'm lookin' for men who can work!"

"Get off my ship!" cried Trask.

Big Beam ignored the captain. "I ain't talkin' about prospectin'. I'm talkin' about honest work. Real work. I need blacksmiths, carpenters, coopers. I pay an ounce a day, sixteen dollars, more than you make in a week back home."

Matt Dooling whispered something to Jacob Foote, a carpenter from Dorchester. Was Dooling tempted? Or Foote?

Trask came down from the quarterdeck, pushed through the company, and growled up at Beam, "Get off my ship."

"Give me another minute, Cap, and I'll save your boys from the perdition of the mines altogether. So"—Beam shouted to the company—"come find me at my sign-up table in Portsmouth Square, and I'll take any women aboard, too—"

Trask pulled a belaying pin from the rail, drove it up into Big Beam's belly, and sent him pinwheeling into the water. The splash reached as high as the mainsail spar, but Trask never even looked down. He slammed the belaying pin so hard on the deck that it bounced. "No one boards my ship without permission."

Meanwhile, the shouting continued on the starboard side as more boats arrived, more promises of fast money filled the air, more Sagamores moved to the rails to listen.

Trask ordered Kearns, "Fetch the four-pounder! Now!"

"Aye, sir!" Kearns scurried to a deck box and, with the help of another crew member, lifted the little cannon onto a mount at the stern.

"You don't frighten me," shouted Slawsby. "That thing ain't even loaded."

"It will be." said Trask. "Loaded with grape enough to clear all you gulls in one shot."

"I'm agent for the biggest merchant in California!" answered Slawsby. "Do business or be damned!"

Hodges nodded to Sloate, who pulled his Colt, and—BAM!—Slawsby's hat flew.

The report of a pistol stunned everyone—on the boats and the ship—into silence.

Except for Hodges. He shouted, "If it's a choice, we'll be damned."

"Damned for sure!" cried Slawsby. "That hat cost ten damn dollars."

"It cost a dollar and a half," answered Willis.

"Not here." Slawsby fished the hat from the water. "Ten dollars, gold."

"See that?" said Willis to the company. "Even the *hats* are overpriced here."

However shocking the gunfire, it was not nearly as shocking as those prices. I actually noticed one man take off his hat and inspect it, as if he might offer it for sale.

No ROWER RELEASED FROM the slavery of a Roman galley was ever as happy debarking from a ship as I was leaving the *William Winter*. To feel solid ground beneath my feet, to escape that vessel, that cauldron of competing interests, that increasingly odiferous refuge for Horn-rounding Boston rats? That was like a cool draft of water after a summer hike up the side of Mount Monadnock.

I wanted nothing more than to get away from the men who had surrounded me for so long, to wander, to observe, to become the all-seeing eye for sights never yet seen. (Yes, I had read my Emerson.) And San Francisco was surely the grandest theater of the new to be found anywhere, a singular place if ever there was one.

So I declined invitations from Christopher Harding and Matt Dooling and let the men of the *William Winter* go barging off in every direction. I went alone.

And by nine o'clock that night, I had seen enough.

But I needed to set it all down because the mail steamer *California* was leaving on the morning tide. If I did not put a dispatch aboard, it would be weeks before I might send out news of our safe arrival.

So I wrote on a barrelhead in front of the solidest building in town, the three-story Parker House. It dominated Portsmouth Square, and at sixty dollars a night, its rooms were surely the most expensive in San Francisco, probably in America, and perhaps in the world. But the hotel did not put a price on the light falling from its windows. So I angled my notebook to catch some of it, pulled out a pencil, and with one eye on the swirl of humanity around me, I began to fill pages.

After posting, I would return to the ship, which seemed much the safest place to sleep, for while San Francisco simmered deliciously with life, bubbling pots often overflow. Everywhere were grifters, gamblers, rapscallions, scoundrels, whoremongers, drunkards, aspiring drunkards, and sharpers of every ilk, the kind of men who come to any conversation as if it were a financial transaction rather than a simple human interaction. And everything was for sale . . . at an outrageous price, of course, whether you hoped to buy a fresh-cooked chicken leg or glimpse a fresh-powdered female leg, which I admit to paying for in the Parker House Saloon.

The lady reclined as a living tableaux above the bar. She wore a satin dress slit at the side to reveal most of her leg and scooped at the neck to show the tops of her breasts. I bought a brandy at the outrageous price of fifty cents, I sipped, I gazed, and when she moved slightly, so that a bit more of her glorious breast revealed itself, I gasped, along with half the men in the room.

I put all this in my dispatch, for I had determined to tell all and let Sam Batchelder decide what to delete in deference to the delicate sensibilities of our Boston ladies.

Thus did I also report on Ah-Toy's House of Happiness, a tent-and-shack arrangement on an alley off Clay Street, just above Portsmouth Square.

A sign listed prices: one ounce of gold for "a two-bittee lookee," two for a "four-bittee touchee," three for a "six-bittee do-ee." I was tempted. I had paid once or twice but had found the experience . . . disappointing. So I stood outside and observed others give their money to a Chinese man, then step under the flap.

When a miner emerged looking as if he had just seen the face of God, I asked him what—or who—was Ah-Toy. He said she was "a Chinese goddess in green and gold silk, prettier than color in the bottom of a pan."

Her husband had died on the voyage from Canton. So Ah-Toy—twenty-one, tall, beautiful—had made herself paramour to the captain. In San Francisco, she had taken an old road to riches, selling something even more treasured than gold. Ah-Toy, however, never engaged in the "do-ee." She left that to the women she hired. She remained, as the miner told me, "an Oriental mystery . . . givin' up no more than a goggle of that silky black-haired China cooch 'fore snappin' her fingers, bringin' down the curtain, and settin' you to diggin' in your pouch for more gold to buy another look."

Yes, women, or the lack of them, seemed to be on every man's mind, including a lawyer named Reese Shipton.

He was a drawling, golden-haired South Carolinian with a trimmed goatee, a white suit, and a sullen Negro slave named Dingus. After reading a law book, he had written the words *Lawyer, Justice of the Peace* on a shingle and hung it on a post in front of a tent on Washington Street. He said that business was good because lawyers made their living off arguments, and human beings were an argumentative species, so business would only get better in a city filling so fast with so many. In July alone, the U.S. Customs House had recorded the arrival of 3,614 souls, bringing the population to almost 6,000. More importantly, only 49 of the new arrivals were female, and their scarcity guaranteed that they would become a lucrative source of argument.

As for religion, it appeared to play little part in the life of this place. I saw no steeples, although I listened to a preacher in Portsmouth Square call down hellfire on all who tempted the Lord's anger. He did not proclaim heavenly displeasure at those of us who had been staring at women. Nor did he abjure against the sin of drunkenness, as common as women were scarce, as evidenced by a fellow who staggered up to him, deposited a bellyful of beery vomit at his feet, and staggered away. No. Greed was this preacher's great evil . . . and this city's great engine.

Greed was everywhere, in every form and every fashion.

So were rats, rats as big as cats, brazen rats scurrying and scuttling about in daylight and dark, rats from Boston and New York and South Carolina, and native rats, too. And many of these rats walked as upright as apes.

Consider Big John Beam, dried and fresh-dressed after his encounter with Captain Trask. He stood at his sign-up table in Portsmouth Square, looking like the big-bellied king of rats, and gave Matt Dooling and Jacob Foote his pitch, after which he dropped a pouch of gold before them, a "bonus" for whoever signed and brought two more along.

Seeing Foote waver, Matt Dooling said he was a fool to give up his share in the Sagamores. But Big Beam dangled another pouch of gold before his nose, telling him that he should have it when he brought four more men with him. This big scheming rat was happy to break our Boston company into pieces so that he could build his own in San Francisco. But Jacob Foote signed and promised to deliver.

Beam then asked them to say honestly if there were women on the *William Winter*. A boatload of women, he said, "would make us all rich."

I drifted away from such base ambitions and wandered until I came upon the Brighton Bulls, all gathered around a miner who was saying that the biggest strikes were to the south, at a place called Sutter's Creek.

The chief Bull, Fat Jack Sawyer, said, "Then that's where we should go."

I had already listened to a similar discussion between Samuel Hodges and two Spaniards in crisp, flat-brimmed hats. These Californios, as the original inhabitants were called, said that they had heard of great strikes in the north, near Mormon's Bar.

Hodges had thanked them in Spanish and asked if there were wagons to let in Sacramento, for that was where the *William Winter* would head.

And in those two conversations, new seeds of dispute were sown.

All that afternoon and into the evening, I observed members of our company lurching from saloons to gambling halls to peddlers' shops, drunk with excitement and rotgut. I watched Sagamores skinned in street-side games of three-card monte. Even sober Attorney Tom Lyons dropped thirty dollars.

I stopped on Kearny Street at a makeshift table—two boards on two barrels. The man behind the table wore a beaver hat, a fine cravat, and a paisley vest. I would have thought him a gambler until he tried to sell me a contraption made of wood and wire resembling a divining rod. He called it a gold finder.

"Guaranteed to point down at the least little glimmer of yellow in the ground, or your money back, friend. Just sixteen dollars."

That amount, or rough multiples of it, seemed to be the cost for just about everything, perhaps because it was the value of an ounce of gold, give or take.

The peddler tried to put his contraption into my hands while looking into my eyes with a kind of forlorn desperation. He had once been someone . . . somewhere. The vest and cravat said as much. But the stains on the vest and the rum blossoms on the face told another tale. Then his eyes widened at something behind me.

A man was approaching, a walking bag of rags, a great mat of beard and hair. He smelled like a ship's hold after the hatches have been battened and the vermin smoked to death. Without a word, he smashed the peddler in the face. The peddler's hat flew off. His head flew back. And his feet flew into the air. When he landed, his wide eyes had rolled back to some faraway place . . . Connecticut, perhaps.

The puncher knelt and extracted a sack of gold dust from the peddler's pocket. He measured out about an ounce and said, "Them things don't work. This feller promised a refund, but he wouldn't give it. So I'm takin' it." Then he disappeared into the crowd.

I looked around to see if someone would detain this man. Only one miner stopped and only to say, "Don't trouble yourself, mister."

I asked where the law was.

"There's a sheriff. The Spaniards call him the *alcalde,* but he does his best to keep out of trouble. And a few judges who spend most of their time drinkin' with the lawyers. Truth is, the only *real* law between here and Missouri is Miner's Law, and by Miner's Law, that peddler got what was comin' to him. He was sellin' bum goods."

Thus ended my introduction to San Francisco and my first dispatch from California. I folded the sheets, stood, and was struck by the ethereal evening light, the glimmer of thousands of lanterns filtering up through the tops of the canvas tents, like votaries to the God of Gold.

IF THAT GOD WAS looking down just then, he saw a gang bursting into Portsmouth Square from the Clay Street corner: five men—an American, a Mexican, and three Chinese—chasing our Negro cook, Pompey, and a fast-moving Irishman whose fast-talking seemed to have failed him.

As they raced toward me, Pompey slipped in a puddle of beery vomit, flew into the air, and landed on his back with an ugly splash.

Michael Flynn stopped, looked over his shoulder, and shouted, "Get up!"

One of the Chinese was swinging a weapon over his head. It looked like a threshing tool, two long sticks held together by a chain.

Flynn glanced at me, and as quick as the glance, he grabbed a pistol from my belt and waved it in the air.

That stopped his pursuers in their tracks, and passersby turned to watch, not because they might intervene but because here was a new form of entertainment.

Flynn told me, "Pull the other one."

"The other what?"

"The other gun. In your belt. Pull it."

"It's not loaded," I said from the corner of my mouth.

"No need to shoot it. Just aim it. Aim it at the Chink with the sticks."

As my hand went to the belt, the white man and the Mexican pulled their guns, too. Hammers clicked and cylinders clacked. Lines were drawn in dust and drunken puke.

I pulled the pistol out and pointed it in the general direction of the Chinese.

The white man put his pistol to Pompey's head and said, "Stand up, nigger."

Pompey did as he was told, professing his innocence all the way.

"You ain't innocent if you run with that Mick," said the white man.

Flynn pulled back the hammer on my pistol. "Just let my friend step away, and we'll *all* be friends."

"We're friends *now*, Mick. 'Cept friends don't cheat friends."

The Mexican, shorter, darker, with a blanket over his shoulder, took two steps up to me and pointed his pistol right at my face. "I am nobody's friend, señor."

Flynn said, "Don't let him scare you, Jamie."

There was advice offered too little too late.

"Just make sure you shoot him first," Flynn added, "not them ignorant Chinks."

"Iggorant? I no iggorant!" said the Chinaman. "You thief!"

"You cheat Keen-Ho," said the white man. "You cheat Miss Ah-Toy herself."

The Chinaman said, "Twenty-four dollar! You gimme twenty-four dollar!" He wore baggy trousers and a long plaited queue down his back. I had heard these Chinamen referred to as "Celestials," since they hailed from what was called the Celestial Empire, and they appeared so other-worldly on these dirty streets that it was as if they had come from some outpost in the heavens. But Keen-Ho Chow was worldly enough to know the value of an ounce and a half of gold.

While keeping an eye—and a pistol—on the Mexican, I said to Flynn, "You owe these men money? Because of a *whore*?"

"No whore," said the Chinaman. "Courtesan. Too good for him. And he cheat her. So no touch-ee for him. And no do-ee. Never do-ee."

The white man said, "If you cheat the Chinks at Ah-Toy's, you cheat the man who sells 'em the whiskey they sell to you. That's me. And you cheat the Mexican who sells 'em tortillas. That's him."

The Mexican grinned, as if he would consider it a pleasure to shoot me to pieces.

I did not grin back. I knew what whiskey was. I did not know what a tortilla was. Perhaps it was Mexican slang for what Ah-Toy was selling.

Flynn said, "I admit to spendin' more than I come with. Some temptin' games of chance around here. But—"

"No sad stories." The white man pointed his pistol at Flynn. "Give over an ounce and a half, or twenty-four dollars in Yankee coin. Otherwise, it's Miner's Law that—"

"If I owe anything," said Flynn, "it's half an ounce. And if I give anything, I want to go back, 'cause I never got to touch her."

"Look-ee one ounce," said Keen-Ho. "Touch-ee one ounce plus one half. You pay one look-ee. You get one look-ee. You try sneak touch-ee, you pay again all over."

"Why, you old swindler," said Flynn. "I'll see you hang."

I feared that we might all hang—those of us who were left—if someone started shooting, so I lowered my gun.

Flynn said, "What are you doing?"

"What civilized men do. Negotiating." I gave the Mexican a nod, but he did not lower his pistol. Then I said to the taller one, "If my friend gives you half an ounce and doesn't demand the touch-ee, can we all be on our way?"

"I ain't doin' it," said Flynn. "Besides, I got no more to give."

"Yeah," said Pompey. "Lost it all bettin' on the game with the wheel. So he borrowed my money to get a look at that Ah-Toy. I was next in line when he come stumblin' out the tent shoutin' for me to run."

Flynn shrugged, as if to say he was a weak man and the temptations were strong.

The white man shook his head. "Can't let boys be sneakin' free touch-ees, or the next thing we know, they'll be sneakin' free drinks."

I swallowed the dryness in my mouth and offered a compromise: I would pay eight dollars, and Flynn would walk away, or I would pay twenty, and Pompey would get his look-ee.

All around us, drinkers and gamblers and walkers were watching, including a few familiar faces from our own company. The sight of them gave me an idea.

"It's a good deal," I said. "But on the other side of the square, there's a man from Boston who's mad at the world. He'd love to use his new gun on something other than a wooden target. He's a friend of mine. Next to him is a man who's nobody's friend but can shoot the eye out of a needle and wouldn't hesitate to shoot yours, just for sport."

The white man looked over his shoulder at Christopher Harding and Deering Sloate.

I raised a finger in Harding's direction, and he tipped his hat. Sloate put his hand on his pistol, as if anticipating a bit of fun.

The white man said, "Bostoños, eh?"

"Hard bargainers," I said. "But fair."

And we made the deal. I delivered twenty dollars from my pouch. Keen-Ho took it and went away grumbling in Chinese, followed by the white man and the Mexican.

As Pompey broke into a grin of pure reprieve, Flynn gushed out congratulations for a man who could so skillfully talk his friends out of trouble.

I suggested that it was my money and the danger of a Boston crossfire that proved more persuasive than my wit. I added that while Pompey could go back and get his reward, the now-penniless Michael Flynn would do well to return with me to the ship.

This Flynn counted a fine idea. So he gave back my pistol and got to talking. He talked all the way to the post office, extolling my skills as a negotiator, complimenting me on my willingness to back up my talk with threats, telling me I might make a good banker, one who carried a pouch filled with ten-dollar Gold Eagles to loan out on the spot.

At the post office, he stood beside me in a long line of homesick miners waiting to send letters that would assure loved ones far away that their Gold Rush adventure continued, even if it didn't. I pulled out my coin pouch and paid the outrageous sum of ten dollars to post my dispatch and a single letter to Janiva. Then we made our way down to the water, where our longboat was arriving with Sean Kearns at the tiller.

Doc Beal stood aloof from a gang of waiting Sagamores, observing various stages of inebriation as if they were stages in the process of infection or healing.

Selwin Gore and Hiram Wilson, the schoolmasters, appeared as drunk as upright men ever had. Scrawny Selwin had a wet stain at his crotch. Wilson was bawling a saloon song: *"What was your name in the States? Was it Thompson or Johnson or Bates?"*

As soon as the boat bumped against the pilings of Long Wharf, about a dozen of us scrambled in, stumbled in, or fell in over the side.

Wilson was so drunk that he almost missed the boat. But he kept singing: *"Did you try to abscond with a beautiful blonde?"*

Doc Beal grabbed Wilson by the belt and pulled him aboard. "You won't be singing in the morning."

Wilson grinned and kept up: *"Such minor offenses we tolerate!"*

Kearns looked into the shadows and said, "All right, push off."

"Wait," I said. "Where's Flynn?"

Kearns called out his name . . . but no answer.

I said, "He was right behind me."

"He ain't now," said Kearns.

Michael Flynn had disappeared into the darkness.

Wilson groaned, *"Oh, what was your name in the States?"* Then he passed out.

As the longboat slipped through the fog, I looked up at the light dancing above all those glowing tents and wondered if I would ever see Flynn again.

As I undressed in my cabin a short time later, I felt for my coin pouch and *knew* that I would never see him again . . . or my coin pouch.

The Irish son of a bitch.

August 3, 1849
Rebellion

I slept fitfully. I had grown used to the rhythmic rocking of a ship under sail, but we were now at anchor. So the *William Winter* rode up slowly, then down, then up, then slowly down, down a bit more, then . . . a movement so intermittent and unpredictable that it vexed rather than soothed.

Add to that my anger at Michael Flynn. I had resolved before falling asleep that I *would* see him again. I would go through the town and find him before he boarded the boat for Sacramento with all the money I had.

And Hiram Wilson's damned song kept running through my head. *So what was my name in the States?*

But each time one of these annoyances woke me, I sensed that something more was amiss. My instincts were no better than any man's. However, the sighs and groans of a ship at anchor were augmented by other sounds . . . the creaking of grates, the clanking of oarlocks, the murmur of voices, the bumps, thumps, and thuds of small boats ferrying men ashore or bringing them back.

Then louder voices roused me from my penumbra: Sloate was saying something, and Hodges was answering, "Goddamn them. Goddamn them all."

I pulled out the watch that Flynn had the decency not to steal and held it to the light slipping through the door slats: ten past six. I tugged on my breeches and boots, tucked in the flannel shirt that I had slept in, and stepped into the saloon.

Hodges loomed before me, looking uncharacteristically unmade, half-dressed, hair askew, nightshirt tucked into his trousers, stubble sprouting on his chin. He said, "We've been sleeping through rebellion, James. Arm yourself." He reached into his cabin and pulled out a well-oiled fowling piece.

THE SKY WAS BRIGHTENING but the fog pressed upon us like cotton batting on a wound.

The cargo grate lay open, and a pallet of barrels, boxes, and hogsheads hung in the air. Three Willis men were holding a line that suspended it above a raft tethered to the side. Charles Collins was ordering that they lower away "and be quick about it."

Hodges blasted his gun into the air, startling the men enough that they let the line slip and the pallet dropped onto the raft, just as Collins wanted.

Hodges shouted at Collins, "Stop! Stop now, or Sloate will put a hole in you."

"Belay that." Captain Trask appeared on the quarterdeck as a splatter of spent birdshot rained down.

Did Willis choose this moment, after the company had enjoyed a night in San Francisco, knowing that drunken stupor would have replaced sleep? Or did he think that the ordinary comings and goings on the ship would mask sounds of deceit? And was Trask part of it, a merchant captain ready to work with the budding San Francisco trading house? Or was he simply trying to maintain order? He said, "Take your disputes ashore or I'll turn the swivel on *you*."

Hodges looked at Collins. "Where's Willis?"

"Ashore," said Collins, "guarding supplies and waiting for you."

Hodges spun back to the captain. "Who opened this hold?"

"Look to your own," said Trask.

"It was Jacob Foote," said Sloate.

"Foote was loyal to us." Hodges seemed more perplexed than angry. "We counted on him to build sluices. We'll need sluices."

"San Francisco needs carpenters," said Collins, "and Big John Beam pays in gold."

Hodges goddamned Collins and Big Beam and appeared ready to god-damn everyone on the ship.

"When Foote and his friends opened the hold and took their supplies," said Collins, "they opened Pandora's Box."

"Willis is waiting for me, is he? Waiting for what?" asked Hodges.

"To talk."

"If I go ashore, I'll do more than talk."

Attorney Tom Lyons asked the captain, "Why didn't your watch stop this?"

"Reduced watch in liberty port," said Trask. "Only two on duty, plus your carpenters, supposedly protecting your goods. They tied up one sailor. The other one deserted with them. My second mate, Mr. Kearns."

"Goddamn them," said Hodges.

"I'll see that God gets the opportunity," answered Trask. "Kearns is a dead man."

More Sagamores were coming on deck now. The Brighton Bulls emerged from the forward companionway. Selwin Gore and Wilson and several others were stumbling up amidships, rubbing eyes, holding heads, blinking stupidly in the brightening fog.

Fat Jack Sawyer came forward and said, "We breakin' apart, Hodges?"

"No, goddamn it. We'll put a stop to this and be on our way."

"To where?"

"The gold fields, you goddamn fool." Hodges said it as if he did not have time for travel planning when there was rebellion to put down. He looked around at the rest of us and said, "I'll brook no opposition, here or ashore."

"Well, sir"—Fat Jack put himself in front of Hodges—"there's fifteen rivers up in them mountains, west-runnin' rivers drainin' along a line that's two hundred and fifty miles long, north to south. A lot of places for diggin'. So I'm askin' you again, which way is this ship goin'? North or south?"

"The big strikes are north," said Hodges. "I have it on good authority."

The conflict had germinated overnight and was already bursting from the soil.

Sawyer said, "We heard the big strikes are in the south. We seen gold nuggets from a place called Sutter's Creek. And seein' the truth is better authority than hearin' it."

"We'll talk about this later," said Hodges, "after I save your goods."

"Mine ain't been stole," said one of the other Bulls. "And I'll be fucked if they are." He shoved two Sagamores aside and made for the hold. "I'm takin' what's mine and headin' south."

"Like hell, you are," said Hodges.

At the same moment, Hiram Wilson got in front of the Bull. "I'm loyal to Sam Hodges, and I say you go no farther."

This Brookline schoolmaster had been a companionable shipmate. The sun had browned his Boston-sallow skin. The sea air and exercise had invigorated him, which had caused him to grow more assertive. He had also drunk so much the night before that he was still drunk, which enhanced his assertiveness but made him weak-legged as well.

All it took was a shove and Wilson went stumbling backward, tripped on the hatch coaming, and fell into the hold.

Scrawny Selwin, standing nearby, took an ill-advised swing, missed, and spun halfway around. Fat Jack grabbed his collar and flung him into half a dozen Hodges men.

Hodges turned to Sloate. "Shoot that bastard."

But Pompey skulled Sloate with a belaying pin. "You heard the cap'n. No more shootin'."

Then another fist flew. It did not matter from whom, because everything was coming suddenly and completely undone. Another body tumbled into the hold. Another man went overboard. Everyone began to shout.

Christopher Harding took a swing at Fat Jack that missed and bounced off the side of Matt Dooling's head, which enraged the blacksmith, who grabbed Christopher and threw him overboard.

Pompey retreated to the quarterdeck, where he and the captain watched the riot erupt among the Hodges men and Willis men and Brighton Bulls and independents, all smashing, punching, pushing, falling into the hold, flying overboard, grappling for goods and . . .

. . . our brave New England experiment came to a swift and ignominious end.

HAD THIS RIOT HAPPENED where there was no Trask or Doctor Beal to exert physical or moral authority, the men might be fighting still. But those two combined to restore order and bring the company to a place where negotiation replaced fisticuffs, cold words supplanted shouts and curses. Trask used musket fire. The doctor spoke common sense.

As the fog burned off, an uneasy peace settled onto the *William Winter*. Men were angry. They were sullen. They were bruised inside and out. But none were for lingering.

The Brighton Bulls demanded their shares. They would go on their own.

Matt Dooling and some of the others formed small groups for the same purpose.

Collins debarked with the pallet of goods and promised to send back for more.

Hodges said that they would *get* nothing more until Willis returned to negotiate. Though he tried to project authority, he seemed stunned, like a man struck on the head by a flowerpot falling from a second-story sill. So he pulled around him his loyalists—Sloate, the soaking Christopher Harding, Attorney Tom Lyons, and the rest—sat on the forward deck, and, most uncharacteristically, listened. But he listened with little or no comment. He did not even notice when I left the ship.

I WALKED THE WHARVES where Sacramento-bound schooners took on passengers and freight. I climbed the hill to the Parker House and watched the men watching the woman above the bar. I watched the table where they played the game with the spinning wheel. I watched a gambler dressed like a New York actor dealing cards to dirty miners. But I spied no Michael Flynn. So I went to Ah-Toy's and asked Keen-Ho if the Irishman had come back. Keen-Ho may have laughed or may have scoffed. But I was sure by then that Flynn and my money were gone, probably on the first boat for Sacramento that morning.

So I went back down the hill and out onto the new wharf at the foot of Washington Street. The planks and pilings, shipped from Oregon, smelled clean, with the fresh-cut tang of green wood. I inhaled and tried to drive

San Francisco out of my nostrils, for on top of everything else, the stench of garbage, tide flat, and human waste was as thick as the fog.

The beach and wharves, connected by a waterfront wagon rut called Montgomery Street, swarmed with boats, carts, and men, as they had swarmed the day before and probably every day since the Rush began. Pallets of goods rose, and barrels formed tight battle squares, and men stood guard around them or within them, and carts clattered up to them and loaded on cargo and went struggling and straining up the hills and down.

The town was booming. But my spirits were not. I sat on a piling, disconsolate and confused, with my elbows on my knees and my chin in my hands and not a coin in my pocket, and I watched the cold fog pouring across the Bay.

Around five o'clock, I noticed Hodges riding the incoming tide with Sloate and half a dozen others. As soon as the longboat struck the shore between two of the wharves, he bounded over the bow and stalked up to a supply pen on Montgomery Street, where Willis had pitched a large tent. He and Willis exchanged a few sharp words in the open, then disappeared into the tent.

My hope rose that they might settle their differences. Being a good distance away, I could not hear what they said. But after a few minutes, they emerged and Hodges stalked back to the longboat, shouting over his shoulder, "This is not the end of it."

Willis shouted back, "We will have the rest of our goods and have them now! And *that* will be the end of it." Then he ordered half a dozen men to seize the longboat.

Hodges spun back. "By God, you won't touch that boat."

"We'll fill it and bring it back," said Willis.

A man named Morrison, a logger from Berkshire County who carried an ax the way other men carried pistols, said, "We'll take what's ours by right." Then, holding the ax at his side, he stepped toward the boat.

What happened next was shocking, sudden, yet somehow appropriate in this brutal new world. As Morrison hefted his ax, I could not tell if he was preparing to place it on his shoulder or deliver it directly into Hodges's head. But a plume of white smoke jetted out of Sloate's gun, and its report reached me half a second later.

Morrison staggered, looked down at a hole in his side, then dropped to his knees.

The waterfront went silent. Everything between the wharves stopped, carpenters in mid-hammer, stevedores in mid-lift, drummers in mid-bark.

Hodges shouted, "You all saw that. Self-defense. He was comin' at us."

Collins rushed forward as Morrison fell facedown in the mud.

Hodges leaped into the longboat. Sloate, still holding the pistol, climbed in after.

"The law will be coming for you!" cried Willis.

"There's no law here but this—" Sloate holstered his pistol.

And a familiar voice whispered in my ear, "Someday, somebody'll have to kill that Sloate. Hodges, too."

I turned and looked into Michael Flynn's face. "You? You Irish son of a bitch."

"Did you know that every company started in the East falls apart in California?"

"I don't give a damn. You stole my money."

"You give a damn. You're sittin' here askin' yourself what to do, now that all your fine Yankee friends is showin' themselves to be no better than anybody else."

Down at the water's edge, Morrison was wailing in pain. Collins and three others picked him up and carried him to the tent.

I said it again. "You stole my money. I did you a favor, and you stole my money."

Flynn pulled my purse from his pocket and dangled it in front of my nose. "I borrowed it." Then he dropped it into my hand. "It's heavier than it was. I pay interest."

I looked into the pouch: gold dust, nuggets, Golden Eagles. "How did you get this?"

"By doin' what everyone does in California, playin' the great game of chance."

"Chance?"

Flynn turned to the sound of Morrison's agony. "That feller's gut shot. But there's a *chance* that he'll live, just like there's a *chance* that Willis gets rich in San Francisco, and a *chance* that minin' pays off for all the fellers headin' for the hills. I took a chance last night that I could hold my own when I took your coin pouch to a card table."

"You gambled my money?"

"And won. Took me all night, but I won yours and mine and then some. Made enough to get more than a look-ee. Even made enough for two of these." He handed me a piece of paper on which was printed: San Fran-cisco Schooner Company, Passage on the *Anne-Marie*, departing

CLAY STREET WHARF FOR SACRAMENTO. And handwritten: *$30. August 4, 1849, 6:30 AM.* Flynn said the ticket was for me.

"But I'm for Hodges."

"Then you're a fool." He snatched the ticket back. "Hodges is a beaten man. And beaten men goes one of two ways. Either they curl up and die, or they get mean and bitter. And he's pretty mean to begin with."

I said that I owed it to my editor to see which way Hodges went.

"Did you like how it went just now, then? Or how it went this mornin', with all them fine Yankee gents havin' their New England town meetin' . . . San Francisco style?"

Morrison's wailing distracted us for a moment, but the rest of the world was already getting back to buying, selling, yelling, hammering, building, hauling.

I said, "I thought we'd be different."

"You thought *you'd* be different." Flynn repeated my words with a fine Irish sneer. "You Yankee boys think too damn much of yourselves. You've heard of the California and Boston Joint Stock and Minin' Company, have you?"

I had. They were mostly Harvard men. They had named their ship the *Edward Everett,* after the college president. He had even given them all Bibles when they sailed.

"Best-equipped company yet," said Flynn. "Sailed all the way up to Sacramento. Got off the ship and lasted a week. The whole company come apart like a rotten wheel."

"How do you know that?"

"I took one of them for a hundred and fifty last night. He said it was all his profit from when the company dissolved . . . his profit on a three-hundred-dollar investment."

"That's only fifty percent."

"Not quite so good as what them harpies was promisin' yesterday, is it?"

"It doesn't matter. My job is to chronicle the Sagamores."

"But there ain't no Sagamores now, just a bunch of squabblin' Yanks who forgot all the high-flown sermons the minute they got here, just like I said they would . . . and got flogged for sayin' it."

"But—"

"Your fat-guts Boston editor don't want stories like that. You need to get out on your own, James, and I need a pardner."

"Pardner? You mean you've jumped ship?"

"The whole damn crew's jumped, but for two . . . the Portagee steward and the nigger Pompey. So there's nobody to sail that ship. So we'll have a mean and bitter captain, too. So I'll be on me way before he can run me down. And you need to be on your way before the law gets round to arrestin' Hodges and Sloate for what we just seen. You don't want to be stuck here, waitin' to witness in some rump court while everyone else is off for the diggin's."

I said nothing. I thought next to nothing. I did not know what to think.

Flynn leaned against a piling and shoved his hands into his pockets. "Loyalty's a fine thing, James, but a man needs somethin' to strive for. He needs a goal, like."

"I can guess yours."

"An easy guess. To find a big strike and sift out every goddamn grain of gold there is. Then go back to Boston, pay me back rent so I get that daguerreotype of me mother, and buy that fuckin' club of yours."

"And mine?"

"A rich boy's dream. To see life . . . lived large and rubbed raw. To see what you'll never see again, once you settle into your Boston parlor with your pretty wife. What you want to see is up there"—he jerked a thumb toward the eastern hills—"up where the gold is, up where the stories are, stories to write down and make you famous."

I did not admit it, but he was right.

"Your dream has its head in a cloud, James. Mine's rock hard. Between the two of us, we could make a fine team. So"—he put the ticket into my breast pocket—"sleep on it. If you see the sense of what I'm sayin', meet me at dawn. Just remember, travelin' is for friends, and Hodges may act like he's your father, but he ain't your friend."

August 4, 1849
Jumping

Some time after midnight, I wrote a note to Samuel Hodges.

I never spoke with him. He was drinking when I returned to the *William Winter*, drinking hard. I had only seen him sip a few glasses of port in the captain's cabin, and these had produced pleasant effects—a looser tongue, a broader laugh, a more relaxed demeanor. But that night, he had worked his way through a bottle of bad whiskey and was starting on a second. He appeared sullen, and beneath that, belligerent, a man of thwarted ambition.

So I chose to write rather than talk. I should have looked him in the eye, but drunk or sober, he was certain to see betrayal in my actions. And he had been betrayed enough.

Besides, it was not only Hodges who radiated anger. Most everyone who remained a Sagamore, twenty-five men in all, seemed in the same state.

My note explained that since the company had dissolved, they no longer formed a clear prism through which I might show this Gold Rush to the people of Boston. It was my job to find a new perspective. I did not expect Hodges to accept my argument. But by the time he read, I hoped to be long gone.

AFTER THE SHIP'S BELL rang once for four-thirty, I waited a few minutes so that anyone bestirred by the sound might slip back to sleep. Then I left the note on the saloon table and tiptoed up to the main deck.

Lanterns burned bow and stern and bled light into the fog. I had my sea bag on my shoulder, my pistols in my belt. I moved quietly and breathed lightly. I was a shadow.

The Negro Pompey and Christopher Harding had the watch. Christopher was asleep on the forecastle deck. That was good. But Pompey's voice cut through the darkness from the stern. He said, "If you's thinkin' of sneakin' off, Mr. Whoever-You-Are, I got the oarlocks. Ain't supposed to let no one leave at night. Not after last night."

"You owe me a favor, Pompey," I said just above a whisper.

His shadow picked up the lantern and came down from the quarterdeck. He held the light to my face. "Mister Spencer?"

"How was that touch-ee?"

"Got a fine yeller woman to stroke my dick, and it—"

"You owe me, then."

Pompey glanced toward Christopher Harding, who was still asleep. I thought, for a moment, that I saw someone asleep behind him, with an arm thrown over him.

"Besides," I said, "after last night, there aren't many left aboard to worry about. Mr. Harding isn't even worried about . . . sleeping on the deck."

Pompey said, "Him and his friend done more than sleepin', when they thought I was asleep. Mr. Harding, he have a ass that shine like moonlight, and—"

I was not surprised to hear that, but I cut him off. "Will you row me in, Pompey?"

"You can't take nothin'. Cap'n'll flog me if you—"

"I want nothing but to get ashore."

Pompey gave another glance toward the two sleeping men on the forecastle deck. Then he blew out his lantern. We lowered ourselves into the small rowboat, Pompey fitted the oarlocks, and we pushed off.

Reverend Winter looked down from beneath the bowsprit, and I fancied that I saw disapproval in his eyes. But with each dip of the oars, I felt growing relief.

Then the voice of Samuel Hodges cut through the night fog. "Goddamn you, James Spencer. You desert me, too?"

Had he gotten up to piss and seen the note? Had Christopher Harding awakened him? Or Sloate? For it was certainly Sloate asleep behind Christopher.

"Don't say nothin'," Pompey told me.

"Come back," said Hodges. "Come back, and I'll forget this ever happened."

Pompey kept pulling, and the oars rocked rhythmically in the locks.

Clink, clank, splash. Clink, clank, splash.

"Turn that boat around or we'll start shooting," cried Hodges.

"Shooting?" I heard Christopher Harding say. "I can't shoot Jamie Spencer."

"I can." That was Sloate's voice.

"Don't say nothin'," Pompey whispered, "Be harder for 'em to figure out where to shoot in the fog. Bad enough I'se makin' noise with the oars." *Clink, clank, splash.*

Hodges shouted, "You came to tell the world my story! *Our* story!"

I felt a pang at that. Hodges was right. I would never have begun this adventure if not for his willingness to take me on.

"Is it that damned Irishman? Are you throwing in with that bog-hopping scum?"

Pompey whispered, "If I'se runnin', I'd run with Flynn, too. He know how to get by."

Hodges's voice grew thicker. A note of defeat seemed to creep in, or perhaps it was the fog, deadening it, "Be careful of him, Spencer. He'll find a noose sooner or later." Then he added, "What will your mother say? Your father?"

And that sealed the matter. My father would tell me to stay. So I was going.

"I won't forget this, James Spencer! You've backstabbed me. You and that Irish son-of-a-bitch will come to grief, by my hand or somebody else's. You mark my words."

But Hodges did not pursue, perhaps because there were not enough awake to pull the big longboat. Soon, our rowboat slid up to the Clay Street Wharf, just forward of the schooner *Anne-Marie*.

Pompey took my hand. "If not for Cap'n Trask, I be jumpin', too, but no man treat me better. He give me a job, give me my own caboose to cook on, give me a chance to make the money for to buy my wife and babies out of North Carolina, so—" He released his grip. "I hope to meet you again, sir."

"Tell them that I put a gun to your head and made you row me in. They'll go easier on you, and . . . I'll pray you make enough to buy your family."

August 9, 1849
Sutter's Fort

This morning, I put into the hands of John Augustus Sutter himself a dispatch which he promised to post when he journeyed to Monterey.

It has been said that in warfare, no plan of battle survives contact with the enemy. I would add that in California, no plan of organization survives the enormity of the landscape or the unleashed ambition of men come to extract their fortune from out of it.

And so, I must report that the Sagamore Mining Company has dissolved. Men have taken their shares and gone on their own, and I have no certainty that I will ever see any of them again. However, if it is any comfort to families, investors, and friends, dissolution is the common fate for all companies soon after debarking in California.

So I have joined with a man named Michael Flynn, and we have struck out on our own.

We left San Francisco on August 4 aboard the schooner *Anne-Marie*, a vessel of fifty feet and twenty ton, with a shallow draft for getting over river bars. We beat across the bay, passed through the Carquinez Straits and Suisun Bay (named for a tribe of Indians that once lived there), and entered a vast delta formed by the confluence of the Sacramento and San Joaquin Rivers, a maze of waterways, marshes, and islands that resemble Eden before the fall (assuming there were sparrow-sized mosquitoes in Eden).

Tall grasses wave in the delta breeze. Oak and willow festoon the water's edge. Salmon roil the streams. Waterfowl darken the sky. Deer and elk graze the banks. And all of these creations of God exist entirely oblivious to us and our ambitions.

A few passengers took pot shots at the deer, but our captain did not stop when one was felled. We protested, as fresh meat is a luxury, but we came to understand his reasoning at the next bend, where we spied on the bank the most enormous four-legged creature that ever I have seen, a silver-brown bear as big as a deck house, his face buried in an elk haunch, his muzzle and claws covered in blood.

Someone said that the bear was called a Grizzly, that he was as ferocious as he was huge, and that it was best to leave the riverbank to him. The man spoke with such confidence that all accepted his judgment.

Indeed, there seemed as much confidence as knowledge on that boat. But in California, a man who speaks with confidence is assumed to have knowledge. I could write a volume about the men aboard who spoke confidently of the riches they would find. They have big dreams and have come to a place big enough to hold their every aspiration.

The vistas, even from the river, are long and broad and big. The river is big, too. Its breadth doubles our Merrimack, just as the mountains that birth it are reputed to reach twice the height of those where the Merrimack takes life. Even the sky is big . . . and hot. No New Englander experiences the kind of baking, bone-drying heat that cooks this California country. The mercury glass on the mast registered near a hundred on the first day, surpassed it on the second, and came a few degrees shy of hellfire on the third.

By the time we reached Sacramento, the chill San Francisco wind was but a fond memory. Aside from the heat, however, this is San Francisco in miniature. A dozen abandoned ships serve as floating storehouses. Scores of shacks and tents line the riverbank. And two structures dominate: the three-story City Hotel and a windowless warehouse with a sign proclaiming "S. Brannan & Co."

This Brannan appears to be everywhere, as are the gamblers, the grog merchants, and the grifters, working their schemes in canvas pavilions or at tables under the trees. Merchants pile their open-air depots high with goods, secure in the knowledge that no rain will fall between May and October. And all of them pile their prices high, too, knowing that men will have to pay or go back to San Francisco for a better price.

Two miles south, on higher ground, stands Sutter's Fort, wise grandfather to this adolescent riverfront, a four-acre compound, enclosed with a fifteen-foot wall of whitewashed adobe, blindingly bright in the afternoon sun. But all is not brightness. It appears a heavily used place, busy and bustling, but in truth, worn to a nub.

Two years ago, John Sutter was a wealthy man, a sort of feudal lord who welcomed wayfarers to an agricultural empire served by hundreds of mechanics, farmhands, and Indian slaves. He grew crops, ran cattle, tanned hides, milled grains, all on a Mexican land grant of 50,000 acres. By most accounts, he was a benevolent despot. But when one of his men found gold at his sawmill, forty miles up in the hills, Sutter tried to keep it quiet, not out of greed but because he knew what would happen. And happen it did.

Portly, courtly, with bushy side whiskers and polished walking stick, Sutter strolls the compound today like a man who has gained all that he sought in California. But his eyes reveal bewilderment, for all that he sought is being swept away, his dreams destroyed by the thousands who have swarmed across his land pursuing dreams of their own.

As his fort stands at the confluence of the Sacramento and American Rivers, it was inevitable that it would become the nexus for thousands of Gold Rushers. But it seems that people who come to draw riches from the earth believe that anything the earth renders is theirs. They have trampled Sutter's wheat fields, stripped his orchards, plucked even green apples for cider. And pens that held cattle are now empty, because rustlers have stolen most of the livestock that grazed on the wide plains around us.

Representing myself as a Boston correspondent, I sought Sutter out. He told me of his misfortunes and said, "I never believed that people could be so mean." He is preparing to leave for Monterey, where a statehood convention may bring a degree of order and give him the authority to put squatters off his land. It is a measure of gold's power that this new possession called California may pass more quickly to statehood than any since the first thirteen.

Despite everything, Sutter's Fort remains a jump-off point for those heading inland. So horse traders, muleteers, and wagon drivers are every-where about. A newspaper called *The Placer Times* is published on a hand press. Brannan & Co. has another store here, to sell to the buyers they miss at the landing. A billiard table and an actual bowling alley compete for amusement. Indeed, there is so much commerce, so much trading, so much buying and selling, that a restaurant serves food here around the clock.

We pitched a tent outside the fort, traded information about San

Francisco and the gold country, and purchased overpriced goods from the Brannan Store. My partner, however, has won steadily in card games on the boat and at the fort, so we have eaten well and provisioned well, and in his final game, he won two horses and a burro from a short, fat, and very unlucky Mexican named Carlos.

This is the way of things in California. Great agrarian empires are wantonly destroyed, livestock and money casually wagered on the turn of a card. But in a country so big, there is always a chance that tomorrow will be better. In a country so fertile with possibility, chance rules, and second chances are plentiful.

And so, we strike out to play the great game.

Yr. Ob't Correspondent,

The Argonaut

By mid-morning, we were riding east across the rolling dry grasslands. About a mile ahead, a cloud of dust floated above a wagon train hauling goods into the hills. To the south, a plume of smoke marked a California prairie fire, a fast-moving beast that seemed to devour both the earth and the air above it. But as the flames were burning south before the breeze, the fire remained a distant spectacle, like the mountains faintly visible beyond the foothills.

We let the horses go at a steady gait, covering not much more than seven or eight miles in an hour. From time to time, we passed groups of miners, most of them moving along on foot. Some had a mule carrying their gear. Others rode in wagons or carts. We exchanged greetings, like ships passing, and kept on. This was the last phase of the rush to the goldfields, but no one seemed to be rushing in the heat.

We reckoned that we would get to the camp called Sutter's Creek by sundown. Sutter had gone there in the spring with a crew of Indians and had done well until the traveling grog shops had opened and enticed his Indians to spend more gold than they mined. Soon they were all in debt or drunk or both. So Sutter had given up mining altogether and left only his name in the diggings.

Flynn allowed as how grog shops would be no distraction to him. I was inclined to believe him, in that I had never seen him drunk. But he was Irish, so I had my dubieties. If he needed drink, however, it would not be to loosen his tongue. For that, he needed nothing but the air in his lungs. Lord but that man could talk.

We had agreed to take only one canteen each and to drink little, so by mid-morning, my mouth was as dry as the grass. But without a sip of water or a swallow from the jug of whiskey he had bought at Sutter's, Flynn talked and talked. He talked about Ireland, about the Fenians, about Boston, about his mother and his sister. He talked about the ceaseless sun, about the men we met on the road, and about our plans for mining, too. He even talked me out of one of the Colt Dragoons, saying that if we were to be partners, best we both were armed. Then he talked as he loaded the gun.

His commentary became like the steady drone of a bug in the heat, except when he chose to sing. Then "The Wild Colonial Boy" or "Billy Broke Locks" or some sea chantey would roll out of him, and I would thank God that he could carry a tune. He even sang the song about all of us bound for this heat-stroked Promised Land.

But a question vexed me: Who was this Irishman? Had I betrayed men of my own background to throw in with a scoundrel? I thought I had been able to gauge his character at sea. How would he perform in a crisis on land?

I would not have long to find out.

AFTER ABOUT TEN MILES, we came to a side trail marked by a sign—whitewash on an old plank—*Sutter's Creek, Twenty Miles.*

We peeled off, moving now in a southeasterly direction, across that sea of yellowed grass and dry brush, dotted here and there with dark clumps of oak that seemed to be floating atop their own black shadows.

The high sun hammered my hats, the one I was wearing and the one Flynn had stolen from me in Boston. But there was something liberating about sailing our saddleback schooners through the heat. We were on our own, away from the cramped ship, the teeming mud ruts of San Francisco, the know-it-all braggarts aboard the Sacramento boat, and the migrants on the trail. If I rode a few paces behind, I did not even hear Michael Flynn . . . going on.

We saw few dwellings. One we glimpsed at great distance, a cluster of white adobe buildings with red tile roofs. It shimmered in the waves of heat like the exotic castle of a Muslim prince.

Around noon, we came to an inviting grove of oaks. With the land beginning to rise and the hottest part of the day still ahead, we decided to stop and rest. We staked the animals on long tethers, took the saddles from the horses, and let them graze. The burro just stood, eyes closed, head nodding. Flynn said that the animals could go without water until we reached the Cosumnes River, which lay somewhere ahead.

I dropped my saddle against the trunk of a big oak and reclined against it.

Flynn dropped his saddle on the other side of the tree.

I took a swallow of water. It was lukewarm after hours of sloshing in a wooden canteen, but I splashed a bit on my face, wet my red and yellow-paisley neckerchief, and discovered that even warm water would cool the broiling skin on the back of my neck.

"And now"—Flynn reached into his saddlebag and extracted a whole pie, wrapped in paper—"a work of art made from the last peaches in the Sutter orchard."

"But ten dollars for a pie?" I said.

"A damn sight better than beef jerky."

I did not disagree, so we enjoyed the sweetness, the texture, the satisfaction that came with . . . pie.

Then Flynn lay back and said, "Only thing to make this better'd be a woman."

"A woman? Out here?"

"Why not? You think women can't handle the heat or the ride?"

I thought of Janiva and how angry she had been when I told her she could not endure this world. I also thought of how much I missed her.

Flynn kept talking. "Like the man said, I'll take *any* woman. Marryin' woman, loose woman, young woman, old, pretty, ugly, it don't matter. Wish I had one as pretty as the one you left back in Boston, though."

I did not answer. I knew that Flynn did not need an answer.

"Ain't you worried that she won't be there when you get home?"

"We haven't been here a week," I said. "I'm not worrying about going home."

"Liar." He laughed. He knew. I was worried. Then he lay back and covered his face with his hat. "I think I'll dream about one."

"A woman?"

"Maybe. Or maybe *a lot* of women. Or maybe the best parts of a few women."

I agreed that a nap would do us well in the heat. Dreaming of women would be an extra benefit. So I stretched out on the other side of the tree.

In a few seconds, Flynn was asleep, leaving me to enjoy the most exquisite silence I'd known in months, such quiet that I could hear a bird, something big like a turkey buzzard, crossing high above, its wings flap-flap-flapping in the still air.

I opened one eye and watched the bird. I closed both eyes and dozed . . .

. . . . UNTIL A DIFFERENT SOUND woke me, a metallic meshing of gears.

I opened my eyes and looked into the barrel of a cocked fowling piece.

"*Buenos dias,* señor."

I raised my head and the barrel came closer.

"Carlos, take his gun."

So there were two, the one called Carlos and the one giving orders, who now gave an order to one called Pedro. So there were three.

Carlos pulled my gun from my belt and gestured for me to stand.

I heard Flynn rouse himself on the other side of the tree. Then I heard the leader say, "Stop, señor. Do not fight. Hand Rodrigo your gun. *Sí.* Very good."

Soon enough, Flynn and I were standing in the bright sun, hatless and bootless.

The one called Carlos, squat and fat, held the fowling piece. Pedro and a boyishly skinny one called Rodrigo went through our things. Pedro poked into our saddlebags with a machete. Rodrigo dismantled the pack we had built on the burro's back.

Two more sat on their horses, close by their leader, whom they called *El Patrón*. He was mounted on a fine chestnut. He wore a fine sombrero that gave him his own shade. He had a saddle with a fine silver pommel. His spurs flashed silver, too. Even his hair and beard were silver.

The one called Rodrigo pulled a shovel out of the mule pack and held it up.

El Patrón shook his head and said something in Spanish.

Rodrigo threw the shovel at my feet. Then he dove into my sea bag and started flinging out the books.

I said, "If you tell me what you're looking for—"

El Patrón said, "You are very polite to Californios like us. But it is too late for polity." The man had been well educated in the English language to use such words.

"We're just crossin' this country," said Flynn, "so polite is the way we go."

"Polite now. Palming aces last night."

Flynn looked at the one named Carlos. "I remember you now. You give me a nasty look when I beat you fair and square on the last cut of the cards."

Carlos did not respond. He let *El Patrón* do his talking:

"He saw you palm the ace. That is cheating."

"That's a lie," said Flynn.

"No Californio calls out the cheater in a room full of Yankees," said *El Patrón*. "He waits until the odds favor him . . . out here, on a ranchero that still belongs to his *patrón*, though for how long, I cannot say, now that we have Yankee masters and every man who crosses my ground thinks that my cattle are free for the taking."

Flynn said, "I ain't a cattle thief, or a Yankee, or a cheater at cards. Neither is my friend . . . well, he is a Yankee, but—"

"We will take back what is ours and a little more." *El Patrón* patted the pocket of his jacket, where he had deposited our coin pouches. "Interest."

I heard the turkey buzzard come flapping over again, as if he sensed that soon, there might be something to eat in this isolated grove.

El Patrón looked up at the bird and the angle of the sun and said, "I would not move again until dusk."

"With no boots?" said Flynn. "Where can we go?"

"I cannot say. It will not be our problem. But we will leave your canteens."

I said, "Can't we talk about this?"

"There is nothing to talk about, *señor*. We are toll collectors, collecting a toll."

"You're horse thieves," I said.

"The horses are your toll. It is a good deal." *El Patrón* leaned on his silver pommel and said, "A few years ago, when California was Spanish, we would have traded like gentlemen. We would have talked, like gentlemen. Sipped brandy and smoked and shaken hands, like gentlemen. But now that we are Americans, we must act more—"

At that instant, I heard the crack of a rifle and saw a puff of smoke on a low rise about thirty yards away.

The rider to the left of *El Patrón* dropped from the saddle.

Everyone turned to the sound, and Carlos swung his fowling piece just enough that Michael Flynn took his chance and jumped onto Carlos's back.

This caused the gun to discharge and blast *El Patrón's* beautiful horse square in the face. The animal screamed and reared and then, after staggering for a moment on its hind legs, it fell over sideways, pinning *El Patrón*.

Flynn grabbed the gun away from Carlos, who pulled a knife and slashed, but Flynn smashed the butt into the Mexican's face.

At the same moment, an American in a short military jacket and bowler hat leapt from behind the rise and ran toward us with a short-barrel blunderbuss at his hip.

The other mounted man drove his horse between this American and *El Patrón* and fired his pistol, but the American kept coming, and as he did, he released a thunderous eruption of buckshot that knocked the man out of his saddle.

Now, the one called Pedro was spinning toward me with the machete over his head, as if driven by the momentum of the moment rather than any real desire to attack.

I will admit that I stood there, making the observation I have just written with almost as much detachment as I have written it, even though I should have been grabbing the shovel at my feet and fighting back. Then I saw the blade in the air, hurtling toward my face, and I flinched.

But Flynn swept down with the gun barrel and knocked the blade from Pedro's hands. And my instinct was correct. Pedro was as frightened as I. He looked at us both, then turned and leapt onto one of the horses.

The American, running amongst us, cried, "Shoot him!"

I looked at Pedro galloping off, then I turned again to the American, who shouted, "He's gettin' away! Shoot him!"

I put up my hands, as if to say, *Shoot him? With what?*

The American ran toward Carlos, who now lay unconscious in the dry yellow grass. He took the pistol that Carlos had taken from me, aimed, and pulled the trigger. *Click.* I could have told him it wasn't loaded.

But Flynn was turning to the one called Rodrigo, who was hunched over with his hands wrapped around his head and his body trembling against the tree. Flynn kicked him to open up, then pulled his own pistol from Rodrigo's belt and fired at the fleeing rider. The shot hit Pedro between the shoulder blades, and he fell off from the saddle.

The American let out with a whistle. The horse stopped and came circling back.

Flynn looked at me and mouthed the words, "His horse?"

The tall American looked at me and said, "Don't like to fight, eh? You won't last long out here." He was older, perhaps fifty, grizzled, gray, all angles and elbows and unpredictable movements.

Flynn held up his pistol. "Mine's loaded. The one in your hand, that's my pardner's. It ain't."

I tried to say that I didn't want to shoot myself accidentally, but I could not get the words out. I was too shocked by what I had just seen.

There were dead bodies in the shade and dead bodies in the sun. Rodrigo trembled by the tree. *El Patrón* lay pinned under his horse, which was breathing in strangled gasps, its huge flanks rising and falling like a bellows, its face an eyeless mess of buckshot and blood.

I felt the pie rise in my throat, but my neckerchief kept it down.

Flynn offered his hand to the stranger. "Thanks, friend."

"No need to thank me. Been trackin' these brigands a good while."

Flynn said, "May I ask your name."

"Cletis Smith, late of the U.S. Army. We took California away from these thievin' Mexican snake fuckers, and now they're tryin' to take it back, one horse at a time." Smith went over to my mount and ran his hand over the haunch. "Didn't either of you damn fools look at the brands?"

"Brands?" I said.

"Shit in a shoe, but there sure is a lot of tenderfeet comin' into this country." Smith pointed to lettering on the horse's rump. It looked like "USA." But the "U" had been rebranded into a "V." "See that? It's supposed to stand for, 'United States Army.' But this feller says it's for 'Vargas, Señor Antonio,' all nice and alphabetical-like."

I gestured to *El Patrón*, groaning under the gasping horse. "Him?"

Cletis took the pistol from Flynn's hand, walked over to *El Patrón*, crouched, and said, "Vargas, you stole my horses and left me out here to die."

"Your horses were your toll. We left you your burro and your boots." Vargas raised his head and looked into Smith's eyes. "What have *you* stolen? A whole country."

"Lose a war, lose a lot, old man." Cletis Smith fished into Vargas's pockets, pulled out our coin pouches, and tossed them to Flynn. "You figure out which is which."

Then Smith stood, cocked the pistol, and pointed it down.

I cried, "Don't shoot him!"

Cletis glanced at me and pulled the trigger. The shot exploded and echoed over the hills. I thought I was witnessing murder, cold blooded and brutal.

Then I heard Vargas say softly, "Thank you, señor."

"Hate to see a good horse suffer. But it's for the best."

"A sad world, señor, when something so bad is for the best." Vargas looked at me. "Thank you, too. You are a merciful man."

I nodded. I did not think I could speak.

"Just remember," Cletis Smith said to me, "out here, too much mercy'll get you killed." He went over to the one called Rodrigo. "Ain't that right, son?"

Tears were pouring down Rodrigo's face, making rivulets in the dust on his cheeks. He was perhaps sixteen, and he cringed from this growling old American.

Cletis Smith studied him a moment, then handed the pistol back to Flynn and moved methodically to his next task: snatching a saddle from off the ground and throwing it onto one of the horses.

"What are you doin'?" asked Flynn.

"These horses are mine."

Flynn said, "I won 'em on a straight-up cut of the cards and—"

"That don't mean dog puke to me."

"Well, it does to me," said Flynn.

I said, "We just killed three men, and all we care about is who owns that horse?"

Cletis Smith said, "You didn't kill anybody, son. But you better learn how if you want to stay alive. Ain't that right, *patrón*?"

"If you are going to kill us," said Vargas, "be done with it. My leg is broken. It hurts very much."

But the trembling Rodrigo said, "Please do not kill us, señor. He is my grandfather. I promised my *mamá* I would look after him."

"Ain't doin' a very good job of it, boy." Cletis looked at Vargas. "And you ain't doin' too good takin' care of your grandson. Is one of these we killed his father?"

"No. These were loyal hands on my ranchero. But my cattle have been stolen. My horses run off. So we do what we can."

"Where's the boy's father?"

"Gone to the diggings." Vargas grit his teeth to hold down the pain in his leg and perhaps in his heart. "Before the gold, we had a good life. But now, some catch the fever, others spread it, and we are all victims of it."

Cletis pulled the cinch on the saddle and seemed to give something a bit of thought, then he said to Rodrigo, "Don't worry, son. There'll be no more killin'."

"Thank God for that," I said.

Cletis told me to pick up the shovel. Then he pulled another from the burro pack and tossed it to Flynn. He told us to dig a shallow hole around the body of Señor Vargas.

I looked at Flynn, as if to ask . . . *Should we do it?* Flynn shrugged. *Why not?*

So we pulled on our boots and got to digging. In the meantime, Cletis Smith resaddled the horses, slid his handsome Kentucky Long Rifle into a custom-made cinch on a saddle, then reloaded the 1808 model Harper's Ferry blunderbuss, a true brute of a weapon. When we were done, he said, "Looks like you know how to work shovels. How much do you know about placer minin'?"

"What we don't know, we'll learn," said Flynn.

"If you promise to go where I go and do what I say till the winter rains, you can ride with me. I'll teach you what I know."

"Why?" I asked.

"I ain't as young as I used to be. And placer minin' is hard work."

We looked at each other. Flynn winked. I nodded. We liked the offers.

With a good hole dug around him, we were able to pull Señor Vargas from under the horse. His leg was bent just above the top of his boot, so Cletis Smith made a splint out of Rodrigo's old musket, set the break, and propped *El Patrón* against the tree. We gave Rodrigo one of the horses to ride for help, but Smith warned him that we would keep this clump of trees in view for at least an hour. If we saw him riding off before that, we would come back and kill his grandfather. And I think he meant it.

I took Señor Vargas's hand and wished him the best.

"Just don't tell him we're sorry," said Cletis. "Out here, apologizin' is a sign of weakness."

CLETIS RODE HIS FAVORITE horse, the chestnut. Flynn took one of the Mexican mounts. I rode the sorrel. The burros followed on a string.

Presently, Flynn offered Cletis a peppermint from the bag he had bought at Sutter's Fort, and they began to talk as if nothing had happened in that bloody grove of trees. Cletis scoffed at our plan to head for Sutter's Creek. Played out, he said. Much better diggin's deeper in the hills, he said, at a place called Broke Neck, on a river that fed the Cosumnes. That was where we would go, he said, and he did not invite our opinions.

Then he turned us back toward the north and the Hangtown Road, the main route into the mountains. Soon we were rising as steadily as the afternoon heat.

Along the trail, we stopped to help a man with a wagon full of mining tools. His rear wheel had snapped, and he was stuck. Three groups of miners had gone past, leaving him helpless. He was a tall, rock-faced fellow with a long beard. He said he was headed to Hangtown to start what he called The New England Trading Company.

This put me in a warmer frame of mind toward him. Although Cletis wanted to keep moving, I prevailed. If a New England man needed help, help we would offer in the form of muscle to lever up the wagon so that he could change out the wheel.

It felt good to do a small bit of good after what we had done a few hours before.

As we rode off the man said, "I don't forget a favor. I'll write your names down."

Flynn laughed. "You do that, Mister—"

"Hopkins," he said. "Mark Hopkins."

By late in the day, we had risen into a different world. The ground remained yellow-brown and paper-dry, but the trees were growing taller. There was black oak and buckeye, and here and there, conifers with crusty red bark standing as straight and reaching as high as the white pines of New Hampshire.

We were riding south along the line of the Logtown Ridge, which offered the most amazing view that ever I had seen. To the west, and well below, rolled the prairie we had just crossed, fading into the mist of a distant sunset. To the east, a few rods from the road, the land dropped hundreds of feet into the steep valley of the Cosumnes River. But our prospect carried across the river, across the pines and oaks on the far side, across a distance of thirty miles or more, all the way to the rim of white that ran along the horizon. Yes, I said, *white*. The white of snow in August, limning the peaks of those distant mountains like sugar on the lip of a holiday glass.

At a promontory, Cletis Smith stopped and swept his arm from left to right. "There it is, boys, La Veta Madre. From away up north, where them Donner folks et each other a while back, all the way south to the desert, there's gold strikes everywhere. Men hittin' paydirt in rivers and streams, in dry gulches and gullies, all of it washin' out of one great big vein of gold somewhere up them mountains."

"A vein?" said Flynn. "How big?"

"Miles wide, miles deep, or so they say, with lots of little veins runnin' out of it."

"Like capillaries," I said.

"What's capillaries?" asked Cletis.

"Pay him no mind," said Flynn. "He went to Harvard."

"So he's what we call an educated fool, then?" said Cletis. "Rides in dangerous country with an unloaded gun. Talks with words so big a simple man don't understand 'em."

"I don't speak Spanish," I said, "so . . . La Veta Madre? What does it mean?"

"The Mother Lode. Greatest goddamn gold strike since Adam told Eve to bite the apple." He gave his reins a tug and we kept going. He said that if our horses had needed water, we would have been traveling on the lower road along the river. But the high trail was better going. So we stayed on it a few miles more. Then, we headed down, down and southeast, down toward the Cosumnes, southeast toward a tributary called the Miwok.

After a time, we crossed the Cosumnes and turned due east, following a crude sign pointing to a place called Fiddletown.

"Fiddletown . . . is that where we go to hear a bit of music, then?" asked Flynn.

"Nope. There's a camp up there where no one's gettin' rich and they ought to clear out, but they just stay, just stay and fiddle around. Fiddle-town."

Before we had a chance to see the fiddling miners of Fiddletown, we broke off south on another road into another east-west–running valley.

WE REACHED BROKE NECK just as the lanterns were flickering to life. Tents and tossed-together shacks lined a narrow, dusty street crowded with miners. A squeeze-box somewhere was pushing out a tune. Men were laughing. Others were jawing. Others, looking glum, were moving on. It seemed a world made for transition, for quick dismantling and migration, all except for three buildings—a general store on a foundation of river stones just north of the road, and on the south side, a combination assay-and-express office next to a big-top saloon.

The ground sloped away gently behind the saloon, rolling a hundred feet to the river that ran shallow and summer-sluggish.

"They call the river the Miwok," said Cletis, "named for the Injuns still slinkin' around here somewhere. The town they named after an old boy who heard men shoutin' on the bank and reckoned he'd best get down there and stake a claim. Went runnin', tripped on a rock, fell on his chin and—"

"Broke his neck?" I said.

"Died like a damn fool after travelin' all the way from Pennsylvania."

"So we've arrived, then?" asked Flynn.

"Arrived at the strike. That's why there's two or three hundred fellers buzzin' around here, and why the gamblers and grog merchants is set up, waitin' to take their gold 'fore it's even assayed. But this ain't for us."

Just then, someone shouted from the side of the road. "Cletis? Cletis Smith?"

"In the flesh," said Cletis.

The man came over to Cletis's horse and offered a hand. "I thought you was dead. Heard you was jumped by a bunch of Greasers down in the valley."

"So I was. They took everything. Called it a toll for crossin' their land. I got it back with the help of my new pardners." Cletis introduced us to Drinkin' Dan Fleener.

Drinkin' Dan squinted at us through his right eye. A patch covered the left and scars radiated out from it. "If Cletis speaks well of you, you must be right fellers."

"Right fellers, for sure," said Flynn.

I took his hand. It was big and gnarled and felt like wood rather than flesh.

"So we got a strike here?" asked Cletis.

"Already pulled out eighteen ounces."

"What's the claim size?"

"Miner's Council done the usual: a hundred square on the flats or the hills, a hundred runnin' feet along a ravine or a dry gulch."

Cletis took a chaw of tobacco and offered the rest of the plug to Drinkin' Dan. "So, this strike is already big enough for a miner's council?"

"Gotta have rules." Drinkin' Dan took the tobacco and stuffed all of it into his mouth. "I'm on the council myself."

Cletis looked at us. "The richer the soil, the smaller the claim, so everybody can get a share."

Drinkin' Dan said, "You're welcome to use my tent for the night, boys."

"Nope. We'll be movin' upstream. But we'll be seein' you."

"Thank you kindly for the chaw," said Drinkin' Dan.

And we rode on, leaving the noise and lanterns of Broke Neck behind.

As deeper we went into the darkening country, Cletis said, "Remember, never give up more news than you get. And if you hear of a big strike, go a mile upstream. Chances are, if there's gold in one bend of the river, there'll be gold in another."

Then he pulled his horse suddenly and raised his hand for quiet.

I felt my mount tense and skitter, but I put a strong hand to him and he held firm.

Slowly, Cletis reached into his saddle pack and pulled out the blunderbuss.

Then I heard something grunting and scuffling in the bushes nearby, something huge, from the sound of it, something powerful from the wide swath of brush that was spreading and cracking before the shadow of it, something moving off to our left and up the hill.

After another silent minute, Cletis whispered, "Grizzly."

"You mean, there's bears around here?" said Flynn.

"Biggest damn bears you ever did see. Don't tangle with 'em, especially the she-bears when they got their cubs with 'em."

Then he gave us a wave, let us go past, and brought up the rear with his gun at the ready, in case the bear decided that we might be worth eating. But the bear went one way, and we went the other, and I was damn glad of it.

WHETHER CLETIS SMITH DECIDED to stop because he had found his spot or because it was too dark to keep going, I could not tell. But after another half mile, he led us down to the riverbed and across to the other side.

"Why are we crossin'?" Flynn asked.

"I like to camp facin' north. Just a way of doin' things. You got any complaints?"

"Not at all." Michael Flynn had a powerful propensity for complaint, but he appeared ready to take whatever Cletis said without dispute. So we followed Cletis up the slope of the south bank, up about thirty feet to a big skull-shaped boulder.

When he dismounted, we did, too.

"Just unpack what you need for the night. We can do a bit of prospectin' in the mornin', but I don't expect to find much around here."

"Why?"

He pointed across the stream to the only other camp in sight. "Chinks."

"Chinks?" said Flynn.

"You mean, Chinese?" I said.

"Chinks," repeated Cletis. "Not many Chinks around, but enough that white miners don't like 'em workin' new claims. The only kind of minin' Chinks get to do is siftin' the tailings that white men leave. If you see Chinks, you won't see fresh gold."

"Do they ever cause trouble?" I asked.

"They're too afraid."

"Just don't touch their women," said Flynn.

"Women?" Cletis Smith spit a bit of tobacco. "No Chink women in the diggin's."

"I had the pleasure of meetin' a few in San Francisco," said Flynn. "Ever heard of a woman named Ah-Toy? She'll give you a flash of her cooch for an ounce of gold."

"Is that a fact?" Cletis broke off another chaw of tobacco and stuffed it into his cheek. "Does China cooch go sideways, like they say?"

"Straight up and down, just like a white woman's, and as pretty as the sunset."

"Well, *that's* somethin' to think about," he said. "A man could get rich sellin' cooch up here, no matter if it was white, red, black, or yellow."

We pitched our tent next to the boulder, under the tall pines.

We ate bacon and flour cakes cooked in the fat. Then we passed Flynn's jug. When we were done, I announced that on the first night, I would wash the dinner pans.

Cletis laughed and said he would be washing no pans, not that night or the next or the one after that. He said that in gold country, you didn't bother with such things. Time spent crouched by the riverbank was best spent swirling a pan, not washing it.

Perhaps, but for tonight, I would wash the dishes in that river rolling down from the mountains.

Though there was still a bit of light in the sky, I carried Cletis's lantern and set it on a rock. Then I crouched and washed, using handfuls of river bottom to scrub away the bacon fat. I rinsed one tin plate and put it aside. Then I scrubbed another and watched the current spread the sandy gravel and grease like a cloud.

Then I sat back on my haunches and listened to the chatter from the camp of Chinamen. It sounded strange, heavily syllabic, tonal yet arrhythmic. I could not imagine myself learning such a language, nor could I imagine one of them learning to speak mine, so clipped and logical, each word comprised of no more than twenty-six sounds.

Then one of them began to play a flute. The sweet trill of it carried above the burble of the running water, a magical sound, almost romantic in its lonely beauty.

I let it wash over me, hoping perhaps that it might cleanse me of the horror I had seen that day. But I sensed already that ugliness and beauty, shocking violence and gentle quiet, existed side by side in this wild country. So I had best prepare myself.

I grabbed another handful of sand and scrubbed the last plate, rinsed it in the river, swirled it, held it to the lantern light to see that it was clean, and saw something flicker.

I leaned closer, and my heart jumped. It almost jumped out of my mouth. If such things could happen, it would have, because my jaw dropped wide open. I had reached into the river and swept up a fistful of gravel laden with gold.

For the second time that day, I could not speak.

And for the rest of the night, I could not sleep. Neither could Michael Flynn or Cletis Smith, U.S. Army retired. We had found "color." We would know in the morning if we had struck it rich.

THREE

Thursday Morning

"Broke Neck was about six miles from the Sturgis vineyard," said Peter.

"You mean it's gone?" asked Evangeline.

"Most of those camps just disappeared when the gold played out." Peter put his finger and thumb on his iPad and swiped so the satellite image zoomed in. "There's the Miwok River, where Spencer found gold washing dishes." He drew his finger south-southwest across the screen. "And *there's* the Sturgis vineyard."

She studied the screen and said, "You're coming with me, then?"

"Sturgis invited me. Wouldn't want to disappoint him."

"I'd rather have you along than have him hitting on me."

"He'll hit on you anyway. But I need to see that country for myself."

They were in the Nob Hill Club, the hotel's downstairs restaurant. Peter wished they served breakfast in the Top of the Mark. Twenty-six bucks wouldn't be so bad for the buffet—coffee, pastries, lox, bagels, yogurt, "assorted" juices—if you got a great view along with it. But San Francisco was a high-priced town. It always had been. Peter didn't need an old Gold Rush journal to remind him of that. So he spread cream cheese on his bagel, layered on the lox, added a few capers, and . . . heaven.

Evangeline had just come down. She was wearing jeans, cowboy boots, a blue silk shirt, and a suede sport coat. Perfect for vineyard walking. Her hair looked blow-dry bouncy. But she seemed a bit groggy.

She had taken coffee and a croissant from the buffet. That's all. That this made them the most expensive coffee and croissant since the Gold Rush was not something Peter pointed out. Sarcasm, like comedy, was all about timing. And with Evangeline, the best timing was *after* she'd had her first cup. When he asked her how she slept, he did not even add, "in your *separate* bed."

"Exhausted enough to fall asleep right off. Agitated enough to wake up at four."

"Jet lag."

"A travel writer knows how to power-sleep through jet lag. You stay up all day and go to bed on local time. But if your after-dinner stroll includes angry Chinese locals and tong-boy Robin Hoods, it might be hard to get back to sleep once you wake up."

"Wine-tasting will be more fun. No Chinese gangsters in Amador County."

"And no Chinese girlfriends introducing you to pissed-off relatives."

"I thought you didn't do sarcasm in the morning."

"That came out wrong." She took a sip of coffee. "I like Mary, like her a lot. But a lot happened yesterday. A lot of moving parts to fit together. Like the ancient Ah-Toy telling tall tales to Mary's grandmother about bags of gold—"

"Or rivers of it."

"—then Ah-Toy pops up in Spencer's journal."

"Did you finish it?"

"I read myself back to sleep. Got to the part where they're going up the river."

"*They're* going up the river, and my son asks me to go with the flow." Peter ate the last of his bagel. "Upstream in 1849, upstream today."

"And I thought you were coming because you're jealous."

"I am." He drained his coffee. "I'm also planning a side trip."

"Side trip?"

"Field research."

Her cell phone vibrated. "It's the driver. He's outside."

IN THE LOBBY, PETER noticed that woman again, the one with the red hair and the blue pantsuit.

He stopped and looked right at her. She was scrolling through her phone. He supposed that if she'd wanted to disguise herself, she could have been reading another newspaper. Much easier to hide behind. So he should not have been so suspicious, but he stood for a moment in the middle of the Mark Hopkins lobby—small but as ornate as a Versailles sitting room— and her eyes met his.

The message in hers: *total disinterest.*

Evangeline tugged Peter's arm and pointed through the front door. A guy in a chauffeur's jacket and cap was standing by a big black SUV. He was holding a sign: "Ms. Carrington/Manion Gold Vineyards."

At the same moment, the concierge called, "Ms. Ryan—"

The redheaded woman put away her phone and made for the concierge's desk as he bragged about the theater tickets he had just scored for her.

Peter whispered to Evangeline, "She was in Portsmouth Square last night."

"I didn't notice her, and the red hair is pretty hard to miss."

"She was wearing a hat. But the sunglasses—"

"She's not wearing sunglasses now."

"She put them on yesterday when she followed us out of the hotel. Then she made a call. Probably bringing in somebody else to follow us, like the guy who jumped onto the cable car after us."

Evangeline gave her a longer look. "You also said she was carrying yesterday. But that jacket is cut to fit. So, no shades, no sidearm. Do you think she's taking today off?"

"By hanging in a hotel lobby?"

"It's a nice lobby. You can stay here and watch the world go by and score a few theater tickets." The heels of Evangeline's boots tick-tocked across the marble floor. "Or you can come with me. Your choice."

Peter was going. He had a plan. He'd stay with it and keep a clear eye. He threw one more look over his shoulder and followed Evangeline out.

Larry Kwan, the chauffeur, was a middle-aged guy with a wide face, a friendly manner, and a roll of belly fat that made him look like he didn't sweat the small stuff. He drove a black Cadillac Escalade with tinted windows, black leather interior, and high clearance for going off-road in the vineyards.

"Welcome aboard, folks. You'll find bottles of water in the cup holders. Good to stay hydrated when you're wine-tasting. We'll be there in two hours and change. Going against the traffic all the way."

Peter took the front seat, Evangeline stretched out in the middle row. They were the only passengers.

Peter glanced in the side mirror as they pulled away.

Objects may be closer than they appear. But there didn't seem to be any objects following them down California Street. That was good. And if anybody tried to hit-and-run this big SUV, they wouldn't be running anywhere.

So he decided to sit back and enjoy the ride.

Larry Kwan said he was excited to be driving to Amador, courtesy of Manion Sturgis. He had done some driving for Sturgis before, he said, but Kwan's Wine Tours usually headed for Napa or Sonoma. "High-end tours for high-end drinkers and classy bachelorette parties."

"Classy?" said Evangeline.

"Where the girls only get a *little* drunk and nobody throws up in the way-back."

"That explains the nice new-car smell," she said.

Larry Kwan looked at Peter. "Your wife is funny."

"She's not my wife."

THEY CROSSED THE BAY Bridge, took Route 80 through Berkeley, cleared the tolls at the Carquinez Straights, and headed inland.

A little over an hour later, they sped through Sacramento.

Peter had been there for a book show once. And of course, he had toured Sutter's Fort, all whitewashed and shining and dwarfed by the hospital next door. It had reminded him of other historical sites, like the Old State House in Boston or the Alamo in San Antonio, tiny places in the modern world that were enormous in the mythology of America.

And he knew they were headed into the heartland of American myth, a place of unfettered freedom, of get-rich-quickdom, of dreamers who did and doers who dreamed, of no man better than another because of his name, his schooling, his father or mother . . . a place of second chances, and third, fourth, and fifth chances, too, because no one failed in this land of myth. They just quit trying. That was California in 1849 and California today.

Even speeding out of Sacramento's suburbs and running across an open range of yellow-brown grass at 75 mph, Peter could see Spencer and Flynn sitting down to eat peach pie under a clump of trees. He could see forty-niners on rutted trails where superhighways now ran. He could see guys like Mark Hopkins, imagining the wealth of empire as they snapped at their reins and urged their mules up the hill. Sometimes, the modern world just faded away for Peter Fallon, and the past emerged like a parallel universe. Then he remembered that the past did not have big Michelins, AC, or Vivaldi on the Bose speakers. Best leave the parallel universe . . . parallel.

Soon the road was rising into piney woods, rising gradually and steadily toward the Sierra.

At a place called Shingle Springs, Larry turned onto Mother Lode Drive and followed that to the Golden Chain Highway, Route 49, two lanes, north-south, connecting all the quiet hamlets, villages, and strip malls that once had been Gold Rush boomtowns.

Larry said that if not for Peter's side trip, he would have taken Route 16 out of Sacramento, a more southerly route, since the Sturgis winery was down near Sutter Creek, "But like they say, six of one, half a mile of another."

"Don't you mean 'half a dozen'?" asked Evangeline.

"I spend my days coming up with new ways to say things about wine. So I like to play with clichés. Keeps me sharp."

"Old wine in new bottles?" said Peter.

"Cliché," answered Larry.

"Touché," said Evangeline.

"That's another one," answered Larry.

Peter gave Evangeline a look. She laughed. They liked their driver.

Peter also liked that nothing had gotten close to them. No one had followed them from San Francisco. No one had picked them up on the freeway.

ABOUT SIX MILES SOUTH, in the township of El Dorado, Peter directed Larry to turn off at a convenience store with a broken Pelton wheel for decoration: Quartzite Road. (They were big on geological terms around here.)

Peter had never been here before, but he had "driven" it on Google after meeting a retired Kern County detective named William Donnelly at the Sacramento Book Fair. He had sold Donnelly first editions of Ian Fleming and John le Carré. And "Wild Bill," as his friends called him, had become a regular customer of Fallon Antiquaria.

Google had prepared Peter for the arid landscape, the blue oak and buckeye, the eclectic three-mile stretch of houses—working spreads with barns and corrals, retirement ranches doing the long, low California contemporary thing, and here and there a rundown place, something that time and the real estate market had forgot. But Google could not do justice to the view. The road ran along the Logtown Ridge. Forty miles to the west, the buildings of Sacramento reflected the midmorning sun. And the easterly views reached across California, all the way to the snowcapped mountains at Lake Tahoe.

Peter said, "James Spencer described this view."

"Bierstadt painted it." Evangeline was seldom quite as moved by connections as Peter, but this time she was awestruck. "It's the picture in the library."

The Donnelly house was on the left, one of the newer places, a handsome ranch with a paving-stone driveway.

Jane Donnelly answered. "Why, Peter Fallon! We meet at last." She looked at the Escalade backing out of the driveway. "Aren't your friends coming in?"

"Previous engagement. We'll catch up with them later."

Jane was in her sixties and seemed happy to be there, easy in her own skin, in her own house, in gardening clothes puffing dirt. "I'd shake, but—" She held up her dirty hands and gave him a wave. *Come on in.*

The house turned to the east, with good reason. Everything flowed through the open sliders to the patio, the small infinity pool, and the spectacular infinity view.

Bill Donnelly was peering through a telescope. He pivoted, shook Peter's hand, and said, "Here's the man who helps me spend my pension on books."

Donnelly hailed from Bakersfield, California, but he had the kind of beefy presence and tomato-red complexion that would have played well on police forces in Boston or Brooklyn, especially with that Irish name. He swung an arm, north to south, and said, "Welcome to the Mother Lode. The remnants of Broke Neck are about ten miles south, as the crow flies." He pointed to the telescope and told Peter to have a look.

Peter squinted into the eyepiece. "What am I looking at?"

"That fourth ridge out there. The Miwok River is just beyond. It joins the Cosumnes, which flows to the flatland and into the Mokolumne, which eventually runs into the San Joaquin. The ground here is as dry as flour this time of year, but these rivers form an incredible drainage system for half of California."

"Bill is always watching for plumes of smoke," said Jane.

Donnelly looked up into the clear blue sky. "We should be seeing rain any week now, but until we do, every puff of smoke is a worry. Some folks down where we're going, they started a fire about three weeks ago. Drove one of their old cars off road. The heat from the exhaust manifold set the grass on fire. Burned a thousand acres."

"The Boyles family," said Jane.

"They've been on the Miwok for a long time," said Wild Bill, "long after the mines played out, long before the vineyards took off. They ran cattle, wrangled horses for weekend dude riders out of San Francisco—"

"Don't forget moonshining." Jane ducked into the house.

"Yeah, until they discovered marijuana. They grow so much weed back in those hills, anytime there's a brush fire, half of Amador County gets high."

Jane came out again, carrying a shoulder holster with a big silvered .44 Magnum. "If you're going to be wandering the hills, bring this."

Peter said, "Are the Boyles folks dangerous?"

Wild Bill laughed. "This is for the rattlesnakes."

"Rattlesnakes?" said Peter. "That gun could kill a car."

"Might not kill one, but it's stopped a few. Put a round right through an engine block once. Guy behind the wheel was trying to run me over."

Jane said, "Bill was not the best shot, but with a gun like this, close counts. So we get to enjoy our retirement together."

WILD BILL DONNELLY DROVE his Chevy pickup back down to Route 49 and turned south, offering commentary all the way: "The miners would go along the ridge unless they had livestock that needed watering. Then they'd take the river route."

"My guys had horses, but they rode along the ridge."

"Must've been cavalry horses. Tougher. Most miners didn't want to worry about horses. They wanted to be mining. So they went on foot."

The river was on their left now. The previous winter had been snowy, so there was still good water in the Cosumnes, and the current was running fast.

Peter noticed cars parked along the road. Down in the river, guys in wetsuits were panning.

"They still find flakes," said Wild Bill. "Sometimes nuggets."

"You mean there's gold that the miners missed?"

"The laws of erosion don't change. But in 1848, you had thousands of years of gold, lying untouched. Today, if a few flakes wash out in June, they're panned out by the Fourth of July."

They went past ranches and corrals, then over a deep gorge where the Cosumnes turned southwest. The Gold Rush had left scars everywhere, Wild Bill said. If you could see the scars, you could imagine the face of the landscape a century and a half before.

On an open hillside, a foot-high ridge of dirt ran at a carefully pitched slope: the Michigan Ditch, carrying water from the upper Cosumnes downstream fifteen miles to Michigan Bar. Wild Bill explained that some miners, who couldn't make it prospecting, started ditching and "got rich from water instead of gold."

Then he pointed out bone-dry gulches, like vertical cuts on the hillsides. Along the edges of any gulch, hillocks covered in straw grass sprouted trees and bushes. "Looks like they've been there forever, right?"

"But?"

"Those are tailing piles. If miners saw a dry gulch where rainwater or flash flood had caused erosion, they'd start digging. If they found gold, they kept digging, turning over, sifting, leaving piles of dirt that became part of the landscape."

After a few miles, they arrived at a strip of businesses in the town of Plymouth. Donnelly turned east onto the Fiddletown Road, with signs for well-known vineyards . . . Renwood, Deaver, Terra d'Oro, Easton. But they weren't stopping to taste.

A few miles more brought them to Miwok Road. It meandered southeast through country dotted with clusters of oak standing stark and dark on the dried-out hillsides, a lonely house here, a vineyard patch there, and livestock grazing everywhere. All the while, off to their right, sometimes visible in the baking sunlight, sometimes buried in a fold of earth or lost behind a line of trees, flowed the Miwok, as it had when Spencer and Flynn rode this way almost a hundred and seventy years before.

Then Wild Bill turned southeast again, onto little single-lane side road marked with a few mailboxes. Another quarter mile brought them to a dirt road running directly south. It had a closed chain-link gate and two signs: Private Property Keep Out and Beware of the Dog.

"The Boyles' land. They own a thousand acres south of the river." Wild Bill kept on another quarter mile, then slowed and pulled onto a patch of dry grass surrounded mostly by . . . nothing. "Welcome to Broke Neck."

Peter got out, threw his sport coat in the backseat, and drank it all in.

Down the gentle slope, through the trees, lay the riverbed, about forty feet wide. A stream of water—decent for the end of dry season—rolled over the rocks. Grass and shrubs greened the bank and grew along the damp edges. On the uphill side of the road, a two-car garage stood on a stone foundation. Behind it, the land rose to a dusty corral that formed the front yard of a little redwood-board ranch house. Two horses were nodding under an old oak tree by the road.

Peter absorbed the heat and the quiet. But it was more than quiet. It was silence. No road sounds, no airplanes, none of the hum of the modern world.

"Doesn't look like much now," said Wild Bill, "but it was a whole town once. We think the garage is built on the foundation of the Broke Neck store. And those stones you're kicking at, they're the foundation of the Abbott Express Office."

"Are there photographs?" asked Peter. "Daguerreotypes?"

"Not of Broke Neck. It came and went too quickly, like most of these places."

They walked down toward the river. It was cooler under the trees. At the edge of the water, Peter listened to its gentle whoosh.

Wild Bill said, "You can see it, can't you?"

"See it?"

"Hundreds of miners working claims, with shovels and pans and rockers. Scraping, cursing, splashing, joshing, maybe fighting."

Peter knew that he had found a kindred spirit.

"They didn't quite understand the geology," said Wild Bill, "but they knew the gold was along the riverbeds, in the sandbars and under the rocks."

Peter squinted upstream. "Spencer writes that they camped the first night near a big boulder, about a mile above the town."

"Can't see that far. The river bends, and the trees and understory are too thick. But . . . what exactly are you looking for?"

Peter almost never admitted this truth, but he had the feeling that a retired detective might understand. "I don't really know."

And he liked Wild Bill Donnelly's answer: "So we just keep looking."

"As long as you look someplace else." The woman's voice was so startling that Wild Bill's hand went into his windbreaker.

"Easy there, big fella," she said. "I'm not armed."

She was about fifty-five and as sun-dried as the landscape. She wore faded jeans and cowboy boots, but they were no affectation. This straight-up, stringy woman looked like she could spend the morning mucking stables, then go into the house and do a little online bond trading just for fun.

Wild Bill introduced himself and Peter as historians.

She said, "Historians, hunh?"

"From Boston," said Peter.

"Must be hard, being a historian if you can't read."

Peter said, "I think we missed a sign."

"A 'No Trespassing' sign." She gestured back up the hill. "So, what are you really? Gold guys? Wine guys? Cops?"

"Retired cop," said Wild Bill. "Now a book collector."

She looked at Peter. "You a book collector, too?"

"He sells them," said Wild Bill, "to me."

"I've been called a wine guy, too," added Peter.

"Well, if you're looking to buy a riverfront vineyard, this isn't it. No volcanic soils on this bank. And the valley's too deep. You want more sun. So you want to look up high."

"Actually, we're looking for—"

Wild Bill interrupted Peter. "Is that your house up there, Ms.—"

"O'Hara. The name's right on the gate. Ginny O'Hara. But you knew that before you came out here. Public record. So is my property assessment. So you knew that, too. But I'm not selling the land on this side of the river, no matter how many bullshit artists come around saying they're *historians* . . . from Boston."

Just then, they heard a high-revving motor whining over the hill on the other side of the river. A four-by-four ATV appeared at the bald crest about a hundred yards above the bank.

Wild Bill Donnelly stiffened, like a well-trained dog sensing danger.

From this distance, all they could tell was that the driver was as big as the grizzly that James Spencer had written about.

Ginny O'Hara shouted up to him, "Did you send these two?"

The guy said nothing. He spat, revved the engine, and sped away. *Point made.* Stay on your own side of the river.

Wild Bill said, "That's Buster, right?"

"Don't pretend you don't know him. Or his mother. If Buster is buzzing around, Mother Marti is usually up on the other side of the hill somewhere."

Peter watched Buster disappear. Then he said to Ginny O'Hara, "We really are who we say we are."

"You mean you weren't sent by the Boyles bunch because they want to buy my land, because they smell big money coming into our forgotten little valley?"

Wild Bill said, "We saw plenty of 'for sale' signs. Ranchland offered as vineyard. Vineyard offered as ranchland. Folks who'd like to sell and can't. Why would your land be so special?"

"It isn't. Lots of folks think making a living from the land might be easy, or at least maybe romantic. Never has been. Never will be."

"Who wants yours?" asked Peter.

"Folks who think there's still gold here. And there are more of them every day."

"Like who?" asked Wild Bill.

"Start with that Jack Cutler guy. If he sent you, it's a fool's errand."

"Jack Cutler?" Peter tried not to sound surprised at mention of his future in-law.

"He calls himself a geologist. Just a glorified prospector. Wanted to do core samples on my land. I said no way. Bad enough we have the Emery

Mine trying to start up again. I don't need people digging holes and starting fires and getting my livestock all riled up."

Peter said, "What's the Emery Mine?"

Ginny O'Hara looked at Wild Bill. "He does it better than you."

"He wouldn't know the Emery Mine from a rare book."

Peter pulled out a business card and handed it to her. She took it, turned on her heels, and headed up the bank. "Drive him by the Emery Mine. Then he'll know."

"Thanks for your time," said Peter.

"You're welcome. Don't come back."

FROM THERE, THEY DROVE a mile upstream, with a swath of blackened trees and burned grass spreading to their right, on the south side of the river.

"This is where they had that fire I was telling you about," said Wild Bill.

As they rounded a bend, Peter looked down and said, "There's the rock!"

"What rock?"

"The rock where Spencer says they camped the first night. Pull over."

The road was closer to the river here, about fifty feet above the bank, which dropped more sharply. On the north side, it was sunburned but not blackened, because the fire had not jumped the stream.

They got out, and Peter said, "See it? About thirty feet up on the other bank? The big rock?"

Wild Bill said, "This is the first time in decades you can really see that rock from here, thanks to the fire."

"It looks like a big skull." Peter took a picture with his iPhone. Then he looked along the bank and tried to figure out where Spencer would have washed dishes that first night. Probably a straight drop from the rock. So he photographed that. Then he asked, "Do you see mining evidence?"

"Tailings everywhere. On both sides."

Peter looked at the piles forty or fifty feet downstream, where the river widened a bit and seemed to settle. "That was where Spencer saw the Chinese camp."

Peter had a hunch that he would want to know more about that rock and all that might have gone on around it. So he plotted a quick river crossing, then he did it.

"Hey!" cried Wild Bill Donnelly. "That's Boyles' property."

"I'll only be a minute." A few hops. Rock to rock. Big rocks. Then a jump, and he landed on the opposite bank, feet as dry as the ground. But his next step brought a sharp crack and an explosion of dirt at his feet.

Wild Bill pulled his .44 and ducked behind a tree.

Peter heard it again, the sound of a small-caliber high-velocity rifle, an AR-15, maybe. Another shot kicked up the dust to his right. And another struck to the left.

"Stand still!" shouted Wild Bill.

"And let him shoot me?"

Then came three, four, five shots, ripping through the trees above them. "*Now* run."

Peter stumbled into the stream, tripped, slipped in the knee-deep water, smacked his shin on a rock. Two more shots struck on his left and right, bracketing him perfectly, sending up splashes and ricocheting off the rocks.

"Come on," said Wild Bill from the other side. "You'll be all right."

So Peter stumbled and splashed back to the bank, scrambled over the last few boulders, and dove behind a tree. "Jesus Christ. I'm soaked. Who the hell—"

"Sun's out. You'll dry in no time." Wild Bill looked up the hillside, into the trees higher up, all blackened from the fire. Then he stepped out and fired his .44 once into the air. "That's just to let him know we got his message."

A moment later, they heard the ATV whining away.

Peter straightened up. "'Stand still. Run. Stop. Now run really fast.' Very confusing when someone's shooting at you."

"Calm yourself, Book Man. That was just a demonstration."

"Of what?"

"The Boyles' commitment to their 'No Trespassing' sign. Or to scaring off competition for the O'Hara place. Buster probably figures that if he takes a few shots at us, we may decide we don't want to buy."

"We don't."

"He doesn't know that." Wild Bill Donnelly headed up the slope. "Seen enough?"

"For now. Do we file a report?"

"About what?"

"Being shot at."

"Can we identify the shooter?"

"You just said it was Buster Boyles."

"Can't say for sure. And if we're planning to keep trespassing around here, we may not want to raise any red flags with the Amador County Sheriff's Office."

Peter followed Wild Bill back up to the Chevy pickup. "Good advice, but—"

"Thirty years of law enforcement talking."

THE ROAD MEANDERED ANOTHER mile through a mostly deserted landscape, in some places heavily treed, in others open and empty. Then they came to a spot where the river turned sharply below them. Wild Bill stopped and said, "There's evidence down there of miners who came in and built a stone-and-log dam. Tried to control all the water right where the Miwok turned."

"Probably pissed off the downstreamers."

"Damn right. There's also evidence that the downstreamers blew up the dam. But when they did, they exposed a gravel bank in the side of the ravine, just loaded with gold. All kinds of stories like that in this country."

Wild Bill took a dirt road to the left that led up to the top of a hill and a chain-link fence enclosing a rusted twenty-foot steel tower. A sign on the fence said KEEP OUT.

"Why are we here?" asked Peter.

"For history. You've seen riverside tailings. You've seen dam builders. You've seen the Michigan Ditch. You need to see hard-rock deep-hole mining. When they put up head frames and dug holes down a mile, it all changed. Big money came in. Hundreds of men took a wage and went into the ground every day. And the gold-bearing rock came up."

"For how long?"

"This place played out in the 1930s, others stopped running in 1942, when Roosevelt closed the mines as a wartime measure. Most of them never reopened." Wild Bill pulled back a cut in the chain-link and gestured for Peter to step through. "Have a look down that shaft."

Peter felt like an explorer who had come upon an ancient Mayan city in the jungle. The ghosts were still here. But the sounds of machinery running above the mine shafts had been replaced by the almost spectral silence of these California hills.

"There's still gold down there," said Wild Bill. "Gold everywhere, if you believe the geologists. They say that the forty-niners only got about twenty percent of it. The low-hanging fruit."

"Is that why everyone around here is so twitchy? Because there's still a lot of gold out there?"

"Gold always makes people twitchy."

Wild Bill led Peter to the far side of the enclosure, through another break in the chain-link, to the edge of the hill and a panoramic view to the south. They could see two more head frames, and the Miwok flickering and glinting, still doing the work that water had been doing since it first flowed through these foothills.

"After it rains," said Wild Bill, "this'll all be as green as Ireland."

Peter looked back to their last stop, above the bend where the dam had been. "When you hear a story of an explosion opening a vein by accident, do you ever think that stories about lost rivers of gold could be true?"

"Lost rivers?"

"And maybe lost bags, and a seven-part journal that could be the treasure map?"

"Sounds like a lot of myth to me, but sometimes, myths have an element of truth." Wild Bill swept his arm across the scene. "Stories from one end of this country to the other. But if the wrong story gets out, well, people like Ginny O'Hara don't want to see this country overrun again. That's really why they're so twitchy."

Peter pointed southwest, to a plateau and a large, flat building, like a warehouse, about three miles away. "Are they the ones overrunning it?"

"That's the Emery Mine. They used to give tours. But a few years ago, new ownership came in. Gold prices were rising so they were starting operations again. It's not open to the public any longer, but maybe we can get a tour. I'm a stockholder. I bought ten thousand shares a while back."

"Big investment."

"It's a gold start-up. Cost me a thousand bucks at a dime a share."

THE MAIN HEAD TOWER for the Emery Mine was about a hundred feet back of the parking lot, near a huge work shed that housed stamping equipment and vehicles. An open pit held a small pond of waste water. And nothing seemed to be happening.

A dozen cars baked on the tarmac. A minivan or two, a few sedans, half a dozen pickups, and one blue Ford Explorer SUV.

Wild Bill pulled his pickup in near the SUV. As they got out, a guy sitting in the SUV—black guy, dark glasses, black suit—looked them over. And he must have seen something he didn't like, because he jumped out.

Wild Bill whispered to Peter, "He knows I'm carrying. Keep walking."

"Hey!" The guy started to follow them.

Then the door of the office swung open and two men were walking toward them from the other direction, walking fast, looking irritated.

One was a big guy, like a linebacker—white, dark glasses, black suit, another hard-assed security type with a bulge under his jacket.

But security for whom?

The other guy, obviously. He was smaller, Asian, better suit, brighter fabric, blue with lighter blue windowpane. And a little triangular lapel pin.

Maybe the white guy noticed the bulge under Donnelly's windbreaker, too, or the double take that Peter did when they passed, because he stepped quickly in front of his man and put a hand inside his jacket.

And for a moment, they all stood there, facing each other down, five guys in sunglasses, some silvered, some wraparounds, and Peter's Cary Grant tortoiseshells. They looked like five bugs, different species.

Wild Bill said with an innocent grin, "Do you gents know if they're giving tours today?"

"Ask inside," said the white guy.

The Asian may have noticed something familiar about Peter, as Peter did about him, but nothing registered behind the dark glasses. Then the two guards led their boss to the SUV, keeping a protective wall of muscle around him until they got him into the backseat and sped away.

Peter said, "I know that guy from somewhere, the one they were guarding."

Wild Bill raised an eyebrow. "I'm not gonna say it."

"If my girlfriend was here, she'd call the P.C. police on you."

INSIDE, PETER FELT AIR conditioning. He liked it. Eighty degrees in October was just . . . wrong, even in the Sierra foothills. Reception area was clean and neat: new file cabinets, two desks. A good first impression meant optimism. But on a whiteboard on the wall, in blue marker: *Today's Stock Price, 0.15.*

A woman looked up from her desk. Her face said, "Now what?" as if it hadn't been a good day and they weren't about to make it any better. She wore a gold golf shirt and khaki trousers. The shirt had the words, EMERY MINE embroidered and beneath, her name: COLLEEN MALONEY. She listened to Wild Bill's spiel and gave the "Boston Historian" a once-over. "No more public tours. Insurance issue."

"I'm a stockholder," said Wild Bill. "On that basis, perhaps—"

Colleen raised a finger and made a call.

A man in his forties emerged from the hall beyond the glass doors. A little paunchy, combed over, wearing the same uniform. His name: Jimmy Maloney. So a family operation. Jimmy was smiling like an emoji.

Wild Bill extended his hand and said, "Hello, Jimmy."

For a moment, the emoji changed to confusion. Jimmy's eyes shifted as if he was trying to place this big red-faced guy. Then he glanced down at his shirt and laughed. "Jimmy Maloney, Community Relations Officer. Can I help you gents?"

Another explanation from Wild Bill Donnelly.

Smiling emoji back in place, Jimmy said it again: tours no longer available. "Insurance issue, you see."

"But my friend here has come all the way from Boston."

"Even if we could, the mine manager, who could authorize it, well, he was just—" Jimmy stopped himself before he said more.

Just what? wondered Peter. Laid off? Fired?

"We had to shut the tours down once we began the permit process," said Jimmy.

Peter asked, "Is that what you told those guys who just left?"

"Excuse me?"

"The guys who were just here. They didn't look too happy. Are they stockholders, too, disappointed that they couldn't get a tour?"

The emoji kept smiling. "I wasn't in their meeting. But . . . you're a historian?"

Wild Bill Donnelly said, "He's interested in gold mining history."

"Well, I can give you our prospectus." He waved them through the doors.

Jimmy Maloney's office was first on the left. Loud voices were coming from the last office on the right. Beyond, a sign on a swinging door read, Hard Hat Area.

Peter and Wild Bill stepped into the windowless cubicle. On the walls were historical pictures of the mine, a whiteboard with a schedule.

Wild Bill kept talking: "This used to be a great take. Anytime I had visitors, I brought them here. We'd all get in carts, go down into the ground, feel the heat. See the veins of gold-bearing quartz. It gave you new respect for mining work."

Jimmy Maloney went to his computer and called up a 3-D image of the mine. "The main shaft reaches four thousand feet, with a dozen others running off of it. Once we pump it out—groundwater fills those deep holes very quickly—we plan to bring three shafts back on line. With a good ore-to-rock ratio, we can be profitable at—"

That was when another guy came in. "Jimmy, you're wanted down the hall. Sorry, gents." The name on his gold shirt said DON BRAVO. He was a big guy with a broad chest and a dark brow. Hard to tell if he was scowling or just looking.

Jimmy's face fell off, as if he was about to lose his job and knew it. He said, "Sure thing, sir," and introduced Mr. Bravo, head of mill security.

Mr. Bravo's eyes went to the bulge under Wild Bill's windbreaker. He said, "Now, who are you and what do you want?"

Wild Bill told the truth: local stockholder and Boston historian.

Don Bravo gave him a "don't bullshit me" look.

Peter pulled out his business card and shoved it into Bravo's hand. He gave one to Jimmy Maloney, too. "Look me up on the internet. And thanks for your time."

FIVE MINUTES LATER, THEY were driving west again, toward Highway 49.

Wild Bill said to Peter, "I wish you'd stop giving out your business card."

"Why?"

"As you say, people are very twitchy here in Amador County. First Ginny O'Hara, then the Boyles—"

"They didn't get a card."

"Something dicey. That Emery Mine spent years getting the permits, satisfying the California DEP over water purification, tailings disposal, and so on, and now . . . the guys in the other offices were reaming each other out."

"About what?

"I heard them talking about the Chinese, the Chinese money, the—"

"Bags and rivers of Chinese gold?"

Wild Bill chuckled. "Lots of Chinese money coming into international gold funds. Chinese government has instructed banks to support gold exploration *and* production. They offer low-interest loans. They employ agents to buy into good-looking gold investments around the globe. Could be that Emery is backed by a Hong Kong bank. And the big investors aren't happy. So somebody just got fired."

"So we got a conflict between the locals and Chinese . . . again?"

"Except now, the Chinese have the power, because they know the golden rule."

"He who has the gold makes the rules."

They arrived at the intersection of the Miwok Road and Highway 49.

Wild Bill Donnelly gave a look around.

Peter said, "You have the light."

"Just making sure nobody's tailing us. Guys who move with heavy security don't always play nice. And maybe that Don Bravo guy called the boys in the blue SUV." Then Wild Bill turned south. Nobody appeared to be following.

As they passed the turn for Highway 88, Peter took out his iPhone.

A text from Evangeline: "Vineyard table set with places for you and your friend. 12:30. Wonderful wines. Come quick, or I may move in."

She's been tasting, he thought. She's half-lit. She should have had a bigger breakfast.

He tapped, "On our way," and asked Wild Bill, "How long to Manion Gold?"

"Fifteen minutes."

Peter added that, sent the text, and said, "I hope you like Zinfandel."

"Almost as much as signed first editions of Robert Ludlum."

"If you help me to reconstruct this journal, I'll see that you get one."

Then Peter texted his son: "More Chinese involvement, at higher levels? More talk of Cutler Exploration at Broke Neck? Upheaval at Emery Mine? More to explain."

Immediately, a text came back. "More tonight. Dinner with Cutler chief investor, Michael Kou. Maybe Cutler, too. Hunan Garden House, 7:30. Before then, read attachment. Just arrived from Montana branch of Spencer family. Three down, four to go."

Peter had questions, but they could wait. He texted: "You're doing good research without me."

LJ answered: "Had good teacher. And the will names most of the heirs. More a matter of persuasion than research."

"Who's left?"

"Manion Sturgis and Sarah Bliss. Maybe Manion's bro, George, the other winemaker."

"And number seven?"

"That's where you come in. Maybe the Sturgis sister in L.A. Not sure yet."

"Answers expected tonight."

"Answers delivered. But work on Manion, and try his Zinfandel."

Peter clicked off the texting function, then clicked to "The Journal of James Spencer—Notebook #3." He asked Donnelly, "Want to hear some of it?"

"Sure."

So, as they wound through the country where the story unfolded, Peter read aloud.

--------------------------------- ❧ ---------------------------------

The Journal of James Spencer—Notebook #3
August 10, 1849
Gold Fever

Before the sun had cleared the treetops, we knew: I had washed our dishes in a gravel bank that rendered a spoonful of gold for every shovelful of dirt we turned.

By eight o'clock, we had learned how to placer mine, a process as repetitive and exhausting as working a loom in a Lowell mill: Dig, dump, clear. Crouch, dip, swirl. Bounce, dip, swirl. Dip, swirl, swirl. And do it all day long.

Dig gravel from the bank or from under the rocks, in the bends and the bars where the river slows and the sediment drops. *Dump* the gravel into the pan. *Clear* the rocks and then the stones. *Crouch* by the river and *dip* the pan. *Swirl* away the lighter sands. *Bounce* to bring out the blackest sands. Then *dip* and *swirl, dip* and *swirl,* down and down, down to the bottom and the beautiful gold, for the only thing heavier than black sand is gold.

By ten o'clock, Michael Flynn was suffering a high-grade case of gold fever, which caused him to work faster and ever faster, filling and swirling, dipping and bouncing, never stopping, seldom breathing, and talking less than ever before.

If it is true that life is no more than an accumulation of dreams and memories, then Flynn that morning was seeing a bright dream burn away his harshest memories . . . all because of gold. He dreamed of going back to Boston, the city that welcomed him with No Irish Need Apply. He imagined squiring beautiful women, downing champagne and oysters, living on Beacon Hill. And the more color he saw in his pan, the brighter grew his dream, the faster moved his hands, the hotter burned his brainpan.

Gold fever may kill in time, but like the hallucinations of a febrile man, it may also clarify his vision before death overtakes him. He knows that gold—so beautiful, so indestructible, so rare—has value and utility. But so, he may tell himself, does iron. And from iron, he can fashion a nail. Then he can build a house. From gold, however, he can fashion a future. So dig fast, dip deep, bounce hard, and swirl and swirl and swirl again.

Every holy Bostonian assembling in the snow aboard the *William Winter*, every unholy soul inhaling the greed-fog of San Francisco, every know-it-all sailing up the Sacramento, every one of them had suffered symptoms of this affliction. Else, they would not have left civilization in the first place. But no man comes down with a killing case of gold fever until he turns his own dirt and finds wealth by the work of his own hand, as we did that first day.

AROUND NOON, CLETIS ANNOUNCED that this was the "richest damn dirt since Jesus threw the Jews out the temple."

"What do we do next?" asked Flynn.

"We remember what I said." Cletis had warned us that if we found gold, we should not cry out or dance a jig or shout loud hallelujahs to heaven. "We keep this quiet, 'cause word'll spread soon enough, and them smelly miners down the road'll come crawlin' all over this hillside like ticks on a curly-haired dog. They'll stake claims and put up tents and dig holes to shit in, and we won't be able to do nothin' about it. Better if it's just us and them yammerin' Chinks across the river."

We staked three claims, following the laws of Broke Neck. One ran along the river, one on the flatland directly above the bank, ten by ten, and one above that, at the base of the big skull-shaped rock, five by twenty. Cletis said, "A big rock makes the water swirl and slosh and drop whatever it's carryin'."

He put a shovel at one corner of his claim, drove sticks to mark the others. "So long as we leave our tools to show we're workin' at least one day a week, nobody can touch this claim. Miner's Law."

I asked Cletis about claim jumpers.

"A year ago, when I got discharged and come prospectin', nobody worried about claim jumpers. But more folks arrivin' every day now. And more folks means less gold. And when there's less of somethin' folks want, it brings out the bad in a lot of 'em. That's a natural law. So there's more claim jumpin'. But Miner's Law still holds."

"Do you think that those Chinks know Miner's Law?" asked Flynn.

"If they don't, we'll teach 'em." Cletis studied the six small men squatting and swirling on the other bank. "But I don't guess they'd be so stupid as to go stealin' from such stalwart Christian sons of bitches as us."

OUR DAY ENDED WITH a take of twenty ounces and total exhaustion. To those who say that I was "soft," one of those silk-stocking boys who never dirtied his hands until he got to California, I would answer that Flynn knew physical labor as well as any man, and he was more drained than I.

We had not the energy to do anything but eat our bacon and beans and share swallows from the jug of whiskey that Flynn had bought at Sutter's.

Then I staggered down the slope to wash my face in the river that flowed toward the last light silvering the August sky and glimmering like oil on the water. I knelt, dipped my red and yellow-paisley neckerchief, and saw a shadow.

Not ten feet away stood one of the Chinamen.

I jumped up, startled. He stepped back, startled.

For a moment, we stared across the stream at each other's shadows, men who had traveled far from opposite compass points to this new land, this alien place, this gold country in the gloaming.

His hair had been razored back, giving him a high forehead. A long braid curled down his back. And his baggy trousers and gown-like shirt made his silhouette appear square and solid, not to be trifled with.

I said, "Good evening," in a gentle manner, as I would to a skittish dog or a small child, since I did not believe he would understand the words themselves.

He shocked me by saying, "A beautiful sunset."

Yes. The Chinaman could speak English. But he did not stay to chat. He said something to another Chinaman who came out of the bushes nearby, and together they scurried back downstream to their little camp.

August 11–16, 1849
Blisters

Every day came in clear and cloudless, with heat rising into the afternoon, then receding toward a cool evening. There was a comforting predictability to it all, but a profound monotony, too.

In the mornings, I warmed my hands around a mug of bitter coffee, brewed from beans that Cletis had bought for the outrageous sum of $4 a pound, put through his grinder, and roasted in his cast-iron frying pan. Then I wrapped my hands with cotton strips cut from one of my shirts to cover the blisters on my palms. Then I got to work. But no matter how I protected them, by day's end, my hands were so bloody and raw that I could barely curl my fingers around a pencil.

Each night, however, I wrote. Writing was my reason for being here, and in truth, my reason for being. I hoped to produce a dispatch for Sam Batchelder every two weeks and a letter a week for Janiva. But on some nights, I fell asleep before writing a word.

ALL THAT WEEK, WE concentrated on the claim just below the big rock, so heavy with gold, going so deep into the bank, that we might all get rich on that claim alone. But to "wash" the gravel, we had to carry water from the river or carry gravel to the water.

We had decided it was more efficient to carry the gravel, and I was elected, since my blisters were too painful to swing a shovel. Cletis made a yoke for my shoulders, allowing me to carry two buckets at once. Flynn's gold fever broke, for no man could sustain the intensity that gripped him the first day. Cletis, steady Cletis, seemed never to change the pace at which he walked or talked or worked, which was a good lesson for us younger men. And thus, with Flynn and Cletis digging and filling or crouching and washing, with me beating a path between them, we got on.

Then, late on the 16th, the English-speaking Chinaman came along the opposite bank and stood, looking over at us.

Flynn said, "What's he thinkin'?"

"Don't know," said Cletis. "But he better not be thinkin' him and his friends can stake claims on this side." He grabbed his blunderbuss and stalked down the bank.

The Chinaman took a step back, but he did not run.

Cletis said, "No crossee river. You hear?"

The Chinaman just looked at him.

Cletis swept the gun up and down the bank. "White men only, this side."

The other Chinamen were watching, though none moved. They reminded me of frightened rabbits, hoping that if they went motionless, the predator would not see them.

But the bold one kept his eyes on Cletis, who said, "Stay your side, we friends."

"Friends?" The Chinaman sounded more puzzled than pleased, as if he did not understand the meaning of the word . . . or perhaps the possibility of it.

"Just . . . just . . . stay over there." Cletis came back up the slope. "Don't want him gettin' ideas. Don't want him leavin', either. Them Chinks are like a painted sign for white miners . . . Nothin' here. Better diggin's elsewhere. Best keep movin'."

August 17, 1849
Visitors

In the late afternoon, Drinkin' Dan Fleener and his partner came up from town. They stopped on the road and watched the Chinamen for a bit. Then they walked down the slope toward Flynn, who was swirling his pan at the river's edge.

Cletis put down his shovel and whispered to me, "Tell 'em nothin'." Then he gave them both a big, "Howdy, boys!"

Drinkin' Dan squinted through his one eye. His partner limped on a bad leg. Together, they made a formidable man, one that no grizzly or claim jumper would challenge—not one with a nose, anyway—in that the partner, John McGinty, also known as Stinkin' McGinty, was the most odiferous man I had ever encountered. His stench foretold him in a way that the common smell of sweating male bodies did not. He could make eyes water. He could make toes curl. Get too close and the ammonia wafting off of him just might make you gag.

Drinkin' Dan shouted, "You boys makin' money?"

"Workin' our arses off is what we are," said Michael Flynn.

"Ask 'em, do they got anything to drink?" said McGinty.

Cletis laughed. "Drinkin' Dan gets a drinkin' partner. Reckon that makes sense. But we drunk all the whiskey. Got some coffee, though. Brewed it up this mornin'."

I wondered why Cletis offered them coffee if he wanted to be rid of them. Then he said, "Or we could ask the Chinks for tea," thereby drawing their attention to our neighbors.

Drinkin' Dan rolled his eye downstream. "You drink tea with Chinks?"

McGinty kicked at the dirt. "Ain't no gold where there's Chinks."

Just then, the English-speaking Chinaman came along the bank. He was carrying a steaming pot of . . . something.

Cletis whispered to me, "What the hell is this?"

The Chinaman ignored Cletis and offered me the pot. "Tea. Hot tea. Tea for eat."

"Eat?" said Cletis. "What the—"

The Chinaman made a gesture to his mouth. "Deal. Make tea for eat. No?"

I knew what the Chinaman was up to, so I went back to our tent and fetched about eight inches of beef jerky, one of the more unpleasant things I had ever chewed. (I never honored the consumption of beef jerky with the word "eat" because I never ate it, only ground it on my molars until the taste of it killed my appetite. Then I spat out the remains.)

Returning to the riverbank, I stepped rock to rock and met the Chinaman halfway. As he extended the pot, I looked into his eyes. This was the first time that we had faced each other in full daylight.

He was in his twenties and handsome for his race, with eyes that did not deviate or defer but met mine straight on, except when he winked, as if to say, "play along." That surprised me almost as much as his skin, which was more sun-browned than yellow. He took the jerky, bowed, and backed away. "Good deal. Good jerky. Good tea for good jerky."

I turned the pot in the direction of our visitors. "Tea?"

"Chink tea? Made by Chinks minin' here?" McGinty spat. "Got to be better diggin's upstream."

"And better drinkin', too," said Drinkin' Dan.

McGinty turned and went limping up the slope toward the road.

Drinkin' Dan said to us, "McGinty's my pard. I have to stay with him."

"Come by anytime," said Cletis. "But if you bring that feller again, see he takes a dunk in the river first."

"Good luck," said Drinkin' Dan. "And be damn careful when you go for a piss at night. Got us a big grizzly sow up in these hills with two new cubs. Not somethin' you want to meet with your dick in your hands."

Cletis said, "Maybe the bear likes the taste of Chink."

Drinkin' Dan laughed and waved and followed his partner.

After they were out of earshot, Cletis said to us, "Well, that Chink's a bold one, steppin' into white man's talk like that."

From the opposite bank, the Chinaman said, "Drink tea. Give back pot."

"Yep, as bold as the ball sack on a big horny bull," said Cletis.

"But you know," said Flynn, "I could do with a bit of tea. After whiskey, it's the Irish national drink."

"After whiskey," said Cletis, "the Irish national drink is more whiskey."

Flynn sipped the tea, rolled it around in his mouth. "Different. Strong. Nice."

He offered it to Cletis, who looked at it, then at Flynn, and counted, "Eight . . . nine . . . ten."

I asked what he was counting for.

"To make sure it ain't poisoned. If I can count to ten and he ain't keeled over, then—"

"You drink my tea," said the Chinaman, "they think we friends. So they go. Good for you, 'cause you no want more white miner. Good for me, 'cause I no want, either."

Flynn chuckled. He was quick to admire any man who showed a sharp sense of the world and the wit to react to it. He said, "There's one sly little Celestial, for you."

The Chinaman gave a bow of the head. He may even have smiled.

Cletis took the tea pot and drank. Then he offered it to me. "It's all right."

It was more than all right. Tea with herbs and a scent of clove. Delicious.

The Chinaman backed away.

Flynn said to us, "I'm thinkin' those Chinks found somethin' over there on that claim that the white miners missed."

"If the whites find out," said Cletis, "they're like to run the Chinks right off."

The Chinaman did not let on that he heard any of this. He just kept backing away.

I called after him. "What's your name?"

"Chin. Wei Chin."

"I'm Spencer. This is Flynn and Cletis."

"Don't be tellin' him our damn names," said Cletis.

August 18, 1849
Routine

We worked the hillside claim, filling buckets with dirt, carrying them down to the river, or the other way round. As my blisters were toughening into callus, we changed positions often, so no man exhausted any one set of muscles. Better to wear them all out equally. One man dug, one carried, one washed. At noon, we stopped for hardtack and a swallow of water. Then we worked until sunset. In the evening, we cooked bacon and beans. And Cletis insisted that we go into the woods and collect berries, roots, and wild mustard greens that we boiled into a soup.

"A fine feast," said Flynn that night. "It ain't the Arbella Club, but it'll do."

Cletis bit off a chaw, settled back against the big rock, and spat tobacco into the dust. "Too many fellers get the glint of gold in their eye, they forget everything else, even their bellies."

We were pulling twenty ounces a day, so we all had the glint and ever-expanding pouches that we kept buried under the big rock.

"May the glint never go," said Flynn.

"It'll go if we get the scurvy," answered Cletis. "That's why I have you boys pickin' green trash and such. Feller I knew, never et a green thing for six months. Scurvy snuck up on him like an Injun in the dark. First he started losin' his energy. Then his skin got all spots. Then his legs took to swellin' . . . when I found him, his teeth was fallin' out. Knew right off what it was. Bought some limes off a Mexican farmer, give him the juice. Saved his life."

"Lime juice. That's why God made grog," said Flynn. "A fine drink and good for you, too. Not so good as Irish whiskey, but—"

"Speakin' of Irish whiskey . . ." Cletis upended our jug. "Time for that trip into Broke Neck." Then he asked me how much coin I had.

"About two hundred in ten-dollar Gold Eagles."

Cletis said we should spend the coin first. "As soon as we start payin' with fresh dust, folks'll start askin' about our claim. Then we'll get neighbors, sure enough."

"Let's hope the Chinks stay, then. But"—Flynn looked at the campfire across the river—"I sure don't like 'em watchin' us."

"They watchin' now?" asked Cletis.

Two Chinese shadows were moving on the bank. One was coming out of the bushes.

Flynn got up and walked halfway down to the river's edge.

"What are they doin?" called Cletis.

"Can't tell." Flynn watched their shadows gliding toward the light of their own campfire. "But I swear, one moves like a girl. Maybe they were after more than an evenin' stroll."

"You been away from females too long." Cletis scratched one foot on the other. "Best thing about gettin' old, you don't dream so much about tastin' salty-sweet snatch."

"Speakin' of which," Flynn said, "you should see Jamie's Boston gal. Pretty enough to make a priest dream of—" Flynn saw the look that I shot at him, and he shrugged, as if to apologize. "Dreamed of her meself a few times."

"You dream of my Janiva?" I said. "What kind of dreams?"

Cletis laughed. "When a man has a good-lookin' woman runnin' through his brain? He dreams the only dream you can grab hold of with one hand in the dark. Ain't that right, there, Galway Bay?"

I ignored that and kept my eyes on Flynn, who said, "Didn't tell you, Jamie. Didn't want you hittin' me with a shovel if I started talkin' in me sleep, but she's worth a dream or two, for sure."

"Dream about one of your own," I said.

Cletis pulled on his boots. "Might as well dream of a featherbed and a fine steak and a jug full of whiskey, too. At least we can do somethin' about the whiskey. Harvard and me, we'll go into town and refill the jug and mail that gal of his a letter."

"What about me?" asked Flynn. "I need to buy more peppermints. If I can't have a girl to kiss, at least I'll have somethin' sweet in me mouth."

"I'll buy 'em if they got 'em," said Cletis. "In the meanwhile, you keep an eye on them Chinks. See if one of 'em squats to pee. If he does, well, maybe *he* is a *she*."

"Chinks squat to do everything," said Flynn.

"Then watch close." Cletis stood. "And watch for them bears."

"Don't be startin' with talk about bears again."

"It's their country, too," said Cletis, "And I seen piles of fresh scat up on the ridge. That big sow smells food, she might come lookin' for some Irish stew."

WE WALKED THE MILE into town leading the burro. The canvas sides of the tents had been raised, so lantern light filled the street, and the squeal of a squeeze-box annoyed the air. We tied the burro in front of the general store. And it was then that Cletis noticed the sign, *Emery's Emporium, No Kredit*. He said, "I'll be damned. Didn't see that the first time we come through." Then he shouted, "Hey, George!" and hopped through the door.

Emery's Emporium was not much larger than a Broke Neck claim, but what a collection of shovels, pans, sacks, jars, tins, boxes, and sundry cans was packed into that space. And what a crowd of miners was doing business.

Cletis pushed up to the counter and called out to a skinny piece of old rawhide named George Emery. The two greeted each other like brothers, then Cletis introduced me to "one of my oldest army friends. One of the smartest, too, considerin' how fine he's set himself up. A fine store, and . . . how's that fine young wife, George?"

"Back in Sacramento, doin' my buyin' off the ships," said Emery, whose beard was as gray as Cletis Smith's but trimmed and combed, as if to complement his clean shirt and leather shopkeeper's apron.

"Be careful someone don't try to buy *her*," said Cletis. "She's worth her weight."

As Cletis and Emery began to jabber, I held up the jug.

Emery said, "No spirits sold here, son. Nothin' against them. Just need room for things that miners need, like navy beans and shovels."

Cletis told me to try the saloon. "And don't pay more than two Eagles."

"Go see the Scotsman," said Emery. "Grouchy Pete McDougall. Tell him I sent you."

I said, "Thanks for the referral."

Emery gave me a quizzical look. "The what?"

Cletis explained, "Smart young feller. Went to Harvard. Smart but awful dumb."

"A lot like that comin' into this country," said Emery. "Educated fools, I call 'em."

Ignoring that, I headed first for Abbott's Assay and Express Office to send my dispatches. Mr. Abbott eyed me warily. He looked to be about forty and had the cleanest hands I had seen in gold country, with nails neatly trimmed and polished as if to proclaim that he spent no time turning over rocks or shoveling gravel. His business was the weighing and measuring of gold and the delivering of dispatches and letters.

On the table in front of him were arrayed a set of scales and weights, a pistol, and a ledger book. A big black safe hulked in the corner. He had written prices on a chalkboard: *Assays, one ounce. Letters carried to San Francisco, $5, mailed from SF, $5. Gold shipped east, 10% commission.*

I paid with two ten-dollar Gold Eagles and asked how long it would take to get my dispatch and letter to Boston.

Abbott promised that his rider would have the letters in San Francisco within two days. He made no promises, however, as to the schedule of the mail steamer *California*. "We do what we can and trust to God for the rest." This was the first time in this country that I had heard a man mention God as if he actually believed in him.

I thanked him and promised more business. That elicited Abbott's first smile.

THEN I TOOK MY jug to Grouchy Pete's, a huge tent fashioned from sail canvas (a common commodity, given all the abandoned ships in California) with a floor fashioned from wooden planks that may once have been deck-boards.

The bar was a pair of long planks supported on upturned barrels. Behind it were more barrels, set on sawhorses, with spigots in the bungholes and words scrawled on each barrel, to be taken on faith: *Whiskey. Rum. Brandy.* Opposite the bar, a dozen or more drinkers lounged, perched, and flopped, some on the floor, others on benches and chairs arranged in configurations best suited for the sharing of jugs and rumors. And over in the far corner, at a round table, six men were playing cards.

A few drinkers gave me a glance, and I thought I might see a Sagamore or two. But in the greasy lantern light, I recognized no one. So I set the jug down.

The barkeep wore a sweat-stained beaver hat and carried an Ethan Allen six-shot pepperbox pistol in a holster at his belt. Considering the popularity of the liquor in the barrels behind him, it was no surprise that he greeted new customers with a suspicious squint and a glimpse of his gun.

I said, "I'm lookin' for Grouchy Pete."

"He's nae lookin' for you."

"George Emery sent me."

"Who in the name of Christ cares?" I heard the accent of the Scottish Highland.

I said, "Even if you aren't Pete, you sure are grouchy."

He pointed to the jug. "You want to fill that?"

"It's empty, ain't it?" I was learning that sarcasm should be met with sarcasm, aggression with aggression, and men said "ain't" for "isn't."

"Don't be smart with me," he said. "You want to fill it, show some dust. One ounce and a quarter." He pointed to the scale at the end of the bar.

Instead, I pulled two Gold Eagles from my pocket. Twenty American dollars.

They improved his attitude considerably. He said, "What's your drink?"

"Whiskey."

"Ain't you the feller with the old soldier and the Irishman, workin' a claim across from those Chinks?"

I said that I was.

He held up a coin. "And you're payin' with your seed money?"

"I'm paying." I did not look away or tell too much or act intimidated. "Paying is what counts, ain't it?" Another *ain't* for emphasis.

"Aye." He swept the jug from the bar and put it under a spigot, then he turned back to me. "Dinna you fellers figure it out when you saw Chinks? You'll nae find gold where there's Chinks."

"We're learning," I said.

"Movin' on soon, then?"

I shrugged. Cletis might have had a better answer but I had never been a good liar, which my father had said would be both a blessing and a curse. . . .

I waited, staring straight ahead, feigning lack of interest in idle chatter until I heard a voice behind me. "So . . . the traitor of the Sagamores."

I did not turn.

Grouchy Pete looked up from the spigot and said, "Trader? You dinna say you were tradin'. What are you tradin'?"

I just shook my head. "Nothing."

He looked beyond me at whoever was standing there, then seemed to lose interest, as if he had heard everything and did not care too much about any of it.

I waited until he put the full jug on the bar, picked it up, told him to keep the change on account, then turned to face two Sagamores who had found their way to Broke Neck, after all: Hiram Wilson and Scrawny Selwin Gore. They did not look as if they had prospered. Wilson had lost a front tooth. Selwin wobbled and smelled of whiskey.

Selwin said, "Hodges told us, if we saw you, we should give you a message."

"Yes?" I held myself very still.

"He marks you a traitor for leaving," said Wilson.

"But *you* left," I said.

"Not in the dead of night," answered Selwin. "Not before Hodges gave us the say-so."

"And here you are." I changed the subject: "Have you struck pay dirt?"

Selwin elbowed Wilson. "He's learned the lingo already. Pay dirt, he asks."

Wilson—a little older, a little slower, a schoolmaster who had perhaps controlled his classes a little better—said, "We tried three places, pulled out a few ounces, but—"

I wanted to be done with them, so I said as I stepped out the door, "Don't get discouraged, boys. It's only been two weeks."

But I sensed them following me across the street. Then I heard the sound of a hammer clicking and a cylinder clacking into place. This caused me some concern, but I kept walking. As I reached our burro in front of Emery's, I noticed Cletis stepping out of the store with a sack on his shoulder. He saw me, saw them, and went straight back inside.

Hiram Wilson, of Brookline, Massachusetts, once the shaper of young minds, stood in the middle of a dusty street in a plank-and-canvas mining camp and held a pistol with far less confidence than he might have held a ruler. He was not even pointing it. The ground appeared to be his target. He said, "I'm sorry, Spencer, but Hodges said if we saw you and held you and got word to him, he would not forget it."

"He's proud of his memory," I said.

Selwin said, "Get to it, Hiram. Put the gun on him. We'll bring him to Hodges—"

"We don't even know where Hodges is," said Wilson.

"Bring him to Hodges and maybe he'll give us another horse, so we can—"

From out of the corner of my eye, I saw Cletis Smith. Then a shovel whizzed past my ear and struck Hiram Wilson flat in the face.

The schoolmaster went down. The gun went off. The bullet struck the ground.

And as fast as the muzzle flash, Cletis was cocking the shovel at Selwin. "Whoever bothers my pardner bothers me. You botherin'?"

Selwin said, "Your pardner is not to be trusted."

"I trust him," said Cletis.

Wilson rolled onto all fours. He wiped the blood from his nose, then wiped tears from his eyes. "I'm . . . I'm sorry, Spencer. I'm not made for this. Not for any of it. Not for gold mining. Not for partnering with a shipboard tee-totaller who takes to whiskey at the first sign of trouble. Not for—"

"A man's got a right to a drink," said Selwin, "'specially if there's no gold."

Cletis picked up Hiram's pistol, dumped the percussion caps into the street, then handed it back to him. "If you ain't made for it, best get on home."

"Don't be listenin' to him." Selwin dragged Hiram up by the armpits.

Hiram shoved the pistol into his belt. Then he wiped more blood from his face.

Cletis said, "Saloon's right behind you. Looks like you could both use a swaller." Then he told me to buy my friends a drink.

Like the country itself, Cletis was a strange mixture of violence and kindness, of brutality and beauty. I had seen it with Señor Vargas. I saw it now. If he told me to buy a drink for two men he had just beaten with a shovel, I would. I pulled a coin from my pocket and flipped it to Hiram.

He said that *he* would not forget me, and he did not mean it as a threat. Then he grabbed Scrawny by the elbow and dragged him back toward Grouchy Pete's.

Cletis asked me, "Are they likely to follow us?"

"They might. They're lost. They're wandering."

"We'll watch out, then. Fellers like that are best sent on their way."

August 19, 1849
The Specter of Samuel Hodges

I did not sleep well. I could not erase from my mind the image of those two broken Bostonians. The dissolution of the Sagamores had put Wilson and Gore in a bad patch, and they had failed their first test. They had met disappointment and could not overcome it. Would they pass the second, learn from failure, and go home?

I half expected to find them at our campfire when I awakened.

I got up and scanned the riverbank. The Chinese were already at work. Flynn and Cletis were still asleep after an extra measure from the new jug.

No Hiram or Scrawny. No Samuel Hodges, either.

But Hodges was out there somewhere. Maybe he had gone to the northern mines, as planned. Maybe he and his loyal men were heading south. But he was out there, feeding his resentments, still dreaming of empire and unfulfilled ambition, still furious that the writer he brought to immortalize his deeds had deserted him for the company of an Irish waiter.

Peter Fallon skimmed through the next few weeks.

Spencer, Flynn, and Cletis Smith built a lean-to roof against the big skull-shaped rock and named their claim after the shape.

Other miners staked claims nearby and worked for a while. Some were friendly, others envious, a few resentful, because "placer mining, like life, proved to be unfair." One miner might find a pocket of gold to work for a week, while another scraped ground not twenty feet away and found nothing.

But Flynn, Spencer, and Cletis kept working, digging steadily in their hundred-square-foot plots, pulling out gold every day.

Then, one morning . . .

---- ❧ ----

September 20, 1849
A Surprising Proposal

The aroma of tea awoke me. Tea?

I grabbed my pistol and stepped out of the tent.

Chin was squatting by our campfire, warming a pot. He stood when he saw me and said, "I help."

"Help? How?"

"Dig more gold."

Flynn and Cletis both crawled out a moment later.

Cletis said, "More gold?"

"Tea, first." Chin offered Cletis the cup. "Then gold."

Cletis scratched his behind through his breeches and took the tea, as if to signal his interest.

Michael Flynn pulled on his boots and joined us, too.

"Now," said Cletis, dropping onto a log by the fire, "what's a Chink know about placer minin' that we don't?"

"No call me 'Chink,' maybe I tell," said Chin.

Cletis sucked in a gulp of air to deliver a stream of insults.

But I stopped him with a question for our visitor: "First, maybe you tell us where you learned English."

"From holy men in black robes," said Chin. "They come China. Tell about white man-god, Christ."

"Missionaries," I said.

"Jesuits," said Flynn.

"They taught him good," said Cletis.

"He learned good," said Flynn. "Now he come to California to prove *how* good."

"I come California to escape. I am Sam He Hui—"

"Sam *Who*?" asked Cletis.

"Sam He Hui. Secret society. Fight Manchu rulers. Manchu kill many, but I escape. I come with Uncle Bao, Friendly Liu, and three cousin, Ng-goh, the big brother, Little Ng, who play flute, and Littler Ng. We come to Gum Saan."

"What's that?" asked Flynn.

"Gold Mountain. Chinee call all this"—he gestured around him—"Gum Saan. We sail on Yankee ship. Work on Yankee ship. In San Francisco, we jump Yankee ship."

"You ain't the first." Flynn laughed. He always laughed easily.

Cletis looked up at the sun and said, "We're burnin' daylight, Sam Who. So . . . how *you* mean to help *us*? And why?"

"I watch every day you."

"Pretty bold about it, too," said Cletis.

"You carry dirt down to water and water up to dirt. I make for you to raise water." Chin drew a circle in the air with his finger.

"A wheel?" Cletis hooted. "You want to build a flutter wheel?"

"Flutter?" said Chin.

"That's what it's called in these parts," said Cletis. "Flutter wheel. Chinese wheel . . . if you don't know what it's called, maybe you don't know how to build one."

"I build one in China to water rice. I build one here. Then maybe you build Long Tom."

"What's that?" asked Flynn.

"A trough with a screen called a riddle," said Cletis. "The riddle catches the heavy junk, lets the little stuff drop onto a run of sheet metal poked with holes called riffles. The riffles catch the gold. Works good, but it needs a steady stream of water."

"That's the *what*," said Flynn. "Now, give us the *why*. Why build it for us and not your pardners over there, squattin' like women in the cold water?"

"What we build for us, white men knock down."

Flynn sipped his tea and nodded. "That's for fuckin' sure."

"So I build for you." Chin stood. "But you pay."

"Pay?" Cletis bit off a chaw of tobacco. "How much?"

"Even share. One fourth." Chin held up his fingers for one and four.

Cletis stood. "Get back across the river. We're in dangerous enough country as it is, just talkin' to you. If it ever gets out that—"

"Pay money for brain. I look. I think. I know. But"—Chin rolled his eyes—"if you know what to call wheel, maybe you know how to build."

"You are tryin' me, Mr. Sam Who." Which meant that Cletis did not know how to build a flutter wheel and was as annoyed at his own ignorance as he was at the Chinaman.

I said, "You haven't answered the second question. Why us?"

"I come America do business, not squat in river. I start here. Do business here."

I looked at my calluses and flexed my sore shoulders. "I think it's a good idea."

Cletis gave that a juicy brown spit. "You think it's a good idea. . . . And what happens when white men hear we're pardnerin' with Chinks? What then?"

"No tell white men. And no call me Chink." Chin kept his voice calm, though it was certain that he had mustered all his nerve to come over here in service to his ambition. "One fourth or you all day carry dirt to water, water to dirt."

"Your friends . . . will they help?" I asked.

"If I say."

"Even the woman?" asked Flynn.

"Woman?" Chin's eyes narrowed. "No woman. No Chinee woman in Gum Saan."

"If you say so." Flynn looked over at the Chinese camp, where two men in stiff straw hats were squatting and panning.

Cletis leaned close to him. "White miners get awful touchy when foreigners are doin' better. Can't say what they'll do if they find out it's Chinks doin' better. Might set this whole damn riverbank on fire."

"They might," said Michael Flynn, "but I don't much appreciate fellers tellin' me who I can work with and who I can't." Flynn squinted through the campfire smoke at Chin. "So . . . will you take a tenth? A tenth is worth it. A fourth is too much."

Cletis Smith lifted a leg and farted.

Chin gave Cletis a glare and said, "I build for one-sixth, but he no do that again."

"That might be hard," Cletis said, "considerin' all the beans we eat around here."

"One-eighth," I said. "Split the difference. It's the best we can do."

And Chin agreed.

Flynn finished his tea and said, "So damn the bully boys. Let's build a wheel."

September 30, 1849
A dispatch

Mr. Jack Abbott was quickly becoming my friend. Letters and dispatches, posted regularly, payment in shiny Gold Eagles . . . those made me one of his best customers and therefore one of his friends.

In the letter, I told Janiva how much I missed her. I did not tell her that my longing was as much physical as emotional. I did not think she would understand the need that came upon men, sometimes at dawn, sometimes before sleep. I told her instead that I dreamed of embracing her. I told her that I still wore her neckerchief. I did not tell her that her fragrance remained in the fabric, a faint but real presence, and sometimes I held it to my face to bring back the memory of her and the sensation of her, too. Instead, I told her yet again that no matter the pain of our separation, it was best that she had stayed in Boston. To inhabit this universe of greed, ambition, elation, and frustration, in tents that stunk of butt sweat and bean-farts, on claims that broiled in the sun and puffed dust into the desiccated air, this was not something that a woman should be asked to endure.

And in the dispatch for the *Transcript*, I told the truth about the Chinamen:

If you could leave your Boston parlors and by some magic fly through the air to the far edge of our continent, you would be pleased to see what we have done on this gentle slope, at the place we call Big Skull Rock.

We—Cletis Smith of Kentucky, Michael Flynn of Galway, and Yr. Ob't. Correspondent—have applied one of the basic principles of New England, that water in motion is a transformative force, able to change the contours of the landscape and the economies of men. With the help of our neighbor, Mr. Wei Chin of Manchu, China, we have built a device similar to the water wheels that irrigate the rice paddies of his native land.

We bought planks from the saw pit in Fiddletown, nails and rope from Emery's Emporium, fittings and sheet metal from the blacksmith in Quartztown (at a cost of $3 a pound for 12 pounds). And we invested a weeks' worth of our own perspiration to construct a "wheel" that is actually two wooden hexagons joined together by three-foot paddles at each angle.

As the current drives the wheel, a wooden box attached to the downstream side of each paddle scoops water to a height of eight feet and dumps it into a trough that feeds a sluice connected to something called a Long Tom, thereby delivering a steady flow of water. We then dump gravel into the upper end of the Long Tom and sift gold at the bottom.

We built the wheel on the north bank, burying its moorings on either side of a pool that, even in late summer, is still hip-deep and well-served by the current. Then we tied ropes from the wheel to the horses on the south bank. Smith gave the count and, with a mighty shout, urged the horses to pull. Meanwhile, on the north bank, Flynn and I and Chin worked levers to lift the top of the ten-foot wheel off ground.

Up, up slowly, but up and up and then . . . it stopped rising. We groaned. The horses strained. But the wheel hung suspended until Chin called to the other Chinese. These "Celestials" provoke curiosity by their peculiar dress and clannish habits and are admired for their industriousness, but they are generally timid, for not all white miners approve of them. Still, two strong young Chinamen, the brothers Ng-goh and Little Ng, came running, put their weight on the levers, and the wheel began moving again.

But we did not want it to move too quickly, lest it topple onto the other bank and shatter. So Flynn and I dropped our levers, leapt to the counter lines, and exerted guiding pressure, thereby letting the wheel settle and drop—with mathematical precision, may I say—into the cradle.

Then we stood in silence, waiting for the water to do its work. But the wheel did not move. So Flynn plunged into the river, grabbed one of the spokes, and pushed a paddle down. The current grabbed, the hub groaned, and our invention began to turn.

A cry of joy arose from both sides of the river, from Cletis Smith, from Flynn and me and Mr. Chin, and yes, from all the Chinese.

The first scoop dipped down and swung up and dumped, just as we had intended. But as the trough at the top of the sluice was not yet built, the sparkling silver water cascaded onto Flynn's head. He whooped like an Indian, pulled off his hat, looked up so that the next scoop poured onto his face, and cried, "I am baptized again, Lord, in a flowin' river of gold!"

Within two days, we had doubled our "take." Our deal with Mr. Chin had paid a fine dividend. So we will be staying at Big Skull Rock.

Yr. Ob't. Correspondent,

The Argonaut

October 4, 1849
Chinese Speculations

Our flutter wheel turned and thumped in the steady current. Sometimes, miners going by would stop to admire it. Some would decide to prospect nearby. Most stayed a few days but were quick to leave because of the Chinese, who kept heads down and backs bent, on a claim that white men had abandoned. Others decided that we had found and claimed the perfect turn in the river, where gold had been dropping for as long as water had been flowing, and it was useless to look nearby.

And in that, they were right, because we found gold day after day, while Michael Flynn talked and talked. On this day, he talked about how well we had built, about what a good idea it was to hire "Sam Who," about how easily the job went. "But when they cheered the raisin' of the wheel, did you not hear a high voice on one of them?"

I admitted that I had not.

"The smallest one. The one called Littler Ng." Flynn looked downstream. "The one comin' down to the river now, movin' with them little girlie steps."

And it was true. The smallest one had a short, mincing gait more appropriate to a subservient female than a male, even a Chinese male

Cletis chuckled. "I swear, Galway, you need a woman 'fore you try to fuck my sorrel mare."

October 6, 1849
A Gift

It was dusk. I was writing by the campfire. Cletis was already snoring.

Michael Flynn was acting bored, frustrated, something. He got up and wandered down to the river. Half an hour later, he scurried back, crouched beside me, and with the firelight flickering in his eyes, he said, "I was right."

"About what?"

"He's a *she*. Littler Ng is a Chinese *girl*."

"How can you tell?"

"I waited in the bushes till Chin come along. Then he waved the all-clear to Littler Ng. Then he—I mean *she*—ducked into the bushes, right in front of me and squatted. Prettiest little ass that ever shone in the moonlight, and, well, that's why Chin stands there every night. He's standin' guard. She's his girl . . . or his sister."

"Sister," came the voice from the darkness. Chin stepped into the firelight and into our conversation. "I bring her Gum Saan to save her. Manchu would make her concubine."

"There's folks here," said Flynn, "might try to do the same."

Chin approached us. "You no tell, I take no more money. Wheel done. Payment done. You promise keep secret."

Flynn looked at me. "I guess he trusts us."

Chin said, "No choice. But you bother sister, I tell Miner's Council you pay Chinee to build wheel. They no like."

"We'll promise," I said.

"So long as you tell us her name," added Flynn.

Chin studied Flynn, as if he thought that giving her name would be a violation of her. The fire crackled. A gang of coyotes woofed and howled somewhere in the night. And through clenched teeth, Chin said, "Mei-Ling."

Flynn said the name and said it again, almost whispering it the second time, and he pronounced it a good name. Then he went into the tent and got the bag of peppermints Cletis had bought for him at Emery's. He tore off a corner of the paper and wrapped three candy drops in it, then tied it with a twist to make a bag. "Give this to Mei-Ling. Tell her it's from an admirer."

Chin looked at Flynn, then at the peppermints, perhaps imagining where such small gifts might lead. Then he took them and turned back into the darkness.

"Now we know why he built the wheel for us," said Flynn. "To keep us quiet."

October 7, 1849
Sabbath Visitors

Sunday in gold country is a day of rest. But as there are no churches, few preachers, and even fewer ladies, keeping holy the California Sabbath entails card-playing, jug-passing, small talk, big talk, loud talk, louder talk, and singing at the top of your lungs. And sometimes it includes a round of stomp-foot dancing, with men drawing lots to determine who leads and who follows. On a California Sabbath, you will hear little talk of Abraham, Isaac, Jacob, and their God but much about Mammon and his.

I was writing. Cletis was mending socks. Flynn was studying the Chinese, who worked on the Sabbath as if they understood how little time they might have before white miners drove them off, or as Cletis suggested, simply because they were heathens.

Around ten o'clock, I felt a wave of nostalgia. It was not something that bothered me except in my quieter hours. "Back home," I said, "the bell of the Park Street Church would be tolling just about now."

"Aye," said Flynn, "and I'd hear it in the dirty damn Hightower House. If me bed was empty, I'd hear the voice of me dear sainted mother sayin', 'Michael, get out to Mass and say a prayer for me.' But if I woke up next to a female, I might slide her nightgown up to her hips, and slip meself in there, and—"

"For a feller who grew up under the sign of the Catholic cross, you sure are a randy—" Cletis stopped in mid-sentence.

Five mounted men turned off the road and descended the bank toward our wheel.

Flynn whispered to Cletis, "You want your blunderbuss?"

"Nope. Whatever this is, we'll brazen our way out of it. Talk and smiles." He pulled on his boots. "I'll do the talkin'. You boys do the smilin'."

They all had the look of miners—stringy, sunburned, long-haired. Two we recognized—Drinkin' Dan and Stinkin' McGinty.

The leader, in a white duster and a beaver hat, dismounted and apologized for coming onto our claim. "My name is Micah Broadback, late of New Orleans."

An ironic name, I thought, for a man so skinny.

"And me and the boys here, Jonas and Edgar Johnson, and—I believe you know McGinty and Drinkin' Dan—we been asked to talk to you about this here wheel."

"You the Miner's Council?" asked Cletis.

"Duly elected last May in Grouchy Pete's"

Cletis looked up at the wheel like a painter proud of his picture. "So . . . what about it?"

"Well, sir, the flow is gettin' pretty low downstream. Some boys think this wheel is cuttin' into it. We're here to ask you, gentleman-like, to shut 'er down."

"Shut 'er down?" cried Michael Flynn. "Now, listen here—"

"Don't mind Galway Bay. He's one of them short-fused Irishmen." Cletis made a gesture to Flynn—calm down—but he kept a smile for Broadback. "Now, considerin' how dry it is, your flow got more to do with the weather than our wheel."

"Besides"—Flynn put his hands on his hips—"if miners go upstream and take the water away from us, we ain't got a word to say about it."

"We ain't askin' you to quit minin'," said Broadback. "It's just that . . . you boys found a spot where the river decided to drop a lot of gold, and you got all the water, too."

"Could be the two things are related," said Flynn.

"Or maybe we're just smart," I said.

Cletis shot me an angry look. In this country, it was all right to be smart but you did not remind people of *how* smart.

"Maybe the *smart* thing," said McGinty, "was gettin' into business with Chinks."

Cletis took a step forward. "Who's sayin' we're in business with Chinks?"

Broadback put up his hands. "It ain't been said out loud. But the Johnsons—" Broadback gestured to the brothers, who had remained on their horses, saying nothing, looking stupid—"they're sailors. They been to China. They seen wheels like this."

"Wheels is wheels," said Michael Flynn.

"White men's wheels is round," said Edgar, "but this here's what you call a hexagon."

"Yeah," added Jonas. "That's a . . . a Chinese shape."

So they *were* as stupid as they appeared.

Flynn pushed his hat onto the back of his head and chuckled. "You know, boys, a man would almost think you're serious."

"They are," said McGinty, whom I was beginning to dislike for more than his smell. "It don't set too good when fellers is doin' straight-up business with Chinks."

"Well, I'm serious, too," answered Flynn. "A serious fuckin' feller I am, and if me or me pardners decides to do business with Chinks, Niggers, or Miwok Injuns, we—"

Cletis interrupted whatever was coming next, directing himself to Broadback, age and reason to age and reason. "What would you like for us to do?"

"Stop the wheel," said Broadback. "Give us better flow downstream."

"All right. We'll do it," said Cletis.

Flynn and I both looked at him as if he had lost his mind.

Then Cletis added, "In exactly one week."

"We was hopin' for a bit sooner," said Micah.

"Now, friend, there ain't nothin' the Miner's Council can do except ask. Upstream men got upstream rights. Still and all, we want to be friends. So we'll shut 'er down in one week. But we spent a lot of time buildin' it. We need to get somethin' back." Through the whole speech, Cletis kept smiling, as if to signal his best intentions.

Broadback gazed up at the wheel. "Sure is a fine-lookin' piece of work."

"Chinks is good builders," said McGinty.

"Yep," said one of the brothers. "In China, they got a wall a thousand miles long."

Cletis offered his hand to Broadback. "One week?"

And the time was set. One week.

McGinty looked over at the Chinese, who had not even raised their heads. "We can't stop the wheel, but we can get them to movin'. Bad enough we got Greasers all over the diggin's. Don't need Chinks, too." And McGinty, who up until then had shown little commitment to anything but whiskey, felt strongly enough about the Chinese that he reached for his gun.

But Broadback grabbed his hand and held the arm as the gun came free. "We move 'em off here, they may come down to where we're workin'. Let 'em be. Let 'em clean up somebody's abandoned claim. That's best for all concerned."

"Yes, sir," added Cletis, "you boys just trust us to keep an eye on 'em. If they get too uppity, we'll drive 'em off ourselves."

As soon as the Miner's Council had gone, Flynn turned to Cletis, "Why in hell did you agree?"

"A little agreein' beats a lot of fightin'. And we ain't givin' up much."

"We ain't . . . aren't?" I said.

Cletis looked up at the sky. "Rains'll come soon. River'll rise faster than beer piss in a chamber pot, and run so fast, it'll sweep them Chinks all the way to the Bay, 'less they put off their heathen ways and start prayin' to Jesus. Won't be able to work. Might not be able to sleep. May even start buildin' that ark that Jesus told Moses about."

"Noah," I said.

"No to what? Can't say no to winter rains," answered Cletis, "even in California."

I decided not to go on with the Bible class. "Rain's better than snow."

"Yep," said Cletis. "But the best part for you boys, once it comes, we won't be able to work. It'll be time to head for the fleshpots to spend some of that gold."

"That'll be a happy day," said Flynn.

We laughed, but something new had come to Big Skull Rock. Men were angry that they were not doing as well as we. In time, their anger might overflow. Would it swamp us, or the Chinese, or both?

October 9–11, 1849
Change at last

The rain began on Tuesday, just before dawn. In all my life, I had never been so happy to hear the sound of droplets pattering. It kept on and off for two days. By Thursday morning, the river was up, running just enough to make riffles on the rocks. Cletis said that now, there would be water flowing for the downstream miners, so we could run our wheel, and no one would complain.

And no one did. For most of a month, Spencer recorded only mundane activities. Soon, green shoots appeared on the brown hillsides. As Spencer wrote for the Transcript, *"The approach of winter in California signifies something far different than in New England, where the earth falls into sleep, frozen and brooding. Here, the moistened ground revives, then brightens and blooms."*

❦

November 3–7, 1849
Raining Harder

On the 3rd, the showers that had been so intermittent and gentle turned to something entirely new, a pelting, punishing all-day downpour. No one worked for four days, not even the Chinese. And the rain that fell on the 7th fell harder and faster than any before, playing its torrential music to the tune of old Niagara.

November 9, 1849
Cutting Timber

Awoke to sunshine and the sound of the Miwok roaring and huffing and hurtling over the rocks like a Boston & Worcester steam engine.

We knew by then that the California climate could turn against us like a Boston January or a disappointed woman (and her Boston father). We would need more than a lean-to for shelter, so we spent the day cutting pine logs and dragging them to a place about ten paces east of the big rock. There we would build a cabin.

The Chinese watched us for a time, then Chin came up the bank and asked us if he could "rent" our ax to begin their cabin.

"A good ax rents for two dollars a day," said Cletis. "Buy one instead."

Flynn said to Chin, "You got three ounces of dust? I'm headin' into town to buy us a second ax and more peppermints. Give me three ounces, I'll buy one for you, too."

Chin pulled out four ounces and asked that we buy tea also, black tea.

November 10, 1849
News of a Strike

The axes arrived in the afternoon, carried through the rain by George Emery himself. He had been sold out the day before but promised a new shipment. And here it came. We were hauling and hammering and welcomed a rest. So Cletis invited Emery into our half-built cabin, bid him sit on a log in the driest corner, and poured him a mug of coffee.

Michael Flynn asked about a new strike at a place called Rainbow Gulch.

"Plenty of fellers movin' down there," said Emery.

"Hurtin' your business?" asked Cletis.

"My store got a stone foundation and a wood floor and stock enough to keep me sellin' for six weeks, no matter how bad the roads get. We got plenty of what them Rainbow Gulch miners need. And come next summer, so will you."

"What would that be?" I asked.

"Water."

"They don't have water?" asked Flynn.

"Right now, they got plenty, down in the ravine that the gulch drops into. But this looks like a strike to last. Come next July, when things dry up, the only way to wash dirt down there'll be to piss on it, unless somebody figures out how to get water in. That's when a flutter wheel in a good-runnin' river could mean a nice profit."

"Run water to Rainbow Gulch?" asked Flynn. "How far?"

"About six miles southwest, as the crow flies," said Emery. "All downhill."

"You mean, dig a trench?" I said.

"You boys got muscles, ain't you? And you got your Chinks. By spring, there'll be a lot more of *them*."

"A lot more of everybody," said Cletis.

"But they ain't exactly *our* Chinks," said Flynn.

"That's not what some fellers think," answered Emery. "Put 'em to work diggin' trenches. Keep 'em out of the diggin's."

Cletis said that we were doing well mining. "Prob'ly better than we could deliverin' water to other miners. But let's talk again come June."

"A man needs to think ahead, is all," said Emery. "It won't be miners that make this country. It'll be them who figure out how to give the miners what they want, get their money and spread it around, so everybody can make some, every feller who knows how to forge a horseshoe or drive a nail or barber a shave. That's how the world works."

And a voice from the doorway said, "In June, if this no Gum Saan, we go. No ditch dig." Chin stood outside, with the rain dripping off his wide-brimmed straw hat.

George Emery said to Cletis, "Is that the head Chink?"

"Yep," said Cletis. "We call him Sam Who."

"And he speaks English?"

"Taught by the Jesuits." Flynn waved for Chin to come in and gave him one of the axes. "As ordered. Now go build yourself a fine cabin."

"I almost forgot." George Emery reached into a pocket under his oil-skin and pulled out a sack of tea. "You asked for this, too. Five dollars a pound."

The Chinaman took the tea and thanked him.

George Emery stood, smoothed his rain gear to his body, and said, "Take a ride down to Rainbow Gulch. See if you don't think we could make a profit runnin' a trench. I'll supply the shovels and the wood for sluicin'. You do the work. We'll make a team. And if you go, you'll see a few friends."

"Friends?" I said.

"The boys who met the backside of Cletis's shovel a few weeks ago."

"Hiram and Scrawny?"

"Scrawnier now, so they say," said Emery. "Plenty of gold down there. Plenty of dysentery, too. Them Boston boys got it bad, so I hear. They been askin' for their friend from Broke Neck."

Cletis jerked a thumb toward me. "That'd be Harvard, here."

Emery pushed past Chin, then stopped in the door. "They say you Chinks know about herbs and medicines and such. If you know how to stop men from shittin' till there's nothin' left inside 'em but white bone, you might make good money in Rainbow Gulch. Damn good money."

After Emery left, Chin said to us, "Medicines? I no doctor. No magic priest."

"Maybe not," said Flynn, "but if you do some good, you might make a few more friends, earn a bit more respect in these parts."

"Respect?" said Chin.

Cletis said, "Don't be gettin' his hopes up."

November 11, 1849
Rainbow Gulch

As the next day was the Sabbath, we took Emery's suggestion and visited Rainbow Gulch. We also brought Chin. It was bold of us, I know, but he wanted to see a bit more of the country, and he thought he might have a remedy for what ailed those loose-bowel miners.

"Bring your sister," said Flynn. "The sight of her would cure anything."

Chin did not even dignify that. But somehow he managed to look dignified riding our burro down the road to Broke Neck, then across the river and onto the muddy trail that ran southwest over the rolling country.

We passed many a miner along the way. Some were heading to Broke Neck in high spirits, intent on a little Sunday spending. Others trudged along, intent on nothing more than the ground in front of them, weighed down by the mud that clung more heavily to their boots with every step and sucked them deeper and deeper into their own disappointment.

Flynn offered each of them a smile, a nod, a greeting. That was why we let him lead. Quick to anger, quick to calm, convivial as the town crier, that was Michael Flynn. A much better face for our trio than a nervous Chinaman or Yr. Ob't Correspondent, who was often accused of being too damn serious for his own good.

After about five miles, we came out of a stand of blue oak and brush on a ridge that looked across a ravine toward an open plateau.

A light rain was falling. The clouds had closed down the vistas. The ravine and the gulch draining down from the plateau appeared as nothing more than gutters running through a crowded neighborhood. Scores of tents and lean-tos hid in the shadows below us. A miasmic fog of campfire smoke trapped all the odors of this tight-packed hill-country slum, a commingling stink of stale food, unwashed bodies, and human waste. And a din rose to assail our ears, the noise of men jawing and laughing, or relaxing to music from harmonica or banjo, or moaning their Sabbath away in some deep yet undefined misery.

A hollow-eyed miner was climbing the path toward us, as if he would escape before he was swallowed by the earth.

I said, "Excuse me, friend. Is this Rainbow Gulch?"

"Not for me, it ain't. No pretty colors here. Just another rainy day. But—" His eyes fell upon Chin. "Is he your pardner, or does he work for you?"

Chin was smart enough to keep quiet.

I said that he was my servant. "And a kind of healer."

I expected an unfriendly response. Instead, the miner asked if I hired white men, too, because he needed a job. I said I had no more work, so he nodded and strode on.

Meanwhile, Chin had dismounted and was staring across the ravine, which was about four times as wide as deep, fifty feet down, two hundred across.

Flynn said, "What's got your slanty Chinese eye now?"

"I look. I think."

"What about?"

"Land. I think, why gold someplace and not other? Why gold there in . . . in—" He made a motion with his hand, describing the slope and the big cut in it.

"The gulch?" I said.

"Many claims along gulch. That mean much gold. But where gold come from? Wash down from flat land above? And why flat land go south then turn west, like river of grass between hills?"

Flynn looked at me. "Fair questions, Jamie."

"Questions for another time," I said.

And down we rode into the ravine. Here it was darker, colder. The gloom of a cloudy November day was an unassailable force, even in California. Here the stream merely trickled, despite a month of rain. I could not imagine how we might keep water coursing through it all summer, even if we *could* dig a trench six miles from Big Skull Rock.

We rode past tents and huts and covered wagons. Then Flynn reined his horse, startled by one of the rarest sights we had seen in gold country. Beside a wagon, a dozen men had lined up, each with a bundle of clothes under his arm. A man was taking their bundles and their gold and writing down their names. Beside him, bent over a washboard in a big metal tub, a woman—skinny, scraggly-haired, worn—did woman's work, and men who had not washed clothes in months paid handsomely.

She glanced at Flynn. He tipped his hat. She looked down again into the suds.

Flynn turned to me. "Do you got any dirty clothes?"

"All of them," I said.

We asked along the ravine for Wilson and Selwin until a hairy miner sitting on a tailing pile pointed to a tent about halfway up the south side. "Might find 'em there or down at the shit pit, down where the streambed straightens. That's where all the quick-steppers try to get to 'fore they let go."

Scrawny Selwin was sitting on a hogshead in front of his tent, his head in his hands, his body curled in on itself. He looked up as we approached, and an emotion crossed his face, but even his features seemed too exhausted to define it. He said, "You come to see the dying? Or to do some gloating?"

I dismounted and said we had come because they had asked for us.

"I didn't. I'd never ask help from a man who took a shovel to me." He slurred his words and smelled of shit, both dried and fresh.

But his stink was as nothing compared to the stench in the tent.

Hiram Wilson lay on a pallet. His cheeks had sunken. His eyes did not focus. His breathing came in short bursts. The air created by his exhalations and other emissions fogged the space with a hot, fetid foulness, strangely sweet, like a rotting rose head.

Chin took it all in, then stepped out.

Michael Flynn listened to Wilson and said, "That's the death rattle."

I said, "How can you be sure?"

"Heard that sound before, and smelled that smell, though it's about as bad in here as—" He took off his hat and fanned the air in front of his face.

I knelt beside Hiram and said his name. He groaned and tried to speak, or so it seemed. Then his brow furrowed and he made a different sound, a liquid sound, followed by a fresh stink. Whatever the mechanism draining him of life, it was working still.

Scrawny came to the flap of the tent. "He's been shitting for a week."

"It looks like a lot of men around here are doing the same," I said. "Dysentery."

"Dysentery, diarrhea, the bloody flux . . . what's it matter?" said Scrawny. "There was cholera in the wagon trains, and—aw, Jesus." Suddenly, he doubled over and went running out of the tent.

So this was the end of the rainbow in Rainbow Gulch.

I put a hand on Hiram's forehead and said, "Can you hear me, lad?"

Chin came back into the tent with a mug in his hand.

"What's that?" I asked.

"Black tea. Black ginger tea. Ginger good for stomach. Black tea good for . . . for . . ." He brought his hand to his belly and the region below.

"Bowels?" I said.

"In China we give. Sometime help." Chin knelt beside Hiram Wilson and gently raised his head, then poured some tea into his mouth.

Wilson gurgled and the tea came out.

"Try again," I said.

So Chin tipped the mug a second time to Hiram's lips. Again the tea fountained out of his throat.

Chin stood. "No good. He die."

"I could've told you that." Scrawny was back, trembling from the exertion of shitting again after shitting all day.

And I was filled with sudden, overwhelming anger at the futility of it all, of potential wasted, of hope lost, of dreams denied, a sense far more oppressive to my mind than the stench in this pitiful tent.

I said, "You should have listened. You should have gone home in August."

Scrawny wobbled, seemed to use all his energy holding himself up. "Home to what? Teaching arithmetic to Boston brats? We couldn't go home . . . as failures."

"Better than dying here, shitting yourself to death or drinking yourself to it." I pushed past him and stepped out into the fresher air.

Scrawny staggered after me. "I haven't had a drink in a week. Too sick."

Chin followed us and handed Scrawny the tin cup of black gingered tea. "You drink this, then. Maybe help you. No help friend."

WE BURIED HIRAM WILSON in the gloomy mist. We wrapped him in his excremental blanket, dug him a deep hole on the rise overlooking Rainbow Gulch, and put him into the ground. At least he was not alone. A dozen lumps of dirt marked a dozen other dreams. Some had a stone or a cross or a crudely lettered sign. Others were as anonymous as the earth itself.

I recited the Twenty-third Psalm. Scrawny Selwin turned the first shovel of dirt and shed a few tears, as much for himself as for his partner. Then we covered Hiram Wilson, tamped the dirt down, and stood for a time on that bald hillside, in the pattering rain, beneath that lowering California sky, and I considered again the waste of it.

I shook Scrawny's hand and told him to keep drinking Chin's tea. I thought to invite him to stay with us until he was better, though I knew that the shits could be catching. And he would not leave because, as he said, they had finally staked a claim that was producing. So he would pan and shit and shit and pan until he took enough gold from the ground that he could go home or shat enough of himself into it that he could do no more than go into it himself.

We mounted, and I noticed Chin gazing again across the ravine.

Flynn said to him, "Still lookin'? Still thinkin'?"

"Someday, I know more, then think more, then look more, then find more."

"Well, that'll be just grand. But as for me"—Flynn took a breath—"I've found enough."

I whipped my head around. "Enough?"

"Thinkin' that the season for gold minin' may be just about over. Time to do some gold-spendin' . . . in Sacramento, maybe, or San Francisco."

"That might be a good idea," said Scrawny.

I whipped around again. "What makes you say that?"

Scrawny looked down, as if embarrassed. "Hodges knows."

"Knows what?" I asked.

"Knows you're in Broke Neck."

"Did you tell him?"

"No, but that blacksmith, that Matt Dooling, he came through. He said that he'd heard Hodges and the Sagamores were looking for a place to set up, and they needed a good man on the anvil. So he was headed north to find them."

"And you told Dooling about us?"

Scrawny trembled and said he was sorry, then he doubled over again and went running for the trees. Even a man with dysentery wants a private place to shit.

If Dooling had carried news to Hodges, who could tell what might come of it? But if we spent the winter below, as Cletis had already suggested, Hodges might find that there was enough to keep him and his friends busy without ever bothering about us.

For a month, the weather varied between too rotten to travel and so nice that they just had to stay and wash a bit more dirt. Then, on December 18th, it began to rain and did not stop for five days. It grew cold, nearly New England cold. And day by day, the river rose ever higher and roared ever louder. It was time. But one more thing . . .

December 24, 1849
A Celebration

We could not leave Cletis on Christmas Eve, of all nights, when men most desired good fellowship. Besides, the rain had left the roads so slick that mule teams were slipping and sinking everywhere between here and San Francisco.

Christmas Eve in Broke Neck meant drinking, gambling, and laughter—all regular nighttime pursuits—to which were added celebratory gunshots to welcome the Infant Jesus. But the most memorable moment came when a bedraggled young man from Maine walked into the middle of the street and began to sing "Adeste Fideles" in a voice so pure that it seemed an angel of the Lord had found this tiny outpost on this holy night.

A man from Virginia joined in. Then a Mexican in a serape added his voice. Flynn took a swallow from his jug, announced that he had been educated by Irish priests, and slipped into the Latin himself. I could not resist, either. And before long, two dozen men were caught up in the ancient carol and thoughts of home.

Never had that song sounded more ethereal yet more assertive in the holy message it sent into the black night sky above us. We may not have found the Promised Land, but each day here heightened my sense of my own existence.

―――――――――――――――――――――――――――――――

On the day after Christmas, Flynn and Spencer headed for Sacramento. Cletis stayed behind to watch the claims. Neither he nor Flynn wished to entrust their gold to Abbott Express, so Cletis kept his in the hiding place beneath Big Skull Rock and Flynn carried his to spend. Only James Spencer was willing to pay 10 percent to Abbott for assurances that the amount would be placed "on account" for him in their Boston office.

They waved to the Chinese as they left, and Michael Flynn placed a bag of peppermints on a flat rock by the river, on the Chinese side.

―――――――――――――――――― ∞ ――――――――――――――――――

December 28, 1849
An Open Cesspool

We reached Sacramento after a day's ride and took lodgings in the relative comfort of Sutter's Fort.

And, wonder of wonders, two letters, both mailed in June, were waiting for me in the satchel of Abbott's rider, whom we happened to meet as he was heading east.

My mother and sister wrote proudly that my seagoing dispatches had made a great splash in Boston.

Janiva wrote of how much she missed me. She said she had filled her days by studying her father's bookkeeping operations, her nights by attending meetings of the Boston Female Antislavery Society. I reread her letter a dozen times, to assure myself there was no hint of a new beau hidden between the lines. But each time I read, she closed with a single word, "Love," and it was as if she had whispered it in my ear.

As for Sacramento, I would not have stayed, had intelligence not reached us of disaster in San Francisco. On Christmas Eve, a fire had erupted near the waterfront and incinerated two thirds of the tents, shacks, and warehouses now proclaiming themselves the first city of the West. Even the Parker House fell in a shower of embers.

So, Sacramento it was, though it promised no pleasure. After six weeks of rain, the city had become a wallow of mud, garbage, animal guts, and human waste. Men had been in such a rush to make money here that they had neglected to dig necessaries, with what consequences for the health of the public, I could not say. Perhaps a lively epidemic of cholera would cause prices to spike and spur outhouse diggers to work.

But there was also a business opportunity: Mark Hopkins, the man we helped on the trail in August, was good to his word. He remembered us. He had retreated from Hangtown, his New England Mining and Trading Company having failed at both, and was determined instead to become a wholesaler of hardware and foodstuffs. So, while Flynn planned for San Francisco, I took a winter position in the Hopkins store.

December 31, 1849
Farewells to Friends

The side-wheel steamer *Senator* now ran a regular route between San Francisco and Sacramento. Laid down in Boston, she had steamed around the Horn and gone into river service in November. Ever since, she had been doing a lively business, ferrying the hopeful upstream and the despairing down, all in twelve hours rather than three days.

This morning, I accompanied Flynn to the landing, where he bought a $30 ticket and got into line with hundreds of others, including a group of Sagamores—three Brighton Bulls, worn, tired, hollow-eyed, and Matt Dooling.

Our eyes met, and I said, "I hear you're reporting my movements to Hodges."

"Hodges?" Dooling laughed. "I've had enough of that son of a bitch."

"A point in your favor," said Flynn.

"I wasn't put on this earth to build his empire. He's up the hills, tellin' men where to stay, where to mine. When he started givin' me orders, I told him he could treat me like an employee if he paid me like one. Otherwise, he could say 'please.'"

I asked, "Did you tell him where we were?"

"He knew already. But it wasn't my doin'. Never my doin'."

I took my hand from my gun and relaxed.

Dooling pointed to the tool bag at his feet. "San Francisco's burned to the ground. They'll need men who know how to make nails and hinges and hardware and have the tools to do it. If not for you, my tools'd be rustin' in Boston Harbor. And like I told you once before, I never forget a favor."

Just then, the *Senator* gave three blasts, and the men at the quayside pressed forward. Had I brought my gear, I might have gone with them. But I knew that if I reached San Francisco, I might keep going. I might climb aboard the next vessel bound for Panama or Patagonia and go home. And my work here was not yet done. So I stayed at the landing and watched the big steamer churn downstream beneath a cloud of its own smoke. Then, I returned to my room at Sutter's Fort and tried to write.

January 28, 1850
News for Boston

Herewith, the first commentary I have written for the *Transcript* in almost a month:

> Ask me about a California winter, and I will say I prefer New England. I prefer dry cold to cool damp. I prefer snow to rain. Yes, snow falling gently on the cobblestones of Boston, snow bending the branches on the white pines of Concord, snow sending husbands and wives to cozy hearthstones of a stormy evening, snow white and pure, blanketing a world reborn when cold sunshine comes again.
>
> California is reborn in winter, too, but in a fashion more biblical than poetic.
>
> Whatever they may tell you of the balmy air flowing over any page of the calendar, they have not told you of the rain. They could not tell you because it is nearly impossible to describe. The gentle showers of October give way to the torrents of November and the downpours of December, and sunny days become as commas in a long, wet sentence.
>
> Your Ob't Correspondent, having made his way to Sacramento with

the intention of wintering, took a position with a merchant named Hopkins, in the belief that it is always best to engage with the world you hope to write about. In his shop, I listened to big talkers and doomsayers alike, all commenting on the relentless rain.

They marveled at the roar of it, thrumming and thundering on Sacramento rooftops. They watched it turn the streets from ankle-deep muck to quick-mud quagmires that could swallow a mule right down to his ears. But the river would never flood, they said. There was no need for a levee, they said. The great Sacramento Valley could soak up every drop that the heavens poured down. No need to do anything but keep to business, always business. All else would take care of itself . . . they said.

Then, on January 8, came a deluge the like of which no one had ever seen, even in California. All day it rained, hard and harder, inches an hour, inches in minutes. Mr. Hopkins sent me home, for there would be no business on such a day. So I trudged through the mud to Sutter's Fort, which sits on the high ground about a mile from the river.

That night, I was awakened by what sounded like distant calls for help. But strange cries at night are common in places where Gold Rushers gather to drink, gamble, and satisfy their baser desires, so I rolled back to sleep. Then, at first light, I heard cries of "Flood! Flood!" I dressed quickly and scrambled up the blockhouse steps for a view.

What I saw was enough to shock me all the way back to Boston. Sacramento lay under a sheet of dirty brown water, afloat with swimming rats and dead cats, with overloaded rowboats and empty packing crates, with all the effluence of a place that had been booming and building far too quickly for its own good.

And the water kept rising for three days more. By January 12, Sutter's Fort was an island in a wilderness of water stretching farther than the eye could reach. No first floor in the city remained uncovered, and the water all around us moved as if pulled by a current that carried off a fortune in ruined merchandise every hour.

It was two weeks before the river finally dropped, while prices for everything began to rise.

By then, however, I was insensible to all but my own misery, as California had done to me what it has done to so many: laid me low. For nearly three weeks, I was abed, suffering from fever, ague, chills, abdominal pains, and other symptoms of dysentery.

I feared that I would end as badly as some of the men I had seen in a sad place called Rainbow Gulch. I might have but for those who brought me sustenance. Despite the meanness that I often describe here, kindness still abides on the precarious edge of the continent, and I have been the beneficiary of it.

Yr. Ob't. Correspondent,

The Argonaut

I did not tell the whole story of my sickness. To describe it would have required that I tell of certain bloody events on the road to Broke Neck the previous August, events I preferred to forget.

After five days of confinement in the Sutter's Fort Hotel, during which time I was barely able to reach the outhouse, a dark-skinned young man appeared in my room. As he leaned over me, he appeared, to my fevered mind, like someone I had known in another world. Harvard perhaps? But there were no such complexions at Harvard.

I propped myself on my elbows and peered at him through aching eye sockets.

He said, "Where are your friends, señor?"

I knew now that he was no classmate. He had come to rob me. I fumbled for my pistol, which I kept in a holster on the bedpost.

But he grabbed it first and asked again, "Your *friends*, señor, where are they?"

I said, "Who are you?"

He brought his face close to mine. "I am Rodrigo Vargas."

Now I remembered. The last time I had seen him, tears were streaming down his face while his grandfather moaned with the pain of a broken leg. Fearing that he had come to extract revenge, I tried to lift myself off the pallet. But he put a hand on my shoulder and said, "I am here to help you."

"Help me?"

"My grandfather visits the fort for doing business. He saw you. He remembered. Then he did not see you. So he asked. Señor Sutter said you were sick. But so many are sick here, there are not enough to help them. So my grandfather sent me to help you."

"But—"

"He remembers that you are a merciful man."

And Rodrigo Vargas proved Cletis Smith wrong: too much mercy would not get you killed. It might save your life. Rodrigo brought me water from a clean well on Vargas land. He brought me beef broth and lime juice. He did this almost every day.

And when he could not, a servant girl from the hacienda visited in his place. She was a pretty, birdlike thing named Maria. But always, I was cared for. When I recovered, Rodrigo said that he and his family owed me no more and the next time I crossed his land, they would tax me. If I did not pay, they would kill me.

I told him I would pay gladly because he had saved me from the miserable fate that put so many into the graveyard above Rainbow Gulch. Then I prayed for spring. . . .

"THE 2013 RAINBOW GULCH old-vine Zinfandel," announced Manion Sturgis, "decanted and ready to pour."

They were sitting at a garden table, beneath a green umbrella. The autumn vineyard glowed. The aromas of grilled meats and mesquite smoke rose from the barbecue pit, where two chefs were preparing lunch. And the wine awaited.

Manion nodded to a waitress and watched her fill the big Reidel glasses, like a proud parent watching a child hit a baseball or play a sonata. "Our finest growth. Old vines, dating back to the Gold Rush."

"These grapes actually grow at Rainbow Gulch?" asked Peter.

"Above it, on the flatland that drains into the gulch. When I bought the place ten years ago, the vines were overgrown and forgotten."

"I can't wait to see them," said Evangeline.

"We'll go out there after we eat," said Manion Sturgis.

"I've seen everything else," she said. "Cellar, tasting room, restaurant. They even have a Gold Rush museum, Peter, with a big lump of gold found down in the gulch."

"And your opinion?" Manion asked her.

She raised her wineglass. "This is why I love my job."

Peter had not seen her so relaxed in a long time. Wine-tasting at midday could do that. And wine cellars could be dark and romantic. But he wasn't hitting the "jealous button," not yet.

Manion said, "'Make your vocation your vacation.' Twain's best quote."

"Twain felt the magic in these foothills," said Wild Bill Donnelly. "They inspired him."

Manion swirled the wine in his glass. "Or maybe it was Amador County Zin that inspired him."

"You sound like a commercial," said Peter. "We'll sell no wine till Twain says it's time."

Evangeline said, "Just taste and enjoy, Peter."

"Yes," added Manion. "Forget Napa and Sonoma and the hot drive from dusty old Broke Neck."

Peter sipped and said, "All is forgotten," because this was one of the best Zins he had ever tasted. He hated to flatter Manion Sturgis, but he had to.

And Manion flattered easily. "We're making something rare here, Fallon. More European. Lower Brix. Still around fourteen percent alcohol but subtler, smoother, more elegant, a term that people don't usually apply to Zinfandel."

Then the meal arrived: three artfully arranged baby-back ribs, dry-rubbed, a pepper-jack cheese polenta, grilled asparagus . . . a bite of rib, a taste of polenta, a swallow of Rainbow Gulch zin and . . . no more calls. They had a winner. Peter was smart enough to know that when food and wine worked this well and the setting was this pretty, you stopped analyzing and enjoyed.

Wild Bill purred like a cat, a big, white-haired, red-faced Irish cat.

"Enjoying the meal, Mr. Donnelly?" asked Manion Sturgis.

"I'd agree with Ms. Carrington that this is why I love my job, if I had a job. But now I'm just a retired detective reading thrillers and enjoying the view."

Evangeline said, "What did you detect around Broke Neck?"

"We were exploring," said Peter, "not detecting."

Evangeline said, "You weren't making him drive all over without a plan, were you?"

Wild Bill sipped the wine. "I know about looking at things without a plan, just looking, not really knowing what I'm looking for . . . or at. Detectives do it all the time."

"That's why we'd love to look at Rainbow Gulch," said Peter.

AFTER LUNCH, THEY HEADED out in a six-passenger electric cart, the kind airports used to ferry old ladies, except this one had a nice hard top to keep off the sun. Manion took the wheel, and they sped past rows of vines that etched the landscape north of the main complex.

Peter rode next to Sturgis and enjoyed California wine country in October, with the grapes harvested, the vines fulfilled, the leaves turning in the soft sun. Over the hum of the motor, he said, "We were reading about Rainbow Gulch on the ride down."

"In a guidebook?" asked Manion.

"In 'The Spencer Journal.' I have three of his notebooks now."

"*Three?*" said Manion. "You're doing well."

"I didn't find them. My son did."

From the middle seat, Evangeline said, "LJ is doing such a good job, I'm wondering why he asked you to come out here."

"You mean you're wondering what you're *really* looking for?" asked Manion.

"Do you know something we don't?" asked Peter.

"I bet you've heard about the bags of Chinese gold," said Manion. "Some people think they're buried someplace around here."

There it was again, thought Peter. Another echo from Spencer and Flynn and ancient Ah-Toy: "'the Chinese gold of Broke Neck, the first trickle from the lost river of gold.'"

"Have you read about this Chinese gold in the journal?" Evangeline asked Peter.

"Spencer's met some Chinese," said Peter. "He thinks they may be finding more gold than they let on."

"Legends from the past," said Manion. "The future is what interests me. And the future is up there." Up where the trail ended, the land dropped into a ravine, then rose to a range of rolling brown hillsides.

Manion stopped the cart, and they got out amidst the gnarled, brown grapevines. "Rainbow Gulch. Tomorrow's best wines from yesterday's best vines."

"How many acres?" asked Evangeline.

"Just four of the old vines." Manion gestured around him. "Zins love the heat. We have heat. Zins love volcanic soil. We have plenty of that. And old vines make the best wines. These may be the oldest vines in California." He looked at Evangeline. "Are you writing this down."

"I'm remembering every word," she said.

Peter thought he heard an extra *something* in her tone, as if she was as taken with the winemaker as she was with the wine.

Manion Sturgis kept talking: "They'll try to tell you that Napa Cabernet is *the* California grape. But it's Zinfandel, sibling of the Primitivo, offspring of the Croatian grape, Crljenak Kaśtelanski, planted right here by thirsty Gold Rushers in ground that defined the Golden State. You feel the soul of the country in every grape. You taste California history in every sip."

"The terroir," said Evangeline. "You taste the terroir."

And you feel the passion, thought Peter. He never faulted passion, even in someone he didn't like. Manion was passionate about his wine, like Peter about history. And for the second time that day, Peter felt history all around him. Rainbow Gulch looked like an open-air theater where the actors had played the matinee, then stepped out for dinner before the evening performance.

The hillsides sloped into the ravine, all covered in dry yellow straw grass, scattered over with brush, blue oak, and buckeye. A natural gutter dropped from the vineyard plateau and still carried off the rains of a thousand years. Rocks and stones along the bottom marked the path of a stream that would flow again the next time it rained. And silence hovered above it all, deepened by the sound of a turkey buzzard flap-flap-flapping overhead.

But Peter saw miners working their claims, cooking their food, lining up to have their clothes washed by the only woman within miles. He saw shacks and tents and covered wagons. In some of them, men were weighing out their gold. In others, they were dying of dysentery. And across the ravine, up on the bald hilltop, a wrought-iron fence marked the graveyard where Spencer and Flynn had buried Hiram Wilson.

"Tailings everywhere," said Wild Bill.

"Tailings?" Evangeline had missed the earlier lesson.

Wild Bill pointed out the grass-covered hummocks lining the gulch.

Manion said, "I've been told that those piles still hold gold today."

"Why don't you get it?" asked Evangeline.

"I'm not letting anyone come onto my land for placer mining or drift mining or heap leach mining, either, dumping pulverized rocks and dirt onto a rubber sheet, then sprinkling it with cyanide."

"Cyanide?" Evangeline wrote that down.

"Good for attracting gold," said Manion, "but not for improving the terroir."

"I can see the reviews now," said Peter. "A great old-vine Zin, with hints of spice and the nutty almond nose of a well-blended cyanide solution."

"Very funny," said Manion. "But if I ever allow heap-leaching here, I'll get bad reviews for the wine and the worst reviews for my life."

Evangeline said, "I think you love this vineyard more than your ex-wives."

"My ex-wives were as useless as the lump of gold on display in the tasting room . . . soft, inanimate, no practical application, nothing more than nourishment for the vanity of human wishes. Flashy women and flashy metals. Not like . . . not like this."

For some guys, thought Peter, why did arriving at self-knowledge always sound like self-congratulation?

"What did Warren Buffet say?" asked Wild Bill. "Something about how we spend our lives digging gold out of holes in the ground called mines, just to put it into holes in the ground called vaults. Better to do something useful with our energies."

"I like your friend, Fallon. He gets it." Manion pulled a bottle of Rainbow Gulch Zinfandel from the basket on the back of the cart. "So he wins a prize. Real California gold . . . the grape, grown with love, refined with care, appreciated like a lover."

"What I don't get," said Peter, "is why you won't help us with the journal."

"Even after seeing all this? After tasting the wine? If you spread legends about bags of Chinese gold, you'll have people crawling all over this land, all over again."

So, thought Peter, Manion Sturgis *had* read a section of this journal.

"Besides"—Manion pointed to the northeast—"just beyond those hills, the Emery Mine is getting back into operation. They'll bring trouble enough."

"And you mean to protect your vineyard?" said Wild Bill.

"I mean to protect my land," said Manion. "That's a story as old as the West."

PETER DIDN'T WANT TO talk about Manion Sturgis in front of Larry Kwan, who had already established his credentials as a talker and was probably a full-fledged gossip, too, especially when it came to gossip about big names in winemaking. Peter really didn't want to talk about Sturgis at all. So, on the ride home, he talked about the Sturgis *wines*.

And Larry knew what he was talking about. He also knew the wine-country driving rule: "Swirl and spit, baby. Swirl and spit. You can't drive the drinkers if you're drinking yourself. But you won't know where to drive them until you've drunk what they're drinking in the places you're driving them to."

Evangeline laughed. "Can I quote you?"

"Just spell it right: Larry Kwan's Wine Country Tours."

"Guaranteed," she said.

"Maybe I'll team up with your detective friend for a new tour. History and wine."

"You know the wine," said Peter. "I'll bet you know the history, too."

"You have to if you want to know the wine. I'll show you."

They were taking Route 16 back to Sacramento, two lanes, undivided, with a 60 mph speed limit. After about ten minutes of gentle descent, Larry pulled off into a little roadside lot with a marker. "Welcome to Michigan Bar, westernmost of the Gold Rush sites, hardly noticed now but a boom town in the 1850s. The Cosumnes River runs about a mile to the north. But it never carried enough water, so they dammed the flow back in the foothills—"

"And dug the Michigan Ditch some fifteen or twenty miles." Peter recited his lesson from earlier.

"Very good," said Larry.

"Ditch?" said Evangeline. "For what?"

Larry explained: "In 1852, a guy figured out the quickest way to get at gold in gravel banks was to wash away the hillsides with high-pressure hoses, wash everything into long sluices lined with mercury, which attracts gold. Every few days, they'd clean the riffles, drop it all into a big still, boil it off, and get molten gold at the bottom. Hydraulic mining."

The land on either side of Route 16 was a moonscape of buttes, cuts, dips, and escarpments. It could have been sculpted by nature over millennia. But hydraulickers had spent less than a generation ravishing this virgin countryside . . . all for gold.

Larry opened the liftgate of the Escalade and pulled out a shiny black drone and said, "One of my kids set this up for me. Very smart boy, applying to Caltech. A drone with a camera connected to my laptop."

Peter and Evangeline watched the screen. Larry drove the drone up and out in an ever-widening arc that revealed patterns in the topography, otherworldly and beautiful now, but evidence of staggering destruction more than a century and a half before.

Peter said, "They sure did make a mess."

Evangeline was awestruck. "Manion is right."

"About what?" said Larry.

"Nothing like this should ever happen again."

After that, Peter and Evangeline snoozed. Midday wine mixed with jet lag. They slept from Sacramento all the way to the bridge across the Carquinez Straits, where the traffic went from bad to Bay Area terrible.

Forty-five minutes later, as they inched through a FasTrak gate on the Bay Bridge, Larry Kwan said, "That's funny."

"What?" asked Peter.

"I got a midnight-blue Ford Explorer about five cars back."

Peter looked behind him.

"A blue Explorer followed us down Highway 49 onto 16. That was half the reason I pulled over at Michigan Bar, to see if he'd go by."

"Did he?" Peter realized that he had let down his guard altogether after lunch.

"Yeah. But . . . you think he's following us?"

"Why?" Peter did not want to give up anything. "Another tour operator wants to learn your secrets?"

"I don't know. But if he follows us into the city, I might have to go all Steve McQueen on his ass."

And yes, the Ford followed them off the downtown exit, right onto Fremont.

As the afternoon traffic inched toward Market Street, Larry said, "Maybe we lose him here, right in the heart of Old San Francisco."

Evangeline said, "Hey, listen, Mr. Bullitt—"

Willie gave the big Escalade a goose and rode the bumper in front of him right across the intersection, with the light turning red behind him. He sped two blocks on Front Street, hung a left on California, drove right up to the rear of a cable car lurching up the hill, and slammed on his brakes.

"That went well," said Evangeline.

Peter looked through the back windscreen as the blue SUV swung round the corner and came toward them with two or three cars in between.

Evangeline said, "Can't you pass the cable car?"

"I got a better idea."

They came up to the light on Grant Street, known to the Gold Rushers as Dupont, the main thoroughfare through Chinatown. The cable car ground to a stop, so Larry Kwan threw the Escalade into park and popped out.

"Not a better idea," said Peter. "Not even a good one."

As quickly as that happened, the Explorer turned left and disappeared. That's what it looked like. Just disappeared into the middle of the block and—gone.

Before the light changed, Larry was back in the driver's seat. "They went down Quincy, a skinny damn alley. We'll never catch them."

"Probably for the best," said Peter.

"You got any idea who they were?" asked Larry.

Peter shook his head. Larry did not need to know that the SUV matched the one in the parking lot of the Emery Mine that morning. The Asian guy and his bodyguards? Had they tracked Peter around the Mother Lode all afternoon? Why?

A few more blocks uphill and they were pulling into the Mark Hopkins turnaround, a graceful circle that covered half the footprint of the fabled property, all in brick as nicely laid as a Beacon Hill patio.

Peter offered a tip, but Larry refused. "Just say the name of my company in your article. And if you need more driving, call me. I live over in Emeryville. I can be here in no time. And this Escalade is armored, in case you didn't know."

"Armored," said Peter. "Why?"

"So I can drive diplomats, businessmen, big deals. You're in good hands with Larry Kwan."

"Good to know." Peter got out, took Evangeline's arm, and whispered, "Someone is watching us."

"Maybe it's because I'm so gorgeous."

"Is that what Manion said?"

"Jealous. I like that." She went in ahead of him.

He watched her go up the stairs and said, "You're playing me. I'm wondering who in the hell is following us, and why, and you are actually playing me. Either that or you're still feeling the wine and those big Manion eyes following every step you took."

LJ SENT HIS FATHER an email before dinner: "Our guest will be Michael Kou, 39. Berkeley B-School. Phi Beta Kappa. Venture capital guy, lots of commodities, drug research. Invested in Cutler Gold Exploration in 2015. Many connections. But Jack Cutler not coming."

LJ and Michael Kou were waiting in a booth when Peter and Evangeline arrived. Howard Ching had set them up with Tsingtaos, pork fried dumplings, fried wontons.

And answers? Would Michael Kou set them up with those?

He looked about ten years younger than he was, thought Evangeline, and very sharp in a gray suit, silver tie, white shirt.

"Nice to meet you," said Peter. "I'm disappointed that your partner isn't here."

"So am I," said Michal Kou. "But Jack Cutler has a core sampling job up in Placerville. And core sampling keeps geologists in business. Can't turn down work."

"Maybe he's looking for buried bags of Chinese gold." Peter decided to toss out the Manion Sturgis rumor right at the start.

LJ laughed, but Evangeline thought he seemed nervous. His eyes kept shifting to the young Chinese guys in the corner booth, half a dozen of them, talking loud, cracking jokes, living large.

Michael Kou, however, kept his eyes on Peter and said in a flat monotone, "Chinese gold?"

If the wise guy who called himself Wonton Willie defined colorful, thought Evangeline, Michael Kou was Chinatown's Prince of Bland.

Peter said to his son, "Remember when I used to ask you what you learned in school every day? I'd ask you to tell me one new thing?"

LJ nodded.

"Well, I learned three things today. One: Broke Neck is a ghost town surrounded by a lot of very touchy locals, some of whom have strong opinions about Jack Cutler. Two: the Emery Mine has a lot of very touchy staffers, especially after a visit from a scowling Chinese businessman who looked very familiar. And three: Manion Sturgis grows very good wine on the edge of an old gold field where legend has it that there's buried bags of Chinese gold."

"Chinese gold?" said Michael Kou again, as if testing the words in his head.

"That's four things," said Evangeline.

"Three and a corollary," said Peter.

"So you don't have to learn anything else for two days, Dad." LJ tried a joke.

"What I want to learn," said Peter, "is how Cutler Gold Exploration fits into this. Or why a guy with a Berkeley MBA would invest in the unpredictable gold business when there are better bets all over the Bay Area."

"I like the romance of gold, the adventure of it," said Michael Kou.

"You don't seem like a romantic," said Evangeline.

"Don't let the gray suit fool you." Michael Kou smiled. "If I'd been around in 1849, I would have sailed for San Francisco with all the other Celestials. But today—"

"Today, you have three kinds of gold miners," LJ jumped in. "The hobbyist, like the mom-and-pop prospector who might belong to a mining club that owns a stretch of riverbank, or the guy who just pulls up at the side of a road and starts placer mining."

"You mean, like, panning?" asked Evangeline.

"Yeah. *Placer* means 'sandbar' in Spanish," said LJ. "You dig into a sandbar, put the sand into a pan, and start washing."

"I thought the placer gold was panned out a long time ago," said Evangeline.

"Most of it was. But every flake counts. Gold is that scarce. In all of human history, we have only mined 160,000 tons of it, just enough, given its amazing density, to fill two Olympic-sized swimming pools."

"That's all?" said Evangeline.

"That's all," said LJ. "Panning today is like fishing. You might catch a big striper. More likely, you'll get skunked. You do it for fun."

"Fun I get," said Evangeline. "But—"

"Then you have what are called 'juniors,'" said LJ. "Professionals. Businessmen."

Michael Kou added, "The pros know that eighty percent of the gold is still out there in the Mother Lode, but most of it is too dispersed to make it economically feasible to mine. If gold prices go up, however, the juniors get attention. They've been out in the field, researching, identifying formations, core sampling, buying claims."

"What constitutes a major?" asked Peter.

LJ said, "A big corporation like Barrick or Newmont. They trade on the Toronto exchange, where most gold stocks get sold. They have real equity valuation, high capitalization, layers of management, all the bells and whistles."

"Like Emery?" said Peter.

"Technically, Emery is a junior," said Kou, "with a low stock price but big dreams and proven reserves."

"Worth fifteen cents as of this afternoon," said Peter.

"If gold prices rise, watch that stock," said Kou. "Emery could go through the roof. A buyout would make a lot of small-time investors happy."

"From what we learned in Chinatown last night," said Peter, "a certain small-time geologist made some Chinese investors very *unhappy* not too long ago."

"You mean Jack Cutler? That stuff about him burning investors?" Michael Kou dipped a wonton in sweet sauce and popped it into his mouth. "They should've read the prospectus."

LJ explained: "Cutler is a loner, a wildcatter, drilling test holes, exploring, selling his services to juniors or acting as one himself. Invest with a guy like him, the risks are enormous. So are the rewards."

"That's why I partnered with him," added Michael Kou.

"Cramer put it best on CNBC," said LJ. "Majors are Big Pharma. Juniors are research labs, looking for the next Viagra. You could add that my future father-in-law is a mad scientist with a lab in his garage."

"Right," said Michael Kou. "Sometimes it's science that makes us money. Sometimes it's dumb luck. Sometimes it's legends about bags of Chinese gold that bring investors to an area like Broke Neck, but legends bring cash, and cash means working capital."

"Have you read these legends in, say, the Spencer Journal?" asked Peter.

"I've heard of the journal," answered Michael Kou, perhaps a bit too innocently, "and the legends."

"I'll bet you have." Peter detected a moment of . . . something . . . that passed between LJ and this smooth businessman. They had been tag-teaming the conversation, finishing each other's thoughts like longtime associates. But there was a twinge of tension.

Then LJ said, "Whatever a lost journal may tell us, any geologist will tell you there are undiscovered ore bodies out there, worth mining in 1849 or tomorrow morning."

"Finding one of them is a junior's dream," said Michael Kou, "But seasoned investors at a place like the Emery Mine live with the reality of fluctuating gold prices and wait. When prices rise enough to pay for operations and for lawyers to wrangle the California regulations—"

"Is Asian money running Emery?" asked Peter.

"Asian?" said Michael Kou, again a bit too innocently.

Peter and Evangeline both felt another little twinge of tension.

Michael Kou said, "Money is money, whether it's from Hong Kong or Iowa. Investors want profit. And the greater the risk, the greater the reward. The Emery Mine is risky. But the work of Cutler and others tells us that there's still gold there, in proven hard-rock reserves and—" Kou glanced at LJ, as if to ask if he should say more.

LJ finished the sentence. "—in other forms as well."

"Exactly," said Michael Kou. "So I wouldn't be surprised if you saw Asian investors, Canadian gold firms . . . even Donald Trump."

That brought a laugh from LJ, a big, broad laugh of the kind that Peter seldom heard from his son, who always held things close.

JUST THEN, THE FRONT door swung open. Wonton Willie was making a big entrance . . . flashing in like he owned the place.

Some diners—mostly tourists who didn't know enough—glanced up, then went back to their dry-cooked shrimp or crispy orange beef. But Chinese diners watched, some surreptitiously, some nervously, a few submissively, with a little smile or a nod, as if to ask, *Now what?* Or to say, *I'm a civilian, so play nice.*

Whenever a Tong tough guy walked into a restaurant, especially a guy like Willie, the people who knew about local power struggles knew enough to be nervous. Was something up? Something going down? Would there be gunplay? It wouldn't be the first time.

Wonton surveyed the room, noticed Peter and Evangeline, and ambled over, with Wraparound and Mullet Man at his heels, all smooth, all smiles, all attitude in his dark shades and black-on-black outfit. He said, "Can't get enough of Chinatown, hey?"

Evangeline said, "I'm writing about it." If she felt threatened, she always called forth the power of the press. Nobody messed with the press, even if her hard-hitting article would run in *Travel & Lifestyle* magazine.

"What you writin' 'bout?" Willie pulled off his shades. "Chinese gold?"

"There it is again," said Peter to LJ.

LJ said nothing, showed nothing.

"I'm writing about Chinese *food*," said Evangeline.

"Yeah," said Peter. "In a Chinese restaurant, you write about Chinese food."

"That's where I get my nickname, hey, from Chinese food. But when you write about it, don't put no hyphen in Wonton." Willie looked at his boys. "*Chronicle* crime writer, he put a hyphen in my name."

"What's a hyphen?" asked Mullet Man.

"Don't know, but he only do it one time." Willie laughed. So all of them laughed.

Peter stood, and Wraparound took a step. Peter suspected he was still angry after Evangeline's Mace threat the night before.

Willie put up a hand. *Relax, boys.*

Peter nodded. *Yeah, relax, boys.* "Want to join us, Willie? Maybe we'll talk about—oh, I don't know—Cutler Gold Exploration."

"See . . . you *are* talkin' 'bout Chinese gold." Willie wagged a finger in Peter's face. "You can't fool Willie. But my friends are waitin'. They don't order without Willie. You and me, we sit down real soon, Mr. Boston. I tell you all about Jack Cutler and what he cost Chinatown peoples. Ain't that right, Michael Kou?"

Kou said nothing, showed nothing, though his eyes shifted to a table nearby, where two older Chinese men ate quietly. One of them had an ankle holster. The other was wearing a loose windbreaker with the *Racing Form* in the pocket and a shoulder holster under the arm.

Willie leaned down and whispered to Michael Kou, loud enough for everyone to hear, "I watch out for my own. That why Chinatown peoples

like me. I don't fuck nobody." Then he gave his boys a flick of the finger—
follow me—and headed for the circular booth in the corner, where the
others slid out to give him the best seat, back to the wall, surveying the
room. Loud voices and big laughs followed.

Evangeline said, "Are we the only ones who don't know about this Chinese gold?"

"That's not why Willie's here," said LJ.

"You mean, he's just hungry?" said Evangeline.

"Maybe," said Michael Kou. "Or maybe marking turf . . . or maybe a
target."

"Target?" said Evangeline.

"Sometimes," said LJ, "Chinese gangs bring a hit man from out of
town—"

"Right." Michael scanned the restaurant. "They bring him to a place
like this to show him the target. Someone in here might be an assassin,
someone eating hoi-sin chicken, pretending to mind his own business.
Maybe Willie just marked someone."

"One of us?" Peter sat again.

Evangeline took the can of Mace from her purse and put it on the seat
beside her.

"Or," said Peter, "one of the guys over there talking about horse racing.
They look like two grandfathers. But they're both carrying."

"I'm a powerful man," said Kou, without a hint of arrogance. "They are
my bodyguards."

"Since when do venture capital guys need bodyguards?" asked Evangeline.

"Since I got interested in something that interests Wonton Willie," answered Kou.

"The Chinese gold?" said Peter.

"Or the Spencer Journal?" said Evangeline.

"Some people think Willie already has the journal," said Michael Kou.
"They think he stole it from the California Historical Society."

"Didn't the society make a copy?" asked Evangeline.

"It was one of those items they hadn't gotten around to digitizing yet,"
said LJ.

Peter was not surprised. "That happens a lot in big libraries."

LJ added, "When they opened the archive box about nine months ago,
the journal was gone."

Peter leaned across the table and looked hard at his son and Michael

Kou. "This is about more than a journal or a mythical bag of gold. And what happened last night in Portsmouth Square is tied into it. So is the hit-and-running of Maryanne Rogers. But how?"

LJ and Michael Kou looked at each other.

"Don't all talk at once," said Peter.

Michael said, "Exploration is an inexact science. Cutler's ventures have lost money for small investors. They've lost me and my big investors money, too. He dreams of finding bags of gold and paying off his debts to the locals, so he can regain respect in the community. He married a Chinese woman, don't forget."

"And fathered a lovely daughter," said Evangeline.

LJ smiled, as if to say he appreciated that.

Evangeline appreciated the smile.

But Peter still had his eyes on Kou. "What do you dream of?"

"Something bigger, Mr. Fallon. Much bigger."

Peter wished he had asked his question another way.

SOMEHOW, DESPITE THE TENSION and that filling vineyard lunch, Peter and Evangeline managed to eat their way through another Chinese feast.

And when Wonton Willie and his boys left in another big flurry, the whole place seemed to breathe a little easier.

Then Evangeline recognized a guy in the corner. She had noticed him earlier, sitting alone, eating a bowl of lo-mein noodles and reading a Chinese language newspaper. When Willie left, this guy got up, put on his Giants cap, and went out right after him.

So Evangeline asked Peter for his phone and scrolled to the selfie Peter had taken on the cable car the day before, the accidental photobomb and . . . was it the same guy, the one from the airport baggage claim, too? She couldn't tell.

The only other sign of trouble came when the front door opened and in walked Uncle Charlie, the angry investor from Portsmouth Square. But he didn't stay. A bag of takeout was waiting for him. He paid, glanced into the dining room, and left.

Peter was glad of that. He sensed that LJ was, too.

Michael Kou grabbed the check. Peter let him pay. It might be the only thing they got out of him. But what Peter got was the sight of something dangling from the key fob that came out of Michael's pocket when he pulled out his wallet, a kind of unfinished triangle.

Peter gestured to it. "What's that, some kind of smart-guy society?"

Michael Kou looked up from the bill. "What? Oh, just an old Chinese organization. Hong Kong businessmen." He signed the bill, and they were done. He clearly knew how to brush off a question he didn't like.

Out on the street, Michael Kou flagged a cab on Washington Street and jumped in.

LJ went to get in the other side, but Peter grabbed him by the elbow. "The man at the Emery Mine today, the Asian guy. He looked familiar. I just made him."

"Made him?" said Evangeline, who homed right in on this little exchange.

"You mean like in the detective novels?" asked LJ. "You recognized him?"

"You know how?" said Peter. "He had a lapel pin like Michael Kou's key ring, and I'd seen him somewhere else."

LJ gave Peter that look again, a little embarrassed, a little apologetic, a little like a twelve-year-old. "At the Arbella Club?"

"He was leaving as I arrived. He looked pissed off then, pissed off this afternoon."

"Are you in danger?" whispered Evangeline to LJ.

"No more than I can handle."

"Are we?" she asked.

"You're civilians. You're okay. And you can go home if you want. I'll understand."

"Go home?" said Evangeline. "Hell no. I have an article to write."

"But what does that mean? Civilians?" asked Peter.

"It means to keep doing what you're good at. Helping to reconstruct this journal. If that's all you do, you'll stay out of trouble."

"You seem to be doing a good job with the journal yourself," said Evangeline.

LJ gave a nervous glance toward the taxi, where Kou was absorbed in his iPhone. Then he whispered, "I have to schmooze a little more. And— oh, shit."

The front door of the Lucky Li Laundromat was banging open, and an old man was stalking across the street, shouting, "I tellin' you now, for last time."

"Good evening, Uncle Charlie." LJ spoke politely to the old man, no matter how unhappy he was to see him.

"Don't give me that. I mad at you. Chinatown no good for you. Get Mary and go."

"Thank you, Uncle Charlie," said LJ. "I appreciate your words, but—"

The window of the cab went down and Michael Kou said, "Tell that crazy old man you're in a hurry."

"Fuck you, too, Michael Kou," said Uncle Charlie, then he waved a finger under LJ's nose. "No buts. That what I say to you and your father. Just go. Go." Uncle Charlie waved his finger in Peter's face, too, then pivoted, and went back to the Laundromat.

As the cab sped away with LJ and Michael Kou, Evangeline said, "I fear that our careful young lawyer has gotten in over his head."

"I may have to do more than what I'm good at to get him back onto dry land."

"But you're good at so many things."

"As many as Manion Sturgis?"

"Well, you can drink wine. But can you *make* it?"

"Touché."

"Cliché."

They thought about having a chat with Uncle Charlie, but he had already disappeared from the Laundromat, as if into thin air. So they decided to work off the big meals with a walk back to the hotel.

AT MASON, THEY TURNED up the hill, as steep as a pitched roof, a dark stretch of apartments and precariously parked cars that led to a San Francisco landmark, the great illuminated American flag fluttering atop the Mark Hopkins Hotel.

Peter took a breath and said, "If you can talk in normal tones while engaged in aerobics, like climbing a hill, you're in good shape. So keep talking."

She was breathing more heavily, too, even though she ran three miles every other day. "Your son and his friend talked a lot, but they didn't say a damn thing."

"LJ usually plays it close, but he's scared—"

"Who do you think is watching him?"

"The same people watching us, leaving me phone messages to watch out for hit-and-runs."

"Phone messages? And you didn't tell me?"

Peter shrugged. "I try not to raise red flags."

"Maybe they're the same people who sent an assassin into the restaurant tonight." She looked over her shoulder, as if he might be following them.

"Assassin?" said Peter. "Now that's a red flag."

"I think it was the same guy I saw at the baggage carousel yesterday, who also followed us on the cable car. He was in the restaurant. He liked lo mein."

"So that's why you wanted my phone?"

"Yes, but the picture on the cable car isn't definitive, so maybe—"

"Maybe he might not be an assassin."

"But somebody's watching us."

"So we'd better be careful." Peter liked it when she said "us."

Before they crossed California Street, they looked in every direction for fast-moving vehicles, cars without headlights, or white panel trucks, the kind that might still be in the hit-and-run business. Then they crossed in front of a cable car and strolled into the turnaround at the Mark Hopkins.

Peter stopped and looked up at the big fluttering flag. "If someone is watching us, how about we show them how well we dance?"

"Dance?" There was an idea she liked and didn't like at the same time.

"There's dancing every night at the Top of the Mark. And we've been dancing around each other for quite a while. Let's see how it feels to dance together again."

But . . . she was still committed to separate beds. And though she hadn't told him, she was seeing Sturgis again tomorrow. And dancing at the Top of the Mark was just too damn romantic. Of course, Peter had been doing the right things so far . . . giving her space, cracking jokes, letting her find her way into another case, which always excited her, whether she wanted to admit it or not. And it *was* the Top of the Mark. So maybe—

The doorman came down the steps and opened the door of an idling black limo.

Peter didn't think anything of it until a familiar voice said, "Let's go for ride."

They both turned to see Wonton Willie leaning out of the limo. "My cousin own. He say, 'You know big-time lady writer? We give tour. Maybe she give limo company nice write-up.'"

Evangeline looked at Peter and whispered, "No fucking way."

"Nice talk for a big-time lady writer," said Peter out of the corner of his mouth, then he tried to see into the front seat, but it was too dark.

"Come on," said Willie. "It'll be fun."

The doorman made a gesture, inviting them to step in.

Peter said, "Big-time lady writer has a deadline."

"Wrong choice of words," she whispered. "Just say, 'I have some work to finish.'"

Wonton extended his hand. "Finish work later."

She slipped her arm around Peter's. A gentle tug, a few steps, and they'd be in the hotel, safe.

"Relax," said Willie in a lower voice, so that the doorman could pretend not to hear. "If I want to kill you, you be dead already."

"How can a girl resist an invitation like that?" said Evangeline.

"Just keep Mace in pocketbook, hey." Willie waved his hand.

Peter decided they should play along. So he nudged Evangeline into the car.

She dropped into the rear seat, as far from Willie as she could get. Then she pulled down the armrest.

Peter climbed into the jump seat facing Willie. But before he said a word, he glanced into the front. Just a driver—unfamiliar, not one of Willie's regular "boys."

Willie said, "So, where you like to go?"

"Someplace safe," said Evangeline.

"You safe right here. My cousin best driver in San Francisco. Car got bulletproof glass, armored door panels, puncture-proof tires. Don't even need seat belt."

So Peter stopped looking for his.

Willie said to the driver, "Go down to Market, then Embarcadero, then bring 'em up Powell. Nice views up Powell." He turned to Evangeline. "You like the nice views?"

"I wish I brought my camera." She peered out the smoked glass window.

Willie pointed to the little bar where the left rear door would have been, if the limo hadn't been tricked out like a high-end party chariot. "Drink? I got Cristal."

Before Evangeline could make a crack about the drug dealer's champagne of choice, Peter asked, "Is it open?"

"Popped and chilled, hey." Willie pulled the clear bottle out of the ice, produced three flutes from his armrest, poured, and toasted, "To my new partners."

If it hadn't been Cristal, Peter might have done a spit-take. "Partners?"

Willie smiled, so that his gold-rimmed tooth glinted. "Drink your drink."

The limo dropped down California Street. Late at night there wasn't much traffic. So they reached Market in no time, with the Ferry Building directly in front of them. Then they turned along the waterfront.

"You like my town?" asked Willie.

"I liked it even before you took possession," said Evangeline.

"When did that happen, exactly?" asked Peter.

"When the Feds took down Wo Hop To. Everybody scramblin' now to see who goes up. Well, Willie and his tong goin' up. You know what the 'tong' mean?"

"Meeting hall," said Peter.

Willie laughed, impressed. He said to Evangeline, "You boyfriend real smart, like his son, hey."

"Like his son."

"Tong also mean 'social group.' That's what me and my boys are. Social group. Sometime tongs do things so people get what they want . . . some gambling, some drink . . . maybe some girls. All nice and social. And if you need protection, you no trust SFPD. You come to your own. Been that way since the Chinese come to Gum Saan, right?"

Gum Saan. Gold Mountain. Peter thought of Wei Chin, Mr. Sam Who, and wondered if he had needed a tong . . . or if he formed his own.

"Do *we* need protection?" asked Evangeline.

That's why Peter liked having her along. She always asked the blunt question.

"Maybe," said Willie. "You no pay me tribute, I no happy. I got to pay, too."

"We all have our bosses," said Peter.

"Who's yours?" Evangeline asked Willie.

"Dai-lo."

"Dai-lo?" she asked.

"Big Brother, from Hong Kong," said Willie. "Triad boss."

"Triad? What's that?" asked Evangeline.

"Chinese organized crime," said Peter. "Heaven, Earth, and Man. The three elements of the universe, operating in synergy for the good of all. The Triad."

"Their symbol is triangle," said Willie.

Like Michael Kou's key fob? thought Peter. The other guy's lapel pin?

"Poetic, hey?" said Willie. "It also stand for Trust, Loyalty, Honor. Those important, too."

Peter said, "The Chinese are a very poetic people, even the ones engaging in extortion, money laundering, drug trafficking, human trafficking, and prostitution."

"Now why you want say that?" Willie scowled with almost theatrical anger, feigning insult. "You talk me down, I no pour you no more Cristal."

Peter held out his glass, as if he sensed that Willie was blustering for show.

Willie grinned and poured. "You know, a lot of guys want to take control in San Francisco. We got big power vacuum. And sometime civilian get caught up, and if you do bad to Triad, no can of Mace gonna help you."

Peter continued to act as if he had heard all this before, from much tougher guys, even if he hadn't. "Does the Dai-lo want the gold journal?"

"Not the journal." Willie made a wave of the hand. "Nobody give shit about old writing. Dai-lo want gold. That what you lookin' for, right? Chinese gold bags? There been talk about Chinese gold bags long time, since Ah-Toy. You know Ah-Toy?"

"Doesn't everyone?" said Evangeline.

Willie gave her a look, as if he was trying to decide if he really liked her or thought she was really annoying, or a little bit of both. "You know, Lady Mace, you bein' watched to see if you get gold bags."

"By you?" she asked.

Willie nodded.

"By a blue Ford Explorer?" Peter asked.

"I don't know about no blue Explorer. I ride with Yee Limo." Willie sipped his Cristal. "Only way to go. But we even watchin' you in your hotel room, lady."

"I'll turn off the light when I shower, then."

Peter liked the wisecrack. Never let them know you were creeped out.

The car turned and headed up the hill at Powell Street.

Suddenly, Willie leaned forward. "I got three day. *Three* day." He pushed three fingers into Peter's face. "Before big sit-down with Dai-lo. You give me something. I get in solid with Dai-lo, you get in solid with Wonton, your son in solid with everybody. Then we have big party when he marry Chinese girl."

"Half," said Peter.

"Half what?"

"Half Chinese."

"Yeah, well, some people don't like that. Some people don't like she marryin' white boy. But the world changin', hey."

"And if I can't deliver in three days?" asked Peter.

"Dai-lo no happy with me. I no happy with you." Willie sat back.

The car climbed Powell Street, turned onto Sacramento. The downtown buildings leaped up in front of them.

"You like view?" said Willie to Evangeline. Then he looked at Peter. "You help Willie, Lady Mace get apartment with great view next time she come San Francisco."

A few more turns, and they were back in front of the hotel.

The doorman opened the door and peered in.

"We all friends now, so"—Willie made a wave—"you can leave."

But something happened . . . or perhaps a dozen things happened, all at once.

Peter heard the driver say, "Oh, shit." Then the Plexiglas separating them from the front seat slammed open.

At the same instant, the doorman went flying, struck by a guy dressed all in black, with a hoodie pulled low over a Giants cap. Then the guy shoved a pistol into the limo.

Before Peter could react, two shots exploded into Wonton Willie's chest. Two muzzle flashes lit the interior of the limo.

Evangeline screamed.

The gun swung in her direction.

Two more muzzle flashes. Two explosions right in Peter's ear.

But these came from the front seat.

Willie's cousin was more than a driver. He was a bodyguard. He put two bullets into the heart of the assassin, who dropped on the paving bricks.

Evangeline looked at Peter. He looked at her. They both looked at Wonton Willie.

After a moment, Willie gasped, then gasped again, then laughed and said, "Kevlar . . . wow . . . good fuckin' idea to wear Kevlar."

DENTS IN KEVLAR, WIND knocked from Willie, no other wounds, except for Peter's ringing ear and Evangeline's shattered nerves, and, of course, one Chinatown hood, dead on the turnaround in front of the world-famous Mark Hopkins Hotel.

Before SFPD got there, Willie said to Peter and Evangeline, "Tell cops truth."

"I'll tell them what happened," said Evangeline.

"You here to write about Chinatown, so you talkin' to all kinds Chinatown character."

"Ain't *that* the truth," she said.

"Damn sure is, hey." Willie was getting back to normal. "And you"—he looked at Peter—"you here to do work for big law firm."

Peter said, "That's the truth, too, hey."

"Just leave Chinese gold out of it."

Peter thought that would also be a good idea.

When the flashing blues appeared, Willie said, "Shit about to get real."

"*Get* real?" said Evangeline.

Detective Patrick Nauseda interviewed Peter and Evangeline, but not separately. That was good. They could keep their stories straight, and since most everything they said was true, keeping stories straight was not difficult. He was young, polite, neatly dressed, the good cop.

The bad cop was named Darcy Immerman, a compact cube of San Francisco kickass female, who got out of the unmarked cruiser with a scowl on her face, glared at everyone in the courtyard, pointed at Willie and his driver, and said, "You and you, dummy up and we go downtown. Answer nice and we do this right here."

"Nothin' but the truth on the hotel steps," said Willie.

And they started the Q & A dance.

Lieutenant Nauseda kept asking questions until Detective Immerman folded her notebook. Then he said to Peter and Evangeline, "I would ask you to stay in town until our investigation is complete. If you must leave, please contact us."

"We're scheduled to fly back east on Monday," said Peter.

The detective wrote that down, then gave Peter and Evangeline his card, "Call me on Sunday. I'll let you know what we've decided."

Evangeline asked him, "Are we in trouble?"

"Hard to say, ma'am. Witnesses to a gang hit. The good news is that the hit man is dead. The bad news is that the gangs are getting restless. If I were you, I'd write about something else the next time you come to San Francisco."

In their room, they dropped onto their separate beds.

"I'm exhausted," said Evangeline. "But I don't think sleep is in the cards without chemical assistance."

"That dead gunman," said Peter. "Was he the one you saw in the restaurant tonight?"

"No. But they were both wearing Giants caps."

"Like I say, half the guys in San Francisco are wearing Giants caps." Peter flipped the bolt on the door. "So there's someone else out there."

"Working for who?"

"Hard to say." Out of habit, Peter looked at his email. "But it appears that your persistence with a certain winemaker came through."

The email from Manion Sturgis arrived with a little paper-clipped attachment. "Read about the Chinese gold. Then make this all go away."

Evangeline said, "Something to entertain us until the melatonin kicks in."

As Peter started to read, the hotel phone rang again, and Evangeline nearly levitated from her bed. They both looked at the phone, then at each other.

"Who the hell is calling us at this hour?" she said. "On the hotel phone?"

This time, Peter answered with his best get-off-my-lawn voice. "Who is it?"

"Somebody who's happy that he missed your limo ride tonight. I'm telling you, this can be a very dangerous town."

Peter decided to engage his mystery caller. He said, "What are you after? The bags of gold, the river, or the journal?"

"I want the journal. All seven parts. It'll answer all the other questions. Then we can all live happily ever after." *Click.*

Evangeline looked at his face. "So . . . another avid reader?"

The Journal of James Spencer—Notebook #4
February 1, 1850
Steam Passage

Samuel Hodges is heading for Broke Neck.

This intelligence reached me shortly after I had settled into a comfortable chair in the saloon of the steamboat *Senator*, bound overnight for San Francisco. I had determined to see how the city had rebuilt, to escape the stench and general awfulness of Sacramento, and, most importantly, to find Michael Flynn, from whom there had been no word since New Year's Day.

I sipped a brandy, my first strong drink in nearly a month, listened to the thumping of the engine, and opened for the hundredth time my letter from Janiva. Would the sight of a Boston-bound ship in Yerba Buena Cove tempt me to buy a ticket and sail back to her? I wondered. Then I sensed someone standing over me.

"Spencer, is it?" He wore a sweat-stained hat and a threadbare tweed suit, and under his arm, he carried a leather satchel as if it was his most valued possession: Tom Lyons, de facto attorney for the Sagamores. He said, "Good to see you, though you look something the worse for wear."

Traveling in style, I was, in my own tweed suit. But I had lost such weight to the dysentery, I looked like a stick in a tweed bag.

"Headed home?" asked Lyons.

"No. Not yet. Not done yet in California. And you?"

"San Jose. The new government is meeting there." He dropped into the chair opposite me. "Hodges has asked me to represent his interests."

"Hodges?" I said the word with what I hoped was concealed trepidation.

Lyons eyed my brandy, although he retained enough dignity not to lick his lips. I offered to buy him one, knowing that nothing lubricated a man like brandy. After that, I needed only to ask how the Sagamores fared, and he began to talk: Hodges had been all over the northern mines searching for a place to build something bigger. Then he heard about Rainbow Gulch, studied the map of the Miwok, and said that was the place to go. But not for the gold. For the water.

"Does he know my claim is on the Miwok?"

"Oh, yes." Lyons toasted me with the brandy. "He speaks of you often."

"Warmly?"

Lyons sipped the brandy. "He said that in Broke Neck, he would show you all that he had predicted. In Broke Neck, he would fulfill his ambition, and you would have to tell the people of Boston."

I was not so foolish as to believe that Hodges was going to the Miwok simply to impress me into writing about him, but that was how Lyons made it sound.

"Hodges means to build that empire, Spencer. He's greedy for it."

"Everyone is greedy in California," I said.

Lyons eyed the crowd—drinkers and gamblers, men of business going between the new hubs of California commerce, flush miners intent on squandering newfound wealth, backtrackers looking sullen and disappointed, and he said, "The greed of most men is for gold. It can be quantified, understood, even satisfied. Hodges is greedy for fame, respect, reputation. That kind of greed is . . . metaphysical."

"Then why are you working for him?"

Lyons patted the satchel. "In a land where men make up the law as they go along, there's great opportunity for one who's been schooled in it."

"Lawyers bring civilization, or so I've been told."

"Hodges aims to bring it, too." Lyons drained the brandy. "But he has joined forces with a company of Missourans, led by brothers named David and Moses Gaw."

"Lawmaking with David and Moses? Sounds more biblical than legal."

"They're Bible thumpers, yes, but the only law they care about is the law of water. And California has no laws regarding downstream rights. Water is power in this country, Spencer. And power is wealth. And wealth guarantees power. Hodges wants water to close the circle."

"Our water? From the Miwok?"

Lyons stood. "Be careful, Spencer. That's my best advice."

February 2, 1850
San Francisco Rebuilds

The *Senator* reached the city at eight the next morning.

Lyons' intelligence lent greater urgency to my mission: find Flynn, then hurry back to Broke Neck and face Hodges.

But my first thought upon debarking was that California was an amazing place, to draw forth such effort from men who had seen their city burn and had built it back up again in six weeks. Bright new frames of wood and clean white canvas covered all that the fire had scoured. And the air smelled of fresh lumber, not the fetid flood-waste of Sacramento or the burnt stink I was expecting.

They were building bigger, better, stronger, and I was filled with confidence in the future of this place, which was bright indeed if the inhabitants could control their baser instincts.

I climbed to Portsmouth Square, mailed a dispatch and a letter for Janiva, then began my hunt. I might have expected to find Flynn at the Parker House, which was rebuilding quickly but not yet ready to reopen. Business being business, however, and drinkers being thirsty, the proprietors had set up a bar outside, where men were buying and backslapping and bending elbows in the bright sunshine. But I found no Michael Flynn quaffing an early brandy.

Nor did I find him at Ah-Toy's, where Keen-Ho Chow was minding the gate. I asked, and Keen-Ho shook his head, as if he did not recognize the name or did not care. So I described the Irishman, and Keen-Ho's eyes narrowed. "You friend?"

Saying I was Flynn's friend did not seem the best course, so I admitted only that I was looking for him.

"You find, you tell him no more come back. He drink too much. Fight too much."

I decided that if anyone knew where to find him, it would be the lawyer, Reese Shipton.

He was working out of a tent on the north side of Portsmouth Square. He offered to give me news. His fee: a pinch of gold dust for fifteen minutes of his time.

I opened my pouch and watched this yellow-haired, honey-drawling Southerner wet his fingertips, then dip them deep. A pinch was the going price for many things not worth an ounce, and a clerk with thick fingers was a valued employee.

Shipton deposited his pinch in a small box on his desk, then gave me a grin.

"So," I said, "what's your news?"

"Your Sagamore friends couldn't take it. Sam Brannan undercut them. And with more ships bringin' more supplies, prices kept droppin'. Then come the Christmas fire. Burned Jason Willis of Boston right out of business. Him and Collins and half a dozen other fast-talkin' Yankee boys up and left on the next steamer, pockets empty and dicks draggin'."

I was not surprised but did not care. I said, "What do you hear of Michael Flynn?"

"Makin' a fine old legend of himself, that one is. Drinkin' and fuckin' and fightin', too. Surprised he didn't generate a few fees. I make plenty gettin' pugnacious drinkers out of the hoosegow."

"Hoosegow?"

"The city jail. It's on an abandoned ship till they build one for good and proper. The brig *Euphemia,* anchored off Long Wharf."

"So . . . Flynn's in jail?"

Shipton shrugged.

"If you keep shrugging, I'll consider that pinch to be money wasted."

"Spoken like a Boston Yankee. Always puttin' a man to the guilt when he asks for an honest fee. No wonder Willis didn't make it, treatin' folks that way."

"Forget him," I said. "What about Flynn?"

"I hear he got in a fight over a card game. A Boston blacksmith rescued him."

"Dooling?"

"That's him. Come after the fire. Went over the burnt ground, siftin' metal . . . old nails, barrel rings, and such. Melted it all down, started makin' new nails at a forge on Montgomery Street. Enterprisin' feller. Nothin' this city needs like nails, considerin' that lumber's not worth a shit without 'em."

"But Flynn. What about Flynn?"

"Oh, Flynn found other whorehouses, other gamblin' tables. And he got into business with Big Beam, of all people."

"Big Beam? The labor broker?"

"Brokerin' a new kind of labor, from what I hear. Go see him."

"Where?"

"Can't really say. They been movin' as the city rebuilds. Ask around." Shipton popped open his pocket watch to signal the end of our time. "But if you need a lawyer, y'all come to ol' Reese."

I stepped into the sunshine and the surging San Francisco crowd, considered my next move, and heard a low voice. Dingus, Shipton's slave, was sitting on a stool by the tent flap, whittling. "I tell you where your friend is, mister. I tell you for two pinches."

I looked at his huge black hands. "One pinch is all your master got."

"He my master till California come in a free state. Then he my *nothin'*. And when it come to your friend, my master *know* nothin'. But I do . . . for *two* pinches."

I scowled and opened my pouch.

Dingus scowled back, but I suppose he had the right, being enslaved in a place where men of so many races had come to prosper, regardless of their class or the bonds that had held them at home. He took the second pinch and gestured toward the harbor. "He's out there. Out on the ship."

"The *William Winter*?"

"If that the ship that brung y'all to California."

"He signed on again?"

"Signed on?" Dingus laughed, though he was careful to look down. He was not yet so defiant as to laugh in a white man's face. "That ship ain't even got a cap'n."

"Trask is gone?"

"The boy, Pompey, he say the cap'n cut half the lines, make nooses of 'em, and take off to find every last desertin' crewman from his ship. Fixin' to hang 'em. Hang all of 'em."

I GOT A BOAT to row me out to the *William Winter*, now just one more derelict in Yerba Buena Cove. The paint was peeling on her false gun ports. Rigging lines swung loose. The upper masts had been stepped down and carried off. Reverend Winter himself had developed a split down his cheek that resembled a great wooden tear. I gave the rower a pinch of gold, told him to wait, climbed the footholds at the side of the ship. The deck, which had pitched and rolled a hundred thousand times on our voyage, lay deserted, bleaching in the sun. Cracks had opened between the boards. Weeds grew in the cracks.

Then female laughter came to me from somewhere aft. I followed it to the quarterdeck, to the skylight in the roof of the captain's cabin. I peered down and saw breasts . . . naked, voluptuous breasts.

A woman was pumping herself on someone who was pumping right back. She said, "Come on, baby, come on, pop one more time for Mama and—"

A deep groan rose from beneath her.

"Yeah, yeah, you know what Mama likes." She pumped harder and threw her head back, perhaps in ecstasy, perhaps not. I was no expert, but as her face turned to the skylight, I saw no contortions of pleasure, only the concentration of someone finishing a job of work. And her eyes were open. When they met mine, she screamed.

A man's face appeared beneath her. He shouted, "You son of a bitch!" And with the woman still astraddle, he grabbed a pistol from somewhere and fired.

The shot shattered the pane at my ear, and a moment later, Michael Flynn, wrapped in a dirty sheet, exploded from the stern companionway. "I told you sons of bitches that— Why, Jamie! What are you doin' here?" He was naked except for the sheet and an enveloping cloud of whiskey.

I said, "I've come to bring you back."

"And leave all this?" He waved his pistol toward the city, as if he owned it.

Then the girl emerged, also in a sheet. "You said no customers 'fore noon."

"It's all right, darlin'. He's my good friend." Flynn gestured to her. "This here's Roberta. Want her?"

"*Want* her?" I said, trying to hide my shock.

In the sunlight, she looked hard and hard used. And she smelled, but in a way that smelly miners didn't. There was something earthy in the air around her, a scent of fecundity, of musk, of sex. I had to admit I found it tempting. She grinned, but a missing tooth did little to diminish the power of her scent. She said, "I don't come cheap, mister."

"You can have her for two ounces," said Flynn. "Or Sheila? She's got a glorious rump and ain't above offerin' it, if your taste runs that way. Hey, Sheila!"

"Not before noon." Sheila, in frilled pantaloons and camisole, was emerging from the forward companionway. She staggered to the rail, held a finger to a nostril, and blew her nose into the water. Then she asked, "Where's the nigger?"

"Drummin' up business," said Flynn.

"What about Big Beam?" she asked.

"Ain't he with you?" asked Flynn.

She scratched at her crotch. "He'll never be with me again, if he give me what I think he did."

Flynn looked at me. "Big Beam's me pardner. He brought three girls. I had two—"

"You're pardners? With Big Beam? In whoredom?"

Flynn put an arm around Roberta. "It may be whoredom, but it's heaven, too."

I said, "Cletis needs us."

"Cletis?" Flynn wobbled, as if he was drunk at ten o'clock in the morning. "These girls need me. They come down from Oregon, lookin' for to make a few dollars. And—"

"And we made plenty from you, Mr. Galway Bay," said Roberta.

"I'm a man who likes to live," said Flynn, "and ain't above payin' for the pleasures we're entitled to while we're on this side of the grass."

"How much?" I asked.

Roberta looked me in the eye, "Say, mister, do you want a poke or not?"

"Oh, he wants one," said Flynn, "but he's too upper-crusty for the likes of you."

My crust had nothing to do with it.

She said, "He ain't *good* enough for me." Then she disappeared down the companionway as Flynn gave her a loud smack on the bottom.

"How much?" I asked Flynn again.

"After roulette and faro and the buyin' of bad liquor, the lasses got all I had left."

"All? You lost it *all*?"

"Makin' it back, though. I get all the cooch I want, while Big Beam and Pompey go about town, tellin' the boyos who'll pay in gold all about our floatin' palace of pudenda. That's Latin for the pussy, the snatch, the cunt itself, the wellspring of life, deeper and richer and way more rewardin' than all the hot holes men are diggin' up in them blasted foothills." He chuckled. "Of course, your Boston investors, they'd fall over dead if they seen the holes we drill on this ship. But—"

"Trask? Where is he?"

Flynn gestured to the east. "Gold country swallowed him up, like it swallows up damn near everybody. Swallows 'em whole, then shits 'em out into the California dirt, and they never even know they been digested. I'll stay here and get fucked when I want and get fifteen percent to protect these gals when they do their business."

"What happened to your dream? Your Boston dream?"

Flynn looked at the hills and islands around us, blinked, and said, "Why, I woke up."

I took a ticket from my pocket and put it into his hand. "The *Senator* is leaving this afternoon. We can be in Broke Neck tomorrow."

"What's so damned important in Broke Neck, now?"

"Hodges. He's gone to the Miwok Valley."

"Let him. I'll stay on the *Willie Winter.* And you'd be smart to take passage on the *Panama,* not the *Senator.* She'll be here in a day or two. You'll be steamin' back to Boston in the time it takes to fuel her up and turn her around. Get on back to civilization, Jamie. It's what you're made for."

"I signed on to tell the story of Hodges. And we owe that old man up there. Without him, we'd be dead. So I'll see you in an hour or goddamn you."

February 3, 1850
Returning

Michael Flynn did not meet me on the dock, so I gave him a good goddamning, then goddamned myself because he was right. I had "seen the elephant." I had faced loaded guns, fought for my life, found a fortune in gold, and met inhabitants of the Celestial Empire itself. I had watched men die and had buried them and had nearly died myself. If all that experience could not make me a writer, nothing could. So I should have taken passage for Panama City and joined the reverse migration across the isthmus to the Atlantic, where a fleet of steamers now ran between Chagres and the East Coast. I would have known the embrace of my beloved before the glaring red rockets of the Glorious Fourth had faded from the Massachusetts sky.

But here I was, riding again toward those distant mountains, crossing countryside now as green as the land of Michael Flynn's birth. While I headed east, backtrackers were streaming west, washed out at last. But for every one of them, two newcomers were trudging or riding or wagon-wheeling along with me. It seemed that the worst of the winter rains were over, so the roads were drying, which made for better going.

It took me two hours to cross what I now recognized as the Vargas ranchero, but no one rode out to demand a tax. And to *El Patrón*, I would have paid.

I did not stop in the grove where Flynn and I had our meeting with him. But about five miles later, I was drawn to another grove, drawn by the need to pay witness, though to what, I was not certain. Turkey buzzards floated in the sky above. Crows cawed in the branches. And the air hung heavy with the stench of rotting flesh, as when we come upon a dead animal in the woods.

Then I saw something hanging from the branch of one of the live oaks. It was a man, hands and feet bound, head to one side, mouth open, tongue like a sausage grotesquely bloated from his mouth. A crow was perched on the corpse's shoulder, pecking at his eye, not bothered in the least by the soul-gagging smell.

I recognized the blue jacket, cut at the waist. Second Mate Sean Kearns had been wearing it when he signed the Sagamores aboard the *William Winter*. Around his neck was a crudely lettered sign: *Deserter*. So the stories about Trask were true.

I would have buried the corpse, but I had no shovel.

I REACHED BROKE NECK as the evening chill settled and felt like a man returned to the ancestral manse, only to find a new family moved in. The camp seemed more crowded yet less busy, as if everyone who had put aside mining for the rainy months had found their way here, to winter where supplies, whiskey, and gambling were easily come by.

And Grouchy Pete could accommodate them. He had been building a proper saloon when we left. Now it was finished, a fine place to escape the rain and occasional snow of the foothill winter. He had even imported a handsome mahogany bar and stand-up piano from San Francisco, so music was rolling out of the saloon, along with loud talk, louder laughter, and a large collection of legless drinkers.

Noticing a familiar sorrel horse tethered outside, I stopped for a swallow of whatever McDougall was passing off as brandy.

Faces turned as I stepped in. Some I recognized through the cigar smoke and lantern light. Some were new. A few I had not seen since the Sagamores broke apart. At two tables in the far corner, a pair of gamblers—one wearing a top hat and satin vest, the other a white suit contrasting with pomaded black hair—were mining more gold than the miners with much less effort. Cletis was standing just inside the door. Micah Broadback and a few others had collected around the wood stove. They were chatting and half listening to a loudmouth by the bar, who was declaiming, "Once a mining camp gets big enough, you need to expand the council."

Cletis seemed in no way surprised to see me. "Did you get my letter?"

"Letter?" I leaned against the wall beside him.

"Wrote you a letter. Brung it to Abbott's three days ago."

"What did it say?"

"'Where the hell are you? I ain't heard a peep out of you.'"

"I was sick."

Cletis gave me the once-over. "I'll say."

"Almost sent for you to help me. But Vargas sent his grandson, the boy Rodrigo."

"Vargas?" Cletis cocked an eyebrow. "Strange country. Friends become enemies. Enemies make friends." He gestured toward the bar. "You got any friends over there?"

"I know a few. Wouldn't call them friends, exactly."

"They been askin' for you. Been doin' a lot of big talkin', too. And speakin' of big talk, where's Galway Bay?"

"In San Francisco."

"What's he doin' there, outside of fuckin'?"

"More fuckin'," I said. "Have you met Hodges?"

"Not yet. But his friends are stirrin' for an election, and—"

The air was ripped by a gunshot. All the jawing and laughing and music stopped. Grouchy Pete waited for the shock to settle, then he lowered his pepperbox and shouted, "I'm done with all this political yammerin'. You're cuttin' into my business. I say we run a new election, then get back to drinkin'."

Micah Broadback jumped up and shouted, "We picked a council nine months ago, agreed on the particulars, and done what needed to be done."

"Damn right," added Stinkin' McGinty from the end of the bar. There was not another drinker within five feet of his smell. Some things did not change.

The big man who had been doing all the talking grinned and put a hand on the bullwhip coiled at his belt. The brown of the leather whip was the only color on him. Shirt, pants, boots, and vest were as black a priest's cassock. "My brother and me and our friends, we just want things on the up-and-up."

Broadback said, "This council been on the up-and-up. Me, the Johnson boys, Drinkin' Dan, Stinkin' McGinty, we've played fair all across this district."

"And we thank you for it," said the man.

"We?" said Broadback. "Who in the hell is *we*?"

"My brother and me—" He gestured to the man standing next to him, who looked like a deflated version of himself and actually wore a minister's collar with his black outfit—"and the men of Triple MW."

"The what?" said McGinty.

"The Massachusetts and Missouri Mining and Water Company," answered a man standing in the shadows near the bar. I had not seen him until now: Deering Sloate.

The big talker approached Broadback. He was still grinning, as if he knew that there was something sinister about flashing white teeth in the nest of a black beard. "My name is Moses Gaw, late of Joplin, Missouri. This here's my brother, David."

"Biblical fellers, are ye?" said Cletis.

"All good names are born in the Bible, sir," answered Moses.

Brother David kept his peace and kept his dark eyes on me. These were the men that Lyons had warned me about.

Cletis said, "If it's biblical names you favor, do you got a *Jesus* Gaw in the family?"

"Basphemy is not our way, sir," said David Gaw.

"Namin' someone *Jesus* ain't blasphemy to the Greasers hereabouts," said Cletis.

"Is that a fact?" Moses Gaw kept grinning. "Well, we won't be worryin' about them too much longer."

Brother David said, "We're just good Christian white men askin' for new rules."

Broadback said, "We agreed on hundred-square-foot claims and a hundred runnin' feet along dry gulches. We hang a man who kills and flog a man who steals. What more rules do we need?"

Moses Gaw said, "We need rules on water, rules on Niggers, Chinks, Greasers, and any others the Lord did not see fit to make white, and rules on whether such as them have the right to work on an equal basis with white miners. We need—"

"Too many rules get confusin'," said Broadback. "'Come and go and do as you please, just so long as you don't bother no one else.' That works just fine."

"A place without rules ain't a place to last, and we mean to last in Broke

Neck." Moses Gaw spread his arms. "So, as claim holders in this district, we're callin' for a new election in due time, as is our right." And out of the corner of his mouth he shot this at Broadback: "You honor the rights of *white* miners, don't you?"

"What's due time?" asked Broadback.

"A week," said Grouchy Pete. "That's fair, 'less you want to step down, Micah."

"Hell no," said Broadback.

"It's settled, then. All candidates gather in front of the saloon at noon a week from Sunday," said McDougall. "You got any complaints, Mr. Moses Gaw?"

"To prove that I have none, I'll stand every man to a drink."

That brought a cheer from the crowd, but from Micah Broadback a plaintive whisper to Cletis: "Ain't I done fair in this district?"

"As fair as Solomon cuttin' his kid in two." Cletis had been Bible-reading again.

The crowd got back to drinking and betting and yakking, but then Stinkin' McGinty shouted, "Who in hell said I *stink*?"

"I did," said Deering Sloate. "And I'm not voting for anyone who stinks."

And the room fell silent. Certain men had a sound to their voice, a timbre of trouble, that could stop any conversation. Sloate practiced it.

"Hell, Sloate," said another Sagamore, "we *all* stink."

"I'm not voting for a man who smells like his own asshole." Sloate kept at it.

"He's goading," I whispered to Cletis, "just to show how dangerous he is."

"McGinty does smell awful bad," said Cletis.

"And he's an easy one to goad," said Broadback.

Everyone was listening now. Even the roulette wheel had clattered to a stop.

McGinty said, "You must've gotten your nose awful close to my asshole to know what it smells like, mister. Are you one of them nancy-boys who like assholes?"

"Am I *what*?"

In point of fact, he was. I must say it honestly.

Moses Gaw said, "This ain't talk for a friendly saloon. Take it outside."

"Yeah," said Grouchy Pete. "Outside."

"If they take it outside," I whispered, "McGinty won't come back."

That seemed to be what Sloate was goading for. He said to McGinty, "If you want to talk more about your asshole, I'll be in the street. Maybe I'll give you another one."

McGinty said, "I ain't afraid of you, you asshole-sniffin' son of a bitch."

I took a step, but Cletis grabbed my arm. "You got a wall at your back. Keep it there."

Micah Broadback did not hear that advice, for he certainly did not heed it. He pushed past us with his hands up high, not threatening, and approached McGinty. "Now, boys, let's don't do nothin' rash."

"He looks at me crosswise," said McGinty, "I'll pull on him, by God."

"That ain't a good idea," said Broadback.

Sloate said, "I'm lookin' at you crosswise right now."

And Micah Broadback made his mistake. I had seen him stop McGinty before for his own good, right at our claim. He reached now for the pistol in McGinty's holster, and McGinty tried to knock Micah's hand away, a simple motion that sealed his fate.

The blast and smoke hit McGinty at the same instant. He looked down at the hole in his belly, then dropped like a hundred pounds of brick.

After a moment, Moses Gaw broke the silence: "He was pullin' on Sloate. You all saw."

"I was takin' his gun," said Micah Broadback. "It was an accident."

"Accident pullin' on Sloate," Moses Gaw looked around. "Ain't that right, Brother David?"

"So saith the Lord."

From somewhere in the shadows, a familiar figure pushed forward and knelt over McGinty. He said, "I'm Doctor Beal."

McGinty was moaning in rhythm to the blood pumping onto the sawdusted floor.

Grouchy Pete leaned over the bar. "Want a whiskey for him, Doc? On the house."

Doc Beal shook his head and told McGinty, "You just lie quiet."

"I . . . I can't feel my legs," said McGinty. "I can't feel my goddamn legs."

Doc Beal reached into his little black leather case and pulled out a bottle of laudanum. "This'll take the pain."

I stepped from the shadows with my hands well away from my sides.

Sloate's eyes shifted but showed not a glimmer of surprise. His gun was back in his holster, and he seemed entirely composed, strangely satisfied, as if he had just finished a good meal or a good . . . something else.

I tried not to look at the wide circle of blood spreading under McGinty.

Sloate spoke as casually and contemptuously as if we were aboard the *William Winter* or back at Boston Latin School. "What is it this week, Spencer? Pencils or pens?"

Now, every eye turned in my direction.

I turned mine to Doc Beal. "Hello, George."

Doc Beal gave me a nod, poured a measure of laudanum into McGinty's mouth, and told him to swallow.

McGinty's eyes were searching the ceiling, as if watching his soul leave his body.

Sloate said, "Write it down for the *Transcript* that I killed a man in self-defense."

"Same excuse as when you shot one in San Francisco?" I said.

Sloate looked at bleeding McGinty. "Same result, too."

McGinty let out a final low groan, a loud fart, and breathed his last.

Moses Gaw stepped between me and Sloate, still grinning like a hungry bear finding a fresh carcass of elk. "So this is the writer."

Cletis stepped up behind me. "And I'm his pardner. Welcome to Broke Neck."

The sight of the blunderbuss crooked in Cletis's arm warmed my heart.

Moses kept grinning. "Glad to be here. Maybe your friend will write a speech for our candidate." He shifted his eyes to me. "You heard of him, I think. Samuel Hodges."

"Tell him to come by and say hello," said Cletis.

February 4, 1850
Morning at the Claim

The cry of a rooster awoke me. *A rooster?*

I had been expecting Hodges or his men, not roosters.

Cletis heard me stir, and from his pallet he said, "That damn rooster's the only bad thing about the Chinks having chickens."

I went to the cabin door and looked across the river.

The Chinese were moving about in the chill morning air. One was gathering firewood. Another was stirring a pot. A third was tossing cornmeal to a dozen pecking birds.

"They spent good gold dust to get a few hens and a rooster. Now they got chickens and eggs. Ever taste egg blossom soup?"

"You mean they *feed* you? You don't even like them."

Cletis scratched at his stubble. "They like me, and I like their soup."

"You liking their soup I understand, but them liking you?"

"I warned 'em when the river was fixin' to rise. Figured it was the Christian thing to do. Saved all their gear. After that, they adopted me. Now, they bring me hot soup, and I give 'em weather wisdom and Bible verses."

"You'll make Christians of them yet." I looked out at the flutter wheel, standing firm in the middle of the stream. "River's gone up and down some since I left."

"It'll come up again with the snowmelt," said Cletis. "Yes, sir, a river's a livin' thing, risin' then fallin', runnin' then walkin', then gettin' up and leapin' like the Lord."

My claim and Flynn's were underwater. So Cletis suggested I stake one a bit above the edge of the river. "Don't want those Triple MW fellers thinkin' there's any room for 'em here." Cletis poked up the fire, greased his pan, cracked four eggs into it. "That was some nasty gunnin' your Boston friend put on last night."

"He's not my friend. Not now. Not when we were in Boston."

It was good to sit again at the rough table with Cletis and swallow strong coffee in the morning. The cabin felt like home now that it had a proper door, which Cletis had built himself and hung with leather hinges.

"I tell you, I worry some about them Chinks." Cletis flopped two fried eggs on my plate. "What that Moses Gaw feller said ain't far from the truth."

"About what?"

"About makin' rules on who can mine where. This country belongs to the United States now, so real Americans should have the say-so."

Cletis had his contradictions, I knew. I ate some egg and sipped some coffee and waited for more wisdom.

He put the frying pan on the table—he still avoided dirtying plates—and sat. "Foreigners catchin' it all over . . . like the French down Mormon's Gulch. They was infringin' considerable on the rights of us Yankees, doin' what they pleased, no matter what the Miner's Council said. Pretty damn saucy—"

"Good term for a Frenchman."

"What?'

"Saucy. The . . . unh . . . the French. They're known for their sauces."

Cletis gave me a long look, as if he was thinking about calling me an educated fool again. Then he returned to the point. "These Frenchies got so troublesome, the local *alcalde* decided to go round to the other diggin's to get some help."

"For what?"

"For drivin' them out," said Cletis. "He come back with a hundred armed Yankees and give that gang of frog-eaters five minutes to pack up and leave, or else they'd run 'em off and sell the tools and tents at auction."

"By what right?"

"Miner's Law and the plain rights of God-fearin' white Americans." Cletis shoveled an egg into his mouth and wiped a dribble of yolk from his chin. "French ran like rats. Then there was that gang of Chili-eaters down Sonora way."

"Chili-eaters?"

"Fellers from Chile. Good miners. Too damn good. Made the whites resentful. So they got chased. And don't forget the Injuns. Over in Woods-ville, them sneak-thieves was stealin' food and tools, even jackasses. White miners had to take a few scalps and send 'em skedaddlin' with their squaws and papooses." Cletis finished his coffee. "Yes, sir, too many dusky folks around here, and more comin' every day."

"So you're for chasing off the Chinese?"

"*I* ain't. But others will be. With less gold to go around, it stands to reason it'll get nasty. But the trouble them Chinks have, it's as old as dirt. Don't make it your trouble, too. Even if you like that little Chinese gal."

"Who said I liked her? Flynn was the one giving her candy all the time."

"I seen how you looked over there last night . . . and just now. She's awful pretty with her little Chinese feet and her little Chinese titties."

"How do you know?"

"I snuck down there one night myself. She was takin' a bath in the river."

"Why, you dirty old man." I said it with admiration, and we got to work.

Mid-morning, Chin came across with two pots. One contained ginger tea, the other soup. "My sister say you look like you been sick. Skinny like handle of shovel. She think you need tea for to make stomach better. Chicken soup for to make full."

"I lost weight. I did not die."

"Good not to die. Where Flynn? She want to know."

"In San Francisco. I don't think he's coming back."

"My sister sorry to hear. Not me."

So Mei-Ling had liked Flynn's peppermints more than my longing gazes. So much the better.

February 7, 1850
Samuel Hodges

There was music in the turning of the wheel. A steady rhythm of push and whoosh, push and whoosh, push and whoosh and splash, all the day through. And nothing brought more focus to a distracted mind. When the wheel was turning and the water was flowing and we were spreading gravel in the Long Tom, Cletis Smith and I were engaged right to the bottom of our souls.

We ignored the weather, the Chinese, and the stream of men now traveling on the road above our piece of river. Miners went on foot, on horseback, and in wagons laden with supplies, all headed for the big up-stream claim of the Triple MW.

At midday, Cletis and I were sitting in the cabin, spooning Chinese chicken soup. I had my back to the open door, so I noticed his reaction first. Then he said, "What the hell is this?"

They had come at last. There were four of them:

Moses Gaw was running his finger along the riffles in the Long Tom. His brother David was standing nearby, holding their horses. And another mounted man was up at the road, watching everything, like a guard.

But the real presence was the big man on the black horse at the edge of the river. His hands were folded on the pommel of his saddle. His head was turned because he was studying the Chinese, who were working hard at pretending he wasn't there.

Samuel Hodges was still as handsome as Byron, though much changed. His hair curled to his collar, his beard had grown full and thick. His black coat had been torn and mended. But one thing had not changed: the square of his shoulders bespoke more power than the turning wheel or the river that drove it.

As Cletis and I came down the bank, Moses Gaw held up a finger covered in dirt and gold dust. "Rich damn diggin's. No wonder you like it here."

Cletis had his scary old blunderbuss crooked politely in his arm, but his tone told everything. "How long you been in this country, mister?"

Moses grinned. "Long enough."

"Not long enough to know you don't touch a man's tools or his pay dirt 'less you're invited. Now wipe that finger on the edge of my sluice and take a step back."

Moses Gaw did as he was told, though by his motions made it plain that he was not ordinarily so compliant.

Hodges gave Cletis a glance, then said to me, "You seem to favor hotheads, James. Where's the Irishman?"

"San Francisco."

"So he deserted you? I hope that this old veteran serves you better."

Cletis said to me, "Is this the Boston windbag? The one who wants to mind everybody's business?"

"I mind my own," said Hodges. "And my friends'. Isn't that right, Mr. Gaw?"

"It's why we threw in with you, Mr. Hodges. Shrewd Boston Yankees and strong-backed Missouri muleskinners. We make a good team."

"What do you want?" asked Cletis.

"Your vote," said Moses. "We're visiting claims in the district, telling what we'll do for you boys, so you'll vote for our slate on Sunday."

Cletis said, "What can you do for me that I can't do for myself?"

David Gaw said, "Guarantee a white district for the white Americans."

I knew that Chin, squatting downstream, was listening while pretending not to.

Hodges swung his big head toward the Chinese. "Things might not go so well for them, but . . . we'll be humane. Maybe we'll hire them to dig a trench to Rainbow Gulch."

"Mindin' Chink business, too?" said Cletis. "A man starts mindin' other men's business, he may get to likin' the idea."

Hodges ignored Cletis and said to me, "I'll count on your vote, Spencer. We want to make this the best damn mining camp in the Mother Lode."

"Why?" I said. "Men mine and make money, or they don't and move on."

"We're after building something more than a camp," said Moses Gaw.

"Much more." Hodges kept his eyes on me. "But you knew that back in Boston."

The rider on the road inched his horse down, "Sir, we've other claims to visit."

I recognized my old friend, Christopher Harding. I waved to him.

He had grown a black goatee and pulled his hat low. "It's good to see you, James."

I said, "Thank you for not shooting me the night I left the ship."

Moses Gaw mounted his horse and said, "Harding wouldn't do that. He's one of them Boston gentlemen. But I ain't."

Samuel Hodges, backing his horse across the stream, said, "We'll take it kindly if you vote for us. Then you may interview us for the *Transcript.*"

February 10, 1849
Election

Too much democracy can be a dangerous thing. That is why the framers of our Constitution chose a republican form of government, with checks and balances to keep the baser instincts of the voter—or of him who would court the vote—in check.

While Californians at the coast had convened a legislature and awaited news of statehood, up here in the hills where such aspirations had been born, democracy functioned on its most basic level. One man, one vote, majority rule.

And would the majority vote for Samuel Hodges?

The miners turned out on that pleasant Sunday to keep holy the California Sabbath in all the usual ways. They came from claims up the river and down. They loaded their wagons and burdened their mules at Emery's. They lined up outside Abbott's Express to post letters. They brought high spirits or got into them soon after they crowded the outdoor bar that Grouchy Pete had set up. And when someone started strumming a banjo, someone else pulled out a harmonica, and a squeeze-box started to wheeze, and soon, miners were jumping about and pounding their feet in a rough imitation of dance, though it appeared more likely that they were trying to stomp an army of roaches.

Micah Broadback and the Johnson brothers came through this crowd, pumping hands all about and promising that things would be as they always had been in the District. But Drinkin' Dan had decided to sit this one out, a decision made after Moses Gaw stood him to a night's worth of whiskey in Grouchy Pete's.

"You got our vote," Cletis told Broadback.

"Thank you," said Micah. "Never seen miners wanted to be on the council so much as these Triple MWs. Most of us is here to dig for gold, but these boys—"

Whatever Broadback was about to say was drowned out by the bang-boom of a big bang-booming kettle drum coming down the road.

All the other music and talk and politicking stopped, and every man turned.

Bang-*boom*-boom-boom-boom!

Into town marched two dozen men of the Massachusetts and Missouri Mining and Water Company. I noticed Sloate and Christopher Harding, Doc Beal, Attorney Tom Lyons, two of the Brighton Bulls, and half a dozen others. The only mounted men in this group were the Gaw brothers, and Samuel Hodges himself.

They paraded through the crowd, and Sloate fired his Walker Colt into the air, all as if it had been planned, stage managed like a Boston play. (For that, I credited Christopher Harding, whose love of amateur theatrics at Harvard was widely known.)

"If this don't beat all," muttered Micah Broadback.

Moses Gaw shouted, "Drinks all around, as soon as the votin' is done!"

That brought a mighty cheer.

Micah Broadback said to Cletis, "My claim ain't rich enough for buyin' drinks."

"The boys'll vote for you still," said Cletis. "They know you done the job."

I knew otherwise. Hodges had won already. If the drinks hadn't done it, his promises would. He asked to speak first, proclaiming that the new-coming challenger should defer to the incumbent.

Cletis and I retreated to the little porch in front of Emery's for a better view of Hodges, who climbed onto the makeshift speaker's platform—a flag-bedecked buckboard in front of Grouchy Pete's—and eyed every man as if he could see into their hearts and know their frustrations. His rock-like presence seemed to comfort men, even calm them. All the disappointments and defeats of the last year had not diminished him, especially when he wore his black coat with a clean white shirt and a red cravat.

He began by telling of our journey from Boston, the collapse of our company, and its rebirth when he met "these good men from Missouri and their God-fearing wives."

"You got wives?" shouted someone.

"We sure do," answered Moses Gaw.

"Are they pretty?" shouted someone else.

"Who cares?" shouted a third.

"They sure are," said David Gaw.

"How come you didn't bring 'em?" shouted another.

"'Cause of how pretty they are," answered Moses Gaw.

And everyone laughed. Oh, but there were high spirits in Broke Neck that afternoon.

"Now, boys," said Hodges. "We have no desire to change any of the good things that Micah Broadback and his council have done. So we'll interfere with none of the hard-working white American miners. But for foreigners, there'll be changes."

And that brought an ear-splitting, jaw-cracking yowl in the dry air.

Hodges raised his hands. "Who denies that white Americans took this place from Mexico?"

"Nobody!" shouted Deering Sloate from the back, bringing a cheer.

"Who denies that white Americans discovered the gold?"

"Nobody!" shouted Christopher Harding, in the middle, bringing a louder cheer.

"So who denies that we have the right, the *right*—"

The cheering was growing so loud that Hodges had to stop, while Moses Gaw walked back and forth on the buckboard, like a bear in a cage, waving his hands for the men to pipe down.

Then Hodges shouted, "Who denies that we have the right to limit the number of Mexicans comin' into our district to look for gold?"

More cheering and general shouting.

Hodges cried over the noise: "God put American gold in American ground so good Americans could dig it up."

"It's prophesied"—Moses Gaw held up a Bible—"in the good book."

And from the booming shouts and gunshots that greeted Gaw's gesture, I knew that his argument was good enough for most of the men of Broke Neck, even though Cletis whispered, "I guarantee there ain't no such prophesy in *my* Bible."

Hodges continued, "Therefore, I speak for all of us, from New England and Missouri and the good states of the South, when I say—"

Cletis whispered in my ear. "Here it comes—"

"—that from this day on, any foreign miner who wants to work a claim in Broke Neck will have to pay a tax of twenty dollars a month at the Abbott Express Office."

The cheer was so loud it brought a chill up the back of my neck.

Micah Broadback leaned over to the Johnson brothers and said something that looked like, "Wish I thought of that." He and the Johnsons conferred a bit more, then he put up his hands and shouted, "I concede. Let the Hodges slate have it by acclamation."

Now came more celebratory gunshots and hats skimming into the air, then Hodges, with a grand air of noblesse oblige, accepted his election and invited Micah Broadback to join him, "for his good counsel and opinions."

"Very smart," said George Emery, standing next to me on his porch. "Bring your rivals into the fold."

Hodges waited for quiet, then said, "I will run the council like a New England town meeting. So I'll ask for a voice vote. Be it written by David Gaw, our secretary."

"Can he write?" shouted one in the crowd.

Yes, spirits were still climbing, and jokes were flying.

"He can write *and* shoot," said Hodges. "Be it written, all Mexicans, Chileans, Chinese, and other non-Americans will have to register and pay or get out of our district." Hodges let another ovation subside, then he said, "I have it on good authority that every miner's district in California will be levying a tax on foreign miners. That's word from the assembly in San Jose. So let Broke Neck show the way."

And the subsequent roar was punctuated by more gunfire and the beating of the big kettle drum.

They say that in 1848, right after the discovery of gold, California was a place of almost religious harmony. The horde had not yet arrived. There was gold enough for everyone. So men tolerated each other, overcame their prejudices, and devoted their energies to rewarding labor. But resentments had begun to simmer with the rising population, and they overflowed before the end of '49.

I should not have been surprised in early 1850, then, that Samuel Hodges would seek to expand his power by playing on the fears of men for whom there was less and less to share with more and more strangers, many of whom looked, spoke, and dressed strangely, too. But I was not merely surprised. I was infuriated. Chinese had become my friends. Californios had threatened me only later to save my life. And what they wanted for themselves and their families was no more than what white men wanted for theirs.

"We don't give a damn about showin' the way," shouted a miner. "We just want better claims for the white men. And free drinks!"

"Before the drinks," answered Hodges, "the vote. All in favor of taxing foreigners, signify by saying, 'Aye.'"

And hundreds of men roared out the word, as if this would solve all their problems in the California diggings.

Hodges nodded, "Any opposed?"

I could see beards shaking, heads turning, eyes shifting. A few Chileans, who had been mining and minding their own business, lowered their heads and discreetly moved off.

I was not by nature a man who separated himself from the crowd. But I was learning to speak out, and I could not stop myself. I called, "Before the vote, a question."

Cletis whispered, "Watch it, Harvard."

I asked, "What do you plan to do with the money this tax brings in?"

"You serve your New England upbringing well," said Hodges. "Your Harvard professors would be proud of your questioning nature. So would your mother."

This brought a big laugh. Mama's boys were a favorite target of the self-styled toughs who strode around any mining camp.

Cletis whispered, "You got 'em laughin'. Let's get the hell out of here."

But once entered upon a thing, I did not know how to back away. So I kept talking, perhaps to my detriment: "You have no right to drive a man off his claim because you don't like the color of his skin."

"The miners of Broke Neck have given me that right," shouted Hodges.

Cletis said it again. "Time to leave."

But everyone was watching. I could not back down. I said, "That's money they worked hard for, just like every man here has worked hard."

"The money will be shared in the district, until the government in San Jose asks for it. We'll use it to dig trenches to keep water flowing to the places where men need it."

"Who will control this water?" I heard my voice echo.

"The laws are clear," said Tom Lyons from the edge of the crowd.

"He who has the water controls it," said Hodges. "The council will mediate disputes."

I was growing bolder. "So you set yourself up on the Miwok, above all our claims, then get control of the government, just to control the water?"

Moses Gaw hopped down from the buckboard. "If you don't like it, you should've stood for the council yourself."

The miners parted before him as he strode into the street and stopped where all could see him. Hodges had surrounded himself with henchmen: Moses Gaw, burly bully from Joplin, Missouri, in front of me, Sloate to my left, Christopher Harding to my right, others all about. I hoped that no one noticed my kneecap shaking.

Moses Gaw told me, "I don't like what you're sayin', mister."

"Then be like me," said Cletis from our perch. "Don't listen."

A few men got a laugh from that.

"If the California assembly says the tax is legal, it's legal," proclaimed Hodges.

"So wait for them to say it," I answered. "It's too big a law for one district."

"These men voted us the power to back the laws up"—Moses Gaw unfurled the bullwhip—"with force, if need be."

I had heard that he could use his whip the way I used a pen. He could snatch a fly from the tail of an ox at twenty paces or put out a man's cigar with the flick of a wrist. And before I could say another word, the whip snapped, wrapped around the pistol in my belt, and pulled it clear out. In another instant, it took the hat off my head.

I came down from the porch, tried to grab my pistol, but the whip snatched it away.

"We're whippin', not shootin'," said Gaw, "so keep your hands off that gun." And he snapped again.

I saw the tip of the whip, heard it, then felt my cheek open and the blood spill down.

At the same moment, Cletis was moving quick and certain toward his saddle and the blunderbuss that could end any argument.

But every other face was turned to me, some twisted with derisive laughter at another Silk Stocking meeting a real man, others contorted in shock or awe at the speed and skill of the whip master, and at least one gratified that Moses Gaw knew just the man to whip. Yes, Hodges was letting it all play out as if there was a lesson here for everyone.

The next snap of the whip went around my ankle and yanked my leg, so that I flew off my feet and hit the ground. When I banged my head, I wished I had my hat.

Gaw yelled, "That's what we do to Chink lovers!"

I rolled over and tried to see where Cletis and his old gun were. But Deering Soate was holding a pistol to Cletis's head. I was on my own.

Moses Gaw was hauling on the whip, dragging me toward him "Come on, Mr. Boston Writer, come and take the lickin' you deserve for insultin' our American democracy."

The men were egging him on, cheering his strength and anger. This was now nothing but great fun and good entertainment at my expense.

But if Moses Gaw thought that calling me a writer would appeal to my sense of myself as a gentleman, he was mistaken. I rolled over and grabbed a handful of dirt, rolled again, and flung it at his face.

Gaw bellowed and brought his hands to his eyes, but he never let go of the whip.

I tried to stand, and he yanked the whip again, slamming me onto my back.

"Now you've bought a real beatin'." Gaw strode toward me to deliver something—a bare knuckles or a boot—while the men closed around him.

Then, as if it had come from the sky, a fist flew from the crowd, a flash-pan left that drove into Gaw's big, broad belly and stopped him in mid-stride. He doubled up around the fist, and looked toward the puncher, just as a right hand shot from shoulder-level into Gaw's face. His nose crunched. He landed on his ass in the middle of the street, looked up dumbly, and a boot took him square in the jaw.

Michael Flynn had come back, and just in time. He spun around, look-ing into the eyes of every miner, and shouted, "If anybody attacks one of me pardners, he attacks me. Fightin' with Jamie Spencer means fightin' with me. Do you understand?"

I got to my feet, wiped the warm blood from my cheek, and grabbed for my pistol and hat.

Flynn shouted it again, with a kind of crazy Irish anger that he could summon when he needed it. "Maybe you sons of bitches didn't hear me. I said, 'Do ye's all understand?' 'Cause I ain't askin' another time."

Deering Sloate turned his pistol onto Flynn.

But I heard George Emery's voice, "Don't you be thinkin' of shootin' any of my friends, there, bub. You pull that trigger, I'll let fly, and it'll be too damn bad for whoever gets hurt." Emery stood in the doorway of his store, with his fowling piece at his hip. The miners downwind of him im-mediately gave way, making a wide berth for the spray of ball and buck that was sure to follow if Emery kept his word.

Hodges made a slight motion of his hand, and Sloate lowered the gun.

"That's better," said Emery, and he shouted, "You need to get control of your men, there, Mr. Samuel Hodges."

Moses Gaw by now had rolled onto all fours, spit blood, and reached for his whip.

Flynn snatched it away and threw it at my feet. "Go ahead, Jamie. Use it on him."

I wiped the blood from my face, picked up the whip, and—when David Gaw made a move, I snapped it. I was shocked by the power I felt at the end of my arm.

David Gaw stopped where he was. "Best put that down. Or it'll go awful bad."

Moses Gaw looked up. "You're bound for trouble, mister. Right now."

And here was the crucial moment. In half a second, we could all be spraying lead and leather and blood, but—

As always, Flynn knew when to throw water on rising flames. "Nobody's bound for trouble, Mr. Whip Man, so long as you stay calm. If you do, I'll give you first crack."

"First crack at what?" said Hodges, as if he was ready to leap down and exact the revenge he had been planning on Flynn since the Arbella Club.

"First crack," Flynn paused like an actor, then shouted, "at the women!"

In that transcendent moment, it was as if a second sun had burst though the blue of the cloudless California sky.

Women? *Women?* The word went flying faster than the tip of the whip, repeated a hundred times, two hundred, all in an instant. Women? *Women! WOMEN!*

Then we heard wild, high-pitched shouts from the west, and a female voice screamed, "Howdy, boys! Howdy! Howdy!"

A covered wagon came pushing up the road into the mob of men. A gang of painted women was waving from behind Pompey, who rode shotgun for Big John Beam. Yes, Big Beam, the two-legged San Francisco rat, was riding to the rescue, whipping the horses, shouting and yahooing in a voice loud enough to call the grizzlies down from the hills.

And among the Broke Neck mob erupted a riot of running, stumbling, rushing, pushing, until Michael Flynn leaped onto the wagon beside Hodges, and fired three times into the air. "You'll all get your turn, boys. We brung some fine ladies, and—"

A miner shouted, "I can smell 'em!"

Another shouted, "Smell 'em? I can taste 'em!"

Another one shouted, "I can't taste 'em, but my mouth's waterin'!"

Concerns about democracy, the taxing of foreigners, and the revenge that I now wanted upon Moses Gaw, which was surely as strong as what he wanted upon Michael Flynn—all of that faded in the cloud of perfume and high-pitched female laughter.

IT IS FAIR TO say that February 10, 1850, brought a greater transfer of wealth in Broke Neck than any day before or since (including the best days of '48, when the earth itself rendered riches to any man who could bend at the waist).

Samuel Hodges proclaimed that the Miner's Council would deliver to every man another free drink while they waited for Big Beam's Traveling

Circus of Earthly Delights to stake its tents and position its wagons on the south side of the road, right next to Grouchy Pete's. Then he sent the Gaw brothers home to their wives, no doubt because they had to appear as virtuous men. He also sent George Beal to see to my face, which would not stop bleeding.

Doc Beal took me to the rear of Emery's store, gave my cheek a look, and said, "Stitches." He then pinched the skin together and challenged my manhood with a curved surgeon's needle and thread, four times, painfully but neatly.

And in a reversal of a long-ago scene aboard the *William Winter,* Flynn appeared with a flask. "You have an awful habit of speakin' your mind, James Spencer. It'll get you into trouble. Ain't that right, Doc?"

"I'm glad he did," said the young doctor. "Honest words take root."

Flynn offered me the flask. "Ain't right, drivin' out foreigners."

I took a drink and said I was grateful for his help.

"Not at all, not at all." He offered us peppermints. "Thank me when I get you laid."

Doc Beal said, "These girls you've brought, are they clean?"

"They all had baths in San Francisco," said Flynn. "I washed Roberta meself."

"That's not what I'm asking," said the doctor.

"Well, come to think of it, I got a bit of an itch, like."

"I don't want a girl," I said, "whether she itches or not."

"Yes, you do, Jamie." Flynn caught Doc Beal's eye. "Don't he, Doc?"

"He's twenty-five. He wants something." The doctor raised an eyebrow, as if to ask if what I wanted was not a woman. "Be careful, both of you, or you'll both end up with the itch."

"Ah, but it'll go away," said Flynn. "Always does."

"If it doesn't," said Doc Beal, "come see me. I'll give you the mercury treatment."

"Shove a big needle up me pecker and shoot me full of quicksilver?" Flynn put his hands over his crotch. "Not on your life."

"That's not how it works. But it's not *my* life I'm worried about," said the doctor. "You both should be worried to start a war with the Triple MW. Hodges has changed."

"He seems like more of the same to me," said Flynn.

"No," said the doctor. "More dangerous."

"Love conquers danger," answered Flynn. "That's what I told Big Beam. I said, 'Too much love in San Francisco. Women arrivin' every day, some a lot better lookin' than what we're offerin' the stiff peckers of Portsmouth Square. So let's head for the hills. Bring some love to lonely miners.'"

I asked, "Are they the girls you had on the ship?"

"And a few more. You remember Señor Vargas? We stopped at his ranchero. He offered two girls, indentures up from Mexico."

"You mean, slaves?" I asked. "Sex slaves?"

The doctor shook his head, as if he did not want to hear more, as if it disgusted him, as if he had seen too much in every direction that disgusted him. He packed his instruments into his leather case and said, "We'll cut those stitches out in a week. I'll come to your claim, just so long as that old man with the blunderbuss doesn't shoot me."

"Once he gets his poke," said Flynn, "he'll be downright docile."

I said, "Cletis? He's in line for a poke?"

"He damn sure is." Flynn took me by the elbow. "And you need one yourself."

FLYNN LED ME OUT onto the porch of Emery's Emporium.

Though the days were getting longer, the lanterns were already ablaze because when dark came to those foothills, it came quickly. George Emery was leaning against a post, looking across the street at a line of miners outside the largest of the new-pitched tents.

Flynn said, "You been over there, Georgie boy? Considerin' all you done for this town, I could get you one on the house."

"My wife would kill me. And don't call me Georgie."

Flynn, always impossible to insult, tipped his hat. "Well, you don't mind if I give Jamie a tour of the titties and bums, do you?" And he led me toward the tent.

I stopped in the middle of the street and said, "I'm not sure about this."

I know how naïve I sounded. But my experience with women was as limited as my experience with life had been when I boarded the *William Winter*. I had gone far toward expanding the latter. I wanted to expand the former. But—

"Come on, lad," Flynn whispered, "Sally Five-Fingers won't make you a man, nor teach you how to love a woman. And there's a long line of fellers who seen you take a beatin' already today. If you don't go into one of them tents with a bulge in your breeches and come out pantin' from the pokin', they'll call you a nancy-boy for sure."

"But—"

"I have someone special for you." And he told me to wait. Then he jumped to the head of the line, ignoring the grousing miners. In the tent, Big Beam had set up a table on which were scales, a loaded fowling piece, and hourglass timers. After a few words, Flynn gestured for me to follow.

And I went. I wanted it as much as any man in Broke Neck. And I decided that what Janiva did not know would not hurt her.

"You got fifteen minutes," said Flynn.

Then he led me through the back flap and down a line of six smaller tents lit by lanterns hung from poles. Beneath one of them stood Pompey, arms folded like a harem guard. All around him rose the sounds of male satisfaction, of female urging, of the grunting of every man desperate to make the most of his time before the sand in his glass ran out.

I said to Pompey, "I see you found something other than cooking."

"Oh, we cookin', Mr. Spencer. And the food be very tasty."

Flynn led me to the last tent and shoved me through the flap.

I expected to see a woman from the ship, like Roberta or Sheila, wrapped in crusty sheets or stained camisole. Instead a small, birdlike girl of dusky complexion sat, head down, on the edge of the cot. Her eyes darted up to me, glistened briefly in the dim light, then turned down. She wore a clean, plain dress, a black ribbon around her neck, and a red ribbon in her hair, which was wet and combed back, as if someone has spruced her up a few moments before I entered.

I did not smell that feral, female aroma that I remembered from the other whores. If I smelled anything, it was fear. I said, "Good evening."

She kept her eyes on her hands in her lap.

Outside, Pompey shouted, "Hey, Number Five. Fifteen minutes up."

In the adjoining tent, a man began to pound harder, the thump of copulation causing our canvas walls to vibrate as if the breeze had just stiffened.

Pompey repeated, "Time's up!"

"But so am I!" said the man in Number Five, then he whispered, "Damned embarrassin' to be explainin' such things to a nigger."

"If you ain't out in sixteen seconds," said Pompey, "you'll pay another ounce."

I heard the man finish, stumble, jump, bump, and fall out of the tent next to ours.

I said to the girl, "He's very clumsy."

She nodded but did not look up.

I sat beside her on her pallet and asked her name.

She said, "It does not matter."

"You are very young."

"I am sixteen, señor." Her accent was thick with the music of Old Mexico. "Please do not hurt me."

I took her hand. I knew what I wanted to do. I was simply mustering the courage to do it. I asked, "Have other men hurt you?"

And she stopped me with this. "There have not been other men."

I was shocked. I said, "I am the first to—"

She took her hand away and folded it on her lap. "This is my new job."

"And before?"

"I work at the Vargas hacienda, washing and cooking. Then Señor Vargas tell me to go with Beam and the Irish man who talk so much. *El Patrón* say times are hard. He need to make more money. So he sell me and—"

"*El Patrón?* With the broken leg?"

"His son. Back from the gold fields with nothing to show. Back now to run what is left of their ranchero. The old señor is dying."

Any lust I felt for her, in my head or my loins, drained quickly away. She did not want to be here, not for desire or commerce. I leaned over and kissed her cheek. She neither rejected nor invited. But when she turned her face, so that a shaft of light fell upon her from the lantern outside, I recognized her.

This was the girl who had cared for me in my sickness at Sutter's Fort. Whenever Rodrigo could not come, she had brought me beef broth and clean water. She had been gentle and kind. I took her hand and reminded her and thanked her for taking mercy on a sick man.

Then Pompey shouted through the canvas flap.

My time was up. I said good-bye.

Maria thanked me for my kindness.

I felt better hearing those words than if I had spent half the night spending myself inside her. I felt better for me . . . but worried for her.

Outside, I made sure to walk with a bit of a strut, so that Flynn would sense a change in me.

"How you feelin'?" he asked.

"Fine, just fine."

"The quiet type, eh? How was she?"

"A nice girl."

He gave me a long look, then said, "I'll be damned, Jamie, but it's the quiet ones who do the best. You could go far with the ladies. But for now, let's go home."

"Home?"

"Back to the claim."

This puzzled me. I thought he had found his life's work in whoredom.

He said, "I woke up the mornin' after you left and thought, damn me, but Jamie's right. I come to here to find a river of gold, not little trickles of it dribblin' from the dicks of randy miners. So I'm splittin' with Beam. Takin' me share, gettin' back to manly work."

There was nothing to say to that, so we walked some in silence. Then I stopped.

"What?" said Flynn. "Do you want to go back? Get another poke already?"

"What would you think of me buying that girl I was just with."

And Flynn laughed in my face. A burst of whiskey breath and bacon, loud and maniacally amused. "By Jesus, you're in love!" And he started walking.

I followed on, saying, "Not in love. But—"

"You spend fifteen minutes in a little Mexican gal—or was it fifteen seconds?—and you think—"

"She's not made for this."

"She got a pussy, ain't she? Besides, the old *Patrón* was worried that his grandson, Rodrigo, was fallin' in love with a girl from a lower class, so they sold her to us."

"For how much?"

Flynn led me to a buckboard beside Beam's covered wagon. He flung back the canvas, revealing a load of supplies—coffee, flour, bacon, brandy, beans, and four hogsheads of gunpowder. "Beam and me, we bought up a lot of supplies, agreed to divvy 'em when we split. *El Patrón* offered us the girl if we'd barter. He didn't need food, but he said he could use some gunpowder. So he took nine hogsheads. We kept the rest."

"Why gunpowder?"

"He's sellin' it to miners. Good for blastin' holes in hard rock. Never know but we might need it ourselves. And with Emery's prices, it's for damn sure we can use the rest of the supplies, too."

February 11, 1850
Chinese Eggs and Chinese Gold

In the morning, I stepped out of the cabin and saw something I had never seen in six months in California: a smile on the face of Wei Chin. He was brewing tea at our campfire, and two large sacks were curled at his feet.

He stood and offered a deep bow. Then the Chinese across the river stood as one from their tasks and raised their hands over their heads and clapped, causing the birds to flutter up from the bushes on the bank above them. Uncle Bao, Friendly Liu, Ng-goh, Little Ng, and Mei-Ling sent their joy echoing up the valley and down.

"They know your words in the town yesterday," said Chin. "They thank you."

I did not say that if I'd had it to do again, I might have held my peace.

The noise brought Flynn and Cletis stumbling out, and I noticed Flynn's eyes brighten. Then he turned and went back into the cabin.

Mei-Ling was crossing the river, climbing for the first time toward Big Skull Rock. She carried a small lacquered box before her with great ceremony until she stopped directly in front of me. She handed the box to her brother. Then she withdrew a tin of salve from her sleeve and, with a delicate gesture, daubed some on my face, which had swelled so that my left eye was all but closed.

I admit that I was filled with warmth and desire both. Had she been the girl in the tent, I would not have held back out of conscience, guilt, or fear of disease. But her brother was watching, and Michael Flynn was returning with a bag of peppermints, which he offered her, saying, "Here you go, darlin'. All the way from San Francisco."

Cletis laughed. "Now we got two fellers wantin' the same pretty Chinese girl."

She did not know what we were saying, but she accepted the candy, which she handed to her brother. Then she took the box and held it forward.

Chin translated as she spoke: "My sister say she make for special times. *Maodan.*"

Flynn looked into the box and said, "Eggs! Hard boiled?"

"Pickled special egg," said Chin. "*Maodan.*"

Flynn reached for one and Mei-Ling slapped his hand.

"First one go for man who speak for us," said Chin.

Mei-Ling now held the box to me. "*Maodan.* Good." She nodded and made a gesture as if to have me take an egg.

I lifted one from the box, looked at Chin, who gestured for his sister to help me. She took the egg and, with a dainty touch, removed its top. I expected to see white, but instead, I saw a beak, and bulbous, blackened eyes, and the little pea-sized brain of a cooked embryo.

Flynn said, "Now that's what I call hard boiled."

"Feathered egg," said Chin. "Great delicacy."

My face must have turned gray at the prospect of eating it.

Cletis whispered, "You turn down their fancy food, and all the good you done speakin' up for them won't mean a damn thing. You'll never get to touch them little titties."

Chin said to Cletis, "That never happen."

"Certainly not by Harvard," said Flynn.

Chin aimed a dagger-eye at Flynn, too.

But Mei-Ling continued to smile and nodded for me to eat.

So I took the egg, then she raised her finger to stop me. I thought I had been saved from my fate. But no. She took a pinch of salt from the box, then a pinch of pepper, then a dash of something red from a bottle. Then she made a drinking motion.

"Down the hatch, Jamie," said Flynn.

I raised the egg in a toast to the Chinese below. Then I brought it to my lips. If I could have held my nose, I would have. But I closed my eyes, and down it went. I refused to gag. Even when the feathers tickled the back of my throat and the beak scratched the roof of my mouth. I concentrated on the salt and pepper masking the taste of cartilage, bone, and cooked organs. I swallowed, breathed hard, held it down, and was done.

Mei-Ling smiled and nodded. *Good, no?*

I took another deep breath and said, "Delicious."

Cletis grinned. "Surest way to a man's heart is through his belly."

"Delicious," said Chin. "And good for man who spend time in fuck tent."

Flynn said, "You mean eatin' them little cooked chicks'll make you stiff?"

Chin nodded.

"In that case." Flynn grabbed the other egg and sucked it down, much to my relief and his distress.

Mei-Ling did not stay. At a look from her brother, she bowed her head and scurried back down the bank.

Wei Chin picked up the two sacks and said, "Inside? We talk? We talk inside?"

So into the cabin we went. I took a swallow of tea to wash out my mouth. Flynn threw back a shot of whiskey.

Chin dropped the sacks onto the table. "I pay you to watch this."

"What is it?" asked Cletis.

"From the way it thumps," said Flynn, "I think it's gold."

"Our gold," said Chin. "Chinee gold from piles white men leave. Sixty pound in two bag. You keep safe. Bury with yours, under big rock."

"How do you know where we bury our gold?" asked Cletis.

"I look. I think. And I think, if Miner Council come, they maybe try take our gold. Like they do to Frenchmens at Mormon Bar. If they give us five minutes to go, how we save our gold?"

"By payin' whatever the tax is," said Cletis.

"No pay. No pay tax. No pay 'less you pay," answered Chin. "Or him." Chin jerked a thumb toward Flynn. "He foreign, too."

"Got a point there." Flynn burped. "Damn feathers." He tapped his chest to coax another burp, then said, "If we bury their gold, we charge five percent."

"Five percent? You rob me," said Chin.

Cletis shook his head, "Don't matter. We ain't doin' it. I don't want any more trouble than what you Chinee boys brought on us yesterday. If not for them gals comin' in, we'd have been in a fight for fair. Nope. This is dangerous damn business. So we all need to agree. We need to be anonymous."

"Unanimous," I said.

"That too." Cletis grabbed his shovel and headed for the door. "So the answer is no. I ain't stickin' my neck out again. I ain't buryin' Chinese gold."

Chin did not wait for us to say more. He threw the sacks over his shoulder and stalked back down the bank.

Flynn said, "I knew they was sittin' on somethin' rich."

"We should protect his gold," I said. "Put it with ours under Big Skull Rock."

"And if somethin' should happen," said Flynn, "like the Chinks get driven out so fast that they can't come get it, well, we'd just have to hold it, and invest it, and—"

"That's not why we'd hold it."

"Why then?"

"It's the right thing to do. If you don't know that, why did you came back?"

"I came back for gold, Jamie. I came back for a river of gold flowin' through this promised land of California. I came back for gold and I mean to get it, however I can."

In the days that followed, the passions of the men dissipated between the legs of Big Beam's women. Moreover, the mining was good, the Chinese were docile,

*and Hodges seemed to have delayed his plan to expel foreigners. But what were
the men of the Triple MW up to? James Spencer decided to find out.*

*Cletis counseled against it, but Spencer considered this his job. And he had
four stitches for Doc Beal to remove. So he made sure that his pistol had fresh
loads, sealed with clean grease. He told Flynn to stay behind, so as not to provoke
Hodges by his presence. And he emptied his bladder, so as to be certain that he
would not piss himself from fear.*

A few hours later, he returned and sat to write:

The Mother Lode runs two hundred and fifty miles, north to south, in a
wide band that begins as the ground rises from the Sacramento valley
and butts at last against the granite wall of the Sierra. There is ample
room for men to come and go and never see each other once they have
separated.

Thus, I had little expectation of encountering the Sagamores again,
but I have the pleasure of reporting that I was wrong. They have united
with others and created the Massachusetts and Missouri Mining and
Water Company, establishing a claim comprised of many contiguous
claims on the upper Miwok, where the river turns north and cuts between
two hills formerly covered in tall pines.

In my capacity as Yr. Ob't Correspondent, I took the road that comes
up from Broke Neck, runs past our claim, then carries across a long ridge,
rising gradually, to a promontory from which you may look down on the
entire Triple MW operation.

I stopped there to take it in: three cabins and a longhouse; fresh
stumps stubbling the landscape; new logs piled in pyramids atop the hills;
muleskinners driving skids of logs along the bank; men in a saw pit cutting logs into boards; others digging a ditch beside the river or collecting
dirt in wheelbarrows and delivering it to a sluice beside a flutter wheel;
half a dozen women, as rock-hard as their men, washing clothes, stirring
pots, sweeping dirt out of the cabins.

Then I heard a ragged volley of pistols, four or five going off nearly at
once. My eyes traced the rising plumes of white smoke to a target range
where Deering Sloate, formerly of Dorchester, was giving pistol lessons to
a handful of men. On the voyage, he had promised, "Every man a marksman." Perhaps by this, he sought to make good.

Then Christopher Harding startled me with his appearance from the
nearby brush. He said that he had been watching me up the road, as it was
his task to guard this approach to the camp. He is an old friend and a true

gentleman, despite the bristle of weapons protruding from his belt, and he bid me follow him.

As we descended, men stopped in their labor to give me a greeting or glance. Some appeared curious. Others glared with open hostility. But I presented a cordial expression, despite the four stitches under my right eye, which gave me a fiercer look than the readers of Boston might remember.

Stopping first at the tent of Doctor George Beal, I sat while he quickly and painlessly removed the stitches, displaying all the skill we would expect from a graduate from Harvard's Medical Annex.

Then Samuel Hodges received me in the biggest cabin. He has seen the inside of many a Boston boardroom and knows how to present himself. So he was sitting behind a table, with a roaring fire on the stone hearth and an American flag hanging over the mantel. But I did not approach him with the awe that he once inspired. Experience in this country has changed us both.

He complimented my courage for riding into a camp where I have more than one antagonist.

I said I did not count Doc Beal in that number and was thankful for his ministrations after my altercation with Moses Gaw, the Missouran now allied with Hodges.

That alliance, announced Hodges, was soon to be affirmed, in that he was betrothed to Moses Gaw's daughter. Yes, you disappointed ladies of Boston, Samuel Hodges intends to take a California wife, a young but plain woman named Hannah Gaw, who will presumably mother his two daughters when Hodges sends for them at last.

He explained that his alliance with the Missourans had strengthened all of them. "And joining with a woman in holy matrimony strengthens any man. That is why we have partnered with family men. They are already strong, reliable, and responsible and seek to settle the land, not merely exploit it."

Was that why they were cutting so many trees, stacking logs, sawing lumber, gathering rocks, piling dirt, and digging a long ditch beside the river, I asked.

"We plan to divert the Miwok and control it," he said. "As the Lord has given us dominion over the birds and the beasts, he wishes us to have dominion over the land and the flow of the rivers."

Hodges explained that soon, they would dam half the river and run the rest through a wooden flume controlled with a sluice gate. And for what purpose, this massive effort of engineering and labor? Why, for gold, of course. To expose the riverbed for mining, to generate a strong, continuous flow to run pumps that would keep the bed dry, and to drive flutter wheels for washing the gravel. The dam would also create an upstream pond from which to sell water to the dry diggings at Rainbow Gulch. It was a measure of how seriously they took this work that they were doing it in March, when the river was far more difficult to control than in August.

I suggested that all this might cause resentment downstream.

Hodges said, "The law favors us. I won't let downstreamers stand in the way of progress. The man who builds a textile mill cannot bow to the woman who runs a loom in her parlor. The corporation that lays iron rails cannot bow to the whims of he who makes wagon wheels. I've told you before, we are remaking the earth here, not just digging for gold."

I asked if he was also hoping to remake our society with his promise to implement a foreign miner's tax.

He gave a sage nod as if to signal how much thought he had given to this matter. "We will be informing the foreigners soon, giving them the chance to leave and avoid paying. But we will implement the tax only when we receive word of its official passage from the assembly in San Jose."

Moses Gaw had joined us by now and said, "In the long run, the law will benefit us. If it doesn't, we'll change it."

Hodges added, "Those who do not pay will be treated like the French at Mormon Bar."

"America for Americans. That's our motto," said Moses Gaw.

Hodges gave another nod, as if to show his approval of such comments, even if he found them to be no more than a film on the surface of his own deep lake of thought. He said, "Tell them in Boston that men who have known disappointment, defeat, and despair have rallied around us and our vision."

My response to my old mentor was that he had become a dangerous man. If this discomfits any who knew and loved him in Boston, I am sorry. But his answer was characteristic of the man I now knew. He told me that if I was not prepared to be dangerous, I should go back to Boston, "where you can believe what you want at ease, because your beliefs will never be tested."

Yr. Ob't Correspondent
The Argonaut

———— ❧ ————

March 1, 1849
Before the Mail

I allowed my pardners to read my dispatch when we broke off work at midday. Our lunch was beans and coffee and the prose of James Spencer, which
I flatter myself had a kind of flow and rhythm not unlike the wheel turning
in the river.

But nothing that Flynn or Cletis read made them happy.

Cletis said, "They're plannin' to take our water."

"Can't take it all," I said. "The whole district will rebel."

"If they clear out the Chinks and Greasers at the same time as they're
takin' the water, it might be enough to keep the boys happy."

"Oldest trick in the book, that," added Flynn. "Offer a little with one
hand while takin' a lot with the other."

"Well, boys, I been thinkin'"—Cletis stood—"gold veins go dry as fast
as youth goes by, and our color's gettin' thin. May be time to pull up stakes."

"Pull up stakes?" said Flynn. "On a payin' claim?"

Cletis spat and went down the bank. "Can't stay here forever."

Flynn and I sat in the midday sun and watched the wheel, thumping
and turning, thumping and turning, as Cletis took to shoveling.

Flynn said, "I think the old boy's losin' his nerve."

I did not answer, perhaps because I was beginning to wonder if pulling
up stakes might not be the best course. Was water really worth a fight? Was
the dwindling supply of gold? Were the Chinese, who would have to learn
to fend for themselves?

Flynn must have sensed my thoughts. He was good at reading people.
He said, "You know, Jamie, Hodges is right."

"About what?"

"About gettin' dangerous, or goin' home."

Flynn was right, too. I had come to write about this world, but I could not
stand aside while others struggled to create a society. Still, I was no fool.

I said, "No matter how dangerous we are, Hodges has twenty men or
more. Those are bad odds."

"Jamie, me lad, odds don't matter to me one damn bit." Flynn stood and
brushed the dust from the back of his breeches. "If they did, I'd be back in
Galway, hoein' spuds. But all me life, I had men tellin' me I couldn't do this
or couldn't say that and best keep me place, no matter who said what to me.
It's why I come to California. Any man can get a piece if luck favors him

here, no matter where he come from and no matter how many stripes he has on his back. And I won't let any one man take that away from me . . . or any twenty."

"So if Hodges takes the water, you'll fight?"

"If I have to. But I been learnin' from you, Jamie. You always think before you fight. It's a fine trait. So"—Flynn tapped his head—"I been doin' my share of thinkin'."

"Thinking can be dangerous, too," I said.

"Especially if you do it right." Flynn disappeared behind the cabin. A few minutes later, he was back, leading our two horses. "Let's go for a ramble."

WE HEADED ACROSS THE roadless hills, traveling south by southwest, studying the terrain, marking the places where the slope would be strong and give weight to water, noting down the places where we would need a wheel, perhaps, to move it along, or a wooden sluice to guide it all the way to Rainbow Gulch.

About halfway there, Flynn said, "I wish we'd brought Chin. He might see things we don't."

"He'd see how hard it is to dig a trench six miles."

"That's for fuckin' sure," said Flynn, "but if we make deals in Rainbow Gulch and get them boys water before Hodges can, we'll have standin' amongst them when Hodges steals our flow."

From what I had seen, miners sided with the men who made it easy for them to mine. And if the Triple MW sluice reached Rainbow Gulch a few weeks after ours, with a better flow at a better price per miner's inch (the measure of water hereabouts), the men of Rainbow Gulch would shift their allegiance to Hodges as easily as they would shift their attention from an old hag to a young beauty. But like two quixotic knights we rode on, seeking salvation in sharp thinking and square dealing with men whose only goal was to wash dirt.

At length, we came to the little graveyard where Hiram Wilson would sleep until the Second Coming. We stopped and looked down on Rainbow Gulch, bathed now in the high, hopeful spring sunshine. Hundreds of miners worked the claims at the bottom and along the gulch. But they would not be working for long, for the water was already drying up.

Some were anticipating this. Half a dozen wagons were rolling west out of the ravine. And over on the plateau on the south side of the gulch, two men were busy with shovels, but they were not mining. They were planting. It looked as if they were planting grapevines.

Flynn said, "Do you reckon they got a Miner's Council here?"

"We can ask Scrawny Selwin, if he isn't dead yet." I spurred my horse, but Flynn remained, staring out across the ravine. I stopped and asked him what he was doing.

He said, "Doin' like Chin. Lookin'. Thinkin'. Wonderin'."

"Wondering what?"

"Why there's so much gold here, so far from any runnin' river. Where did it come from? Another river, maybe? A river that dried up?"

"We could ask Chin, if he wasn't still angry that we wouldn't bury the Chinese gold with our own."

"If that's all it takes for him to give us that sharp Chinese eye, then we should hold his gold for nothin'."

"And give it back to him when he asks."

"My only thought," said Flynn. "Bury it. Bury it deep. Bury it safe. Just like our own."

"So . . . did they bury the Chinese gold?" Evangeline dipped her spoon into the tiny jar of strawberry jam and spread it on her croissant. "Or did Manion show us his section of the journal just to prove that they *didn't* bury it, so we should stop bothering him?"

"Not sure." Peter sipped his coffee. "But I think he likes it when *you* bother him."

"Please." She took a bite of croissant.

"I think *you* like it when he bothers *you*."

"Right now, you're the one bothering me."

They were eating breakfast by their window. They liked the view of Nob Hill. And she liked to luxuriate over room service in a hotel bathrobe, with wet hair wrapped in a plush towel. He liked his robe, too. He also liked looking at her in terrycloth.

He held up a piece of bacon. "Ever wonder why they call these rashers?"

"Focus, Peter. The journal. The gold. The big rock."

"Big Skull Rock?"

"Do you think you can find it?"

"I found it. Yesterday."

"You found it? Why didn't you tell me?"

"Yesterday, I didn't know the Chinese wanted to bury their gold under it."

They had both stayed awake to read. Neither of them could sleep. Not surprising after a bad night in the back of Wonton Willie's limo or another cryptic phone call. Evangeline drifted off around two. Peter kept reading till the end.

Evangeline popped the last of the croissant into her mouth. "Two bags of Chinese gold, each weighing thirty pounds. What would a bag be worth in today's dollars?"

"Precious metals are measured in troy ounces. Twelve troy ounces to a pound, almost half a million a bag at thirteen hundred an ounce."

"Nice haul," she said. "But enough?"

"For what?" He dipped the bacon into his fried egg.

"For all this trouble." She poured more coffee. "For the Spencers to get all twisted over . . . for your son to drag you out here over . . . for Chinese gangsters to start whacking each other over."

"Have your ears stopped ringing from the gunshots?" asked Peter.

"I have tinnitus. I hear hissing, not ringing."

"Too many rock clubs in your twenties."

"I ran a flower shop, remember? I was dreaming of a nice, quiet life."

"Boring." He finished his egg, took a sip of coffee.

"*Your* lifestyle was not what I signed up for." She unwrapped the towel. Her hair dropped down, wet and stringy. She saw his look and said, "I know what you're thinking."

"What?"

"Gray hairs. You see gray hairs up under the blond."

"Even gray hairs look good on you."

"You'd better say that. You gave me most of them."

"You know . . . this is what couples do best."

"Give each other gray hairs?"

"Know what they're thinking across the breakfast table."

She finished her coffee. "So what am I thinking now?"

"I should shave. Male-model stubble looks lousy on me."

"Wrong." She stood and toweled her hair. "I'm thinking you need to get this Wonton Willie off our backs, because I don't want any more gray hairs."

He put an arm around her waist.

She allowed the arm, but she knew just how to stand to tell him she wasn't interested in anything but conversation.

And he knew the signals: *don't push*. He said, "It looks like we're back in it."

"So, focus. What's your plan?"

"Have another chat with my son."

"LJ has become a very evasive young man."

"He didn't pick up when I called him last night. He just texted, 'Stay the course.'"

"We need to know the course before we can stay it."

"We start by visiting the California Historical Society."

"Why? You think they have answers?" She finished toweling.

"We need a baseline. Who was looking at the journal transcription? How often was it requested? That kind of thing." Peter put his face against her robe and inhaled.

She let him enjoy the moment. She enjoyed it herself . . . for a moment.

But he knew enough to keep talking business, no matter how good she smelled after a shower. "The reading history of the transcription can tell us a lot."

"Not us. *You*." She slipped out of his grasp.

"Are you quitting?" He sat back, sensing that the moment was slipping away, too. "It's all right if you're quitting. It's dangerous. And I hate giving you gray hairs."

"No matter how many times we get into these things, I never quit on you, do I? And I wouldn't quit on LJ. But I'm not letting some Chinese thug stop my work out here."

"What work could be more important than finding Spencer's journal, and Flynn's lost river of gold, and the bags of Chinese gold? In no particular order?"

"A helicopter ride with Manion Sturgis."

"Sturgis? In a helicopter? What the—"

"I brokered a meeting between Manion and his brother in Napa." She headed for the bathroom. "Relax, Peter. It's research. The brother makes Cabernets. My editor told me to write about Cabernets. So I'll take the ferry to Alcatraz, then—"

"Alcatraz?"

"The National Park Service lets Manion land there. Pretty cool."

"Yeah. Cool as hell." He watched her go padding off to the bathroom. No chance now that they'd finish breakfast in one of the single beds. He finished his coffee instead.

THE DAY WAS DANK and overcast. Sometimes it began that way in San Francisco and ended in sunshine. Sometimes it began in sunshine and ended in cold fog. And sometimes you got all four seasons in a single day.

Downstairs, everything seemed back to normal. No police tape. No one paying attention to Peter Fallon. No Ms. Ryan in the lobby. He even asked for her at the concierge's desk, but no, she had checked out. And no one followed him across the traffic turnaround or noticed him pounding past the Fairmont, down Mason, moving like a man who was very pissed off.

Helicopter ride with Manion Sturgis? *Jesus.*

Breakfast table chitchat clearly hadn't worked with Evangeline. Maybe a little fatherly talk would work with LJ. The boy had always hidden his emotions, even during the divorce, but he was playing things way too close now. Time for a face-to-face.

And it was early enough that LJ might still be at home.

So Peter followed Mason's drop down to the corner by the Cable Car Museum, where he stopped and texted his son: "I am right outside. I need answers."

LJ texted back. "On the way to L.A. Following journal lead. At airport now."

Peter answered, "BS. I can see you in your bay window."

LJ: "Not me. Maybe Mary forgot something and came back. Talk tonight. Cocktail Reception, NPS Maritime Museum. Big SF history event. 5:30–7PM."

Peter decided to back off. "Okay." But now what?

Somebody was up in that apartment, and it did not look like Mary Ching Cutler.

Best find out who it was . . . and maybe find a few more answers.

Peter knew that his son always kept a hiding place for an extra key—in Cambridge, in his apartment in Berkeley—always where Peter could find it. Force of habit from back when LJ was a latchkey kid and he feared that on visitation days, Dad might get to the house early and leave if no one was home. Peter had always promised that he'd wait in the car all afternoon if need be. Still, the key was always there.

Why should it be any different in San Francisco? So Peter turned onto Jackson and climbed his son's stoop. The building was a post-earthquake classic: wood frame, blue and white paint, big windows with a bay hanging out over the intersection, two sets of names on the buzzer box. Apartment B, top floor: Fallon/Ching-Cutler.

But . . . an inner door and an outer door. This might be harder than he thought.

He looked around. No pedestrians, but over on the downhill corner of Mason and Jackson, three Chinese guys, talking and smoking and laughing. Two of them were wearing hoodies over ball caps. One of them was circling idly on one of those bikes with undersized wheels, curb-jumping, spinning, killing time. Were they waiting for a ride? Or a meet-up? Or were they on a stakeout? Of what? LJ's apartment?

Peter was happy that Evangeline wasn't with him. Sometimes, it was easier to go solo. It attracted less attention. He took his own keys out of his pocket, pretended to fumble with them, dropped them, all so that he could kneel. While he was down there, he ran his hand along the threshold. And . . . right where he had expected it: the key, duct-taped to the underside. LJ really *was* a creature of habit.

But a single key . . . for three doors?

Give it a try. Into the main lock and . . . pop. Open. The same with the inner door. He let it close softly behind him. Then he slipped off his loafers. No footfalls on the stairs. And up he went . . . to the landing at Apartment A. He stopped and listened. No TV or radio. No movement. Nothing.

So on to Apartment B, stairs leading right up to the door. He listened: silence and city sounds. Would the same key work? No. But he found another duct-taped to the underside of that threshold. Into the lock and . . . pop again.

He pushed the door open but did not step in, just looked. Everything he saw was rehab modern: a galley kitchen across from the door, with counter and stools opening on a living area and that big window with its view down Jackson all the way to the Bay Bridge. Everything high-end, well-chosen, sleek . . . leather furnishings, leather window seat, glass tables, granite this, stainless that. To his right, a hallway, open doors, a window at the end.

The clanging of a cable car startled him in the silence, but he stayed where he was, right on the threshold, listening. Then he heard movement in one of the bedrooms, then a door opening, and a draft blowing down the long hallway.

Someone was running. He dropped his shoes and followed the draft to the end, to a pair of doors: one led to the bathroom, the other onto a service porch. He stepped onto the porch. Stairs led down to an alley and up to the roof. A gate on the downside appeared locked. So . . . above? To a trap door that opened to the roof? Or back into the apartment? Or stand still and listen for footfalls?

Hard decisions in a place he'd never been. He heard muffled traffic. Somewhere a radio was playing.

He took the lid from a rubber trash can on the landing and held it like a shield. He wished he had his shoes, too.

He led with the lid and climbed until he could just poke his head above the roof line: Right, left, nothing, nothing. He turned toward the front of the house: a fire escape dropping down between two windows. No one hiding. No one running. No one coming at him with a knife. He was glad of that, and glad that no one saw him with the trash can lid. He looked pretty stupid.

He dropped back down, replaced the lid, went back into the apartment, to a room along the hallway that had caught his eye: the office. At dinner, the kids had talked about the office. They worked in the same room, which Evangeline thought was cute.

Peter stopped in the doorway and looked in at a mess.

Then a tight, nervous voice surprised him: "I am licensed for concealed carry in California, and you are a home invader. I can blow your brains all over the wall. So put your hands behind your head and turn very slowly."

Peter did as he was told and was greeted by the barrel of a small handgun, a Walther PPK, maybe, and a widening set of eyes. "Oh, shit. Are you LJ's dad?"

Peter said, "You first."

"I'm Jack Cutler"—he lowered the gun and made a gesture for Peter to put down his arms—"your future in-law."

He was a tall guy, skinny, sunburned, dressed in a tan bush jacket and cargo shorts and big boots for tromping across dry fields or old vineyards in search of gold-bearing quartz veins. The adventuring geologist . . . or the host on a wild animal show.

Peter asked, "What are you doing in their apartment?"

Cutler gave a jerk of the head and led Peter back to a spot in the living room where they could look out the bay window without being seen. "Notice the three Chinese guys."

"We're on the edge of Chinatown," said Peter. "It's the white guys who stand out. But yeah. I noticed them. They didn't even look at me."

They were still smokin' and jokin' on that corner, with cable cars bumping past and street life flowing like a river around them.

"They may not have looked, but they were watching. And they're watching right now. I figured it out after I let myself in."

Peter asked, "Wonton Willie's boys?"

"Willie? Willie's small-time. A pimp." Jack Cutler put the gun back into the side pocket of his cargo shorts. "But if those guys cross the street, we ought to run. I think they work for the Dai-lo."

"The Dai-lo? The Big Dragon from the Triad?"

"Word is that he's coming to town. He might even be here." Cutler went into the kitchen, poured coffee for himself, and gestured with the pot. *Want a cup?*

Peter shook his head.

"I need some. Glad it's hot. You gave me the jitters. You and the Dai-lo."

"Is he why you're waving a gun around in our kids' apartment? The Dai-lo?"

"I need a little armament. I'm not really a civilian."

"What are you, then?"

"Long story. Google my name and 'gold fraud.'" Cutler went to another window and looked again into the street.

Peter didn't like the evasion, and he'd been getting a lot of it, lately. He said, "What were you doing in their office?"

Cutler's face got long, then longer. "Who said I was in their office?"

"My son's desk drawers are open. He never leaves his drawers open. He's a neat freak. And the computer is on. He never leaves his computer on. He's a green freak, too."

Cutler backed away from the window but kept his eyes on the street. "They're coming. We better go."

Peter snapped at Cutler, "Stop playing games. They're nobody."

"Hey, fuck you, Pete."

"Just tell me what the hell you're doing here. And don't call me Pete."

"Okay, *Mister* Fallon."

This was not going well, thought Peter. Meeting the future in-laws was supposed to be more civilized.

Cutler moved to a side window, above Jackson, and tracked the movement of one of the Chinese guys. "We got one coming up to the stoop, one still standing watch, and"—Cutler looked up—"if I hear anyone up on the roof—"

"Just tell me this: why is my son's desk ripped apart?"

"I wouldn't know."

"LJ does a thing as if he's choreographed it." Peter had believed that until the last few days. "He considers every move and doesn't move until he considers every option."

"Like marrying my daughter?"

"A very good move."

The compliment seemed to soften Jack Cutler. He said, "Yeah, well, they make a nice couple, but your kid's tap dancing right now."

"Why?"

"He's in trouble over this journal. He's helping the wrong people."

"Who?"

"You've met a few of them. Unfortunately, I'm in business with them."

"Are you in trouble, too?"

Cutler gestured to the window, "Half the people in Chinatown hate me, so, yeah."

"What are you doing here?"

"Research I should have done years ago, before that damn journal disappeared. I could have put all this business to bed before it started. But if the right guy puts it back together again now, he can—" Cutler caught himself, as if he did not want to say more.

"He can what?"

Just then, the buzzer rang. The electric sound snapped through the apartment and right through Peter's spine. Through Cutler's, too, from his reaction. Without another word, he drained his coffee and headed down the hallway.

"Where are you going?" said Peter.

"Back to my place in Placerville. It's safer there. I have a shotgun there. I should have stayed there."

Peter went after him. "What were you looking for in the desk?"

"The journal pages that tell where the goddamn Chinese gold is hidden."

"Bags of it? Or a lost river?"

"Everybody says the lost river is a myth. But the bags are real. If I find them, maybe I can have dinner in Chinatown again." Cutler disappeared around the corner.

Peter would have followed, but he wasn't wearing shoes. So he went back to where he had left them, by the front door, slipped a foot into one, and . . . the stairs creaked in the hallway. Somebody was out there. One shoe on, one shoe off, Peter listened, motionless.

On the street, a cable car clanged. In the kitchen, the coffee maker hissed. On the other side of the door, a person took a breath.

Peter reached for the dead bolt . . . an instant too late.

The door burst open and slammed into him and sent him flying into the stools, which went flying into the living area, with Peter Fallon flying right after them.

The guy was short and square and as solid as a fireplug. He reminded Peter of Oddjob, the James Bond villain.

"Where'd Cutler go." Perfect English.

"Cutler?" Peter played dumb. "What the hell are you talking about?"

"Fuck that. Where is he?" The guy came at Peter.

Peter rolled to his feet, grabbed a stool for protection, and retreated.

Could he talk his way out or would he have to fight?

Talk was always better. But if he had to fight, best know the ground. He shifted his eyes from point to point. Behind him: the bay window. Before him: the front door and the hallway to the bedrooms, blocked by Mr. Oddjob. To his left, through the dining area: the galley kitchen, with two entrances, one a few feet away, and the other opposite the front door. That would be his route.

He said, "Do you work for the Dai-lo?"

The guy scowled and reached into his jacket—black leather, a fashion statement in the Tong tough-guy community—and pulled a pistol with a silencer, also a statement.

The time for talk was over. Peter moved left, into the narrow kitchen, putting the countertop between himself and Oddjob.

"I count three, then shoot."

Peter pulled out the coffee pot and said, "Want a cup?"

"Fuck the fuckin'—"

Peter gave him hot coffee, right in the face.

The guy bellowed and brought his hands to his eyes.

Peter fired the pot right after the coffee, right at the guy's forehead, then he leaped for the front door.

But Oddjob grabbed him by the sleeve and spun him around.

Peter tore away and—oh, shit!—the front door was opening. Someone else!

LJ? Mary. The other Tongsters? Who ever it was, Peter didn't want them stepping into this, so he slammed the door as it opened, flipped the dead bolt, and sprinted down the hallway. He got to the doors at the end: one to the bathroom, one to the back steps. He stopped. Which way? And Oddjob caught him with a vicious flat hand into a kidney.

The pain made stars explode in Peter's head, and he hit the cold bathroom floor. Then a knee was dropping onto the middle of his back, pinning him to the tile.

This was no contest. Peter was a Boston brawler, who always ran if he could, up against a martial arts master who grabbed a fistful of Peter's hair and pulled back so hard that Peter thought his neck might snap.

"Where's fuckin' Cutler and what are you doin' here?"

Peter tried to mumble something while also reaching for something, anything—hair dryer, toilet brush, anything—to fight with.

Oddjob slapped his hand. "You talk or I put a bullet in your brain." And with his free hand, he pulled another pistol from an ankle holster and jammed it against Peter's temple.

Peter heard a pop. His neck vertebra? No. He could still feel hands and feet.

The guy released Peter's hair, gurgled, and slumped over. His head struck the edge of the tub with a *thwang* that made the whole room vibrate.

A woman in a blue pantsuit was squared in the doorway, in perfect two-hand pistol-range stance. Her gun had a silencer, too. She looked at the thug, then her eyes shifted to Peter. "Why did you flip the goddamn dead bolt? I had to shoot the door open."

Peter rolled, pushed Oddjob off, brought a hand to his neck.

She gave the thug a poke with the tip of her high heel. "Did he say anything?"

Peter recognized the woman who had been stalking him from the Mark Hopkins lobby. "You're the one the concierge called Ms. Ryan."

She ignored that. "Did he say anything?"

"About what?"

"About any goddamn thing? And in what language?"

"He spoke English."

"Good English?"

"Like a TV weatherman."

"That means they're using local talent."

Peter sat up and rubbed the back of his neck. "Now, who are you?"

"Your new best friend." She disappeared down the hallway and returned a moment later with his other shoe. "Put this on and get the hell out of here."

He asked it again. "Who *are* you?"

She pulled her wallet from her back pocket and flashed her identification. "Christine Ryan, FBI Special Agent."

He looked at the picture, looked at her, and said, "FBI? What's going on here?"

"Nothing good." She crouched and looked at the thug more closely. "Don't recognize him. At least he died in the bathroom. Easier to clean up." The way that she looked—red hair and long legs—reminded Peter of an old girlfriend. The way she acted—all business and attitude—reminded him of his current girlfriend.

"My son and his—"

"We're doing our best to keep them safe," she said as she rifled the dead man's pockets. "You, too. Just play your part."

"My part? In what?" Peter sat on the toilet and put on his other loafer.

"What did our friend here say?"

"He was looking for Cutler. But he didn't like it when I mentioned the Dai-lo."

"That's no surprise." She went to the back door and pulled it open. "Up the stairs. Do as you're told when you get up to the roof."

"Can't you help me out a little?"

"'Need to know.' And the less you know, the better. Just keep doing what you're doing, playing the dad with the special skill helping his son."

"What about Cutler?"

"He's on his own. We can't cover everybody." She gestured with her gun up the back stairs. "Louis is waiting for you."

Peter did as he was told. He had no other options. At least he had both shoes.

On the roof, an Asian guy in a Giants cap called from a fire escape four roofs away.

Peter climbed out and glanced toward Mason Street, just as a black SUV was stopping, and two big guys were bursting out, but the hoodies on the corner were scattering.

The guy in the cap said, "That's us, trying to clean this up. Come on."

So Peter went. Across one roof, two, three, finally to the fire escape next to the Cable Car Museum. He asked for the guy's ID.

Mr. Giants Cap flipped open his wallet: Agent Louis Lee. "Call me Louie."

"All right, Louie"—Peter climbed onto the fire escape—"you got any answers?"

"Miss Redhead is the answer lady. I'm all about the legwork."

Louie led Peter down to the alley. "I'm going one way, you're going the other."

"Then what?"

"Then get back to helping your son. You help him. He helps us. We all help the American people."

"The American people?" said Peter.

"That's our constituency." Louie started up the alley.

"Hey," said Peter.

"Yeah?"

"Tell your boss we made her in the Mark Hopkins lobby. We made *you*, too, at the airport and at the cable stop on California and in Hunan Garden last night."

"That's great, but I wasn't at the cable stop."

* * *

MANION STURGIS WOULD HIT on her.

Evangeline was sure of it. As the Robinson R44 Raven rotored in and touched down in the Alcatraz exercise yard, her expectation became anticipation.

This was a lot more than a vineyard tour. This was over-the-top chick charming. A helicopter ride, a sit-down between rival brothers, brokered by the chick in question, a sampling of some of the finest Cabernets in California. And a great story.

Manion Sturgis hopped out into the swirl of dust and helped her aboard, then he jumped in right after her, gestured to her seat belt, and gave her a headset.

The ground guy, an NPS Ranger holding his stiff brim with one hand, gave the thumbs-up, and the helo rose over that dank hive of concrete, the ruins of the legendary prison that now drew tourists and Hollywood location managers like acolytes to a shrine.

Manion bragged that he had some "juice" with the NPS. He also admitted to promising an article by Evangeline Carrington, the famous travel writer, about how well the NPS ran the San Francisco Bay Marine Park, if they'd just let him land.

And now the helo was airborne.

Manion clicked on his microphone and said, "Can you hear me?"

She gave a thumbs-up. She could feel the rotors thumping through the seat and right up her spine. Outside, the blue of the bay was widening and brightening. She had to admit that she liked the excitement. She liked Manion, too. Always had. And here he was, doing something he said he'd never do, just to make her happy. He was going to see his brother. She decided that she'd be disappointed if he *didn't* hit on her.

He introduced the pilot, mostly ball cap, shades, and headset. "Enjoy the flight, ma'am. If there's anything special to see, I'll point it out. We should be in Napa in about thirty-five minutes." *Click.*

Manion said, "If you want to talk to him, just press that button on your armrest." He reached across her body and showed her.

She did not pull back. There wasn't room. And she liked him. She liked the air about him. She liked his confidence and ambition and the speech he had made the day before. And maybe she was just a free market capitalist when it came to love. Competition made everyone better.

But she was too old for little brush-and-flutters—a man "accidentally" brushes across your breasts and you get all fluttery—so she said, "I know how it works. I've been in helicopters before."

"I'll bet you've never flown up the Napa Valley before."

The helo angled north, with the magnificent bridges bracketing them. "We'll follow 101 for a while toward Sonoma, then cut over to Napa."

"Like flying from Burgundy to Bordeaux," she said.

Manion nodded, "From the cool climate of Chardonnay and Pinot Noir to the heat of Cabernet and all its cousins. But I still grow the best Zinfandel."

Twenty minutes later, they were passing over Domaine Chandon in Yountville, and across the road, the restaurant called The French Laundry, or as Evangeline had once written, "a Bay Area shrine to the pilgrims of the palate."

Manion pointed it out. "Do you remember our meal?"

"How could I forget? Fantastic."

"I was trying to impress you. Meeting you after twenty-five years . . . that was the best part of our Harvard reunion. I was thrilled when you said you'd come out and visit."

"I was working. The Laundry was expensed."

"Ah, yes. Too pricey even for me." He patted her on the knee.

The pilot clicked on and said, "Opus One coming up on the right."

They saw the long allée leading up to the big house, and the glorious fields of grapes that one day would become Cabernet Sauvignon for a c-note a bottle.

He said, "Happy memories . . . a loaf of bread, a wedge of cheese, a bottle of '07."

"Maybe the best bottle of wine I ever had," she said.

"Too expensive. Not like my Zins. Wines for the people."

"Can I quote you?"

"I sure hope so." And he squeezed her hand.

She did not pull it away, but she did not squeeze back.

He said, "For the first time since our first wine competition, I'm nervous."

Oh, God, she thought, he's acting vulnerable.

"I wouldn't be doing this for anyone else," he said. "Really."

That was bullshit, made all the more bullish in that she was hearing it through the little speakers in her headset.

But he kept squeezing her hand. "I want to thank you for getting us together."

And she thought, *Now what?*

* * *

PETER NEEDED TO PROCESS what had just happened. He needed a shot of something strong and some coffee, too. And there was a place where he could get both in one cup. So he jumped on the Powell Street cable car at Jackson and headed for the waterfront. From what he could tell, no one followed him.

He got a seat on the outside and texted Evangeline. "Careful. Things heating up."

She texted back, "Tell me about it."

What? "Danger everywhere. Even in LJ's apartment. Not sure who friends are."

She repeated: "Tell me about it."

What did she mean by that? He decided he would worry later.

He texted LJ: "Jack Cutler in your apartment? FBI, too? WTF?"

Answer: "Keep doing what you're doing. Really AM in L.A. Remember, tonight, NPS Maritime Visitor Center. Cocktails and food. Appearances to keep up."

Peter jumped off in the waterfront park at the end of the line and bounded across to the Buena Vista. He ordered an Irish coffee at the bar where they claimed they invented it, then took a stool and watched it materialize: bartender pours hot water into shaped glass, warms glass, discards water, follows with sugar cube, generous shot of Tullamore Dew, coffee, then heavy cream poured over back of a spoon so it spreads and floats. The first sip—the cool cream, the hot coffee, the sweet whiskey—calmed him like a Sinatra torch song.

He wished that he'd skipped his son's apartment and started his day here instead, with eggs Benedict to accompany the Irish coffee.

He thought about a second, which would leave him feeling like he could handle anything. In his younger days, he sometimes drank too much, took pride in "going on a bender" once in a while to prove how tough—or how Irish—he was. But not now. What he wanted now was a clear head. So one Irish coffee, then hail a cab for the next stop, to keep doing what he was doing.

THE CALIFORNIA HISTORICAL SOCIETY had once occupied the Whittier Mansion in Pacific Heights. But real estate had grown so valuable up there that they sold and moved down to Mission Street, where they repurposed the old Merchants Exchange Building—gutted it, rehabbed it, quake-proofed it, and installed a climate-controlled storage area to protect the treasures.

Peter preferred the mansion. He liked the Oriental carpets and the Victorian flourishes. He liked the big tables and the high windows in the reading room. He liked the librarian who invited him to come back the next time he was in "the City," as if there was no other. He liked the civilized, old-school San Francisco tradition.

But the new building screamed "San Francisco," too, an evolution of today from yesterday, of cool from utilitarian. It looked like one of those celebrated Painted Ladies, two stories, with puce-colored blocks offsetting gray stone trim, big windows showing off new books and trumpeting new exhibits. Inside, it was all modern—shiny floors, glassed gallery spaces, big reception area. A docent directed Peter to the rear, into . . .

. . . a perfect rare-book room: steady 68 degrees, low humidity, windowless but well lit, though not too bright, so as not to overexpose delicate materials, a librarian's desk with clear sight lines, and on every worktable, little receptacles of sharpened pencils because, as in all rare book rooms, no pens allowed.

But what about other sharp objects, like matte knives or scissors? Stories of thefts in rare book libraries abounded, from Boston to Yale to the far shores of the Pacific. How easy would it be to lift something from the California Historical Society?

The room was empty but for a librarian at her computer. A slow day. She finished typing, then came over. Horn-rims: all-business. Name tag: MEG MILLER. Discreet *Ph.d* tattoo on the inside of her wrist: show-off.

Peter said, "Dr. Miller, I presume."

"What? Oh." She looked at the wrist and pulled down the sleeve of the black cashmere sweater, perfectly matched to the black of the horn rims.

He was hoping for a laugh, but it was a lame joke.

She gave him a level look. "How can I help you."

He played it straight. "I'm a dealer in rare books and documents. I'm purchasing some Gold Rush materials. So I'd like to familiarize myself with the collection—"

"Like what, in particular?"

"I'm just getting started."

And from the look she gave him, she was just getting annoyed.

He said, "I've read J. S. Holliday's book—"

"*Rush for Riches.*"

He really had. He had even sold a few in his catalogue. "I love the image on the cover. It comes from a daguerreotype—"

"*Group of Miners.* We have it. What else?"

He couldn't think of anything, so he leaned his elbow on the counter and said, "When I go to a restaurant, sometimes I trust the server's judgment about the menu."

"There's no daily special at the historical society, sir."

"How about a recent acquisition, then? Something that amazed you."

She gave him a longer look, as if she was intrigued, and told him to fill out a card. When she saw his name, she looked up with eyes wide behind the horn rims. "Peter Fallon? *The* Peter Fallon?"

He could not tell if she was angry or impressed or both. He tried to recall an auction where he outbid the California Historical Society. Nothing. So he said, "That's me. Cofounder and owner of Fallon Antiquaria."

She extended her hand. "I read your catalogue all the time. I love the essays on your offerings. You write like a historian."

So, he had found a friend. He said, "My doctorate is in history."

"Mine, too. Along with a degree in library science. And you just made the best request I ever heard. 'Something that amazed me.' Wait here."

Peter took a seat at the reading table and looked around. If there were cameras, he didn't see them. But given that Ms. Miller called in her assistant—name tag: Kim Hally—it was clear that they were always monitoring the reading room. Best practices.

He nodded. Kim Hally smiled and looked at her computer screen, even though her job was to watch him from the corner of her eye.

Meg Miller returned shortly with two archival boxes.

The first contained the original daguerreotype of *Group of Miners,* one of the most famous Gold Rush images: nine men, five seated, four standing, and all leaping from the plate. The first clumsy photographic process produced pictures that, in the original, were as three-dimensional as holograms. Peter moved his head, and it was as if their eyes followed him.

They looked cocky and confident. One balanced a shovel like a walking stick. Another cradled a Bible as if to proclaim that no matter how much trouble they got into, a mighty fortress was their God. One wore a neckerchief and held his chin just so. Another wore a kepi with a leather brim and glared, challenging you to insult him. And the center was held by an older man with a fringe of chin whiskers, a placket-fronted shirt, and the weathered confidence of one who had seen it all. Those last three reminded Peter of Spencer, Flynn, and Cletis Smith. And seeing those faces drew him a little closer to them.

Then, item two: a long ledger.

Meg Miller set it down on a foam backing, to prop it up, and opened in.

"This was recently discovered in a private collection. The Sacramento Death Registry for 1850."

It was the very definition of a primary source, research on the most granular level: the names of the dead, with ages, places of birth, causes of death. Early in the year, many things carried away the Gold Rushers, like pneumonia, scurvy, gunshots, gangrene. But as the year went on, more and more seemed to be dying from diarrhea or other bowel complaints. And by fall, those deaths had coalesced around a single cause: cholera.

"An epidemic," said Meg Miller. "Most were males in their twenties and thirties. Half came from New England."

"A lot from Massachusetts." Peter pointed out three or four names. Then he saw *Christopher Harding, age 26, Boston, Mass. Cholera.* And he felt a chill. The past was reaching right off the page. He said, "That's what a guy gets for killing an albatross."

"Albatross?" said Meg Miller.

"Like the poem. Christopher Harding killed an albatross and was cursed."

Meg Miller gave him a long look, as if wondering how he knew this.

But aside from Christopher Harding, there was no mention of any other Sagamore, no way to get beneath the surface of that daguerreotype or cross the bridge of time to James Spencer and the major players of 1849.

So what next? Peter Fallon was on a fishing expedition. So he threw out a bit of bait. "A lot of these guys left journals or diaries, right?"

"A literate generation, having their grand adventure. They called it 'seeing the elephant.' We actually have dozens of their journals."

"Back in the Arbella Club in Boston, there's a portrait of a man named Thaddeus Spencer. He had a son who—"

"So *that's* why you're here."

"What do you mean?" Peter made an innocent, wide-eyed face, but he could tell, from the way she folded her arms, that she saw right through him.

"Big-time Boston dealer with a rep for finding things that lots of people are looking for? You don't just wander in off the streets of San Francisco."

"Busted."

Kim Hally came through the room again, stopped to check something, gave them a sidelong glance, as if to ask her boss if she needed any help, then returned to the stacks.

Meg Miller waited until she was gone, then she said, "If you're trying to find the lost journal, remember, it's ours. If it surfaces, the historical society lays claim to it."

"The family would be happy to find it and return it. So would I."

She pulled out the chair and sat next to him. "All right, how can I help you."

"How was the disappearance discovered?"

"We received a grant to digitize a lot of the old journals, including the Spencer transcription, which came to us right after the earthquake. About nine months ago, we went to the box where it had been stored, and it was gone."

"And the last time it was seen?"

"A woman named Maryanne Rogers doddered in here one day about a year ago and wanted to read it. This was a few days after the *Proud Pilgrim* had been uncovered in the landfill during excavations on Clay Street."

"What's the *Proud Pilgrim*?"

"A Gold Rush ship. It sank into the Bay, and the city was built over it."

Landfill burying history? Peter Fallon had been down this road before. He said, "So it disappeared after she saw it? Do you keep records of who looks at what material?"

"Only for six weeks. I remember Mrs. Rogers because she was a big donor. But San Franciscans are protective of their privacy. Who reads what in any library—that's a sensitive area."

"Do you remember anyone else? Any other names? Manion Sturgis?"

"The wine guy?" She shook her head.

"Johnson Barber, the lawyer? Or LJ Fallon, his assistant, who is also my son?"

No and no.

Here was one that Peter had been thinking a lot about: "Willie Ling?"

"Wonton Willie, the Tong guy? Wasn't he shot last night at the Mark Hopkins?"

Peter nodded. "Why would Chinese tongs start shooting each other over this?"

Meg Miller thought a bit, chewed her lip, stumped.

The names Michael Kou and Jack Cutler got the same answer.

He asked, "Did you ever read the document?"

"Only the first chapter. There's so much material here that—"

Then he threw out a name. "Did a woman named Sarah Bliss ever ask for it?"

"Bliss. . . . Bliss. . . ."

"A great San Francisco name for a woman who looks like an old hippie and happens to be the heir to a nice chunk of the Spencer estate."

And that one worked. Meg Miller remembered the lady in the peasant skirt.

Next stop, Sausalito.

PETER TOOK THE FERRY from Pier 33.

Lots of folks heading home. Business people, shoppers, a few tourists, even a Chinese kid wearing a hoodie and carrying—yes—a small-wheeled Dahon folding bike. But . . . there are kids like that everywhere. And it was a nice way to commute, especially when your destination was the upscale town under the Golden Gate Bridge.

Peter followed the Gate 5 Road along the waterfront to Waldo Point Harbor, then walked out onto the Liberty Dock, named for all the Liberty Ships built there during World War II. Now it was lined with places that ranged from center-entrance colonials on barges to converted railroad cars to ramshackle collections of this and that cadged from whatever was floating around.

In the old days, all the houseboats could come and go under their own power. They took their water from hoses and got their sewage treatment courtesy of the twice-daily tide. Now water and sewage lines were permanent hookups. Nobody had engines. And the houseboats, known to their inhabitants as "floating homes," formed a fine exhibit in the living museum of California funk.

At the corner of the wharf, Peter saw the sign TREE HUGGER. As he expected, it was one of the more eclectic vessels, a ramshackle thing that looked like three or four other things all nailed and spliced and welded together.

He had called ahead, so Sarah Bliss was waiting outside with her Giants cap pulled low, shielding her eyes from an outbreak of afternoon sun. She was reading *National Geographic*. She looked up, "It says here that we used to have grizzly bears, right along the shores of San Francisco Bay."

"Hence the beast on the state flag." Peter looked around. "Nice neighborhood."

"Great scenery. Friendly people. We all keep keys under the doormats so neighbors can come in and borrow sugar or salt or rolling papers when we're not home." She waddled to the door. "Where's the pretty lady?"

"Doing her own thing."

"That's good." Sarah gestured for him to follow her. "That's the way relationships last, when you let the lady do her own thing. Isn't that right, Brother?"

A voice from within said, "Oh, yeah, baby. Whatever you say."

"I didn't know you had a brother," said Peter.

"I don't."

Peter followed her into the cool interior, a single giant space, a multi-level collection of dining areas, sitting areas, and sleeping areas, with windows popped in here and there like cookie cutters hanging on the walls of a bakery.

Everything had a kind of Dumpster chic about it . . . the 1950s kitchen set with the red vinyl seats, the coffee table made from an old cable spool, two recliners from a 1970s La-Z-Boy ad, posters of Che Guevara and Jimi Hendrix—Che on a red background, Jimi the centerpiece of a psychedelic pinwheel that was supposed to make the heavy drugs that killed him look mind-bendingly cool. And speaking of drugs, three marijuana plants thrived beneath a skylight.

Sarah introduced her husband. She actually called him her "old man," as if this was some kind of Sixties commune. But he really was old. His tie-dyed shirt covered a big belly, and his bushy beard and glasses made him look like Jerry Garcia, if Mr. Grateful Dead had been in a wheelchair, tethered to an oxygen tank, and angled so he could see out the open slider onto the boat channel.

He turned the chair. "I'm Benson Bliss. But people call me 'Brother,' Brother B., for Brother Bliss, brother of the downtrodden man, the rising-up *wo*man, and the nature-loving *hu*man." Then he chuckled, as if he liked his own wordplay.

And Peter knew already that he was going to like this guy.

Sarah offered Peter a cup of tea. "Or something stronger?"

Peter said, "I have a feeling that the tea is stronger."

"She makes a great marijuana tea," said Brother B. "I drink it all the time now, but let the record show that I never once appeared high before a judge."

Sarah chuckled. "That you know of."

"We fought the good fight to keep the city for the people, not the developers, and to protect the California environment from here to the High Sierra." Brother Bliss gestured to another photograph that Peter had missed: two men standing on a cliff above the Yosemite Valley: John Muir and Teddy Roosevelt.

"America's greatest naturalist and the conservation president. Aside from Lincoln, TR's the only Republican I ever let in the house." Brother B. gave Peter a scowl. "You're not a Republican, are you?"

"Unenrolled," said Peter.

"Even if he's a Republican," said Sarah, "he's from Massachusetts, and you know what they call a Massachusetts Republican in Texas?"

"What?"

"A Democrat."

Sarah and Brother B. had a chuckle over that. Nothing like an old couple laughing together. They probably needed to entertain each other, considering that he saw no pictures of children around. No sons or daughters. No nieces or nephews.

Peter said, "So you two have been fighting the good fight for a long time?"

"Too long," said Brother B. "I just wish my heart hadn't given out. Congestive bullshit. That's why I got ankles like baloney rolls."

Sarah jumped up and said, "Tea time." A pot on the stove was staying hot. She went over and grabbed it and brought back three mugs. She poured for her husband and herself, then waved a cup at Peter. "You won't regret it. I use a nice coconut oil to extract the THC from the leaves. I even add a little raw sugar."

"It makes me happy," said Brother B., "and not much does these days."

What the hell, thought Peter. If he joined them, it might loosen them all up.

And yeah, Sarah's marijuana tea was delicious, even if Peter didn't feel a thing after a cup.

She refilled it and said, "You're here because of that Gold Rush journal, right?"

"The codicil is bullshit," said Brother B. "Holding up everybody from getting their money is a cheap game."

Peter sipped the tea. "Whose game?"

"Barber's. And *you're* helping him," said Sarah. "Why?"

"My son asked me."

"Good dad," she said. "But who asked him?"

Peter said, "Barber."

"So Barber asked *your* son to play *his* game and *your* son asked *you*," said Sarah.

"So you're helping Barber to screw us," added Brother B.

Peter sipped some more tea. "Unh. . . . yeah. I . . . I . . ."

"Have you asked yourself why?" asked Brother B.

"Why what?" Peter felt his buzz growing buzzier, and the circularity of the conversation wasn't helping. Maybe that tea was stronger than he thought.

It didn't seem to be bothering the old folks, though.

Sarah said, "Why would a shithead like Barber, with a long list of nasty clients like big chem companies that make insecticides that kill bees and soft-drink companies that pump California groundwater in the middle of a drought, so they can bottle the water and sell it back to Californians at a thousand-percent profit, why would—"

"Don't forget the Chinese banks," said Brother B.

"Yeah, them, too," answered Sarah. "Why would he want to reconstruct an old Gold Rush diary, Mr. Famous Boston Bookseller? Why? Answer me that."

"Wait . . . what?" said Peter. "Did you say Chinese banks?"

"He damn sure did."

Brother B. said, "The banks are the tools of the Chinese government, and they're funding Chinese companies that are on a commodity-buying spree all over the world."

"The Chinese are no fools," said Sarah Bliss. "They know that if they buy the ground that holds the minerals, and leave them there, the minerals only rise in value."

"Like gold," said Peter.

"Gold, oil, iron, manganese, copper. They're into everything."

Peter felt things getting away from him. He tried to pull them back. "All I know is that somebody stole the diary out of the California Historical Society, and you, Miss Sarah the Teamaker—"

Sarah snickered. Her own tea was getting to her.

"—you were maybe the last to see it. That makes me think you're the one who stole it and doesn't want anyone else to read it."

"You feelin' a little buzz?" said Brother B.

Peter nodded. He liked the buzz. And he liked that he felt safe with these two. It was the first time he'd felt safe outside of the hotel room since he got to San Francisco.

"A little buzz is nice," said Sarah.

"At some point, it's all we got," said Brother B. "So why deny us? Why delay us with this journal business? I want that estate money so I can hire a few more lawyers to fight another good fight for weed against the Feds."

"A high goal," said Peter, and they all laughed a lot harder than the joke warranted, as if any of them, straight, would dignify it as a joke.

And the laughter must have put Sarah in a better mood because she went over to a messy, paper-piled desk in the corner and came back with an ancient notebook. She dropped it on the table in front of Peter. "Drink your tea, then read this. It's the only part of James Spencer's Gold Rush journal that I know a damned thing about. And I don't care if it sends you off lookin' for gold that isn't there."

"You mean, this is the section that starts another gold rush?"

"That's bullshit. Geologists have been over every last square foot of the Mother Lode. There's no more easy gold, no matter what Jack Cutler wants you to believe."

That name again, thought Peter, the rogue geologist.

"No more getting rich quick." Sarah gestured to the folder. "Read all about it."

Peter knew right away, even with a little buzz, that he was looking at the original article, in James Spencer's own hand, written on rag bond, folio'd foolscap, in ink that splotched as Spencer wrote, with few misspellings or scratch-outs, without the filter of transcription or Microsoft Word, a real bridge into the past. So he took another sip of the tea and started reading.

He still wasn't sure what he was looking for, but wandering the hills with James Spencer was like exploring them with Wild Bill Donnelly. Peter would know what he was looking for when he found it.

The entries for March 1850 spoke of calming tensions. Men moved up and down the Miwok, following strikes from below Broke Neck all the way upstream to the valley where the Miwok turned and the Triple MW was building a dam. Anti-foreign sentiments seemed to calm, too, especially when half a dozen Chileans packed up and left of their own accord. Now, only a few Mexicans were working west of town and, of course, the stubborn Wei Chin and his relatives, still squatting upstream of Broke Neck.

By late March, the claims at Big Skull Rock were playing out. But the river flow was good. So Cletis bought into the plan for selling water to Rainbow Gulch, as it "might be worth more than gold." Then the new government in San Jose issued a decree. . . .

The Journal of James Spencer—Notebook #5
March 27, 1850
The New Law

Today—beneath a cool blue sky—they brought the law to Big Skull Rock.

They rode down the north bank, crossed the river by the first flutter wheel, climbed past the second flutter wheel and the new sluice, climbed all the way to the trench we were digging at the top of the hill.

We had made deals at Rainbow Gulch. We had given Scrawny Selwin a commission on every miner he signed to buy Big Skull water. And the race was on. If Flynn believed that by bringing water to Rainbow Gulch, we could gain allies and avoid violence, I would try it. And Cletis, for the moment, was going along.

I had followed a deer trail over the hills to spy on the Triple MW camp. Even as one shovel gang was building the wing dam, another was digging two trenches, one southwest toward Rainbow Gulch, another due south in the direction of Broke Neck.

I had no doubt that they had spied on us, too. They might even have heard us because we had used Flynn's gunpowder to blow rocks out of our path, and the echoes had rolled like thunder up the valley and down.

But our progress had been slow. Wei Chin, who saw this as a safe way to prospect, had overcome his anger and brought Little Ng along, too, all for a price. But as we dug, Chin would stop often to reconnoiter the route or puzzle over the presence of random gold flakes in some dry gulch. And Flynn would repeat his suspicion that there must be a lost river of gold somewhere nearby, an underground river, just flowing and flowing. And it would fall to me to urge the work forward.

In college, I had read about the Roman aqueducts that delivered water across hundreds of miles. So I knew that in a slope of just one foot per mile, in a conduit three feet wide and three feet deep, we could create a velocity of seventy cubic feet of water per second. Even Cletis was impressed. But before we went too far, we needed to test our design.

That was what we were doing when the men from the Miner's Council came riding up the bank.

Cletis and Chin had paced out eighth-of-a-mile increments along the trench. Little Ng, shirtless and shoeless, stood below, waiting for our signal to engage the second flutter wheel, which would lift water from the old sluice and drop it into the new one, which ran ten feet above the ground on skinny stilt legs, like a giant, wooden centipede. Flynn and I stood at the crest of the hill, well above Big Skull Rock, and waited to open the gates on the trough that would fill from the upper sluice. If we could raise water from the river, then start it running downhill with the requisite force, it would run all the way to Rainbow Gulch.

Little Ng was playing his flute when the Council men approached. His sweet tune ended like the song of a dying bird, and he crouched, as if he could hide behind the wheel.

The horses snorted and snuffled and came crunching over our tailing piles, the Gaw brothers in the lead, followed by Sloate and Attorney Tom Lyons. When they reached the top of the hill, they stopped with the sun behind them.

Flynn squinted and said, "If you come to baptize us, Moses, we'll have water as soon as we pull the chocks."

Moses Gaw studied the flutter wheels, the elaborate sluice works and the trench, and he said, "What's that Chink down there fixin' to do?"

"That's Little Ng," said Flynn. "Give 'em a wave, Ng."

Ng stood reluctantly, as if expecting a blow, though he was fifty feet away. Then he tentatively raised his hand.

"Muscular little rat, ain't he?" said David Gaw.

"Little *yellow* rat," said Sloate.

"Don't stand too close," said Flynn, "or he might start the wheel and baptize *you*."

Moses Gaw leaned forward. "We been baptized. Not like these heathens."

Attorney Lyons said, "You know why we're here, Spencer."

"You'd best tell us." Cletis had picked up his blunderbuss and come from his spot along the trench.

Lyons dismounted. He was gentleman enough that he would meet us eye-to-eye. He said, "I've brought the new law. Read out at San Jose on March twentieth."

"We're spreadin' the word," said Moses Gaw.

"Fulfillin' our promise to the miners of Broke Neck," added David Gaw, always finishing his brother's thoughts.

Lyons looked at Flynn the way a man might look at a dog he was about to poke with a stick, then read, "'By order of the California Senate, under recommendation of the Finance Committee, foreigners are now obliged to pay twenty dollars a month for the privilege of taking from our country the vast treasure to which they have no right.'"

"No right?" said Flynn. "No right?"

Deering Sloate put his hand on his pistol.

"Easy, Michael." I had seen enough of Sloate to know that the boy from Boston Latin, who would pour lamp oil on a cat and strike a match, or find cause to pummel anyone who did not stand up to him, or find followers enough to pummel anyone who did, that boy had not matured. He had merely intensified.

Sloate said, "Don't pull your pen, Spencer, or I might have to shoot you."

Lyons kept reading: "'We expect that said foreigners will cheerfully pay this fee to tax collectors appointed by the state. Effective on April 1.'"

"Cheerfully?" Flynn looked at me. "They're out of their fuckin' minds."

Lyons ignored him and kept reading: "'Foreigners are generally considered to be the worst population of the Mexican and South American States, Australia, and the Sandwich Islands, including the convicts of Mexico, Chile, and Botany Bay who are daily turned upon our shores.'"

"It don't say Chinks or Irishmen," said Cletis. "That's what we got here."

"It says Australians," answered Moses Gaw. "They're just Irish convicts. And if Chinks ain't mentioned, they should be. They will be. That's how we read this law."

"But if it ain't written," said Cletis, "how can you read it?"

"It's implied," said Tom Lyons.

"Implied?" I said. "It's a *law*. It says what it says. You know that, Tom."

"It implies what we say it does." Moses lifted his whip from the pommel of his saddle. "And we say that the Broke Neck miners want no foreigners takin' treasure they ain't entitled to, unless they pay a tax. So"—he looked around—"I count six Chinks. The one by the wheel, the four down by the claim, and this one comin' down the hill."

Chin was striding toward us, showing not a shred of subservience. I put myself in his way and said to Tom Lyons, "You want a hundred and twenty dollars a month from these people, just so they can work?"

"Plus one Irishman. Twenty dollars for him, too." Moses Gaw pointed the whip handle at Flynn, all but daring him to make a move.

"And," said David Gaw, "if you're hirin' Chinks, you'll pay a tax of ten dollars for each. So saith the Lord."

"The Lord got nothin' to do with it," said Cletis.

"You'll hang a long time before I pay any tax," said Flynn.

"You'll hang first, Mick," answered Moses Gaw.

Lyons put up his hands, "Now, boys, let's calm down. This is the law. We waited till it was read out in the senate. We've been fair about this."

Cletis cocked the blunderbuss. "Here's my law. Get off our claim."

Sloate kept his hand on his gun and his eyes on Cletis.

Lyons blanched, backed away, got on his horse. "I'll be back in four days as the state-appointed tax man."

"You keep talkin' about the 'state,'" said Cletis, "but I ain't heard news about no California statehood."

"California has petitioned," said Lyons. "So we'll conduct our business in the appropriate way." He turned his horse and started down the slope.

But Moses Gaw did not turn. He backed his horse down, telling the others, "Don't take your eyes off that crazy old man."

"Good advice. Just keep watchin' all the way off our claim," said Cletis.

Moses kept his big, black horse moving backward but his eyes on Cletis. That way, he could deny any intent over what happened when his horse bumped against his brother's, and his brother's horse lost its back hoof and stumbled.

David Gaw whipped the horse around, as if to get control of him, and all but threw him into a nine-foot-high stilt. Flynn tried to grab the stilt, to stop it from tipping and taking the sluice with it.

Sloate, seeing the chance to shoot Flynn, reached for his gun, so I drove my shoulder into the flank of Sloate's mare. Sloate tried to hold his horse on the steep bank, but the mare screamed and fell over sideways.

David Gaw's horse was now caught under the sluice, flailing and whinnying as its rider frantically—and, I thought, purposely—whipped its head back and forth.

Flynn smacked Gaw's horse on the rump, sending him shooting out from under the sluice, but right into another support, so that half the structure came crashing.

And now Moses Gaw went to work with his whip. He fired it at one of the wobbling stilts and pulled another section of sluice down. Then he fired it at Flynn, caught him by the neck, and pulled. But Chin sprang forward with his knife and slashed down on the whip, cutting it in half and freeing Flynn.

Moses Gaw almost fell off his horse, he had put so much weight behind the whip.

Meanwhile, David Gaw swung his horse back, got control, and turned on Chin.

Cletis cried. "Sam, get down!"

The Chinaman dropped, giving Cletis a clear shot at both Gaws.

But instead of shooting, Cletis shouted, "We're done!"

"Done." Lyons waved his hands to get the attention of Judge Blunderbuss. "Done."

"Just remember, old man, you all got taxes to pay," said Moses Gaw. "If you shirk 'em, this whole camp may get ruined, just like we ruined your sluices."

"Get out," said Cletis.

The only gunfire came when Deering Sloate, uninjured but for his pride, put down his horse, which had managed to stand and was hobbling about on three legs. The animal crashed to the right, onto the broken foreleg, dead before it hit the ground.

Sloate said, "That horse cost two hundred dollars."

"So did that sluice," I answered. "So we're even."

As Sloate doubled up with Lyons, Flynn said to me, "Someday, somebody'll have to shoot that Sloate feller. Mark my words."

Around sunset, Flynn and I sat on stumps, listening to the river and looking at the destruction. Weeks of hard work shattered in minutes . . .

Sloate's dead horse was already beginning to bloat. At least the Chinese had cut the meat from the haunches. But we would have to burn the carcass.

Flynn said, "I'll be payin' no taxes to men who'd put me out of business."

Cletis loped up the bank, bringing the jug and a bad mood. He sat on a stump, took a swallow, and offered the jug to me, all before he said to Flynn, "You don't pay that tax, we'll all pay. Us and the Chinks, too."

I sipped—I could not drink Grouchy Pete's rotgut like water—and passed to Flynn, who said, "They won't go. They've taken sixty pounds out of them diggin's."

"Then they can pay," said Cletis. "So can we. But I'm for movin' on."

Flynn swallowed and passed the jug to Cletis. "If you go, who'll burn our coffee? Who'll hold the claim while we get to diggin' this trench again?"

"Diggin' a six-mile trench is fool's work, even if we hire *all* them Chinks." Cletis took the jug again. "Look at them, workin' down there like there's no tomorrow."

"Maybe for them, there ain't." Flynn rubbed at the welt that had risen around his neck, where Gaw's whip had grabbed him.

"Ain't our problem," said Cletis. "Time to move on. We made enough."

"And I been chased enough," said Flynn. "Chased out of Ireland. Chased out of Boston. Even deserted some fine wet cooch to come back to my claim . . . so I ain't bein' chased off of it, and that's for damn sure."

"Then get ready to fight." Cletis pointed his whiskered chin at me. "You, too. You proved you can take a whuppin'. You need to prove you can give one."

Perhaps Cletis was right. He was right about most things that he opinionated upon.

But again, I chose what I hoped was the more civilized course, to prove something better about myself and the men who had come to this valley.

March 29, 1850
More Civilized?

And so, I went in search of help and good counsel. On a chilly Wednesday night in Broke Neck, the best place to find such things, along with plenty of unsolicited opinions, was at Grouchy Pete's.

The saloon was quiet. Only a dozen or so stood at the bar. Another dozen worked the gambling tables. The murmur of voices was low, the mist of cigar smoke light.

I spied Drinkin' Dan and bought him a whiskey. I bought myself a brandy, which tasted suspiciously like the whiskey, which I am told tasted like the rum, which I never drank. After a few swallows, I asked him if he had heard that the new law had been passed.

"About damn time. Makin' the district safe for white miners."

"The law says nothing about Chinamen or Irishmen, but the Council—"

"The Council's doin' right." Drinkin' Dan drained his glass.

I'd get no moral support from him, so I turned to Grouchy Pete, who wore a shiny new vest, unstained, and a new beaver hat, jauntily perched, offsetting the old steady scowl.

I said, "Have you read the new law?"

"Do I look like a man with time for readin'?"

Someone at the end of the bar called, and Grouchy Pete went grumbling away.

So I ambled over to the woodstove, where Micah Broadback hunched on his customary bench, close to the warmth.

"Whip scar healed up nice," he said. "See you don't lose your eye next time."

"There'll be no next time, if you take my part on this Foreign Miner's Tax."

"Can't choose you over the law."

"The Broke Neck Council is overreaching."

"Hodges has promises to keep, and the Gaws will see they're kept. So saith the Lord."

"The Lord has nothing to do with it," I said.

"The Gaws outvote me, too." Micah spat on the wood stove. "I come to California for gold. But I seen the need for fair dealin' in a place where law and order is wantin'. Somebody had to make a council. So I did, me and Drinkin' Dan and the others. Now, these Triple MWs, they take the business a lot more serious. If they want to do the work, I'll vote what they want."

Grouchy Pete came over, picked up a split of wood, shoved it into the stove, which caused a shower of sparks to pop. He stamped them out, then slammed the stove door. "See what I done to them sparks? That's what Hodges and Gaw will do to you if you dinna stand down, young Spencer."

Most of the drinkers at the bar, most of the gamblers at the tables, most of the loud talkers all around, most of them were white. But here and there, I saw a serape, a dark complexion, a different demeanor. And foreigners paid in dust, too. I told him as much.

"Foreigners dinna sell shares in water companies," answered Grouchy Pete. "But Hodges, he means to build somethin' that'll last. So I bought four preferred shares of the Triple MW. So long as they stay in business, so does Peter McDougall."

I had not anticipated this. But it made sense. If Hodges was going to take control of our water, he should make sure that the most powerful men in the Miwok Valley were slaked with money . . . or the chance to make some.

I said to Micah, "They're working like beavers up there, building that dam."

"It'll be the fellers in Rainbow Gulch who'll pay the price, and you boys, too, if you think you can win a shovelin' race against two dozen men."

Deterred in the saloon, I crossed the street to Emery's Emporium. It was quiet, but I sensed a new presence. I even smelled it, something clean, like soap, and then I saw it, not merely a presence but a whole human female. She looked up and smiled. A slender, sunburned woman she was, younger than George Emery by a decade. She was cutting carrots into little slices, bright orange carrots, the first carrots I had seen in a long time. I was not sure if I was more impressed to see her or the carrots.

Then Emery himself appeared from the back with an armload of potatoes. He dropped them on the counter and said, "Spencer, meet the little lady. Meet Mrs. Patricia Emery."

She wiped her hands on her apron and extended one to me. "They call me 'Miz Pat.'" And her smile warmed me as nothing had in a long time.

"Yes, sir," said Emery. "We're together now for good."

"Didn't like being apart," she said. "So we made a deal with Sam Brannan.

Buy wholesale in Sacramento, sell retail in Broke Neck. And live like a husband and wife should."

She had to be a formidable woman, to have run her husband's operation in Sacramento. She had to be a loving woman to have joined him here. And she had to be a woman unafraid to work because, as Emery said, "Maybe you seen the big tent I just strung out along the road. Hammered some tables and benches together, too, all so tomorrow, Pat can start cookin' her famous beef stew. Plannin' to sell it for one dollar or one pinch per bowl."

"Smart women are settin' up food tents all over the Mother Lode," added Miz Pat. "Makin' more money than the miners."

Emery threw his arm around his wife's waist. "Yes, sir, ain't she somethin'? Come across on a wagon train in forty-eight. Lost her first husband, then found this old soldier when he was mustered out. She can do sums, bargain a Connecticut Yankee out of his breeches, and grease a wheelhub or a bread pan, dependin' on what kind of lubricatin' you need. I swear, my Pat can do anything." He was in an ebullient mood, and why not? A warm body beside him in bed, a hot meal to look forward to, and big money to be made if his wife could cook even passably well.

"Now," he said, "what can I do you for?"

"It's about the Triple MW." I twitched my eyes toward the wife, who wisely sensed private talk and returned to her carrots. Then I said, "You and Grouchy Pete and Mr. Abbott, you're all voices of reason. But Pete bought stock, and—"

"Hodges came to me, too. I told him my money's tied up in my goods and the eatin' tent. So—"

Shouting in the street interrupted our talk: "Howdy, howdy, howdy!"

And someone in the saloon yelled, "The nigger's here!"

Another voice cried out, "Has he brung the women?"

Across the street, my old friend Pompey was standing in front of Grouchy Pete's. He shouted again, up and down the street, then turned and strode into the saloon.

George Emery said, "Spencer, you should've started diggin' that trench to Rainbow Gulch four months ago, when I told you to. I'd have invested. I wanted to be in business with you. But not now . . ." Then he reached under the counter and put a paper bag on the table in front of me. "Peppermints for Flynn. He sure does like them peppermints."

I snatched the bag and headed back to Grouchy Pete's.

Pompey was standing near the entrance, proclaiming, "I come to tell you boys that we'll be back tomorrow night. We'll be pitchin' our tents like before, wettin' the pussy, like before. Doin' it all like before but better than ever. So save your dust!"

This brought shouts, backslaps, raised glasses, even a few gunshots.

"Stop the damn shootin'!" cried Grouchy Pete. "You're puttin' holes in me roof."

Pompey said to Grouchy Pete, "Thank you, sir."

The gambler in the corner spun his wheel. As it started to rattle, he gave a shout. "Place your bets, boys. Place your bets. The little ball bounces wild but fair."

And Pompey added this: "But y'all just remember, you lose your money at them tables, you'll get no credit when you line up for a fuck. Gold dust only."

And the gambler who wore the white coat and hair pomade put a hand on his spinning wheel and stopped it. His name was Carl Becker, and men who had been in Broke Neck any length of time knew well not to trust him. He said, "You talk awful big for a nigger."

"I got a big man backin' me up," said Pompey. "A man named Big John Beam."

The other gambler, the one who favored silk vests and top hat, looked up from his faro shoe. His name was Tector Bunche, and in any dispute, he backed Becker or Becker backed him. He said, "I just want to know, where does a nigger get a fancy vest as that?"

Pompey pulled back his coat to reveal the grip of an ivory-handled Colt pocket revolver. "Same place he gets one of these."

"Well, this goddamn country's goin' straight to hell," said Bunche, "when a nigger can get his hands on such a pretty gun."

"An honest black man," said Pompey. "Better than a dishonest white man."

Oh, but Pompey was treading dangerous ground. If he had not brought the promise of women, he might have found himself in a noose right then.

Becker said, "You better hope California comes in a free state, boy, or I just might decide to buy you."

"Or shoot you," said Bunche.

Becker stepped away from his wheel. Bunche stood from the faro shoe. The others in the saloon all took a step back.

I was behind Pompey, close enough to whisper, "The one on the left keeps a knife in his boot. The one on the right will distract you, then the knife will fly."

Pompey flashed a grin. "Why, howdy, Mr. Spencer." He had grown.

Not physically—he was big enough already—but in the way he carried himself. A new suit of clothes and a pocketful of money can make any man walk a bit taller, no matter his race.

Becker said to me, "So you're a nigger lover, too."

"And now that I know your trick," Pompey said, "why don't you boys get back to business. But remember, a man who feel good down in his balls is a man who feel lucky all over. So you gamblers, y'all gonna thank me after the girls come through."

And that was a bit of sophistry fine enough for a Boston lawyer, never mind an uneducated Negro. He had negotiated his way right out the door and even left a few men laughing.

On the street I said, "You're looking prosperous. You'll be able to buy your family soon if you keep this up."

He patted the money belt at his waist. "Once I have enough, I'll git on back to North Carolina. And. . . . you know, you one of the few men ever ask me 'bout my family. I 'preciate that. So I got a nice woman for you. That little Mexican gal. She got some 'sperience on her now."

I did not like the sound of that.

"She didn't take to this work straight off, but we kept her at it, and, well, y'all get in line tomorrow night. You git a free poke, doin' what you just done for ol' Pompey. Nothin' so sneaky as a fancy-dressed white man with a knife in his boot."

I had no interest in mounting a frightened girl. But perhaps I could help her. Perhaps I could get her out, get her back to a decent life. Perhaps in this I was still naïve.

As I started out of town, Mr. Abbott called to me from his Express Office.

I asked him, "What about you? Will you speak for us against the tax?"

"I'm neutral. I'm a businessman. And here is my business." He put a letter into my hands. It came from Janiva.

I took it into his office and tore it open.

When I saw just four lines, I thought that she was telling me it was over, that she had found someone else. And the first sentence was not promising: "I cannot live like this any longer." But she followed with, "I am on the verge of doing something amazing. And no one will be more amazed than yourself, sir. Your Love, Janiva."

That was all. I reread, puzzled, and must have shown it, because Abbott said, "It's my business to be discreet. So I will not ask you what's in that letter that just turned you as white as new canvas. I will only tell you to be careful on the trail."

"Why?"

"When a man asks me a question about the deposits of another, I say nothing."

"Fair enough."

"So I said nothing to your friend, Harding, when he came by today, paid for a few letters, and started asking about you."

"Me personally?"

"You . . . and your friends. Your white friends and your Chinese friends, too." He brushed his hand up and down his vest, polishing those neat nails. "It's like they're trying to find out where you're keeping your gold."

"What did you tell him?"

"I told him nothing. There's loose lips in this camp. But not inside these walls, rough hewn though they might be."

I thanked him for his discretion.

I saw one more thing that night in Broke Neck that I must report:

As I was leaving Abbott's, a man was riding up the road. He looked like a professional mourner. He wore a long black frock and a top hat in the shape of an upturned plant pot. He rode with his eyes straight ahead, as if fixed on some dark, distant star. He reined up in front of Grouchy Pete's and dismounted. Then I saw the length of rope draped over his saddle. It terminated in a noose.

Captain Nathan Trask had come looking for deserters.

He glanced in my direction, but I withdrew into the shadows.

My senses were sharp as I rode home.

There was a good moon, so the road ahead was well-lit, and the darkness beneath the trees did not threaten. Nor did the distant woofing and crying of the coyotes.

And I did not fear the Triple MWs. They had gone to such lengths to assure the legality of their predations that an ambush would be out of the question. Nor did I fear Mexican phantoms, though there were stories of banditos riding in the night, robbing the Yankees who had driven them from their claims. And I did not fear the grizzlies that Cletis said were awakening now in late March and wandering the hills, ravenous and dangerous.

No. It was that cryptic letter from Janiva that vexed me. What on earth would be so amazing? And how, this far away, could I be amazed by what she was doing in Boston?

I dismounted at the road above our claim and led my horse down the bank, toward the flutter wheel that stood like a sentinel in the night. For a moment, I stopped on the north bank and watched the water, running with a steady rush and swish, doing its springtime business day and night.

Then, over its burble, I heard a voice:

"Trouble comes." Chin's shadow stood to my right, on the narrow bank between the bushes and the water. The moonlight shone off his forehead.

"Trouble. Yes." I saw the bags of gold dust over his shoulders. "When it comes, it may come as quickly for us as it does for you."

"So bury gold." He spoke just loudly enough to be heard over the water. "Bury one bag. We bury the other on this side. That way—"

And I made a decision. Chin had earned our friendship. He deserved our help, no matter what Cletis said. I took one of the bags and told him, "Nine o'clock."

He furrowed his brow, as if he did not understand.

"Big Skull Rock is round, like a clock. Flynn's gold is buried at two o'clock, Cletis's at noon. Mine is at ten o'clock. I will bury yours at nine o'clock, three feet down."

But I would not tell Cletis. In this, I would remain anonymous.

March 30, 1850
A meeting

Sunlight streamed like warm liquid through the east window and awoke me for the first time since we had lived there. A week after the vernal equinox, a man could feel the turning of the earth, hear "the music of the spheres," as Professor Agassiz had described the celestial hum of the planets around the sun. Such were the thoughts that filled my mind for a moment or two before consciousness came upon me. Then I heard the simpler music of the river. Then I heard the crowing of one of the Chinese roosters. Then I heard something—or someone—else.

Flynn was stumbling through the door, bootless and bottomless, naked from the waist down. I asked him what he was doing.

He said, "Takin' a piss. Go back to sleep."

But I was awake with the sun in my eyes. So I got up, pulled on my breeches, and slid on the soft moccasins I had bought at Sutter's Fort. Even a hillside in the California wilderness can seem more like home when you have soft footwear in the morning.

I stepped outside, grabbed a few splits of wood, and threw them on the embers smoldering within the circle of campfire rocks. The ground had not yet dried to a crispy brown, so we did not worry about our campfire, and we preferred to cook outdoors, where smoke and smells dissipated readily. I was puzzled to see Flynn's wet smallclothes hung to dry on the grate, but I poked a bit until the flames began to jump, then I grabbed the coffeepot and went down to the river. I knelt, dipped the pot, and over the rush of water, came a voice:

"I've been here since first light, hoping to catch you alone."

On a boulder on the other side, shielded from the downstream view by shrubs and deep shadows, sat Samuel Hodges. He pulled a white handkerchief from his pocket, almost like a flag of truce. "I've come to talk, James."

I left the coffeepot and stepped across from rock to rock.

With the handkerchief, he brushed off the boulder next to him and invited me to sit. As I did, I remembered the power in his bulk.

He said, "I'm sorry for what happened. You and your partners worked hard to build that sluice."

"Your partners did not have to work at all to destroy it."

"I won't deny that I've made common cause with rough men. This is rough country. But I'll build a legacy here, however I must."

"If the legacy means that you drive away men because of their skin color—"

"We are white men of European descent, James. We are builders." He spoke calmly, as a counselor. "Mexican sneak thieves, Digger Indians, spineless Chinese claim squatters . . . they block the path of progress. You should have learned that by now."

"I've learned that it's easy to unite beaten men against an enemy that doesn't exist, then use them for your own purpose."

"My purpose is to build something I could never have built in Boston."

"You were well respected in Boston."

"My father kept ledgers. He moved from one shipping house to another. It would have taken two generations for Hodges sons to rise to the level of the Spencers or for daughters to know the comforts that Spencer women know."

"Sons? Is Gaw's girl-child with a child of her own? Have you married her?"

This comment unnerved him. He was making a larger point, but in this elemental place, with the river at our feet and the sun slanting through the trees, I would take no larger points. What was in front of us was what mattered.

He stared at me, as if trying to decide whether to submit to his anger or continue to conciliate. He chose the latter. "In California, I can make a future. Then I can bring my little girls. Then perhaps I will marry. But first must come the building. So I come to you as a friend. We are days from completion of the dam. I come to propose an arrangement."

The rooster crowed again, and the hens began to gabble and cluck.

Hodges looked toward the sound and said, "We are ringed by enemies, James. Best know who your friends are. I'm yours, as I was in Boston, as I will be forever if you commit to us. In exchange, I will give you and your partners ten shares of stock."

"Do you include Flynn?"

"He can stay. As the new law is written, a foreigner is anyone who has come directly from another country. Flynn came from Boston. And he's white. But not the Chinese. I cannot go back on my word to the men of this district."

"I cannot go back on my word to my friends."

"You went back on your word to me. You were one of the few men on that ship that I trusted. I'm proud of what you've done here. But you betrayed my trust."

Those words gave me a pang of sorrow for denying him, a burst of pride for earning his admiration. I had proven myself.

Just then, Michael Flynn stumbled out of the cabin, pantless and oblivious, and headed for the outhouse.

Hodges said, "I watched your Irish friend this morning. He was down here before dawn, down here with one of the Chinamen. Is he that sort? Like Sloate and Harding?"

I shook my head, but in shock that Flynn was meeting Mei-Ling.

Hodges waited for a response to the larger question.

I fixed my eyes on the water forming V-shaped riffles as it cut over the rocks.

Hodges watched the water himself for a time, then clapped his hands on his knees and stood. "All right, then. Let me tell you what will happen if I go up that hill without an arrangement."

I stood and looked him in the eye. I would not let him intimidate me.

He said, "We will divert your water at our dam. Then we will finish the trenches. The first will carry water to Broke Neck. Once those claims are supplied, we will run another to Rainbow Gulch. Your complaints to the Miner's Council will be denied. I will win. And it's all legal. Ask Lyons."

By damming the water, he could create a reservoir and keep sluices flowing all season, at a volume that would not be affected by the meandering watercourse, the natural absorption of the streambed, or evaporation in the summer heat. That his trench bypassed Big Skull Rock would bother most miners not at all.

But I did not give him an answer. And he did not offer his hand. He simply turned and stalked off.

FLYNN BY NOW WAS sitting at the campfire, with his pants on, warming his stocking feet. "What did *he* want?"

"A son. Or an arrangement."

"I hope you told him to go and fuck himself."

"In so many words." I put the coffeepot on the grate and recounted my conversation. Cletis came out, scratched his rear end, listened, and said, "So we got trouble comin'." Then he went up to the outhouse.

I waited until he was beyond earshot before telling Flynn, "Trouble coming downstream and trouble across the river, if you're shaking the shrubs with Mei-Ling."

"Did Hodges—?"

"He thinks you were doing it with a China*man*, which could get you hanged on general principle."

Flynn gave a nervous laugh. "I got up to piss before dawn. I looked down at the river and saw somethin' movin' in the water. So I went, very quiet-like, till I was close. And it was Mei-Ling, cleanin' herself. She looked up, looked right at me. I figured, now you've done it. She'll scream and all the Chinks'll come runnin' and—"

Was I envious? I suppose. I could not take my eyes from Mei-Ling. But as I had told myself before, if her eyes were for Flynn, I would be grateful for a temptation eliminated.

"You know what she done?" Flynn looked off into space, as if reliving the wonder. "She smiled. I swear to God, Jamie, she smiled like she was invitin' me. She covered her titties with one hand and her little black snatch with the other, and she smiled. Then she climbed onto a rock and disappeared into the bushes. Oh, but the sight of her sweet little ass was like lookin' at honey made flesh. Me dick went as stiff as—"

"What did you do?"

"I crossed the river. That's how I got all wet. I followed her into a little hollow in the bushes. She was sittin' there, holdin' her black gown up in front of her."

"Did she say anything?"

"She just looked at me."

"Did you say anything?"

"Wasn't the time for talkin'. I knelt to kiss her. Then she heard somethin', and she tensed like water freezin' to ice. I thought, what's that? A grizzly? A Chink? Felt like I was back in New York, standing outside that window—"

"You never did finish that story."

"Someday . . . But faster than a fairy, she put that gown back on and shooed me away, sayin', 'Go. Go.'"

"She can speak English?"

"Maybe the most important things. So . . . even with an extra bit between me legs, I scrambled across the river and stumbled back to bed bareassed and ballocky, which must've been a bad way for you to wake. Oh, but I tell you, Jamie, I think I'm in love."

"In lust at least."

"Always that. But she was so delicate . . . so innocent when she looked at me . . . I guess them peppermints worked."

"So you won't be coming to town tonight? Big Beam's bringing the girls back."

"Like hell. I'll lead the way."

"When you do, keep a clear eye. Watch for a man in a top hat and black frock."

"A sea captain with a noose instead of a ship?" said Flynn. "He don't frighten me."

AROUND MIDDAY, CLETIS BEGAN to pile his goods on the back of the burro, and as we watched like deserted children, he said, "Damn good little beast, this burro. Works all day, carries more than his weight, goes where no horse could. Gotta have my Miguel."

"You call him *Miguel*?" said Flynn, as if this was the greatest insult of all. "Miguel's Spanish for Michael."

"Boys, we made a deal to hang together till the winter rains. Now, it's, it's—" He gestured up at the sun arcing ever higher into the sky, as if he could not finish the sentence. He tightened the cinches on his saddle and said, "I ain't stickin this old neck out no more. I got enough gold to live like a king. Could never get a woman to love me, but now I can pay for all the women I want, so . . . I hear they got some fine ones in San Francisco."

I felt deserted, deprived. Cletis was more than just a friend. He had become a counselor and guide, with a view of the world that was narrow but always clear.

I said, "You were right about the men in town. None of them want to stick their necks out. Not even George Emery."

"Good faith plays out fast. Just like a claim. You boys can keep the black fryin' pan." He shook our hands solemnly, wished us luck, then swung a leg and rode past the shattered remnants of the second sluice. At the river's edge, he stopped and looked back, "Are you sure you won't come along to Frisco?"

"We been there," answered Flynn.

"Suit yourself, then." Cletis gave his horse a kick and headed up to the road.

"Now what?" I said to Flynn.

He stood. "We clean up and go to town. I got an yearnin' for Sheila's round rump."

That night, the town smelled of sex. It was in the air, something copulative, creative, a commingling of scents to excite the spirit and then the loins. Big Beam squirted perfume onto the tents so that if there was a breeze, the aroma took life. And the sweet smell of anticipation, of men finished with their labors looking forward to fulfillment, that was so strong, it almost hummed. And if anticipation was keen enough, cleanliness might follow, so that the smells of soap, hair pomade, and bay rum danced on the currents of air, too.

Or was I confusing the smell of sex with the smell of stew? Almost as many men had trooped into town to get themselves a bowl at the huge steaming kettle that Pat Emery was stirring in the tent beside Emery's Emporium.

Flynn said we could have stew later, so we made for the line on the south side of the street. A dozen men stood in front of us, all waiting to get into the big top of Big Beam's Traveling Circus of Earthly Delights, where every man stopped before heading to one of the smaller tents that led to fulfillment. We waited our turn. We would have been in a fight otherwise. There was almost a fight anyway, as the two men ahead of us—two from the Triple MW, a skinny, hairy specimen named Vinegar Miller and his rat-like partner

Charlie Boles—offered us crosswise looks as soon as we ambled up behind them.

But Flynn answered with a smile. "Boys, as the unofficial Irish mayor of Big Skull Rock, I proclaim all hostilities suspended for the night, since we're all after one thing: the best fuck of our life."

And that seemed sufficient. Without a crosswise word to match their looks, they turned back to the night's plan.

Things had grown more organized since Big Beam's first visit. Just inside the flap, at a table under a lantern, he greeted each man. A chalkboard behind him showed the names of seven girls. And yes, *Maria* was one of them. Big Beam wrote the name of each man on the board, next to the name of the girl he requested, either for herself or for her particular specialty. Some men liked to ask for Sheila. Others cared only to know that they were getting a "round rump" or "smooth-shaved legs." Big Beam promised to fulfill requests, if he could, then demanded an ounce for fifteen minutes, two for thirty, and so forth, but *No Kredit Accepted,* as the sign said. So men dutifully measured out their dust, then sat on benches, like schoolboys awaiting dismissal into the June sunshine. When a girl came ready, she would ring a bell and another miner would go through the back flap. If there was romance in any of this, I did not see it. But romance was not the point.

I requested Maria. Flynn made a joke of my request, something about me being in love. Then he and Big Beam went to jawing about all the whoremongering competition coming into the gold country. Meanwhile, men kept streaming through the back flap, toward the smaller tents until only two remained ahead of me.

Then Big Beam called for Vinegar Miller, who popped up, cried, "Here I be."

The other miner, Charlie Boles shouted, "Hey, we come in together."

"One of you has to wait," said Big Beam. "There'll be another girl soon."

"I waited all day. I ain't waitin' no more," said Boles.

"Me neither," said Miller.

Big Beam said, "But there's only one girl."

Raised voices brought Pompey to the back flap, ready to exert himself.

But when it came to sex, the men of the Triple MW were downright cooperative. Boles said, "We'll both take her, then. We'll give you four—no five!—five ounces for half an hour. That ought to give us some extra fun. Right, pardner?"

Vinegar Miller got a devilish glint in his eye, pulled out his pouch, and dropped it on the table. "Take what you want out of there. Then let's get to her."

"Well, I don't know." Big Beam scratched the back of his neck.

Charlie Boles pulled out his pouch and offered three more ounces.

It was all too much for Big Beam to turn down. "The girl is Maria, in tent six."

I made a strange, strangled sound, and Flynn asked if I was all right.

I said to Beam, "I'll pay six ounces for her, right now."

Miller and Boles looked at me. Then Miller said to Big Beam, "Tell that son of a bitch to wait his turn." Then he and his friend went through the back flap.

I thought to follow them, to stop them. I even took a step, but Pompey put himself in front of me. "Sorry, Mr. Spencer, but once the boys pays their gold and go down the line, ain't nothin' we can do. You get her for free, like I promised. But they gettin' what they want first."

Big Beam said, "If you wasn't friends with my old pardner, I'd throw you out on your thick head. Just sit quiet and wait. You'll have the little Mexican filly in half an hour."

I called him a fat son of a bitch and would have called him more, but Flynn grabbed my elbow and pulled me away, whispering, "Either you found something good or you're in love. Want to let me in on it?"

Before I could speak, Big Beam shouted, "Flynn! Roberta's free. And she been talkin' about you all day. Says she powdered up nice, just for you."

Flynn said, "I'm here for Sheila, but I missed Roberta, too. Maybe I'll have her, then pay another ounce for Sheila." And that was the end of my talk with Flynn. He told me, "You be careful, Jamie, and wait your turn." Then he headed for the back flap.

More men were coming in, loud men swinging jugs, spreading laughter and the scatology of minds made up for fucking.

One of them shouted, "We hit it big, and we all want a poke!"

"That's right. Poke anything that ain't nailed down."

"One ounce for fifteen minutes," said Beam. "Gold dust up front. Leave your guns with me."

"You want my pistol or my gun?" shouted another, and they laughed and burped and farted and eyed me as if they remembered me from somewhere. One of them dropped down beside me, his breeches already bulging, and offered me a swallow of whiskey.

I took it. I could use it, and refusing it would only bring bad feelings, of which there were already enough in that tent.

Then, to my surprise Deering Sloate came in, approached Big Beam, and asked for Sheila. "I hear she'll take it in the rump."

"You'll have to pay her a bit more," said Beam. "Leave your pistol with me."

Sloate seemed to be a man who followed his stiff dick in any direction it took him. He paid his money, dropped his gun and holster, looked around, and his eye fell on me. "Writing with your other pen, Spencer? What'll that girl back in Boston think?"

"What would your mother think?"

In response, his hand went to his hip. I was glad he was unarmed.

I decided to step out of the tent, away from Sloate, away from the cloying smells of perfumed canvas and whiskey breath, away from the close stink of miners in rut. Another fifteen minutes in that tent and I'd be gagging.

I walked a little ways up the street, past the crowd slopping down in Emery's eating tent, and I took a perch on the stoop of Emery's store.

Miz Pat came out, aproned and sweating, to take a small rest. She lit a cigar, which did not shock me as once it might have, and she leaned against the porch post.

I said, "The boys like your stew."

"They'd eat anything that didn't eat them first, so long as it had a sauce." She took a deep inhalation of smoke and said, "Sure is rowdy tonight. Are you headin' for the girlie-tents?"

"Yes, but not for the purpose you might be thinking."

"My husband said you were a strange young man."

I suppose that I was, given such an answer as that. And she had no more talk to offer. So she turned and went back inside, muttering about more carrots for the stew.

I stayed on the stoop, watching the men surging through the streets. I heard laughter from the eating tent. I listened to the piano in Grouchy Pete's pounding out "Oh, Susanna." The fucking and eating and carousing would go on all night beneath the sputtering torches of this transitory little town in the middle of the wilderness, and—

—a scream pierced the air like the shattering of a window. It came from the line of whoring tents. A moment later, Maria burst from the last of them, running, running as if she had just seen hell and wanted to escape before she fell into the abyss, running as I had never seen a woman run before, running completely and utterly naked, and screaming as she ran, wordless and terrified.

Vinegar Miller lurched out of the tent after her and cried, "Murder! Murder!"

Pompey burst from the main tent. "Murder? Who been murdered?"

Then Boles staggered out behind Miller, looked down at his chest, reached for the handle of the knife now protruding from it, and collapsed.

"Murder! Right here!" cried Miller. "That Mexican whore just killed my pardner!"

Two miners came out of Grouchy Pete's. One fired his gun into the air. The other shouted into the saloon, "Hey, come see the naked whore!"

Pompey grabbed Miller and threw him back. "You just wait, now. Wait."

I ran into the street, and as she came toward me, I tried to grab her. "Maria, stop! It's me. Spencer."

She gouged at my eyes and kept running, the innocent nakedness of her shining in the torchlight.

Now dozens of men were running and lurching and staggering from everywhere, shouting for us to grab her, stop her, get the Mexican whore.

The man in the top hat and black frock stalked out of Grouchy Pete's. He had a noose over his shoulder. He saw the young woman go by. He saw the body of the miner. He stepped off the porch and strode after her.

Pompey tried to put himself in front of the crowd. He threw up his hands and shouted, "Y'all wait one damn minute, now. Let me get her. She trust me. She—"

I heard a gunshot, and the crowd surged over the falling Pompey, all except for one in a white suit, who rifled Pompey's pockets, pulled off his money belt, grabbed his pistol. As he ran off, I saw the pomade shining in his hair. The gambler named Becker, making good on a threat, which meant Bunche was sure to be lurking nearby.

Now the Gaws burst from the saloon. Moses was unfurling his new whip. David was carrying the leg of a chair like a club.

I put myself between Maria and the men and cried, "Stop! She's just a girl! Stop!"

But the mob did not stop for me, either. They were an angry wave rolling right at me, right over me. When the chair leg hit me, the world went black.

THEY HANGED HER FROM the oak tree beside Emery's Emporium.

Her pendent body was my first sight when I came to. Pain was my first sensation . . . for her and for the throbbing inside my skull.

Flynn had dragged me unconscious out of the riot, to the safety of Emery's porch.

I tried to go to her, but Flynn held me, held me down, held me in place.

"Goddamn them," I said. "She was just a girl."

"She killed a man," said George Emery.

I looked over toward the line of whoring tents, to where Boles had fallen. They had carried him off, but Pompey still lay there, in a pool of blood that glistened darkly in the torchlight.

Flynn said, "I reckon our black friend won't be buyin' that family, after all."

My mind, fogged by confusion and pain, kept going from the girl to Pompey and back. I said, "Who hanged her?"

Miz Pat put a mug of tea into my hands. "Moses Gaw got her with his whip, tripped her, dragged her. Then his brother started in to screamin' hellfire and damnation on a murderess. Then a tall man in black frock and top hat stepped up, said he'd do the work of the Lord and the law."

I said to Flynn, "Trask? He hanged her?"

"I'm thinkin' he'll hang anybody."

"Sure did kill the appetites in the eatin' tent," said George Emery.

Miz Pat told her husband, "If that's all you have to say, get inside."

The town had gone quiet. Even the randiest of miners left after the hanging. The only sound came from the hissing and sputtering of the torches that lit the street.

Then Big Beam appeared from his big tent and hurried toward us like a man late for work. He carried a ladder on his shoulder and was muttering, "Terrible thing. Terrible thing to have to see. Terrible. Terrible."

George Emery said, "At least justice was swift."

Miz Pat turned to him, "I swear, George—"

As Maria twisted in the night breeze, so that her breasts and bottom were displayed for any who passed, Big Beam fitted the ladder beneath her and called over to us, "Does anybody got a knife?"

I said, "Why don't you use the one she fought them off with?"

Big Beam said, "Why don't you just stay out of it?"

"I stayed out of it." I came down off the porch and strode toward the ladder. "I let you use her, you and those dirty miners, and now—" I looked up at her and felt something explode inside me. It was in my mind, and suddenly, it was in my whole being.

I flew at Big Beam and smashed into the ladder and sent him sprawling onto his fat, food-filled belly. When he tried to get up, I kicked him in that belly, then kicked him again, then again, kicked out all the fury I had in me, all the anger building for months, anger at the ease with which men slipped the bonds of civility and civilization, kicked out all the anger at letting those bonds slip in myself, kicked and kicked and smashed my boot into his face, so that his nose crunched, then kicked again so that his teeth flew and then, Flynn flashed from somewhere . . . and the world went black once more.

March 31, 1850
Swift Justice

Morning sunlight brought no joy when it struck my face.

Flynn was sitting on the edge of his pallet. He said, "Sorry I had to hit you. I thought you might kill Big Beam."

"She was sixteen. He let two miners have her at once. Damn him, damn them, and damn this place." I was lost, cut loose from anchor and mooring. The mob had left me unnerved, unwound, and unmanned. I stared at the wall, saw her naked breasts and blackened face twisting obscenely, then saw the black bulk of Pompey, bleeding in street.

Flynn brought me coffee.

I did not want it.

He suggested I step outside.

I wanted to stay in the dark of the cabin, stay and hold my head, keep it motionless and empty.

Flynn brought me my journal and suggested I write. "Might make you feel better."

I said, "I'll write about Pompey, shot down like a dog—"

"Pompey got no more rights here than in South Carolina. It was one of them gamblers killed him. A low brace of cowards, them two."

I took the pen and dipped into the ink and stared at the page. They say that after a blow to the head, a man can go wobbly for days . . . or months. I had taken two, and though I scratched a few things, I could not focus. I closed my eyes and held my head. I heard Flynn working outside. I heard the Chinese down by the river. I heard Chin talking to Flynn. I could not hear what they were saying. I did not care. Then, late in the day, I heard horses coming down the opposite bank. Whoever they were, let them come.

Then I heard Samuel Hodges say, "Who you boys speak-ee English?"

Moses Gaw said, "The tallest one, the one scowlin'."

Chin said, "I know your language."

"You tell others boys, we no like-ee fight, so they move, chop chop."

"But tax?" said Chin. "If we pay tax?"

"The council met last night," said Hodges. "We've decided to move you all out. No more Chinks or Niggers or Mexicans murdering white men."

I went to the window. The sunlight made my head throb.

Hodges had brought half a dozen Sagamores, including the Gaws, Tom Lyons, Sloate, Vinegar Miller, and Christopher Harding. Up on the road, in white duster and top hat, Miner's Councilor Micah Broadback sat his horse. Next to him, a perfect contrast in black, sat Nathan Trask. Broadback looked like he did not want to take any part in this. Trask looked like he was yearning to use the noose again.

Tom Lyons said, "From now on, foreigners can pass through, but they'll stake no claims in Broke Neck, not even on tailing piles like this."

Stepping into the cabin, Flynn watched through the open door. "Might be trouble." For all his volubility, he understated things when they were at their worst.

Little Ng, shirtless in the hot sun, had moved close to Chin. The other three, in their baggy clothes and straw hats, had formed a half circle around Mei-Ling. Uncle Bao held a hoe, Little Ng's big brother, Ng-goh, stood with a shovel, and Friendly Liu had produced a pair of threshing sticks chained together.

Flynn said, "I don't like it, Jamie. If them Triple MWs find out about Mei-Ling—"

Hodges was saying, "We'll give you fifteen minutes."

"Fifteen minutes?" Chin just stood there.

Hodges pulled out his watch. "Starting now."

Flynn said to me, "Last night is an excuse. No talk. No tax. Just go. He'll steal every foreign claim, give it to some white miner."

Chin was saying, "We do no bad thing. We no move." Then he took a few steps toward the other Chinese.

Hodges looked up toward our cabin, to see if we were watching, then he said to Moses Gaw, "Seize him up. Tie him to the wheel."

Two men grabbed Chin, who kept his eyes fiercely on Hodges . . .

. . . who leaned down from his horse and said, "A dozen lashes, Mr. Chinee man. Then you leave. If you stay, we give a dozen to every Chink here."

They dragged him to the wheel, which was chocked and motionless above the current.

I moved toward the door.

Flynn stepped into my way. "No, Jamie. They have to face this themselves."

Four of Hodges's men tied Chin, hand and foot. He said nothing and did not struggle, as if by taking the punishment he could protect the rest.

But David Gaw had dismounted and was walking among the Chinese. He stopped in front of the smallest of them, gave a long look, and said, "Brother Moses, let's flog this one instead." He was pointing at Mei-Ling.

And Flynn forgot his own advice. He flew out the door and down the hill with his Colt drawn and fury in his stride.

Sloate pulled his pistol and swung it toward Flynn, but Hodges stopped him and said, "No. No. Not yet." Then he shouted at Flynn, "Keep that gun pointed down."

"These people had nothin' to do with last night," answered Flynn. "You got no right to be punishin' them. If they pay the tax, take it, and ride on."

"Did you hear that," said Moses Gaw. "This arrogant Mick says ride on. To us?"

Hodges looked at him, "Arrogant in Boston, arrogant in Broke Neck."

Sloate laughed as if he knew that a bully's laughter was just the thing to provoke an Irishman's anger. "You think you can drive all of us off yourself, Mick?"

"No, but I can kill you, you son of a bitch, and two or three others."

Moses uncoiled his bullwhip and said to Flynn, "Where are your pardners?"

Sloate leaned back in his saddle. "One of them is up there writing all this down. That's all he's good for."

I watched as if this were a play unfolding in a Boston theater. But through the fog in my brain, I could see that Flynn was right. Exposing myself to their guns would do no one any good. Standing ready to fire from cover might keep them at bay. So I pointed my pistol out the window, aiming it at the men who had hanged Maria like a dog and done it as self-righteously as a New England jury.

David Gaw shouted up at me, "Write it down that we hanged a whore who murdered a white man." Then he turned to Mei-Ling, "And if my eyes don't deceive me, we got another whore right here, of the Chink species. A woman breakin' the rules of Leviticus by dressin' as a man." He knocked

Mei-Ling's straw hat off her head. Then he put his hand under her chin and turned her face to him.

From his spread-eagle on the wheel, Chin shouted something in Chinese.

Ng-goh, the biggest and strongest of all the Chinese, let out a bellow and swung a shovel into the back of David Gaw's head. And the uprising began.

Friendly Liu swung his threshing sticks as he put himself between the girl and the other whites. Little Ng leapt foward with a wild cry. Uncle Bao raised his hoe like a club.

These Chinese men had protected Mei-Ling across thousands of miles and most of a year, and they would fight for her now, lest she be violated.

Deering Sloate, however, was unmoved by their anger. He pulled his gun and coldly shot Uncle Bao, just as the Chinaman was turning his hoe onto Moses Gaw.

Flynn fired at Sloate. But once, twice, he pulled his trigger in frustration. Two haphazard loads, two misfires, so he shouted, "Run, Mei-Ling! Run!" And before Sloate could swing his pistol again, Flynn leapt at him and pulled him off his horse.

As Flynn and Sloate went at it, Mei-Ling scrambled into the bushes and up the bank.

Ng-goh swung the shovel at two Sagamores who came flying from his right.

Moses Gaw looked at Chin and said, "See what you done?" Then he kicked out the chock, so the wheel started to turn with Chin tethered to it, down into the water then up, around, and down again . . . Wei Chin, tortured by his own handiwork.

Uncle Bao had fallen and was screaming in pain, his body curling around the hole in his belly. But Friendly Liu, who always seemed to be smiling, even when he wasn't, backed toward the bushes, keeping himself between the white men and Mei-Ling.

David Gaw got to his feet and pointed his pistol at Friendly Liu.

And a rifle shot cracked from somewhere downstream.

David Gaw cried out as his elbow seemed to explode in blood.

Another shot came right after, from the bushes on the north bank. Were two men shooting from cover? Had Emery and Abbott come to our rescue?

Christopher Harding turned his gun toward the trees and loosed two or three rounds. He was answered with a rifle shot that took off his hat, which was followed by the high-pitched cackle of Cletis Smith. "I wasn't aimin' for the hat!"

And for a moment, there was silence, punctuated by the steady thump of the flutter wheel, turning Chin up, around, and down, while David Gaw sat on the ground and moaned, and dying Uncle Bao whimpered in agony.

Then the disembodied voice of Cletis Smith echoed again, "Hey, Harvard! Rest that hog leg on the windowsill. Aim good. And shoot Hodges first."

Realizing his predicament, Hodges shouted up to me. "Our arrangement still holds, James. If you want it—"

Moses Gaw was tightening his belt around his brother's arm to stop the bleeding. He said, "Arrangement? What goddamn arrangement?"

Cletis delivered another shot that cut the reins on Samuel Hodges's horse.

"That's *my* arrangement." Then he shouted, "Now, we got two muskets and a rifle up here, and a big old blunderbuss, too. Every time I shoot, I get another gun right in my hands. So I've got you in a crossfire, boys."

Vinegar Miller emerged from the bushes, dragging Mei-Ling by the hair, shouting, "And we got the China whore."

Chin, still turning up, around, and down, cried out to his sister, then splashed into the water again.

Flynn, who had left off grappling with Sloate, ran toward her, but Moses Gaw fired his whip, took out Flynn's legs, and dropped him on his face. Someone else drove a knee into Flynn's back. Sloate pinned his arms. And two more took Ng-goh.

Hodges ordered Miller, "Put a gun to her head." Then he shouted up at the hills, "There'll be no more shooting. We're arresting the big Chink for assault on a white man, and Flynn's a deserter from the *William Winter*. His fate is sealed."

I hadn't fired my pistol yet. I knew that if I did, I was likely to hit someone I cared about. And Cletis had gone silent.

Hodges ordered his people to mount. Then he shouted up at the hills again. "You can have the Chinaman riding the wheel. You can have the girl, too."

Tom Lyons looked up at our cabin. "We'll give them a fair trial,

Spencer. I promise. In town, tomorrow, as prescribed by the council. You can testify."

"Then we'll hang them," added Moses Gaw.

CLETIS DID NOT DESCEND until after the Triple MWs had disappeared up the road with Flynn and Ng-goh, hands tied and tethered to saddle pommels, running along behind the horses.

By then, I had chocked the wheel and was untying Chin, while Mei-Ling and Friendly Liu comforted the dying Uncle Bao.

Cletis led his horse and burro into the clearing, followed by a young man leading a horse of his own. I recognized Rodrigo Vargas. The frightened boy who had waylaid us in August, the angel of mercy who had nursed me in January, had once again been the agent of our rescue.

Cletis said, "I met him on the road. He was comin' up. I was goin' down. He said he was lookin' for the girl he loved. The girl named—"

"Maria?" I said.

"I told him I'd help him find her."

"Why?"

"Well, Harvard, I could never get a woman to love me, so I reckoned I'd help a young feller who could." Cletis bit a chaw of tobacco. "Then we heard that she'd been hanged, most likely by them who just left."

Rodrigo looked from under the brim of his straw hat. His face had been a river of tears when first I gazed upon it in that bloody grove of trees. It was now a mask of grief. But his jaw was set, as if he would never cry another tear. He told me he would bring Maria back to the ranchero to bury her, and he would avenge her. "It does not matter in what order I do these things. I will do them."

I said, "They may have buried her already."

"Then I will help you," he said. "Help you kill the men who killed her."

"You helped plenty already," said Cletis. "Damn good loader."

Chin, soaked and exhausted, half drowned and disoriented from his riverine crucifixion, dragged himself to his feet, listened as Little Ng unleashed a stream of Chinese, then said, "He wants to know . . . what will happen to his brother."

"They're supposed to wait for the law," I said. "But if they promise a trial tomorrow—"

Cletis said, "Elected head of the Miner's Council does the job when you don't have a real *alcalde* nearby. That's Hodges. So, if there's a trial, it'll be quick."

"We can't just leave them," I said.

"We can fight," said Rodrigo with a sudden, adolescent ferocity.

"Hodges has two dozen men, boy, all armed," said Cletis.

"I will fight," said Rodrigo. "I will fight them myself if you will not."

Chin added, "We not let them hang Ng-goh."

Mei-Ling came toward us, standing straight, head high, as if something had happened within her, something that overcame her natural subservience. "Uncle Bao dead. No hang Flynn and Ng-goh, too."

Chin said, "No hang. I help. Little Ng, Friendly Liu, they help, too."

Little Ng scowled. Friendly Liu smiled and nodded.

I remembered the body of Sean Kearns hanging in a grove of trees and the corpse of Maria twisting above Broke Neck. I would not let them do that to Michael Flynn, too. No man worth his manhood would let them hang his friend. I said, "A small, dedicated group of fighters can win by catching an enemy in his bed."

Cletis spat tobacco. "When did you become a military expert?"

I massaged my aching head. "I'm a student of history. George Washington led a surprise attack in a sleet storm at Trenton and changed history."

"Is that a fact? Well, whatever we do, we'll change history, too. Our own." Cletis led the animals across the river, up toward the cabin.

Chin called after him, "Ng-goh not be hanged."

Cletis looked at Chin. "No matter what happens, you'll have to go. Make for San Francisco, get on a boat, go home."

"Gum Saan home, now," said Chin. "We go Chinese camp or San Francisco."

Cletis looked at me. "You ought to go home, too. You ain't made for this."

"Get Flynn first," I said.

Cletis leaned on the burro's back and appeared to think it over. "Well, they'll never expect us. They think we're too frightened."

"We are," I said.

"Can you draw a map of the camp, the log piles, the sluices, the dam? All of it?"

Around nine o'clock, in the midst of our plotting, we heard someone crossing the river below. The moon was up, so we could see him clear. He reined about twenty feet from our cabin and called my name.

Cletis pointed his blunderbuss out the window. Then he nodded to me. *Go ahead.*

I stepped into the moonlight as the rider dismounted and came closer: Christopher Harding, no more than a shadow beneath the brim of his hat. He said he was leaving.

"Why?" I asked.

"Hodges has no . . . no conscience. Neither does Sloate." And I saw a flash of the boy I had known in our school days—honest, principled, perhaps a bit naïve—not the man who had taken abuse on the boat, taken a predator like Sloate as a pardner, and taken to doing the work of Samuel Hodges in the Mother Lode.

He said, "Flynn will be hanged at dawn."

"Without a trial? Tom Lyons said there'd be a trial."

"Trask says deserters get hanged. They don't need a trial. That's the argument."

"And Hodges won't stop it?" I said.

"Hodges wants him dead. Moses Gaw hates him. Sloate wanted to shoot him. They've all gone mad with their own power and ambition up there, Jamie. They think you men down here threaten it. So they'll hang him and come after you."

"We were here first," said Cletis from the window.

"Doc Beal cut off David Gaw's arm tonight," Christopher told him. "Your shot shattered his elbow. He's gone feverish. If he dies, they'll hang you first."

Cletis came out of the cabin. "Where they keepin' Flynn."

"They put him and the Chinaman in the saw pit."

"I know the saw pit," I said. "Right in the middle of the encampment."

Christopher Harding said, "It's about six feet deep so a man can work a ripsaw and turn tree trunks into planks. They cover it at night so animals won't fall into it. That's all I know."

"That's enough," I said.

As Christopher mounted again, I asked if he was going home.

He said, "After all I've seen? All I've done? No . . . . but California is a big place. A man can get lost."

I watched him go and thought, yes, a man could get lost, or find himself, even a man who had killed an albatross. Then I told Cletis that I could draw the sawpit on a map.

"That's good," said Cletis. "Good that you can draw. But can you kill?"

I showed him my Colt Dragoon. I could. I would. I had seen enough death to know that, sometimes, violence was the only answer.

Cletis nodded. "Then we have to go tonight, whether they're expectin' us or not." But we'll leave the girl and Friendly Liu here.

April 1, 1850
The Dams

Gunpowder is not a weapon. It merely allows a weapon to work. The weapon is a pistol or a musket, or in our case, a door. Yes, the door that Cletis Smith had made so proudly for our cabin. He had always said that an honest door must be thick enough to shut out the weather yet wide enough to admit a friend. He might also have said that it should be solid enough to float two hogsheads of gunpowder on a river.

I had scouted an overland trail to the Triple MW dam, so I went in the lead, Chin and Little Ng following, with Rodrigo and Cletis at the rear, leading the burro that carried the door and gunpowder. What a strange vision we must have made in the moonlight, moving though the brush and over the hilltops, following deer paths and rabbit runs, angry and aggrieved men, bent on rescuing our friends and securing vengeance. Around three in the morning, we came onto an open patch overlooking the Triple MW camp and the dam . . .

. . . that marvel of primitive engineering, eight feet high, three feet wide, built of stone and wood and earth, reaching halfway across the stream, turning at ninety degrees, running fifty feet downstream, then turning back to the bank, all to expose a portion of riverbed. At the upstream end, they had built a footbridge all the way across the stream, and they had installed a sliding-log sluice gate, so that they could allow more water or shut off the flow entirely. That would be our escape route, the last step in a four-part plan that began with diversion, destruction, and extraction.

Cletis would stay on this side of the river. There was not much cover, a few rocks here, an outcropping there, a dozen three-foot stumps where a blue oak grove had stood not that long ago. He could do his best work with his Kentucky Long Rifle and musket, sowing fear and confusion, while Rodrigo did his loading and fired off a few potshots of his own.

I would climb the hill on the other bank, above the road, to play my part.

Torches burned on the dam and in front of the longhouse where the men slept. Someone was moving through the night to the outhouse near the edge of the settlement.

"Figures they'd put the shithouse downstream," said Cletis. "About the only thing they want flowin' down to us."

We could hear the river running and a wheel turning, driving a shaft attached to a pump that removed water from the exposed riverbed so that in the morning, men could get at the gold in the bottom.

Most dam building did not happen till late summer, the driest time of year. But as soon as the rains of January and February had subsided, the current had slackened enough to make it possible for determined men to work until the snowmelt began. And they had made remarkable progress, damming and fluming and slowing the Miwok right where it bent.

But we cared nothing for their ambition. We cared only about saving our friends.

Chin and Little Ng took the burro. If the animal honked, it would sound as if he was just another beast in the Triple MW corral, which lay unguarded at the upstream end of the camp. Just before the attack, Chin would open the corral gate because frightened mounts were sure to scatter, raising more confusion.

I moved downstream, well below the camp, where I was certain there would be no lookouts, and I slipped across. Then I scrambled up the bank. There were more stumps and fewer trees than on my last visit, so there was less cover in the moonlight. But I moved from stump to shrub, stopping, looking, waiting, until I had found good cover, near a pyramid of logs.

From here, the camp spread below me, covering perhaps two acres of flat riverbank: three large structures, scattered tents, sluices, and wheels. The saw pit lay near the base of the hill. Two men were playing cards at a table atop the planks covering the pit. The glare of their lantern made it difficult to see much around them, but I knew that Flynn was beneath them.

He probably knew that somewhere in the camp, Nathan Trask was tightening a noose just for him. Could he have known that somewhere in the dark, an old man was picking targets? Or that somewhere upstream, two Chinamen were lashing a hogshead of gunpowder to a door, piling branches on top of it to disguise it, preparing to light the fuse and launch their device? Or that I was here, waiting to loose the logs?

I looked at the moon, which had passed its apex but still shone bright.

Chin had said, "When the moon dips below the trees, I will light the fuse. Then you will hear Little Ng's flute, like a bird awakening. Then send the logs."

It was not yet time, so I leaned back and I listened to the music of the

river. And I wondered at this Mother Lode night. I had dreamed of showing Janiva our brilliant sky, with Mars and the other planets wheeling
above me. And I told myself I would do it . . . a year from now, in Italy or
the Alps. But not here. Never here.

Then I heard a door bang open below. A man strode out of one of the
smaller cabins, lumbering like Moses Gaw. I could track him across the
clearing because the moonlight caught the white of his nightshirt. He muttered a few words to the men guarding the saw pit, then went into the outhouse and slammed the door.

Then I heard something in the bushes nearby, something big, coming
my way. I pulled my Bowie knife. Could I kill a man hand-to-hand, especially a man who sounded as if he might be bigger than Moses Gaw? And
what was he doing up here? Was he with someone? A woman perhaps?
Someone's wife?

I waited and listened. And yes, there were others with him. It sounded
like two, moving off to my left. I held my breath.

Then I caught the smell, oily and earthy, like a dirty fur collar. I heard
a deep-throated grunt and snuffle. I moved my head so that I could see
around the branches, and there, rising on its haunches in the middle of the
road, stood a huge grizzly bear. The silvering moonlight struck her back, and
it was as if she shone in the dark.

I would have preferred Moses Gaw.

But here I was, if not eye-to-eye, close enough to be terrified. Then one
of the cubs emerged from the brush, followed by the other.

This hillside in the night was their domain. We gold seekers were inter-
lopers, all of us with our sluices and flutter wheels and high-minded con-
ceits. The sow came to within ten feet of me, then stopped, rose on her
haunches again, and snorted. Was it me she smelled in the still air? The salty,
pickled stink of white meat, dirty clothes, and abject fear? Or was it the
garbage down in the slops pit beside the outhouse?

I wanted to sheathe the knife and pull my pistol, but any motion would
attract her. Bullets would only anger her and alarm the camp, too. So . . .
sit, hold my breath, and hope she moved away.

Down below, a woman came out of the longhouse. She was carrying a
bucket. She chattered some at the men guarding the saw pit, then went
over and dumped the bucket. Fresh slops.

The grizzly snuffed, liked what she smelled, and down the hill she went,
pushing through the bushes, down toward the sleeping camp, down toward

the sweet aroma of garbage, down with her two yearling cubs tumbling after her.

I exhaled, then I unbuttoned my trousers and took the piss that had almost poured out of me unbidden a few moments before.

Then I heard one of the guards say, "What the hell is that?"

The other said, "You wait here."

His surprise was not long in coming. He shouted, "Oh, Jesus! Jesus!" And boom! A gun went off. The other man leaped up.

Now, the saw pit was unguarded.

In an instant, doors were banging, men were running and shouting, and the great mama bear was rising onto her hind legs. When the outhouse door swung open and all but slammed into one of the cubs, she turned to deliver a mighty swat that caught Moses Gaw in the side of the head.

Someone else shot into her huge back, which only enraged her. She whipped her paws about in a great arc as the terrified cubs scurried around her.

Moses Gaw tried to stand. The bear turned to the movement and with thunderous bellow and another swat, all but ripped his face off.

I heard him scream, saw him turn and stumble into the slops pit.

For a moment, I wondered if I should let this confusion unfold or take advantage of it. Then Cletis made the decision for me. He started shooting. His rifle flashed in the dark on the opposite bank, then his musket, then his rifle again.

Meanwhile, the men in the clearing did not seem to know where to shoot . . . at the grizzly now lumbering and bellowing and swatting at anything that came near, or at the terrified cubs, or at the hillside where muzzle flashes were flaming like starbursts in the night.

I ran to the front of the log pile. Two heavy stakes kept the pyramid in place. I kicked one out, then ran around to the other side and did the same. The pyramid held for a moment. Then, with a roar, it collapsed into a moving wall of two dozen logs . . . pounding and thundering down the hill, bouncing over their own stumps, flattening canvas tents, knocking down work stations, destroying sluices, and making a perfect diversion as I dove after them, down into the shooting and shouting, while the bears bellowed and the horses and mules that Chin had loosed came galloping into this scene of riverside chaos.

Hodges was at the door of the main building, shouting, "Not the bear. We're under attack. Forget the bear."

A rifle shot from the hillside whizzed past him and ricocheted off into the dark. He stopped shouting so abruptly that I thought he was hit.

I went straight to the saw pit. The logs had shattered the table and chairs, and the guards were running around with all the other Triple MWs, trying to make sense of what was happening in the torchlight. I grabbed the boards and threw them aside.

Flynn and Ng-goh looked up, and Flynn said, "What kept you?"

A bullet flew past my ear.

Flynn said, "We can't climb. They got our hands tied."

One of the Missourans saw me and pulled a pistol. I reached for mine, but a shot from the far bank took him in the side and sent him spinning away.

Flynn held up his hands and cried, "Cut the bonds! Cut the bonds!"

I took my knife and slashed through the rope. Then I cut Ng-goh's bonds. Meanwhile, the bear was still bellowing, and men were shooting at it, and the cubs were yowling, and Cletis was still firing. All was confusion, just as we had hoped.

Hodges shouted, "Stop shooting! Stop! Or we'll be shooting ourselves." Then he called, "Moses! Moses!" and was answered with a strangled cry from the slops pit.

The bear stood up in the moonlight, and the noise that rose from her made the ground shake.

Flynn bounded out of the hole, then grabbed one of the shattered chair legs for a weapon. Ng-goh sprang up after him.

I said, "Come on!" and turned.

And there stood Nathan Trask, in his long frock coat and hat, with a noose in his hands. "Going somewhere?"

"Straight to hell," said Michael Flynn, and he delivered a blow with the chair leg that squashed Trask's top hat and maybe split his skull. Down went the captain, and away went three fugitives from angry justice.

A woman on the bunkhouse porch was waving in our direction. "Samuel! Samuel, they're by the saw pit! The saw pit!"

Hodges came stumbling out again with a musket at his hip, shouting, "Stop! Stop in the name of the Miner's Council!"

"Where are we goin'?" said Flynn.

"The dam!" I pointed him and Ng-goh across the river.

And we raced through the confusion, past men who saw us and started to give chase, others who were still trying to chase the bears or grab the panicked livestock now galloping about.

And all the while, I could hear the crack of Cletis's rifle, then the report of his smoothbore musket, and in between, the peppering shots of Rodrigo's pistol. Then came the boom of Hodges's gun and Ng-goh spun down. I grabbed him and dragged him to his feet. But he had taken it in the belly, the worst place for a musket ball.

Hodges threw down the musket, pulled a pistol, and shouted for us to stop. As he raised it to fire, a shot from the trees hit him in the leg and took him down.

"Keep running," I said to Flynn. "Across the dam and up the hill."

Then I heard the shrill warning of Little Ng's whistle. No tune, no birdsong, just a scream above the shouting of men and the bellowing of animals and the crying of women.

Chin and Little Ng had risen from the water on the far bank, and Chin was shouting, "Run! Run!"

We kept dragging Ng-Goh behind us. He was losing strength, but we had almost reached the planked walkway across the dam when Sloate came out of the shadows. He did not tell us to stop. He did not warn us. He raised his gun and fired. The bullet went over our heads. Then he lowered, pointed at me, but before he shot, he fell to his knees, dropping the gun and grabbing at the back of his head.

Chin had hit him with a perfectly aimed rock that knocked him senseless. Then Chin cried for us to hurry because Hodges was up again, limping toward us. Two or three others had broken off chasing the bear and were coming, too.

I kicked Sloate's gun away and leapt onto the dam. Flynn kicked Sloate in the face and leaped after me. But Sloate grabbed Ng-goh by the leg.

I turned to grab Ng-goh and then I saw the brush-covered door floating toward the dam and the hidden fuse burning in the brush.

Chin screamed, "Run!"

I pushed Flynn ahead and stumbled after him. We both tumbled onto the bank as a flash lit the world. An invisible fist knocked me sideways, knocked me down, and punched through the air with a burst of sound that sent the dam flying into the sky.

Rocks and chunks of wood rained down everywhere. And a torrent of water swept through the breach, shooting down the ravine, slamming up and over the bank where the river turned, and roaring down the valley.

* * *

WE MADE IT BACK to our camp before dawn. But the water had made it well before us, racing down the little narrow gorge with enough force to knock the flutter wheel off its supports and somehow deposit it right against Big Skull Rock.

But our concern was Rodrigo. He was dying. He had sent pistol shots into the night, drawing wild gunfire back, and one of the shots had hit him in the gut. Now he was bleeding out, and there was nothing we could do.

We got him off his horse and into the cabin, where we laid him on the pallet.

"I'll stay," said Cletis.

"He won't be alive for long," said Flynn.

"Then he needs a friendly face, even if it ain't a pretty one." Cletis studied Rodrigo and listened to his breathing and said to us, "You boys best be goin'."

"What about you?" I asked.

"I can brazen my way out of anything." Cletis spit tobacco and laughed at his predicament. "Strange country. Friends become enemies. Enemies get to be friends. And too much mercy, well—"

"Too much mercy'll get you killed," I said. "You need to come with us."

Then we heard commotion outside.

Chin, Mei-Ling, Little Ng, and Friendly Liu were coming up the hill. They looked somber, sad, frightened, as gray as the pre-dawn light. They were leaving with everything on their backs but without Uncle Bao and Ng-goh, both now dead.

And there was something else. Half their gold was still buried under Big Skull Rock. Chin had insisted that they not dig it up until our attack was over. That way, if we failed and our claims were raided, the gold would still be safe for Mei-Ling to find later. But they would not be digging now, because the flutter wheel lay wedged in the way.

Chin grabbed at it, tried to move it, let out with a great bellow of frustration, then called for the ax, which Friendly Liu carried.

While the others watched, he began to swing the ax, swing hard and angry, but as soon as it began to echo off the hillsides, Cletis stalked out of our cabin and said, "That gold won't be worth a damn if the Miner's Council hangs you Chinks. I knew you planted it there and never touched it. I'll never tell anyone. So git. Come back for it later."

Chin stopped straining, as if he knew that Cletis was right and was a man of his word, too.

Then, from inside, Rodrigo cried, "Señor Smith. Please."

Flynn stepped toward Mei-Ling. She stepped toward him.

Chin stepped over the wheel and put himself between them. "You go north, Irish. We go south."

Flynn gave a long look at Chin, a longer look at Mei-Ling. Then he pulled a bag of peppermints from his pocket and put them into her hand. "We will see each other again."

She looked down at the bag, looked into Flynn's eyes, and tears filled her own.

Her brother grabbed her by the arm and said, "Never see again."

Cletis shouted from inside the cabin. "Y'all better be gone 'fore that sun gets up and those boys get their livestock together and come ridin'."

I headed west for San Francisco and the first Boston boat, even though my gold from the last four months was now pinned under the rock, like Chin's.

The Chinese aimed south for the Chinese camp, where such as they would be welcome, and where they might lose themselves in the anonymity of their race.

And Flynn, with his gold in his saddlebags, took one of the horses and headed north.

April 2, 1850
Shocking Intelligences

I reached Sacramento late in the afternoon of April 1 and checked into the Sutter's Fort Hotel, as there was no passage aboard the *Senator* until the afternoon of the second. I slept with my pistol loaded on my lap, expecting a posse of Triple MWs at any moment.

Then, this morning, two backtracking miners stopped for breakfast in the fort and discussed the events they had seen in Broke Neck. I ate and listened . . . and listened.

The Miner's Council had arrested Cletis in the morning. They tried him in the afternoon in Grouchy Pete's with Hodges as judge.

Cletis testified that he had slept through the night. Then a Mexican boy had come to him before dawn. Cletis explained that he had tried to help, but the boy had died. He may have thought these were good lies, but Samuel Hodges did not believe any of them.

Then they asked Cletis about his friends.

Cletis said that they had all left late the night before, played out, disappointed, and fearful of the Miner's Council.

Hodges did not believe this, either, and said that he had dispatched Sloate to find Flynn. The Chinese he did not care so much about. He could round them up anytime.

George Emery had corroborated Cletis with more believable lies: "Spencer came through about ten o'clock last night. He bought provisions and said he was headed for San Francisco. The Chinese came through a while later."

Pat Emery said the same, and who did not trust a woman who could make such a fine beef stew?

"And all the while," said one of these overheard miners, "a feller in black clothes and crumpled top hat was tyin' nooses to pass the time, like a woman knittin'."

I continued to listen with growing trepidation for the fate of my friend.

Hodges had his men carry the corpse of lawyer Tom Lyons into the saloon and showed the hole in his side, then the .45 caliber bullet they dug out of it. Hodges said to Cletis, "That's a ball from a Kentucky Long Rifle. Not many men in this district have such a weapon. But you do. You shot me, and Lyons, and three others. Moses Gaw is dead from the bear attack. His brother is dyin' from fever after you put a ball through his elbow. You did that, didn't you?"

Cletis did not lie. Yes. He had shot David Gaw. So saith the Lord.

Hodges told him that if he confessed to everything, they would go easy on the Chinese and his pardners. So, as a last gesture of friendship for us, that is what Cletis Smith did.

They hanged him from the same tree where they hanged Maria two nights before.

As the backtracker described it, "The old boy took a final chaw of tobacco, thanked the Emerys for being good friends, and swung off into space."

I could not finish my meal. I paid and hurried for the riverfront, more determined than ever to make it as quickly as I could to San Francisco and thence to Boston.

But something made me stop at Abbott's Sacramento office. If there was mail bound for me in Broke Neck, I might catch it. And a letter was waiting. It came from Janiva. My heart leapt, then fell, then leapt again.

Dear James,
I have accomplished something amazing. I am in San Francisco! By the time you read this, I will have been here more than a week. You will find me in the harbor, aboard the ship Proud Pilgrim . . .

Good Lord.
Without reading the rest of it, I ran for the boat.

PETER FALLON FELT LIKE he had lived it . . . or dreamed it . . . or drunk so much marijuana tea that he hallucinated it. But he knew those guys now. He had looked into their eyes . . . and maybe their souls. And . . . oh, man, why did they have to hang Cletis?

He was glad that Spencer didn't see it.

But was Janiva *really* waiting for Spencer in San Francisco? And Flynn, riding north with Sloate on his tail? Did he get away? Did he turn and kill Sloate? Did he find that river of gold? And what about the Chinese? This much was certain: if their gold was still buried, Peter Fallon knew exactly where it was, and he was going to go and get it. And . . .

How long had he been reading? He looked through the slider at the fog and said, "Wow."

"Great stuff, eh?" said Sarah Bliss.

"Spencer sure learns a lot about himself up in those hills."

"I meant the tea." Sarah was puttering in the kitchen area.

Brother B. was snoozing in his chair, which Sarah had turned again to the slider, so that he would be looking out on the water when he awoke.

She invited Peter to stay for dinner. "I'm making a nice quinona with tofu chunks."

Tofu chunks? Even if he didn't have plans, Peter would have declined.

"We're vegans," she said. "No food with a face. It's the ethical thing to do."

"Oysters and clams may disagree."

"Aren't you hungry? Munchies, you know . . ."

Brother B. raised his head. "THC bonds to the olfactory bulb and makes everything smell better, taste better, too. That's why you get munchies."

Peter *was* getting hungry, but he had to go. He gestured to the pages. "Let me take these. Then we'll be close to ending this."

"You'll end nothing." She dropped the pot on the stove. "You'll just cause more trouble."

"By telling a story of Gold Rush prejudice and the Foreign Miner's Tax?"

"Always blame the immigrants," said Sarah. "A story as old as humans."

Brother B. looked up and said, "They dropped the tax, then revived it a few years later, but only on the Chinese. Easy to pick on the yellow folks. California collected on them for a lot of years."

"But this journal shows the Chinese fighting back." Peter thought that might appeal to these two Sixties relics.

Wrong. Sarah swept her arm at all the pictures on the walls. "We've spent our *lives* fighting back . . . against racism, sexism, the Vietnam War, the draft, the big corporations that sucked our blood in sixty-eight and the bigger corporations that are sucking our bone marrow today. We have enough stories to tell."

"So you've sided with Manion Sturgis. But the only thing he ever grew besides a grape was a hedge . . . as in hedge *fund*."

"The enemy of my enemy is my friend," said Sarah.

"When the earth asked him, he gave the right answer," said Brother B. "What's your choice? A vine or a mine?"

"Nice rhyme," said Peter. "But he grows Zinfandel, a wine for grilled meats."

"Now you're just messing with us." Sarah chuckled. She could take a joke. But she still wouldn't let him take the journal. And she wouldn't admit that she had ever read any other part of it.

"We'd rather contest the will," said Brother B. "I will be filing a motion on Monday to have this codicil struck."

EVANGELINE HAD DONE IT.

That's what she was thinking. She had brought the Sturgis brothers together to discuss their work, their rivalry, and the wonderful world of wine. A hell of a story . . . at least for the people who read *Travel and Lifestyle Magazine.*

They were meeting on the Silverado Trail, a legendary two-lane blacktop that wound through Napa like the aortic artery of California Cabernet. Unless you came by helicopter, you approached the Sturgis House under a long allée of palm trees that ran past visitor parking and the tasting room, the winemaking and bottling facility, then up the hill to the Victorian mansion that the family bought out of a Prohibition bankruptcy in 1931.

Evangeline and the Sturgis brothers were sitting on the veranda, over-looking the golden sea of grapevines that rolled toward Caymus, Mumm Napa, and Joseph Phelps. Six bottles sat on the table, along with a few cheeses, a sourdough baguette, water flask, waste bucket, and three Riedel glasses for each drinker. They had tasted their way from the Chardonnays to the single vineyard Pinot Noir to the three mighty Cabernet Sauvignons.

Manion was playing his best-behavior card. But Evangeline knew it was getting harder for him as the day wore on and the alcohol content in the wine went up.

Where he was expansive and boastful, always aware of his own pres-ence, the balding, pot-bellied George was soft-spoken and distracted, like an accountant planning on nine holes after he finished the morning audit. But he made terrific wines. Evangeline had taken notes on all of them. She had also gotten the brothers to talk, and she had taken notes on that, too, prodding them about their passions and the sources of their fraternal con-flict.

Manion had made his fortune on Wall Street and come home to make wines, just as his brother was hatching plans to expand the sales of his lower-end Chardonnays and Pinots. This should have meant a perfect match, the serious older brother and the playboy money manager, wine smarts and business experience, U.C. Davis and Harvard B. School. But the conflict that arose—not for the first time in a California winemaking family—pitted a grand vision for boosting the bottom line against an arti-san's dream of beauty in a glass, or, as George once described it, the "Char-donnay realist" and the "Zinfandel dilettante."

George and Manion had a younger sister named Rebecca. The three of them had inherited the Napa property from their father, a cousin of Mary-anne Rogers. But Rebecca spent her time chasing acting jobs in L.A., seldom visited, and always voted with George.

So, when George decided to go big, Manion went to Rainbow Gulch. George turned to the venture capital firm called Sierra Rock, announcing, "We'll grow cheap Chardonnay for the guzzlers and Arbella Reserve for the connoisseurs. Let my brother grow Zinfandel. It's a lowbrow grape, no matter how you grow it."

From such condescensions were family feuds born, and you did not condescend to Manion Sturgis. When it came to condescending, if anyone was doing it, it was going to be him. But all afternoon, he kept smiling.

Then George said to Evangeline, "What did you think of Arbella House?"

"A home, a museum . . . beautiful," she said.

"A pity that the new will mandates a sale," said Manion.

"Is that why you're stalling?" asked George. "Because you love the house and want to hold on to it a while longer?"

"Now, boys"—Evangeline tried to keep it light—"Peter Fallon came to California to appraise the Arbella books. I came to taste the wines and—"

"—reconstruct the Spencer journal?" asked George. "That's what Barber said."

"Barber." Manion spit the word but not the Reserve Cabernet. He said the wine was too good to spit, which made him envious. But since he wasn't driving—he had a designated pilot—he was swallowing, which made him more outspoken, despite his good behavior.

George told Evangeline, "Barber called you the 'on-again off-again' girlfriend. If I know Manion, he's hoping you're off-again. Why else would he be impressing you with helicopter rides?"

Manion poured himself a little more of the Reserve.

George said, "I'd rent a helicopter to impress you, too." He was not as smooth as Manion, but he was genuine, perhaps because he was widowed.

Evangeline liked him. She said, "The wine was enough."

Manion stopped swirling and gave her a look.

She said to him, "Your brother must love you. He pours you his best wines and plays wingman, in case I missed the helicopter come-on."

"I don't need a wingman," said Manion, "and I make my own wines."

"And you're very good at both." She knew it was time to flatter. "But—"

"—I bet you'd love my section of 'The Spencer Journal,'" said George.

"An added bonus, after the wines," she said.

"All you have to do is ask." George excused himself for a moment.

And Manion taunted Evangeline in a high voice. "'The wine was enough.' I bet you tell that to all the vintners."

"Don't get jealous. Two jealous men is more than I can handle."

"Peter? Jealous of me? Cool." Manion finished the wine.

George returned with a leather folder. "My gift to the on-again off-again girlfriend of the famous Peter Fallon."

Manion said, with sudden anger, "Was she *compos*?"

"Was who what?" asked George.

"*Compos mentis*? It's legalese for 'Did Maryanne Rogers have all—or any—of her marbles when Barber manipulated her into signing the new will?'"

"Why would Barber manipulate her?" asked Evangeline.

"Because he manipulates everyone," said Manion, "including Peter Fallon's son."

"You got the kid the job," she said.

"As a favor to you. Against my better judgment." Manion looked at his brother. "Why did Barber get this codicil into the will? Or was it you?"

"You can blame me because Barber brought Sierra Rock to us and because I brought Barber to Maryanne. But don't blame me for undue influence. She knew what she was doing. She wanted to divide her cash among her heirs, sell Arbella House and its contents for charity, and reconstitute the journal that tells the creation myth of California. She was planning for all of it, long before Barber came along."

"And the hit-and-run? Was she planning for that?" asked Manion.

"Drink your wine," said George, as if he would not dignify that remark.

"Drinking your wines almost makes up for your bullshit." Manion's phone pinged. He read: "A text from the pilot. 'San Francisco fogging in. Need to leave now or unable to land on Alc.'"

PETER FALLON SENSED THAT someone followed him through the fog from the *Tree Hugger* to the five thirty ferry. If he hadn't passed so damn many kids in hoodies, he would have thought it was one of them. But kids like that were everywhere, or so it seemed when you were looking for them . . . and you were still a little . . . *high*.

He texted LJ. "Leaving Sausalito. Know location of Chinese gold."

LJ popped right back. "Take ferry to Pier 41. Come to SF Maritime Visitor Center. Drinks, answers, more Barber, too. Appearances to keep up."

Peter hoped they had hors d'oeuvres, because . . . well, he had the munchies after all, and the aromas from the restaurants on the Sausalito waterfront weren't helping.

As the ferry rumbled into the fog, he took a seat and checked the link LJ had sent: "Tonight, at the National Park Visitor Center on Jefferson St., Friends of the San Francisco Maritime District invite you to partake of history, cocktails, and conversation."

A fund-raiser, one of dozens every week in a city like San Francisco. And one of the major sponsors: Van Valen and Prescott. So yeah, appearances.

EVANGELINE AND MANION STURGIS buckled in, and Napa was soon spreading below them, while the sun steamed into the blanket of fog out beyond the coastal range.

Through the earphones, Manion said, "Sorry I got pissy back there."

Click. "You're forgiven."

"I hoped the pages I gave you would end the questions about 'Chinese Gold.'"

"They didn't," said Evangeline. "The questions multiply."

"Such as?"

"If your brother insists there was no undue influence, why do you disagree?"

"Because my brother is in business with Sierra Rock, which is in business with Barber. And I don't trust Barber."

"Neither does Peter."

"I'm surprised he stayed on the case. He seems like a bottom-line kind of guy."

Evangeline was enjoying the wine, the flirtation, the helicopter rides. But she didn't like loose talk behind Peter's back. She said, "I guess you don't know him very well."

The pilot clicked on, "Hey, boss, I can't land in San Francisco, not in the fog."

"Oh, darn," said Manion.

"We're not cleared anywhere else in the Bay Area," said the pilot.

"Nothing to do then," said Manion, "but make for Amador."

"Amador?" said Evangeline.

THE SAUSALITO FERRY REACHED Pier 41 at 6:05.

The fog lay so thick over Fisherman's Wharf that it looked like the neon signs were bleeding liquid color into the atmosphere.

Peter glanced at his phone as he came off.

A text from Evangeline: "Fog. Must land in Amador. Back tomorrow via Larry Kwan. Don't worry."

He texted back. "DON'T WORRY? Spending night in Amador - with Sturgis? - and don't worry? WTF?" SEND. He hurried along Jefferson until his phone pinged. He stopped to read under the famous FISHERMAN'S WHARF sign with the big red crab.

Evangeline: "Staying in guesthouse. Locking door."

Peter: "Make sure he's on other side when you do." SEND. Then he pressed her number. Time to *talk* to her, the way people used to when they had something to say. Talk and walk at the same time because he had to get away from the sights and smells of all the open-air seafood counters—God, he was hungry.

The phone rang five times before another text came in: "I'm in effing helicopter! Wearing ear protection! Can't hear myself think let alone HEAR YOU on phone! Do. Not. Worry. And Manion says, do not trust Barber. Ties to something called Sierra Rock."

ON THE HELICOPTER, MANION said to Evangeline, "'Do. Not. Worry.' You never have to worry with me." His voice was seduction soft.

Thank God for headsets, she thought, or he would have been nibbling her ear.

She turned off her iPhone and said, "Please don't read over my shoulder."

She really hoped that the guesthouse had a lock.

AFTER THAT TEXT, PETER tried to calm down. Not easy to do with low blood sugar and a hyperstimulated olfactory bulb. He hurried past the high-end art galleries and high-tack souvenir shops and—oh, God—the In-N-Out Burger. But all he bought was a bottle of water, which he sipped while Googling Sierra Rock:

"A private equity firm focused on Pacific Rim investments—leveraged buyouts, growth capital, associated investment funds—across a broad range of mineral and resource-based industries." The article mentioned investments on both sides of the Pacific—mines, vineyards, and other U.S. investments. Most important: Michael Kou was listed as one of the principals. Beyond that: "U.S. legal representation by Van Valen and Prescott, San Francisco, Ca. Contact Johnson Barber."

The circles were tightening. Peter decided to go into that party with a plan. The best he could come up with: blow things up. But hydrate first. So he drank down the bottle of water and kept going.

PETER LOVED CITIES THAT loved their history, so he felt right at home walking into the National Park Visitor Center, in the repurposed cannery building on the corner of Hyde and Jefferson. He got a name tag and looked around: a six-foot-tall antique lighthouse lens dominated the space, surrounded by ship models, two bars, and running toward the back, a long exhibit hall.

Over in a corner, appearing to take in the exhibits while taking in everything else from the corner of her eye, was Christine Ryan, of all people. As soon as she saw Peter, she disappeared.

But the power crowd was filling fast: young lawyers and business people, creative types and . . . in San Francisco, it wasn't always easy to tell who was business and who was creative. A guy in dreadlocks could be the best software engineer in town. The young woman in the conservative Hillary pantsuit might be working at some cool think tank down by the Bay Bridge. And the Gen Xer in the bushy beard and stocking cap might have access to more venture capital than half the bespoke hustlers in Manhattan. So . . . not a bit like New York or DC or . . . yeah, here came a platter.

Peter went after it.

The server, a young Asian woman in a tuxedo shirt and black bow tie, said, "*Croque m'sieur,* sir?"

Little grilled ham-and-cheese sandwiches with a fancy French name. Peter grabbed two and inhaled them.

"Where's your girlfriend?" Johnson "Jack" Barber sidled up. "Off-again?"

"Off on business," said Peter. "And you know, you don't have much skill at winning friends and influencing people. The minute she met you, she put you on her shit list."

"I'm on a lot of shit lists. That's why I have your son working for me." He pointed to LJ, in the midst of a group of older men, chatting and charming. "Smart boy, nice personality, good looking."

"Like his father." Peter grabbed a couple of coconut shrimp from a passing tray and dipped them into the sweet sauce.

Barber said, "Hungry?"

"Starving." Peter stuffed one into his mouth.

Barber watched like an annoyed prosecutor. "Any luck with the Spencer journal?"

A drink tray was coming—red, white, and sparkling water.

Peter said, "You're drinking red. Is that a preference or a statement on the white."

"Sturgis Napa makes a nice Pinot."

"In that case—" Peter snatched a glass of red.

The party photographer came by, told them to smile.

Barber gave a big fake grin.

Peter held up his glass and said, "Fancy party."

"This is an important charity for us," said Barber. "We're one of the city's oldest firms. We understand history."

"I wish I did." Peter downed half the wine. "And I've been studying it all my life."

The camera flashed a few times, and Peter was sure that at least one shot caught Barber glaring at him, because as soon as the photographer slipped off, Barber said, "You appear to be thirsty, Mr. Fallon."

"Dry as a bone." Peter grinned.

Barber took a breath, as if to move past annoyance, as if he hadn't pegged LJ Fallon's father for a drinker. "I appreciate that you've been working without portfolio. It speaks well of your commitment to your son and to the historical truth of the journal. If we can put it back together, we can liquidate the estate and move on. That's all I want to do for the family, yet they're resisting."

"Why would they resist? As you say in the law, *cui bono*?"

"Who benefits? From doing what the law prescribes?"

"Who benefits from reading the story of James Spencer and the Chinese with their bags of gold and Michael Flynn with his river of it?"

"Michael Flynn? I don't know who that is," said Barber.

Peter didn't believe him for a second. But here came more shrimp, and Peter couldn't resist. He grabbed, dipped, ate, but what to do with the tail?

Barber said, "You might use your pocket."

"Or"—Peter knocked back the rest of the wine—"my empty glass." He dropped the tail into the glass and grabbed a Chardonnay from another tray. "Let's try the white."

"Yes, do . . . before they run out."

"Well, you know, Jack—they call you 'Jack,' right?"

Barber gave him a thin smile. Peter half expected him to say that only his friends called him "Jack," but a Boston Book Man could call him Mr. Barber.

"You know, Jack, all this business with wiseass tongsters like Wonton Willie is driving me to drink. I came out here to help my son, and—"

"Smart boy, as we have agreed."

"—all of a sudden, I'm in a Chinatown gang war over this journal."

Barber pretended to laugh, though he wasn't amused. "A war? I doubt it."

"Doubt it all you want." Peter swallowed half the wine and saw that he was getting where he wanted to go—under Barber's skin. "But Wonton Willie asked me to find the Chinese gold that Spencer writes about, so he can give it to the Dai-lo, the big man from the Hong Kong Triad. You know the Triad, right? Chinese organized crime, like the Mafia."

Barber sipped his wine. "This worldwide Chinese crime stuff, it's out of the Nineties. Whatever's happening on the streets today is local and petty.

My Chinese contacts are businessmen. Very important. Very upright. Just look around this room. Many of them are here."

The noise level was rising. But it swirled around Barber. A powerful man power-talking, even in the middle of a party, got all the power-space he needed.

Peter said, "You seem to know a lot about the Chinese."

"And you're learning. But remember"—Barber kept smiling like a baseball fan imagining a World Series between the Red Sox and Giants—"your allegiance is to your son, and his is to me, and ours is to our late client, last great-granddaughter of James Spencer. Help your son, and—ah, here's the young man now."

LJ was coming toward them, wineglass in hand.

Peter said, "Back so soon? You can't be too serious about this Spencer journal if you're running off to L.A."

Barber glared into Peter's glass, then at Peter. "I sent your son to L.A. because we thought the Sturgis sister had one of the notebooks."

Peter looked at LJ and winked. *Play along.* "Did she?"

LJ said, "We were misinformed."

"That's how I feel right now." Peter raised his voice a little. "Johnson 'Jack' here can't even give me good information about the local Chinese community."

LJ's eyes shifted, as if he was embarrassed at his father's familiarity. "Mr. Barber is an expert, Dad."

"Expert?" Peter finished his white wine and grabbed another. He toasted to Barber, who watched disapprovingly as Peter drained half the glass in a single swallow.

Barber looked at LJ. "Perhaps you should educate your father to the important Chinese interests we represent in America."

"Like, unh, Michael Kou's Sierra Rock?" asked Peter in a loud voice.

And for a moment, conversation stopped all around, as if someone had dropped a glass on the floor. Heads turned. Eyes shifted. Even Christine Ryan looked from behind the giant lighthouse lens. Michael Kou, of all people, pulled his head out of a conversation halfway into the main gallery. *Bingo,* thought Peter. And was that one of the bodyguards from the Arbella Club steps and the Emery Mine parking lot? *Bingo!* And where was the bodyguard's boss? Right there, talking to Michael Kou. *Triple Bingo!*

"Here's to Sierra Rock." Peter took down half the wine still in his glass. "Whatever they're up to."

Barber said to LJ, "Your father likes wine."

"I sure do," said Peter.

Barber's head veins were pulsating. He scowled at Peter as if he had just smelled a lie in a deposition, then he pretended to see someone on the other side of the room, made a phony wave, and left the Fallons alone.

LJ whispered, "Come on, Dad. Don't embarrass me."

"Don't worry," said Peter. "I hydrated and filled up on hors d'oeuvres. I just wanted your boss to think I'm a little bit more of a loose cannon than I am, just to see how he'd react."

"And?"

"Half the room hopped a foot into the air when I mentioned Sierra Rock, but don't tell me whether they're investors in Cutler or the Emery Mine. That would be too easy. Let me guess."

"'Need to know,' Dad. 'Need to know.'"

The partiers were again raising the volume so high that Peter and LJ were talking out loud, and no one else could hear them. This event had achieved the definition of what Peter called a "full stand-and-shout."

"Behave yourself for ten minutes," said LJ. "I have to work the room and calm a few nerves you just frayed."

"Keeping up appearances?"

"Right. And when I talk to Michael Kou, keep your distance."

"What about the guy he's talking to now?"

"Him, too."

"Is he the Dai-lo?"

"Later, Dad. Promise. Now, you need to know about the ship that got this thing started. The *Proud Pilgrim*." LJ pointed his father into the exhibit hall. "Follow the timeline."

So PETER SNATCHED A glass of sparkling water and retreated into a corridor lined with exhibits, including a multimedia presentation about the Bay, from native fisherman to the Bostoños to the Transamerica Pyramid, an interactive map showing the building of the Gold Rush wharves and the filling of Yerba Buena Cove, a mock-up of the Sam Brannan storefront . . .

Then, the noise and swirl of the party dropped away, because Peter came to this: a life-sized photo of workers in modern San Francisco, excavating an old ship. Displayed in front of the photo—a rusted kedging anchor, a cognac bottle, an old Ames shovel, and projecting out of the image like a 3-D extension of it, a piece of the ship's keel.

The placard read: "Workers uncover the infamous Gold Rush Murder Ship. The *Proud Pilgrim*, out of Boston, arrived in San Francisco in March,

1850, scuttled in May, 1850, rediscovered during an excavation along Clay Street in July, 2016." This was the ship that Janiva mentioned in her letter to Spencer, dated March 28, 1850. Peter felt the historical synapses firing in his head. Past and present were reaching toward each other, right here in this exhibit. And shortly after this story broke, the Spencer Journal disappeared. Why? Perhaps because . . .

. . . a smaller photo showed what the excavators found when they cleared the mud from the bones of the *Proud Pilgrim*: bones of another kind, six human skeletons chained in the keel. For days, the story had been huge in San Francisco. How did the skeletons get there? And why? One had a bullet hole in its forehead and the back of the skull blown out. Another had been pierced by some kind of two-pronged object.

Was this the great scandal the journal thief was hiding, the black blot on the Spencer name?

Then Peter sensed someone standing beside him. Red hair, red lipstick, expensive blue pantsuit. A great combination.

She said, "Amazing to think that there are ships like this buried all over the financial district."

He whispered, "Is that supposed to be an icebreaker, so that anyone noticing thinks we're just having a random conversation?"

"But it *is* amazing," said Christine Ryan.

"At most parties, if a beautiful redhead seeks me out in a quiet corner and makes small talk, I start thinking about the age-old question, 'My place or yours.'"

"If you're thinking that now, Mr. Fallon, you're drunker than I think you are."

"Not drunk at all." He sipped the sparkling water. "Are you really FBI?"

"No. I just go around shooting assassins in random apartments."

Sarcasm. Why did he always like women with a taste for sarcasm?

He looked toward the brighter lights of the outer gallery, where LJ was in conversation with the big players. "What do you suppose they're talking about?"

"That's what your son will be reporting to me later."

"Reporting to you?"

"That's why I'm watching over him. That's also why you are still alive."

LJ, Kou, the sleek-tailed Asian man with the black and white bodyguards, and Johnson "Jack" Barber all threw their heads back, enjoying a big laugh.

"I'm surprised they're willing to be seen together in public," said Peter.

"Good P.R. Van Valen and Prescott trots out its biggest clients for this fund-raiser. Those guys know that appearing as pillars of the community is a good way to deflect attention. It also builds goodwill in case the shit hits the fan."

"Is it about to?"

Christine Ryan leaned forward, as if to read the display card more closely and to tell him that she wasn't answering that question.

So Peter said, "Let me put it another way. Is my son an agent?"

"Call him an asset. But remember, you're not helping anyone if you start sticking your nose too far into his work. Try not to keep blundering the way you just did."

"The Boston blunderer. That's me."

"Your Sierra Rock remark set off alarm bells." She straightened up and leaned close, so she could be heard in the din of conversation. "Just remember, your son is not alone in this. We have other assets."

"On the inside?"

"Everywhere." And she was gone. Just like that. So yeah, FBI . . . or maybe a phantom from the Gold Rush.

LJ MUST HAVE SEEN that conversation because he waited a few minutes, then approached. "Talking to all the players, I see."

"She started talking to me," said Peter.

LJ took his father by the elbow. "Talking to her leads to trouble. And you've ruffled enough feathers for one night."

"Sorry, but—"

"With friends like her, you don't need enemies."

"She was on our side this morning in your apartment."

"She's using me, and you, and she wants to turn my future father-in-law."

"Using us?"

LJ jerked his head for Peter to follow along. "I'll tell you outside."

Halfway through the crowd, Peter noticed the black and white bodyguards, watching. The white guy pulled out his cell phone. Bad sign.

LJ kept leading Peter with excuse me's and polite nods and friendly words.

But when they were a few feet from the door, Michael Kou stepped out of a conversation and into their path, looking prosperous in his expensive suit, and relaxed in a roomful of peers. "Evening, Mr. Fallon. Still hot on the trail of the Chinese gold?"

"Just like your partner, Jack Cutler. I met him today."

"You went to Placerville?" Kou asked, as if he did not already know the answer.

LJ jumped in: "Dad's looking everywhere, just as he said he would."

Peter played along. "Chasing myths, tracking journal pages. That's my job."

"Whatever you find, we'll be interested." Michael Kou shook Peter's hand a little longer, pulled him a little closer, "I want to help your son with his new in-laws." Then he gave Peter a wink, like they all were pals, which Peter knew they most definitely were not.

As an NPS ranger stepped to the podium in the corner of the room, tapped the microphone, and called for attention, LJ whispered to his father, "Let's get out of here."

OUTSIDE, THEY TURNED THE corner onto Hyde Street. A block ahead, the neon sign for the Buena Vista lit the fog, and the cable car clanged its bell in the turnaround.

LJ pointed his father toward the car. "Hop on."

Peter said, "Let's hop into the Buena Vista instead. I could do with a hamburger."

"Just go."

Peter took a seat at the front, on the right, in the outside section. LJ stood on the little platform beside him and held the handrail.

"Okay. Where are we going?" said Peter.

"A safe house."

"Safe house? Why?"

The car grabbed the cable and lurched across Beach Street.

LJ said, "That Sierra Rock business . . . where did you hear about that?"

"Evangeline brought the Sturgis brothers together for an article. Brother George mentioned Sierra Rock. So I decided to shine some light into that corner."

"You shined plenty. That's why we need a safe house."

"Time for you to shine some on a certain Asian guy I keep running into, along with his bodyguards . . . on the Arbella Club steps . . . in the Emery parking lot . . . at this cocktail party."

"That's Mr. Lum. And yeah, he's the Dai-lo, the Big Dragon."

"A gangster?"

"A very classy gangster, come from Hong Kong—" LJ glanced at two hooded figures on small-wheeled bicycles rounding the corner of Beach Street.

"I've been seeing a lot of those Dahon bikes around town," said Peter. "Just kids?"

"Maybe. Maybe not. Maybe good guys. Maybe bad guys."

Even with the wind blowing cold fog, Peter felt the heat rise at his neck. "If they're bad guys, why did you put us on a cable car that doesn't go much faster than a dog trot? And who sent them?"

"First answer, we're not going far, getting off at Lombard Street, so cable car is the way to go. Second, a lot of people could have sent them. But I think it's Michael Kou."

"Aren't you guys on the same side—"

"That's what I've had him believing. But something may have tipped him. Maybe it's because his people made Christine Ryan."

"I made Christine Ryan the day I got here."

"Or maybe it's because my father just outed me over Sierra Rock."

"Sorry."

"Don't always think you're digging deep by doing it alone."

"Well, don't be so goddamn mysterious and I won't do it alone."

The gripman was chatting with another rider. The conductor was in the rear, taking tickets. Everyone else seemed to be tourists, laughing, joking, ignoring the father and son at the front.

As the car climbed Russian Hill, LJ glanced at the guys on bicycles, who were pumping hard about a hundred feet back. Then he leaned close and said, "The Triad Dragons of Hong Kong want to go legit in the U.S. Much better than running prostitutes and protection scams. Berkeley MBAs trump street pimps like Wonton Willie any day."

"So Lum comes to San Francisco to work with Kou but . . . why was Lum in Boston?"

"Mending fences with the Boston boss. And if you want to meet venture capital guys in this country, you always go to Boston."

"So you went with him to hold his hand?"

"Part of the job. Barber bills big hours from Sierra Rock, and Lum is using Sierra Rock for his commodity buys. I was also tracking down a Spencer notebook, because no matter what happens, the journal's the thing."

"That's what people keep telling me. But why?"

"Because of the fucking river of gold, Dad. Come on."

"Don't swear at your father. But . . . is it really a river?"

"Well, not an actual river, but—" LJ stopped talking for a moment and watched a pair of guys in black leather jackets come out of the trees in Russian Hill park, about fifty yards behind the cable car. They were moving with purpose, loping like a pair of Dobermans, heads turning, heels clicking.

LJ took out his phone, texted something, kept talking. "When the Chinese government decided to offer low-interest loans for mineral exploration, Sierra Rock jumped in. So I introduced Kou to the only gold explorer I knew, Jack Cutler, who'd bought a piece of land up in Amador, up in a gulch between the Miwok River and Manion Gold Vineyards. Kou pitched local Chinese investors on Cutler, just to stir up some excitement. Then he took that excitement to the boys in Hong Kong."

"But?"

"The rumor has always been that Cutler's test holes were 'seeded.'"

"Seeded? How?"

"A geologist can create false results by sprinkling gold into test holes. A good test brings investors running. If the mine turns out to be a bust, as Cutler's did on further exploration, well, at least somebody makes money."

"That's why they hate Jack Cutler in Chinatown?"

"The Hong Kong Triad should have put Cutler down like an old dog, but Michael Kou wanted to put him to work instead. Always good to own a guy right down to his boots. So they told him they'd back him. Told him to keep hunting for that lost river. Also told him they'd kill him and his daughter and her fiancé if he blew the whistle on them."

The bell clanged out the San Francisco beat as the car crossed Chestnut: *BANG-ba-bang-bang. BANG-ba-bang-bang. BANG-ba-bang-bang.*

And somewhere between the bangs, Peter said to LJ, "So . . . you're fucked."

"Don't swear at your son."

"Where's Mary?"

"She's safe."

The cable car seemed to be rising at a forty-five-degree angle, lurching to a stop at the Chestnut Street corner.

Peter asked, "Where does Christine Ryan come into all this?"

"One Saturday, I drove up to Tilden Park to hit a bucket of golf balls at the driving range, and this woman takes the tee beside me. I'm a lefty, she's a righty, so she's looking me right in the eye. She compliments my swing, so I think she's hitting on me. Then she says, 'Do you know you are involved in a criminal enterprise with Cutler Gold Exploration?'"

"I bet that messed up your backswing," said Peter. "Did she offer you a deal?"

"I could go down myself or help take down the San Francisco players in an international money-laundering scheme involving a prominent San Francisco attorney and a venture capital firm called Sierra Rock, which funnels dirty Triad dollars through various gold mining operations—"

"Including Cutler's?"

"And turns it all into a nice clean commodity."

"A gold mine."

"A *lot* of gold mines. Deep rock mines like Emery with proven reserves, and long shots, too, like Cutler's river of gold. That's Michael Kou's idea. And Lum likes having Kou. He likes having a B-school butt boy—"

"—who now has a Boalt Hall butt boy of his own?"

"I've been working hard to make it seem that way. Then along comes my father, pretending he's had too much wine, outing Barber and Sierra Rock over cocktails."

"I'm sorry."

"Dad, I just want to be a corporate guy, do my deals, live my life with Mary, and—shit." LJ watched the shadows moving along the sidewalk. "They're getting closer."

The dark mass of George Sterling Park rose on the right, a high bank of trees and ivy on the hill between Lombard and Filbert. At the top was a tennis court fence, but no lights. Not in a nice neighborhood like this.

LJ looked up Lombard Street and cursed. "Backup's not here." His phone pinged again, he read, then said, "Okay. We jump off at the next corner, take the steps up to the tennis courts. Run like hell. We go along the fence, then back down to Lombard. They'll be there by then."

"Who? The Feds?"

"You'll know when you see them. Are you in shape?"

"I can outrun you but not a bullet."

"Get ready. Another half block, at the corner of Greenwich." LJ looked down the street at the Dahon bikes, which were also closing in.

The cable car herked and jerked.

"On three." LJ gripped his father's shoulder. "Stay with me, Dad."

"I've never quit on you yet."

"We'll talk about the divorce later. One, two—"

And they jumped.

Across the dark sidewalk, up the stairs, two steps at a time.

As he reached the top, Peter felt something zip past his ear. He yelled to LJ, "You were right. Bad guys."

They sprinted toward the end of the chain-link fence, then raced along the pathway through the trees.

Another bullet hit a redwood and sent up an explosion of bark.

Then a bike burst through the shrubbery and slammed into LJ, knocking him off balance. Peter barreled into the bike, sent the rider flying, grabbed LJ by the collar.

And both of them kept running, with the guys in black leather coming through the shadows.

Peter and LJ cut across the little switchbacks in the path, racing for the opposite corner of the park, for more stairs—wider, nicer, better lit—dropping down to Larkin and Lombard. As they trampled through the shrubs, they heard the bikes racing after them and the guys in black pushing ahead like hunters working the underbrush.

At the steps, they saw the limo idling, lights out, rear door open.

"That's it."

A shot hit the concrete right by Peter's leg and ricocheted. Peter ducked. LJ grabbed him. And—*Ping! Ping!*—the driver of the limo was out, his hands balanced on the roof, his pistol pointed up the stairs as Peter Fallon and his son pounded down.

Peter reached the limo and dove onto a rear-facing jump seat.

LJ jumped in after, right onto Peter, with the door slamming behind them.

And *bang*! A shot hit the window on the right side, starring the glass.

Someone shouted, "Go! Go! Go!"

And *bang*! The limo slammed into a second bike as it flew off the hillside. No stopping for that hit-and-run. They burned rubber up the street, scraping bottom on the crest of the hill, grabbing some air, shooting across Hyde, onto the famous stretch of Lombard with all the wild S-curves.

The car slammed left, then right, then left, then right, hitting the curbs on both sides, throwing Peter and his son back and forth and then . . .

. . . they got to Leavenworth and the ride smoothed.

That was when Peter could finally look up.

Waving in front of his face was a champagne bottle.

Wonton Willie said, "Tonight, we drinkin' Dom Pérignon."

IT COOLED QUICKLY IN the Sierra foothills, so Manion and Evangeline ate in the dining room of Manion Gold, at the A-table by the fireplace.

A fine crowd had followed the mountain roads from Jackson and Fiddle-town, Columbia and Calaveras, couples and families, foliage tourists who stayed in little guesthouses, Tahoe-bound travelers planning to jump off early for the run up Route 88, all filling the place with high Friday night spirits.

California modern was the theme: a wall of glass looking out on the illuminated vineyards, an open kitchen with a roaring grill, stainless-and-glass décor with redwood accents. The piano stayed quiet, just the right cool jazz tone. And the food was delicious: Braised lamb shanks. Rainbow Gulch zin. Truffled baked macaroni for soaking up the wine. Salad from greens grown right outside the door.

Evangeline took a taste of lamb and said, "This was a set-up."

"Heavy fog in San Francisco, I swear. I just hope I haven't gotten you into trouble with Peter. Although"—he leaned forward—"it's great to spend time with you like this."

Evangeline changed the subject. "Crowded on a Friday night, but on Tuesdays?'

"We're closed for dinner, Mondays through Wednesdays. But if we make Amador another Napa, well . . ."

"Stiff competition."

"Our wine is as good. We have more history. Route 88 runs right up to Carson Pass, where the wagon trains came through, and 49 goes down to the giant Sequoia grove at Calaveras. Few places as beautiful." He clinked her glass. "Few women as beautiful."

She liked that, but not enough to take it seriously. "You're working too hard."

"You mean if I back off, I might have a chance?"

"Talk about wine, not the effect of my strong Yankee bone structure on your—"

"On my what?"

She shook her head and cut the meat off the lamb shank. . . .

She was surprised that they still had plenty to talk about.

After the crème brûlée, he offered to walk her out to the little guest cottage, a few hundred feet back of the big house. The path wound through California palms and evergreens, past a gazebo where they had weddings, into an area displaying more Gold Rush artifacts, big stuff like a Pelton wheel, a Long Tom, an old miner's tipcart . . .

The full moon threw their shadows ahead of them. The little guest-house was already lit from within like a greeting card. And a move was imminent. She knew it. But she had decided there would be no full-on-the-mouth kiss.

Then Manion stopped in front of a huge, heavy, iron nozzle, about six feet long, propped nicely for visitors to study. He said, "Do you know what that is?"

"No, but it's very symbolic."

"That tool caused a lot of damage in California."

"Tools shaped like that often do."

"I'm serious. It's a monitor, the nozzle of a hydraulic mining hose. They ran water through these things from a great height, delivering enough pressure to knock a man over at two hundred feet. They could cut away whole hillsides in an afternoon to get at ancient riverbeds. You can still see scars all over the Mother Lode. But not here." Manion looked up at the moon and out at the vineyard. "This land was saved. But if they thought there was gold here today, they'd do anything to get it."

"Who's they?"

"*They.*" Manion made a wave of his hand. "Whoever they are, out there. The ones who destroy. The ones who don't care what they take and what they break. *They.*"

And she asked a question that suddenly seemed pertinent. "Do *they* think there's gold here . . . or do they *know* there's gold here?"

"No one knows anything."

"But a lot of people think that Spencer knew something, right? So they're trying to find the journal, and you don't want anyone to know any more than they do now."

"This is sacred ground, Evangeline. Ground I've been given to protect. I thank God for that chance." He took both of her hands in his. "And I thank you for understanding."

Oh, Lord, she thought, he was playing vulnerable again. That could be sexier than all the *smooth* in the world.

So she said, "Do you have an internet password in the guesthouse? I want to scan the journal pages from your brother and send them to Peter."

"Internet? Peter? I'm showing you my soul, and this is your answer?"

"I'm sorry, Manion." She kissed him on the cheek.

And he kissed her on the mouth. Not hard or aggressive. But enough . . .

She pulled back, looked into his eyes in the moonlight, looked for something, and said, "Just this once." She wrapped a hand around his neck and pulled him toward her and kissed him like a lover.

She wasn't sure why she did it. But she did it. And before he could pull her toward him, she was pulling away, catching her breath. The first words she could think of were, "The password?"

He looked at her as if to say, *You can't be serious.* Instead, he said, "You'll find everything in the cottage." Then he went off into the night.

"WHAT?" WONTON WILLIE FLASHED the gold tooth. "You think I have safe house in some crummy Chinatown basement, with all old grandpas and grandmas playing mah-jongg upstair and cigarette smoke floatin' down?"

They were on the eighteenth floor of a luxury high-rise on Mission Street, a block from the California Historical Society. Two bedrooms, nice furniture, in-your-face view of the Bay Bridge.

Mary Ching Cutler was waiting for them. She was sitting on the sofa, surfing the internet, when they got off the elevator. She gave LJ a hug. "I ordered from In-N-Out."

"My California dream," said Peter.

"Mine, too," said Willie. "Better than dim sum."

In the limo, LJ had given his father the backstory: He first met Willie four years earlier, as a young lawyer doing summer work in the public defender's office. He helped two of Willie's boys, in trouble for extorting a coin-op laundry. Ever since, Willie had kept a back channel open.

"And now, we all in the same boat," said Willie. "We all know each other business. I even know what you thinkin', Dad. Do Willie know about Feds?"

"Well, do you?" asked Peter.

"Hell yeah. Like I tell you." Willie walked over and waved his hand from one side of the vista to the other. "This Willie's town. I know everything. Feds watchin' me, Michael Kou, Mr. Lum. But they always watchin' someone."

Peter was watching the stream of headlights and taillights crossing the Bay. As safe houses went, this one was pretty nice, but he didn't think it was particularly safe. Eighteenth floor, no back door, access only through elevators.

"You know why I save you, hey?"

"You like my Boston accent?" said Peter.

"Because you still on the case for Willie. We got two day before big sitdown. You still goin' after Chinese gold. And that's what wins this fight." Willie looked over his shoulder. "Ain't that right, LJ?"

LJ nodded and told Willie, "Dad thinks he knows where it is."

"And tomorrow," said Peter, "I will go and get it."

"I like you father. He make a good soldier." Willie turned to Peter. "And you son, maybe secret agent, hey, 'cause nobody know just what his game is."

"What's *your* game," asked Peter.

"Like I tell you, I here to make Chinatown peoples happy and give Dai-lo nice gift, so he know who on his side. Mr. Lum want Michael Kou to run San Francisco. Smart boy, Kou. But book smart. Not like me. Not street smart. Streets tougher than books."

"So those were Lum's guys chasing us?" asked Peter.

Willie said, "Lum or Kou. Lum fly in from Hong Kong, do business, fly out again. When he want to scare somebody, like today in LJ apartment, he use tough guys from LA. Not San Francisco, or my boys know. Right, boys?"

Peter looked at Mullet Man and Wraparound, who were standing in the corners with their arms folded. Mullet Man nodded. Wraparound chewed on his toothpick.

Willie's phone chimed. He looked and said, "Burgers comin' up. Double Double Animal Style. You like? Animal fries, too, hey."

"I like," said Peter. "Whenever I'm in California."

Willie laughed. "Sometime, you gotta have a hamburger."

Mullet Man headed for the door. Wraparound went into the kitchen for beer.

"But I don't save you to eat no hamburger, Mr. Treasure Hunter Man." Willie came over to Peter. "I save you to find Chinese gold. When I give gold to Mr. Lum, everybody happy, even Mary Ching father."

"Don't do us any favors," said Mary, who was still scrolling on her iPad, feigning disinterest in all of this, perhaps as a defense against it.

"Get the gold, leave a good impression, squeeze Michael Kou out." Peter could not believe that Willie was in the dark about the deeper issue, the river of gold.

As the burgers arrived, distracting Willie, LJ whispered to his father, "Play along."

Wraparound brought in beers and handed them out. Everyone sat on the big sectional sofa, facing the floor-to-ceilings.

Willie said, "So where the gold?"

Peter said, "If I told you, I'd have to kill you."

"Kill?" Willie scowled. His burger quivered in front of him, dripping juice.

"Gotcha," said Peter. "A joke."

LJ muttered, "Old joke, seldom funny."

But Willie laughed. It would never do for the big man to miss the joke. He asked, "You need ride to get to gold?"

"Ride? No. A big deal like you attracts too much attention," said Peter.

Willie seemed to like that. "True. True. You do like you do."

Mary said, "He means that you should do it your way. He's giving you permission. He's a real gentleman."

Willie said, "Yeah, yeah. I no care how you do it, but I want Chinese gold. You get, give me, we all okay. After that, I look out for your son and girlfriend all time."

"I got friends," said Peter, thinking of Wild Bill Donnelly's .44 Magnum and Larry Kwan's bulletproof winery wagon. "My guy can carry the three of us in comfort."

Willie took a big bite of his hamburger and said, "What three?"

Peter gestured to himself, his son, and Mary.

Willie shook his head. "Oh, no. Mary like it here. She like view. She like Wi-Fi." He looked at Mary. "Real fast, hey?"

"Like lightning," she said.

"And she like how she order anything she want from anywhere in San Francisco and we go get it for her. But she stay here till I get Chinese gold."

That changed things, thought Peter.

His phone pinged in his pocket. He had a look.

Evangeline wrote, "Door locked. Guesthouse quiet. New journal pages scanned and sent from George Sturgis, who appears to be an innocent bystander to whatever is going on. Read this. Read about the *Proud Pilgrim*."

❧

The Journal of James Spencer—Notebook #6
April 3, 1850
Janiva and the Proud Pilgrim

I could not sleep on the overnight boat.

I paced the deck, gazed into the blackness, felt every slam of the giant piston, and wondered . . . what had driven Janiva to San Francisco?

And when I was not thinking about her, I saw Cletis, urging us to go, assuring us that he could brazen his way out of anything. I lamented now that I had not told him how much I appreciated what he had done for us, that I had not offered him a good word to light his way into the overarching darkness, or off to the stars, or up to whatever heavenly place he imagined in his fractured interpretations of Scripture.

My plan had been to get to San Francisco and board the first Boston-bound vessel. I had little doubt but that Hodges would come after me, despite the sacrifices of Cletis and Rodrigo Vargas and the bravely sworn (though perjured) testimony of the Emerys. Far better to face Hodges at home, in a court with rules of evidence, where witnesses would be few and defense attorneys more skilled than noose-makers.

Of course, they might get to Flynn first. Sloate would gladly shoot him in the back. Or Trask would claim maritime law and hang him. Or they might scoop up Wei Chin and his family at the Chinese camp. Still, I should have been proceeding as if they were coming after me . . . until I read Janiva's letter, then read it again and again.

March 28, 1850

Dear James,

I have accomplished something amazing. I am in San Francisco! By the time you read this, I will have been here more than a week. You will find me aboard the ship Proud Pilgrim, *anchored in the Bay. I have secured a commitment from Ames and Company of Easton and bought 2,000 shovels, with the promise of a partnership. Mr. Slawsby, of Brannan & Co., comes to the ship every day and offers to buy them all. But I will enter into no agreement until you appear. There is more to tell, but I will leave it for our meeting. Please hurry.*

Your Love, Janiva

In six weeks, San Francisco had expanded and solidified, like some confection left to set in the sun. It seemed now as if there were twice as many ships, twice as many buildings, and the population had doubled since August. I was told that it might double again by the end of the year.

And every time the city burned, they built it back up again, bigger, better, stronger. New wharfs reached out over the tide flats. Old wharfs reached toward the ships. And all of them advanced to the steady beat of steam-powered pile-drivers and men pounding nails. Meanwhile work gangs were hauling logs to build docks at right angles to the wharfs, so that tipcart drivers could fill behind them with sand from the hills and ballast from the abandoned ships. And as some created new land, others were throwing up storehouses, saloons, and gimcrack firetrap hotels. And every day, ships brought even more houses, pre-built in the East to hammer up as soon as there was land to set them on.

The *Proud Pilgrim* lay at anchor two hundred yards from the end of the Clay Street Wharf. A rowboat was leaving as mine arrived. A passenger was grousing about the way "that damned woman" did business.

Did he mean Janiva? I would not be surprised.

Stepping aboard, I was met by a man at a table. Before him lay an array of weapons: two Colts, a pepperbox, a Bowie knife. He said, in a grating English accent, "Name and purchase. Foodstuffs at the bow. Manufactures at the stern. Gold dust only."

I glanced forward: another table, another big man, another harsh accent.

Then I heard a female voice coming from the stern, from a table by the aft deck house, where half a dozen men clustered over a woman, either to gawk or do business. I could not quite tell as I could not quite see her, but I knew that voice, confident and smart. And I knew that silhouette, trim and serenely motionless.

I smoothed the red and yellow-paisley silk neckerchief that I had put on for our meeting and stepped toward her.

The man at the table almost knocked it over, he jumped up so quickly. "Did you hear what I said, mate? You go nowhere on my ship without statin' your name."

I had learned from Cletis Smith to answer a challenge with one of my own. So I said, "Are you the captain? And if you're not, why should I give you my name?"

The man picked up the Bowie knife. His face was sunburned, except where scars held it together with jagged white lines. He stood a head taller than I and seemed twice as wide, now that he was on his feet. He said, "State your name or step back."

Challenge met, turf marked, I consented: "My name is James Spencer."

He lowered the knife. "So you'd be the one she's waitin' for?"

"The very one." And here I had a choice. I could threaten this man who threatened me with the tip of his knife, threaten him with a bullet if he ever brandished a blade in front of me again. Or, I could conciliate. "You guard the ship well, sir. I thank you for being so assiduous in seeing to the safety of Miss Toler and the *Proud Pilgrim*."

He gave me a squint. "So *what*? So ass—"

"So *assiduous*. It means so dedicated. Thank you for being so dedicated." I also remembered Cletis's warnings about showing off my book learning.

"She said you was a smart one. Too damn smart. Well, here's the rule of the—"

"Is that James Spencer that I hear?" Janiva was pushing back from her table.

"Miss Toler." I headed aft, paying no further mind to the gatekeeper.

Janiva gestured for the others to give me room, and as they parted, the vision of my dreams appeared. She wore a prim crimson dress of gingham with a white collar, a gray shawl, and a broad-brimmed straw hat that made her look almost girlish. Her posture and tone were as formal as if we were meeting at a Boston cotillion. But from beneath the yellow brim, her eyes met mine, and she smiled.

Yes, she had done something more extraordinary than I could ever have imagined. And she was proud of herself. I could tell. Seeing her like this, holding the center of this circle of businessmen, in the bright San Francisco sun, I was proud of her, too.

Then she offered her hand.

I feared taking it, feared the merest touch of her after so long apart, feared that it might cause me to respond as I had when I thought about her on lonely nights in the high country. But I reached out and said, "Welcome to California."

She told the other gentlemen to complete their transactions with Mr. McLaws, who had taken their weapons when they came aboard.

The largest of these, wearing the blackest coat and beaver hat, looked me over as though I still had the dysentery. "If this man offers you fifteen dollars a shovel, miss, I'll offer sixteen." From the mended bullethole in the hat. I recognized Jonathan Slawsby, the man who had greeted us from his rowboat that first day.

I said, "Sixteen? The Ames shovel is the best made."

Slawsby played the high dudgeon that men of business sometimes affect when met by unexpected opposition. "Just who in hell do you think you are, mister?"

"I know exactly who I am, sir. Who do *you* think I am?"

Janiva said, "This is James Spencer, my partner."

Slawsby said, "Partner? I thought those Aussies were your partners."

"They're my bodyguards. A Boston lady can't go about San Francisco without physical protection, now can she?"

Slawsby said, "The gentlemen of San Francisco will do their utmost to protect your virtue, ma'am."

"I worry less for my virtue than for my two thousand Ames shovels and the license to import more—"

Slawsby's jaw flopped open, so that his beard dropped down over his shirtfront. "You hold an Ames *license*?"

She produced it from a sheaf of papers on the table.

Slawsby took off his hat, wiped the sweat from his forehead, and read the first few sentences before she pulled it away. He said, "May I bring this to Mr. Brannan?"

Janiva raised her finger for silence. In that she had met my father, perhaps she had learned the gesture from him. She certainly understood its impact, because Slawsby stopped in mid-sentence. She said, "You may bring Mr. Brannan here." She then excused us with this: "My partner and I have business to discuss."

She led me down the gangway to the saloon, where we were suddenly, exquisitely alone. She stepped into the shaft of incandescent gold falling through the skylight, took off her hat, took a deep breath, and hurled herself into my arms.

My whole being ignited, as if the skylight were a magnifying glass focusing all the sunshine of that April morning.

I shall avoid the most intimate details of our reunion, except that I could not stop from pressing against her, absorbing the softness of her, inhaling the sweet perfume of her. And she responded with a passion that bespoke her willingness to endure a six-month voyage just to be with me.

How much farther we would have gone at that moment, I cannot tell, because a voice dropped down the gangway: "Miss Toler. Miss Toler!"

It was the first time that the Australian accent of Tom McLaws invaded our privacy, but already I sensed that it would not be the last.

He and his partner, I learned later, had signed on to the *Proud Pilgrim* when she put in at Valparaiso, Chile and attached themselves to Janiva's cousin, John Toler Dutton, who had sailed as her protector and business partner. While the rest of the crew had deserted in San Francisco, along with the captain, these two had offered their services as bodyguards for Dutton, his goods, and "the lovely lady." But their protection had not been enough. On his second day, Dutton had wandered down the wrong street, only to be found the next morning beneath a boardwalk, skull stove in and pockets turned out.

McLaws' partner, Mr. Henderson, had accompanied Dutton and had brought the bad news, while admitting that he had fallen into a drunken stupor himself. McLaws had chastised Henderson with a belaying pin and promised that they would be vigilant in Miss Toler's services henceforth. Vigilance, on the part of McLaws, appeared to have grown into jealousy, perhaps for Janiva, perhaps for her supplies.

I sensed this from the moment of that first interruption, as Janiva withdrew from my embrace and said, "What is it, Mr. McLaws?"

"Beggin' your pardon, but will your friend be stayin' aboard this afternoon?"

"Yes, he will."

"In that case—" McLaws descended backward, big boots followed by big ass, then big, red face ducking under the beam.

"In that case—*what*?" Janiva smoothed her hair and the front of her dress.

"I didn't tell him the rules." McLaws spoke with the false friendliness of a man talking a child out of a sweetmeat.

"Rules?" I said, "About what?"

"About weapons on board. I take charge of all arms, so I'll take the Colt Dragoon I spied under your coat."

Here was another test. I said, "The Colt stays with me."

"I been lookin' after this lady's safety for ten days now, sir, and not a bit of harm has come to her. But for me and me mate, she'd have been all alone after the demise of Mr. Dutton. You should be thankin' me for that."

"I did," I said mildly.

"Well, then—" He held out his hand and gave me a grin, secure in the knowledge that his bulk intimidated most men.

I said, "You missed your chance when I came aboard."

His smile fell off, and the blood drained from his face, almost as if he had willed it. "Miss Toler was so happy to see you, I didn't want to spoil your reunion."

Janiva, whose emotions played on her face like projections from a camera obscura, showed sudden and surprising fear. She said, "James, it's a good rule, I think."

"He can have his gun when he leaves, miss," said McLaws, turning to me. "Stayin' at the El Dorado, are you? They ain't finished rebuildin' the Parker House yet."

I kicked open the shuttered door behind me and threw my sea bag onto one of the berths. "I'll be staying right here."

McLaws looked at me with no expression, which was more unsettling than his grins and scowls. Then he said to Janiva, "I can protect you, ma'am, from them who knows enough to fear me. But I can't protect you from every man you bring below."

It was as if he was leaving me out of this, as if this was only between them.

So I asserted myself: "I'll keep my gun, and you will give us our privacy."

"Is that your wish, ma'am?" asked McLaws

Janiva said, "We have business to discuss."

"When you do, remember our deal." Then he climbed the gangway.

"Deal?" I said to her after he was gone.

"He and Henderson are promised ten percent of the profits for security."

"Each?" I asked.

"I'm not sure. I was so upset when my cousin died, but . . . oh, James, I'm glad you're here." She led me to the stern, to the captain's cabin, which extended the width of the ship and was an even finer space than Trask's on the *William Winter*.

As soon as we had closed the door, I said, "I'm going home."

She folded her hands in front of her, lowered her head in that way she had of expressing disappointment, so that she seemed to be looking at you from under the darkest, angriest eyebrows God ever gave a woman, and she said, "I have come all this way to build something with you, and you would go home?"

"I was going home to build something with *you*," I said.

Her answer was simply to stand, still and silent, framed by the four windows of the stern gallery, with the blue of the bay and the light of the day pouring in around her.

So I told her of all that had happened, from finding the first gold to the final good-byes a few days earlier. And with each detail, her posture relaxed a bit, her expression blossomed slowly from anger to surprise to awe to shock, and when I was done, she said, "Did you leave your gold?"

"Five pounds, safe under Big Skull Rock."

"And the rest?"

"On account with Abbott Express. The value of twenty pounds was shipped to Boston in January. Following it home seems the safest course."

"But is it the *right* course? You fought for something up in those hills, James. You helped the weak confront the strong. Running can't be the right course."

"I'm tired of deciding the right course," I admitted.

She turned to the windows. "So you'd go home to Boston, where your family, your friendships, and your standing among your peers will speak more loudly than Samuel Hodges?"

"Isn't that why we live in a society?" I said. "To have the trust of neighbors and the benefit of reputation?" I realized that I sounded like my father.

"To have the benefit of the doubt, you mean?" She pivoted back, crossed the cabin, came close, looked into my eyes.

A week earlier, beside the Miwok, I could only have dreamed this moment, alone in a clean, well-furnished place, with Janiva's eyes on mine.

She said, "What you seek in Boston, you can have right here."

What I sought was her. But she was not offering herself. She was talking about something grander. She said, "You just need to build it, James. Build it through business, through relationships, as my father and your father and their fathers did it in Boston."

"You would"—I searched for a word—"*replicate* Boston in San Francisco?"

"I would remind you of how the world works."

"I've seen how the world works. It works harshly."

"Then let us set about changing it."

"You mean, civilizing it?"

"We start with Slawsby and his boss, the famous Sam Brannan. We make a deal for the shovels and other Ames equipment. We establish ourselves, so that if Hodges comes to extract vengeance, he's assailing a man of business, a man with friends, a man with a reputation."

It was good sense, though tinted with more hope than realism. I said, "*When* Hodges appears."

She went to the desk and wrote a note. "You sign first. The male in the partnership should sign first."

And I think that in the sudden intensity of her dedication, I loved her even more, no matter that her litany left out the most important leg on the stool of reputation: a man with a wife. A wife gave a man the stability of a rock in any corner of the world, and surely in wild and wifeless San Francisco.

I read the letter: "Dear Mr. Slawsby, Please inform Samuel Brannan that we shall await his visit aboard the *Proud Pilgrim* tomorrow, Saturday, at 11:00 a.m."

After I signed, she snatched the paper and scratched her signature beneath mine, then said, "What shall we call our partnership?"

I said, "Is it a full partnership?"

But before I could answer, we were distracted by an ear-piercing whistle as the steamer *Panama* came thumpering past, so close that her side filled the stern gallery, and her wake caused us to rise and rock and dip.

Janiva grabbed the table for balance and must have seen something on my face, something that reflected my uncertainty, because this exploded out of her:

"James Spencer, I did not endure my parents' shock, my friends' derision, and the leering looks of passengers and sailors alike, nor did I suffer awful food, cramped quarters, and water so layered with green slime that it smelled like a millpond, nor did I torture myself with seasickness, boredom, storms, and the death of my own cousin, all so that you could look longingly at the steamer that might take you back to Boston. I am here, James. I am here for you. I expect you to be here for me."

I let her words hang in the air for a moment, to lessen their impact as the ship stopped rocking, then I said, "If I look longingly, miss, it is only at you."

She lowered her chin and gave me that angled eye, from under that dark brow. "Then you *are* staying? It's your name on the Ames license. They're your cousins, not mine. Tell me that you are staying."

"Tell me that you did not come all this way just to sell shovels. Tell me that and I'll stay. Stay to build something more, out there"—I gestured to the stern gallery—"and in here"—I gestured to the space between us.

"Soon, James. Soon. If we can build a company, we can build a life. But the company first. The shovels. The deal with Brannan."

Such ambition she had, for a woman. But what she said was enough. Soon was enough.

Since we were not yet joining our names, I suggested we find a title for our partnership that bespoke our Boston background. We tried "Union," after the Union Oyster House. No. "Atheneum." Too bookish. "Beacon," for Beacon Hill? No, but what held memories on Beacon Hill? The Arbella Club. So . . . Arbella Shipping and Mercantile.

Janiva wrote it on the letter, beneath our signatures, then put the letter in an envelope. "We need to get this up to Sam Brannan straight away."

On the deck, I called for the rowboat.

McLaws said, "Me and me mate, Muggs Henderson, we'll do the rowin', sir."

Henderson was shorter than McLaws and carried a belly that protruded over his belt like a flour sack flopped over the edge of a buckboard. He gave a touch of his knuckles to his forehead, like a sullen seaman. "Pleasure to meet you, sir."

I had known Janiva's cousin, J. T. Dutton, and had never thought much of his judgment. I thought even less of it now that he was dead. Looking at these two, I thought that perhaps his judgment was the reason he *was* dead.

I told them I could row myself. The Clay Street Wharf was not far. But they insisted. They said that the day's business appeared to be done on the *Proud Pilgrim*, so Miss Toler would be safe aboard. And they had business of their own in town.

"Yeah," said Muggs, positioning himself on one of the thwarts and gripping the oars. "Ah-Toy's Palace of Pleasure is a good place to work off the stiffies."

"You heard of Ah-Toy?" said Tom McLaws, stepping into the boat after me.

"The Chinese princess of whores," said Henderson.

"And we're two randy kangaroos," said McLaws.

"We sure is, and protectin' a pretty lady like Miss Toler, it strains the loins."

"But don't worry, mate." McLaws patted my leg. "We been good boys."

I just looked at them. I had learned that sometimes, just looking was enough to unnerve a man, force him into saying what was really on his mind.

"So," said McLaws, pushing off, "how's the whores up in gold country?"

I said nothing.

Muggs chuckled. Maybe they would not be unnerved. "The quiet type, Trub."

They said no more until we looped a line around a piling on the wharf and started walking. They positioned themselves on either side of me, more as a threat than as bodyguards. After we had gone a short distance, sidestepping stevedores and piles of goods and scatterings of garbage and debris, McLaws said, "Did you hear what Muggsy called me? 'Trub'?"

I did not answer, as if I was not in the least interested.

"It stands for 'Trouble.' I'm known as Trouble Tom. Trub for short. 'Cause I'm nothin' but trouble for them as gives me such."

"Do I call you Trub, then, or Mr. McLaws?" I picked up my pace. I could imagine one of them stabbing me and leaving me to drop in the swirling confusion of dockhands and cargo and carts, so I wanted to be off this wharf as quickly as possible.

But McLaws kept pace. "You can call me Tom, so long as there's no trouble."

"Don't make trouble," I said, "and there won't be any."

McLaws looked at his partner. "Now there's a right answer, Muggsy, me lad."

I pointed to the dirty old brig *Euphemia,* anchored between the Clay Street and Long Wharfs. "Wouldn't want you to end up on the jail ship."

Their laughter told me that they underestimated me. Let them.

Now we approached one of those sights only seen in San Francisco: the whaleship *Niantic,* run onto the mudflat, propped with huge redwood supports, and surrounded with a fine new dock. They had covered her deck with what resembled a New England barn, cut a doorway in her side, and put up a sign: REST FOR THE WEARY AND STORAGE FOR TRUNKS. A larger sign along the ridge beam announced, NIANTIC STOREHOUSE.

"Amazin', it is," said Muggs, "doin' all that to a ship."

"What's amazin'," said Trub, "is the things people thinks of to make money. Some men makes things. Some makes the space to store things. Some digs things out of the ground. And some serves the rest."

"It takes all kinds," I said.

"Me and Muggsy, we serve. Don't you think it was good of us, stayin' on like we done to serve Miss Toler in her hour of need."

"Aye," added Muggs, puffing his beery breath, "'fore you was anywhere to be seen, Mr. Spencer of Boston."

"So true, Muggsy, me lad, so true." Like a bad actor, McLaws took off his hat and placed it over his heart. "Kept her safe from all manner of evil fate in a dangerous place."

"Damn dangerous, Trub. As dangerous as the hairy-faced Australian fucksnake."

"Ever heard of him, Mr. Spencer?" Trub McLaws put his hat back on.

"Not a snake I'd worry about, so long as it stays in Australia."

We crossed over one of those long docks running at right angles to the wharfs, following the line of Sansome Street. On the landward side, tip carters were dumping fill and shovelers were spreading it, creating new-made ground on which buildings rose as quickly as the land dried. But dry land was more hoped-for ideal than *terra firma* reality. When the tide rose, the new ground might still take on the consistency of buttered oat gruel, as I discovered when I stepped off the wharf into the ankle-deep mud.

McLaws and Henderson had a great guffaw at my expense.

Yes, I was stuck and damned embarrassed about it, too.

McLaws shouted, "So, our new pardner ain't smart enough to step 'round a big puddle when it's right in front of him."

I was not their pardner, but now was not the time to argue, stuck as I was with the mob of San Francisco—the walkers and hawkers, the workers and wagoneers, the muleteers and drivers and barking dogs—all sloshing and splashing around me, all oblivious to this little exchange of insults and threats.

McLaws came close and offered his hand. Reluctantly, I took it, preferring his help to falling facedown in the mud.

He said, "See how good we treat them we works for? A pair of stout blokes, we are. But we'll be paid fair. Ten percent of everything that comes out of your partnership. You understand? Ten percent. Each."

"I hope you got that in writing," I said.

"Ooh. In writin', he says. We'll give you writin'." He let go my hand, sloshed over to the boardwalk, and said to Muggs, "Let's go get fucked."

April 4, 1850
A Man of Business

I lay awake half the night trying to decide how to handle McLaws and his pardner. I spent the other half wondering how to bring Janiva into my bed.

With the Australians, it seemed best to act as the boss. So in the morning, I ordered them not to insult Mr. Brannan and his assistant by asking for their weapons when they came aboard. McLaws tried to contradict me, but I cut him off. "No arguments." And before he could answer, I turned on my heels and went below.

We had decided to receive Brannan and Slawsby in the captain's cabin, at the fine cherrywood table by the stern gallery, with the bustle of San Francisco as our backdrop. We would appear as part of the fabric of the city, part of its future.

Presently, we could hear them descending.

Janiva squeezed my hand and said, "Thank you. I have dreamed of this."

"I am shocked by this," I said. "By all of it."

Some big men shriveled when they drew closer. Some small men expanded to fill a room. Sam Brannan was a big man in fine crimson coat and luxuriant side whiskers, and he filled every bit of vacant space in the cabin, so much so that we barely noticed the blustering Mr. Slawsby coming in after him.

We exchanged pleasantries and took our places at the table.

Brannan had single-handedly started the Gold Rush two years before. Learning of the discovery at Sutter's Mill, he had quickly and quietly bought up all the shovels, picks, and pans he could find. Then he traveled to San Francisco, strode into the sleepy adobe settlement at Portsmouth Square, held up a bottle filled with glittering yellow dust, and shouted, "Gold! Gold! Gold from the American River!"

He might have sounded like a cheap barker in a country carnival. But his cries awoke the nation. And no one had ever called San Francisco "sleepy" again.

He was now reputed to be the wealthiest man in California. He was also a Mormon, one of the so-called Latter-Day Saints, though there was little saintly about him. I had heard that he could be crude, impatient, and outspoken, but his opinion was solicited on every matter. Such is the power of the money-made man . . . here or anywhere.

He looked at Janiva and smiled. "A lovely lady is a pleasure."

I was reminded of an old word, "lickerous," to describe the look in his eyes. He was eager, lustful, but constrained for the moment.

He turned to me. "Will the lady be negotiating with us?"

Before I could say anything, she said, "Yes. I will."

Brannan raised an eyebrow, as if asking me, *Are you in charge here or is she?*

But Slawsby jumped in, eager to assert himself. "Mr. Brannan has little time. You know of his reputation. You know it will speak well of you to be in business with him. Eleven dollars a shovel."

"Is this fair?" Janiva said to me.

Slawsby said, "Fifty percent, wholesale to retail, standard here and in the East."

Brannan's eyes offered me a challenge: Did I have anything to say, or was the woman going to do all the talking?

Janiva said, "We would do better to sell them ourselves."

Slawsby said, "That will require a warehouse, a store, a paid staff."

Brannan kept his eyes on me.

So I slid our licensing agreement across the table. "Ames and Sons make the best shovels in America. They invented the back-strap shovel. They make other fine implements, too. *And* they are my cousins."

He inclined his eyes, read, raised a brow. "You come from fine stock, sir."

"They promise a second ship with another two thousand shovels and two thousand picks. The *Madeleine M.* left a month after the *Proud Pilgrim,* but she's a fast brig, so the semaphore on Telegraph Hill will be announcing her any day now." This was all as Janiva had described it to me.

At a look from Brannan, Slawsby said, "Let's not quibble, then. We'll sell these shovels in Sacramento for twenty-two dollars apiece. But we'll offer you twelve, a dollar more than wholesale."

I said, "I've been in a camp called Broke Neck."

"We've heard of Broke Neck," said Brannan. "We've heard of trouble there."

I felt Janiva tensing beside me.

But I remained calm and offered my prepared answer: "The Miner's Council overreached their power. Trouble always follows when men seek to inflict their will unfairly on others."

"True in the mines," said Janiva. "True at this table."

I had not expected that, but it was the perfect point. We made a good team.

Slawsby huffed, "How does Broke Neck affect wholesale on your shovels?"

"Traveling from Broke Neck, one goes through Sacramento, so one may visit Mr. Brannan's fine store there, where a shovel much inferior to the Massachusetts-made Ames shovel goes for twenty-*five* dollars."

Slawsby reddened, scowled, picked a bit at his beard.

But Brannan seemed to brighten, as if sensing he was in the presence of someone more formidable than he had first thought, and while he might not have liked that fact, he liked the challenge. So he sliced to the bone of the matter: "We'll offer you fourteen."

I looked at Slawsby. "Yesterday, you offered sixteen."

"Sixteen?" Brannan turned his bushy side whiskers to Slawsby.

"I heard a rumor that someone was planning to bid fifteen and sell at thirty," said Slawsby. "I wanted them to know we'd be prepared to top it. But—"

I cut him off. Time for the kill. Time for the deal. "If you would pay sixteen against fifteen, it means you think our shovels are worth seventeen. So—"

"Do you see that city behind you?" Brannan slid his hands into his waistcoat pockets and pointed his chin at the stern gallery windows. "Do you know how much of it I own?"

Intimidation by means of wealth and power was a game I had seen my father play.

Before I could think of a response, Janiva said, "If you own as much as we've heard, you'll need shovels to dig foundations. Many, many shovels."

Brannan almost smiled. "But if you hope to get more than thirteen, you'll need to find another bidder. Who will bid against me?" Despite his reputation as a blowhard, he spoke softly when he spoke from power.

But I had to earn his respect now. If I did not, I'd best flee on the *Panama* at the next trill of her whistle, because these men knew about Broke Neck. That meant the story was spreading and would soon swell into a nasty carbuncle, one that a man without the respect of his peers might never be able to drain.

So I said, "Are you familiar with my friend, Mark Hopkins?"

"Hopkins, the hardware man?" said Slawsby.

"A license to sell Ames shovels would benefit Hopkins, undercut you, and develop a business relationship for me in Sacramento."

And competition made all the difference. Our back-and-forthing went on for a time, but we agreed. Arbella Shipping and Mercantile would sell 75 percent to Brannan for two years, shovels and picks at a firm price of sixteen dollars. But because I was loyal to my friends, I had to give Mark Hopkins a chance in Sacramento. And that might have been the most important position I took, for Brannan said, "A man who is loyal to his friends, even if they are my competitors, is a man I can trust." I knew then that I would have an ally in Sam Brannan.

He stood and shook hands and told Janiva, "You have chosen well, miss."

Civilized business, conducted in a civil manner. We closed the deal with a bottle of the departed captain's De Luze cognac. Though Sam Brannan espoused Mormonism, he did not decline a good cognac.

GETTING RID OF TOM MCLAWS and Muggs Henderson proved more difficult. After we had signed the papers with Brannan in the new office of Reese Shipton on Portsmouth Square, I returned to the *Proud Pilgrim*, went to the table by the aft deck house, put my pistol next to the inkwell, and called our Australians aft.

When they were looming over me, I produced two sacks containing eight pounds of gold dust each—sixteen hundred dollars times two.

"There's your ten percent," I said. "Good luck and thank you."

Trub said, "Ten percent? Each? That don't look like ten percent each."

"Miss Toler tells me it was ten to split," I said. "Five apiece."

Janiva stood behind me, hands folded, eyes shadowed by her straw bonnet.

"Well, beggin' your pardons, but Miss Toler's as wrong as rottin' fish."

McLaws pulled from his pocket a sheet covered in pencil scratchings, and read, "'I hereby authorize Tom McLaws and Muggs Henderson, to receive payment of ten percent *each* for the total value of our shipment of Ames shovels upon completion of a sale in exchange for services. J. P. Dutton.'"

I snatched the sheet, glanced at it, showed it to Janiva.

She nodded. "That's my cousin's signature."

"Well, then," said Trub, "it's a contract, gen-u-ine."

"The signature may be genuine. But"—I held the paper between two fingers—"the document has been altered. Someone inserted the word 'each' in a darker pencil, and it's not initialed. If a caret is not initialed, it's invalid."

"Carrot?" said Muggs, about whom I worried less each time he opened his mouth. "We ain't talking about bloody vegetables. We're—"

Trub raised a hand for his partner to be quiet. Then he looked at Janiva and jerked his head at me. "Is he a lawyer? Because he talks like one."

"I'm not, but up on Portsmouth Square, there's a lawyer named Shipton. We can ask him." I stood and picked up my pistol.

McLaws kept his eyes on Janiva, as if to express an unspoken attachment, as if to say that the real man to protect her was himself. "This is how you'd treat us? Men who've tooken care of you and—"

She said, "I won't let you cheat me, Tom. You're released from your contract."

After a moment, Trub McLaws picked up one of the sacks of gold.

I said, "That's the full amount, though we've only contracted the sale of three-quarters of the shipment. Take it, or we can go see that lawyer."

McLaws hefted the gold. "Outside of a few police and some weak-kneed judges, there ain't much law in San Francisco. Men comes and goes and does as they please, and them as has the strongest hand has the strongest chance."

"That's why I never give up my pistol," I said.

"But that little popgun won't stop the Sydney Ducks. Ever heard of them?"

"If he ain't, he should," said Henderson.

"Right you are, Muggsy, me boy." Trub leaned on the table. "They live in Sydney Town, over by Telegraph Hill. They ain't the nicest blokes, and they been comin' in bunches, ever since word reached Down Under about this here Gold Rush."

"Aye." Muggs laughed. "More hairy-faced Australian fucksnakes every week."

I was looking for a chance to take this conversation back, and Muggs gave it to me. I picked up the pistol and jammed it against his red, vein-streaked nose. "Miss Toler is a lady. Use those words in front of her again, I'll put a bullet right through your pudding pot of a brain."

"Easy," said Trub. "What Muggs is sayin', in a crude way, is that we got bad Australians in San Francisco, and we got worse Australians. We come from a penal colony, you know. So most of us is escaped convicts, or former convicts, or the sons of such."

"So what?"

"So some folks say the big Christmas fire was set by them Sydney Ducks, lookin' to do some lootin' while the city burned. Considerin' that you two are settin' up a tradin' outfit, with your own warehouse and all, you'll need some lads who know how to fight fire with fire." Trub McLaws could sound quite logical when he wanted to.

Even so, I pretended not to understand his meaning. "Fire with fire?"

"In a manner of speakin'. So let's forget the lawyers and such. For one ounce of gold per day, per man, we'll protect you from the Ducks, the Chinks, the Greasers, and all other comers, whether you're here on the *Proud Pilgrim* or in a warehouse ashore. And from what I heard, you got another ship comin' any day now. You need our help."

So, this hairy-faced Australian fucksnake was an eavesdropper, too.

Janiva and I went below to talk it over, and we agreed that once the second ship arrived, we would need storage on land, and storage would need protection.

"Besides," Janiva added, "better to have these 'fucksnakes' inside the tent pissing out than outside pissing in."

I laughed. "Such language."

"I'm not Hallie Batchelder, James. I'm a woman of the world."

So she was. She was also right. We were stuck with these two. We could never trust them. But if we dispensed with them, they could make even more trouble. So I would let them enhance our presence—if not our respectability—in San Francisco. Arbella Shipping and Mercantile would have its own protection force. They would protect our goods and, by association, Sam Brannan's. And they would be well paid. That ounce of gold a day would be an investment in our safety . . . or a deal with the devil.

But I told them that if something happened to me, all agreements would end and Miss Toler would return to Boston.

"On a journey like that, I'd go with her meself," said Trouble Tom McLaws.

Such an answer gave me the resolve to sleep every night with my cabin locked, and my pistol or Janiva—or both—at my side.

And that night, to my everlasting joy, it was both.

April 5, 1850
A New Day

Janiva awoke with these words: "I cannot believe that San Francisco is ever anything but the most beautiful place on earth."

"If it isn't," I whispered, "we will make it so."

She rolled toward me. "But if we hope to bring our new city a bit of respectability, we're doing a rather poor job of it."

I told her I respected her more with every caress of her hand and touch of her leg.

So she pressed her leg against mine and ran her hand along my arm.

In all my imaginings of this morning, I had never anticipated the transformation it would make in me. I was drained of all but pleasure by the softness of her flesh, by the satisfaction of my own, by the salt-sweet aroma of our bodies filling my lungs and soul.

The captain's narrow berth, built into the little gallery that bowed out on the larboard side, was just wide enough for two, if two slept entwined as one.

"You're different than when we embraced after musicales at the Atheneum." She touched my cheek, just below the whip scar. "You look harder."

"The men who made the scar made me harder." I got up and pulled on my breeches. "Before we're done, we may both have to grow harder still."

"But not today. Today, I prefer to be a wanton." She threw her arm over her head, giving me a frankest yet most innocent view of her sweet breasts that I could ever have hoped for. Her sudden smile lit the room. Her brown hair, which she had never unpinned for me before, spread across the pillow and framed her face in a dark halo.

But I could hear the Australians moving about. They had hired another pair, known only as Brizzie and Bludger, so now they were four. And they were making breakfast. I smelled coffee brewing, bacon cooking. Time to take control, a task that I expected I would have to perform every day for as long as they were in my employ.

I bent to put on my boots, glanced out the stern gallery, and noticed the semaphore on Telegraph Hill. A new signal had appeared: arms extended, at two o'clock and three: *A brig.* They were signaling the arrival of a brig.

I said, "Isn't the *Madeleine M.* a brig?"

"A brig, yes, and fast."

"This could be her, then." I looked at Janiva, half-wrapped in the sheet. "But the wind is from the east. It will take her an hour to work her way onto an anchorage."

"An hour can be a long time."

I undid my galluses and dropped my breeches, then I knelt beside the berth and touched her leg, slid my hand along the smooth skin, kissed her again. . . .

And a voice in my head whispered my prayer, that Samuel Hodges forget me.

April 9, 1850
A Pre-Dawn Visitor

First entry since the arrival of the *Madeleine M.:*

Our brig brought all that we expected and more: Ames shovels, picks, and pans; flannel shirts, boots, hats; a hundred pipes of rum; a hundred cases of French champagne; a hundred crates of salt cod; a hundred other foods in every kind of container from tin to sack to hogshead; and four pianos manufactured by Chickering & Company of Boston.

Why had we received all of this?

My brother Thaddeus had decided that my California adventure might have merit after all. At the insistence of his wife, Katherine (surely meddlesome but perhaps not the ninny I thought), he had been a great help to Janiva, first by persuading her father that she had the fortitude to endure a long sea journey, then by aiding her in the Ames negotiations. Of course, I suspected that he acted for his own benefit as well as mine. Opening a new market in San Francisco or quieting a querulous wife in Boston were high ideals for any man of business. But I was glad that he had decided, in his fashion, to throw in with us.

And I was glad that, in addition to her other assets, Janiva Toler had the backbone to push my brother, confront her father, and challenge me.

Unloading our treasures took most of three days.

Brannan brought a crew to take three-quarters of the Ames shipment. He paid for the shovels, picks, and pans with 99.9 percent gold dust, which we left on deposit in the safe in his warehouse on Sansome Street. He gave us space in the warehouse—for a price, of course, but a fair one.

Until our goods were properly stored, the papers signed, and the

Madeleine M. on her way back to Boston for more, I had no time to ask Janiva if it was time to marry.

So, unmarried, we slept as if we were. And the captain's berth became our Bower of Bliss, until . . .

THE EASTERN SKY WAS just glimmering when the knock came.

I grabbed my pistol and bounded for the door. "Who is it?"

"You got some deep-sleepin' guards on this boat, Jamie, that's for sure."

I undid the latch and pulled open the door. "Michael!"

Janiva half rose from the bed. "Who is it?"

"Your Irish waiter," I said over my shoulder.

Michael Flynn peered in at her. "So it *is* true? She came to you after all."

I pushed him into the saloon, struck a match, lit a lantern. He had a black beard now. But he still wore my old visored hat and seemed little changed.

I whispered, "Is Hodges after you?"

"Hell no." Flynn laughed. "He's still at Broke Neck. Seems we done him a favor. He was looking for a way to get rid of the Gaw brothers. Gettin' too big, they was, tryin' to take over. And when we blew up the dam, we opened a gravel bank like a river deposit, halfway up the hill and loaded with gold."

"A lost river of gold?"

"Don't know about that. But Hodges and the rest, they're minin' and bankin' and not givin' two damns about us."

"We're in the clear, then?"

"Don't know about that, either." Flynn picked at his beard. "Hodges may be downright cordial, but you got problems of your own."

The cabin door opened and Janiva stepped out, neatly dressed, hair pinned.

Michael Flynn swept off his hat and bowed. "A pleasure to see that the lovely lady followed my advice after all."

She gave a little half curtsy. "You were the only man to encourage me."

"And damn glad to do it."

She liked Flynn. She had liked him from that first day in the Arbella Club. She said, "I'm damn glad, too. And I'd be damn glad for a cup of coffee."

"Coffee?" said Flynn. "Why? Is it morning already? I ain't even been to bed."

"Brandy, then," I said.

"In your coffee." Janiva went forward to the caboose, where we always kept a pot bubbling.

And Flynn whispered to me, "Good lookin', feisty, curtsies like a lady and curses like a lad. Oh, Jamie, you're a lucky man."

We sat at the captain's table and watched the morning light brighten the April-greened hills. I sweetened three mugs with brandy, and Flynn told of his travels. He had begun by leaving tracks to the north mines, to throw off Sloate. Once he was certain that Sloate was deceived, Flynn had turned south for the Chinese camp.

Janiva asked him why.

To find Mei-Ling, he admitted. But when he got there, he learned that she and her brother and their friends, fearing vengeance from Broke Neck, had already moved on. To where? No one knew. So Flynn had come looking in San Francisco.

Janiva understood. She had sailed seventeen thousand miles for much the same reason. She said, "Love will make you journey far."

Flynn said he wasn't sure if it was love, but he sure missed Mei-Ling.

Janiva told him that we all have our dreams and must do what God tells us, even when he tells us to pursue the love of a heathen. She spoke with what I knew she considered a liberality of spirit about the Chinese. And Flynn, well-supplied with a liberality of his own, took no offense.

He explained that he had not found Mei-Ling in San Francisco, so he had gone to Ah-Toy's, to satisfy his urges. And there, he had overheard the conversation of a man called Trub with three others named Muggs, Bludger, and Brizz.

At first, Flynn was surprised to hear our names bandied about in a Chinese whorehouse. Then he was astonished to hear the one called Muggs say, "You know, Trub, she's a bird worth pluckin'." To which Trub responded, "I thought of it. And from the way she makes eyes at me, she thought of it, too."

Janiva said, "Eyes? At him? He frightens me."

"Some women like to be frightened," said Flynn. "And some men think frightenin' is what women want."

"I am not *some women*," she said.

I poured Flynn more brandy and told him to keep talking.

"The one called Muggs, he said if you was out of the way, Jamie, this Trub could have it clear with Miss Janiva and her goods." Flynn sipped. "Amazin' the things you hear waitin' for your name to be called in a whorehouse. We need to see that this Trub McLaws don't call yours . . . in a manner of speakin'."

"We can fire him," said Janiva after a moment.

"No," I said. "We've agreed that if we do that, he'll just make more trouble."

"It ain't firin' you should be thinkin' of," said Flynn. "It's killin'."

"Killing?" said Janiva. "Killing McLaws?"

"But first, you two get married if you ain't already, so the likes of him can't be braggin' in the whorehouses about havin' a chance with a proper Boston lady." Flynn drained his cup, got up, and unlatched a gallery window, which swung out on its hinge. "I'll come and go by the stern. Better them Aussies don't know when I'm about." Then he put a leg out and dropped down a rope into a rowboat tethered to the rudder.

Janiva leaned out the window and asked, "Where are you going?"

"To find that Chinese girl. And if not her, *any* girl."

"Where are you sleeping?" I asked.

"Nobody on the *Willie Winter* but rats. I'll sleep with them." He pointed to the figurehead of the North Shore minister, rotting and lonely, a few hundred yards away.

And I said, surprising myself and Janiva both, "Will you witness our wedding?"

Janiva looked at me. "Wedding?"

"Day after tomorrow!" I said. "Shipton's at eleven o'clock."

"I'll be there, but ask that Brannan feller to be your witness. Make friends with the powerful, not the Irish."

April 11, 1850
Man and Wife

It was not the nuptial that we would have planned in Boston. It was in no way traditional, since we had spent the night before in the same bed. But we knew as our wedding day unfolded that we would never forget it.

Janiva wore her best dress, maroon, with four petticoats, a dark blue half jacket, matching hat. I wore my last white shirt and red cravat with the brown tweed suit, and I arranged my red and yellow-paisley neckerchief as a bit of color in my breast pocket.

We let Muggs and Trub row us in. Trub offered to escort us to Portsmouth Square, but I told him we had someone else watching over us. Who? The man waiting for us at the end of the Washington Street Wharf. He wore polished boots and a new gray flannel shirt with a black neckerchief. He was holding a bouquet of orange California poppies.

Trub said, "Who's he?"

"My friend, Michael Flynn," I said. "Expert with pistol or fists."

The boat bumped against the wharf, and Flynn handed Janiva the flowers, then helped her up. "Ah, but it's a grand sunny day for the most beautiful bride in California."

Trub whispered, "You don't invite your faithful Aussies . . . but a Mick?"

I knew the old adage about keeping your friends close and your enemies closer. But this was our wedding day. We would invite who we would. If the Aussies wanted to loot the ship while we were ashore? I had goods in the Brannan warehouse. I would not be impoverished. So I put McLaws out of my mind, took Janiva's arm, and together we walked up Washington Street with Michael Flynn clearing the way.

There was no plan to our procession, but up ahead, Reese Shipton's slave, Dingus, was standing on the boardwalk. When he saw us cross Kearny Street, he put bow to fiddle and delivered the most beautiful rendition of the old Pilgrim hymn, "We Gather Together," that ever we had heard.

Now, the mob around Portsmouth Square made way, as if all of them, engaged in all their forms of commerce, construction, and conversation, remembered for a moment what a wedding had meant back home, in Joplin or Savannah or Boston, Massachusetts.

Men doffed hats and bowed. Women, many of them what we might have called "soiled doves," offered us a "God bless" or "you look beautiful, dear" or even "make him pay, darlin', pay every day," which made Janiva laugh out loud.

Dingus played us right into the office, where Reese Shipton awaited in a suit so white that I could not believe he had ever worn it in California before.

As our official witnesses, Sam Brannan came with his wife, a delicate woman named Ann Eliza, who greeted Janiva with a motherly embrace and told her that she would always remember this day, "even if it's not a church wedding."

I sensed that Janiva liked her from the start.

Jonathan Slawsby and his wife also attended, as did a woman named Sally Tucker, who was associated with Shipton, but who appeared as if she had been associated with other men. Indeed, as I thought about it, I realized she had been the living tableau above the bar at the Parker House.

After Shipton pronounced us man and wife, we paraded to the Brannans' home at Stockton and Washington, on the uphill outskirt of town. The green slopes above were dotted about with houses, and the streets faded into sandy paths crisscrossing their way toward the top. But the Brannans' house reminded us of a pleasant dwelling in Concord or Lexington, and as the day was warm—April being one of the nicest months in these parts—they had laid out a collation on the veranda. We feasted on oysters and champagne and fresh sliced beef prepared with chilis and Mexican spices, all with a glorious view over the city and across the bay to the distant hills.

Though our small talk was genteel, as spirits rose, so did the volume of our laughter and sense of good fellowship. And in San Francisco, there was a distinct lack of the caste consciousness that we would have found in the environs of old Boston. When I introduced Flynn as "my good friend from Galway," Brannan did no more than look him over, take the measure of him, and offer his hand. "If Spencer vouches for you, you must be all right." When Flynn asked Sally Tucker if she had any friends, no one acted insulted or appalled. Social boundaries here were fluid, and Sally said she would be happy to introduce Flynn to a few "unattached" San Francisco ladies.

At sundown, Janiva and I bid our farewells and retreated to the St. Francis, the red-painted, twin-gabled, three-story hotel at the corner of Dupont and Clay. In that few marriages were celebrated in these parts, the hotel lacked a bridal suite, so they gave us a double room on the third floor, beneath the gables, from which we could see the ramshackle city expanding in every direction. And a bottle of champagne awaited us, chilled in shaved ice shipped round the Horn from Boston.

Alone together, we toasted to the great wonder of our lives, that in little less than two weeks we had come so far. We toasted to a future that we viewed now with new optimism, no matter the dangers around us. We put the distant spectre of Samuel Hodges and the nearby threat of Trub McLaws out of our minds. And we agreed that Mrs. Brannan was right. We would always remember this day.

Then we fell together into the enormous featherbed.

April 14, 1850
Doing Business

After four nights of bliss in the Drake and four days of meals in the restaurants around Portsmouth Square, including an exotic Chinese dinner (which did not feature *maodan*) in a restaurant called Jon-Ling's Canton House, we returned to the ship, where we immediately felt a distinct sense of resentment from our hirelings.

I resolved to be on my guard around Trub and Muggs and their equally hairy associates, Brizzie, short for "Brisbane," and Bludger, which is Australian slang for lazy.

But I lowered it the first night back as I strolled the deck after dinner. I liked to watch the sky darken from east to west. And here, as we raced toward the longest days of the year, I liked the lingering of the light. I also wanted the stern lanterns lit, so that the *Proud Pilgrim* looked like a storeship rather than a derelict.

As Janiva preferred to stay in the warmth below, I brought a cognac for company. I leaned on the rail and sipped and considered the ways in which my life had changed. Boston was no longer my destination. It was something much closer, up on those San Francisco hills . . . and something far away and unknown, a distant future . . .

. . . until my contemplation was interrupted by, "Evenin', Mr. Spencer." The voice of Trub McLaws preceded him. He sauntered along the rail, mug in his hand, and the thought skittered through my head that a man who enjoyed an evening stroll must have some good in him, after all.

So I offered a bit of friendly talk: "Marvelous night."

"Aye, Marvelous." Trub tipped his mug.

I asked him what he was drinking.

"Rotgut rum."

"Would you like some cognac?"

"Is that like brandy?"

I told him to drain the mug, then I poured him a healthy measure from my glass.

He sipped and smiled, as if his whole being had been illuminated by such a magnificent drink as the De Luze. He said, "You know, runnin' with the likes of you is a good way to get an education in the finer things . . . and another in knowin' when your betters is lookin' down on you."

"Betters? Lookin' down?"

"Me and Muggsy was awful hurt you didn't invite us to your weddin'."

Though I had an answer, Trub was not interested. He kept talking. "But something tells me you ain't so high and mighty, seein' as you're friends with that Irish whoremonger—"

"Whoremonger?" I sipped my brandy and feigned amusement.

"An honorable callin' in my world, but not in yours." Trouble Tom turned and headed toward the bow. "Maybe he'll come round tonight and tell some Irish tales. A tall teller, that one is, with a big mouth for the tellin' and some mad men on his own tail, too."

On his tail? Hodges? Trask? Had Flynn led them to us? If so, they would be more trouble than Trouble Tom.

April 18, 1850
A Ship Sinks

Michael Flynn did not come round that night or for days afterward. Neither, I was happy to say, did Hodges or Trask.

And our fledgling company kept growing, despite my fears of revenge. We made another wholesale deal and awaited word from Hopkins in Sacramento. We also considered the purchase of land. We had come late to the sale of so-called water lots. The city council had run an auction on January 3 for four hundred and thirty-four prime plots. But by spring, men were developing new means to lay claims, as I observed that morning.

I happened to glance toward the storeship *Elizabeth,* anchored between us and the Washington Street Wharf. I had noticed her crew dismasting her and removing anything—binnacle, bright work, lines—they might carry. Now, they were rowing frantically away, because she was sinking, going down on an even keel, as if they were scuttling her right there in Yerba Buena Cove.

But why?

McLaws came by, stopped, looked out, and said, "Fine smart fellers, them hulk undertakers, buryin' dead ships like dead bodies."

If Trub McLaws admired them, dishonesty was afoot.

"What's a hulk undertaker?" I asked.

"The city sells 'water lots' for tax money and the buyers agrees to fill the land, all as if it's the very thing to make this canvas-and-sand shithill a right honest city. But hulk undertakers kedge their vessels into prime spots and scuttle 'em. That way they owns the land without payin'."

The air was bubbling up through the hatches of the *Elizabeth* and roiling the water as she settled onto the bottom.

"How do they own it?" I asked.

"Laws of maritime salvage. Shipowner can claim the bottom his hulk is sittin' on. That's what they done with the *Elizabeth* and the *Niantic* and a dozen more."

"Sounds like a good line of work."

"Aye." Trub scratched at his stubble. "But not so good as what we got here. And my price is goin' up. Two ounces a day for all four of us. And a monthly bonus for me, to keep me mouth shut."

I was almost afraid to ask: "About what?"

"About what you and that Irish whoremonger done in a place called Broke Neck. Blew up a dam, killed men . . . that's the talk, anyway."

"The talk? The humbug, you mean."

"It's what they're sayin'." He studied me, as if waiting to see fear's shadow cross my face, then he turned and headed for the fo'c'sle, casting this over his shoulder: "New arrangement starts next week and the first bonus on May 1."

THAT NIGHT, I FOUND Flynn at Ah-Toy's. I warned him that if he was to spend time there, he had best not drink beforehand. Too much drink caused his gums to flap.

He assured me that he had said nothing, that word must be spreading by other means. He also warned against paying McLaws to keep quiet, as it would lead only to more demands. Having heard talk of an actual lake of gold, he was planning on leaving. "But I'll stay a bit longer. You might need help with this Trub. And I might still find Mei-Ling."

I looked around at the men, sitting on benches, waiting for their "look-ees," "touch-ees," and "do-ees." I said, "Just so long as you don't find her in here."

May 1, 1850
No Pay

When we handed out the week's wages, the gold share was as it had been, an ounce a day, one of the best salaries in San Francisco. But no bonus for Trub McLaws.

When he said nothing, I told Janiva that he was planning something. But I could not imagine what lay ahead.

May 4, 1850
Fifty-dollar shovels

Even San Francisco slept at four in the morning, but I lay awake.

Most of the worries afflicting me since Broke Neck afflicted me now. But they were calmed by the quiet breathing of the woman beside me. She lay on her stomach, her face turned to the window, her hair cascading onto us both. I touched her sweet bottom, but lightly so as not to wake her. The rising sun would do that within the hour.

I would simply enjoy the quiet and her presence and our existence together.

Then I heard the sound of a distant bell. It clanged once or twice, then it began to ring as furiously as a scream in the night. I sat up, looked toward the city, and saw flames leaping near Portsmouth Square.

I jumped into my breeches and boots and ran to rouse the Aussies, for we had goods to protect in the Brannan Warehouse. Past the long table in the saloon I ran, past the caboose, into the forecastle, and—where were they? Their berths were empty. Could they still be carousing at this hour?

I raced back to our cabin, where Janiva was already dressed, striking a match, lighting a lantern, and screaming at the sight of a face appearing at the stern gallery.

But it was Flynn, once more clean shaven. He pulled open the window and said, "It's a bad one, Jamie."

I told him the Aussies were gone.

"Probably out lootin'." He climbed in. "Them Sydney Ducks been braggin' they could torch the city and loot the hell out of it whilst it burned."

I said, "If the Brannan Warehouse goes—"

Janiva said, "If it goes, the five hundred shovels we're holding on this ship will become the most valuable shovels in California."

"So we'd best stay and protect them," I said.

"It'll take a long time to steal five hundred shovels," said Flynn. "You got a lot more in that warehouse you need to protect. But the lady—"

"Don't worry about me," said Janiva.

"I don't, darlin', not at all, not with a woman who can sail seventeen thousand miles on her own hook, all for the glories of love and commerce. But I worry for your goods. So your husband should stay with you to protect 'em on this ship, and I'll go protect 'em in your warehouse."

Janiva said, "They won't even know who you are, Michael. They'll shoot you for a looter. So both of you, go. I'll stay with the shovels."

And before I could protest, she grabbed a fistful of my shirt and looked at me fiercely. "This is our future, James."

"She's right about that," said Flynn.

Then she went to the locker in the corner and pulled out the seven-barrel Nock gun that the captain of the *Proud Pilgrim* had left behind when he headed for the gold fields. It was like a small cannon, perfect for sweeping a deck of mutineers or pirates. She said, "I have shot duck on the Row-ley Marshes and partridge in the Berkshire Hills. I can shoot anyone who comes aboard this ship."

And I relented. She was right. Our future lay crated and priced in that warehouse, not to mention the gold in Brannan's safe.

I said, "Stay here, then. Bolt the door. If anyone tries to get in, shoot through the door. Seven barrels will make an awful mess, no matter what's on the other side. Then use this." I put my pistol on the table. "It's fresh-loaded and capped." I kissed her and followed Flynn out the window, down the rope, into the rowboat.

The red glow of dawn was expanding to the east. But we were headed toward the redder glow of the flames spreading over San Francisco.

"The wind is up," I said.

"Bad sign." Flynn took the oars. "But there's a good sign behind you."

I looked over my shoulder at Janiva, standing in the side gallery, watch-ing us, with the big gun in her hand. I waved to her, but she could not see me in the dim light.

Flynn pulled a few times—*clink, clank, splash*—and said, "I was hopin' you'd come with me. Help me find my river of gold. But you found your gold right here."

WE TIED UP AT the foot of the Clay Street Wharf and ran.

We passed four men dipping buckets and filling a canvas-lined cart. One of them was shouting, "Hurry up, damn you. They're giving sixty dollars a cart for water. If we can keep it comin', we'll be rich before the city burns down."

"Does your heart proud to see men doin' their civic duty," said Flynn.

We ran past the *Niantic,* its balcony crowded with gawkers watching the flames on the hill. We ran all the way to the end of the wharf and dove into a torrent of people and carts and animals flooding Sansome Street.

A month ago, this had been a dock. Now it was a thoroughfare, lined with one- and two-story buildings, sheds, canvas tents, saloons. And it might all soon be gone. Everywhere, men were running and stumbling, in and out of buildings or off toward the wharfs. Some were saving what they could carry. Others were stealing what they could grab. And a noble few were pre-paring to fight the fire, filling buckets and daubing walls with great gobs of insulating black mud.

Meanwhile, more fire bells were clanging. And in one of the saloons, someone was pounding on a piano, perhaps for the last time.

The whole east side of Portsmouth Square, the downhill side, was now ablaze, including the magnificent new Parker House, scheduled to reopen that very night with a grand ball. And the wind was pumping the smoke and firebrands in our direction, so that everywhere, sparks were flickering on rooftops and boardwalks.

"If that wind keeps up," said Flynn, "Frisco's fucked."

A gang of men came along, hauling a red fire pump. The words Martin Van Buren were painted on the side. It had once belonged to the former president, who used it to water his lawn. Saving San Francisco on this night would be a far greater challenge.

"Hey, lads, tail on," shouted one of the volunteers. "We could use a push."

"We got things to do," answered Flynn.

Another volunteer shouted to a gang of men milling about on the corner of Clay Street. "You! What about you? We need help gettin' up the hill."

"Three dollars an hour!" said one of the men.

"Why, you son of a bitch," shouted the brigade captain. "We got a fire to fight and a city to save. If that fire gets goin'—"

"It's already goin', mate," cried one of the corner hangers. "The Exchange is gone. The new Parker House is goin'. It's all bloody goin'."

Flynn grabbed me by the elbow. "Sydney Ducks. Keep clear of 'em."

The captain looked from the Ducks to us, then back. "So none of you'll help?"

"Three dollars an hour!" shouted one of the Ducks. "Each!"

"Well, fuck you all!" The fire captain made a swooping wave and got his men going again to push the Martin Van Buren up Clay Street.

The Ducks went in the other direction on Sansome, moving like gangs always seemed to, all dark shadow and bobbing hats, swaying shoulders and swagger. One of them was carrying a wooden club. Another pulled a sap from his pocket. A set of brass knuckles flashed. Trouble Tom was nowhere in sight. But trouble was everywhere.

Flynn said, "Do you recognize any of them."

"None on our payroll." I noticed, however, that two of them broke off and went running up Clay Street. I figured later that they went in search of McLaws, because I saw them again. But we were distracted just then by the shouts of Reese Shipton, who came rushing along in his white suit, with Dingus at his heels.

"Shipton! Where are you going?" I asked.

"To my office, if I can get there. Get my papers."

"Ain't you got a fireproof safe?" asked Flynn.

"Yeah, and the last fire cooked everything in it right down to a fine powder."

I told him I'd help, but we had worries of our own, and he understood. I shouted after him, "The papers aren't worth your life."

Shipton went one way into the surge. We went the other, dodging carts and crowds and clots of thuggish toughs bent on nothing but trouble. The Australians weren't the only bad ones in town. We knew that. Society's bonds could easily be loosed in the kind of panic now rising like dawn in the eastern sky.

When a group of Chinese came scurrying by, their backs laden with whatever they had saved from their huts and hovels, Flynn studied them in the orange firelight, as if hoping that he might see Chin or Mei-Ling. And . . . did he see a female? I could not tell. But someone, a Celestial shadow, turned as if startled to see us. Flynn took two or three steps, and the shadow disappeared into the throng. Then I grabbed him and dragged him ahead. We had a job to do.

Off to my left, I heard a window shatter and saw two men run from a hardware store carrying—yes—shovels.

"Ignore that." Flynn pulled his pistol. "Keep goin'."

Up ahead, on the right side of Sansome Street, stood Brannan's barn-like warehouse. A gang of men had gathered in front of it, dark men with muskets, hulking in the heat and strange burning light. Were they looting? Would we have a fight? As we drew closer, we saw that they were surrounding Sam Brannan himself. They barred my way, but Brannan said, "It's all right, boys. It's *his* goods we're protectin'."

"And we're damn glad of it," I said.

"We learned our lesson at Christmas." Brannan looked up at the flames leaping a few blocks away. "Somebody set fire to the U.S. Exchange just to get us stirred up."

Jonathan Slawsby stood next to him. "We'll be fine, sir, with the help of God."

Flynn said, "We come to help you hold off the looters."

"I got my Mormons," said Brannan. "I promised them a percentage. They know our goods are worth more with every hardware store that goes up. We could be holdin' fifty-dollar shovels by dawn. So we'll wet the roof and shoot the looters."

A ladder was leaning against the side of the warehouse, and a bucket brigade was lifting from one of the water-filled carts.

Brannan said, "The son of a bitch who owns that cart is gettin' sixty dollars a load. But I'll pay, Spencer. I'll pay, and you'll get the benefit."

From up the hill came a great, explosive *whoosh* of sparks as a building fell in on itself. Brannan said, "Get back to your ship. Protect the shovels you kept aboard. They're the real gold."

"Have you seen my men," I asked. "McLaws and Henderson?"

"They were here when we got here, takin' positions around the doors. The big one, McLaws, he said they were here to protect your goods."

"They'd been drinkin' some," said Slawsby, "and one of them had a crowbar. Strange tool for protectin' a warehouse."

IF THE WIND SWEPT the fire toward the Brannan warehouse, nothing would stop it. But if my Australians were disappointed that they could not plunder on land, they might decide to steal the fifty-dollar shovels from the *Proud Pilgrim*.

So we rushed back onto the wharf, only to discover that our boat was gone. I cursed and looked toward our ship, and what I saw froze my blood. Men were moving about on the deck, looking furtive in the pre-dawn light, doing nefarious business for certain.

"They're lootin'," said Flynn. "Probably usin' me own damn rowboat, the bastards. Probably tied her up on the other side, so nobody sees what they're up to."

I began looking for another boat. Some were chained and padlocked. Some were without oarlocks. And—

I heard a voice behind me. "Is that Spencer? Mr. Spencer?"

He was wearing a plug hat and leather vest. He was carrying a big canvas bag full of tools, just as the first time I had seen him on the wharf in Boston.

"Matt Dooling! Where are you going?"

"Burned out," he said. "Nothin' left but my anvil and my rowboat. I'll get the anvil when it cools, but—"

Flynn said, "You have a boat?"

"Right here." He went to the side of the wharf and dropped his bag into a boat chained below. "Goin' back to join a bucket brigade."

"Can we borrow the boat?" I asked. "Somebody stole ours, and—"

"They're lootin' the Spencer ship," said Flynn.

"Lootin'?" said Dooling, almost indignantly. "From you?"

I pointed to the *Proud Pilgrim*. As I did, I heard a muffled shot and saw the windows of the starboard gallery, our Bower of Bliss, lit by a muzzle flash.

Good Lord, but Janiva had just fired that monstrous Nock.

I said, "We need that boat, Matt. Right now."

"You need help?" asked Dooling.

"Do you got a gun?" said Flynn.

"Nope. But I got a big claw hammer. And this!" He pulled a fine Bowie knife. "And Matt Dooling never forgets a favor."

In an instant, all three of us were in his rowboat, with powerful Matt Dooling pulling hard for the *Proud Pilgrim*.

The next few minutes were pure agony for me, knowing that intruders were aboard with Janiva.

Dooling said, "You want to go right up to the side? Or do we surprise 'em?"

I heard myself say, "Surprise or not, if they've hurt her, we kill them all."

"We might have to," said Flynn. "But we need to see what's happened in the cabin before we start shootin'."

Behind us an explosion rocked the city. The fire had reached something flammable—paint, turpentine, gunpowder—and a huge red-orange ball roiled into the sky. The brigands on the deck glanced toward the eruption, but with all the boats full of panicked people fleeing the flames, we attracted none of their attention as they got back to pillaging our stores.

Flynn told Matt Dooling, "Make like you're pullin for the *Willie Winter* over there, then get in close to the stern."

In a few minutes, we bumped unseen under the gallery of the *Proud Pilgrim*.

Flynn borrowed Dooling's Bowie knife, slipped it into his belt, threw his hat into the boat, then lifted himself onto his rope ladder, up to the windows of the stern gallery. He peered in and made a gesture: nothing. Then, he lifted himself to the taffrail, beside one of the glowing stern lanterns. Another gesture: two fingers for two men. He dropped back, pulled out the unlocked gallery window, and climbed in. Then he stuck his head out and, with his finger to his lips for quiet, he gestured for us to follow.

I could not imagine what I would see. But what I heard pierced my soul. As soon as I dropped through the window, the sound of gasping, moaning, and crying struck me. It was echoing down the passage from the saloon amidships.

Flynn grabbed me and whispered, "If you want to end this right, be quiet."

A second later, Matt Dooling followed me through the window with his big shoulders and his big ass and his big feet tripping on the sill. He dropped his hammer. But Flynn, with a flash of his hand, caught it before it hit the floor.

We all stopped, motionless, in fear that we had been heard. Instead, we heard Trub McLaws say, "Come on, Muggs, finish up. Then Brizz gets a bit."

"Aye," said another voice. "My dick's fixin' to explode."

Janiva groaned out a cry that sounded more like a growl.

Again I fought the impulse to race down the short passage and burst into the saloon, where these slugs were raping the woman I loved.

Flynn pointed at the deck. The body of the one called Bludger, face and upper torso shot to pieces. Splinters of the door were shattered and blood was splattered all around him.

Then I heard a groan, met by higher-pitched screams, a male voice and female response. Muggs Henderson was finishing his obscene business.

Flynn raised a finger and whispered, "We kill them all. Nobody gets away. Not in there, not—" He pointed above. Then he asked Dooling, "Are you with us?"

Dooling held up his pound-and-a-half hammer—octagonal head, long nasty claw. "Goddamn them all to hell."

In the saloon, Trub laughed, "Get off her, Muggs. Time for Brizz. And I'm gettin' another stiffy just watchin'. I'll have her again 'fore we call Brizz's baby brother down."

"He's sixteen," said Brizz. "Awful randy."

"Let him keep loadin' shovels. It'll make him tired so's he don't pop off so fast."

Janiva whimpered, then she growled, "When my husband gets back—"

"When your husband gets back, we'll kill him," said Trub. "All we wanted was a signature, sayin' we was takin' them shovels all nice and legal-like. Then we would've been gone for good. Them shovels was our payment for keepin' quiet about Broke Neck. But your smart husband wouldn't pay in gold. Instead, he told you to shoot through the door."

"I'm glad I did."

"So now," said Trub, "we'll kill him. We'll lure him aboard. Give him a look at what we done, then kill him."

"Aye," Muggs said, "him and that smart-mouthed Irish prick."

"Should've killed 'em the first time we set eyes on 'em," Trub went on. "But too many watchin'. So we had to act like gents. Like proper poopers—"

All the rapists laughed at that.

Trub kept talking. "Now them damn fools is off fightin' our fire. Maybe they'll burn up in it. Then we'll take the ship, too. Bring Lady Boston here along with us, fuck her all the way to Sacramento. Would you like that, darlin'?"

I heard Janiva spit. Then I heard a slap.

Flynn's hand went across my chest. *Wait. Wait.* He pointed to himself and said, in gestures, "I'll look." He slipped down the passage as it began again, and the sound of my wife's pain tore at my soul.

A moment later, Flynn scuttled back and whispered, "Trub is at her head, with a knife to her throat. They got her legs tied on the table."

Trub said, "That's a fine big cock you got there, Brizzy boy."

I heard poor Janiva scream.

Trub cheered him on. "Get it all the way in lad, all the way."

Now we heard another man coming down the gangway from the main deck. "Oi, when's it my turn?"

"After me," said Trub.

And that was all I could take. I grabbed my Colt from the table, cocked it, and rushed down the hallway.

Janiva lay there, legs splayed in my direction, Brizz between them, his back and bare ass to me and his pants at his ankles. I could have killed him, but it was Trub that I wanted. Trub stood at her head, holding a knife. And Trub would kill her.

But I gave him only enough time to see me, see the muzzle of my pistol, and see it flash in his face. The ball went through his forehead, and the back of his skull blew out, splattering brains all over Muggs, who was just then pulling up his pants.

And that was my plan. Kill Trub while one man had his pants half off, another had his half on, and a third was halfway down the companionway steps.

But Flynn and Matt Dooling followed right after me, and they knew what to do.

Flynn grabbed Brizz by the shoulders, pulled him off Janiva, sent him stumbling back with a look of shock on his hairy face and a white dick standing stiff and wet. He drove the Bowie knife so deep into Brizz's belly that it came out his back.

Muggs turned to run, but Dooling drove the hammer claw right into the top of his skull. Muggs sank to his knees, stood and stumbled forward, then collapsed with the hammer in his head.

The one on the companionway steps—he looked about sixteen—stood frozen in shock.

Flynn tried to pull the knife out of Brizz, who was still twisting and struggling and squirting blood, but the knife would not budge. So Flynn shouted at me, "Shoot him."

And for a moment, I hesitated.

He was a boy. He raised his hand, cried, "No!"

Then Janiva sat up and looked at me fiercely and said, "Kill him."

And I did. I went up straight and hard, and before he could turn, I put a bullet under his rib cage. It came out his back and cut his spine, because his legs collapsed and his young body flopped down the steps like a sack of clams.

Another voice cried down from above, "Oi, what's goin' on? Did you fuckers shoot her before I fucked her?"

Fucked her? Another one? He would get no hesitation, no mercy. As he came down, I went up, shot him once, chased him out onto the deck, and shot him again.

Dawn covered the sky. Fire covered the dawn. And blood covered the *Proud Pilgrim*.

BY NOW, JANIVA WAS standing, trembling. She seemed not to notice the dead bodies. Trub and McLaws, Brizz and the boy. She was saying, "Seven barrels for six men. That's what I had. Seven for six. One shot should have killed them all."

"Don't worry, darlin'," said Flynn, wiping the blade on the shirttail of the dead boy. "Big gun like that, sometimes, it ain't so accurate. Ain't that right, Matt?"

"Right for sure. You done good, missus."

She looked around at the mess of blood and gore and said, "It stinks in here."

I tried to lead her back to the captain's cabin. But she pulled away, smoothed the front of her dress as if it would make everything all right. "It's time for breakfast." She started forward, to the caboose.

I reached out to her again, and she screamed, "Don't touch me! Do *not* touch me." But there was no anger on her face, no fear, just a cold, affectless stare, the expression I had seen that day in the Arbella Club, when I announced I was leaving.

Flynn said to her, "Let me cook, darlin'. You go back to your cabin and rest."

"Yes," said Matt Dooling. "We'll protect you."

After a moment, I reached out again, though I did not touch her, and she allowed me to lead her to the stern, to our Bower of Bliss, which felt as violated as she.

While the city burned beyond the windows, we three tried to comfort her. We gave her brandy. We had some ourselves. We made coffee, too. We brought her hot water and cloths from the ship's store so that she could clean herself. Then she retreated to the captain's private necessary in the gallery on the larboard side, a single-holed seat dropping straight into the sea. There, she spent twenty minutes, behind a louver.

Flynn, Dooling, and I sat at the table, watched the flames leaping on the hill between the waterfront and Portsmouth Square, and debated our next move.

Finally, I said, "We go to the law. We take Brannan. We plead self-defense."

And from behind the louver I heard her voice, cool and rational. "We do nothing of the sort." Then she emerged, hair pinned, dress smoothed, the front of the bodice covered with a clean white apron, and powder makeup, which I did not know she possessed, covering the bruise under her eye.

She poured another brandy, and brought the glass to her mouth. Though she could hide the bruise, she could not hide the shaking hand. But after a swallow, she said, "Seven barrels and only one man went down. I grabbed for the pistol on the table, but—"

"We'll plead self-defense," I said. "No shame—"

"No," she said softly, then furiously, "No! I never want to speak of this again. I never want to answer a question. And they will ask. Six dead men? How many raped you? How many times? Two? Three? Why are there six dead men? How did they get aboard? Were they invited? Where was your husband? Where were his friends? Weren't some of these men in his employ? And six dead? Why did you kill them all? And wasn't the Irishman a whoremonger? Could it be that the men were confused, or were you one of his girls? Couldn't you just—just—no. No!" She looked out at the burning city.

After a time, as the truth of what we had done sank in, I said, "We still need to answer for their bodies."

She said, "Let the crabs eat them."

And Michael Flynn, who had been uncharacteristically quiet, said, "You know, she's right."

"I know I will not suffer another indignity," she said.

Flynn asked Dooling, "Can you lend us that strong arm a while longer?"

Matt Dooling nodded and made a fist.

"Good," said Flynn. "If we can row an anchor about a hundred yards, we'll turn something bad into good. We'll sink the *Proud Pilgrim* with all six bodies."

"And claim a water lot," I added.

SAN FRANCISCO BURNED UNTIL eleven o'clock that morning.

The fire consumed everything from Kearny down to Montgomery, from Clay to Washington. It jumped Portsmouth Square and started burning up the hill, but John Geary, the strong-browed young man whose appointment as U.S. postmaster had positioned him to win the city's first mayoral election, ordered the destruction of all buildings on Dupont, thereby creating a firebreak. It was easy because some of the buildings were made of canvas, and others had been thrown up in a few days. Now they were all gone, making room for another round, bigger, better, stronger, perhaps built of brick.

But the Brannan warehouse survived. So did all our goods, which would now leap in price. Once we could swallow down the horror of what had happened on the *Proud Pilgrim,* we would be in business for as long as we wanted.

By afternoon, we had carried the six bodies deep into the ship, chained them along the keel, and closed the hatches of the orlop deck. I tried not to look at the faces. I tried not to consider the lives. We had done what needed to be done. Even the boy had earned his fate. I felt better once the bodies were out of sight. But while we could wash the blood from the decks, we could never wash it from our souls.

I told Janiva to stay in the cabin while we did this dirty work. I told her to read the Bible or Shakespeare. She chose *MacBeth*. She said that she admired the backbone of that fierce, flawed wife. I admired hers.

Later, Michael made beef stew, and we ate, though none of us had much appetite.

As night came on, we moved the last of the shovels off the ship. It took five trips in the rowboat. We loaded half of them onto a cart. And while

Matt Dooling waited on the wharf with the other half, Flynn and I brought the cart to Brannan's warehouse. The night fog had rolled in. The smell of smoke hung thick and wet.

Brannan was doing an inventory, re-pricing while the city smoldered. I told him that it would be best if he sold all our shovels in San Francisco. As I had not heard from Hopkins in Sacramento, and as Brannan had done such a loyal job of protecting our goods, I would honor the price I had given him on all the other shovels. And our partnership grew stronger.

Then, as we were leaving, I saw Wei Chin. I was not certain at first. He was hunkered in a shadow in an alley across the street. He pulled back at the sight of me.

I did not think that Flynn noticed him, so I said that I had left something behind, that he should continue down to the wharf. Then I stepped into the shadow and looked into the eyes of the Chinaman, filled with fear and defiance.

Yes, he and the others had been in the crowd of Chinese we had passed during the fire. He had been watching the Brannan warehouse ever since, hoping to see me. He said he had brought his people to San Francisco, and here they would stay. Then he asked about Flynn. "Does he come to stay?"

And a voice cut through the darkness. "I come to find Mei-Ling." Flynn had not been fooled. He was never fooled. He knew I had seen something, so he doubled back.

Chin looked at him. "She no see you."

"Why not?"

"She marry. She marry Jon-Ling."

"The one with the restaurant?" I said.

Chin nodded. "She no love white man. Too much trouble white man. No white man for brother. No white Irish man. No peppermint. She never want see you."

Flynn blustered and threatened and said he would follow Chin back to wherever they were living or spy on the restaurant until he saw her.

Chin, with cold calm, said he would kill the Irishman if he interfered with Mei-Ling's marriage to a man of business, one of the Celestial leaders of the town.

And for one of the few times that I knew him, Michael Flynn took no for an answer.

Something came over him for days after that. He stopped smiling. He stopped talking. He stopped making light of serious matters and waxing serious about trivial things. And I knew that he had more than mere lust for the Chinese girl named Mei-Ling.

I MUST RECORD ONE more thing about that terrible day, illustrative of the deep wellspring of strength in Janiva Toler Spencer.

Torn by the horrors of the dawn, she rolled to me late in the night and told me to love her. She did not ask, nor did she seduce. She spoke bluntly, as if telling me that it was a necessary task. After all she had gone through? I hesitated. So she said, "If something more comes of this, we will always believe it is *your* child." I admired her bravery even more. And somehow, we affirmed our life together.

May 8, 1850
Good-bye, Proud Pilgrim

In the succeeding days, Janiva did not smile and seldom spoke. But if she had a task, she went to it willingly. Prepare coffee. Wash her "rape dress." Repeat the process of procreation with her husband. Sink the *Proud Pilgrim*.

We waited for the morning when the tide took flood at four o'clock, then we got to work. While Flynn and Dooling rowed the kedging anchor to a spot about two hundred feet away, we detached the main anchor and let slip the *Proud Pilgrim*.

We had the help of Wei Chin and Little Ng in this. They did not know our exact purpose, only that we needed muscle. Chin said they would provide it, if Flynn would promise not to see his sister again. And Flynn agreed. I asked him why, and he said, "So your wife never has to answer a bad question about a terrible thing."

Yes, I thought, he was a true friend.

With the tide running, Wei Chin, Little Ng, Janiva, and I wrapped hands around the capstan bars and waited for Flynn to sing out, a signal that the kedging anchor had taken hold. When the first lines of "The Wild Colonial Boy" rose from the darkness, we threw our strength forward and began to crank. By six o'clock, we had accomplished the amazing task of kedging the eight-hundred-ton vessel into a spot directly in line with the end of the Clay Street Wharf. Whoever laid claim to the mud beneath her keel would now have to contend with us.

Then I told the Chinese to leave.

Chin said, "You no want us to see blood?"

"What blood?"

"Blood everywhere, James Spencer." He tapped his nose. "Get nothing without spill blood. This ship make you rich where you sink it. I be rich, too. Spill blood, too, if need. Spill blood to make good place for Chinese."

Flynn, who had come back aboard, must now have felt the weight of his promise, for he said, "I love your sister, Sam Who. I can make a good place for her right now, if she'll have me, if you'll let me."

"Stay away, Irish. If you my friend, stay away," said Chin. Then he and Little Ng went over the side.

While Matt Dooling rowed the Chinese and my silent wife ashore, Flynn and I went below and lifted the hatches of the orlop deck, then dropped down into the cramped space beneath. Our torches did little to burn away the stench of rotting flesh but were a great weapon in warding off the swarm of rats that scurried everywhere, except for those still feasting on the bodies of the six men we had killed.

Flynn to the bow and I to the stern, we hunched and crab-walked through the bilge. With chisels and six-pound hammers borrowed from Dooling's tool bag, we set to cutting the boards close by the keel.

As water seeped in, the rats started squealing and darting and slithering around my legs. I waved the torch to ward them off, and for an instant, saw the half-eaten face of Trub McLaws in the light. Goddamn him, I thought, for what he had done to my wife and for what he had made me do to him.

I hammered harder and faster until I had opened a six-by-six-inch hole. When I struck the final blow and knocked the square of plank free, a column of water fountained up.

An instant later, Flynn shouted, "Get out, Jamie. Get out now."

I lifted myself through that hatch, but Flynn was not following. I stopped, waited, listened to the rush of water and the noise of the rats. Was he so despondent that he would stay and drown with them, mourning Mei-Ling? A moment after that thought crossed my mind, he emerged, holding a pouch of gold dust. He said it belonged to Trub. But now it belonged to him. The old Flynn was not gone altogether.

By full sunrise, the *Proud Pilgrim* had sunk into twenty feet of water, masts and upper works still visible at low tide, hull sitting on a bottom that would one day be worth a fortune.

May 15, 1850
Good News

We live now in the St. Francis Hotel. We exchanged the water rights we claimed with the *Proud Pilgrim* for a piece of land on Market Street, at the edge of town, where Dupont runs in. We will build a warehouse there and a business, too. It is a good deal.

And this evening Janiva gave me news that we had prayed for. Yes, we pray regularly, having joined the new Congregational Church. And what we prayed for we have been given: Her monthlies have arrived. We will never wonder who fathers our first child. For the first time in ten days, a glimmer of smile has appeared on her face. And so I write my last dispatch for the *Boston Transcript*:

A new James Spencer emerges from the cocoon of the callow young Sagamore, one of a hundred such who sailed through the Golden Gate just nine months ago.

The Sagamores have dispersed, like birds before the hurricane. Some still work the Miwok, where the mining is good and the water flows fast. Others wander, still searching. Some are happy. Others, heads hung, make for home. And sadly, some have now passed to another plain.

The only truth we can offer is that in California, opportunity abounds. But it is an unforgiving place. Hard work is essential, but good fortune trumps labor. Life can be beautiful or it can be brutal, but it is seldom fair.

As for me, I have seen the elephant. I have seen beauty and brutality on the shores of this bay, and out on the browning plains, and along the rivers that drain the beckoning hills. So I will now set about civilizing this place, creating a new order, where the fickle mistress of fortune will give way to a caring and reliable mother.

I thank God that in this purpose, I have a true helpmate, Janiva Toler, daughter of Joshua of the Toler Ropewalks. We are business partners, shipping goods from Boston for wholesale in the city where, we are told, more cash and gold are in circulation than anywhere else in America. We are also life partners, man and wife. I apologize to any for whom this news is a shock, but our American distances are great, so we must live the adventure of life as it unfolds before us. And be assured that our prospects are bright.

As for my old partner, Michael Flynn has heard stories of an actual lake of gold near the headwaters of the Yuba River. He says that there may lie the great source of the Mother Lode, the strike to make all others pale. A general migration has begun in that direction, and he has joined it. I will miss his friendship, as I miss the mentorship of Samuel Hodges and the companionship of so many I sailed with and so many I met in the gold country.

I wish them all Godspeed and good luck. And never fear word of another San Francisco fire, for each time it burns, we build it back up, bigger, better, stronger.

"FIFTY DOLLARS A SHOVEL." Peter Fallon stepped onto the elevator after his son. "About sixteen hundred bucks in today's dollars."

LJ pressed G. "I keep telling you, Dad, San Francisco is an expensive town."

Mary was still in the apartment, alternately scrolling through Facebook, then staring out at the bright day and the light weekend traffic on the Bay Bridge. Wraparound was guarding the door.

LJ said, "Do you think we should be going out to Amador?"

"Willie wants the bags of gold. We satisfy Willie, while we keep looking for the real prize, the last chapter of the journal."

"So the bags of gold are the bridge?"

"I don't know, but finding them will get Willie off our back."

In the lobby, the desk manager gave them a look, then went back to thumbing his phone. Probably on Willie's payroll, too. Like all big cities, San Francisco could be a very small town.

Through the plate-glass windows, they saw Larry Kwan, waiting beside his Escalade.

Peter told his son, "You're not coming."

"What?"

"Bill Donnelly has a big gun. Jack Cutler has a metal detector. And Larry Kwan can talk a dog off a meat wagon, so I won't be bored on the drive."

"But I got you into this, Dad."

"I'm glad I can help."

"You make it sound like you're having fun."

"There's fun, then there's fulfillment. I thought I taught you that."

"Fulfillment, as long as you don't get killed," LJ said.

"So in the interests of fulfillment and keeping us all alive, stay by a computer. I may need research. And stay close to Mary, in case Willie or his boys get fresh."

"It's not Willie I worry about," said LJ.

Peter looked up the street and down. "I don't see any FBI surveillance teams."

"I'm not sure if that's a good thing or a bad thing."

"Christine Ryan seems to be letting this play out as if we're all bugs in an experiment."

"Undercover bugs," said LJ.

"As long as no one steps on us." Peter wrapped an arm around his son's shoulders and pivoted him back toward the elevator. "Stay close, kid."

"Go easy on Jack Cutler, Dad. He's scared."

"Sure." Peter did not add that he was scared, too.

PETER HOPPED IN NEXT to Larry Kwan and said, "Anybody following you?"

"Nope, and I been watchin'. No blue SUVs, no cable cars, no rickshaws, nothing." Larry pulled into the Mission Street traffic and started talking. "You know, I Googled Peter Fallon, and I have to say, you're big-time. Rare books . . . Revere tea sets . . . Lincoln diaries . . . And you sure do get into a lot of trouble for a historian."

Peter patted the dashboard. "That's why I like riding in an armored Escalade."

Larry laughed. "The Escalade's armored, but I'm not."

"I have one rule in life, Larry. If somebody pulls a gun, run."

"Nice rhyme. Like, 'If you go for the history, you may get a mystery.'"

"Sometimes it happens that way."

"So, are you going to tell me what our history-mystery is this time?"

Peter decided to trust Larry. He needed friends, and Larry had bought in. "A Gold Rush journal, stolen from right there." Peter pointed to the puce-and-white California Historical Society, half a block up the street.

And as if it was just popping into his head, Larry said, "Hey, remember, I told you I went out to Amador a few times before?"

"Yeah."

"I picked up somebody at that society about a year ago and drove them out to Manion Gold Vineyards."

"One person? For a tasting?"

"I don't know if they were tasting, but Manion Sturgis called, asked me to pick up a lady, right there."

"Who was she?"

"Oh, hell, what was her name?" Larry was distracted by the lefts and rights, the stops and goes, the beepings and creepings that led to the Bay Bridge. Then they were merging and swinging west, with downtown on their left, all those enormous buildings sitting on the landfill of Yerba Buena Cove, ancient graveyard of the Gold Rush fleet.

"Try to think," said Peter.

"I am. But when I drive across the Bay Bridge, I think about *driving*."

They shot through the tunnel on Yerba Buena Island and onto the new section of bridge, rebuilt for billions to withstand the "Big One," the San Andreas quake lurking out there somewhere, maybe tomorrow, maybe in a century, a massive shake to dwarf the Richter-scale bomb of 1906.

Once they were rolling through Oakland, Larry said, "OK. No more lane changes. *Now* I can think. But I don't think I can remember her name. I can remember wines and vintages from fifteen years ago, but names? Not so much."

Peter said, "It was just one person, though?"

"Yeah."

"Did she carry anything?"

"I don't remember. I drove her out. And—"

"Was anybody else at this lunch?"

Larry snapped a finger. So he remembered something else. "Her mother. Yeah. We stopped to pick up her mother on one of the back roads in Amador."

"Was this woman's name Meg Miller?"

"The mother?"

"No. The one you picked up at the historical society."

"Nah, no, but—"

"Did she have a tattoo?"

"Maybe on her ass. But I didn't see it."

As they sped up Route 80, Peter went to the historical society website and read Larry the names of everyone on the masthead.

Larry didn't recognize any of them.

But there was something here. Sometimes things happened because of research, sometimes because of dumb luck, but however they happened . . .

He sent Evangeline a text. He told her to ask Manion about a visit from someone from the California Historical Society a year ago. Then he added, "You'll need something to talk about over breakfast. Larry Kwan on the way. Me, too."

EVANGELINE WAS SITTING ON the porch of the guest cottage when her phone pinged.

It was around nine o'clock, so the sun was up full, warming nicely. She had her hands wrapped around her coffee cup and was admiring the way the light sculpted the landscape rolling south from Rainbow Gulch and bending gracefully southwest, out where one of the brown hills seemed to redirect the golden river of grapevines.

She loved a quiet morning coming in fresh and clean, even if her underwear wasn't. She was in such a good mood, she didn't bother to text Peter the big "F-U" for that "over breakfast" remark.

But breakfast was coming, too. Up the garden path, past the picnic tables, through the outdoor display of Gold Rush rockers and sluices and monitor nozzles, two tasting-room workers were carrying trays, led by Manion Sturgis, in jeans, white shirt, and yellow sweater draped over his shoulders like a late-in-life prepster.

Trying too hard again.

But she was enjoying the pampering . . . the helicopters, the meals, the little discoveries in this fairy-tale world of wine, the undisturbed night in the sweet little cottage, with nothing but the adventures of James Spencer to keep her company. She had to admit that it all tempted her . . . a retreat in the California hills, a refuge from the passage of time, an oasis overseen by a man who had sanded off all his hard edges.

Peter always told her that hard edges were part of his appeal.

So why had she and Peter continued to swing toward each other, then away, toward, then away, across all the years since they reconnected? Why couldn't they settle down and do it? Just get married and move in together?

She had always been the one more reluctant. She had always been the one constantly moving, constantly pitching editors on stories of new and exotic places. And her love of New York over Boston was a good excuse to keep them lovers at long-range.

But there was something deeper. She was past the age to have children. She would not live on through another generation. So she traveled. Even if she had not carved a place for herself in the shrinking world of travel magazining, she would have traveled. To see how other people lived and to live something different right along with them, she traveled. To taste all the tastes, hear all the sounds, see all the colors, she traveled. To live, she traveled. Then she went home and wrote about it all. Then she traveled again. And she read a lot, because reading was a kind of travel, too, as real as taking to the road.

And for some people, having an affair was also a kind of travel. With all the excitement, drama, and inevitable pain, an affair let you live another life, if only for a short time. It let you escape whatever it was about yourself that kept you running, let you see someone else's horizon and, maybe, someone else's heart.

Evangeline liked to think she was happy with who she was, running from nothing, comfortable with the long-range deal that she and Peter had worked out. But there were so many lives to live, so many futures to embrace, and so little time to gather it all in. Maybe that was why she had kissed Manion Sturgis the night before. But she had locked the door of the cottage and spent the night alone.

Now, as Manion came up the pathway, she let herself wonder.

"Huevos rancheros and a sparkling Chardonnay from my brother's vineyard," he announced. "We don't make sparkling. But this retails at twelve ninety-five. Good for mimosas."

She leaned back, stretched, and said, "I'd love a mimosa."

The servers left them alone with their breakfast. And for yet another meal, Evangeline and Manion Sturgis did not run out of things to talk about.

But before she brought up the vineyard visit of a woman from the California Historical Society, Evangeline caught the glint of a windshield down the hill. A blue Ford Explorer was turning off the main road into the parking lot.

"That's funny," said Manion.

"What?"

"Larry Kwan drives an Escalade." He poured her another mimosa, as if he thought nothing more of it.

Evangeline sipped hers and asked Peter's question.

"A woman from the California Historical Society?" said Manion. "A year ago? I'd have to think about that." Just then, his cell phone buzzed. He said, "It's the office. I told them I did not want to be disturbed." He answered: "What?"

And Evangeline saw something new cross his face. Shock. Surprise. Fear.

He said, "On their way? Up here? But—no, no. No police."

A golf cart was following the path that breakfast had taken.

A black guy in a dark suit was driving. A white guy in a dark suit was riding shotgun. Both wore sunglasses. Both looked about as big as the guest cottage.

Riding in the rear seat was a smaller Asian man in an expensive suit and tie.

The golf cart pulled up. The white guy got off and extended a hand so the Asian man could step off gracefully.

Manion Sturgis said, "Good morning, Mr. Lum."

"A pleasure to see you again, Mr. Sturgis." Lum spoke with, of all things, a BBC British accent, learned perhaps in Hong Kong. He looked at Evangeline. "And a pleasure to meet the lovely lady. Mr. Barber told me all about you."

"Did he tell you I am not selling?" Manion Sturgis gestured at Lum to have a seat.

"I am here to make a new offer." Mr. Lum was as smooth as his suit.

"I've told you, there's no amount of money that will induce me to sell this land."

Lum looked at Evangeline. "The two of you could travel far and wide on what I am prepared to offer. First class everywhere."

Evangeline did not correct Mr. Lum's assumptions about their relationship. It was none of his business. He did not seem that interested, anyway.

Manion said, "I travel first class as it is."

"I do not propose to buy the whole property. Just the mineral rights." Mr. Lum opened the folder he was carrying. He had none of that clichéd Asian inscrutability. No gamesmanship. No dance. He pointed to a figure. "Our research shows that ten years ago, you paid five hundred thousand dollars to your family estate for this land, including patented mineral rights."

Manion said, "I bought a vineyard that lay dormant since Prohibition. I revived it. I worked with the oldest vines in California, out at the edge of the gulch. I grafted other varieties. I worked miracles here. Why would I sell the mineral rights so you could exploit them and, no matter how careful you might be, damage this wonderful valley?"

Mr. Lum fingered his triangle lapel pin. "There will be no damage. We will engage in drift mining, working from the other side of Rainbow Gulch."

"Jack Cutler owns that land."

"Leave Cutler to me." Mr. Lum's half smile fell off. "This is a special offer, a final offer. It will please men on both sides of the Pacific if you accept."

Evangeline looked over at the two bodyguards. The black guy was staring out at the vineyard. The white guy was studying his phone.

Lum said to Sturgis, "Your land is now assessed at five million dollars. High for this county, but we will give you six, with surface rights remaining in your possession."

"I'd rather turn it over to the Mother Lode Land Trust."

"I would not grant conservation or agricultural easements here. We think there's gold under this ground, Mr. Sturgis. It is my job to make the best deal for it." He looked at Evangeline. "Do you have any opinions?"

"I like it as it is," she said.

"Then enjoy it." He stood and put a paper on the table. "Sierra Rock wants to own it by the end of this weekend. We are also purchasing land along the Miwok, owned by the Boyles Family and the O'Hara Family."

"Sierra Rock owns the Emery Mine. It's right in the middle of all those properties. What else do they need?" said Sturgis.

"Diversification. Different kinds of gold require different kinds of ownership." Mr. Lum got back onto the golf cart. "I will see you tomorrow."

IN A LITTLE OVER two hours Larry Kwan delivered Peter Fallon to Placerville, the crossroads of gold country.

Route 50 slowed here to a traffic-light crawl. If you stayed on it, you'd soon be climbing toward Lake Tahoe. A left onto 49 sent you toward Sutter's Mill and the deepening valleys and rising slopes of the northern mines. A right took you into the dry, gentle countryside of the southern mines, dotted with towns like Angels Camp, Calaveras, and Sutter's Creek.

Placerville had been born as Old Dry Diggins, a place with gold in all the gulches but barely a trickle of water to wash it. So miners hauled the dirt to the only creek, which was bone dry for half the year. After they hanged three desperadoes in the center of town, they started calling it Hangtown. But respectability had turned it to Placerville.

Google's early photos showed dense-packed ramshackle cabins, a miserable damn place like the hundreds of others that sprang up during the Gold Rush. Most of them had disappeared, but Placerville still stood at the crossroads. Modern images showed a thriving Main Street with the feel of an Old West town. Add parking places instead of hitching posts, a Shell station, Jimboy's Tacos, banks, a used bookstore, and restaurants, and you had all the comforts.

Cutler Gold Exploration was on a side street, a little building with a plate-glass front and five parking spaces, three occupied by a pickup, a compressor, and a trailer holding a Bobcat front-end loader.

Peter went up to the window and peered in: two desks, Cutler sitting behind one, deep in the shadows. Motionless. Drunk? Asleep? Dead?

Peter knocked, then opened the door.

Cutler looked up. He had not shaved, combed his hair, or changed his clothes since the day before. A double-barreled shotgun lay on the desk.

Peter said, "What's with the cannon?"

"I don't know if anyone's told you, Peter Fallon, but this shit is getting real."

"Oh, they've told me. More than once."

"Did you get away over the apartment roof, once you got your shoes on?"

Peter was still trying to figure this guy out. He did not trust him. He did not especially like him. But LJ and Mary had asked Peter to work with him, so Peter told him they needed picks, shovels, metal detector. "Shotgun, too, if you want to bring it."

Cutler said, "The Chinese are coming."

"Coming where?"

"To the Mother Lode. To Placerville. To my fucking office."

As jittery as a man trying to push a wheelbarrow across a freeway, thought Peter. "Are you on something, Cutler?"

"Caffeine. Lots of caffeine since Michael Kou called and told me to expect a visit from the Dai-lo himself, bringing a P&S on my land. I own everything between the Emery Mine and Rainbow Gulch. You know Rainbow Gulch?"

"Manion Sturgis makes his wines on the plateau above."

"That's no plateau." Cutler scoffed, like an annoying IT guy one-upping the office Luddite. "It's an ancient riverbed."

"Listen, Jack, I think I know where there's half a million dollars in gold. You want it. I want it. If we find it, we can get Wonton Willie off our kids' backs. Let's focus on that."

"Half a million? Chump change." Cutler tapped his computer. "Look at this."

Peter looked at his watch instead.

Cutler waved him over. "Come on. It'll just take a minute."

Peter stepped around the desk, stepped closer. And yeah, Cutler smelled as bad as he looked. "You must be really nervous."

"I've been nervous ever since that old lady got hit-and-run on Van Ness. But no one's murdering me. Not without a fight." He gestured to the shotgun.

"But what are you fighting for? Yourself or our kids?"

"The truth . . . and my own reputation. Everything else follows from that."

Outside, Larry Kwan honked his horn.

"And here's the truth." Cutler jabbed a finger at the screen. "U.S. Geological Survey map from 1911, compiled by a guy named Waldemar Lindgren. It shows all of California's ancient rivers from the Tertiary Period."

Another honk.

Peter looked toward the window. "We have to go."

"These rivers flowed west long before the Sierra rose in the east. The earth was warmer and wetter. The landscape was gentler, with low mountains that had already gone through eons of erosion. A shallow sea reached as far inland as Sacramento. But the laws of geology, physics, and hydrodynamics still pertained, so—"

"—those rivers were already eroding gold?"

"From the moment the quartz veins extruded into the crevices. But—"

"—a lot can happen in sixty million years?"

"Like the subduction of one tectonic plate under another, causing the upthrust of a mountain range, which generates heat, which generates magma, which means volcanoes."

"Fascinating," said Peter, "But—"

"There were eruptions all over this area." Cutler gestured toward the window, as if a big vent was steaming away in the parking lot. "Volcanoes spew lava. And lava is liquid, right?"

"Hot liquid."

"Which follows the path of least resistance, like water. Those eruptions sent lava right down the riverbeds. Find old lava flows or andesitic soils, you'll often find a nice defined layer of alluvial gravel, sometimes a few feet down, sometimes hundreds."

"Where the ancient rivers flowed?"

"Right. Most of those rivers were found before we were born." He pointed at the screen. "There's the bed of the ancient Calaveras. There's the Yuba. They produced a steady stream of gold, back when prospectors could come across a layer of exposed gravel, run a little test, then turn a big hose onto it."

"Hydraulic mining?" said Peter.

"The most environmentally destructive thing ever done in California."

Cutler had Peter's attention now. The lost rivers of gold weren't just a metaphor. They were real, but they were underground, and made of gravel, not water. Peter pointed to the tributaries of a stream that seemed to surround Broke Neck.

"That's the ancient Mokolumne," said Cutler. "It's been mapped from the El Dorado National Forest down to Route 49. I've plotted all the places where auriferous deposits were found."

"Auriferous. That means gold-bearing, right?"

"Right." Cutler pointed here and there. "Irish Hill, Indian Diggs, Volcano, Fiddletown."

"Why those places?"

"Ancient rivers dropped their deposits just like modern rivers, at turns and bends in the landscape. Most of those spots have all been mined. But I still believe in undiscovered ore bodies. That's what keeps me going." He grabbed the paper cup beside the computer and took a swallow. "That and coffee."

Peter pointed to another line, in a different color, like a modern overlay.

"That's the ancient Miwok," said Cutler. "My river."

"*Your* river?"

"Lindgren missed it, so did everyone else. But one day, I was a few miles north of the Broke Neck site, inspecting a gravel bank in a hillside, above the ruins of an old wing dam some miners blew up. That was the legend, anyway—"

"The legend is true. It's in the journal."

"Now you see why I was in your son's apartment looking for it. I'd love to get my hands on it. Does it talk about Rainbow Gulch?"

Peter nodded. Larry honked again.

Cutler kept talking. "At the old dam, I found an overlay of volcanic soil atop a gravel bank. But discontinuous."

"What does that mean, discontinuous?"

"Sometimes, an ancient river deposit appears, then you lose it, then it shows up again a mile away, in a place where logic suggests it's part of the same flow. Lindgren shows a lot of discontinuous streams on his map. The ancient Miwok just stopped on land owned by the Boyles family. You couldn't trace it beyond there."

"Not that they'd let you."

"Very stubborn folks. But as far as I can tell, it runs southwest through their land, then around the Emery Mine property, then pops up on a four-hundred-acre plot of rangeland with Rainbow Gulch as its southern boundary. Across the millennia, water cut a ravine fifty feet deep and two hundred wide, right across this ancient stream, and released a lot of gold in a short time. That's why Rainbow Gulch was so rich. But it didn't last long because the deposits were so—"

"Discontinuous?" Peter was getting it now. "But across the ravine, you have Manion Gold Vineyard—"

"Where I am sure that there are other discontinuous deposits. There's even a bump in the land, about a quarter mile back, a bend where a river could have turned and dropped its gravel. Sturgis won't let me do core samples. But there's nothing Zinfandel likes better than volcanic soil."

"So . . . an ancient river of gold?"

"I bought the property north of the gulch as speculation. It's what small timers do. Develop gold reserves, proven and unproven, then pitch investors. My core sample showed a belt of auriferous gravel at twenty-six feet. So, the lost river the Irishman—"

"Michael Flynn?"

"—told Ah-Toy about. Ah-Toy told my wife's grandmother, who told my wife, who told me."

"And your daughter told my son?"

"Yeah." Jack Cutler ran his hands through his hair. "Although, my daughter is not very happy with me these days."

"Because you cheated so many people in Chinatown?"

"I was having trouble paying the mortgage on my Rainbow Gulch acreage. Then your son brought Michael Kou to me, and Kou said it would mean a lot to the big-money Hong Kong boys if we could produce a good report. I got blamed, but Kou and his boys did the seeding."

"How?"

"Core samples are supposed to go into bags that are sealed until they arrive at the assayer. Kou could have gotten into them en route. He wanted the big loans from China. But he also wanted the support of certain elements in the community, just to show the Hong Kong bosses that he could spread the wealth."

"Certain elements like, say, Wonton Willie?"

"I told you. Willie's a pimp. Someone with more juice."

"Who?"

"Not sure. All I know is that Kou might think big and act smooth, but he's still a hood, and hoods are all the same. They hurt their own people first. Some do it with gambling, drugs, protection scams. Squeezing people over a bad gold investment . . . eh."

"So he seeded the test holes, and you benefited?"

Cutler shrugged, as if he had come to terms with it. "The locals lost money, but Kou stayed with me because I kept my mouth shut and proved my loyalty. With some of these guys, it's all about respect and loyalty."

"Even when you know a guy is dirty?"

"Especially then. Michael Kou told Hong Kong that we'd found a modern Gum Saan, so Sierra Rock got investment loans from Chinese banks. I paid my mortgage."

"Gum Saan," said Peter. "Gold Mountain."

"The Chinese came here looking for Gum Saan. But most of them figured out that the only way to get to it is to work your ass off."

"Like the guy they call Uncle Charlie?"

"It's guys like him I'd love to make whole. I never went bankrupt. So if they held onto their stock, they may have lost money, but their shares are still worth five cents each."

"Down from what?"

Cutler looked at the floor, shamefaced. "An initial offering of five dollars."

The door opened and Larry Kwan said, "Mr. Peter, I have a pickup scheduled at Manion Gold. Your girlfriend, remember? We keep her waiting, she won't be happy."

Peter took the shotgun off the table and said, "Then let's go."

Larry Kwan said, "Hey, I'm a peaceable guy. I like wine. I don't like shotguns."

"You drive an armored Escalade," said Peter. "You've been waiting for this."

"Well"—Larry flashed his smile—"I guess so."

CUTLER BROUGHT OUT PICKS, shovels, and a Minelab GPX 5000 gold prospecting metal detector. He put them into the back of the Escalade and told Peter, "About this half million in Chinese gold. I think people like Uncle Charlie have first dibs on it."

Peter turned on him. "The only reason you're along is because you have the tools, and my son loves your daughter. And I told you, our first problem is Wonton Willie. We'll worry about your reputation later."

Twenty minutes south, they picked up Wild Bill Donnelly. He was waiting in his driveway, wearing his windbreaker, with something bulky under his arm. He hopped into the back next to Jack Cutler and said, "I've heard of you."

"He's a geologist," said Larry. "Knows a lot."

"He also has a Minelab GPX 5000," said Peter.

"Then let's go get the legendary Chinese gold," said Wild Bill.

BACK TOWARD BROKE NECK, a turn down the Fiddletown Road, another to the southeast, then another, deeper and deeper into the rolling dry-grass savannah.

They passed the No Trespassing sign by the dirt road leading to the Boyles' property, then bumped along until Ginny O'Hara's little ranch house appeared on the left, above the corral.

Larry Kwan noticed the house and said, "Hey, this is it."

"What?" said Peter.

"This is where the mom lived. When I brought that woman from the historical society, we stopped here and picked up her mom."

"Then stop now, for Chrissakes!" said Peter. There was no telling when dumb luck would play its part. That was why he always fell back on research, legwork, and careful dot-connecting. Sometimes, dumb luck came first, sometimes later. But he was always ready for it. He had done the research and legwork on the last trip. Time now to connect some dots.

He told the others to stay in the car. He went past the garage that sat on Emery's foundation, under an old oak tree that might have served for the hangings he had read about, then up the hill to the screen door of the little ranch house. The television was tuned to CNBC. The Dow Jones was up. Gold prices were down. The front room looked comfortable, sparse, arrayed around a hearth that faced the door.

On the mantel: a picture of a young couple. The girl looked . . . familiar.

He rang the bell.

From somewhere in the house the voice of Ginny O'Hara trilled, "Who is it?" as if she was expecting someone else, someone she would be glad to see.

"It's Peter Fallon, the historian from Boston."

Ginny O'Hara's face appeared. "I thought I told you to stay away from here."

"Could I ask you a few questions?"'

She looked over his shoulder at the Escalade. "Is that Jack Cutler in the backseat? You tell him there'll be no core sampling. There's no gold here. And even if there was—"

"I don't care about your gold or your land."

That stopped her. "Then what?"

"Can I step in for a moment?" He wanted a closer look at the picture on the mantel.

"Say what you want to say right there. Then be on your way."

"I was at the California Historical Society yesterday. I met your daughter." He threw that out. He did not know if it was true or not.

"Kim?"

"Yes. Kim." And his mind started to spin: from the girl who greeted him at reception to Meg Miller, the librarian, to the assistant who kept coming in and out and watched the room when Meg Miller wasn't there. And her name was—yes—Kim.

Ginny O'Hara stepped out, all sun-dried, denim-wrapped, no-nonsense and plenty suspicious, too.

Peter said, "It's Kim O'Hara, right? She works with Meg Miller?"

"Kim O'Hara Hally. Her husband's name is Hally. She works in the library. What's this about?"

Peter could recall Kim Hally now. Taller than her mother, more bookish, not so skilled at the eye-to-eye glare. He decided to go straight for the truth. Ginny might appreciate that, even after being tricked into giving up her daughter's name.

So he said bluntly, "Do you have it?"

"Have what?"

"The James Spencer Journal. Or did you bring it to Manion Sturgis?"

She nailed him with that glare, nailed him like the horseshoe nailed above her door, and said, "You, sir, are a son of a bitch." Then she slammed the door so hard that the horseshoe fell off.

BACK IN THE CAR, Wild Bill Donnelly said, "Sounds like it went well."

"Yeah," cracked Larry Kwan. "Lady says 'son of a bitch' and slams a door . . . means you're doing something right."

Peter told Larry to drive on. When he saw the blackened hillside appearing through the cottonwoods, he started looking. When he saw the cut that led down to the river and to Big Skull Rock, he told Larry to stop.

Cutler said, "There's a famous old landmark."

"More famous than you know."

"Hell of a fire," said Larry Kwan. "Burned all the way up to the top of the south ridge."

Wild Bill said, "If we spend too long here, expect the Boyles to start burning, too."

Peter said, "We'll be quick. The Chinese gold is there, or it's not."

"If it's there, the Boyles will lay claim," said Jack Cutler.

"Then we take pictures for Wonton Willie," answered Peter, "and give the bags to the proper owners, even if it means the Boyles."

Now that he had read of the events here, Peter could see everything on this burnt-over ground . . . the wheels and sluices, the Chinese camp and the cabin near Big Skull Rock. Anything made of wood was long gone, burned, carried off, or rotted away after a hundred and seventy years. But the spirits of Spencer, Flynn, Cletis, Wei Chin, Mei-Ling, and the rest were watching right then. That's how Peter Fallon felt.

Larry Kwan said, "What should I do?"

"Stay in the car. Keep it running." Peter grabbed a shovel.

"Just make sure you're not idling on any dry grass or you'll start another fire." Wild Bill pulled his .44, held it at his leg, walked down the embankment, across the stream onto the burned ground, with Peter and Cutler close behind.

Peter said, "You're making yourself quite a target, Bill. Remember last time?"

"Last time was for show. I let Buster play his scene. This is for real."

"Keep a clear eye," said Jack Cutler. "That Buster's bad-tempered."

"Nine o'clock," said Peter to Cutler.

"What?"

"Imagine that Big Skull Rock is a clock. Dig at nine o'clock. That's what Spencer told Chin. And Spencer's gold would be at ten o'clock."

Wild Bill said, "Do you really think you're going to find anything there?"

"I told you the last time," said Peter, "I'm not sure what I'll find. But sometimes, you go to the place where the thing happened and—"

Again, the detective got it. "—you can find your way to what's happening now."

Cutler looked around. "A great spot for precipitating gold."

"That's what the journal says," answered Peter.

And they went to work.

Cutler pointed the gold finder down. "Nothing. Nothing. Nothing. At nine, ten, or eleven o'clock."

Peter said, "How deep does that thing read?"

"Five feet."

"Spencer said they buried the gold three feet down." Peter started to dig. Maybe the bags had broken and mixed with the surrounding dirt. Maybe Chin had come back with a saw and cut up the flutter wheel. Maybe Flynn had gotten to it. But maybe, just maybe, it was there, as it had been for a century and a half.

They dug two thirds of the way around the rock, tossing the rough dirt and gravel into a pile until they heard the whine of the ATVs on the ridge above them.

With a note of professional cool, Wild Bill said, "You boys just about done?"

"No gold here," said Peter.

"Chinese or otherwise," said Cutler.

Peter put down his shovel and took a few photographs for Wonton Willie. With the journal pages and the photographs, he could now put the bags-of-gold scenario to bed.

The whine of the ATVs was growing louder. This time there were four of them. They burst over the crest of the hill, fifty feet above Big Skull Rock, each leaving its own contrail of black ash-dust.

Three of them skidded to a stop on the crest, up where Spencer and his friends had tried to dig the trench to Rainbow Gulch.

But Buster revved his engine and shot down, blasting through the black-twig remnants of a few bushes.

"More shit, getting realer," said Cutler.

"Stop talking like you're a rapper," said Peter. "You're a white guy in cargo shorts and a bush jacket."

Wild Bill said, "Let me do the talking."

Buster Boyles cut his wheel and kicked up another puff of black dust. He wore his AR-15 military-style, slung across his chest on a flexible strap so that he could bring it into action in an instant. He dressed in blue jeans, camo T-shirt, and a black ball cap with the Oakland Raiders insignia. "Didn't you fuckers see the signs? I could have you arrested. Or shoot you."

"We got no good answers," said Wild Bill, "except this." He gestured with the gun to the hole around the rock.

Then Marti Boyles came riding down, as if she could not resist an argument. She was the matriarch, the Mother Lode marijuana grandma, the dam of all the big-bellied Boyles boys, the bane of her neighbors, too, a small, white-haired bird-like woman who squawked like an angry crow. "What are you son of a bitches after on my land?"

"Chinese gold," said Wild Bill.

"You find it, it's ours," said Buster. "You take anything from this land, you'll have hell to pay. Right, Ma?"

"We're goddamn sick of people comin' on our land, and—" She scooted closer and studied Cutler. "You again? We told you never to come back, sniffin' around here like a bear at a birdfeeder."

Cutler shrugged. "I had an old girlfriend, once, called me her hurly-burly bear."

Marti looked at Peter. "This fuckin' guy's crazy. Comin' around with stories about an underground river of gold."

Buster said, "All the gold was sucked out of here a long time ago. Just tailing piles left, and an old trench that runs away toward Rainbow Gulch."

Marti said to Cutler, "Are you the one who called that Chink, that Lum guy?"

"Stupid goddamn name, Lum," said Buster.

"Is he coming?" asked Cutler.

"He says he's comin' to offer us more than our wildest dreams for our land," Marti Boyles went on. "But this land is our dream. We like it just the way it is. Tell him that when you see him."

"I'll do that," said Cutler.

Buster pulled a high-capacity magazine from his belt and popped it into his gun. "Maybe we'll tell him ourselves."

Yes, thought Peter. Maybe the Boyles family would have a big surprise for Lum's bodyguards.

Wild Bill said, "Since we didn't find anything, Marti, it's time for us to leave." He cradled the .44 in the crook of his elbow.

The sons up on the crest of the hill raised their AR-15s.

More target practice? wondered Peter. Or something worse.

And a little engine began to hum behind them. Then something small and black, like a four-winged bug, rose over the river, a shiny black drone that went up to the crest of the hill and looked down on the ATVs.

Buster said, "What the fuck?"

Marti Boyles turned to the hilltop and jerked her thumb. *Shoot it down.* And from under the Escalade lift gate, Larry Kwan shouted, "Anything happens to my nice new drone, all this video's going right out onto the internet. I got a son who can make it go viral in no time."

At that moment, Peter was very glad that he had brought Larry Kwan along.

Wild Bill said, "So let's end this like friends, and Larry won't take that drone for a ride over your grove of wacky tobacky, the one that's growing a lot more than the state allows. Okay? And given my close relationship with members of the Amador County police force, I could serve as a character reference if you ever need it."

"Don't do us any favors," said Marti.

"Not a favor, a deal. You wave good-bye, we stay out of your business." Wild Bill holstered his .44.

Marti Boyles gestured for her sons to lower their guns. Then she said, "You bastards remember, we know where you live. Get out, but tell that bitch across the way, that Ginny O'Hara, tell her and her friend Sturgis and that old fuckin' hippie from Sausalito that the answer is 'no.' We ain't sellin' to anyone. No to them, no to the Chinks, no to anybody else."

And Peter Fallon almost kissed that grouchy old woman. She had just connected dots all over the place, with a single long, squawked, sarcastic sentence. Ginny O'Hara, whose daughter may have stolen the transcription, was in cahoots with Manion Sturgis and . . . Sarah Bliss? Strange, strange allies. He said, "If the Asian investors visit—"

"They won't stay for long," said Buster.

"Nobody fucks with a woman who has three armed sons," said Marti. "Now get."

As Peter, Wild Bill, and Jack Cutler climbed the other side of the bank, Larry Kwan shouted, "You guys like my toy?"

Cutler said, "I want one."

And Peter's phone pinged. A text. It came from Ginny O'Hara and made him very glad that he had given her his card. It read: "Sturgis has the journal."

So, she had changed her mind before Peter tried to change it for her.

Larry Kwan asked, "Where to, boss?"

Peter said, "Manion Gold Vineyards, as scheduled." Then he forwarded Ginny O'Hara's text to Evangeline, adding, "Ask Manion, where is it?"

An hour later, Peter Fallon was holding the transcribed "Journal of James Spencer." And his hands were perspiring.

It had sheepskin leather covers, marbled end papers, and inside, long sheets of careful handwriting, the steady work of an old man who had less and less to do with his business, so he could concentrate more and more on his Palmer Method loops and dips.

"This is what we've been looking for the whole time," said Peter. Then he gave Manion Sturgis the best withering, sidelong glare he could muster. He almost hurt his eyes, he withered so hard.

But Manion wasn't having it. He said, "You can take the boy out of Boston, but you can't take that Boston stink-eye out of the boy."

"You could have made this easier on all of us," answered Peter.

He, Wild Bill, and Jack Cutler had joined Sturgis and Evangeline on the veranda of the little guest cottage, while Larry Kwan flew his drone around the vineyard. A pot of coffee and a plate of scones sat on the table. Only Cutler was eating.

Manion Sturgis said, "This thing has never been about bags of Chinese gold under a rock. Cutler knows . . . with his core sampling augur and his cheap metal detector."

"Mine's not cheap," said Cutler.

"And that's not an explanation." Peter held his glare.

Sturgis glared right back. "This has always been about protecting our countryside from mining."

"Protecting it?" Wild Bill laughed. "But Amador County is built on mining."

"Not today," answered Sturgis. "Sarah Bliss and her husband agree on general principle. That's why they opposed reconstructing the journal. And Ginny O'Hara has always agreed. That's why she had her daughter remove the journal from the historical society. When Cutler called about it—"

Peter looked at Cutler. "You?"

Cutler took a bite of croissant. "In my business, research precedes field work. The story of the *Proud Pilgrim* got my attention, just like it got the attention of old Maryanne Rogers."

"But," said Manion, "Cutler had already gotten our attention out here in Amador. We knew what he was after. Dumb luck that Ginny's daughter, Kim Hally, fielded his call to the library. She told him the journal could not be located."

Cutler shook his head, stuffed another croissant. "And I believed her."

"I might, too," said Peter, "because documents disappear in the best of libraries."

"The next day, Kim Hally walked out the door with the transcription, and brought it to her mother, who gave it to me," said Sturgis as proudly as if he had planned the whole thing. "Simple, clean, elegant."

"You took the journal to protect the land?" said Evangeline.

"To keep it open, quiet, and productive," said Sturgis, "because we produce something that matters here. But Kou's company, backed by Chinese money, dirty money, laundered money, whatever kind of money—"

"Are you sure it's all Chinese?" asked Peter.

Sturgis said, "Who do you think Sierra Rock really is? You've been to the Emery operation. You saw Lum making everyone nervous. Evangeline told me the whole story."

Peter swallowed his jealousy and said to her, "What else did you tell him?"

She said, "I told him to come up with Spencer's journal or I'd never speak to him again. Keep taking that tone with me, and I may never speak to you again, either."

Wild Bill refreshed everyone's cup, just to do a little distracting.

Manion Sturgis said, "If Sierra Rock gets the Emery operation going, they'll do hard rock mining. They'll haul up quartz, pulverize it, heap-leach it right on the property. The sound of the rolling mill will echo all across the countryside. And if they control the surrounding lands, where the ancient Miwok is supposed to run—"

"Discontinuously," said Jack Cutler.

"—they can drift mine. Run side shafts into gravel banks. Bring men, trucks, noise. I won't let them get at gravels beneath the vines that have been growing on this plateau—"

"Ancient riverbed," Cutler corrected.

Peter said, "Cutler, you are being a pain in the ass."

"It's my nature," said Cutler.

"—for a century and a half." Manion Sturgis finished his thought.

Peter flipped through the journal. "What did you learn from this that you didn't know before?"

"We learned that myths aren't truths," answered Sturgis. "But dreams never die."

Evangeline nodded. She liked the sound of that, liked how it was phrased.

But Peter missed the poetry. He was thinking about the practicalities. He said, "This has to go back, you know. I can't tell you what it's worth, but Kim Hally is guilty of grand theft. You and Ginny O'Hara are guilty of receiving stolen property."

"But this"—Manion Sturgis gestured to the vine-covered landscape— "the productivity of it, the beauty, the quiet, this has to be protected, no matter the cost."

As if to make the point, a turkey buzzard came flap-flap-flapping over. They all stopped and looked up. They actually could hear the wings.

Evangeline said, "That's a fine inspiration."

Peter watched her, the way she was looking at Manion, to see if she inclined herself toward him or touched his arm. But she did not change her posture in any way.

So Peter said, "I've returned materials to libraries anonymously before.

I can probably do it now. But why would Ginny O'Hara choose this morning to tell me about this?"

"Because you asked," said Evangeline. "You figured it out and she was busted."

"No," said Sturgis. "Because Sierra Rock is here this weekend, pushing to buy us all out, so they'll own the proven reserves at the Emery Mine and all the twists and turns of the ancient Miwok, too. They'll do what they have to and get signatures on P&S agreements on my land, Ginny's, the Boyles', even Cutler's here."

Just then, they heard gunfire off in the distance.

"Sounds like the Boyles are shooting at targets," said Manion Sturgis.

"Or maybe at Mr. Lum," said Wild Bill.

Above them, Larry Kwan's little drone growled and buzzed off toward the sound.

"I never liked those Boyles people too much," said Cutler. "But I'm glad they're ready to shoot first and ask questions later when the Triad comes around."

"Which the Triad will continue to do," said Wild Bill, "until this is over."

"And it won't be over," said Manion Sturgis, "until you find the original of Notebook Seven. Otherwise the requirements of the will are not met, and the Spencer estate remains in escrow. That's what Attorney Barber would tell you. And that's fine by me. I hate the idea of breaking that grand old house into its component parts."

Just then, Peter's phone pinged. A text from LJ: "They hit Willie an hour ago. Willie and Mullet Man. Wraparound disappeared. We're still in safe house. Next move?"

Peter looked at the others. "We need to get to San Francisco right away. I hear there's a helicopter."

"It comes with its own pilot," said Manion, "but it only carries three passengers."

Wild Bill glanced at Peter's phone and said, "You may need me and Mr. Magnum and my SFPD connections."

"Okay," said Peter. "It's me, Wild Bill, and who else?"

Evangeline said, "You can be a bull in a china shop, Peter. You might need a delicate touch."

Peter said to Manion, "Is that OK with you?"

Evangeline stood. "No need to ask him." Then she told Manion, "Call the helo."

Peter texted LJ: "Sit tight. On our way. Do not have Chinese gold. Do have journal transcription." SEND. Then he put the completed journal into its archival box and said, "I'll be taking this with me."

THE KEY WAS SOMEWHERE in these last pages. It had to be. That's what Peter Fallon was thinking as the helicopter rose over the irrigated vines and the brown, baked landscape, because nothing he had read in the first six notebooks was enough to trigger "a new gold rush."

He began to flip, then read aloud to Evangeline and Wild Bill.

But the last section did not unfold day-by-day. Once Spencer gave up the *Boston Transcript* gig, he stopped keeping a detailed record of his days. The 1906 rewrite covered broader spans of time, a longer perspective. Rather than an impatient youth discovering who he was in a violent new world, Peter sensed the old man, experienced, observant, melancholy, reflecting as he rewrote. . . .

———— ⬭ ————

The Journal of James Spencer—Notebook #7
September, 1850
The Sea Captain

In a moment of weakness, Janiva admitted that she wanted to go home.

It was not because she feared Samuel Hodges or Nathan Trask, whose expected vengeance kept me vigilant, nor because she missed her family, as any young woman would, nor because the soul-deadening horror of that awful night had destroyed her natural optimism and for weeks had rendered her all but mute.

To understand, one needed to spend a summer on this peninsula.

In New England, July fills us with a sense that we may live forever. August reminds us to enjoy life's gifts, for all is fleeting. September brings the gentle wisdom of old age. But San Francisco saves its most miserable days for summer, which may provoke homesickness in even the hardest of hearts.

A cold ocean rolls through the Golden Gate. A valley hot as hellfire lies beyond the eastern hills. And as with all of nature, one thing balances the other. When the inland heat rises, cold air rushes in. Thus is born the wind that brings the fog that chills the wind that brings the fog . . . in a cycle as regular as the tides.

Add to the weather our weekly earthquakes—some small, some large— and any of them enough to shake the deepest sleeper awake. Add to the earthquakes the relentless tension of living in a tinderbox town where any errant flame or ill-intentioned looter might start the next conflagration. And anyone might be tempted to leave.

But Janiva was made of stronger stuff. Her time of weakness came and went. She knew that fall would bring warmer winds. She knew what we were making here. And she showed, as the weeks went by, that she was like her new home. With every assault, every insult, every arson fire in our city or upon her soul, she committed to building again, bigger, better, stronger.

Five weeks after the May fire, another conflagration consumed three hundred buildings and an astonishing five million dollars in property. But we were unscathed, having moved our goods into our new warehouse at the edge of the city, on Market at Dupont. And as with earlier fires, those who built things or sold the tools to build with or owned the land to build upon enjoyed the boon of prices rising ever higher. Those who had a steady flow of goods, even manufactured seventeen thousand miles and seven months away, were best positioned to bring civilization and stability to a city that now numbered twenty-five thousand souls, with thousands more passing on to the diggings every week.

But like any city, we needed cheap labor. So we looked to the Chinese, who came on ships from Canton, drawn by the myths of Gum Saan and driven by the upheavals of their ancient land, or on foot from the diggings, driven by prejudice and drawn by a growing community of their own kind. But from wherever they came, they worked. No race was so industrious or so clannish, and both qualities we appreciated.

Chinese women like Ah-Toy provided an essential service to the mostly male population. Chinese laborers who hammered nails, dug ditches, and did a thousand backbreaking tasks brought honor to the most menial job. And Chinese cooks knew of herbs and spices to tenderize the tough roosters running through our streets or flavorize the stringy cattle driven up the peninsula, thereby enriching us all, thrice daily.

So Mayor Geary decreed a ceremony to honor our Chinese. On a bright August day, a platform was raised at the plaza in Portsmouth Square, before the old adobe city hall, and a great assemblage of citizens ascended, including the Brannans, Reese Shipton and his wife, Sally, U.S. Vice-Consul Woodworth, and all the ministers of San Francisco.

Meanwhile, a skinny old Celestial named Ah-Sing was assembling two hundred "China boys" at his apothecary on Clay Street. He comported himself like the leading Chinaman of the city, a great Mandarin who wore a fine fur mantle, a red silken hat with two tassels, and, as if to add a touch of ancient wisdom, a huge pair of spectacles, the glasses of which were about the thickness of a telescope lens. At his signal, with a cacophonous banging of drums and clanging of cymbals, and accompanied by the raucous roaring of the crowd that came to watch, the China boys paraded down Clay, around the square, and up Washington Street to the platform.

Janiva was much impressed by the native dress, the pigtails, and the singularly picturesque appearance of these men, especially as so many of them carried colorful fans to shield their faces from the dust and wind. But we looked in vain for Wei Chin, who had promised to march with his brother-in-law, Jon-Ling . . . in vain, that is, until we noticed one who never took his fan from his face, as if trying to hide. We both wondered why.

We also wondered at the peculiar effect of the sermon by our minister, Reverend Hunt, upon the China boys. He told them, as Ah-Sing translated, that though they came from a so-called "Celestial Empire," there was a higher place, much better and bigger, and while they were "sometimes taken sick and suffered in California, then died and were seen no more, all good China boys went to that celestial place to live forever in perfect harmony."

This Christian vision of heaven caused the Chinese to laugh heartily, but I was not laughing, because by then I knew why Chin was hiding his face. On the other side of the crowd rose the plant-pot crown and curved brim of Nathan Trask's hat. And his eyes were boring straight into me.

Vengeance had arrived.

My enjoyment of the ceremony ended as abruptly as a gunshot. It was a humbug anyway, indoctrinating heathens into childish knowledge of divine truths. Surely the ministers believed they were saving souls, but this talk of a happy afterlife was meant to make docile citizens, nothing more. After a benediction, the China Boys formed a parade to honor the American president and did it with great glee upon hearing that the president was "all the same" as their emperor. As Chinese cymbals and drums began to beat and clang again, Janiva and I paraded right out of Portsmouth Square.

OUR OFFICE LOOKED ONTO Market Street. My desk and Janiva's flanked a double door that led to three thousand feet of storage space, currently half-filled. A fireproof safe in the corner held our papers, gold, and specie. We lived in a small apartment above, accessed by an outside staircase. But for the dangers of looting, we might have chosen to live in the Drake. However, close to our goods was the place to be.

I was alone at my desk when Trask's silhouette appeared in the window.

Janiva had gone upstairs to make afternoon tea, one of the soothing Boston routines that she had come to rely upon since the terrible events of May. And Matt Dooling, who kept his shop in a lean-to built onto our warehouse, must have been elsewhere, as I heard no clanging of hammer on anvil. But a man who has a Colt Dragoon for a friend is never entirely alone. And mine lay in plain sight on my desk.

Nathan Trask pushed open the door and stood in the square of light. He carried only a length of rope coiled around his shoulder. His eye went to my pistol as my hand did, and he said, "You are in no danger, sir. Samuel Hodges has absolved you and the Chinese. The death of the old man was penalty enough."

"Especially since we opened a vein of gold for him."

"I would not have forgiven so easily." He approached my desk.

"Then why are you here?" I asked.

"I want Seaman Flynn. He's a deserter."

I had considered this moment for weeks. But until now, I had not thought of the appropriate lie: "I bid good-bye to him three months ago, when he boarded the *California*. He's bound for Boston."

Trask fingered the noose. "I'll not take kindly to learn otherwise."

"He took ten thousand dollars out of the Miwok. He reckoned he had enough."

Trask's brow dropped below the brim of his hat. His sallow face turned a deeper shade of yellow, as if that was how salt-cured skin showed anger. Sharp lines descended from the corners of his mouth and followed stripes of gray through his beard. Black circles bagged under his eyes like bruises. He looked as if he had been absorbing all the sins of all the men he had been punishing all across California. He said, "Those drunk on gold are no better than tosspots pissing away their lives in Boston alleys. Yet here, we propose to make a society out of them."

"Flynn has gone back to Boston, I tell you, to make a society there."

Trask said, "And what if I tell you I do not believe you?"

"He will tell you that he does not care."

While watching the sea change in Trask's face, I had not noticed Janiva slip in the side door, holding the mighty Nock at her hip.

Trask shifted his eyes toward her, but wisely did not move. "Is this the young woman whose arrival on Long Wharf disrupted Reverend Stone's benediction?"

Janiva said, "You have an excellent memory, sir."

"I do not forget affronts to the dignity of my ship or my command."

I said, "Would you flog her, too, as you did Michael Flynn that day?"

"I would never flog a woman, no matter how much she deserved it."

"In that case—" I gestured for Janiva to put down the gun. I had no wish to see Trask splattered all over me, and if all seven barrels were loaded, I had no wish to be splattered myself . . . all over the wall.

She said, "First, make him promise that he's not here to use that rope . . . on anyone."

"You do not trust me?" asked Trask.

"I may never trust another man again, save my husband."

Piece by piece, bit by bit, Janiva had been restoring the equanimity ripped from her on that awful night. But her trust had always been a hard-earned thing. Now, even I felt the challenge.

Trask studied her from the corner of his eye and said, "If Flynn has gone back to Boston, you can trust that it's a promise I'll keep, until I get to Boston. He was the last crewman at large."

I hoped that Janiva had caught my ruse, and of course, she had.

I said to Trask, "You've hanged nineteen men?"

"Sixteen. The others received permission to leave my service."

"And you now have our permission," said Janiva, "to leave our presence."

Trask turned to face her, appraising her from the hem of her skirt to the top of her head. He looked and said nothing, looked for so long that she began to grow uneasy under his gaze. At length, he asked, "What do you bring?"

"Bring?"

"To this city. To this society. What do you bring of yourself, ma'am?"

Janiva looked at me, plainly undone by this line of question.

Trask had just as plainly gone crazy, but in a fashion that reflected deep, disappointed sanity. He saw concentric circles of chaos around him and sought to bring order to each of them, from greedy ship owners to shirking seamen to the roiling, storm-dark sea itself. His neat cabin had reflected his belief that only through order and discipline could we navigate life. He hated the quick-wealth ambition of the men passing our office windows or streaming up to gold country. And those who transgressed laws of personal discipline deserved public discipline from men of stronger character, men like himself. In such a cosmos, his question made perfect sense, because he believed that by restoring discipline, he guaranteed order, and order gave structure to hope.

He said to Janiva, "A married woman bespeaks stability. She promises the future." He turned to me, "Would you have a family?"

"We would," she said.

"My crew were my family. Like a father, I loved them. And so have I punished them." Then this calmly crazy man left the office and headed down Market Street.

WEI CHIN AND I had agreed that we would share news if the vengeance of Broke Neck followed us to San Francisco. So I went the next morning to Ah-Sing's Apothecary, a small, wood-frame storefront above Portsmouth Square. Over the door hung a green sign with gold Chinese characters. The English words, *Chinese herbs*, were scrawled on a chalkboard in the window.

By marrying his sister to one of the leading Chinese businessmen of San Francisco, Chin had earned favor in his community. By distributing loans from his stash of gold, half of which he believed was still buried beneath Big Skull Rock, he had earned loyalty. By taking as a bodyguard his cousin, Little Ng, who now carried a knife in the baggy sleeve that once held a flute, he had earned respect.

Chin also understood the preparation and application of Chinese herbal potions, skills that had earned him the position of Number Two in Ah-Sing's Apothecary. He offered remedies and opinions on afflictions ranging from fever to flaccidity of the male member, while he and Little Ng kept the peace and collected the fees in Ah-Sing's mah-jongg parlor, accessed through the rattling bead-curtain at the side of the apothecary shop.

I had visited many times. Ah-Sing himself had given me ginseng tea, promising, "It make stiff you root and make swell you wife's belly." At my age, I had no difficulties with the former, and the latter, Janiva and I were certain, would happen in God's good time, another layer of tissue to cover the wound in her soul. But we liked ginseng tea, and I loved the sensation of stepping off Clay Street into a cloud of cinnamon and clove and a dozen other spices.

Chin was behind the counter, talking to a tall, exotic Chinese woman who wore her hair in what appeared to be a black fan spreading from either side of her face, making her appear all the more dreamlike, which was fitting in that she was a source of dreams for white men and yellow, both here by the Bay and far up in the gold fields. She was the glorious Ah-Toy herself, wrapped in a robe of green-and-gold silk.

Wei Chin introduced us and added for Ah-Toy, "Spencer friend of Flynn-man."

She said, in surprisingly good English, "Flynn-man, Irish. Big dreamer, him."

"Most men are big dreamers," I said.

"Most men dream what I give. What Wei Chin and Ah-Sing soon bring from China."

Chin scowled, as if he did not want me to know his business.

That made Ah-Toy giggle. Her lips, painted into the shape of a little red bee sting, seemed to embrace her words: "Yes, yes. China girls they bring. Pretty ones, I take. Ugly ones go street cribs or up to mountains, where white mans make fuck with any girl-cooch. I pay forty dollar each, pretty or ugly. Ah-Sing pay ten dollar in China."

Now I understood. Chin had fled China to escape oppression. But he was not above indenturing Chinese women to whoredom in California. He must have sensed my thoughts by the look I gave him, as he said, "Most men in California dream of Gum Saan."

"Gum Saan. Gold Mountain." Ah-Toy gave another giggle and brought her fan to her face. "Flynn-man, he no dream gold mountain. He dream gold *river*. He like-ee China girl swim bum-naked in gold river. He find?"

"The river?" I said. "I don't know. I have not heard from him in months."

"If do, tell him China girl him like-ee. He spend gold at Ah-Toy's, he get look-ees from me, do-ees from girls. And talk. Much talk, that Flynn-man. You talk?"

I shook my head, as if to prove the point, though I was as intoxicated as most men by the painted lips, the regal height, the long legs balanced on open-toed platform shoes.

Ah-Toy said, "You quiet man. Quiet man deep river. Maybe you find gold river?"

"There is no such thing," I said.

Ancient Ah-Sing came from the back, placed a package on the counter, and looked at Ah-Toy with eyes of longing behind thick spectacles. No man, young or old, escaped her allure. "Cinnamon Bark. Oil of jasmine. Alkanet root. One pinch."

She opened her purse and offered her pouch to the old man.

He gestured for Chin to do the dipping. "Bigger fingers."

Chin dipped and deposited the gold dust in a little box.

Ah-Toy spoke to Chin in Chinese, then smiled at me, said "Good-bye," and stepped outside, where Keen-ho Chow held an umbrella to shield her from the sun.

Chin said, "Cinnamon bark tea, good for woman cramp. Oil of jasmine and alkanet root, mix with mutton fat, make red paint for lips. Red lips make women very fucky, even ugly woman."

Ah-Sing grunted, as if this talk was beneath him, and he disappeared again into his back room.

Chin said, "He pretend no like. But he know men in China, sell slave girls. Put on ship, send here. Big profit. Ah-Toy promise to pay and give me my pick, too."

"Is that what she just said?"

"That what always she say, then always she say to make my sister courtesan."

"But your sister is married."

"Ah-Toy know we mix ginseng for husband. Ah-Toy say ginseng no work. She say Jon-Ling come see her to make him hard. But no good. Ah-Toy say pretty sister need stiffer thing than what Jon-Ling have."

"And what do you say?"

"I say leave sister alone. Ah-Toy just want to make money off her."

"While you make money off other girls."

Chin held up eight fingers. "In all California, eight China girl. No one get rich off China girl. Not Ah-Toy. Not me. Now, you here tell me you see Trask?"

"He's living on his ship. He says you're in the clear, but be careful."

"If he come Clay Street"—Chin looked around—"we send him forever home."

I lowered my voice. "You mean, kill him?"

"Maybe. Maybe I chain him in ship and sink him if he try hurt family. I kill for family, kill for friend, keep quiet for friend, too, if friend ask. And you always friend." Yes, he had figured out our *Proud Pilgrim* secret.

"You always friend, too," I answered.

"Some day, Mr. Always Friend, we go back to Big Skull Rock and get gold."

I did not tell Chin something I had known for weeks: the gold was gone. I had written to George Emery, the only man I trusted in the Mother Lode, and told him to move the wheel and dig at nine and ten o'clock. But he had found nothing. My loss had not hurt my finances too deeply. And the knowledge of his loss would not help Chin. But someone had taken the gold. I had my suspicions.

NATHAN TRASK SURPRISED US a few weeks later with what, for him, amounted to an expression of friendship.

Around four o'clock on a September morning, another great blaze exploded, this time at the Philadelphia House on Jackson Street. As the fire bells rang, Janiva and I leapt into our clothes. She grabbed the Nock gun and took a position on the outdoor landing. I went down to the street, and Matt Dooling came to stand next to me, with a claw hammer in one hand and a six-pound sledge in the other.

Though the smoke and embers were blowing away from us, we had to be vigilant, for every fire brought out looters who took advantage of the confusion to break into storefronts. And the dark gangs came, slowed, saw my pistol or Dooling's hammers or Janiva's seven barrels, and kept going.

Soon after the alarm, Janiva shouted, "One man, coming fast from the water."

It was the dark silhouette in a plant-pot hat. Trask looked more yellowed and stooped, as if disappointment or loneliness in the ruined cabin of his ship had worn him down. But he tipped his hat to Janiva and said, "Would you need help in the chaos?"

"All the help we can get," I said.

"Then we will teach San Francisco about the simple physics of fear." He turned to the street, lay a noose over his shoulder, pressed the shoulder to mine, and gave every passerby the hangman's glare. Trouble did not even stop to chat.

Around six, as the sky was brightening, another gang surged up Market, but led by Sam Brannan. He shouted, "I come to see how you fared. It looks as if you three need no help."

"Four," said Janiva from the landing above.

Oh, but she made me proud. Those were hard days, much harder for her—but with such a helpmate, how could a man do anything but stand firm?

Brannan gave her a tip of the hat. Then he noticed the rope over Trask's shoulder. "Are you the hangin' captain we've heard about?"

"I've served justice on deserters and murderers. I'll serve it on looters, too."

Just then, half a dozen men rumbled down Dupont, splashing bottles and spitting insults, the Sydney Ducks, the king villains. They stopped in the street and threw their dark looks at us, but there were too many of us to bull rush. So the leader shouted, "Oi, Spencer! Have you seen me old mate Trub McLaws?"

I said nothing, but Matt Dooling clanged his hammers together.

"Damn funny, that," said this tough. "Feller used to work for you, just up and disappears one night along with his whole crew, and you know nothin'?"

"Look for him in the Mother Lode," I said.

"Nah. I like prospectin' right here. C'mon, lads." And off went the Ducks.

"That's Jenkins," said Brannan, "they call him the Miscreant."

"They're all miscreants," said Trask.

Brannan nodded. "You know, Captain, if they cause more trouble, we may need a hangman. The law around here is too lenient."

"If I find a crew, I'll leave you my nooses. If not, I'll do your hanging."

Brannan fingered the heavy knot. "You make a fine noose."

He had much practice at making them, but I did not say so. When a man stood at your shoulder, you called him a friend. And this country, as Cletis had said so often, made strange friendships.

October, 1850
Statehood

On the 18th, the steamer *Oregon* blasted her whistle before she cleared the Golden Gate, blasted and blasted all the way to her anchorage, for she carried glorious intelligence: California had been admitted to the Union!

We celebrated with parades, a grand ball, and a fine expression of our American dream, as written by an Englishman in the *Alta California*: "A community of thousands, collected from all quarters of the world, Polynesians and Peruvians, Englishmen and Mexicans, Germans and New Englanders, Spaniards and Chinese, all organized under old Saxon institutions and marching under command of a mayor and alderman, celebrated admission—which they had literally *demanded*—into the most powerful federation on earth, the American union, thereby creating a state with a territory as large as Great Britain, a population difficult to number, and a destiny which none can foresee."

Such a bright ideal, I thought, so beautifully expressed. But I wondered about those who had seen a darker vision, men like Samuel Hodges.

And Janiva wondered what Michael Flynn might think of such a glowing encomium to our young nation, considering all that he had endured.

I admitted that I worried about him, in that I had heard not a word in five months. There were even times I considered a trip into the high country to find him, but she could not understand why.

"Because he is my friend," I told her. He had saved me more than once.

He had saved her, too. And he had helped me in the Mother Lode to discover the man I was, so that I could now be the husband she deserved. For such a friend, a man stood up, even if he had stolen our gold from under Big Skull Rock.

December, 1850
Christmas in California

Christmas in San Francisco brought celebration and sadness, too.

We enjoyed dinners with the Brannans and other friends, but pleasant times reminded us both of home, of the joy of reunions with those whose smiles were the light of past happy hours, blest now in our imagination. We might see them all present—but only by looking into our hearts, or following with fancy's eye the rail track of memory to behold parents and sisters, brothers and loved ones. At least she and I were together, and in the long run, that was what mattered.

On Christmas Eve, Reverend T. Dwight Hunt gathered his congregation in the Jackson Street meetinghouse. There we experienced a powerful sense of community, as we enjoyed the Nativity in the Gospel of Luke, followed by a fine sermon, then ringing carols that overrode—for us at least—the noise of gunshots, shouts, and raucous caterwauling that signified the celebration of any holiday in Gold Rush California.

Then, on New Year's Day, Reverend Hunt paid us a visit. He came to ask our assistance in starting the San Francisco Orphan Asylum Society. And it was as if Janiva Toler Spencer had found a purpose. And in finding it, she regained something that had been taken from her eight months before.

It might seem odd that a city with so few females would produce so many orphans. Some had lost parents to cholera on the wagon trains or to accidents at sea, and without oversight, they might be victimized by the army of unscrupulous shavers who surged each day through the streets. Others were the offspring of "soiled doves" and anonymous miners paying for pleasure, and as such, were likely to become the jetsam of a harsh place. Janiva insisted that it was simply un-Christian either to punish them for the sins of their parents or leave them to the predations of evil.

So I paid for a building prefabricated in Boston and put up on the corner of Second and Folsom. And Janiva poured forth her energy, going about the city identifying children in need and prevailing upon our friend, Dr. Coit, to tend to their ailments. We did not do any of this to enhance our standing in the community or gain capital in the currency of public opinion. We did it simply because it was the right thing to do.

February–March, 1851
A New Law

But in San Francisco, knowing the right thing to do was not always easy, for as men impose order in a new place, the wheels of justice may grind too slowly . . . or too harshly.

In February, when the shop of dry goods merchant C. J. Jansen & Company was robbed and Jansen mercilessly beaten, a pair of troublemakers named Stuart and Windred were arrested and charged in the Recorder's Courtroom on Portsmouth Square. An angry crowd gathered, and with the cry of "Now's the time," they made a general rush for the prisoners. Doors and windows were smashed, desks and railings broken to pieces, and the mob would certainly have dragged the prisoners out and hanged them right there, but for a company of Washington Guards, U.S. Military, who had been parading on the Plaza.

Righteous anger had been rising against unpunished criminality in San Francisco, so it was not only the rowdies who rioted. Our best citizens had come to believe that the law afforded no protection and thus should we take matters into our own hands. Having seen a lynching, I retreated from this demonstration of mobocracy, of shattering glass, of a crowd's deep-throated angry roar, and returned to the quiet company of my wife.

But that evening, a handbill was slipped under our door, addressed to the Citizens of San Francisco: "For too long, murders, robberies, and arsons committed in this city, without the least redress from the law, have brought anarchy! When thieves are left to rob and kill, the honest traveler must fear each bush a thief! Are we to be attacked and assassinated in our domiciles while the law allows aggressors to perambulate the streets merely for the payment of straw bail? If so, let each man heed the remedy of OLD JUDGE LYNCH!"

I was reading this screed and Janiva was knitting by the woodstove when there came a knock. I greeted it with a cracked door and Colt Dragoon. But it was our friend, Sam Brannan, come to persuade me to join his new committee, to consult with authorities, and report to the mob.

Before I could refuse, Janiva said, "James, you cannot turn this down."

But I smelled violence, no matter that the committee was comprised of men from all the best walks of city life, attorneys, merchants, bankers.

Brannan said, "There's too much lawlessness here, James. The police and courts are enfeebled, so our committee will make an investigation and report to the citizens. If the report is of guilt, I say we hang the guilty. And are you pouring brandy this evening?"

I filled three snifters. Then I said, "You would hang men for robbery?"

"For attempted murder. They beat Jansen half to death."

Janiva, focused again on her knitting, gave me that look from under her brow. "We've lived long enough with these outrages, James. How many more nights do we stand guard with guns loaded while the city burns?"

She could put steel in your spine for certain, especially if you knew of the steel in hers. But I sipped the brandy and sought a path to mediation, for I knew how easily anger could grow into the kind of violence that left a girl named Maria twisting from an oak tree in the mining camp called Broke Neck.

Our American freedoms were protected by thin veneers of law and civility. In places like New England, many layers had been applied across many decades. But here, society had so recently been set down that no more than a light shellac covered it. Each bow to legality, each nod to public decency, each gesture of mercy, represented a fresh coat. So I suggested that we call upon the mayor to convene a grand jury.

Brannan's snifter was halfway to his nose. "Grand Jury? Good Lord, man, but I'm sick of such talk. The courts have never yet hung a man in California—unlike your friend the sea captain."

"He's not my friend."

"He treats you as if he is," said Brannan.

"And so must we treat him," said Janiva, "for there are men outside the circle of civilization who do society great favor by doing the distasteful and the dangerous. He's one of them."

"Indeed, ma'am," said Brannan. "And the captain would agree that some old-fashioned noose-knotting would concentrate a lot of minds."

"You're talking about lynching?" I said.

"I'm talking about honest punishment. Hanging without mercy *or* technicalities. The committee should hear evidence and let the decision be final. If we find those vagabonds guilty, let Trask fashion two nooses and hang them within the hour."

THE NEXT MORNING, WE heard evidence before the terrified and tearful defendants. Then Brannan made a recommendation for hanging . . . without technicalities.

The ayes and nays were called. Ayes—four, including Brannan. Nays—eight, including Spencer. One man was pardoned outright, since Jansen could not identify him. The other was taken to Sacramento to face new charges. And the mob, after some remonstrance, accepted our deliberation and dispersed. The veneer had not cracked.

Brannan was angry with me, I knew. But I demanded proof of guilt before punishment. What could be worse than knowing we had consigned an innocent to ignominious death? Outside the courthouse, he said, "The time is coming, James."

"Coming for what?"

"For him." Brannan pointed toward the middle of Portsmouth Square, toward the grassy plot where the city well promised to slake the thirst of any man.

There stood Nathan Trask, a dark sentinel with a noose draped over his shoulder.

"The time must come when we make of ourselves true vigilantes," Brannan said, "when we take the law into our own hands and execute it promptly."

BUT IT WAS A bad law that was soon executed: the Foreign Miner's Tax, perhaps because it was so hard to enforce. Soon, hundreds of Chinese were going back to the diggings, unaware that within a year, the tax would be levied again, but only on them. Wei Chin and many others stayed, however, because they were becoming great somebodies in the eyes of their countrymen and solid, if second-class, citizens in the eyes of white San Franciscans.

As I passed along Clay Street one night, I saw Chin escorting one of the more beautiful Chinese doves back to Ah-Toy's.

We exchanged bows, and I asked how he fared.

He gestured to the girl. "I fare well with one like her."

"And your sister?"

"There are none like her," he said.

I agreed, as would Flynn, I thought. Then I asked if Mei-Ling was happy.

"She live in house of Jon-Ling, live better than any other China girl."

In that there were few Chinese girls, the truth of this was not easily disputed. Neither was Chin's growing power. His reputation as a former member of Sam He Hui had spread among his countrymen, many of whom came to him for advice, protection, or loans. As other Chinese passed by that night, they offered deep bows, which Chin returned with a dismissive nod. He had learned how to conduct himself in the Mandarin fashion, too. And loyal Little Ng—silent, unsmiling, angry—was always nearby.

April, 1851
Good News, Vengeful Visitors

The sun was high and bright on the morning that Janiva and I headed to the daguerreotype studio of H. W. Bradley. Almost a year after the darkest day a woman might endure, I would capture her beauty after she gave me the greatest news a man can hope for. We were so young, so much in love, so happily conjoined in the certainty of our purpose. And now she was with child.

Dressed in our wedding outfits, we stepped into the reception area—a table, a worn carpet, two hard-back chairs, and a stairway leading up to the studio. As we were early, Bradley called down that he had other clients and would be with us presently.

We entertained ourselves by studying the daguerreotypes on his walls: images of our growing city, our ship-filled harbor, our friends and neighbors, all captured in mercury vapor on a polished silver plate.

Janiva liked *Group of Miners*—nine men, five seated, four standing. She said, "This is how I imagined the Sagamores back in Boston."

Above us, feet and chairs were moving and scraping, voices were rumbling. I said, "It sounds as if they are almost finished."

To which Janiva responded, "I have to vomit."

I took her arm to lead her outside.

But she pulled away. "Not in public. I can't be seen vomiting in public."

"It wouldn't be the first time on Montgomery Street." Then I called up the stairs to Mr. Bradley. "Do you have a bucket, sir?"

"I will be with you in a moment," said Bradley from above.

Janiva gasped and told me to hurry. It would be a great embarrassment for her to leave her breakfast on Bradley's floor, so I looked about frantically for a basin, a waste basket, and—yes—the spittoon.

But before I could fetch the tobacco-stained tureen of saliva, Janiva made a gulping sound, brought a hand to her mouth to hold in a burst of morning sickness, and rushed outside. Passersby stepped around her as she left a deposit in the mud. A few rats scuttled from under the boardwalk to inspect her leavings. I shielded her from the rats and led her back inside, reminding her that every woman with child suffered from this sickness.

But she would have none of it. Home we should go. Home, she insisted, to clean the splatter from the front of her dress and the back of her glove.

So I ran up the stairs to inform Mr. Bradley.

He was finishing a session with four men, while a fifth watched.

The four were arranged—one in a chair, three standing—before a gray canvas backdrop, with the skylight illuminating them. Mr. Bradley, an officious man in a long white coat, stood beside a polished wooden box mounted on a tripod. An assistant was moving mirrors to fill the stage with reflected light. The subjects appeared as actors playing a scene, their weapons shining, their hair pomaded, their beards combed. And actors is what I wished they were, for when I recognized them, I nearly vomited myself.

Samuel Hodges, in a fine black suit, occupied the position of power in the chair. Behind him, with his Walker Colt cradled in his arm, expressing power of its own, stood Deering Sloate. Doctor Beal stood to Sloate's left, and one I did not recognize, a slender, sleek-featured young man with yellow hair and a petulant expression, stood to the right, his hands perched on the pistols in his belt.

From the shadows, Sam Brannan said, "Why, Spencer! You were to be our next stop."

Hodges, whose head was held by a metal brace at the back of the chair, thereby to keep him from moving and spoiling "the exposure," rolled his eyes in my direction and said, "Spencer, is it? *James* Spencer? Late of Broke Neck?"

"The very one," offered Brannan. "A leading businessman of the town." And those words were the most important that Brannan could have uttered on my behalf.

But Mr. Bradley was growing impatient. "Gentlemen! Hold still. One more exposure. Now look at the camera eye and . . . hold . . ." He removed the cap from the brass-necked lens, studied his watch, counted, "Hold . . . still . . . another fifteen seconds . . ."

. . . which seemed like five minutes before Bradley replaced the cap and said, "Done. Please wait to be sure the image took. Meanwhile, we'll have the Spencers—"

"We must cancel," I said. "My wife is ill."

"Wife?" said Deering Sloate. "What will the girl from Long Wharf say?"

"You may ask her yourself," I said. "She's downstairs."

"Spencer," said Brannan, "you *know* these men?"

When recalling a conversation, we often inflate our acumen and wit. But a wise man thinks on what he will say and anticipates exchanges before they happen, like a playwright. I did not, just then, feel like a wise man or a playwright, for I was struck speechless.

"Yes." Hodges came over. "We sailed together. We knew each other."

Brannan looked at me, perhaps for signs of weakness, as he did in any conversation. "Knew each other? Without much liking, I sense."

"Or too much," said Hodges.

Brannan said, "I'd include Spencer in your stock offering, Hodges."

I tried to drop my voice to the businesslike baritone I had used in my first negotiation with Brannan. But it cracked like a schoolboy's. "Selling stock? Again?"

Janiva's retching broke the tension beneath the skylight.

And Deering Sloate showed that he still knew how to needle. "Your wife is calling, Spencer." Then he pursed his lips in a kiss.

Doctor Beal stepped forward. "May I offer her my help, Spencer?"

Bradley said, "Gentlemen, back to your places, please. Another image."

But Hodges kept his eyes on me. "What about it, James? I'm prepared to do business with you. Business is business."

"I prefer to do my business here in San Francisco." I hurried down the stairs with Brannan close behind.

Janiva stood in the middle of the room, a miserable look on her face, vomit on her dress, spittoon at her feet.

Brannan said to me, "I thought you'd appreciate a new opportunity, Spencer."

"I usually do. But not—"

The heavy step of Samuel Hodges clumped down after us. He walked now with a distinct limp, thanks no doubt to a bullet from Cletis Smith.

At the sight of him, Janiva's face filled with such shock, I thought she might vomit again.

But Hodges greeted her like a beloved uncle, asked after her health, and said, "I've come to offer an olive branch to your husband, Mrs. Spencer."

"Olive branch?" Her voice trembled, whether from her "episode" or shock, I could not tell.

"The Sagamore Water Company is growing, despite earlier setbacks." He shot me a look loaded with buckshot. "Water is our first order of business. But we mean to start a line of small river steamers to navigate above Sacramento, to capture the market where the streams narrow and the bigger

boats cannot go. We'd welcome partnership with a trading house that has
Boston roots."

Sloate came down and stood in the shadows, followed by the doctor,
then by the young pistoleer, who managed to look both somnolent and
arrogant at the same time.

Janiva glanced at them, at Brannan, then at me, as if for direction.

I said nothing. I wanted to be out of this conversation and out of the
gunsights of Deering Sloate and his silent friend as quickly as possible.

But Hodges continued to charm Janiva, in his fashion. He said, "I will
offer this opportunity only once, ma'am. Business may be business, but pride
is still pride."

She looked around this room of men, some presenting a distinct threat,
and for a moment I thought she might flee from them and the memories
they must have inspired. But as I have written, she had steel in her. She
fixed her eyes on Hodges and said, "My husband understands pride, sir.
He is a proud man." Her words made me proud of her and of how well she
knew me and of how nimbly she phrased things.

"Perhaps you can persuade him to overcome his pride, as I have mine."
Hodges took her hand in both of his. "May I count on the help of such a
beautiful Boston treasure?"

Janiva smiled. Then her smile turned to shock at what was suddenly
rising. And it rose right out of her, right onto his black suit.

THAT EVENING, DOCTOR BEAL came to visit us at Market Street and
offer his ministrations. After examining Janiva, he stepped into our little
parlor and told me how well she was doing, despite the morning sickness.
"I'd say you'll be a father in November."

I did not tell him that from time to time she slipped into a blue funk
that lasted for days. I did not think there was much he could do for that. So
I thanked him and asked how he fared in his foothill practice.

"I make my rounds from Hangtown to Sonora . . . Fix broken bones,
treat venereal diseases, patch up gunshots unless they're too severe."

"Like the one that killed Stinkin' McGinty?" I poured two brandies.

"The Walker Colt makes a terrible hole." Doc Beal took a brandy, sat by
our woodstove, and offered this: "So be careful of Sloate. His appetites are
different from most, but he considers the merest whim of Samuel Hodges
an order to fulfill."

"And what is Hodges's whim at the moment?"

"You rejected him today in front of the richest man in California."

"Rejected him and vomited on him."

At that, the straight-faced doctor cracked a smile. "We return to the gold country tomorrow, but if you answer the door tonight, lead with your pistol. Hodges will be drinking. When he drinks . . . Do you remember Jack Abbott of Broke Neck?"

"A good man."

"He fell into a dispute with Hodges over the amount of gold that Hodges had deposited with him. Abbott made good on the shortfall, but Hodges remained angry. Then, one quiet night, an errant gunshot killed Abbott in his office."

So many men who had passed through my life had died violently, I found it hard to keep count. I hid my shock behind the snifter and said, "Sloate?"

"Or his acolyte, young Hilly Deane."

"The yellow-haired boy?"

"Yes. Very dangerous. Meaner than Sloate. That's why Sloate likes him."

We froze at the sound of men on the outside staircase. I led with my pistol, but again, it was Brannan, who took off his top hat and stepped in. As I have said, Brannan was known for gruff manners and blunt talk and both were on display as he bellowed, "You blew up a dam? You blew up the Hodges *dam*?"

I stammered, glanced at the doctor, then at Janiva, who had just joined us.

And Brannan gave a booming laugh. "Good Lord. The man wants to dig sluices across gold country and run steamboats, too, and he wants my money to do it. But he lets Harvard toffs and China boys blow up his dam? I may demand harsher terms."

"He won't be happy about that." The doctor finished his brandy and made for the door. "He'll blame you, Spencer. So remember. Until tomorrow keep a sharp eye—"

Brannan said, "My Mormons will be on the stairs all night. That man with the Walker Colt has the look of murder about him. So does his blond friend."

"You are very perceptive," said Doc Beal. "Goodnight."

Brannan said to me, "I didn't think you had it in you, Spencer."

Hodges left without further incident the next morning, but I knew that I had not heard the last of him.

May–June, 1851
Communication from Gold Country

At the beginning of May, I received a letter at last from my truest friend:

> *Dear Jamie,*
>
> *The Lake of Gold turned out to be bollocks, a yarn spun by digger Injuns and spread by Yankee sharpers. Water so clear you could see gold nuggets on the bottom and flakes on the shore? Ha! But the papers printed the tale, and the gulls come flocking. And where there's gulls, there's sharpers. For two hundred dollars a man, they led the gulls up into the mountains, up between the headwaters of the Feather and Yuba, up where that lake was supposed to be, and left them to find their own stupid way home.*
>
> *I smelled a rat, so I stopped at a place called French Corral, on the San Juan Ridge. That's where I found something better than a faker's lake of gold. I found a feller who showed me how to look for rivers of it, which I've always told you are as real as the rocks.*
>
> *His name was Nathan Knapik. He come from Europe someplace, come to California on a wagon train with his wife. He done some prospecting, but seeing as how men liked looking at his wife, a round-faced yellow-haired girl who could cook up a sausage called kill-bassa and mix it with cabbage and carry a man right up to heaven, well, he decided to set up an eatin' tent, like the Emerys done in Broke Neck.*
>
> *Me and a lot of other men went there to eat but stayed to look at the missus, named Anna. And I visisted so regular that the mister offered me a job. He studied geology in Europe, so he knew about old volcanic flows in California and how they covered rivers from way back when Adam and Eve was naked as jaybirds. To find these rivers, he looked for layers of gravel in the sides of hills or in dry gulches. Just like Rainbow Gulch.*
>
> *Now, he'd already tried drift mining, where you dig sideways into the hill, with timbers and planks, shoring up as you go and praying that the mountain don't collapse on you. He'd also gone coyote holing, where two men dig straight down till they reach gravel, then send it up by the bucket. And he knew the thing to use was water.*
>
> *There's plentiful water up here and companies digging trenches and building flumes everywhere to deliver flow for "ground sluicing," which is glorified ditch-digging, at which nobody's better at than the Irish. So he*

offered me a salary and all the mining knowledge I could pick up, which I reckoned was better than picking up gold.

Ground sluicers dig v-shaped trenches through "the overburden," down toward the gravel. Then they run water, which widens that V and deepens it fast. Arses get broke shoveling the loose gravel into sluices below. Big boulders crush fingers and toes. Skin gets so wet it curdles. But you wash a lot of gravel a lot faster than we ever did, even with a flutter wheel.

Now, things was working fine 'til one evening, I look along the ridge as I'm going in to supper, and guess who I see? Hodges and that rat Sloate and a skinny, yellow-haired feller in a white duster called Hilly Deane.

Hodges come into the eatin' tent in his black suit, and the important goddamn bulk of him just about filled it. Sloate stood behind him, eying the eaters, which included me, who kept his head down and his hat pulled low. Musta been a hundred men—twenty working for Knapik, the rest just hungry, smelly miners—all hunched over their bowls or gazing like lonely deer at Anna Knapik. Whilst I et, I tried to hear the talk. Seems Hodges had bought the water rights thereabouts, and he was doubling the price on a miner's inch. Knapik could pay or cut Hodges in for half his profits.

I wanted to warn Knapik. But Sloate had his Walker, and that Hilly Deane stood there all shifty-eyed and twitchy-fingered, like a second Sloate. And . . . you know, someday, somebody'll have to shoot that Sloate. But not me, not that night. I was outgunned. So I give a last look at Anna's blond hair, all patched to the sides of her face with work sweat, and I packed me things and left for Marysville, where I heard the placers were givin' a good yield.

Here the main body of the letter ended. But there was more, written on a different kind of paper, written in pencil, written in greater haste and thus harder to read:

I have one more thing to tell, but keep it quiet:

Knapik made his deal with Hodges, and things went so well that Hodges left Sloate in charge and headed back to the Miwok with Hilly Deane. Then Knapik got himself shot in his own outhouse. His wife found him the next morning with his breeches at his ankles and a bullet hole in his forehead, dead as the wooden seat.

This news come to me from a woman who worked in Knapik's tent. Said she couldn't stand it, once Knapik was gone, how Sloate come sniffing around the cooking women day and night. (That Sloate'll put his pecker wherever he finds a friendly hole, male or female.) I figured he must have killed Knapik so the Sagamores could take over and that pretty widow would go up for grabs. So, considering that her husband had treated me so well, I decided I owed her a visit.

Got there early one morning, an hour before sun-up.

Knapiks' cabin was about forty feet from the edge of the sluice trench. I tethered me horse in the trees and took cover in that wet trench, just downwind of the outhouse. But there wasn't much stink. The air smelled of bread. Anna made bread every day, and even with the sides of the cook tent down, that smell was heaven.

Then, just after a rooster crowed, I saw Sloate. And damn me but didn't he come out of Knapik's cabin, just as if he spent the night. He was holding up his breeches with one hand and carrying his Walker with the other, ready to shoot any snakes he found curled up in the outhouse. But halfway across the clearing, he stopped like he smelled something other than fresh bread or stale shit. Then he come all suspicious-like toward the trench.

And I done it. I popped up and pulled the trigger, but all I heard was a "snap" because I'd let the loads get too much moisture. A misfire, which surprised the hell out of me.

Sloate, just as surprised, looked at me and me gun and said, "You! You worthless Irish bastard."

But men who hold their dicks with their right hand usually hold up their breeches with the same hand. So he had the Walker in his left hand. So I knew his aim would be off when he pointed at me and told me to get on me knees. "Down where you belong."

So I cocked again. And he shot at me, but I was right. The bullet flew by. Then he let go his breeches to change gun hands. And whilst he was doing that, I walked up to him and killed that son of a bitch with a bullet right into his black heart.

Then the damnedest thing happened. Anna Knapik come to her cabin door in a white nightgown, like an angel in the rising sun. She saw me. Then she saw Sloate, with his pants down around his ankles and his blood sluicing toward the trench, and . . . she screamed. Damn me, but he was her man, her lover, and I'd killed him.

As I rode away, I kept hearing her scream and scream. Once I was in the clear, I took to wondering about love and lust and how they get all mixed up in folks. And that got me to thinking about another woman who took a protector instead of a lover. Mei-Ling. Do you ever see her? Is she happy? Tell her I asked for her. And tell Janiva I asked for her, too, because Jamie, you are a lucky man.

So Flynn had never given up his dream of the Chinese girl. I feared that he and his unbridled Irish desires would someday soon be the cause of fresh trouble.

But my concerns faded as the anniversary of the first May fire approached. The Sydney Ducks had been bragging it about that they might "celebrate" with another fire and follow that with some old-fashioned looting. And sure enough, on the very night, a fire destroyed eighteen blocks and two thousand buildings, a staggering loss of $12,000,000. It started around 11:00 in a paint store on the south side of Portsmouth Square and burned for 10 hours. But once again, our Market Street location saved us.

Anger simmered for weeks across San Francisco. Men talked of solving our problems once and for all. And in June, Sam Brannan published an article in the *Alta California,* calling for a new citizens' committee of safety: "Desperate diseases require desperate remedies, and though the remedies may not be in strict accordance with law, the time has come that we must be a law unto ourselves!" I was reading this when my door open. I expected Brannan, come to enlist me in his cause. Instead, something thudded onto my desk, something gleaming, oiled, and enormous: a Walker Colt.

Then the leather visor of a familiar old hat appeared over the top of my paper and Michael Flynn gave me a grin. "I would have brought you Sloate's head, but I didn't have time to take it off his shoulders."

"You always said that somebody would have to shoot that bastard."

"I'm glad it was me."

My old friend had come back. My heart filled with joy at the sight of him. I leapt up, embraced him as I had never embraced a man before.

Then he held me at arm's length, and said, "I found my river of gold."

"At Rainbow Gulch?"

"I ain't done any prospecting yet. But it's there. I know it."

"When did you get to town?"

"Last night." He gave a wink. "Had a grand dinner in the Canton House."

That was our first sour moment. I said, "Have you been sniffing around Mei-Ling?"

And straight away, he changed the subject. "How's Janiva?"

"Stronger every day." I did not tell our happy news. I would let her have the pleasure. "Come for dinner. You'll see."

Then he patted the saddlebags slung over his shoulder and said that he was carrying a bottle of wine he had promised to deliver.

"Wine? You'll have to explain that."

"On the way."

We stepped out and turned toward the water. It was one of those early summer days that men remember when they wish themselves boys again: warm, balmy, hopeful, a fine day to walk across a city that never ceased to grow. Off to our left, the burnt district was rebuilding, almost as if it was routine. All the debris was rolling down to the landfill, while fresh lumber and pre-made houses came off the ships and climbed the hill. Hammers rang, and men shouted, and the din of rebirth filled the air.

Flynn was in his usual expansive mood. "When I got down to Rainbow Gulch, I went by the little graveyard where we buried the schoolteacher, that Hiram feller."

"I remember."

"Scrawny Selwin's name is on a grave, too. Heard somebody shot him when we couldn't deliver water."

We both agreed, it was a hard country, but there was little we could do after the fight at the dam. We had not taken money from the Rainbow Gulch miners, just promises. Scrawny might have asked for more, which might have cost him his life.

"At least him and the others have a good view for eternity." Flynn stopped in mid-stride, as if suddenly enveloped by a cloud as black as the one that swamped us at Cape Horn. "If I die before you, Jamie, promise you'll bury me there."

Yes, death sometimes came as an unexpected guest, but certain men had a way of inviting it even when living life to the top. And for all his love of it, Flynn always seemed to walk a knife ridge with life on one side and death on the other. But of course, I promised, then laughed.

And as quickly as it came, the dark mood was gone, and Flynn was striding again. "Anyway, there was a few miners down in the ravine, pannin', scratchin', turnin' over tailin's, goin' nowhere and gettin' nothin'. Amazin' how fast some strikes peter out."

"But the wine?" I said.

"Across the ravine, on the flatland beyond, I seen rows of grapes."

"I remember from last year."

"They was a pair of brothers, by the name Gasparich. They come for gold, but they knew grapes, and when they saw that soil, they knew they could grow what they call Kastelanski grapes." He pulled a bottle from his saddlebag. "And by damn but here's the first of the wine."

Wine was one of the few subjects I actually wanted to learn that my father had taken the time to teach. So I knew that such a young bottling, from such young grapes, would be sharp and acidic. But someone would drink it. In San Francisco, there was always someone who would drink anything.

Flynn said the Gasparich brothers did not stake a claim. They just started planting. "And guess who owned the land? The Vargas family. It was part of their land grant. Señor Vargas's son didn't have much fight left. So he sold for a dime on the dollar. Figured some Yankee lawyer might get it otherwise."

"Too many lawyers in California already," I said.

"That's for fuckin' sure. Too many lawyers and too much civilization."

We went along Sansome and turned onto Long Wharf, which was lined with huts and warehouses and piles of goods, and we followed a cloud of swirling gulls to a corrugated metal shed about halfway out. It had a white-splattered roof, courtesy of the gulls, and a simple sign: Coffee Stand. Men crowded the counter, and the aroma of roasted beans was enough to make a man drunk, but Coffee Stand sold more than coffee. On a charcoal fire in the back, great slabs of halibut and neat little sand dabs sizzled, while California crabs steamed away in a cast-iron kettle.

Flynn called to a burly, dark-browed man sweating at the grill, "I'm looking for Nikola Budrovich."

"Who you?"

Flynn held up the bottle. "I have a gift from his cousins."

When Budrovich heard the name "Gasparich," he handed off the grill duties, came around, and accepted the wine with great reverence.

Like his relatives at Rainbow Gulch, Budrovich and his partners had decided there were better ways to make money in California than panning for gold, though it surely appeared that they were working as hard as men could behind that counter. (In truth, when they sold to another Croatian immigrant named Tadich years later, their hard work had made them wealthy men.)

After we enjoyed their fare and drank some young wine, sweet and raw as grape juice, Flynn and I walked to the end of the wharf and looked back at the city.

"Ah, Jamie, you can burn it a dozen times, and it still keeps boomin'."

"I do love it, Michael."

"Yes, but"—he turned and peered into the water—"it won't be long before the landfill reaches the *Proud Pilgrim*. If somebody goes below at low tide to scavenge, it could bring some hard questions."

I assured him the hulk was always covered. "But we should have told the authorities that day."

"We done the right thing by Janiva, sinkin' that ship, feedin' them bastards to the crabs."

"I suppose. But the ship you need to worry about is still afloat." I pointed toward deeper water. "The *William Winter*. Trask lives aboard. He's hanging deserters. It's his way of bringing civilization."

"Like I was sayin', Jamie, too much civilization. To hell with it. Come on back with me, up there"—Flynn jerked his thumb toward the hills—"up where the gold is, up where the stories are. Come back and see life lived large and rubbed raw. You won't get many more chances, now that you're settlin' in with your pretty wife."

Though I tried to interrupt him, he kept talking, swept away by his vision of what had once been and could be again. "With your high-flown palaver and me dangerous presence, we'll talk them Croatians right out of that vineyard. Then we'll get to prospectin', because—"

I tried to again to interrupt but failed.

"—there's a bend in the land about a quarter mile back from the south rim of Rainbow Gulch." He walked to the edge of the wharf and gazed east, as if he could see all the way to gold country. "I'm thinkin' it's right where the ancient river turned, right where she dropped gold enough to make us kings of the world. But—"

"Michael—"

"—I need a pardner. Hodges'll kill me. But you? You're the son he never had. Offer him your hand, and you'll be the prodigal, come home. Then we can start in with a few coyote holes, and—"

"Michael, Janiva is—"

"What?"

"I'm going to be a father. There'll be no more running off."

A flicker of disappointment crossed his face, then he let out with a hoot and slapped me on the back. "Well, there's a thing to make a man feel good, James Spencer. Good about the world. And good about life."

"I thought you always felt good about life."

"I been givin' more thought to it, to the meanin' of it, to the meanin' of love . . . and lust, too, ever since that mornin' I killed Sloate, only to find that he'd been shackin' up with the wife of the one he killed. And, you know, I'm thinkin' that while we may mix up the meanin' of love and lust a lot of the time, a man needs someone to love, or he ain't worth much at all."

"I agree."

"So"—he winked—"I had Mei-Ling last night. Had her like it was a dream. If I can get her away from that limp-dick husband, I'll have her every night for the rest of me life."

"She's another man's wife, Michael. Chin won't stand for it. And a white man taking up with a Chinese woman? This civilization won't stand for it."

"I just said to hell with civilization, didn't I?"

"But where would you go?"

"You leave that to me." He patted the saddlebags on his shoulder.

"What's in there?"

"Never you mind." Then he started walking toward the city. Or perhaps I should say strutting. He was a creature of life, my Irish friend, explosive, expansive, unfiltered, unfettered. Even when he courted death in the bed of a Chinese beauty, he was reaching for life's greatest gifts.

So together we strode past the grog shops and storehouses on the wharf, past Coffee Stand, still pumping aromas of fresh roast and charcoaled fish, and I inhaled the sense of optimism and possibility everywhere around me.

We parted on the corner of Sansome and Clay. I had an appointment with Sam Brannan. Michael Flynn wanted to visit Ah-Sing's Apothecary and get a little ginseng tea. I told him to be careful, because Chin might kill him. He laughed, patted the bag again, and said, "You leave Chin to me, too."

SAM BRANNAN WAS IN his second-floor office, gazing out at the harbor. Without turning, he said, "When does it end?"

I glanced at Slawsby, who rolled his eyes, a warning that the boss was in a mood.

Brannan gave Slawsby a jerk of the head, shooing him from the room. Then he told me, "They picked up another arsonist last night. He set six fires. None of them spread, thank God. They slapped him in jail, and he escaped, just like a wisp of smoke from one of his fires. I tell you, Spencer, there's no crime in this city that a man can't erase with a pouch of gold."

"But why did you want to see me?"

"Come to the meeting tonight, at the Monumental Company Firehouse."

The city had many volunteer fire companies, all competing for men, money, and when fire erupted, for the water to fight it with. Brannan said he wanted to stop the fires before they began. "And the presence of a young father-to-be, a businessman, will go a long way to legitimizing a committee of vigilance."

"You mean I'll bring out the *polite* hangmen?" I did not like being used.

Brannan poured two brandies and gave one to me. His face was flushed. He had already had a few. "We'll form companies of twenty men in each ward to hunt out the hardened villains, the robbers, the arsonists."

"The Australians, you mean?"

"Anyone. We'll give them five days to leave. Then it's a war of extermination."

"Extermination? A powerful word."

"We tell them if they stand against us, we'll shoot them down like dogs." He drained another glass, refilled it, gave me a look, as if to ask, *Are you with me?*

I said, "I've seen mob violence . . . and the violence of retribution."

"You've even committed it." Brannan brought his brandy breath close. "If Hodges didn't love you like a disappointed father, he'd have hunted you down and hanged you for blowing up his dam and destroying his operation."

He stepped back and waited for a response. I remained silent. I did not like where this was headed.

Then Brannan laughed. "Oh, hell, I don't give a damn about Hodges. But what goes on in San Francisco? That I care about. When you kill men in my city—"

"Who says I've killed men here?"

"Anyone who knows that Trub McLaws and his bunch disappeared one night, without a trace." Brannan went back to the window.

I said, "It was the night of the first May fire. Maybe they all burned to ash."

"You know"—Brannan gazed out—"when the dock's built between Clay and Long Wharf, along the line of Battery Street, the landfillers will reach the *Proud Pilgrim*. Pray no one goes looking for salvage."

Sam Brannan could bully, sometimes with a word or a fist, sometimes with a threat or a lawyer, sometimes with the grin he gave me now. "We need a committee of vigilance, James. If there's no spirit for it, we should let the city burn next time. Let the streets flow with the blood of murdered men. And murdered women, too, murdered *pregnant* women, all because the judges are lily-livered technicality men and what police we have are too busy taking bribes."

I finished the brandy and made for the door.

Brannan said, "I'll count on your presence tonight." It sounded like a threat.

BUT IN THE INTERESTS of maintaining the friendship I had built with the most powerful man in San Francisco, I went to the meeting. I joined the two hundred who crowded that night into the brick firehouse, passed bottles of rotgut, and filled the air with shouts and the whiskey-mist sweat of long-sustained anger. Sam Brannan stood on the engine and made a speech as angry as the sweat. The men roared and cheered and committed to his brotherhood of vigilance, all except for Nathan Trask. He stood by the stable door, holding a noose on each shoulder, speaking without words.

Then the committee's constitution was passed, man to man, binding all signers to perform "every lawful act for the maintenance of law and order and to sustain laws when faithfully administered, but we are determined that no thief, burglar, incendiary, or assassin shall escape punishment, either by quibbles of the law, the insecurity of prisons, the carelessness of the police, or the corruption of those who administer justice."

We were above all that. We were the citizens of San Francisco. Good men and true.

Mr. Woodworth, the Vice-Consul, signed first, followed by Brannan. I was the twenty-fifth to sign and told to remember that number, because henceforth, it would be my identification when we were summoned to action with the tolling of the Monumental Company bell: two clangs, then a minute's silence, two clangs, and so on.

I did not like any of this. But I could not say no. Appearing as the solidest of citizens was always my defense against the acts I had performed aboard the *Proud Pilgrim* and along the Miwok. And solid citizens, as Brannan proclaimed that night, should prove themselves by signing.

We dispersed, sure in the knowledge that something bad would happen soon and the perpetrator, or someone who looked like him, would meet the kind of fate that makes an example of one man for all men to see.

I knew a man with a propensity for trouble, a man never above making an example of himself. I knew I had to get him off the street and out of town as quickly as I could, because the anger in this firehouse could explode in any direction.

So I headed for the Canton Restaurant, far enough up Jackson Street to have been spared in the fires.

Jon-Ling was welcoming diners, leading them to the long tables or to the counter at the back. A chalkboard read: *6 Dumpling pork–$1. 6 Dumpling soup–$2.* Steam was billowing from the kitchen. If Mei-Ling was there, she was lost in those clouds.

Jon-Ling spied me in the doorway and scurried over, small and stooped, scowling and growling. "What you want?"

"I am looking for—"

"I tell Irish to leave." Jon-Ling pushed me out into the street, so the dumpling-eaters would not hear. "He come last night. He talk Mei-Ling." The small man made a fist and held it in front of my nose. "She my wife."

"Can I talk to her? Is she in the kitchen."

He snorted at me, causing his gray mustaches to puff in the air. "She no here. I no make her work. She lady. So you go. You see Irish, you tell never come back. Or I kill him. Go!"

I decided after that to cover the circuit of gambling halls and hotels around Portsmouth Square. I stopped first at the Bella Union on Washington. Flynn was not holding forth in any of the public rooms, nor was he registered. The story was the same next door in the Louisiana House.

Then I headed for the east side of the square, where the proprietors of the El Dorado had reopened under a shed roof while they reconstructed the huge and oft-incinerated gambling hall. Though the city had banned the use of canvas as building material, someone had passed a bribe, because canvas sides had been dropped all around to hold in the heat, the noise, and the crushing crowd. A new bar served dozens of drinkers. A girl on a velvet swing flew back and forth above them, offering indiscreet flashes of leg as she passed. And a group of Negro minstrels, Dingus Reese and his Music Men, played banjo, piano, guitar, fiddle, and jew's-harp, keeping up a racket that drowned out the roar of the drinkers and the chatter of the gamblers, and the cooing of the soiled doves.

Here was San Francisco in full cry.

I stood near the entrance and scanned the hall through the fog of whiskey fumes and cigar smoke.

A woman, strong smelling but not unpleasant, sidled up and propositioned me.

I told her I was looking for someone.

She said, "Who, mister? Who you looking for? Maybe I can help." A missing canine tooth did nothing to lessen the effect of her smile. To a man who had been in the mines, womanless, she would have been an intoxicant. Then I remembered her, or perhaps her aroma. I had spied her first aboard the *William Winter,* riding Michael Flynn's loins, and then in Broke Neck, riding Big Beam's wagon.

I said her name—Roberta—and added, "I am looking for Flynn—"

"You!" she whispered. "I'd watch it if I was you. You beat Big Beam so bad, he never been quite right in the head since."

That struck me hard. I saw Big Beam sitting off in a corner, sipping from a mug of beer, watching a familiar gambler dealing cards onto green felt. It seemed that Big Beam had cut in Becker and Bunche, white suit and top hat, from Grouchy Pete's. Now they were stepping up in class, or at least in the size of their stakes.

I told Roberta, "I need to find Flynn."

She said, "He got into a game at Bunche's table last night. Almost pulled on him. Then he saw Becker across the room, and Flynn knew how they worked, so he stood back."

Now Becker, the one in the white suit and pomaded-hair ringlets, noticed me.

Roberta said, "Flynn should've shot them both. He was a lot better to me than them bastards are. A right charmer with his pants on, a real lover with his pants off, and a fine singin' voice, too."

"A good epitaph for any man."

"But now," she said, "we're bound for work with that Sam Hodges. He's come to get his new riverboat to start the run above Sacramento. We're goin' back with him tomorrow night . . . as entertainment."

Here was an even worse development. Hodges was back in town.

"Said he's come to *do* some business and *settle* some, too," added Roberta. "I think he means Flynn."

Becker had just finished a hand. He gave the deck to Big Beam, who sat dumbly and looked at the cards. Then he came through the crowd, more suspicious than a jealous husband, but not recognizing me in my tweed suit. "Hey, friend, you tie up these gals, you'll have to pay. Now, either— You! What are you doin' here? There's no niggers to stick up for in here. They're all freedmen. No Chinks, neither."

"Fine pistol." I pointed to his ivory-handle Colt. "Matches your white suit."

"What's it to you?"

"I remember a Negro with a fine pistol like that."

"Niggers are nothin' to me," said the gambler. "Now are you payin' for this lady, or am I tellin' Big Beam that the man who beat him senseless just come by to laugh at him?"

I looked at Roberta. "If you see my friend, tell him I have an important message." Then I said to Becker, "Take care of that pistol. See nobody steals it."

So if Flynn was not among the gamblers, I feared he was with Mei-Ling again. Considering all his talk of love, life, and lust, he might even have tried to run off with her.

What a swirl of trouble, I thought, as back into the dark streets I went.

A marquee in front of the Parker House proclaimed, TONIGHT, *OTHELLO*. Yes, such entertainments came to us regularly now . . . the Masquerade, French vaudeville, and at the Jenny Lind Theatre above the Parker House, regular visits from Hamlet, Lady Macbeth, and wicked Iago himself, all alive in creations of genius that moved Janiva and me with their insights into the human heart and the soul's sympathies. But not tonight.

I peered into the Parker House saloon and a few of the other recently reopened grog shops, but there was no sign of Flynn, so I hurried up Clay Street to Ah-Sing's.

Keen-Ho Chow blocked the door. "Private party."

I pushed past and stepped through the beaded curtains into the mahjongg parlor. The lamps hung low. The dirt floor softened the sound of rattling tiles and murmuring voices. The air floated with smoke and sweet, spicy smells that could calm you as easily as Chinese tea. But I was not calmed, and I sensed tension floating in the smoke.

Chin, Ah-Sing, Friendly Liu, and another were playing the game, while Little Ng stood guard, arms folded, watching everything.

Chin saw me out of the corner of his eye and said, "Flynn come back."

"I know," I said. "I'm looking for him."

"He come here today. He offer me gold for my sister. He offer buy my sister. I tell him leave my sister. Leave San Francisco.

"But he no leave, I don't think." Off in a corner, Ah-Toy was puffing on a pipe. Her eyes seemed glassy, her demeanor dreamy. She said, "I think Flynn-man make do-ee with Mei-Ling."

Chin angrily told her to be quiet.

But Ah-Toy seemed oblivious. She said, "So why Jon-Ling so mad, eh? Something bad happen, I think. He come, ask me make him hard, but he too mad to get hard . . . and too old. Not like yellow-haired man or big Boston Hodges-man."

Ah-Sing looked over his spectacles. "You know Hodges?"

"He come, too," said Chin. "Bring nasty yellow-haired man."

"Yeah, yeah," said Ah-Toy. "He want women business with us."

"Here?" I said.

"Up rivers. On boats." Ah-Toy gestured with her fan toward the bay. "He want all China girls, pretty, ugly, all, go him."

I looked at Chin. "I hope you told him to go and make do-ee with himself."

And Ah-Toy gave a silly giggle. "Quiet man very funny."

Then ancient Ah-Sing stood. He seemed angry, almost insulted. "Hodges say if we no supply girls, he send San Francisco law after Chin and Little Ng."

"Yeah, yeah," said Ah-Toy. "He say they do bad in gold country." She took a draw on the pipe. The air around her smelled scorched but sweet, like burning flowers. "He say Chin and Little Ng bad China boys."

"He want us fear him," said Chin. "But I no fear in Broke Neck. No fear now."

Ah-Sing glared through his thick spectacles. "No more fear anywhere." And he began to speak in English so profoundly that I was left flabbergasted. "White men call this republic, but only for one race. They say Constitution admits of only the pale face. But declaration of your independence, and all acts of your government and your history are against you. This country for all who work. And there will be no fear. *No fear!*"

(He would put these words into an eloquent letter a year later, when the new governor sought to reinstate the unfair taxes on the Chinese. People would question if the old man had even written it. I can attest that he spoke it, so he must have written it.)

"Tell that to Hodges," said Chin. "Tell him we do not fear him."

But I feared Samuel Hodges. I had since that night I left the *William Winter*.

That fear almost split my chest when I came down Dupont Street and saw Hilly Deane leaning against the front door of my office. I did not bother to speak to him. I leapt to the steps and bounded up, two at a time, tore open the door, and found Hodges, sitting in our parlor, sipping tea. He was wearing his black suit and balancing his teacup on his knee, as if this were all unfolding in a Beacon Hill parlor rather than on the lawless edge of our American continent.

Janiva sat on a straight-backed chair as far away from him as she could get.

He said, "I've been discussing our adventures in the Mother Lode, James."

"Things not going well in the water business?" I asked. "You're trying to cut yourself into the female slave trade."

Hodges glanced toward Janiva. "I would not discuss such indelicate subjects in the presence of your wife."

"Speak plainly in front of her, Samuel. And speak quickly."

"It is all happening as I predicted, James."

"Your empire?" I remembered his grand vision. I had once been impressed.

"I'm here to take possession of a riverboat, bought with profits from my water business, which I started with profits from my gold operation, which you started when you ripped open a hillside on the Miwok." Hodges set the teacup down on the saucer with a polite clink. "I'm also here for Flynn. I know he ambushed Sloate. I know he passed through Broke Neck on his way to Rainbow Gulch. I know he's run for San Francisco. I know you can find him. He might even be under this roof right now."

Janiva picked up the teapot and refilled Hodges's cup, then filled one for me.

Hodges said, "Flynn killed the man more loyal to me than anyone on earth."

"Send for your children," I answered. "They'll be as loyal. They might even love you."

Hodges cast his eyes on Janiva's belly, which felt like an intrusion, almost physical, into her being. Instinctively, she put a hand across her midsection.

Hodges said, "Give me Flynn, or things may go badly for you, James."

I picked up his hat and handed it to him.

Hodges stood and changed his tone. "I've contracted for three boats, shipped in sections around the Horn, assembled here at Rincon Point. If I was your Ames distributor above Sacramento, we could—"

I said, "I won't have anything to do with female slavery, not with you, not with Chin."

"Let Chin make his own decisions. Just give me Flynn and I'll let you be. Clay Street Wharf, tomorrow night. We steam at eleven o'clock."

"I don't know where he is."

"That's why I'm giving you twenty-four hours. Bring him to us. We'll take him up the Yuba to French Corral, try him, and hang him for Sloate's murder, so the beautiful Mrs. Knapik can be avenged."

"I won't betray my friends," I said.

"You betrayed me to ride with that Irishman."

"My husband is no Judas, sir," said Janiva.

"Perhaps not. But in this little parable, who is Jesus?" Hodges opened the door. "If I don't see you, I may decide to inspect the wreck of the *Proud Pilgrim*. There are rumors. The new Committee of Vigilance might want to know that one of their own executed the law on six Australians. They might be pleased. Or they might decide to execute you."

NEITHER JANIVA NOR I slept that night. We lay awake wondering how we had gotten into this, and how we could get out. We lay awake until dawn, when there came a banging that caused me to grab the Nock gun and bound for the door.

Chin was squared on the landing, as if ready to fight. "Mei-Ling gone. She here?"

"Why would she be here?" I asked.

"Flynn steal her. We find." He gestured to Little Ng, standing behind him.

Janiva emerged from the bedroom, saying, "James, invite your friends in."

And the softness of her voice softened Chin. He gave her and her swelling belly a look, then he gave a bow and backed away.

"Where are you going?" I asked him.

"The wharfs. Sacramento steamers. Morning sail."

As soon as Chin left, I dressed and hurried for the docks. If Flynn was leaving, all the better, but he needed warning, because if Mei-Ling was with him, Chin would kill him. And if she wasn't, Hodges might.

IT WAS ANOTHER DAY to put a man in a good mood if his worries were small. But mine had taken on the weight of six dead bodies in a water-filled ship. Up and down the docks I went, talking myself aboard the *Senator* and the other boats or begging a look at the manifests for the morning departures. But I found no sign of Michael Flynn.

So, around nine o'clock, I went to the Coffee Stand. A few breakfast-eaters lingered at the counter, but Budrovich took time to talk, because yes, he had seen Flynn. He said that he always arrived early to start his coffee, but he always walked first to the end of the wharf. "To stop and think."

"About what?"

"About the beautiful bay, the big chance we get here. Do you stop and think?"

"Not enough," I admitted, then I turned him back to the subject.

That morning, at about five o'clock, as the eastern sky brightened, he looked from Long Wharf over at Howison Pier, and he saw them, Flynn and the Chinese girl, walking arm in arm to the end.

"I hear them talking. I see them kissing. I watch. They hug. They kiss. Very nice. I think, I wish I had nice Croatian girl for to hug and kiss."

Seeing their pre-dawn embrace had touched something in him, as it would in any man, especially a lonely man far from home. He said, "You have woman?"

"I have a wife."

"Nice." He got back to the story. "Then come whistle of steamboat. Overnight from Sacramento puffing around Yerba Buena Island, headed for Howison Pier. But Chinese girl step back. Whistle blow again. She step back more. Your friend reach out to her, but whistle blow again, and poof! She turn and run. Your friend go after, but he limp. Hard for him to move."

"Limp?" That surprised me. "Was he hurt?"

"Limp very bad. He try to follow. But she go. He call to her. I can hear him call her name. 'Mei, Mei.' But she running, like afraid, then gone. So he look around, like maybe he don't know *what* to do. Stay. Go. What? I feel very bad. Then he just limp off the dock. I think maybe I go over, say hello, but time to make the coffee."

I LOOKED FOR TWO hours more. I tracked droplets of blood that led into the mud off Howison Pier. I visited the grog shops along the water. I watched the crowds collecting for the steamers. Around eleven, once the boats were all gone, I headed back to Market Street. As I approached our warehouse, I heard Matt Dooling's hammer ringing, so he was in his shop, but I sensed something else, something out of place. I stopped and peered through our office window.

Janiva was at her desk, fidgeting with papers, pen, and the positioning of her inkwell. And she was no fidget. I stepped in and saw Hilly Deane leaning against the interior door between our office and Dooling's shop. He was chewing a toothpick and chatting so amiably, it was as if he hoped to make a tryst with my wife. His canvas duster was tucked back around the grips of his pistols, as if he hoped they would impress her if his chatter failed. He gave me the merest shifting of the eyes and said, "Mornin'."

I asked him what he wanted, no niceties observed.

"Mr. Deering said you wasn't very friendly. Right from childhood."

"He wasn't too friendly himself."

"Damn good to me. Taught me to shoot. Taught me how to act after I lost my folks to cholera on the Gaws' wagon train. Taught me a lot." He rested his hands on the grips of his pistols. "But that Irishman killed Mr. Deering, and before that—"

I noticed Janiva move her foot to cover something on the floor. Blood.

"—somebody killed Moses Gaw to save the Irishman from hangin'. And David Gaw, he died from fever after losin' his arm. The Gaws was damn good to me, too."

"I heard it was a bear killed Moses Gaw. Now . . . what do you want?"

"Just bringin' a reminder from Mr. Hodges. We want the Irishman to-night. No better way to impress a woman than to hang the man who killed her lover. And Mr. Hodges, he's sweet on that Knapik woman, up there at French Corral."

I said, "I thought he married Gaw's daughter."

Hilly Deane just laughed, as if that could never have happened. Then he tipped his hat to Janiva and left, white duster fluttering behind him like a priest's cape.

Janiva seemed to release a great gust of breath. She moved her foot to reveal a trail of blood running from the desk to the warehouse door at the back of the office.

MICHAEL FLYNN LAY ON the floor, behind a piano crate, in the far corner of the warehouse. He was propped up on his saddlebags, holding the Walker Colt. He said, "Is that little shit gone?"

Janiva came up behind me and said, "His leg is broken."

"Not at all it isn't. Just fractured a bit." Flynn tried to laugh at his troubles. "A big pistol ball can do that. Who thought Jon-Ling would be carryin' a Colt Dragoon when he caught me on top of his wife?"

I said, "Jon-Ling did this?"

"I tried to wrestle the gun away, and we both went through a window, a second-floor window. At least the Chinaman broke me fall, along with his neck, almost the way it happened in New York that time."

"You never did finish that story," I said.

"You need a doctor, Michael," said Janiva.

"No doctors." Flynn was perspiring and ash-colored. "The leg hurts like hell, but I can hobble. Bullet went through and through, just chipped the bone. Still and all, some sawbones might try to take me whole damn leg off. They love doin' that, you know."

Matt Dooling came in with a medical kit. He had cotton lint to pack the wound, an outer dressing to wrap it, some kind of salve, and scissors.

"You a doctor, Matt?" asked Flynn.

"I can doctor a horse. And you ain't much more than the ass of a horse, so—"

Flynn tried to laugh. Then he locked his eyes on the scissors. "What's them for?"

"Cuttin' away torn flesh," said Dooling. "Helps the healin'."

Flynn rolled his eyes to Janiva. "Do you have a bit of whiskey?"

"I have brandy. I'll go get it." And she scurried off.

As Dooling worked, Flynn asked, "How do they figure to get me onto the wharf?"

"You heard him? So you know you're in trouble. You have Chin angry. You have the Committee of Vigilance to worry about if they decide to hang a man for killing a Chinaman. And you have Hodges."

"Three aces in a marked deck," said Flynn.

Janiva returned with a bottle. Flynn took a drink, then Matt Dooling grabbed the bottle and poured a shot onto Flynn's leg.

Flynn cried out in pain "What did you do that for? Wastin' good brandy?"

"Damn fool to leave dirt around a wound like that," said the blacksmith.

And yes, the bullet had gone in the back of the calf and clipped the shinbone going out. You could see pieces of it, white and teeming, like insects nibbling. Dooling wrapped his big hands around the leg and, with his thumbs, manipulated. "If we seal it, then splint it, you might have a chance. I'll be right back." Then he went into his shop.

And Janiva went to meet a customer, leaving me alone with my friend.

Flynn shook his head. He knew the predicament he was in. "Promise me you won't let them take me leg off, Jamie. A man's no good without a leg."

"Don't worry." I took the brandy bottle and sloshed down a swallow. Then I said, "Was it worth it? Taking another man's wife?"

"Worth it?" Flynn laughed. "Was it worth it to you to have Janiva wrapped around you on the *Proud Pilgrim*, even when you knew them Australians was somewhere forward, horned-up and jealous as cuckolds?"

"You've got me there."

"Damn right, but . . . ah, Jamie, we're nothin' without love, are we? Even old Cletis knew that. Why else would he come back that day, with young Rodrigo? He knew. He always knew, even if he never loved anyone."

I said, "I think he loved us."

Flynn snatched the bottle and downed another swallow. "All the gold in the world ain't enough if you got no one to share it with. I been chasin' a river of it, but I been dreamin' of Mei-Ling, dreamin' of havin' her by me side, the two of us lookin' out on Rainbow Gulch."

"It's a fine dream, Michael." But I knew it would never come true.

We patched his wound as best we could. Matt Dooling brought two metal rods for a splint and fashioned a crutch, too. Then we pulled the crate away from the wall to make more room for Flynn behind it. We brought him some bedding and barricaded him with a second piano crate, which Janiva had saved, because in a city where materials were scarce, a big crate had many uses. And we told him to rest.

THEN JANIVA AND I spent an hour in the outer office, meeting customers, doing business, acting as if all was well, all the while wondering what to do with Flynn. If he had killed Jon-Ling, would he be arrested? Would anyone even care? Chinamen were in general not so valued as white men, here or in gold country or even in China.

But around noon, we had a surprising visitor: Mei-Ling herself, dressed as she had been every day in the Mother Lode, in men's clothes, with a stiff-brimmed straw hat pulled low. She came in by Dooling's blacksmith shop, and he brought her through the adjoining door. She shocked us first by her presence, then by her insistence that we were hiding Michael Flynn and by her demand to see him.

I gave Janiva the eye and told Mei-Ling, "I heard that he took passage on one of the Sacramento boats."

She studied us both, looking for signs of deceit, and said, "If you see him, tell him . . . tell him I love him. But tell him I no go with him. Tell him my brother too angry. Tell him my brother kill him now."

"And what of your husband?" I asked, as if I knew nothing.

"My brother say to tell anyone Jon-Ling jump out window. They say why, I say Jon-Ling have young wife but he old. Never say Flynn make fuck with me."

"Good of your brother," said Janiva.

Mei-Ling looked down at the floor and wiped a tear from her eye.

And Janiva understood, because she took Mei-Ling by the hand and led her into the warehouse, to Flynn's hiding place.

I did not follow. Let them have their moment. Let them embrace, say good-bye, pledge eternal love, or—

Janiva came rushing back, more angry than surprised, and said, "He's gone."

JANIVA COULD NOT HOLD down her evening meal. The tensions of the day were too great. And she feared that the night would be no better. I knew, every time she looked at me, that her stomach tightened and squeezed the baby, because I had determined to meet Samuel Hodges. I would tell him that Flynn had disappeared, and if I told him the truth, perhaps he might put profits ahead of revenge, steam for Sacramento, and leave us in peace.

Janiva did not want me to go. But once it became clear that she could not dissuade me, she took the Nock gun from the closet, checked the primes on all seven barrels, and said, "Then I'll go with you. We made this baby together. We'll protect its future together."

I insisted that the way to protect our baby was to stay close, stay safe.

She answered with a dark look from under her dark brow.

I went to my chair and picked up Installment IV of *David Copperfield*. She sat in hers with Installment VI. This is what amounted to an argument between us. Quiet page-flipping, cold silence. I was going and she was not. Or she was coming and bringing the Nock gun. Which would it be? The answer lay not in Dickens.

Then, just after ten o'clock, the bell rang at the Monumental Firehouse. Two fast rings, then a minute's silence. Then two, then a minute.

The Committee of Vigilance had found their example. I prayed it was not Flynn.

I told Janiva that I had to answer that summons, or it would go badly for me among the important men of the town.

And she said the right thing. "For that, you must go."

"For the baby, you must stay." I grabbed the Nock gun, went onto the landing, and fired it into the air. Seven barrels erupted. The recoil almost threw me down the stairs. As a rain of shot came skittering back to earth, I took the flint and threw it into the night, so she would have no weapon.

Drawn by the thunderous report, Matt Dooling appeared at the bottom of the stairs. I gave him the gun and said, "See that she stays put."

APPROACHING BRANNAN'S WAREHOUSE ON Sansome and Bush, I saw a crowd gathering under the streetlamps and torches. Somebody said that a certain Sydney Duck was "in for it now," having robbed a shipping office and absconded with a safe. "The whole damn safe!" said another man in amazement. "Then he tried to steal a rowboat to get on to Sydney Town. But they caught him and beat him. Now they're goin' to try him and hang him."

I should have been taking my place in this tribunal of the mob, as I had promised both Janiva and Sam Brannan I would. But here was the moment to confront Samuel Hodges, when so many henchmen for law and good order were swirling around the waterfront, providing me protection by their angry presence.

So I headed to Clay Street and turned onto the wharf. I hurried past the grog shops that were still doing business, no matter the noise of the clanging bell and the roaring of the crowd a few blocks away. I strode past a new hotel rising on the site of the old *Niantic,* past food sheds and storehouses, deeper into the darkness, toward the shadowed mass of the steamboat at the end of the wharf.

Hodges and Hilly Deane were waiting, as if they had anticipated that I would come early, or that the Monumental bell would draw me out.

At my approach, their shadows separated. Hodges, in black, limped to the end, making himself a silhouette against the moonlit waters of the bay. Hilly Deane, easier to see in his canvas duster, crossed to the opposite piling, so that he was on my left and the big steamboat was on my right. A yellow shaft of light fell dimly from the pilothouse window. The huge engine vented once, like an exhalation. But no passengers or dockhands were about. It was plain that Hodges had no intention of leaving until morning.

His voice leaped from the shadow under his hat brim. "I knew you'd come, James. Always doing the right thing. Your father taught you well."

"I'm learning to appreciate him."

The Monumental bell clanged twice.

Hodges said, "The Committee of Vigilance is vigilant tonight."

"There are vigilant men everywhere tonight," I answered.

"So there are." Hodges looked up at the steamer. "Do you like it? Eighty feet long, broad in the beam, shallow in the draft. We'll move cargo and passengers, provide gambling and women. Imagine a fleet of them, James, running on all the inland rivers. But for a fleet, I would need partners. Trusted partners, like you."

Another offer of alliance, no matter what had gone before. I was tempted. Perhaps extending my hand might calm his anger, soften his hate, make things better for me, for Flynn, for the future of my young family, even for the Chinese. But in the Mother Lode, his hate had appeared as a tool or a means to an end. Now it burned hot and pure for Michael Flynn.

I heard footsteps coming along the wharf.

Hodges looked past me. "Ah, my new associates."

I glanced over my shoulder: a white suit and a top hat with a shiny vest, Becker and Bunche, bad and worse.

Hilly said to them, "Where are the girls?"

"Disappeared, the bitches," said Becker.

"Must think San Francisco is better for sellin' cooch," said Bunche.

And I knew, if Hodges was accommodating these pomaded killers, I could have no dealings with him. I said, "An empire built on cards and whores, Samuel? What will they say back in the Arbella Club?"

"We won't know, unless you tell our story for the readers of Boston."

So there it was. He wanted me to fulfill my role as hagiographer, so that Bostonians would see what they had lost when they blocked the rise of Samuel Hodges.

I said, "I'm afraid that this country has revealed too many truths about you, Samuel. The readers of Boston might be surprised."

"Then to hell with them." Hodges took a step toward me. "Let us breed Hodges money to the Spencer line right here in California. We'll watch the dollars multiply. We'll change the minds of all the Boston bankers and countinghouse crooks who wanted men like us to dance to their jig, all because of where we landed on life's ladder."

"Men like us?"

"Both blocked from fulfilling our dreams by men like your father."

Becker and Bunche were closer now. I could smell the whiskey-and-cigar stink of them. I was just about surrounded.

"Take the deal," said Hilly Deane. "Throw in with new Americans. Throw in with men who know that the future belongs to those who grab it."

I said to Hodges, "You've taught him well."

Hodges said, "I taught Sloate. Sloate taught Hilly. But the lesson is plain."

I tried to gauge my best course out of this. I realized that I should have heeded my wife and stayed away. But here I was. I decided that if talk failed, I could jump for one of the rowboats tethered to the wharf.

The big steam engine gave another mighty exhalation.

Hodges said, "Make the choice, James. Friends forever, or enemies for life."

"Just give us Flynn." Hilly Deane put his hands on the grips of his pistols.

"He has a debt to pay," said Hodges.

"He has lots of debts to pay," said Becker.

But I said nothing to any of them.

So Hodges tugged at his vest and spat into the water, as if he had talked enough. "You won't give me Flynn. You won't invest. You won't write my story, which could be ours together. You're not a real friend in any way, James. I've been as patient as I can be."

The Monumental bell clanged again, and I said, "I need to join the Committee."

Hodges said, "Are you planning to tell them about the *Proud Pilgrim*?"

Hilly Deane looked out into the water. "Tide's droppin'."

Then from somewhere near the other end of the wharf came a burst of female laughter, and two women began to sing in high, dry-gear voices. My first horrified thought was that Janiva had followed me to play some diversionary game. But it was not her voice screeching the song that I had first heard in the Arbella Club. "There was a wild colonial boy!"

Becker said, "So the bitches came back. Both drunk."

"Singin' them fuckin' Irish songs again." Bunche looked at Hilly. "We told 'em if they sang them songs again, they had to suck us off. Both of us. Hilly, you want—"

But Hilly must have sensed something else happening, because he was already pulling when the canvas came flapping off a rowboat tied up at my left. A dark figure sat up in the boat, and the flash of the Walker Colt lit the night, sending Hilly Dean spinning into the water.

Then two more shots, two more thunderous reports, two more night-to-day flashes. The first took off Bunche's top hat and half his head. The second hit Becker, who answered with two wild shots from Pompey's ivory-handled Colt. Then a shot hit him in the chest and turned his white coat blood red.

All while this was happening, Samuel Hodges was pulling his pistol, pointing at me, hesitating, then swinging toward the rowboat.

Michael Flynn, the shadow in the boat, cried, "Kill him!"

My gun was in my hand but—again, the old hesitation. Could I shoot him?

Hodges swung back to me, perhaps asking himself the same question.

Flynn was struggling to stand on one bad leg in a rocking boat, because from where he sat, he had no angle on Hodges. He fell back and shouted it again. "Kill him!"

Hodges fired three times at Flynn's shadow. Wood chips flew as the shots ricocheted off the planking. The boat rocked. Flynn almost went over—had he been hit? And I fired. I could not tell where my bullet struck Hodges, only that it drove him back and he hit the water with a tremendous splash.

Then I turned to Flynn. Before I could ask if he was hit, he laughed. "That son of a bitch better be dead, because I can't stay in this fuckin' rowboat another minute."

I reached down and pulled him up by the crutch.

"Ah, Jamie, but you had me worried. I thought you was about to prove Cletis right."

"About what?"

"About too much mercy gettin' you killed." Then he shouted to the girls, who stood about twenty feet up the dock, "Run, gals! Run! Get on back to Big Beam. And never let cheatin' gamblers pimp you again."

"We love ya, Michael," shouted one of them, who sounded like Roberta.

"Keep singin'!" cried the other, who had to be Sheila.

Flynn said to me, "I knew you'd need help. But I couldn't move around. So I rowed out here a few hours ago. The girls was in on it, too. They hated their new whoremasters more than I hate Hodges, and if singin' was enough to get them in the clear, well—"

The Monumental bell clanged twice more.

Then a voice rang out, "Murder! Murder! Clay Street Wharf!"

Suddenly, torches and lanterns were appearing up where the wharf met Sansome Street.

"I hope the girls get through the mob," said Flynn. "As for you, go home. Get dry. Then get on to the Committee meetin', or they'll suspect you for certain."

"Get dry?" I said. "But I'm not wet."

Flynn glanced at the torches coming toward us, then he hit me in the gut with the crutch, driving me into the water. "You're wet now."

The shock of the black cold stunned me. The weight of it filled my boots and soaked my trousers and tweed coat. And the rumble of footfalls on the wharf above filled me with dread. I could hear the crowd shouting: "Murders!" "Lay hold!" "Hang him!" "No, bring him to the committee!"

The tide was ebbing, pulling me out, and the farther it carried me, the stronger it grew. But I was afraid to splash because the torches were probing the dark in every direction.

Someone shouted at Flynn, "Is there anyone else with you?"

"Not at all," answered Flynn. "I killed all four, I did. And fine act of self-defense it was."

The cold current now seemed strong enough to sweep me all the way to the Golden Gate. I resolved to ride it well into the dark before I began to swim. I went twenty or thirty yards through the water, then struck a hard surface, bounced along, bounced and rolled, and realized that I had struck the *Proud Pilgrim*, emerging as the tide dropped. I grabbed for the rail, held on, then flipped over. From water to water I went, from the pulling current running around the hull to the still water inside it. My feet found the hard deck.

Waist deep in water, I gripped the top rail and hunkered down so that the men on the wharf could not see, and I stayed like that for five minutes or more, waiting, shivering, while six dead bodies lay like unforgiven sins below, and all the while, the Monumental bell kept ringing, two clangs, a minute's silence, then two more clangs . . . tolling the dead and calling the Vigilantes.

Finally I heard a man shout, "There's no one else."

"I told you that, you damn fools," said Flynn.

I watched them go, all bobbing torches and burning anger. Then I turned my cold-fogged brain to the business at hand—survival. Could I swim against the current, swim off to the left, to the little stub of a wharf at the end of Market Street? Did I have the strength? I might drown first, even if I took off my boots and trousers. But I could not stay in the icy water. I was already shivering, and the cold seemed to be digging down to the very marrow of me.

I looked for something floating, anything by which I might gauge the speed of the current. What I saw was large and dark, off to my left. It was a man, floating facedown, the body of Samuel Hodges, riding the waters toward oblivion.

Then I heard a voice calling my name. *A voice?*

Instinctively, I looked toward the stern companionway, to see if the ghost of Trub McLaws was rising with his rat-eaten face.

Then I heard it again and thought, yes, there are ghosts in the dark cold of this sunken hulk. This one said, "I no come that side. You come here."

I turned to starboard and saw a shadow that seemed to stand on top of the moonbeams that lit the water, as a ghost would do. It was looking in at me. But standing? How could that be? My God, was I going crazy with the cold and the dark?

Then it said, "Spencer! I no swim. I no get wet. You wet already. Come."

Chin? *Chin*. He was standing in a rowboat next to the hull. He said, "I come find Mei-Ling. I think, maybe she go with him tonight. He try buy her, so maybe she go with him."

"Buy her? But I thought you told him—"

"Ah-Toy give me note from Flynn. It say, Flynn take my sister to Rainbow Gulch but leave me 'the Chinese gold of Broke Neck, first trickle from lost river of gold.' That what he say. He say gold in Brannan Warehouse safe, put in the name of Chin."

"Is it?"

"Brannan office not open." Chin reached out his hand. "Now come."

I shivered and waded toward them.

They pulled me aboard, and I said, "So you've forgiven Flynn?"

"For giving back my own gold? No forgive. Never forgive. He dirty my sister, kill her husband." Chin gestured to Little Ng to start rowing. Then he said to me, "You friend. Always friend. But if they no hang Flynn tonight, I kill tomorrow."

AN HOUR LATER, JANIVA insisted that I go to the meeting of the Vigilance Committee. She said it would be the best way to deflect suspicion. And she reminded me that until the *Proud Pilgrim* was filled in and covered over, we had much to deflect. So, dried, warmed, fortified with a brandy, dressed in a new black suit, I hurried back to Sansome Street and the huge mob milling and gossiping in the torchlight outside the Brannan Warehouse.

I gave the sergeant at arms my name and the number 25, which were checked against the master list, and I was duly admitted into the crowd of San Francisco men ready to distribute angry justice to the pair who stood before a committee of "judges," including Sam Brannan and Reese Shipton.

Brannan was shouting, "John Jenkins, also known as the Miscreant, is accused of stealing a safe. Who saw him do it?"

"We saw him run!" shouted someone in the crowd.

"Yeah, run with a big sack over his shoulder. Then he stole a rowboat, and when we caught up to him, he threw that sack into the water!"

"Sounds like guilt to me," said Sam Brannan. "What do you say, Jenkins?"

"It wasn't me," answered the accused, all split lip and blackened eye.

"But you're a solid, big man, the kind just able to carry off a safe," answered Brannan.

As this "interrogation" was unfolding, I got to the side of the room and worked my way toward the front. Those who knew that I was Flynn's friend kept an eye on me, as if I might try to rescue him or some such foolishness. I could feel the gaze of suspicion all around me, but as I reached the front, Flynn saw me and winked.

By now, they had heard all the "evidence" against John Jenkins, Sydney Duck, so Brannan called for a verdict. "A voice vote, if you please. All in favor of guilty?" This was answered with a roar of *ayes*. And opposed? Not a voice.

John Jenkins hung his head.

Michael Flynn, however, held his head high.

"What about you?" Brannan stalked over and looked Flynn in the eye. "Four dead. Two on the dock, two in the water."

"Self-defense," said Flynn, with an air of disdain so obvious that he knew no one would believe him.

"There's a story that two of the men, the two gamblers . . . you had an altercation with them night before last."

"The son of a bitch Tector Bunche was palmin' aces," said Flynn.

"So you followed him back to his boat and shot him?"

"Cowards is what they were. I went down to see if I could get me money back. They called for Hodges to tell his little yellow-haired squint of a bodyguard to shoot me."

"How do you explain this?" Brannan held up the Walker Colt.

"A damn fine gun, good for killin' mad grizzlies or bad men."

"Only fourteen hundred made in the whole world. And only one man in the Mother Lode ever carried one that I knew of. Hodges's man, Deering Sloate."

"And a rotten mean son of a bitch he was," said Flynn.

"Did you kill him, too?"

"No. I just borrowed his gun."

Some in the audience laughed at that. I sensed grudging admiration for a man who faced death with such spirit. Would it save him?

Reese Shipton looked again in my direction, "Is there anyone who would like to speak for the defendant's good character?"

I pushed forward. I would do it. I had to do it. I did not know what I would say. No playwright had written this scene. But—

Flynn saw me coming and cut me off. "No need for any of that. I killed them four. And I killed the Chinaman named Jon-Ling last night."

"You did that, too?" said Brannan, genuinely surprised. "But why?"

"He give me the wrong dumplings. Pan fried instead of steamed."

"Goddamn you," shouted someone in the crowd. "I loved them dumplin's."

And many of the men in the room began to shout angrily, perhaps because they loved dumplings, too.

Brannan had heard enough. He called out, "All right, same as with the Aussie. Give me a voice vote. He's confessed, but all in favor of finding him guilty—"

"AYE!"

And opposed? Eyes turned to me. The words caught in my throat.

Flynn again made it easy for me. "Nay to all of you. I done you all a favor. I killed cheatin' gamblers and bad cooks."

Brannan called, "What's the sentence of this body, gathered here, June 10, 1851?"

And something surprising happened. These angry men, sensing what was now being asked of them, quieted and seemed to draw back. I saw eyes shifting, heads turning toward the floor. Death was not something they were so willing to serve, after all.

But Sam Brannan believed that this had to be done, or our city would never stop burning and our society would never grow strong. Why else would he be so determined? He said, "All right, then. I tell you all that the punishment for murder is hanging. And for you, John Jenkins, Sydney incendiary, the punishment for grand theft is"—here he paused, as if thinking it through—"also hanging."

Now, the crowd murmured rather than roared. Was conscience afflicting them? Did they see that they were taking the law into their own hands, which would soon be covered in blood?

Brannan said, "For the Irishman? All in favor of hanging?"

The *ayes* came through, though with less force than before.

"Opposed?

Flynn looked at me and shook his head. *Don't fight this. It's a scrape no man gets out of.*

Feeling as low as ever I had, but knowing I had no choice and no chance to change the outcome, I closed my mouth.

Flynn nodded. He may even have smiled.

For Jenkins, the *ayes* had it, but fewer men voted . . . and less loudly.

Brannan put his hands on his hips. "You seem to be losing your spirit."

And from the back of the room came a voice that was high and harsh, sharpened by years of cutting through stiff winds. "As I understand it, we came here to hang somebody. Now it's my right to hang that Irish deserter, and—"

Nathan Trask never finished the sentence. Whatever he said, it struck the right nerve. The room seemed to explode. In an instant, men were shouting for execution. Others came forward to lay hold of the prisoners. Brannan himself carried word out to the street, where more shouting erupted. Lord, but the mob could be a fickle thing.

Meanwhile, Reese Shipton was asking Jenkins and Flynn if they had any last requests.

Jenkins asked for a cigar and a glass of brandy, both of which were quickly brought.

Flynn said, "No tobacco. Bad for the health. Just a whole damn bottle of brandy."

And the bottle, minus one glass for Jenkins, was put into his hand.

Flynn drank down two or three swallows, looked at me with tears in his eyes, and offered it to me. For the last time, I drank with him. Then he took another swallow and fired the bottle against the wall.

They bound Jenkins' hands in front of him and led him out, but this was a task more difficult with Flynn, since he needed the crutch to walk up the hill. So someone came forward with a wheelbarrow. "Here you go, Mick, a final ride in a Irish schooner."

Flynn looked at the man, then at the wheelbarrow, and said, "Fuck you and the horse you rode in on." Then he pulled himself up straight on the crutch and whispered to me, "Stay close, and I'll show these bastards what kind of man they're hangin'."

OUT INTO THE STREET we all went, surrounded by a cordon of stern-faced Vigilantes, the best and best-armed men in San Francisco. And though it was near one-thirty in the morning, the crowd seemed to come from everywhere to witness this new form of justice, to jeer and cheer, to surge and swirl as we started up the hill to Portsmouth Square.

I knew it would be a brutal climb for a man with a gunshot leg. So I would stay close to him on his final walk, no matter what the town thought, go with him, help him, support him. In truth, I would have done it even if he had been moving on two good legs.

But after a block, he wobbled and fell to one knee. As I tried to lift him, he said, "Don't worry, Jamie. If I go a little slower I get a few more minutes of life."

"Damn, Michael, but I'm sorry," I whispered.

"I'm sorry, too, lad, sorry that when I circled back that day—with everyone in town to hang Cletis, with Sloate gone the wrong way lookin' for me—sorry that I took your gold, too. Dug it up and spent it. But I held on to the Chinese gold, held it to swap for Mei-Ling. But now . . . ah, Jamie, what a bollocks. I'll never live to pay you back."

I told him I forgave him.

He patted may arm, then said, "Ah . . .'t'would have been a bollocks if I lived, too. I'd have had to kill Chin. Then Mei-Ling, she'd have hated me forever." Flynn raised his head to the dark night sky, thought some dark thought, then turned to me, his eyes glistening in the torchlight. "At least you're in the clear, Jamie. I killed Hodges. Never say otherwise to anyone. I pulled the trigger. Just stay strong, and . . . and stay merciful."

I helped him to his feet, he leaned one arm on the crutch and the other on me, and we kept on. Just before we came to the square, he said, "Whatever happens, you have that baby. Bring him up strong and straight, and tell him about his Uncle Michael."

Then the mob in the square saw our moving clump of men approaching. Voices rose. Angry faces pressed in from every direction. Someone shouted that they shouldn't hang criminals from the liberty pole. That was a symbol of America's greatness and "too great for the likes of these bastards!"

Someone else shouted that they should find a tree instead.

Another pointed toward the old adobe city hall, where an exposed beam and support formed a huge wooden cross. "Do it there!"

Michael Flynn did not seem to care. He was losing strength, and blood, too, in a long trail that traced all the way back to the waterfront. When he tripped and sank to his knees again, Matt Dooling appeared from the crowd and lifted him gently.

"Ah, Matt. Grand to see you. You're a grand friend," said Flynn. "Even if you *are* helpin' me to a noose."

"This is a terrible thing, Michael." Matt Dooling was crying big unabashed tears. "Just terrible."

Flynn tried to wipe the sweat from his eyes, hunching his face to his shoulder.

And there came Roberta, the whore, pushing forward, tearing one of her dirty petticoats, and wiping the sweat from Flynn's face.

She said, "I hope it wasn't me singin' that Irish song that got you in this trouble."

He said, "You done a grand thing, darlin'. And the voice of an angel you have."

Then Janiva's hand reached through the crowd to grab mine.

Matt Dooling said, "I couldn't keep her at home."

I gripped her and pulled her close, glad for her presence but fearful at the same time, and angry that she would expose our unborn child to such a mob. But when she touched Flynn's face and kissed his cheek and he smiled as if she had given him his freedom, I thanked God that she had come.

Reese Shipton said, "We need to move, folks, I'm sorry." And we started across the wide greensward, toward the old adobe city hall lit now by furious torchlight. Jenkins walked ahead of us, calmly smoking his cigar, but I could feel the emotion boiling in Flynn, as it was boiling in my own belly, and in Janiva, and in the ravening crowd itself.

Then someone stepped in front of us and ordered us to stop. His name was James Kenney, a state senator. Half a dozen others surged in behind him, as if they would oppose the lynching by force.

Sam Brannan shouted, "We are duly authorized and will not be stopped!" Duly authorized by themselves, perhaps, but a dozen committee men raised their guns, and the Kenney men backed off. The Vigilantes were now the law of San Francisco.

I said, "Sam, we don't have to do this."

Brannan turned on me. "We damn well do. It's set in stone. Tonight we take back our city."

There were others swirling around, too, dark men, thugs and growlers, the Sydney Ducks, threatening our committee men, shouting from the shadows, "We have your names!" "We know who you are!" "You hang our boy, Jenkins, we'll find you out, and kill you, then burn down the fuckin' city!"

Brannan shouted into the darkness at them, "We'll kill every last one of you sons of bitches. Every last one, so get back to Sydney Town or die tonight."

Off at the edge of this mob, a scuffle started. Then the Ducks were running down Kearny. Someone shouted, "Chase them! Get them! See they don't start another fire!"

And Flynn fell again, unable to keep up on his splintered leg. So Matt Dooling, all powerful arms and shoulders, lifted him to help him along.

Flynn whispered, "Remember, Matt, Michael Flynn never forgets a favor."

"Just put in a good word for me when you get where you're goin'," said Dooling.

Then Flynn sang a few bars of that hymn from the day we sailed, *"I am bound for the Promised Land. Oh, who will come and go with me? I am—"*

I held Janiva's hand to keep her close. I would not lose her in the crowd pushing and surging across the greensward, up to the front of the city hall and those convenient cruciform beams.

Then the ropes flew up and over the arms of the cross, bringing a roar from the crowd. John Jenkins started shouting that he was innocent. Reverend Hunt appeared from somewhere with the Bible in his hands and the 23rd Psalm on his lips. But Flynn had gone silent.

He was looking out over the crowd, out beyond us to something that made his eyes brighten. I followed his gaze to find Chin, Little Ng, and Mr. Ah-Sing. And . . . did Flynn see Mei-Ling? Hope may have filled his heart, for he loved her as surely as I loved Janiva, and the sight of her would have given him a last moment of happiness. But after searching, his eyes lowered, his hopes faded.

Then he looked at me and gave a bitter laugh. "Like I was sayin' . . . there I was, standin' on that windowsill, overlookin' the great Broadway in New York, kind of like tonight, with the crowd shoutin', and the, the . . . ah, Jamie, what a fuckin' waste."

Half a dozen men grabbed for Jenkins, but Nathan Trask would admit of no interference in noosing Flynn. He pushed me aside, knocked off Flynn's hat, and passed the rope over his head. His sallow face, yellowed all the more in the torchlight, was a cold mask, a completed work. He yanked the noose and said, "Michael Flynn, for the crime of desertion, I execute the sentence of death. May God have mercy on your soul."

To which Flynn responded, "Better than servin' chowder to a lot of Yankee swells in some snooty Boston club."

Then, suddenly, Kenney and that gang of political men came rushing back with reinforcements, so Brannan shouted, "Every lover of liberty and good order, lay on!"

Vigilantes pressed forward and grabbed for the ropes as Trask raised his hand, then dropped it. In an instant, Michael Flynn and an Australian criminal known as the Miscreant rose into the air, their legs reaching for the earth that would soon cover them.

I turned Janiva away, dragged her through the crowd, and we never looked back. Only later did I see that, somehow, she had picked up Flynn's hat and brought it with her.

I PAID TO BURY my friend in the graveyard at the end of Powell Street, where Filbert ran in. Reverend Hunt gave a reading and led us in the Lord's Prayer. He was reluctant, considering that the following Sunday, he preached cold justification of the Vigilantes: "Actual incapacity, or gross corruption on the part of rulers, may sometimes justify, or even require, a people to take power into their own hands. . . ."

I threw dirt onto Michael Flynn's grave, as did Janiva, Matt Dooling, and two "soiled doves" named Roberta and Sheila.

Turning away, I happened to glance up toward Telegraph Hill and the semaphore that had announced our arrival eighteen months before. And there, standing beside the skeletal tower like a skeleton himself, stood the black figure of Nathan Trask.

THE NEXT MORNING, NIKOLAI Budrovich arrived at Coffee Stand to roast the beans that began the day for San Francisco. And as was his custom, he walked first to the end of the wharf, there to contemplate his great good fortune in California.

And in the rising light, Budrovich noticed something strange on one of the ships. When he realized what it was, this Roman Catholic blessed himself and wished that he had a crucifix to hold up, so as to ward off the evil spirit he felt floating over the bay.

A black-shrouded figure was hanging by the neck from the bowsprit of the *William Winter*, dangling like a lure before the wooden face of the good reverend himself. The bringer of death had died.

We would never know what strange misery Nathan Trask inhabited in the stern cabin of his rat-infested ship. But for him, the death of Michael Flynn must have seemed the end of his work in California and in the world. He would never sail the *William Winter* back into Boston, never round the Horn, never command again, so he hanged himself, alone and unmourned.

April, 1853
A Journey

For two years after that, business consumed me. It is fair to say that I became my father. But with Janiva at my side, and a daughter arriving a year after James, Jr., I became the proudest father that ever had been.

From time to time, I thought about Flynn and his dreams. But my river of gold was like the Gulf Stream or the great Pacific Gyre, a mighty ocean current carrying goods south from Boston, north to San Francisco. Shovels, picks, pans, Ames plows, and all the other products of New England manufacture . . . these were the nuggets and dust giving color to our sluices and fulfillment to our dreams.

SAN FRANCISCO GREW SO fast that by 1853, the city fathers decided to extend Powell Street through the old cemetery, thereby to enhance the neighborhood known as North Beach. It was reported that a contractor, hired to move the interred bodies, had treated them with marked disrespect, exhuming them haphazardly and shoveling them into carts to be hauled like mere carrion across town to another burial ground. Rotting coffins were burned, good ones sold for firewood.

I determined that Michael Flynn would not be so badly treated. He should spend eternity in a place he had dreamed about, the place where I had once jokingly promised to bury him.

So, a few days later, I stood amidst the piles of dirt, the open graves, and the burning coffin boards, enveloped in the gaseous exhalations of the ground itself, and watched his coffin rise from the earth. To my relief, it was intact with few signs of rot.

I had authorized the building of an outer box—oak and copper lined—into which his was deposited directly, along with sprigs of sagebrush that would reduce escaping odors. Then the outer box was sealed before my eyes and brought by wagon to Long Wharf, to be loaded aboard the *Senator*.

Leaving our children in the tender care of Matt Dooling and his wife, now arrived from Massachusetts, Janiva and I steamed for Sacramento. We spent much of the night on the bow, enjoying the breeze and submitting to our awe at the starscape above us, an expanse of existence that could not but make a man or woman feel insignificant, while reminding them at the same time of their place at the center of the moral universe, especially if fortune had offered them each a hand to entwine with their own.

We reached Sacramento in the morning and hired a team and a driver. I promised Janiva that I would introduce her to Mark Hopkins when we headed back. But we could not linger, for no matter how well sealed, Flynn's coffin must not be exposed to the elements too long. So we passed through the town, went by Sutter's Fort, now fallen to ruin without the benevolent presence of Sutter himself, and soon were riding east through the country I had dreamed of so often in my San Francisco bed.

The sun was gentle and warm, the vista green and glowing, awash with great orange lakes of California poppy. When we came to a dip in the road and Janiva glimpsed the distant white mountains for the first time, she gasped, for in all her New England days, she had never seen anything so majestic.

It was spring, and we were in the very springtime of our lives, with the brightest days yet ahead. So I did not point out the bloody clump of oaks where we first met Cletis Smith. Nor did I mention the hanging tree some distance beyond, from which still dangled a long strand of rope. But I did direct her gaze to the south, to the red tiles and white adobe walls of a distant hacienda, no longer strange and exotic to my New England eyes, but a natural part of this landscape, just as Señor Vargas had been.

From time to time, we passed groups of miners. Most went afoot. Some piled their gear on the backs of burros or mules. Others rode in wagons or carts. But the rush to the diggings was over. These men would get there when they got there. So we moved steadily with the Cosumnes on our right, then passed over the river and approached the sprawling town of Michigan Bar, most westerly of the placer mining sites.

A plume of water was arcing into the sky above the road. It glimmered and shimmered in the bright sun, but there was little of beauty in it, for it was shooting from a great nozzle called a monitor, and while some men directed the stream that cut like a liquid knife into a hillside, others worked below the flow of cascading debris, forcing the mud, muck, and mess into long sluices that ran into the gullies that ran back to the river.

This was my introduction to a new form of devastation called hydraulic mining. It would take hold here because men had discovered the gravel of an ancient river winding through these low, grassy hills, and the easiest way to get at it was to wash away the ground that covered it. The Cosumnes River by itself could not deliver enough pressure. So an enterprising water company had dug the Michigan Ditch down from the high country, thereby empowering men to destroy the work of eons in an afternoon, all to get at the gold in the gravel.

In time, hydraulic mining would choke our vast deltas with mud and silt. Rich bottomland would flood because our rivers were no longer deep enough to carry off the rains. Collapsing hillsides would bring down trees and boulders and destroy the watershed itself. And dams, built to hold back a foul after-product called "slickens" would burst, releasing their filth into the valleys in horrible avalanches of ruined earth, rock, and mercury-laced effluent.

But all this lay in the future on the day we carried Michael Flynn's body through Michigan Bar. We had planned to stop here for a meal, but Janiva insisted we keep going. She said she could not stay an hour in a place of such destruction.

BY SUNSET, WE REACHED Broke Neck, now a small hamlet that seemed no longer to spin on the axis of a turning earth. No miners swarmed Grouchy Pete's. No warm aromas of sex or stew floated in the air. No pack mules stood before Emery's Emporium awaiting a burden of beans and bacon. The assay office was gone, as were both the assayer and the gold.

But the Emerys seemed happy for the quiet. We found them sitting on their porch, rocking, humming, enjoying their own company and the shade of the big oak beside their store. They invited us to stay with them in the cabin that George had built up behind the Emporium, and we gladly accepted. I had no desire to travel to our claim and old cabin, for too many harsh memories remained.

Over dinner, Janiva and I described the hydraulic operations we had seen.

George Emery suggested that Rainbow Gulch might be a good place to prospect for similar gravel deposits. I told him about a turn in the land, where Flynn had thought there might be gold. And George told me about an assay he had done on a quartz outcropping he had found just three miles south of Broke Neck.

He was ready to stake a claim and sink a hard rock mine. He offered to cut me in, if I would do the same at the place we soon took to calling Flynn's Bend, above Rainbow Gulch. So we agreed. If we could get the permission of the Croatian winemakers, we would prospect on their land.

But Janiva made us promise never to engage in hydraulic mining, no matter what. And in some things, she was not to be argued with.

The next morning, well rested and hopeful, we turned southwest, and in company with the Emerys, we took the little-used road. We followed the rolling path across hills and through stands of trees. We bumped over the Rainbow Gulch water trench and came finally to the north rim of the ravine . . .

"AND THAT'S WHERE IT ends," said Peter Fallon through the headset.

The helicopter was veering south over the San Rafael Bridge, cleared for landing on a perfectly blue October day.

"Just ends?" said Evangeline. "Before they bury Flynn, the journal just . . . ends?"

Peter had skimmed much of it on the ride, noting all the references to Rainbow Gulch, the bags of Chinese gold, and the ancient rivers of it.

"Why didn't Spencer finish it?" she asked.

Peter's voice dropped with the helicopter. "Maybe he ran out of energy."

"Or died," said Wild Bill Donnelly.

"So," said Evangeline, "Barber asked you to find the original because the last notebook answers some unanswered question that the transcription apparently doesn't?"

"But he couldn't just say, find Notebook Seven. That would have been too obvious," said Wild Bill.

Peter said, "Spencer and Emery may have done the only real prospecting at the so-called Flynn's Bend, especially if Janiva was against hydraulic mining."

"Also possible," said Evangeline, "that the whole journal is just a good story. A tale of immigrants making their way."

"Well, it's no treasure map," said Wild Bill. "Geologists keep telling us about undiscovered ore bodies—"

"Geologists like Jack Cutler," said Peter.

"But he never discovers them," said Wild Bill. "And he could never convince Manion Sturgis to allow core sampling."

"Can't disturb the precious grapevines," said Peter.

"Manion doesn't care about gold," said Evangeline, "or money."

"Easy not to care about money if you have a lot of it," said Peter.

"I'm on the goddamn helicopter with you, Peter. Kill it with the sarcasm."

Peter knew enough to back down, always the best course, epecially in the midst of a crisis. "Yes, Ms. Carrington. You're the common sense on this whirlybird."

"You'd better say that." She turned back to the transcription in the gray archival box. "And common sense says we have what everyone's fighting for, so—"

"So the question is," said Wild Bill, "how do we use it to help your son and his future wife?" And he started running down the names: "We got LJ Fallon, Johnson 'Jack' Barber, Wonton Willie—"

"I'm sorry he's gone," said Evangeline. "He was a character."

"Too much character will get you killed in Chinatown," said Wild Bill. "You stand out, people notice. They don't like it. They frown on flamboyance."

"What about Kou?" asked Peter. "Nice, conservative. The perfect m.o."

Wild Bill nodded. "And Christine Ryan, FBI, who says there's someone on the inside, other than your son, so—"

As the helicopter touched down, Peter received a text from LJ: "On the move. Call ASAP." He hurried out of the prop wash and placed the call.

It went to voice mail. *Voice mail.*

Wild Bill said, "They're probably moving quickly. Stay calm."

"But why are they on the move at all? I told them to stay put."

JUST BEFORE THEY BOARDED the ferry, Wild Bill got a callback from his SFPD contact, listened, clicked off. "They whacked Willie in front of Good Mong Kok on Stockton. Every Saturday morning, he buys a pork bun, an egg tart, and a cup of black tea. He sits on the hood of his limo, meets his peeps, buys the local kids dumplings, and just as he bites into his pork bun, two guys come by on those Dahon folding bikes, both in hoodies—"

"Hoodies on Dahons," said Peter, "all over town."

"One comes up the street, distracts the bodyguard, pops him. And as Willie turns, the other guy rockets down the sidewalk, gives him two in the hat, and zips away."

"Bulletproof vest is no good against a head shot," said Peter.

"A Detective Immerman on the case."

"We met her the other night, the first time they tried to whack Willie."

"The question is," said Wild Bill, "who is *they*?"

Once aboard, seated on the lower deck, Peter checked his phone. No texts from LJ. He called again. *Voice mail.*

Evangeline saw the look on his face. She gave his hand a squeeze.

"Stay calm," said Wild Bill, which he did by flipping through his emails.

Then Peter got the text he'd been waiting for: "We're OK. Will call soon." That made everyone feel better.

Then Wild Bill got an email and said, "Wow."

That made everyone feel worse.

"What?" said Evangeline over the roar of the ferry engine.

"Check your email from Larry Kwan, subject line: 'Dai-lo laid low.'"

"That Larry . . . such a jokester," said Evangeline.

The email read: "Driving back with Cutler. Before we left, saw smoke north of Rainbow Gulch. Sent drone to investigate. Watch."

On the attached video, the drone flew over Rainbow Gulch, past the little fenced-in cemetery, then northwest toward a column of smoke rising from what Wild Bill said was Lost Gulch Road. It cut along the southern boundary of the Boyles' property and meandered around the Emery Mine, tracing the twists and dips of that timeless, brown-grass nowhere. Just another back road in the rolling hills of Amador County . . .

. . . except for the big blue SUV on its side about half a mile from Highway 49. It was burning. And the landscape around it was spreading into one of those scary late-season brush fires. But Amador emergency vehicles were everywhere, red-and-yellow, black-and-white, flashing lights, water streams.

The drone hovered above the wreck, then cruised over two bodies by the side of the road: an African American in a black suit, an Asian in a blue suit. It zoomed closer on the Asian: Mr. Lum, the Dai-lo, the man from the Arbella Club steps and the Emery Mine parking lot, head wound gaping. The video ended.

Peter said, "Did the Boyles do that?"

"They might have," said Wild Bill. "But the white guy isn't there. More likely, he tapped the other two."

"But who ordered it?" said Peter.

"The field is narrowing. Michael Kou is my guess," said Wild Bill.

"Whacking a Triad boss?" said Peter. "Very bold."

"Flamboyant, even," said Evangeline, "for such a smooth guy."

"Smoothly washing dirty money," said Wild Bill, "using Attorney Barber to help, mixing dirty stuff in with clean venture capital, like the M&A money—"

"M&A," said Evangeline. "What's that?"

"Mergers and Acquisitions. I'm betting Sierra Rock is like a Laundromat, washing cash from extortion, prostitution, weapons trafficking, crystal meth, all as a down payment for clean loans from Chinese banks, then—"

Peter's phone vibrated. Caller ID: Name Withheld. He answered.

It was LJ, calling from someone else's phone. Peter didn't like that.

LJ said, "We're on the move."

"On the move where?"

"Chinatown. The building super came up in the service elevator and told us we had to get out. He said Michael Kou's men had pulled up out front."

"And you went with him? People getting whacked all over the place and you just *went*? Jesus." Peter sensed that the kid had no choice. "Where are you now? Who are you with?"

"You'll never believe it, Dad. We're with Uncle Charlie."

"Uncle Charlie from Portsmouth Square?"

"He's taking us to another safe house . . . Family Happiness Herbs and Tea, on Spofford Street, in the eight-hundred block of Clay."

"Why aren't you calling on your own phone?"

"Unh . . . it's being inspected."

"Inspected? What the—"

Uncle Charlie came on: "Hello? Mr. Fallon Peter? You son say you got journal. You bring. Maybe we get out of big trouble."

"Hey," said Peter, "put my—"

The phone went dead.

The October sun did not touch Spofford Street, an alley that might have been there since the Gold Rush, lined with acupuncturists, beauty parlors, a benevolent association, and halfway down the block, the red-painted exterior of Family Happiness Herbs and Tea.

Peter, Evangeline, and Wild Bill Donnelly stepped into a cloud of five-spice powder, ginseng, incense, and . . . cigarette smoke?

But the old Chinese man behind the counter wasn't smoking. He glanced at them, looked down at his laptop, looked back at them, then pressed a button by the register. A section of shelving, containing teas from all over China—boxed, bagged, or bricked—swung open to reveal the Family Happiness gambling parlor.

And a cloud of smoke rolled out. At every table, players were puffing away, while conversation buzzed and mah-jongg tiles clattered, and ugly fluorescent lights—which no gambler noticed, whether on a win streak or losing every nickel—gave out a faint but audible hum.

A stairway to the left led down to the basement. Wraparound was sitting at the top of the stairs, arms folded, face impassive.

This surprised Peter. He said, "You made it?"

"I'm sitting here, ain't I? Uncle Charlie told me to get out, soon as they whacked Willie. He said he'd take care of the rest." Wraparound held out his hand to Evangeline.

"What?"

"Mace. Give it, or you don't go down."

Wild Bill nodded.

So Evangeline pulled the Mace from her purse and surrendered it.

Then Wraparound gestured to the bulge under Wild Bill's windbreaker.

Wild Bill, a head taller and half a lifetime older, whispered, "No fuckin' way."

This brought a glare that burned right through the wraparounds.

So Wild Bill reached up and removed them, a gesture performed with such calm confidence that Wraparound appeared shocked rather than violated. He blinked in the fluorescent light, then scowled.

"I keep my gun," said Wild Bill. "Want to see my badge?"

"Badge?" Wraparound looked at Peter. "You brought a fuckin' badge?"

"Retired badge, but he has friends." Without another word, Peter bounded down the stairs. He always told his son to walk into any room like he owned it. Walk into trouble the same way. But he didn't see trouble in the basement. This was no bare-bulb dungeon with leaking pipes overhead. It was clean, well-lit, with gray walls and new linoleum, and everybody seemed pretty relaxed.

LJ and Mary were sitting on a sofa to the left, holding mugs of tea.

LJ stood and said, "Hi, Dad. Glad you could make it."

Peter gauged his son's expression. Was that the boyishly guilty look-away eye-shift, as if to say, *Sorry about all this?*

Evangeline tried to gauge Mary's look, but Mary just smiled and went back to scrolling through her iPad, as though it was therapy . . . or escape.

At a card table on the side, two grandfather types were playing gin rummy. One had a beer. Both were smoking. They looked familiar. Maybe it was the ankle holster under one guy's trouser cuff or the *Racing Form* in the other guy's jacket: Michael Kou's bodyguards. Did that mean Kou was about to make an entrance?

If so, he'd have to move Uncle Charlie out of the power seat, behind the metal desk, beneath the street-level window with the feet flipping past. The old man was wearing his usual uniform—windbreaker, plaid shirt, khaki trousers—but he seemed . . . different. He looked Wild Bill over and said, "You got big gun."

"I'm not good enough to hit a target with a little Walther," said Wild Bill, "especially if I have to bend over to pull it from an ankle holster."

"Me neither." The guy with the ankle holster threw a card down, then reached around and pulled a Ruger .327 out of his waistband. "That's why I carry this."

Peter said to the card players, "Aren't you Kou's bodyguards?"

"We let him think so," said the other guy, squinting above the cigarette in the corner of his mouth. "But we work for Uncle Charlie."

"Cousins," said Uncle Charlie. "Long time. That why they look so old. One got gray hair. One need bifocal. But both very tough. So no be bad, 'cause they badder."

Wild Bill leaned over the one with bifocals and pointed to a card. "Play the jack."

The guy threw it down. The other guy picked it up. Wild Bill got a dirty look.

Uncle Charlie said, "That Bobby Lee with ankle holster. We call Cousin Rebel."

"Like the general," said Peter. "Very historical."

"Bifocal guy, we call Rice Balls. One day he play horse called Rice Ball. Daily double, perfecta, trifecta . . . play all over. Rice Ball come in. Big payday."

Wild Bill said, "I've heard of a Chinese hit man named after a horse that used to run at Golden Gate. He has a bigger reputation than the horse."

"Horse gone for glue," said Uncle Charlie, "but Rice Balls right here."

"You want my autograph?" said Rice Balls.

Uncle Charlie got up, put folding chairs in front of his desk, and said to his visitors, "Sit. Sit. You like-ee tea? Tsingtao? Smoke?"

"Tea would be nice," said Peter, being polite.

"But no smokes," said Evangeline. "I'm getting a nicotine rush just breathing."

Uncle Charlie said to Rice Balls, "Bring hot tea. Three cup."

Peter and Evangeline sat in the chairs and took the tea.

Wild Bill folded his arms and leaned against the doorframe.

"Now," said Uncle Charlie, dropping back behind the desk and dropping both the accent and the act, "the Dai-lo would like to know if you have 'The Spencer Journal.'"

"But the Dai-lo was just killed." Peter shot a look at LJ. *What's going on here?*

LJ said, "We're learning a lot about Uncle Charlie today, Dad."

"Yes." Mary looked up from her iPad. "Things that even I didn't know."

Uncle Charlie glanced at LJ. "Good that you've always treated me with respect, young man, despite my apparent low station. The Dai-lo appreciates respect."

"My father always taught me to treat everyone with respect," said LJ, "until they proved they didn't deserve it."

"Your father taught you well." Uncle Charlie looked at Peter. "We all owe each other respect. That's a lesson we've been trying to teach here since the Gold Rush, no?"

"Wait," said Evangeline. "You're the Dai-lo?"

"Who appreciates respect." Peter gave Uncle Charlie a nod, respect and admiration for a fine performance.

Uncle Charlie said, "Respect makes it easier for me to protect a conflicted young man like LJ, and to bless his marriage to my niece."

"Wow," said Evangeline, "that's almost poetic."

Uncle Charlie smiled. He did not seem like a laugher. "You should hear it in the original Cantonese."

Peter looked at LJ and mouthed the word, "Conflicted?"

"I think he means the FBI business, Dad."

"The FBI," said Uncle Charlie. "Usually our nemesis but sometimes . . . useful."

"Remember what we said about flamboyance?" asked Wild Bill.

"The less of it the better?" said Peter.

"That's why I appear as what I am," said Uncle Charlie, "an old uncle who runs a tea store and a few mah-jongg tables. But the tong boys, they know not to bother me."

"Smart, those tong boys," said Peter.

"So, I tried to warn you without giving anything up, like an old uncle, warn you out of this business, warn you twice. The less you know, the less you can get hurt."

Rice Balls looked up from his cards. "'Watch out for hit-and-run drivers. This can be a dangerous town.' Sound familiar?"

"That was you?" said Peter. "But—"

"If we couldn't get you out of the way, we wanted you to be careful," said Uncle Charlie. "Then Kou tried to kill both Fallons after the father called out Sierra Rock—"

Peter said, "Were you there?"

"The waitress serving the wine said you could drink a lot and keep your head." Uncle Charlie lit a cigarette from the one he was finishing. "After you mentioned Sierra Rock, she saw Kou signal the white bodyguard, the one who worked for Lum . . . until he killed him."

Cousin Rebel looked up. "Who lets a white guy guard him? No honor with the white guys."

"I did some work with that guy," said Rice Balls. "Never liked him. His name's Steele, or so he says. Used to be a D-one linebacker, or so he says. Always works for the highest bidder."

"Which was Kou"—Cousin Rebel threw down a card—"not Lum."

Evangeline's eyes were watering from the smoke. She blinked and said, "When Lum came to see Sturgis at the vineyard this morning, the white guy spent the whole time texting."

"Probably giving Kou a play-by-play," said Rice Balls. "Getting permission for the hit."

"Lum was on his last rounds." Uncle Charlie took two or three quick drags of nicotine. "If he could not make good deals, he would advise the Triad to pull all its money out of Sierra Rock, call loans on mining operations, take losses, move on."

"Why?" asked Peter.

"Too much regulation in California," said Uncle Charlie. "Not enough gold. There are places to put our money where the FBI won't follow. Poorer countries with more gold. Gold is the long play, but not here."

"A few years ago," said LJ, "when the Chinese government told banks to invest in gold mining operations around the world, certain Triad Dragons of Hong Kong—"

"—whom I serve," said Uncle Charlie.

"—grabbed for low-interest loans through banks where their business is welcomed. Then they started looking for gold investments."

Uncle Charlie flicked an ash. "Once China has gold supplies in the same proportion to GDP as the U.S., they can accelerate the movement away from the dollar as the world's reserve currency."

"That's the idea on a macro level," said LJ. "The long play."

"When you have four thousand years of history, you know the long play is the best play." Uncle Charlie puffed up a cloud. "But the Chinese play the game on every level. They encourage every Chinese family to own a kilo of gold."

"A lot of families." Evangeline made a futile wave at the air in front of her face. "So a lot of gold. But why?"

"Because the U.S. Fed may eventually let inflation take hold as a way of reducing the deficit," said LJ. "Inflation erodes savings, but it also erodes debt. The Chinese hold trillions in U.S. debt. So they want hedges. In an inflationary world, gold could run to $10,000 an ounce. If China accumulates enough gold, Chinese debt holders will be safe."

"Like kung-fu fighting," said Peter, "using your enemy's strength—in this case his gold resources—against him."

Rice Balls hummed the old tune, "Kung-Fu Fighting."

"But Kou?" said Peter.

"He wanted to impress the Triad by bringing them a U.S. gold deal," said Uncle Charlie. "He also knows Hong Kong is consolidating U.S. control, from here to Boston—"

"So, he wants to prove he can play dirty," said Wild Bill. "Taking out Wonton Willie for the street cred, I get. But whacking Lum?"

"Hong Kong sent Mr. Lum to 'appreciate the situation,' as the Brits would say. Once it became obvious that the Emery Mine may never be profitable—"

"A conclusion he came to this week," said LJ.

"I know," said Peter. "We were there."

"Lum wanted to make a last-ditch effort to save the investment and show Michael Kou good faith." Uncle Charlie took a slower puff on his cigarette.

"Good faith?" said Wild Bill. "Trust, loyalty, honor?"

"The definition of the Triad," answered Uncle Charlie. "We got Kou's family out of China after Tiananmen Square. He never forgot. Always loyal. Always a team player. As soon as he heard that we wanted to get into gold, he told us about Ah-Toy and the journal and the lost river."

Peter was getting it now. He said, "Jack Cutler told me that Kou was trying to impress 'certain elements in the Chinatown community.' Would that be you?"

Uncle Charlie kept puffing between words. "He gave me a chance to invest. Obeying the chain of command, like a good soldier. I said give the same chance to all the Chinatown people."

"Yeah," said Cousin Rebel. "You're a regular Chinese Robin Hood."

"But somebody tried too hard, seeding holes, cheating people. Still the Triad bosses liked Kou's scheme to use gold mines for money laundering. Elegant way to kill two birds with one stone, so Cutler—"

Rice Balls looked up from his cards. "When are we going to kill Cutler?"

"Kill my father?" Mary looked up from scrolling.

"He's a fuck-up who cost us a lot of money," said Rice Balls.

Uncle Charlie told her, "Your mother loved him, so he's protected." Then he gave Rice Balls a scowl, as if to remind him who was in charge, then he turned back at Peter: "Kou and Sierra Rock had a smart lawyer named Barber who also did work for some old San Francisco families, like the Spencers."

"Did Kou and Barber know about the Spencer journal when Sierra Rock bought the Emery mine?" Peter asked his son.

"What they knew," said LJ, "was what Cutler had told them about proven reserves in the Emery Mine and alluvial gold in an unproven gravel band six or eight miles long, running discontinuously from the ruins of an old Miwok dam, through the Boyles' land, down across Rainbow Gulch. Cutler's version of the lost river."

"Alluvial means river." Uncle Charlie stubbed out the cigarette and lit another.

LJ said, "It was big news all across the Mother Lode when Sierra Rock bought the Emery Mine. Some folks loved it. But retirees and ranchers and vinters felt differently."

"Like Manion Sturgis and Ginny O'Hara," said Evangeline.

"Then comes the story of the *Proud Pilgrim*. It's all over the papers, the Gold Rush death ship with six bodies chained to the keel. Maryanne Rogers goes and reads about it at the historical society. Then she tells Barber about it over one of their dinners at House of Prime Rib. He tells Kou, who tells Cutler to look into it."

"But when Cutler goes looking," said Evangeline, "he's told it's gone."

"Right," said Uncle Charlie. "So Kou got Barber to put that codicil into the will. He figured all seven sections would pop right out if it was the only way to satisfy the terms of the will. Then he'd learn exactly where to look for that discontinuous river of gold."

"But Maryanne Rogers had to die first," said Peter.

"Now you know who did the hit-and-run," said Cousin Rebel. "Kou's guys."

"Surprised they didn't run her over with one of those little fuckin' bikes," said Rice Balls, and he threw down a card. "Gin."

Cousin Rebel tossed in his hand and looked at Uncle Charlie, as if to ask, *Can we get on with this?*

Uncle Charlie pulled out a briefcase, put it on his desk, and said to Peter. "Your son's get-out-of-jail-free card. Notes, thumb drives, documents . . . showing how Kou collects his dirty money and how it gets washed through Sierra Rock via gold purchases and other investments. The Triad has decided it's time to shut him down. And I want to insulate our little operation, which is mostly gambling, protection, immigration work."

Peter guessed he meant "immigration fraud," but no correcting Uncle Charlie . . .

. . . who went on, "Kou is a big liability to our more *traditional* tong. Give me the journal, then your son delivers this to the FBI, and all debts are paid."

That, thought Peter, was a no-brainer. So he put the gray box on the desk.

Uncle Charlie opened it, took out the journal with great care, like a man who respected history, flipped through it, read here, grunted there, made a few comments, flipped to the end and read: "We bumped over the Rainbow Gulch water trench and came finally to the north rim of the ravine . . ." He flipped back as if he had missed something, then flipped again, almost frantically.

Then he looked up. "Where's the ending?"

Peter said, "We think Spencer died before he transcribed it."

Uncle Charlie slammed the book down and raised his hand to slam it again.

Peter said, "Ah . . . could you go easy on that? We hope to return it to its rightful owner. It's very fragile."

"Very fuckin' worthless, too." Uncle Charlie put the book back in the box and the briefcase back on the floor. "Hong Kong wants the ending. Cutler said the ending might have core sample results, so we know for sure if there's gold under the vineyard."

Peter looked at LJ and Mary. "How would Cutler know that?"

Mary said, "Speculation. It's what he does."

"If there's gold there," said Uncle Charlie, "we can still recoup our losses."

"Manion Sturgis won't sell," said Evangeline.

"We'll make him an offer like in the movies," said Rice Balls.

Uncle Charlie fished out his pack of Lucky Strikes. Empty. So he went over to the card table, pulled a butt from the pack offered by Rice Balls, lit, took a long draw, told Peter, "You need to find that original. And fast, because now that Kou has cut loose, there's no more time for watching and waiting. He sent L.A. muscle to kill Cutler in the apartment and found you instead . . . he hit Lum in gold country . . . he's spilling lots of blood so he can be the new blood."

Rice Balls said, "Not happenin'."

"Right." Uncle Charlie exhaled smoke through his nose. "Nothing in this briefcase incriminates me or my people. You get it if you find last section. Otherwise, appraise the library, then go back to Boston, all of you, because I can't protect you."

Peter looked at LJ.

LJ said, "Maybe that's what we should do, Dad."

"What?"

"Appraise the library. I didn't look there. I've looked everywhere else."

He said, "Do you think we can get into the library?"

LJ said, "Mr. Yung is—"

"Don't trust Yung," said Uncle Charlie. "He's on Barber's payroll. But he also takes Saturday off. Usually visits his big-time architect son in Palo Alto."

"How do you know that?" asked LJ.

"I know many things. I also know the house is alarmed. Hard to get in."

So, THE FIRST PLACE to look for the key: Sarah Bliss, the executor. Peter called her.

She answered with: "Even if you allow me to see your caller ID, the answer is still no."

"To what?"

"I just told you. I'm giving up nothing."

"Just told me?" Peter looked at the others. "I didn't call you—"

But she kept talking, "You aren't getting to go through my things here. And you aren't getting the key to Arbella House. You aren't on our side."

"Listen, Sarah," said Peter, "I didn't call you. Somebody is using my name. Don't let anyone in. Don't talk to anyone. Don't do anything until we get there."

Peter clicked off. "Somebody's after her notebook. Should we call the cops?"

"No cops, for fuck's sake," said Uncle Charlie.

"She's in Sausalito, right?" said Rice Balls. "So we go rescue her. Go by boat."

"Good idea," said LJ, and he and Mary stood.

"You're not going, either of you. Too dangerous." Uncle Charlie pointed at Mary. "You're my closest relative. And the next Charlie Chan generation comes from—"

"Wait," said Peter. "Your name is Charlie *Chan*? Like in the movies?"

"You should be the detective here, not me," said Wild Bill.

"Stop with the jokes. I'm out on a limb as it is," said Charlie. "Nobody in Hong Kong knows that my future nephew is working for the FBI. Mary stays here. Your son stays with her. As soon as you get the rest of chapter seven, scan it and send it to me. I send it on to Hong Kong. And your son gets the briefcase. I'm good for my word. Right, Rice?"

"It's why we been with you forever."

"Then Barber and Kou go down for wire fraud, money laundering, SEC violations, and the Triad knows all there is to know about the lost river of gold. The young people can go live their lives so long as—" He looked at Mary and LJ.

"So long as what?" said Mary.

"So long as you name the first kid Charles Chan Fallon. Not Peter."

LJ put an arm around Mary. "You have my word."

FIFTEEN MINUTES LATER, A Grady-White Fisherman 257 rocketed across San Francisco Bay, with Peter, Evangeline, and Wild Bill Donnelly aboard and Rice Balls, whose real name was Hector Chan, at the helm.

He shouted over the roar of twin Yamaha 200s, "Sausalito is about three miles. We'll be there in no time. A little bumpy but it beats the traffic all to hell."

"Nice boat," said Wild Bill.

"Won it on a dice roll. Good bulk, displacement hull to cut through the chop, fast as a Jet Ski . . ."

The Bay, thought Peter, remained one of the wonders of the natural world—just as James Spencer had written when the *William Winter* ran through the Golden Gate—no matter how it had been used and abused for a hundred and fifty years.

The boat bounced and the cold spray showered everyone.

"Sorry," shouted Rice Balls, "but I need all the power I got with that current tryin' to suck us out through the Golden Gate. Up inside Sausalito, it'll smooth out nice. And there's a twelve-foot channel right along the houseboat wharf, so we can get close."

After a few minutes, they tucked under the north footing of the Golden Gate Bridge, all grand and orange above them, and made for Waldo Bay, dropping to "No Wake" speed when they came up on the channel marker.

Rice Balls said to Peter, "Do you want binoculars?"

"How close can you get?"

"As close as you want. This channel was dredged for the Liberty ships they built up in here."

"Get close, then. Binoculars might be too obvious." Peter grabbed a red ball cap with a San Francisco 49ers logo from the forward locker, pulled it low, and took off the sport coat he had been wearing since the day before.

Rice Balls cruised slowly ahead, about twelve feet from the decks of the houseboats. At low RPMs, the four-stroke engines quieted to a whisper.

"Keep up some chatter," said Peter, "like we're out on a sunset cruise."

"I got a better idea," said Rice Balls. "There's cold Buds in the cooler. Grab a few."

"Beer?" said Evangeline. "At a time like this?"

"It's a fucking *disguise,* lady. Drink beer, look casual."

Wild Bill flipped her one. She popped it, and the suds fountained out all over her. Rice and Wild Bill laughed like boaters having big fun. Perfect cover.

The slider was closed but the drapes were open aboard the *Tree Hugger,* and Peter knew right away that something was wrong. A big guy was standing over Brother Bliss's wheelchair, holding the tube from the oxygen generator. Holding, releasing, holding, releasing. But that was all the view they had as the boat went past.

Peter said, "Black leather . . . could be one of the guys who chased us last night."

"If they work for Kou," said Rice Balls, "they shoot first and ask questions later, or they get their questions answered, then they shoot. But they always shoot."

Wild Bill said to Rice Balls, "What are you carrying?"

"I got a Walther with a silencer and a nine-millimeter."

Wild Bill patted his holster. "I'll stay with the cannon. The .44 will go through the glass."

The plan: Peter would jump off on the dock, a hundred yards up the channel, then walk back and knock on the front door to distract the guys inside. Wild Bill and Rice Balls would go in shooting, right through the sliders . . . so long as Evangeline could drive the boat.

"I can handle a yacht," she said. "I'll put this little thing up against that sun deck like I was parking a Toyota Corolla."

"All right," said Peter. "When you hear me yell Sarah's name, come fast."

The boat swung and dropped Peter. Then he started back along the dock toward the *Tree Hugger*. A few people were out, working on their window boxes or sitting in the late-afternoon sun. Some nodded. A few gave this stranger the once-over.

Peter started whistling, as though he was part of the scenery, just moving to his own inner beat. But as he went, he was setting his speed to the Grady-White moving back down the channel, slowly, almost silently.

At the *Tree Hugger,* Peter stopped, took a deep breath, knocked on the door. No answer. Bad sign.

He tried the handle. Locked. Worse sign.

He lifted the welcome mat. The key was right where Sarah said it would be. He put it into the lock, turned, heard the door click open, and cried, "Hello! Sarah! Sarah Bliss! It's Peter!" He pushed the door open and stepped inside.

And a guy in black leather pressed a pistol to his head. The other guy in black leather was standing over Brother B., who lay on the floor by the slider.

Sarah Bliss said, "Fallon! What the hell are you—"

And the whole houseboat shook with the impact of the Grady-White, knocking everyone off balance.

The guy by the slider turned his face right into a blast from the .44 Magnum that tore through the glass, then through his forehead, then threw him backward onto the deck.

Sarah screamed.

The guy covering Peter swung his pistol toward the slider, so Peter swung his hand, knocked the pistol loose, sent it skittering across the floor.

Then a switchblade popped and slashed at Peter, who jumped back.

And that was all the slashing he did . . .

. . . because Sarah Bliss grabbed the pistol from the floor and put two shots through the black leather. Then she pivoted as Wild Bill pulled at the slider.

"No!" cried Peter. "He's one of us."

She didn't put the gun down.

"Don't fuck with Sarah," said Brother B., rising to his elbows. "She might be an old hippie broad, but she's licensed to carry and—"

"Don't fuck with my husband, either," she said.

Peter looked at the two: black leather, both Asian. "These guys chased us last night. What were they after?"

Sarah Bliss said, "The journal. They didn't believe me when I told them I didn't have it."

"So they were chokin' me," said Brother Bliss, "the motherfuckers."

"Relax," said Peter. "Make some tea." Then he and Wild Bill helped Brother Bliss back into his wheelchair.

Sarah lowered the gun and said to Peter, "7-5-4-4-4-7."

"What's that?"

"The code for the burglar alarm once you're in the foyer at Arbella House."

"Is Notebook Seven there?"

"How in the hell should I know? But it makes sense to look." She pulled two keys off her ring. "These will get you in the outer door, then the inner. Yung won't be there. He—"

"—visits his son in Palo Alto?"

"You know a lot," said Sarah. "So . . . once you're in the foyer, it's 9-9-9-7-1-9 to unlock the pocket doors on the library."

Peter pulled out his phone and wrote those codes on the Notes page.

"Now scram," said Sarah. "The cops are coming. And you, Mr. Peter Fallon, need to end this. I don't give a damn who does what anymore. Whether there's gold under that vineyard or not, this world has gone too crazy for me."

On the boat, Rice Balls was leaning over the side, inspecting the hull where it had hit the dock. He was growling at Evangeline, "Like parking a Corolla?"

"It'll buff out," she said. "A little rubbing compound. Good as new."

"Rubbing compound, my ass." Rice Balls took the helm and said, "Hang on."

Peter handed Evangeline a beer. "You've earned one. You did fine."

She took a sip and gave it back to him. "You, too."

He put his arm around her.

Wild Bill gave a shove off the dock, and Rice Balls said, "We're out of here."

It was just after dark when they turned onto California Street, which was always a Whole Foods traffic jam at dinner hour on a Saturday.

Rice Balls was driving a blue Nissan Rogue. He made one pass by the house and said he'd dropped them on the next pass, then park around the block, so as not to attract attention. On the second pass, they hopped out right in front of Arbella House, went through the gate, onto the porch, without anyone noticing.

One key and they were in the vestibule. Punch the code, then the second key, and they were in the foyer. They waited a moment, listened, then Peter called, "Mr. Yung!"

No answer.

"Uncle Charlie was right." Peter turned to the library, punched in the code on the keypad beside the pocket doors, heard a pop, and the doors slid open, revealing the room where this had begun a few nights before.

The drapes were pulled. Peter flipped on the lights.

Wild Bill said, "Wow. Is that a Tiffany pendant lamp?"

"You have a good eye." Evangeline pointed to the Bierstadt. "Recognize that?"

Wild Bill looked, went closer, and said, "That's the view from my patio."

"Spencer commissioned it, we think," said Evangeline. "His first view of the Mother Lode."

Their plan was simple. Go through every book and hope that no one came to interrupt them, although Michael Kou's team was surely closing in.

Peter said, "Look first for leather bindings without title. Spencer wrote on folio'd foolscap, eight and a half by thirteen and a half. Look for taller items and skinny bindings because the notebooks aren't more than sixty or seventy pages each."

"And if it's not here?" said Evangeline.

"We're fucked. Or shot. Or arrested. Or all three."

"I'll take the first," she whispered.

And they dug in.

Before long, Peter was reminded of something he had heard when he was searching for a Shakespeare manuscript in the Harvard library: "A man will be known by his books."

James Spencer still lived in his library, and he showed himself to be a man of breadth, depth, erudition, and patriotism. But they were not stopping to appraise or admire. They were looking quickly, not even reshelving. And after forty-five minutes . . . nothing.

That was when Wild Bill found a section of books marked with Chinese characters, down near the floor. "There are a couple of skinny ones over here, but—"

Peter knelt and pulled one: a children's book in Chinese, illustrated. Then two or three thicker volumes. Then, at the very end, something long and skinny . . . the right size, the right vintage, but . . . an empty notebook. Peter sat back. "For a minute there, I thought we had it."

And a voice behind them said, "You don't."

John Yung was standing in the doorway. As on the day that he first guided them into the library, he wore his white jacket, smoothed his black hair straight back, and offered a presence so preternaturally composed as to appear either disconnected from reality or in complete command of it. Given the cannon he held at his hip, it could go either way.

Wild Bill looked at Yung, then at the gun. "What the hell is that?"

Peter counted seven barrels. "It's a Nock gun. Named after the inventor. Load it with buckshot, and you can sweep the deck of a wooden ship in a battle or knock down a dozen mutineers with a single pull of the trigger. Very rare."

"I can sweep this room, too," said Mr. Yung.

"That gun is ancient," said Peter. "It could blow up in your face."

"You'll hit the rare books," said Evangeline, "the Tiffany, the Bierstadt. Think of the mess you'll make."

Yung looked at the books on the floor. "You've already made a start on that. Glad I stayed home today, or you might have torn the house apart."

"We'd never do that," said Peter. "But what would Maryanne Rogers say if—"

"She'd be happy, if we could bring an end to this madness."

"Madness?" Peter sensed that Mr. Yung was hiding something.

"Mr. Barber calling her, bothering her, even telling her he loved her."

"Loved her? Barber?" said Evangeline. "He's about fifty. She was—"

"Seventy-six." Yung lowered the Nock gun.

Wild Bill let out a deep breath, "Not the first May–December romance."

Peter chalked up another reason to dislike Johnson "Jack" Barber.

"How do you know what he told her?" Evangeline stepped closer.

Mr. Yung gestured to the console telephone in the corner. "Intercom to the kitchen. Once the height of high-tech."

"Still a good eavesdropper if you leave the switch on," said Wild Bill.

"I heard Barber say, 'If you love me, sign the new will.' He had brought George Sturgis to witness. She always trusted George more than Manion."

"Most people do," said Evangeline.

Yung nodded. "So she signed. But as Mr. Manion said, undue influence."

"Why didn't you speak up?" asked Peter.

"Barber saw the hit-and-run. He was waiting in front of the restaurant. He said it looked like I pushed her. But he said if I kept his secrets, he would keep mine."

"What were his secrets?" asked Peter.

"He did not specify. He only wanted me to keep my mouth shut."

"But you didn't push her?" said Wild Bill.

"My people have worked for the Spencers since Mickey Chang. Why would I push her? Besides, I know things no one else does."

That got everyone's attention, but then they heard something outside, in the driveway beside the house.

Wild Bill stepped to the curtains and peered out. "Two guys, out on the sidewalk. And one of them just jumped the gate."

"I'm surprised it took Kou's boys this long," said Peter.

Then they heard footfalls on the porch.

Peter said to Yung, "The guys out there are a lot worse than Barber."

The doorbell rang.

Wild Bill said, "But polite assassins always ring first."

"Maybe they think I'm off at my son's," said Yung. "Or alone."

"Alone with the seven-barrel Nock gun," said Peter.

"It's not loaded," answered Yung. "And it has no flint."

The bell rang again.

Wild Bill went to another window, peered onto the porch, and whispered, "Big white guy. Dark suit."

"The bodyguard who turned on Lum?" said Evangeline. "The one named Steele?"

Wild Bill reached for his shoulder holster. "Mr. Steele may meet Mr. Magnum."

Peter said, "Are you sure we can't run, instead?"

"Running is preferable," said Wild Bill. "But to where?"

Then they heard a different doorbell, a sharper buzzer.

Yung said, "The back door."

"And we're surrounded," said Peter, as if he was expecting it.

"I wish I had my Mace," said Evangeline.

"Relax, miss," said Yung. "This house is a fortress."

Wild Bill said, "The white guy is leaving. Down the steps . . . back onto the sidewalk . . . crossing the street . . . taking up a spot at the lamppost . . . making a call."

Peter looked out. "Lamppost becomes command post?"

Three hoodies, riding Dahon bikes, appeared from the shadows.

"Calling in the reinforcements," said Wild Bill.

Yung gave them a jerk of the head, had them step out of the library. Then he punched in the code and the pocket doors rolled shut with a thunk. "Those are steel, clad in wood. The windows are impenetrable. If there's a fire, halon gas will extinguish it. So the books and the Bierstadt are safe. Come on."

He led them up the stairs, past the portrait of Maryanne Rogers in the sitting room, past James Spencer's master bedroom in the turret, to another flight that rose to the servants' quarters. Yung bolted the door behind them and pointed them up the stairs to a beautiful circular room, with a 180-degree view of California Street below.

"We'll be safe up here," he said, "until help arrives."

"Very cozy," said Evangeline.

Yung said, "After our children went to college, my wife and I moved in. When she passed, I stayed to care for Mrs. Rogers. She was like family. And this is my home."

"And you don't want to lose your home?" said Evangeline.

"Would you?"

Wild Bill went over to a window and looked down. "White guy is still by the lamppost, still on the cell."

From somewhere down in the house, they heard pounding on the door.

"They should know that the house is alarmed," said Yung.

"So am I," said Evangeline.

Yung took out his cell phone.

"Who are you calling?" asked Peter.

"The police."

"No police," said Wild Bill. "Not yet. I'll text Rice Balls first. See what he suggests."

"Rice Balls wants the journal," said Peter. "Finding it is what he suggests."

"Rice Balls?" said John Yung, pure deadpan. "How . . . *Oriental*."

Evangeline said to Yung, "Mrs. Rogers was killed for those notebooks, probably by one of the guys trying to get into this house right now."

"But once the journal is complete," said John Yung, "they will sell this house and all its history. And my ancestors have a past here, too, just like the Spencers. It says so, right in the last notebook."

That caused Peter's heart to pop toward the back of his throat. "*Last notebook? Then you've read it?*"

Mr. Yung led them from the turret bedroom into the sitting room under the eaves, to a steamer trunk with oak strapping. "The Spencers gave this trunk to Mickey Chang when he was a boy in an orphanage. He kept it all his life. Others who lived in these rooms have added things. But it started with gifts from the Spencers."

"Like the Nock gun?" said Peter. "That was Mrs. Spencer's."

"I found the Nock gun here . . . and this." Yung pulled out a wooden box that contained a Walker Colt, wrapped in an oiled rag. The initials M.F. had been scratched into the grip. *Michael Flynn.* Then came an ancient hat, all moth-eaten and squashed, with a cracked leather brim.

"My God," said Peter. "Flynn stole this from Spencer the day they met. Janiva picked it up the night they hanged him."

Yung nodded. It was hard to tell if he was impressed with Peter Fallon's knowledge or feeling smug about how much more there was for him to see.

Then came an envelope out of which Yung removed a rag of red and yellow-paisley neckerchief . . . then a back strap shovel, manufactured by Ames & Co., Easton, Massachusetts . . . a rusted pan that looked like a deep-dish pie plate . . . a crumbling copy of the *Alta California* from June 11, 1851, the day after Flynn's hanging, with the headline, "Justice Is Served!"

Then came other items from other generations: a tasseled silk mandarin hat, an unopened bag of ginseng, a framed photograph of a Chinese man in dark, padded jacket and fedora, seated behind the wheel of an ancient automobile, and a well-dressed white man beside him. On the back: *October, 1905—Mickey Chang drives Mr. Spencer in new Ariel autocar.*

And from the bottom, John Yung brought forth a long notebook that he put reverently into Peter's hands.

Peter took it just as reverently, opened it, and read the inscription, "'To be given to Mickey Chang for his years of service, so that he may know his family and his father.'"

Peter felt the synapses firing again across the decades, between himself and James Spencer and the Chinese man who had been given this notebook. The feeling never got old. He muttered, "My God."

"My God," said Evangeline. "But why?"

"Read on," said John Yung.

"Before you read"—Evangeline waved her phone at Peter—"remember why we're here."

"Right." Peter pulled out his iPhone and scanned every page while Evangeline turned them. It didn't take long. Another wonder of modern technology. Then he emailed it all to LJ and Uncle Charlie as a single document.

"That should do it," said Wild Bill, who was looking out from a little porthole window under the eaves, watching the movement in the street.

"Do you see anything?" asked Peter.

"Steele is still at the lamppost. The bike boys are down in the shadows around the driveway, trying to open the gate, it looks like."

"Do you have other security?" Evangeline asked Mr. Yung.

"Of course. But if I'm here, I don't always turn on the cameras." He grabbed his iPad and brought up a screen. "I can start everything with this. I can have police here in four minutes."

Wild Bill put out his hand. "Wait, at least until I hear from my friend—"

"Mr. Balls?" said John Yung.

"That's Mr. *Rice* Balls to you," said Evangeline.

"No middle initial," said Peter, and he flipped through the notebook.

Not a lot changed from the final version . . . some phrasing here, bits of the story there, until he came to a passage not in the final transcription. It was entered about nine months after Michael Flynn's death:

One cool March eve, as Janiva rocked the baby and I read by the wood stove, there came a pounding on the door. Despite the retreat of the Sydney Ducks and other gangs, I never answered the door at night without my pistol, so I armed myself and asked who was there.

Receiving no answer, I cautiously opened and heard someone leaping down the stairs, running off into the night. Then I heard the mewling cry of a baby in a basket left on the landing. I brought it into the warmth, and upon closer examination, discovered a child, male, newborn, with a Chinese cast to his features and skin color. Had someone left him here because we had helped establish the orphanage? Or was there another reason? I determined to get answers the next morning.

Chin was behind the counter at Ah-Sing's. When he saw me, he spoke without prelude, angrily, almost in mid-emotion, as if he had been expecting me. He said, "Mei-Ling dead." And the anger in his voice implied that, somehow, he blamed me.

"In childbirth?" I asked.

He did not answer directly. He said, "I try protect her. I try find happiness for her. But white man's world destroy her."

I said I had not seen her in some time. "Did she go into hiding?"

He said she went to work for Ah-Toy. "Where else woman work with no husband and swelling belly, thanks to Flynn? But Mei-Ling no make fuck at Ah-Toy's. Never fuck."

So there it was. Michael Flynn was the father.

Chin said he could not raise Flynn's child. His bitterness toward the Irishman, for all the hurt he had brought them, all to plant his seed in Mei-Ling, was a thing that would never die. So Chin had left the child with us. "Skin light enough, maybe he pass."

But I told him I could not take this child into my house.

"Flynn your friend. You loyal to your friends. Be loyal to their seed."

I said that the child was his blood. He should be loyal, too.

"Then who raise him? Ah-Toy? No real Chinese mothers here."

I did not mention Chin's dabbling in female slavery. Instead, I looked into his eyes and gave him the answer I had been considering since the night before. "My wife cannot take in another child. It will kill her."

"Kill?" he said, puzzled.

And I considered telling him the truth. He knew nothing of the rape, nothing of the deep well of pain bored into Janiva on that awful day almost two years before. As I have written, she did her best to cover it, to ignore it, to rely on her straight spine and fierce will to bring her through. But sometimes, that well overflowed. When it did, I had no answers. I could only wait in quiet understanding and wish silently that we lived closer to family, for a wise mother might offer the surcease that a young husband could not.

Then our son was born. And when Janiva should have been overflowing with love, an even greater sadness bubbled out of her. And its dark waters threatened to drown us all. She could barely bring herself to suckle, to comfort, even to love our innocent babe.

Mrs. Brannan explained that this sadness sometimes afflicted women who had given birth, and she suggested a wet nurse. But where? The answer betook me to the establishment recently opened by the two soiled doves who sang so sweetly the night I killed Hodges, Sheila and Roberta. Rumor had it that Roberta had given birth to a stillborn. So I offered her an ounce of gold a day to wet nurse my son.

And little by little, with the help of Roberta and the steady rise of the sun toward the equinox, Janiva emerged from despair. Her strong spine held her upright. The lead of sorrow melted from her jaw. In time, she smiled again. But I feared that at any moment, sadness might swamp her once more, especially if we overwhelmed her now with a foundling.

But I did not tell any of this to Wei Chin. I said only, "We have an infant of our own. We cannot take another. If you cannot take your sister's child, I will see to his care in the orphanage."

Janiva felt considerable remorse at turning Flynn's child away. I felt it myself. But we agreed. As for Wei Chin, he was a man in whom pride and anger were stirred in equal measures, making for a volatile mix, and in this matter, anger seemed to have won. So we placed the child in the orphanage we had helped to establish at Second and Folsom.

Then I sent Roberta to suckle him. Soon she was wet-nurse and mother to half a dozen motherless infants. And she pronounced herself happier than she had ever been.

"Wow," whispered Evangeline. "Postpartum depression."

"Did they even have a name for it back then?" asked Peter.

"Whether they did or not," said Evangeline, "Janiva had it."

"Not surprising, after all she had been through," said Peter.

And for a few moments, they were silent in the attic, absorbing the pain of those lives, lived so long ago on those San Francisco hills.

Then they heard a vehicle pull up out front.

Wild Bill peered down. "Our friends have figured out how to get the gate open. A black panel truck is now in the driveway."

Peter said, "Is it the truck that hit Maryanne Rogers?"

"That one was white," said John Yung.

"They could have painted it," said Wild Bill.

"They have ladders," said Evangeline, peering out. "What do they want with ladders?"

"Maybe they're planning to try the second-floor windows," said Yung. "They will be disappointed."

"Or maybe," said Wild Bill, "they're thinking of cutting the power."

"There are back-up systems," said Yung.

"And"—Wild Bill looked at his phone—"Rice Balls just texted. The cavalry's on the way. We should sit tight."

"Sit tight and keep reading," said Peter. "Nothing ends until we finish."

He flipped to the last pages, looking for answers there in James Spencer's attic, and for the last time, he felt the persistence of Spencer's humanity, the decency of his character, sometimes flawed but always positive:

. . . We followed the rolling path across hills and through stands of trees. We bumped over the Rainbow Gulch water trench and came finally to the north rim of the ravine, where the graveyard had grown, filling with so many who had come to California in pursuit of a dream that life promises but seldom delivers.

There are tales of gold country burials in which actual gold nuggets appeared in the turned earth of a fresh grave, but no such miracle occurred when we dug for Michael Flynn that day. We lowered him, said a few psalms, and prayed for his orphan child.

The boy's uncle, Wei Chin, had become a great Mandarin by then, a "ticket broker" bringing cheap labor from China, and he had recently imported a childless couple named Chang. They had agreed to raise young Mickey, as he is called, with the financial support of Uncle Wei. As the Changs had worked "in service" to British officials in Hong Kong, I hired them for the new home we were building on California Street. So Mickey would grow under our roof, after all.

We stayed a few days with the Emerys in Broke Neck and negotiated with the Gasparich brothers, who owned the stretch of land which in April was a river of budding vines. These brothers had been diligent and hard working, but they had far to go to make wine that would last. So we offered to partner with them in wine if they would partner with us in gold.

Then we prospected for alluvial deposits, following the volcanic soils from the north-facing slope of the ravine all the way to the turn in the landscape that we now call Flynn's Bend. We dug a coyote hole and hit gravel at twenty-six feet. But there was no gold. In the next few days, we dug a dozen other holes with the same results. Whatever ore this ancient river had been carrying, it dropped elsewhere, into Rainbow Gulch, perhaps, or at the site that we exposed on the night we blew up the Sagamore dam.

So I decided that the best I could do for my old friend would be to buy that vineyard, and from its profits, establish a trust for Mickey Chang. Janiva approved. And thus did our Gold Rush come to an end.

Machines and mighty jets of water were doing the work that independent men once did with shovels and pans. The adventure and romance, the misery and heartbreak, the joy and sorrow of those early days were becoming no more than memory, as evanescent as the fog on the bay.

But we learned much in those hills, from great friends, from resolute enemies, and from those who began as one and ended as the other. I can close my eyes and see a hundred faces flying past, feel a thousand emotions pouring forth, and remember how brilliantly gold illuminated every dream and base instinct in all of them.

I have come to believe that human nature may appear to change, but in its hatreds and obsessions, in its hopes and generosities, in the bedrock places where decency and deceit reside, people never change. Gold cannot turn a man from one thing to another, from good to evil, from miser to philanthropist. Gold and the getting of it can only reveal him, as it did so many of us. And yet any man can be raised up with fair treatment. No matter the words of Cletis Smith, there is no such thing as too much mercy.

So we build our society in California, at once the promised land of the grand old song and yet another American paradise lost. Janiva and I will strive to make of this city a golden place, bright and hopeful, not because it will profit us but because it is the right thing to do.

FOR A MOMENT AFTER that, the four people in James Spencer's ancient attic sat in silence, considering his words.

Then John Yung nodded and gave a laugh.

Evangeline said, "What? What's so funny."

"That trust. It helped pay for my son's education at Stanford."

But that was a glow that no one had time to bask in, because a ladder thunked against the side of the house. The whole building shook.

John Yung said, "They are very stupid, whoever they are."

Wild Bill pulled the Magnum. "They're in for a helluva surprise."

Peter unwrapped the Walker Colt and popped the cylinder. Empty.

Evangeline said, "It would take you twenty minutes to load that thing, and you might still end up with a misfire."

"In that case"—Peter pointed to the iPad and told John Yung—"light her up."

John Yung tapped, swiped, tapped, swiped, and outside lights came on all around the grand old Victorian mansion.

Dark shadows scrambled in every direction. Dahon bikes went speeding toward Van Ness. The panel truck rocketed up California Street.

And across the street, the big white guy in the dark suit started down California, moving as casually as if he was on the way to Whole Foods. Then he stopped, because someone was walking up the hill toward him, a shadow of a small man in a windbreaker.

Mr. Steele reached for his gun. But the other man raised a pistol and fired once. Mr. Steele's head snapped back and he dropped onto the sidewalk. The shooter shoved the pistol into his windbreaker and kept going up the hill. Hector Chang, aka Rice Balls, disappeared onto Pacific Heights.

And the flashing blues arrived.

JAMES SPENCER'S LIBRARY BECAME an interview room with Detectives Immerman and Nauseda interrogating two young toughs in hoodies, caught on ladders outside the house, along with Peter Fallon, Evangeline Carrington, and former detective William "Wild Bill" Donnelly.

Immerman looked at Peter and said, "So this is where you're working?"

"With the permission of the family, yes. We're appraising the books."

"That was the story they told me the other night," offered Detective Nauseda.

Immerman said, "Somebody called us, said we might have trouble here. They said these boys may have wacked Wonton Willie, and if we look around out in the shrubs, we might even find their getaway vehicles, a pair of folding Dahon bikes. Do you know anything about that, Mr. Fallon?"

"It's a long story," said Wild Bill.

"I have all night," said Darcy Immerman.

Peter figured that once the pages had gone to Hong Kong, Rice Balls had been given the okay and called in the SFPD "cavalry."

Darcy Immerman said, "I always liked Wonton Willie, even if he was a lot of trouble. A real character. But too much character will get you killed."

"Too much mercy won't," said Peter.

Detective Immerman gave him a look. She didn't get it. But some people did.

Detective Nauseda got a text, then said to the guys in hoodies, "Who knows Michael Kou?"

"No talkin' till we get a lawyer," said one of them.

"Well, don't count on Kou to get one for you. Somebody just whacked him."

"Gang wars," said Detective Immerman. "I hate gang wars."

Peter recognized one of these kids now. He had been the accidental photobomb, that first day on the cable car. So Michael Kou had been following them from the start.

Then came more commotion at the door, and in walked a redheaded woman in a blue pantsuit, followed by an Asian guy wearing an FBI windbreaker.

Darcy Immerman said, "Who the hell are you?"

Evangeline whispered to Peter, "Your girlfriend from the Mark Hopkins lobby."

"And other places."

"Along with the guy who was watching us in the restaurant the other night," Evangeline added.

"And other places," Peter repeated.

The redhead showed her badge. "Special Agent Christine Ryan, and I have a Federal warrant to search this house and library."

Peter's stomach dropped. "In the case against—"

"Johnson 'Jack' Barber. You can read the complaint online, as soon as it's filed."

Darcy Immerman looked at Ryan's badge. "You can have the house, but the collars are mine."

Christine Ryan said, "They're yours, so long as I can question them."

"I want a lawyer," said one of them.

"Anyone else in the complaint?" Peter asked Agent Ryan.

"The bureau does not anticipate that any of Barber's legal associates will be under indictment, if that's what you're asking." Then Christine Ryan stalked into the library and looked around, saw the painting, and said, "Wow, is that a Bierstadt?"

Evangeline whispered to Peter, "Our work here is done."

No one would ever know who eliminated Michael Kou, although LJ told his father that Cousin Rebel and Uncle Charlie had a long talk in Cantonese, just after Notebook Seven was emailed to Hong Kong. Then Cousin Rebel slipped out and never came back.

As for Johnson "Jack" Barber and the late Michael Kou, their scheme to launder millions through Sierra Rock, by repaying Chinese gold purchase loans with dirty money, would earn Barber extended time as a guest of the U.S. government.

When the Federal indictment was handed down, there were numerous references to an informer. And he was named. But it was not James "LJ" Fallon. The informer was William Ling, aka Wonton Willie, of Jackson Street in San Francisco, formerly of Hong Kong.

He had been the other asset on the inside.

Three months later, Peter Fallon returned to complete the appraisal.

And Manion Sturgis invited everyone to Amador for the weekend. He set the table at the edge of the patio, in the warm sun.

Sarah Bliss and Brother B. came out from Sausalito and drank wine instead of their usual tea.

Wild Bill Donnelly brought his wife, Jane. Peter delivered him a signed first edition of Robert Ludlum's *The Bourne Identity*.

Jack Cutler, enjoying his anonymity in Amador County, came to toast his daughter. Since Uncle Charlie had put word out on the street that Cutler was okay, he no longer had to worry in Chinese restaurants.

And Mary Ching Cutler finally seemed as happy as any young bride-to-be. The only one more relaxed was LJ.

Manion raised the first glass. "To Peter Fallon of Boston, who found the seven notebooks."

"It was LJ who found them," said Peter. "I was just along for moral support."

"I couldn't have done it without you, Dad," said LJ.

"In some things, Fallon," said Manion, "no one is your equal."

"Why, Manion, so much Mr. Nice Guy," said Evangeline. "What's come over you?"

"That." He gestured to a pickup truck pulling into the parking lot.

A woman in her late fifties got out and came up the path, moving with straight-up confidence in a nice pair of jeans, a silk blouse, and leather jacket: Ginny O'Hara.

She took a seat next to Manion and said, "Sorry I'm late. I had animals to tend."

They drank the best Manion Gold old-vine Zinfandel with bacon-wrapped petit filets, hot-house tomatoes, and garlic-grilled bread.

"Perfect for lunch or dinner."

That was the pronouncement of brother George. And Manion gave him the honor of announcing that the brothers would be buying Arbella House from the estate and creating a new trust to keep it in the family.

Then they toasted John Yung, who had come out with his son. "He will continue as our caretaker."

They drank and talked and laughed in the warming sun. They admired the way the land rolled up from Rainbow Gulch, then turned at that bump that Flynn had first noticed and Spencer had named after him.

But when Cutler suggested "just a little" core sampling, Manion said he was planning to grow Chardonnay grapes out there, and if the wine was good, they would call it Flynn's Bend Chardonnay.

"That will be the gold," said Peter.

"The best gold of all," said Evangeline.

"Gold in the glass," said Jack Cutler.

"And gold in the future." Peter raised his glass toward LJ and Mary. "To the golden future of two fine young people."

"Here, here," said Jack Cutler.

"I'd love to host a wedding," said Manion. "Or two?"

"Or two?" said Evangeline. "I don't know."

"I was talking about us," said Manion, and he took Ginny's hand.

AFTER LUNCH, MANION GAVE a vineyard tour to the newcomers.

But Peter and Evangeline went off on their own in a golf cart, off to Rainbow Gulch. They parked amidst the first ancient vines planted by two Croatian brothers. They clambered down into the dark bottom of the ravine, then climbed again, up into the afternoon sunlight, up to the little graveyard where so many dreams, the fulfilled and the forgotten, lay forever in the earth.

They combed through the markers, some blank or weatherbeaten, a few identifying the remains beneath, until they found it, overgrown and brush-covered: MICHAEL FLYNN, 1823–1851. A RIGHT CHARMER, A REAL LOVER, AND A FINE SINGING VOICE, TOO.

"A fine epitaph," said Peter.

Evangeline knelt to touch the stone. "You can feel the ghosts."

"They're always here." Peter looked along the ravine that once had throbbed with so much life, then he gazed south along the river of grapevines. "Always showing us the way."

Evangeline stood and took his arm. "Maybe they can show us the way back to the guesthouse."

"Separate beds?"

"No. As James Spencer would call it, our Bower of Bliss."

JAMES SPENCER DID NOT sleep well in the two days before his death. He lay abed, afloat on waves of consciousness and thought that rolled, then ebbed, that swirled, then eddied, then dragged him down again toward insensibility.

When he raised his head from the pillow and looked out, he saw billowing smoke. Or was it fog? The recurring San Francisco fog, the rhythm of it defining the life of the city he loved. But if it was fog, why was it blowing from east to west?

And so many other questions swirled in his head. Why did the air smell acrid and burnt? Why were people shouting in the street, right under his windows, like Vigilantes. And why was he hearing explosions? Some were dull thumps. Others were sharp, almost painful blasts followed by thunderous collapses. In that, the explosions were like the pains in his chest, dull and steady and deep but punctuated by sharp, shattering outbursts.

He must ask one of his visitors. So many had come to visit. So many. Why?

Old Doc Beal had placed a stethoscope on his chest, had listened, had shaken his head and prescribed digitalis.

Matt Dooling had sat with him and talked about the good times.

His faithful daughter, Amanda, loving wife and mother of the Rogers clan, had come over the hill and sat with him for hours. She had read the Psalms, knowing that he had always liked the Psalms. She had read Shakespeare, knowing that he liked Shakespeare even more. She had soothed him with the sound of her voice, so much like her mother's. She had promised that his other children were coming, too, but getting to San Francisco was almost impossible, and some had so far to travel, from Boston, Los Angeles, Amador, Calistoga.

And why again were they coming?

He yearned to stand so that he could piss, so that he could look out the window, so that he could get in the autocar and drive down to the office at the corner of Market and Dupont, where his business and his family had both begun, so that he could save the papers, save the journal transcription, save the seven notebooks.

Or had Mickey Chang done it already? Mickey. Loyal Mickey. Foundling, orphan, nephew of Uncle Chin, who finally found a Chinese family to raise him.

But Spencer's mind spun away from all that as an explosion shook the house.

Then he felt Janiva's hand gripping his. Yes, Janiva . . . no, Amanda . . . or Janiva . . . her touch gave him strength, as it had so long ago.

And now, Mickey Chang was looking over her shoulder, looking down on him. He whispered, "We put out food, Miz Mandy. Go down and eat. I'll sit with him."

She brought her face close and said, "Papa, I'll be right back."

A sharp pain caused him to grimace, gag, grab for his chest.

Amanda dropped to her knees by the bedside.

James Spencer reached out to stroke her beautiful hair. He called her Janiva. And she became his wife, smiling through her tears, beckoning him home.

Another explosion shook the house.

Amanda looked up at Mickey. "Will they make us leave?"

"They're stopping the fire at Van Ness," said Mickey. "Blowing up houses with gunpowder and cannons, blowing up other people's houses to save ours."

And clarity came suddenly upon James Spencer. He said, "Mickey, my journal."

"I got it, boss. I went up and got everything before the fire got it. You remember. The box is on the table, in the bay window, so you can write again when you feel better."

Very good, thought James Spencer. He could not tell if the words "very good" made it out. He could not tell much. But he said, "About your trust."

And Mickey laughed. He laughed as easily as his real father and almost as often. "Don't you worry, boss. I trust you. You trust me. Just like you trust Mom and Dad Chang before me."

James Spencer nodded. Then he tried to hold up fingers. Seven fingers. Then he pointed to the box and gestured for someone to fetch it to him.

Mickey brought it back and gave it to Amanda.

She flipped through it and said, "There are seven notebooks, Papa. Each written with a name. Your six children and"—she looked up—"Mickey. His folder says, 'To be given to Mickey Chang for his good service, so that he may know his family and his father.'"

Mickey gasped, "Father?" And his eyes filled with tears. "Father?" Then he said to James Spencer, "The Chang family raise me, Mr. James. They my parents. And . . . and you been like a father, too."

James Spencer nodded. Then a great exhaustion came over him. He put his head back. He felt sleep coming on. He heard the explosions, some far away, some nearby, as intermittent as the beating of his heart.

A FEW HOURS LATER, Amanda and Mickey stood on the porch and looked down California Street.

The bestial fire was not far away, chewing relentlessly on the hills and valleys of San Francisco, on the hopes and dreams and mementoes and keepsakes of a hundred thousand lives.

But a fire engine had moved into position at the corner of Franklin and California. So the fight to save what was left would go on.

Mickey said, "If the fire jump Van Ness, we gotta move."

"But not yet," she said. "Let Father lay a while longer in peace."

Mickey wiped his tears. "I gonna miss him, Miz Mandy."

"We all will." Amanda took him by the arm. "But he bequeathed a different property to each of his children. Arbella House will be mine. And his will includes positions for you and your family under this roof, forever."

"Can we stay upstairs, in the apartment under the eaves? With our trunks and things? We like it there."

"Always."

"But—" Mickey wrinkled his brow. "My father? Does that book tell who my real father was?"

"Whoever he was, know that my father loved you like a son."

"Yes, yes."

"So you can stay, and welcome your grandchildren to Arbella House anytime. We'll put books in the library for them, in English and Chinese both."

"They will learn both. Chinese to know where they came from, American to know where they're going, both to always be friends."

And for a time, James Spencer's daughter and his servant stood on the veranda looking at the distant ruins and the approaching flames.

Then Amanda said, "Whatever happens, when the fire is out, we'll have to get back to work. As my father always said, next time, build it bigger, better, stronger."

"Yeah," said Mickey. "Like Americans always do."